Anne of Green Gables

THREE VOLUMES IN ONE

ANNE BALANCED HERSELF UPRIGHTLY ON THAT PRECARIOUS FOOTING. (*ANNE OF GREEN GABLES*, CHAPTER 23)

Anne of Green Gables

Three Volumes in One

Anne of Green Gables
Anne of Avonlea
Anne's House of Dreams

By Lucy Maud Montgomery

PORTLAND HOUSE

This volume contains the complete and unabridged texts of the original editions. They have been completely reset for this volume.

This 2001 edition is published by Portland House, an imprint of Random House Value Publishing, Inc., a division of Random House Inc. 280 Park Avenue, New York, NY 10017.

Random House

New York • Toronto • London • Sydney • Auckland

http://www.randomhouse.com/

Printed and bound in the United States of America

ISBN 0-517-21447-4

8 7 6 5 4 3 2 1

The good stars met in your horoscope,
Made you of spirit and fire and dew.
                    —BROWNING

DEDICATORY NOTE

Lucy Maud Montgomery, not surprisingly, dedicated each of these three books to different people, all important in her life.

Anne of Green Gables was a tribute "to the memory of my father and mother." *Anne of Avonlea* recalled "my former teacher, Hattie Gordon Smith, in grateful remembrance of her sympathy and encouragement." And *Anne's House of Dreams* was dedicated "to Laura, in memory of the olden time."

CONTENTS

INTRODUCTION

THE *Anne of Green Gables* books, written by Lucy Maud Montgomery, are threaded through with delight at the unexpected sweetness of human life and of nature, together with an appreciation for the comedy to be found in the matter-of-fact reality of Prince Edward Island village life in Canada. Anne's character, on that first wagon ride to Green Gables, shows the presence of these two qualities: her appreciation of beauty, often expressed in the flowery phrases she remembers from romantic novels, and the uncomplaining humor with which she accepts the harsh, love-starved reality of her past life.

The writer's underlying feeling that the universe has a soul, expressed in nature, goes hand in hand with her humor and compassion towards her characters. She has a feeling for the particularity and eccentricity of the real world that puts a limit on too far a flight of fancy. Yet as romance gives meaning to the world, so the quirks of the real world give flavor to romance. By the interplay of beauty and comedy, Maud Montgomery creates the tension that moves the rhythm of the *Anne* books along. (The writer was always called Maud by those who knew her.)

The skimpy dress given to Anne at the orphan asylum clings to her angular, skinny frame just as Anne clings to her determination to experience and savor the joy of being alive. Following her romantic ideals often leads Anne into mishaps. "I wouldn't mind my misfortunes so much if they were romantic...but they are always just simply ridiculous." Anne finds encouragement, however, in that

> "I never make the same mistake twice. There *must* be a limit to the mistakes one person can make, and when I get to the end of them, then I'll be through with them. That's a very comforting thought."

Maud underscores the absurdity that lies in the juxtaposition of our daydreams to our everyday life. She sees humor as "a sense of the fitness of things." Anne wears her red hair as a banner from which she wants to, but cannot, escape. When Matthew Cuthbert, who with his sister Marilla will later adopt her, first meets Anne, she tells him,

> "...I *cannot* imagine that red hair away. I do my best. I think to myself, 'Now my hair is a glorious black, black as the raven's wing.' But all the time I *know* it is just plain red, and it breaks my heart. It will be my lifelong sorrow."

Years later, she buys a hair dye that is promised to turn her hair that "beautiful raven black," but finds instead that

> "I thought nothing could be as bad as red hair. But now I know it's ten times worse to have green hair. Oh, Marilla, you little know how utterly wretched I am."

Maud herself had reason to know how often hopes and dreams were dulled by the relentlessness of real life. She was raised by her maternal grandparents because her mother died when Maud was twenty-one months old. Her grandmother raised her according to strict, old-fashioned principles. Maud envied her peers' small freedoms. Yet she gave up both a two-year teaching career and a winter stint at a newspaper to live with her grandmother after her grandfather died, delaying her marriage until she was thirty-six, after the death of her grandmother. Although her grandmother's rigid religious views left Maud with the sense that organized religion made the individual "feel ashamed," Maud married a minister. She spent much of her later life living up to her ideal of a minister's wife. For years, she dealt uncomplainingly with what was then diagnosed as her husband's "melancholia," and only at the end of her life, when her health fell apart, did she admit that these pressures had become too much for her.

We may wonder at the contrast between the freedom Maud allowed her characters, and the roles to which she confined herself in real life. We remember Anne's feeling that "saying one's prayers isn't exactly the same thing as praying."

> "…If I really wanted to pray…I'd go out into a great big field all alone or into the deep, deep woods, and I'd look up into the sky—up—up—up—into that lovely blue sky that looks as if there was no end to its blueness. And then I'd just *feel* a prayer."

We may wonder also at Maud's feelings as she involved herself in the duties of minister's wife. In *Anne's House of Dreams,* the fifth and most philosophical in the *Anne* series, Anne, talking to a writer, contemplates the "queer ache" she experiences when she sees something beautiful and perfect. "Perhaps," responds the writer, "it is the prisoned infinite in us calling out to its kindred infinite as expressed in that visible perfection." Looking at the pale reflection of a sunset in the eastern sky, Anne wonders, "if the spirit of color looked like that." She speaks of mayflowers as "the souls of the flowers that died last summer." Seeing a mossy log struck by a solitary shaft of sunshine, Anne calls it a "poem," and explains to an unbelieving friend who calls a poem "lines and verses," that "the real poem is the soul within" the lines and verses. "I like to fancy souls [of people] being made of light." In *Anne's House of Dreams,* Captain Jim says,

> "When I ponder on them seeds I don't find it nowise hard to believe that we've got souls that'll live in other worlds. You couldn't hardly believe that there was life in them tiny things, some no bigger than grains of dust, let alone color and scent, if you hadn't seen the miracle, could you?"

Captain Jim later asks, "How'd we stand living if it wasn't for our dream of immortality?"

In her short autobiography, *The Alpine Path, The Story of My Career* (published by Fitzhenry & Whiteside Limited, in Canada, 1917), Maud writes,

> It has always seemed to me, ever since early childhood, amid all the commonplaces of life, I was very near to a kingdom of ideal beauty. Between it and me hung only a thin veil. I could

> never draw it quite aside, but sometimes a wind fluttered it and I caught a glimpse of the enchanting realm beyond—only a glimpse—but those glimpses have always made life worth while.

Additionally, Maud displays a love for the eccentricities of the village people. She relishes the quirk of character that lends individuality to seemingly ordinary village folk. Though they might not indulge in Anne's flights of imagination, they had their own ways of expressing their needs and wishes. In one sentence, Maud describes the relationship of two elderly sisters who live together,

> Eliza was sewing patchwork, not because it was needed but simply as a protest against the frivolous lace Catherine was crocheting.

Maud introduces Marilla, who with Matthew will adopt Anne, by exposing her vulnerability, telling us that she is a woman who is "always slightly distrustful of sunshine." She tells us of "Mrs. Jasper Bell, whose family was said to be the only one in the world in which accidents never occurred."

Maud was a prodigious writer. In *The Alpine Path*, she says, "I cannot remember the time when I was not writing." When teaching, Maud would rise early to write, "with fingers so cramped [from cold] that I could scarcely hold the pen..." As a newspaper woman, she found she had to make time for her own creative writing in the midst of a busy and interrupted day,

> ...in a newspaper office, with rolls of proof shooting down every ten minutes, people coming and conversing, telephones ringing, and machines being thumped and dragged overhead....

In the spring of 1904, after returning to live with her grandmother, Maud began *Anne of Green Gables,* finding the germ of the idea for the plot in a notebook of jottings she had written years before: "Elderly couple apply to orphan asylum for a boy. By mistake a girl is sent them." Maud intended to write only a short serial for a Sunday school paper. As she developed the character, "she soon seemed very real to me and took possession of me to an unusual extent." Maud realized that here was a character who could sustain a full-length book. Completing the novel in October 1905, Maud sent it in turn to five publishers, all of whom rejected it. She put the manuscript away in a hatbox, but, rereading it one winter day, decided to try again. It was accepted by L. C. Page and Company of Boston and published in 1908.

Maud would go on to write seven more books about Anne, but, because she found taking Anne into adulthood a burden, she began these only at the insistence of her publisher. This volume contains three of the novels: *Anne of Green Gables,* the first in the series, *Anne of Avonlea,* the second, and *Anne's House of Dreams,* the fifth. *Anne of Green Gables* introduces Anne, chronicling her passage from the beguiling, freckled "witch" of a child into teenager. She meets Gilbert Blythe, who soon changes from tormentor into admirer. In *Anne of Avonlea,* we see Anne as the teen-age village "schoolma'am," bringing together the lives of the "kindred spirits" she discovers in her community. Gilbert continues to show his interest in Anne, and together, with Anne's inspiration, they form a village improvement society. *Anne of the Island* follows Anne in college with her first serious experiences with real-life romance. Anne becomes engaged to Gilbert. *Anne of Windy Poplars* consists of Anne's letters to Gilbert, written during the three years she is principal of Summerside High School while he is studying medicine. *Anne's House of Dreams* begins with Anne's wedding and describes the memorable characters she meets during her early married years.

Maud was to write other novels about young heroines: Emily, Jane, Pat, and Marigold. Like Maud herself, several of these are fatherless. Maud wrote many potboilers, both poems and short stories. Like the people in whose lives Anne involves herself, many of the characters in the short stories search for a lost love—father, mother, lover—and always find it. Maud wrote two novels for adults as well.

For forty years, Maud had pen-friendships with two men she met only briefly: Ephraim Weber, a self-educated homesteader in Alberta who later became a teacher, and George Boyd MacMillan, a writer in Scotland. In her correspondence with both men, as well as in her diary, Maud revealed many of her feelings that lay hidden beneath her masks of conscientious granddaughter and wife. As Mollie Gillen quotes in her biography of Maud, *The Wheel of Things* (Fitzhenry & Whiteside Limited, Canada, 1975), Maud wrote in 1906,

> I used to be a most impulsive, passionate creature....But I
> used always to *rush to extremes* in any emotion, whether of
> hatred, affection, ambition, or what not, that came upper-

most....I fear that, given favorable circumstances, it might blaze up as strongly as ever.

As with Anne, "The pleasures and pains of life came to her with trebled intensity." Truly, Maud could have said of herself, as Anne did, "There's such a lot of Annes in me."

ELLEN S. SHAPIRO

New York City
1986

────────────────── EDITORIAL NOTE ──────────────────

The editions that were chosen for this anthology are the early or first ones, published in the first quarter of this century. The modern reader may be surprised to discover certain old-fashioned styles of punctuation and spelling, as well as some archaic references and descriptions, but these have been retained in order to convey the flavor of the originals.

Anne of Green Gables

THREE VOLUMES IN ONE

Anne
Of Green Gables

CHAPTER 1

MRS. RACHEL LYNDE IS SURPRISED

MRS. RACHEL LYNDE lived just where the Avonlea main road dipped down into a little hollow, fringed with alders and ladies' eardrops and traversed by a brook that had its source away back in the woods of the old Cuthbert place; it was reputed to be an intricate, headlong brook in its earlier course through those woods, with dark secrets of pool and cascade; but by the time it reached Lynde's Hollow it was a quiet, well-conducted little stream, for not even a brook could run past Mrs. Rachel Lynde's door without due regard for decency and decorum; it probably was conscious that Mrs. Rachel was sitting at her window, keeping a sharp eye on everything that passed, from brooks and children up, and that if she noticed anything odd or out of place she would never rest until she had ferreted out the whys and wherefores thereof.

There are plenty of people, in Avonlea and out of it, who can attend closely to their neighbors' business by dint of neglecting their own; but Mrs. Rachel Lynde was one of those capable creatures who can manage their own concerns and those of other folks into the bargain. She was a notable housewife; her work was always done and well done; she "ran" the Sewing Circle, helped run the Sunday school, and was the strongest prop of the Church Aid Society and Foreign Missions Auxiliary. Yet with all this Mrs. Rachel found abundant time to sit for hours at her kitchen window, knitting "cotton warp" quilts—she had knitted sixteen of them, as Avonlea

3

housekeepers were wont to tell in awed voices—and keeping a sharp eye on the main road that crossed the hollow and wound up the steep red hill beyond. Since Avonlea occupied a little triangular peninsula jutting out into the Gulf of St. Lawrence, with water on two sides of it, anybody who went out of it or into it had to pass over that hill road and so run the unseen gauntlet of Mrs. Rachel's all-seeing eye.

She was sitting there one afernoon in early June. The sun was coming in at the window warm and bright; the orchard on the slope below the house was in a bridal flush of pinky-white bloom, hummed over by a myriad of bees. Thomas Lynde—a meek little man whom Avonlea people called ''Rachel Lynde's husband''—was sowing his late turnip seed on the hill field beyond the barn; and Matthew Cuthbert ought to have been sowing his on the big red brook field away over by Green Gables. Mrs. Rachel knew that he ought because she had heard him tell Peter Morrison the evening before in William J. Blair's store over at Carmody that he meant to sow his turnip seed the next afternoon. Peter had asked him, of course, for Matthew Cuthbert had never been known to volunteer information about anything in his whole life.

And yet here was Matthew Cuthbert, at half-past three on the afternoon of a busy day, placidly driving over the hollow and up the hill; moreover, he wore a white collar and his best suit of clothes, which was plain proof that he was going out of Avonlea; and he had the buggy and the sorrel mare, which betokened that he was going a considerable distance. Now, where was Matthew Cuthbert going and why was he going there?

Had it been any other man in Avonlea Mrs. Rachel, deftly putting this and that together, might have given a pretty good guess as to both questions. But Matthew so rarely went from home that it must be something pressing and unusual which was taking him; he was the shyest man alive and hated to have to go among strangers or to any place where he might have to talk. Matthew, dressed up with a white collar and driving in a buggy, was something that didn't happen often. Mrs. Rachel, ponder as she might, could make nothing of it and her afternoon's enjoyment was spoiled.

''I'll just step over to Green Gables after tea and find out from Marilla where he's gone and why,'' the worthy woman finally concluded. ''He doesn't generally go to town this time of year and he *never* visits; if he'd run out of turnip seed he wouldn't dress up and take the buggy to go for more; he wasn't driving fast enough to be going for a doctor. Yet something must have happened since last night to start him off. I'm clean puzzled, that's what, and I won't know a minute's peace of mind or conscience until I know what has taken Matthew Cuthbert out of Avonlea today.''

Accordingly after tea Mrs. Rachel set out; she had not far to go; the big, rambling, orchard-embowered house where the Cuthberts lived was a scant quarter of a mile up the road from Lynde's Hollow. To be sure, the long lane made it a good deal further. Matthew Cuthbert's father, as shy and silent as his son after him, had got as far away as he possibly could from his fellow men without actually retreating into the woods when he founded his homestead. Green Gables was built at the furthest edge of his cleared land and there it was to this day, barely visible from the main road along which all the other Avonlea houses were so sociably situated. Mrs. Rachel Lynde did not call living in such a place *living* at all.

''It's just *staying*, that's what,'' she said as she stepped along the deep-rutted, grassy lane bordered with wild rose bushes. ''It's no wonder Matthew and Marilla were both a little odd, living away back here by themselves. Trees aren't much company, though dear knows if they were there'd be enough of them. I'd ruther look at people. To be sure, they seem contented enough; but then, I suppose, they're used to it. A body can get used to anything, even to being hanged, as the Irishman said.''

With this Mrs. Rachel stepped out of the lane into the backyard of Green Gables. Very green and neat and precise was that yard, set about on one side with great patriarchal willows and on the other with prim Lombardies. Not a stray stick nor stone was to be seen, for Mrs. Rachel would have seen it if there had been. Privately she was of the opinion that Marilla Cuthbert swept that yard over as often as she swept her house. One could have eaten a meal off the ground without overbrimming the proverbial peck of dirt.

Mrs. Rachel rapped smartly at the kitchen door and stepped in when bidden to do so. The kitchen at Green Gables was a cheerful apartment—or would have been cheerful if it had not been so painfully clean as to give it something of the appearance of an unused parlour. Its windows looked east and west; through the west one, looking out on the backyard, came a flood of mellow June sunlight; but the east one, whence you got a glimpse of the bloom white cherry-trees in the left orchard and nodding, slender birches down in the hollow by the brook, was greened over by a tangle of vines. Here sat Marilla Cuthbert, when she sat at all, always slightly distrustful of sunshine, which seemed to her too dancing and irresponsible a thing for a world which was meant to be taken seriously; and here she sat now, knitting, and the table behind her was laid for supper.

Mrs. Rachel, before she had fairly closed the door, had taken mental note of everything that was on that table. There were three plates laid, so that Marilla must be expecting some one home with Matthew to tea; but the dishes were every-day dishes and there was only crab-apple preserves and one kind of cake, so that the expected company could not be any particular company. Yet what of Matthew's white collar and the sorrel mare? Mrs. Rachel was getting fairly dizzy with this unusual mystery about quiet, unmysterious Green Gables.

"Good evening, Rachel," Marilla said briskly. "This is a real fine evening, isn't it? Won't you sit down? How are all your folks?"

Something that for lack of any other name might be called friendship existed and always had existed between Marilla Cuthbert and Mrs. Rachel, in spite of—or perhaps because of—their dissimilarity.

Marilla was a tall, thin woman, with angles and without curves; her dark hair showed some gray streaks and was always twisted up in a hard little knot behind with two wire hairpins stuck aggressively through it. She looked like a woman of narrow experience and rigid conscience, which she was; but there was a saving something about her mouth which, if it had been ever so slightly developed, might have been considered indicative of a sense of humour.

"We're all pretty well," said Mrs. Rachel. "I was kind of afraid *you* weren't, though, when I saw Matthew starting off today. I thought maybe he was going to the doctor's."

Marilla's lips twitched understandingly. She had expected Mrs. Rachel up; she had known that the sight of Matthew jaunting off so unaccountably would be too much for her neighbour's curiosity.

"Oh, no, I'm quite well although I had a bad headache yesterday," she said. "Matthew went to Bright River. We're getting a little boy from an orphan asylum in Nova Scotia and he's coming on the train tonight."

If Marilla had said that Matthew had gone to Bright River to meet a kangaroo from Australia Mrs. Rachel could not have been more astonished. She was actually stricken dumb for five seconds. It was unsupposable that Marilla was making fun of her, but Mrs. Rachel was almost forced to suppose it.

"Are you in earnest, Marilla?" she demanded when voice returned to her.

"Yes, of course," said Marilla, as if getting boys from orphan asylums in Nova Scotia were part of the usual spring work on any well-regulated Avonlea farm instead of being an unheard of innovation.

Mrs. Rachel felt that she had received a severe mental jolt. She thought in exclamation points. A boy! Marilla and Matthew Cuthbert of all people adopting a boy! From an orphan asylum! Well, the world was certainly turning upside down! She would be surprised at nothing after this! Nothing!

"What on earth put such a notion into your head?" she demanded disapprovingly.

This had been done without her advice being asked, and must perforce be disapproved.

"Well, we've been thinking about it for some time—all winter in fact," returned Marilla. "Mrs. Alexander Spencer was up here one day before Christmas and she said she was going to get a little girl from the asylum over in Hopetown in the spring. Her cousin lives there and Mrs. Spencer has visited her and knows all about it. So Matthew and I have talked it over off and on ever since. We thought we'd get a boy. Matthew is getting up in years, you know—he's sixty—and he isn't so spry as he once was. His heart troubles him a good deal. And you know how desperate hard it's got to be to get hired help. There's never anybody to be had but those stupid, half-grown little French boys; and as soon as you do get one broke into your ways and taught something he's up and off to the lobster canneries or the States. At first Matthew suggested getting a Barnado boy. But I said 'no' flat to that. 'They may be all right—I'm not saying they're not—but no London street Arabs for me,' I said. 'Give me a native born at least. There'll be a risk, no matter who we get. But I'll feel easier in my mind and sleep sounder at nights if we get a born Canadian.' So in the end we decided to ask Mrs. Spencer to pick us out one when she went over to get her little girl. We heard last week she was going, so we sent her word by Richard Spencer's folks at Carmody to bring us a smart, likely boy of about ten or eleven. We decided that would be the best age—old enough to be of some use in doing chores right off and young enough to be trained up proper. We mean to give him a good home and schooling. We had a telegram from Mrs. Alexander Spencer today—the mailman brought it from the station—saying they were coming on the five-thirty train tonight. So Matthew went to Bright River to meet him. Mrs. Spencer will drop him off there. Of course she goes on to White Sands station herself."

Mrs. Rachel prided herself on always speaking her mind; she proceeded to speak it now, having adjusted her mental attitude to this amazing piece of news.

"Well, Marilla, I'll just tell you plain that I think you're doing a mighty foolish thing—a risky thing, that's what. You don't know what you're getting. You're bringing a strange child into your house and home and you don't know a single thing about him nor what his disposition is like nor what sort of parents he had nor how he's likely to turn out. Why, it was only last week I read in the paper how a man and his wife up west of the Island took a boy out of an orphan asylum and he set fire to the house at night—set it *on purpose*, Marilla—and nearly burnt them to a crisp in their beds. And I know another case where an adopted boy used to suck the eggs—they couldn't break him of it. If you had asked my advice in the matter—which you didn't do, Marilla—I'd have said for mercy's sake not to think of such a thing, that's what."

This Job's comforting seemed neither to offend nor alarm Marilla. She knitted steadily on.

"I don't deny there's something in what you say, Rachel. I've had some qualms myself. But Matthew was terrible set on it. I could see that, so I gave in. It's so seldom Matthew sets his mind on anything that when he does I always feel it's my duty to give in. And as for the risk, there's risks in pretty near everything a body does in this world. There's risks in people's having children of their own if it comes to that—they don't always turn out well. And then Nova Scotia is right close to the Island. It isn't as if we were getting him from England or the States. He can't be much different from ourselves."

"Well, I hope it will turn out all right," said Mrs. Rachel in a tone that plainly indicated her painful doubts. "Only don't say I didn't warn you if he burns Green Gables down or puts strychnine in the well—I heard of a case over in New Brunswick where an orphan asylum child did that and the whole family died in fearful agonies. Only, it was a girl in that instance."

"Well, we're not getting a girl," said Marilla, as if poisoning wells were a purely feminine accomplishment and not to be dreaded in the case of a boy. "I'd never dream of taking a girl to bring up. I wonder at Mrs. Alexander Spencer for doing it. But there, *she* wouldn't shrink from adopting a whole orphan asylum if she took it into her head."

Mrs. Rachel would have liked to stay until Matthew came home with his imported orphan. But reflecting that it would be a good two hours at least before his arrival she concluded to go up the road to Robert Bell's and tell them the news. It would certainly make a sensation second to none, and Mrs. Rachel dearly loved to make a sensation. So she took herself away, somewhat to Marilla's relief, for the latter felt her doubts and fears reviving under the influence of Mrs. Rachel's pessimism.

"Well, of all things that every were or will be!" ejaculated Mrs. Rachel when she was safely out in the lane. "It does really seem as if I must be dreaming. Well, I'm sorry for that poor young one and no mistake. Matthew and Marilla don't know anything about children and they'll expect him to be wiser and steadier than his own grandfather, if so be's he ever had a grandfather, which is doubtful. It seems uncanny to think of a child at Green Gables somehow; there's never been one there, for Matthew and Marilla were grown up when the new house was built—if they ever *were* children, which is hard to believe when one looks at them. I wouldn't be in that orphan's shoes for anything. My, but I pity him, that's what."

So said Mrs. Rachel to the wild rose bushes out of the fulness of her heart; but if she could have seen the child who was waiting patiently at the Bright River station at that very moment her pity would have been still deeper and more profound.

CHAPTER 2

MATTHEW CUTHBERT IS SURPRISED

MATTHEW CUTHBERT and the sorrel mare jogged comfortably over the eight miles to Bright River. It was a pretty road, running along between snug farmsteads, with now and again a bit of balsamy fir wood to drive through or a hollow where wild plums hung out their filmy bloom. The air was sweet with the breath of many apple orchards and the meadows sloped away in the distance to horizon mists of pearl and purple; while

> *The little birds sang as if it were*
> *The one day of summer in all the year.*

Matthew enjoyed the drive after his own fashion, except during the moments when he met women and had to nod to them—for in Prince Edward Island you are supposed to nod to all and sundry you meet on the road whether you know them or not.

Matthew dreaded all women except Marilla and Mrs. Rachel; he had an uncomfortable feeling that the mysterious creatures were secretly laughing at him. He may have been quite right in thinking so, for he was an odd-looking personage, with an ungainly figure and long iron-gray hair that touched his stooping shoulders, and a full, soft brown beard which he had worn ever since he was twenty. In fact, he had looked at twenty very much as he looked at sixty, lacking a little of the grayness.

When he reached Bright River there was no sign of any train; he thought he was too early, so he tied his horse in the yard of the small Bright River hotel and went over to the station-house. The long platform was almost deserted; the only living creature in sight being a girl who was sitting on a pile of shingles at the extreme end. Matthew, barely noting that it *was* a girl, sidled past her as quickly as possible without looking at her. Had he looked he could hardly have failed to notice the tense rigidity and expectation of her attitude and expression. She was sitting there waiting for something or somebody and, since sitting and waiting was the only thing to do just then, she sat and waited with all her might and main.

Matthew encountered the station-master locking up the ticket-office preparatory to going home for supper, and asked him if the five-thirty train would soon be long.

"The five-thirty train has been in and gone half an hour ago," answered that brisk official. "But there was a passenger dropped off for you—a little girl. She's sitting out there on the shingles. I asked her to go into the ladies' waiting-room, but she informed me gravely that she preferred to stay outside. 'There was more scope for imagination,' she said. She's a case, I should say."

"I'm not expecting a girl," said Matthew blankly. "It's a boy I've come for. He should be here. Mrs. Alexander Spencer was to bring him over from Nova Scotia for me."

The station-master whistled.

"Guess there's some mistake," he said. "Mrs. Spencer came off the train with that girl and gave her into my charge. Said you and your sister were adopting her from an orphan asylum and that you would be along for her presently. That's all *I* know about it—and I haven't got any more orphans concealed hereabouts."

"I don't understand," said Matthew helplessly, wishing that

Marilla was at hand to cope with the situation.

"Well, you'd better question the girl," said the station-master carelessly. "I dare say she'll be able to explain—she's got a tongue of her own, that's certain. Maybe they were out of boys of the brand you wanted."

He walked jauntily away, being hungry, and the unfortunate Matthew was left to do that which was harder for him than bearding a lion in its den—walk up to a girl—a strange girl—an orphan girl—and demand of her why she wasn't a boy. Matthew groaned in spirit as he turned about and shuffled gently down the platform towards her.

She had been watching him ever since he had passed her and she had her eyes on him now. Matthew was not looking at her and would not have seen what she was really like if he had been, but an ordinary observer would have seen this:

A child of about eleven, garbed in a very short, very tight, very ugly dress of yellowish gray wincey. She wore a faded brown sailor hat and beneath the hat, extending down her back, were two braids of very thick, decidedly red hair. Her face was small, white and thin, also much freckled; her mouth was large and so were her eyes, that looked green in some lights and moods and gray in others.

So far, the ordinary observer; an extraordinary observer might have seen that the chin was very pointed and pronounced; that the bug eyes were full of spirit and vivacity; that the mouth was sweet-lipped and expressive; that the forehead was broad and full; in short, our discerning extraordinary observer might have concluded that no commonplace soul inhabited the body of this stray woman-child of whom shy Matthew Cuthbert was so ludicrously afraid.

Matthew, however, was spared the ordeal of speaking first, for as soon as she concluded that he was coming to her she stood up, grasping with one thin brown hand the handle of a shabby, old-fashioned carpet-bag; the other she held out to him.

"I suppose you are Mr. Matthew Cuthbert of Green Gables?" she said in a peculiarly clear, sweet voice. "I'm very glad to see you. I was beginning to be afraid you weren't coming for me and I was imagining all the things that might have happened to prevent you. I had made up my mind that if you didn't come for me tonight I'd go down the track to that big wild cherry-tree at the bend, and climb up into it to stay all night. I wouldn't be a bit afraid, and it would be lovely to sleep in a wild cherry-tree all white with bloom in the moonshine, don't you think? You could imagine you were dwelling in marble halls, couldn't you? And I was quite sure you would come for me in the morning, if you didn't tonight.''

Matthew had taken the scrawny little hand awkwardly in his; then and there he decided what to do. He could not tell this child with the glowing eyes that there had been a mistake; he would take her home and let Marilla do that. She couldn't be left at Bright River anyhow, no matter what mistake had been made, so all questions and explanations might as well be deferred until he was safely back at Green Gables.

''I'm sorry I was late,'' he said shyly. ''Come along. The horse is over in the yard. Give me your bag.''

''Oh, I can carry it,'' the child responded cheerfully. ''It isn't heavy. I've got all my worldly goods in it, but it isn't heavy. And if it isn't carried in just a certain way the handle pulls out—so I'd better keep it because I know the exact knack of it. It's an extremely old carpet-bag. Oh, I'm very glad you've come, even if it would have been nice to sleep in a wild cherry-tree. We've got to drive a long piece, haven't we? Mrs. Spencer said it was eight miles. I'm glad because I love driving. Oh, it seems so wonderful that I'm going to live with you and belong to you. I've never belonged to anybody— not really. But the asylum was the worst. I've only been in it four months, but that was enough. I don't suppose you ever were an orphan in an asylum, so you can't possibly understand what it is like. It's worse than anything you could imagine. Mrs. Spencer said it was wicked of me to talk like that, but I didn't mean to be wicked. It's so easy to be wicked without knowing it, isn't it? They were good, you know—the asylum people. But there is so little scope for the imagination in an asylum—only just in the other orphans. It *was* pretty interesting to imagine things about them—to imagine that perhaps the girl who sat next to you was really the daughter of a belted earl, who had been stolen away from her parents in her infancy by a cruel nurse who died before she could confess. I used to lie awake at nights and imagine things like that, because I didn't have time in the day. I guess that's why I'm so thin—I *am* dreadful thin, ain't I? There isn't a pick on my bones. I do love to imagine I'm nice and plump, with dimples in my elbows.''

With this Matthew's companion stopped talking, partly because she was out of breath and partly because they had reached the buggy. Not another word did she say until they had left the village and were driving down a steep little hill, the road part of which had been cut so deeply into the soft soil that the banks, fringed with blooming wild cherry trees and slim white birches, were several feet above their heads.

The child put out her hand and broke off a branch of wild plum that brushed against the side of the buggy.

"Isn't that beautiful? What did that tree, leaning out from the bank, all white and lacy, make you think of?" she asked.

"Well now, I dunno," said Matthew.

"Why, a bride, of course—a bride all in white with a lovely misty veil. I've never seen one, but I can imagine what she would look like. I don't ever expect to be a bride myself. I'm so homely nobody will ever want to marry me—unless it might be a foreign missionary. I suppose a foreign missionary mightn't be very particular. But I do hope that some day I shall have a white dress. That is my highest ideal of earthly bliss. I just love pretty clothes. And I've never had a pretty dress in my life that I can remember—but of course it's all the more to look forward to, isn't it? And then I can imagine that I'm dressed gorgeously. This morning when I left the asylum I felt so ashamed because I had to wear this horrid old wincey dress. All the orphans had to wear them, you know. A merchant in Hopetown last winter donated three hundred yards of wincey to the asylum. Some people said it was because he couldn't sell it, but I'd rather believe that it was out of the kindness of his heart, wouldn't you? When we got on the train I felt as if everybody must be looking at me and pitying me. But I just went to work and imagined that I had on the most beautiful pale blue silk dress—because when you *are* imagining you might as well imagine something worth while—and a big hat all flowers and nodding plumes, and a gold watch, and kid gloves and boots. I felt cheered up right away and I enjoyed my trip to the Island with all my might. I wasn't a bit sick coming over in the boat. Neither was Mrs. Spencer, although she generally is. She said she hadn't time to get sick, watching to see that I didn't fall overboard. She said she never saw the beat of me for prowling about. But if it kept her from being seasick it's a mercy I did prowl, isn't it? And I wanted to see everything that was to be seen on that boat, because I didn't know whether I'd ever have another opportunity. Oh, there are a lot more cherry-trees all in bloom! This Island is the bloomiest place. I just love it already, and I'm so glad I'm going to live here. I've always heard that Prince Edward Island was the prettiest place in the world, and I used to imagine I was living here, but I never really expected I would. It's delightful when your imaginations come true, isn't it? But those red roads are so funny. When we got into the train at Charlottetown and the red roads began to flash past I asked Mrs. Spencer what made them red and she said she didn't know and for pity's sake not to ask her any more questions. She said I must have asked her a thousand already. I suppose I had, too, but how are you going to find out about things if you don't ask questions? And what *does* make the roads red?''

"Well now, I dunno," said Matthew.

"Well, that is one of the things to find out sometime. Isn't it splendid to think of all the things there are to find out about? It just makes me feel good to be alive—it's such an interesting world. It wouldn't be half so interesting if we knew all about everything, would it? There'd be no scope for imagination then, would there? But am I talking too much? People are always telling me I do. Would you rather I didn't talk? If you say so I'll stop. I *can* stop when I make up my mind to it, although it's difficult."

Matthew, much to his own surprise, was enjoying himself. Like most quiet folks he liked talkative people when they were willing to do the talking themselves and did not expect him to keep up his end of it. But he had never expected to enjoy the society of a little girl. Women were bad enough in all conscience, but little girls were worse. He detested the way they had of sidling past him timidly, with sidewise glances, as if they expected him to gobble them up at a mouthful if they ventured to say a word. This was the Avonlea type of well-bred little girl. But this freckled witch was very different, and although he found it rather difficult for his slower intelligence to keep up with her brisk mental processes he thought that he ''kind of liked her chatter.'' So he said as shyly as usual:

"Oh, you can talk as much as you like. I don't mind."

"Oh, I'm so glad. I know you and I are going to get along together fine. It's such a relief to talk when one wants to and not be told that children should be seen and not heard. I've had that said to me a million times if I have once. And people laugh at me because I use big words. But if you have big ideas you have to use big words to express them, haven't you?"

"Well now, that seems reasonable," said Matthew.

"Mrs. Spencer said that my tongue must be hung in the middle. But it isn't—it's firmly fastened at one end. Mrs. Spencer said your place was named Green Gables. I asked her all about it. And she said there were trees all around it. I was gladder than ever. I just love trees. And there weren't any at all about the asylum, only a few poor weeny-teeny things out in front with little whitewashed cagey things about them. They just looked like orphans themselves, those trees did. It used to make me want to cry to look at them. I used to say to them, 'Oh, you *poor* little things! If you were out in a great big woods with other trees all around you and little mosses and Junebells growing over your roots and a brook not far away and birds singing in your branches, you could grow, couldn't you? But you can't where you are. I know just exactly how you feel, little trees.' I felt sorry to leave them behind this morning. You do get so attached to things like that, don't you? Is there a brook anywhere near Green Gables? I forgot to ask Mrs. Spencer that.''

''Well now, yes, there's one right below the house.''

''Fancy! It's always been one of my dreams to live near a brook. I never expected I would, though. Dreams don't often come true, do they? Wouldn't it be nice if they did? But just now I feel pretty nearly perfectly happy. I can't feel exactly perfectly happy because—well, what color would you call this?''

She twitched one of her long glossy braids over her thin shoulder and held it up before Matthew's eyes. Matthew was not used to deciding on the tints of ladies' tresses but in this case there couldn't be much doubt.

''It's red, ain't it?'' he said.

The girl let the braid drop back with a sigh that seemed to come from her very toes and to exhale forth all the sorrows of the ages.

''Yes, it's red,'' she said resignedly. ''Now you see why I can't be perfectly happy. Nobody could who had red hair. I don't mind the other things so much—the freckles and the green eyes and my skinniness. I can imagine them away. I can imagine that I have a beautiful rose-leaf complexion and lovely starry violet eyes. But I *cannot* imagine that red hair away. I do my best. I think to myself, 'Now my hair is a glorious black, black as the raven's wing.' But all the time I *know* it is just plain red, and it breaks my heart. It will be my lifelong sorrow. I read of a girl once in a novel who had a lifelong sorrow, but it wasn't red hair. Her hair was pure gold rippling back from her alabaster brow. What is an alabaster brow? I never could find out. Can you tell me?''

''Well now, I'm afraid I can't,'' said Matthew, who was getting a little dizzy. He felt as he had once felt in his rash youth when another boy had enticed him on the merry-go-round at a picnic.

''Well, whatever it was it must have been something nice because she was divinely beautiful. Have you ever imagined what it must feel like to be divinely beautiful?''

''Well now, no, I haven't,'' confessed Matthew ingenuously.

''I have, often. Which would you rather be if you had the choice—divinely beautiful or dazzlingly clever or angelically good?''

"Well now, I—I don't know exactly."

"Neither do I. I can never decide. But it doesn't make much real difference for it isn't likely I'll ever be either. It's certain I'll never be angelically good. Mrs. Spencer says—oh, Mr. Cuthbert! Oh, Mr. Cuthbert!! Oh, Mr. Cuthbert!!!"

That was not what Mrs. Spencer had said; neither had the child tumbled out of the buggy nor had Matthew done anything astonishing. They had simply rounded a curve in the road and found themselves in the "Avenue."

The "Avenue," so called by the Newbridge people, was a stretch of road four or five hundred yards long, completely arched over with huge, wide-spreading apple-trees, planted years ago by an eccentric old farmer. Overhead was one long canopy of snowy fragrant bloom. Below the boughs the air was full of a purple twilight and far ahead a glimpse of painted sunset sky shone like a great rose window at the end of a cathedral aisle.

Its beauty seemed to strike the child dumb. She leaned back in the buggy, her thin hands clasped before her, her face lifted rapturously to the white splendor above. Even when they had passed out and were driving down the long slope to Newbridge she never moved or spoke. Still with rapt face she gazed afar into the sunset west, with eyes that saw visions trooping splendidly across that glowing background. Through Newbridge, a bustling little village where dogs barked at them and small boys hooted and curious faces peered from the windows, they drove, still in silence. When three more miles had dropped away behind them the child had not spoken. She could keep silence, it was evident, as energetically as she could talk.

"I guess you're feeling pretty tired and hungry," Matthew ventured at last, accounting for her long visitation of dumbness with the only reason he could think of. "But we haven't very far to go now—only another mile."

She came out of her reverie with a deep sigh and looked at him with the dreamy gaze of a soul that had been wandering afar, star-led.

"Oh, Mr. Cuthbert," she whispered, "that place we came through—that white place—what was it?"

"Well now, you must mean the Avenue," said Matthew after a few moments' profound reflection. "It is a kind of pretty place."

"Pretty? Oh, *pretty* doesn't seem the right word to use. Nor beautiful, either. They don't go far enough. Oh, it was wonderful—wonderful. It's the first thing I ever saw that couldn't be improved upon by imagination. It just satisfied me here''—she put one hand on her breast—''it made a queer funny ache and yet it was a pleasant ache. Did you ever have an ache like that Mr. Cuthbert?''

''Well now, I just can't recollect that I ever had.''

''I have it lots of times—whenever I see anything royally beautiful. But they shouldn't call that lovely place the Avenue. There is no meaning in a name like that. They should call it—let me see—the White Way of Delight. Isn't that a nice imaginative name? When I don't like the name of a place or a person I always imagine a new one and always think of them so. There was a girl at the asylum whose name was Hepzibah Jenkins, but I always imagined her as Rosalie DeVere. Other people may call that place the Avenue, but I shall always call it the White Way of Delight. Have we really only another mile to go before we get home? I'm glad and I'm sorry. I'm sorry because this drive has been so pleasant and I'm always sorry when pleasant things end. Something still pleasanter may come after, but you can never be sure. And it's so often the case that it isn't pleasanter. That has been my experience anyhow. But I'm glad to think of getting home. You see, I've never had a real home since I can remember. It gives me that pleasant ache again just to think of coming to a really truly home. Oh, isn't that pretty!''

They had driven over the crest of a hill. Below them was a pond, looking almost like a river so long and winding was it. A bridge spanned it midway and from there to its lower end, where an amber-hued belt of sand hills shut it in from the dark blue gulf beyond, the water was a glory of many shifting hues—the most spiritual shadings of crocus and rose and ethereal green, with other elusive tintings for which no name has ever been found. Above the bridge the pond ran up into fringing groves of fir and maple and lay all darkly translucent in their wavering shadows. Here and there a wild plum leaned out from the bank like a white-clad girl tiptoeing to her own reflection. From the marsh at the head of the pond came the clear, mournfully-sweet chorus of the frogs. There was a little gray house peering around a white apple orchard on a slope beyond and, although it was not yet quite dark, a light was shining from one of its windows.

''That's Barry's pond,'' said Matthew.

''Oh, I don't like that name, either. I shall call it—let me see—the Lake of Shining Waters. Yes, that is the right name for it. I know because of the thrill. When I hit on a name that suits exactly it gives me a thrill. Do things ever give you a thrill?''

Matthew ruminated.

"Well now, yes. It always kind of gives me a thrill to see them ugly white grubs that spade up in the cucumber beds. I hate the look of them."

"Oh, I don't think that can be exactly the same kind of a thrill. Do you think it can? There doesn't seem to be much connection between grubs and lakes of shining waters, does there? But why do other people call it Barry's pond?"

"I reckon because Mr. Barry lives up there in that house. Orchard Slope's the name of his place. If it wasn't for that big bush behind it you could see Green Gables from here. But we have to go over the bridge and round by the road, so it's near half a mile further."

"Has Mr. Barry any little girls? Well, not so very little either—about my size.

"He's got one about eleven. Her name is Diana."

"Oh!" with a long indrawing of breath. "What a perfectly lovely name!"

"Well now, I dunno. There's something dreadful heathenish about it, seems to me. I'd ruther Jane or Mary or some sensible name like that. But when Diana was born there was a schoolmaster boarding there and they gave him the naming of her and he called her Diana"

"I wish there had been a schoolmaster like that around when *I* was born, then. Oh, here we are at the bridge. I'm going to shut my eyes tight. I'm always afraid going over bridges. I can't help imagining that perhaps, just as we get to the middle, they'll crumple up like a jack-knife and nip us. So I shut my eyes. But I always have to open them for all when I think we're getting near the middle. Because, you see, if the bridge *did* crumple up I'd want to *see* it crumple. What a jolly rumble it makes! I always like the rumble part of it. Isn't it splendid there are so many things to like in this world? There, we're over. Now I'll look back. Good night, dear Lake of Shining Waters. I always say good night to the things I love, just as I would to people. I think they like it. That water looks as if it was smiling at me."

When they had driven up the further hill and around a corner Matthew said:

"We're pretty near home now. That's Green Gables over—"

"Oh, don't tell me," she interrupted breathlessly, clutching at his partially raised arm and shutting her eyes that she might not see his gesture. "Let me guess. I'm sure I'll guess right."

She opened her eyes and looked about her. They were on the crest of a hill. The sun had set some time since, but the landscape was still clear in the mellow afterlight. To the west a dark church spire rose up against a marigold sky. Below was a little valley and beyond a long, gently-rising slope with snug farmsteads scattered along it. From one to another the child's eyes darted, eager and wistful. At last they lingered on one away to the left, far back from the road, dimly white with blossoming trees in the twilight of the surrounding woods. Over it, in the stainless southwest sky, a great crystal-white star was shining like a lamp of guidance and promise.

"That's it, isn't it?" she said, pointing.

Matthew slapped the reins on the sorrel's back delightedly.

"Well now, you've guessed it! But I reckon Mrs. Spencer described it so's you could tell."

"No, she didn't—really she didn't. All she said might just as well have been about most of those other places. I hadn't any real idea what it looked like. But just as soon as I saw it I felt it was home. Oh, it seems as if I must be in a dream. Do you know, my arm must be black and blue from the elbow up, for I've pinched myself so many times today. Every little while a horrible sickening feeling would come over me and I'd be so afraid it was all a dream. Then I'd pinch myself to see if it was real—until suddenly I remembered that even supposing it was only a dream I'd better go on dreaming as long as I could; so I stopped pinching. But it *is* real and we're nearly home."

With a sigh of rapture she relapsed into silence. Matthew stirred uneasily. He felt glad that it would be Marilla and not he who would have to tell this waif of the world that the home she longed for was not to be hers after all. They drove over Lynde's Hollow, where it was already quite dark, but not so dark that Mrs. Rachel could not see them from her window vantage, and up the hill and into the long lane of Green Gables. By the time they arrived at the house Matthew was shrinking from the approaching revelation with an energy he did not understand. It was not of Marilla or himself he was thinking or of the trouble this mistake was probably going to make for them, but of the child's disappointment. When he thought of that rapt light being quenched in her eyes he had an uncomfortable feeling that he was going to assist at murdering something—much the same feeling that came over him when he had to kill a lamb or calf or any other innocent little creature.

The yard was quite dark as they turned into it and the poplar leaves were rustling silkily all round it.

"Listen to the trees talking in their sleep," she whispered, as he lifted her to the ground. "What nice dreams they must have!"

Then, holding tightly to the carpetbag which contained "all her worldly goods," she followed him into the house.

CHAPTER 3

MARILLA CUTHBERT IS SURPRISED

MARILLA CAME briskly forward as Matthew opened the door. But when her eyes fell on the odd little figure in the stiff, ugly dress, with the long braids of red hair and the eager, luminous eyes, she stopped short in amazement.

"Matthew Cuthbert, who's that?" she ejaculated. "Where is the boy?"

"There wasn't any boy," said Matthew wretchedly. "There was only *her*."

He nodded at the child, remembering that he had never even asked her name.

"No boy! But there *must* have been a boy," insisted Marilla. "We sent word to Mrs. Spencer to bring a boy."

"Well, she didn't. She brought *her*. I asked the station-master. And I had to bring her home. She couldn't be left there, no matter where the mistake had come in."

" Well, this is a pretty piece of business!" ejaculated Marilla.

During this dialogue the child had remained silent, her eyes roving from one to the other, all the animation fading out of her face. Suddenly she seemed to grasp the full meaning of what had been said. Dropping her precious carpetbag she sprang forward a step and clasped her hands.

"You don't want me!" she cried. "You don't want me because I'm not a boy! I might have known it was all too beautiful to last. I might have known nobody really did want me. Oh, what shall I do? I'm going to burst into tears!"

Burst into tears she did. Sitting down on a chair by the table, flinging her arms out upon it, and burying her face in them, she proceeded to cry stormily. Marilla and Matthew looked at each other deprecatingly across the stove. Neither of them knew what to say or do. Finally Marilla stepped lamely into the breach.

"Well, well, there's no need to cry so about it."

"Yes, there *is* need!" The child raised her head quickly, revealing a tear-stained face and trembling lips. "*You* would cry, too, if you were an orphan and had come to a place you thought was going to be home and found that they didn't want you because you weren't a boy. Oh, this is the most *tragical* thing that ever happened to me!"

Something like a reluctant smile, rather rusty from long disuse, mellowed Marilla's grim expression.

"Well, don't cry any more. We're not going to turn you out-of-doors tonight. You'll have to stay here until we investigate this affair. What's your name?"

The child hesitated for a moment.

"Will you please call me Cordelia?" she said eagerly.

"*Call* you Cordelia! Is that your name?"

"No-o-o, it's not exactly my name, but I would love to be called Cordelia. It's such a perfectly elegant name."

"I don't know what on earth you mean. If Cordelia isn't your name, what is?"

"Anne Shirley," reluctantly faltered forth the owner of that name, "but oh, please do call me Cordelia. It can't matter much to you what you call me if I'm only going to be here a little while, can it? And Anne is such an unromantic name."

"Unromantic fiddlesticks!" said the unsympathetic Marilla. "Anne is a real good plain sensible name. You've no need to be ashamed of it."

"Oh, I'm not ashamed of it," explained Anne, "only I like Cordelia better. I've always imagined that my name was Cordelia— at least, I always have of late years. When I was young I used to imagine it was Geraldine, but I like Cordelia better now. But if you call me Anne please call me Anne spelled with an *e*."

"What difference does it make how it's spelled?" asked Marilla with another rusty smile as she picked up the teapot.

"Oh, it makes *such* a difference. It *looks* so much nicer. When you hear a name pronounced can't you always see it in your mind, just as if it was printed out? I can; and A-n-n looks dreadful, but A-n-n-e looks so much more distinguished. If you'll only call me Anne spelled with an *e* I shall try to reconcile myself to not being called Cordelia."

"Very well, then, Anne spelled with an *e*, can you tell us how this mistake came to be made? We sent word to Mrs. Spencer to bring us a boy. Were there no boys at the asylum?''

''Oh, yes, there was an abundance of them. But Mrs. Spencer said *distinctly* that you wanted a girl about eleven years old. And the matron said she thought I would do. You don't know how delighted I was. I couldn't sleep all last night for joy. Oh,'' she added reproachfully, turning to Matthew, ''why didn't you tell me at the station that you didn't want me and leave me there? If I hadn't seen the White Way of Delight and the Lake of Shining Waters it wouldn't be so hard.''

''What on earth does she mean?'' demanded Marilla, staring at Matthew.

''She—she's just referring to some conversation we had on the road,'' said Matthew hastily. ''I'm going out to put the mare in, Marilla. Have tea ready when I come back.''

''Did Mrs. Spencer bring anybody over besides you?'' continued Marilla when Matthew had gone out.

''She brought Lily Jones for herself. Lily is only five years old and she is very beautiful. She has nut-brown hair. If I was very beautiful and had nut-brown hair would you keep me?''

''No. We want a boy to help Matthew on the farm. A girl would be of no use to us. Take off your hat. I'll lay it and your bag on the hall table.''

Anne took off her hat meekly. Matthew came back presently and they sat down to supper. But Anne could not eat. In vain she nibbled at the bread and butter and pecked at the crab-apple preserve out of the little scalloped glass dish by her plate. She did not really make any headway at all.

''You're not eating anything,'' said Marilla sharply, eyeing her as if it were a serious shortcoming.

Anne sighed.

''I can't. I'm in the depths of despair. Can you eat when you are in the depths of despair?''

''I've never been in the depths of despair, so I can't say,'' responded Marilla.

''Weren't you? Well, did you ever try to *imagine* you were in the depths of despair?''

''No, I didn't.''

''Then I don't think you can understand what it's like. It's a very uncomfortable feeling indeed. When you try to eat a lump comes right up in your throat and you can't swallow anything, not even if it was a chocolate caramel. I had one chocolate caramel once two years ago and it was simply delicious. I've often dreamed since then that I had a lot of chocolate caramels, but I always wake up just when I'm going to eat them. I do hope you won't be offended because I can't eat. Everything is extremely nice , but still I cannot eat.''

"I guess she's tired,'' said Matthew, who hadn't spoken since his return from the barn. "Best put her to bed, Marilla.''

Marilla had been wondering where Anne should be put to bed. She had prepared a couch in the kitchen chamber for the desired and expected boy. But, although it was neat and clean, it did not seem quite the thing to put a girl there somehow. But the spare room was out of the question for such a stray waif, so there remained only the east gable room. Marilla lighted a candle and told Anne to follow her, which Anne spiritlessly did, taking her hat and carpetbag from the hall table as she passed. The hall was fearsomely clean; the little gable chamber in which she presently found herself seemed still cleaner.

Marilla set the candle on a three-legged, three-cornered table and turned down the bedclothes.

"I supose you have a nightgown?'' she questioned.

Anne nodded.

"Yes, I have two. The matron of the asylum made them for me. They're fearfully skimpy. There is never enough to go around in an asylum, so things are always skimpy—at least in a poor asylum like ours. I hate skimpy night-dresses. But one can dream just as well in them as in lovely trailing ones, with frills around the neck, that's one consolation.''

"Well, undress as quick as you can and go to bed. I'll come back in a few minutes for the candle. I daren't trust you to put it out yourself. You'd likely set the place on fire.''

"When Marilla had gone Anne looked around her wistfully. The whitewashed walls were so painfully bare and staring that she thought they must ache over their own bareness. The floor was bare, too, except for a round braided mat in the middle such as Anne had never seen before. In one corner was the bed, a high, old-fashioned one, with four dark, low-turned posts. In the other corner was the aforesaid three-cornered table adorned with a fat, red velvet pincushion hard enough to turn the point of the most adventurous pin. Above it hung a little six-by-eight mirror. Midway between table and bed was the window, with an icy white muslin frill over it, and opposite it was the washstand. The whole apartment was of a rigidity not to be described in words, but which sent a shiver to the very marrow of Anne's bones. With a sob she hastily discarded her garments, put on the skimpy nightgown and sprang into bed where she burrowed face downward into the pillow and pulled the clothes over her head. When Marilla came up for the light various skimpy articles of raiment scattered most untidily over the floor and a certain tempestuous appearance of the bed were the only indications of any presence save her own.

She deliberately picked up Anne's clothes, placed them neatly on a prim yellow chair, and then, taking up the candle, went over to the bed.

"Good night," she said, a little awkwardly, but not unkindly.

Anne's white face and big eyes appeared over the bedclothes with a startling suddenness.

"How can you call it a *good* night when you know it must be the very worst night I've ever had?" she said reproachfully.

Then she dived down into invisibility again.

Marilla went slowly down to the kitchen and proceeded to wash the supper dishes. Matthew was smoking—a sure sign of perturbation of mind. He seldom smoked, for Marilla set her face against it as a filthy habit; but at certain times and seasons he felt driven to it and then Marilla winked at the practice, realizing that a mere man must have some vent for his emotions.

"Well, this is a pretty kettle of fish," she said wrathfully. "This is what comes of sending word instead of going ourselves. Robert Spencer's folks have twisted that message somehow. One of us will have to drive over and see Mrs. Spencer tomorrow, that's certain. This girl will have to be sent back to the asylum."

"Yes, I suppose so," said Matthew reluctantly.

"You *suppose* so! Don't you know it?"

"Well now, she's a real nice little thing, Marilla. It's kind of a pity to send her back when she's so set on staying here."

"Matthew Cuthbert, you don't mean to say you think we ought to keep her!"

Marilla's astonishment could not have been greater if Matthew had expressed a predilection for standing on his head.

"Well now, no, I suppose not—not exactly," stammered Matthew, uncomfortably driven into a corner for his precise meaning. "I suppose—we could hardly be expected to keep her."

"I should say not. What good would she be to us?"

"We might be some good to her," said Matthew suddenly and unexpectedly.

"Matthew Cuthbert, I believe that child has bewitched you! I can see as plain as plain that you want to keep her."

"Well now, she's a real interesting little thing," persisted Matthew. "You should have heard her talk coming from the station."

"Oh, she can talk fast enough. I saw that at once. It's nothing in her favor, either. I don't like children who have so much to say. I don't want an orphan girl and if I did she isn't the style I'd pick out. There's something I don't understand about her. No, she's got to be despatched straightway back to where she came from."

"I could hire a French boy to help me," said Matthew, "and she'd be company for you."

"I'm not suffering for company," said Marilla shortly. "And I'm not going to keep her."

"Well now, it's just as you say, of course, Marilla," said Matthew rising and putting his pipe away. "I'm going to bed."

To bed went Matthew. And to bed, when she had put her dishes away, went Marilla, frowning most resolutely. And upstairs, in the east gable, a lonely, heart-hungry, friendless child cried herself to sleep.

CHAPTER 4

MORNING AT GREEN GABLES

IT WAS broad daylight when Anne awoke and sat up in bed, staring confusedly at the window through which a flood of cheery sunshine was pouring and outside of which something white and feathery waved across glimpses of blue sky.

For a moment she could not remember where she was. First came a delightful thrill, as of something very pleasant; then a horrible remembrance. This was Green Gables and they didn't want her because she wasn't a boy!

But it was morning and, yes, it was a cherry tree in full bloom outside of her window. With a bound she was out of bed and across the floor. She pushed up the sash—it went up stiffly and creakily, as if it hadn't been opened for a long time, which was the case; and it stuck so tight that nothing was needed to hold it up.

Anne dropped on her knees and gazed out into the June morning, her eyes glistening with delight. Oh, wasn't it beautiful? Wasn't it a lovely place? Suppose she wasn't really going to stay here! She would imagine she was. There was scope for imagination here.

A huge cherry tree grew outside, so close that its bough tapped against the house, and it was so thick-set with blossoms that hardly a leaf was to be seen. On both sides of the house was a big orchard, one of apple trees and one of cherry trees, also showered over with blossoms; and their grass was all sprinkled with dandelions. In the garden below were lilac trees purple with flowers, and their dizzily sweet fragrance drifted up to the window on the morning wind.

Below the garden a green field lush with clover sloped down to the hollow where the brook ran and where scores of white birches grew, upspringing airily out of an undergrowth suggestive of delightful possibilities in ferns and mosses and woodsy things generally. Beyond it was a hill, green and feathery with spruce and fir; there was a gap in it where the gray gable end of the little house she had seen from the other side of the Lake of Shining Waters was visible.

Off to the left were the big barns and beyond them, away down over green, low-sloping fields, was a sparkling blue glimpse of sea.

Anne's beauty-loving eyes lingered on it all, taking everything greedily in; she had looked on so many unlovely places in her life, poor child; but this was as lovely as anything she had ever dreamed.

She knelt there, lost to everything but the loveliness around her, until she was startled by a hand on her shoulder. Marilla had come in unheard by the small dreamer.

"It's time you were dressed," she said curtly.

Marilla really did not know how to talk to the child, and her uncomfortable ignorance made her crisp and curt when she did not mean to be.

Anne stood up and drew a long breath.

"Oh, isn't it wonderful?" she said, waving her hand comprehensively at the good world outside.

"It's a big tree," said Marilla, "and it blooms great, but the fruit don't amount to much never—small and wormy."

"Oh, I don't mean just the tree; of course it's lovely—yes, it's *radiantly* lovely—it blooms as if it meant it—but I meant everything, the garden and the orchard and the brook and the woods, the whole big dear world. Don't you feel as if you just loved the world on a morning like this? And I can hear the brook laughing all the way up here. Have you ever noticed what cheerful things brooks are?

They're always laughing. Even in wintertime I've heard them under the ice. I'm so glad there's a brook near Green Gables. Perhaps you think it doesn't make any difference to me when you're not going to keep me, but it does. I shall always like to remember that there is a brook at Green Gables even if I never see it again. If there wasn't a brook I'd be *haunted* by the uncomfortable feeling that there ought to be one. I'm not in the depths of despair this morning. I never can be in the morning. Isn't it a splendid thing that there are mornings? But I feel very sad. I've just been imagining that it was really me you wanted after all and that I was to stay here for ever and ever. It was a great comfort while it lasted. But the worst of imagining things is that the time comes when you have to stop and that hurts.''

"You'd better get dressed and come downstairs and never mind your imaginings," said Marilla as soon as she could get a word in edgewise. "Breakfast is waiting. Wash your face and comb your hair. Leave the window up and turn your bedclothes back over the foot of the bed. Be as smart as you can."

Anne could evidently be smart to some purpose for she was downstairs in ten minutes' time, with her clothes neatly on, her hair brushed and braided, her face washed, and a comfortable consciousness pervading her soul that she had fulfilled all Marilla's requirements. As a matter of fact, however, she had forgotten to turn back the bedclothes.

"I'm pretty hungry this morning," she announced, as she slipped into the chair Marilla placed for her. "The world doesn't seem such a howling wilderness as it did last night. I'm so glad it's a sunshiny morning. But I like rainy mornings real well, too. All sorts of mornings are interesting, don't you think? You don't know what's going to happen through the day, and there's so much scope for imagination. But I'm glad it's not rainy today because it's easier to be cheerful and bear up under affliction on a sunshiny day. I feel that I have a good deal to bear up under. It's all very well to read about sorrows and imagine yourself living through them heroically, but it's not so nice when you really come to have them, is it?''

"For pity's sake hold your tongue," said Marilla. "You talk entirely too much for a little girl."

Thereupon Anne held her tongue so obediently and thoroughly that her continued silence made Marilla rather nervous, as if in the presence of something not exactly natural. Matthew also held his tongue,—but this at least was natural,—so that the meal was a very silent one.

As it progressed Anne became more and more abstracted, eating mechanically, with her big eyes fixed unswervingly and unseeingly on the sky outside the window. This made Marilla more nervous than ever; she had an uncomfortable feeling that while this odd child's body might be there at the table her spirit was far away in some remote airy cloudland, borne aloft on the wings of imagination. Who would want such a child about the place?

Yet Matthew wished to keep her, of all unaccountable things! Marilla felt that he wanted it just as much this morning as he had the night before, and that he would go on wanting it. That was Matthew's way—take a whim into his head and cling to it with the most amazing silent persistency—a persistency ten times more potent and effectual in its very silence than if he had talked it out.

When the meal was ended Anne came out of her reverie and offered to wash the dishes.

"Can you wash dishes right?" asked Marilla distrustfully.

"Pretty well. I'm better at looking after children, though. I've had so much experience at that. It's such a pity you haven't any here for me to look after."

"I don't feel as if I wanted any more children to look after than I've got at present. *You*'re probably enough in all conscience. What's to be done with you I don't know. Matthew is a most ridiculous man."

"I think he's lovely," said Anne reproachfully. "He is so very sympathetic. He didn't mind how much I talked—he seemed to like it. I felt that he was a kindred spirit as soon as ever I saw him."

"You're both queer enough, if that's what you mean by kindred spirits," said Marilla with a sniff. "Yes, you may wash the dishes. Take plenty of hot water, and be sure you dry them well. I've got enough to attend to this morning for I'll have to drive over to White Sands in the afternoon and see Mrs. Spencer. You'll come with me and we'll settle what's to be done with you. After you've finished the dishes go upstairs and make your bed."

Anne washed the dishes deftly enough, as Marilla, who kept a sharp eye on the process, discerned. Later on she made her bed less successfully, for she had never learned the art of wrestling with a feather tick. But it was done somehow and smoothed down; and then Marilla, to get rid of her, told her she might go out-of-doors and amuse herself until dinnertime.

Anne flew to the door, face alight, eyes glowing. On the very threshold she stopped short, wheeled about, came back and sat down by the table, light and glow as effectually blotted out as if some one had clapped an extinguisher on her.

"What's the matter now?" demanded Marilla.

"I don't dare go out," said Anne, in the tone of a martyr relinquishing all earthly joys. "If I can't stay here there is no use in my loving Green Gables. And if I go out there and get acquainted with all those trees and flowers and the orchard and the brook I'll not be able to help loving it. It's hard enough now, so I won't make it any harder. I want to go out so much—everything seems to be calling to me, 'Anne, Anne, come out to us. Anne, Anne, we want a playmate'— but it's better not. There is no use in loving things if you have to be torn from them, is there? And it's *so* hard to keep from loving things, isn't it? That was why I was so glad when I thought I was going to live here. I thought I'd have so many things to love and nothing to hinder me. But that brief dream is over. I am resigned to my fate now, so I don't think I'll go out for fear I'll get unresigned again. What is the name of that geranium on the window-sill, please?"

"That's the apple-scented geranium."

"Oh, I don't mean that sort of a name. I mean just a name you gave it yourself. Didn't you give it a name? May I give it one then? May I call it—let me see—Bonny would do—may I call it Bonny while I'm here? Oh, do let me!"

"Goodness, I don't care. But where on earth is the sense of naming a geranium?"

"Oh, I like things to have handles even if they are only geraniums. It makes them seem more like people. How do you know but that it hurts a geranium's feelings just to be called a geranium and nothing else? You wouldn't like to be called nothing but a woman all the time. Yes, I shall call it Bonny. I named that cherry tree outside my bedroom window this morning. I called it Snow Queen because it was so white. Of course, it won't always be in blossom, but one can imagine that it is, can't one?"

"I never in all my life saw or heard anything to equal her," muttered Marilla, beating a retreat down cellar after potatoes. "She *is* kind of interesting, as Matthew says. I can feel already that I'm wondering what on earth she'll say next. She'll be casting a spell over me, too. She's cast it over Matthew. That look he gave me when he went out said everything he said or hinted last night over again. I wish he was like other men and would talk things out. A body could answer back then and argue him into reason. But what's to be done with a man who just *looks*?"

Anne had relapsed into reverie, with her chin in her hands and her eyes on the sky, when Marilla returned from her cellar pilgrimage. There Marilla left her until the early dinner was on the table.

"I suppose I can have the mare and buggy this afternoon, Matthew?" said Marilla.

Matthew nodded and looked wistfully at Anne. Marilla intercepted the look and said grimly:

"I'm going to drive over to White Sands and settle this thing. I'll take Anne with me and Mrs. Spencer will probably make arrangments to send her back to Nova Scotia at once. I'll set your tea out for you and I'll be home in time to milk the cows."

Still Matthew said nothing and Marilla had a sense of having wasted words and breath. There is nothing more aggravating than a man who won't talk back—unless it is a woman who won't.

Matthew hitched the sorrel into the buggy in due time and Marilla and Anne set off. Matthew opened the yard gate for them, and as they drove slowly through, he said, to nobody in particular as it seemed:

"Little Jerry Buote from the Creek was here this morning, and I told him I guessed I'd hire him for the summer."

Marilla made no reply, but she hit the unlucky sorrel such a vicious clip with the whip that the fat mare, unused to such treatment, whizzed indignantly down the lane at an alarming pace. Marilla looked back once as the buggy bounced along and saw that aggravating Matthew leaning over the gate, looking wistfully after them.

CHAPTER 5

ANNE'S HISTORY

"DO YOU know," said Anne confidentially, "I've made up my mind to enjoy this drive. It's been my experience that you can nearly always enjoy things if you make up your mind firmly that you will. Of course, you must make it up *firmly*. I am not going to think about going back to the asylum while we're having our drive. I'm just going to think about the drive. Oh, look, there's one little early wild rose out! Isn't it lovely? Don't you think it must be glad to be a rose?

Wouldn't it be nice if roses could talk? I'm sure they could tell us such lovely things. And isn't pink the most bewitching color in the world? I love it, but I can't wear it. Redheaded people can't wear pink, not even in imagination. Did you ever know of anybody whose hair was red when she was young, but got to be another color when she grew up?''

"No, I don't know as I ever did," said Marilla mercilessly, "and I shouldn't think it likely to happen in your case, either."

Anne sighed.

"Well, that is another hope gone. My life is a perfect graveyard of buried hopes. That's a sentence I read in a book once, and I say it over to comfort myself whenever I'm disappointed in anything."

"I don't see where the comforting comes in myself," said Marilla.

"Why, because it sounds so nice and romantic, just as if I were a heroine in a book, you know. I am so fond of romantic things, and a graveyard full of buried hopes is about as romantic a thing as one can imagine, isn't it? I'm rather glad I have one. Are we going across the Lake of Shining Waters today?"

"We're not going over Barry's pond, if that's what you mean by your Lake of Shining Waters. We're going by the shore road."

"Shore road sounds nice," said Anne dreamily. "Is it as nice as it sounds? Just when you said 'shore road' I saw it in a picture in my mind, as quick as that! And White Sands is a pretty name, too; but I don't like it as well as Avonlea. Avonlea is a lovely name. It just sounds like music. How far is it to White Sands?"

"It's five miles; and as you're evidently bent on talking you might as well talk to some purpose by telling me what you know about yourself."

"Oh, what I *know* about myself isn't really worth telling," said Anne eagerly. "If you'll only let me tell you what I *imagine* about myself you'll think it ever so much more interesting."

"No, I don't want any of your imaginings. Just you stick to bald facts. Begin at the beginning. Where were you born and how old are you?"

"I was eleven last March," said Anne, resigning herself to bald facts with a little sigh. "And I was born in Bolingbroke, Nova Scotia. My father's name was Walter Shirley, and he was a teacher in the Bolingbroke High School. My mother's name was Bertha Shirley. Aren't Walter and Bertha lovely names. I'm so glad my parents had nice names. It would be a real disgrace to have a father named— well, say Jedediah, wouldn't it?''

"I guess it doesn't matter what a person's name is as long as he behaves himself," said Marilla, feeling herself called upon to inculcate a good and useful moral.

"Well, I don't know." Anne looked thoughtful. "I read in a book once that a rose by any other name would smell as sweet, but I've never been able to believe it. I don't believe a rose *would* be as nice if it was called a thistle or a skunk cabbage. I suppose my father could have been a good man even if he had been called Jedediah; but I'm sure it would have been a cross. Well, my mother was a teacher in the High School, too, but when she married father she gave up teaching, of course. A husband was enough responsibility. Mrs. Thomas said that they were a pair of babies and as poor as church mice. They went to live in a weeny-teeny little yellow house in Bolingbroke. I've never seen that house, but I've imagined it thousands of times. I think it must have had honeysuckle over the parlor window and lilacs in the front yard and lilies of the valley just inside the gate. Yes, and muslin curtains in all the windows. Muslin curtains give a house such an air. I was born in that house. Mrs. Thomas said I was the homeliest baby she ever saw, I was so scrawny and tiny and nothing but eyes, but that mother thought I was perfectly beautiful. I should think a mother would be a better judge than a poor woman who came in to scrub, wouldn't you? I'm glad she was satisfied with me anyhow; I would feel so sad if I thought I was a disappointment to her—because she didn't live very long after that, you see. She died of fever when I was just three months old. I do wish she'd lived long enough for me to remember calling her mother. I think it would be so sweet to say 'mother,' don't you? And father died four days afterwards from fever, too. That left me an orphan and folks were at their wits' end, so Mrs. Thomas said, what to do with me. You see, nobody wanted me even then. It seems to be my fate. Father and mother had both come from places far away and it was well known they hadn't any relatives living. Finally Mrs. Thomas said she'd take me, though she was poor and had a drunken husband. She brought me up by hand. Do you know if there is anything in being brought up by hand that ought to make people who are brought up that way better than other people? Because whenever I was naughty Mrs. Thomas would ask me how I could be such a bad girl when she had brought me up by hand—reproachful-like.

"Mr. and Mrs. Thomas moved away from Bolingbroke to Marysville, and I lived with them until I was eight years old. I helped look after the Thomas children—there were four of them younger than me—and I can tell you they took a lot of looking after. Then Mr. Thomas was killed falling under a train and his mother offered to take Mrs. Thomas and the children, but she didn't want me. Mrs. Thomas was at *her* wits' end, so she said, what to do with me. Then Mrs. Hammond from up the river came down and said she'd take me, seeing I was handy with children, and I went up the river to live with her in a little clearing among the stumps. It was a very lonesome place. I'm sure I could never have lived there if I hadn't had an imagination. Mr. Hammond worked a little saw-mill up there, and Mrs. Hammond had eight children. She had twins three times. I like babies in moderation, but twins three times in succession is *too much*. I told Mrs. Hammond so firmly, when the last pair came. I used to get so dreadfully tired carrying them about.

"I lived up river with Mrs. Hammond over two years, and then Mr. Hammond died and Mrs. Hammond broke up housekeeping. She divided her children among her relatives and went to the States. I had to go to the asylum at Hopeton, because nobody would take me. They didn't want me at the asylum, either; they said they were overcrowded as it was. But they had to take me and I was there four months until Mrs. Spencer came."

Anne finished up with another sigh, of relief this time. Evidently she did not like talking about her experiences in a world that had not wanted her.

"Did you ever go to school?" demanded Marilla, turning the sorrel mare down the shore road.

"Not a great deal. I went a little the last year I stayed with Mrs. Thomas. When I went up river we were so far from a school that I couldn't walk it in winter and there was vacation in summer, so I could only go in the spring and fall. But of course I went while I was at the asylum. I can read pretty well and I know ever so many pieces of poetry off by heart—'The Battle of Hohenlinden' and 'Edinburgh after Flodden,' and 'Bingen on the Rhine,' and lots of the 'Lady of the Lake' and most of 'The Seasons,' by James Thompson. Don't you just love poetry that gives you a crinkly feeling up and down your back? There is a piece in the Fifth Reader—'The Downfall of Poland'—that is just full of thrills. Of course, I wasn't in the Fifth Reader—I was only in the Fourth—but the big girls used to lend me theirs to read."

"Were those women—Mrs. Thomas and Mrs. Hammond—good to you?" asked Marilla, looking at Anne out of the corner of her eye.

"O-o-o-h," faltered Anne. Her sensitive little face suddenly flushed scarlet and embarrassment sat on her brow. "Oh, they *meant* to be—I know they meant to be just as good and kind as possible. And when people mean to be good to you, you don't mind very much when they're not quite—always. They had a good deal to worry them, you know. It's very trying to have a drunken husband, you see; and it must be very trying to have twins three times in succession, don't you think? But I feel sure they meant to be good to me."

Marilla asked no more questions. Anne gave herself up to a silent rapture over the shore road and Marilla guided the sorrel abstractedly while she pondered deeply. Pity was suddenly stirring in her heart for the child. What a starved, unloved life she had had—a life of drudgery and poverty and neglect; for Marilla was shrewd enough to read between the lines of Anne's history and divine the truth. No wonder she had been so delighted at the prospect of a real home. It was a pity she had to be sent back. What if she, Marilla, should indulge Matthew's unaccountable whim and let her stay? He was set on it; and the child seemed a nice, teachable little thing.

"She's got too much to say," thought Marilla, "but she might be trained out of that. And there's nothing rude or slangy in what she does say. She's ladylike. It's likely her people were nice folks."

The shore road was "woodsy and wild and lonesome." On the right hand, scrub firs, their spirits quite unbroken by long years of tussle with the gulf winds, grew thickly. On the left were the steep red sandstone cliffs, so near the track in places that a mare of less steadiness than the sorrel might have tried the nerves of the people behind her. Down at the base of the cliffs were heaps of surf-worn rocks or little sandy coves inlaid with pebbles as with ocean jewels; beyond lay the sea, shimmering and blue, and over it soared the gulls, their pinions flashing silvery in the sunlight.

"Isn't the sea wonderful?" said Anne, rousing from a long, wide-eyed silence. "Once, when I lived in Marysville, Mr. Thomas hired an express-wagon and took us all to spend the day at the shore ten miles away. I enjoyed every moment of that day, even if I had to look after the children all the time. I lived it over in happy dreams for years. But this shore is nicer than the Marysville shore. Aren't those gulls splendid? Would you like to be a gull? I think I would—that is, if I couldn't be a human girl. Don't you think it would be nice to wake up at sunrise and swoop down over the water and away out over that lovely blue all day; and then at night to fly back to one's nest? Oh, I can just imagine myself doing it. What big house is that just ahead, please?"

"That's the White Sands Hotel. Mr. Kirke runs it, but the season hasn't begun yet. There are heaps of Americans come there for the summer. They think this shore is just about right."

"I was afraid it might be Mrs. Spencer's place," said Anne mournfully. "I don't want to get there. Somehow, it will seem like the end of everything."

CHAPTER 6

MARILLA MAKES UP HER MIND

GET THERE they did, however, in due season. Mrs. Spencer lived in a big yellow house at White Sands Cove, and she came to the door with surprise and welcome mingled on her benevolent face.

"Dear, dear," she exclaimed, "you're the last folks I was looking for today, but I'm glad to see you. You'll put your horse in? And how are you, Anne?"

"I'm as well as can be expected, thank you," said Anne smilelessly. A blight seemed to have descended on her.

"I suppose we'll stay a little while to rest the mare," said Marilla, "but I promised Matthew I'd be home early. The fact is, Mrs. Spencer, there's been a queer mistake somewhere, and I've come over to see where it is. We sent word, Matthew and I, for you to bring us a boy from the asylum. We told your brother Robert to tell you we wanted a boy ten or eleven years old."

"Marilla Cuthbert, you don't say so!" said Mrs. Spencer in distress. "Why, Robert sent the word down by his daughter Nancy and said you wanted a girl—didn't she, Flora Jane?" appealing to her daughter who had come out to the steps.

"She certainly did, Miss Cuthbert," corroborated Flora Jane earnestly.

"I'm dreadful sorry," said Mrs. Spencer. "It is too bad; but it certainly wasn't my fault, you see, Miss Cuthbert. I did the best I could and I thought I was following your instructions. Nancy is a terrible flighty thing. I've often had to scold her well for her heedlessness."

hope; her eyes grew deep and bright as morning stars. The child was quite transfigured; and, a moment later, when Mrs. Spencer and Mrs. Blewett went out in quest of a recipe the latter had come to borrow, she sprang up and flew across the room to Marilla.

"Oh, Miss Cuthbert, did you really say that perhaps you would let me stay at Green Gables?" she said, in a breathless whisper, as if speaking aloud might shatter the glorious possibility. "Did you really say it? Or did I only imagine that you did?"

"I think you'd better learn to control that imagination of yours, Anne, if you can't distinguish between what is real and what isn't," said Marilla crossly. "Yes, you did hear me say just that and no more. It isn't decided yet and perhaps we will conclude to let Mrs. Blewett take you after all. She certainly needs you much more than I do."

"I'd rather go back to the asylum than go to live with her," said Anne passionately. "She looks exactly like a—like a gimlet."

Marilla smothered a smile under the conviction that Anne must be reproved for such a speech.

"A little girl like you should be ashamed of talking so about a lady and a stranger," she said severely. "Go back and sit down quietly and hold your tongue and behave as a good girl should."

"I'll try to do and be anything you want me, if you'll only keep me," said Anne, returning meekly to her ottoman.

When they arrived back at Green Gables that evening Matthew met them in the lane. Marilla from afar had noted him prowling along it and guessed his motive. She was prepared for the relief she read in his face when he saw that she had at least brought Anne back with her. But she said nothing to him, relative to the affair, until they were both out in the yard behind the barn milking the cows. Then she briefly told him Anne's history and the result of the interview with Mrs. Spencer.

"I wouldn't give a dog I liked to that Blewett woman," said Matthew with unusual vim.

"I don't fancy her style myself," admitted Marilla, "but it's that or keeping her ourselves, Matthew. And, since you seem to want her, I suppose I'm willing—or have to be. I've been thinking over the idea until I've got kind of used to it. It seems a sort of duty. I've never brought up a child, especially a girl, and I dare say I'll make a terrible mess of it. But I'll do my best. So far as I'm concerned, Matthew, she may stay."

Matthew's shy face was a glow of delight.

"Well now, I reckoned you'd come to see it in that light, Marilla," he said. "She's such an interesting little thing."

"It'd be more to the point if you could say she was a useful little thing," retorted Marilla, "but I'll make it my business to see she's trained to be that. And mind, Matthew, you're not to go interfering with my methods. Perhaps an old maid doesn't know much about bringing up a child, but I guess she knows more than an old bachelor. So you just leave me to manage her. When I fail it'll be time enough to put your oar in."

"There, there, Marilla, you can have your own way," said Matthew reassuringly. "Only be as good and kind to her as you can without spoiling her. I kind of think she's one of the sort you can do anything with if you only get her to love you."

Marilla sniffed, to express her contempt for Matthew's opinions concerning anything feminine, and walked off to the dairy with the pails.

"I won't tell her tonight that she can stay," she reflected, as she strained the milk into the creamers. "She'd be so excited that she wouldn't sleep a wink. Marilla Cuthbert, you're fairly in for it. Did you ever suppose you'd see the day when you'd be adopting an orphan girl? It's surprising enough; but not so surprising as that Matthew should be at the bottom of it, him that always seemed to have such a mortal dread of little girls. Anyhow, we've decided on the experiment and goodness only knows what will come of it."

CHAPTER 7

ANNE SAYS HER PRAYERS

WHEN MARILLA took Anne up to bed that night she said stiffly:

"Now, Anne, I noticed last night that you threw your clothes all about the floor when you took them off. That is a very untidy habit, and I can't allow it at all. As soon as you take off any article of clothing fold it neatly and place it on the chair. I haven't any use at all for little girls who aren't neat."

"I was so harrowed up in my mind last night that I didn't think about my clothes at all,'' said Anne. "I'll fold them nicely tonight. They always made us do that at the asylum. Half the time, though, I'd forget, I'd be in such a hurry to get into bed nice and quiet and imagine things.''

"You'll have to remember a little better if you stay here,'' admonished Marilla. "There, that looks something like. Say your prayers now and get into bed.''

"I never say any prayers,'' announced Anne.

Marilla looked horrified astonishment.

"Why, Anne, what do you mean? Were you never taught to say your prayers? God always wants little girls to say their prayers. Don't you know who God is, Anne?''

"'God is a spirit, infinite, eternal and unchangeable, in His being, wisdom, power, holiness, justice, goodness, and truth,''' responded Anne promptly and glibly.

Marilla looked rather relieved.

"So you do know something then, thank goodness! You're not quite a heathen. Where did you learn that?''

"Oh, at the asylum Sunday-school. They made us learn the whole catechism. I liked it pretty well. There's something splendid about some of the words. 'Infinite, eternal and unchangeable.' Isn't that grand? It has such a roll to it—just like a big organ playing. You couldn't quite call it poetry, I suppose, but it sounds a lot like it, doesn't it?''

"We're not talking about poetry, Anne—we are talking about saying prayers. Don't you know it's a terrible wicked thing not to say your prayers every night? I'm afraid you are a very bad little girl.''

"You'd find it easier to be bad than good if you had red hair,'' said Anne reproachfully. "People who haven't red hair don't know what trouble is. Mrs. Thomas told me that God made my hair red *on purpose,* and I've never cared about Him since. And anyhow I'd always be too tired at night to bother saying prayers. People who have to look after twins can't be expected to say their prayers. Now, do you honestly think they can?''

Marilla decided that Anne's religious training must be begun at once. Plainly there was no time to be lost.

"You must say your prayers while you are under my roof, Anne.''

"Why, of course, if you want me to,'' assented Anne cheerfully. "I'd do anything to oblige you. But you'll have to tell me what to say for this once. After I get into bed I'll imagine out a real nice prayer to say always. I believe that it will be interesting, now that I come to think of it.''

"You must kneel down," said Marilla in embarrassment.

Anne knelt at Marilla's knee and looked up gravely.

"Why must people kneel to pray? If I really wanted to pray I'll tell you what I'd do. I'd go out into the great big field all alone or into the deep, deep woods, and I'd look up into the sky—up—up—up—into that lovely blue sky that looks as if there was no end to its blueness. And then I'd just *feel* a prayer. Well, I'm ready. What am I to say?"

Marilla felt more embarrassed than ever. She had intended to teach Anne the childish classic, "Now I lay me down to sleep." But she had, as I have told you, the glimmerings of a sense of humor—which is simply another name for the fitness of things; and it suddenly occurred to her that that simple little prayer, sacred to white-robed childhood lisping at motherly knees, was entirely un-suited to this freckled witch of a girl who knew and cared nothing about God's love, since she had never had it translated to her through the medium of human love.

"You're old enough to pray for yourself, Anne," she said finally. "Just thank God for your blessings and ask Him humbly for the things you want."

"Well, I'll do my best,' promised Anne, burying her face in Marilla's lap. "Gracious heavenly Father—that's the way the min-isters say it in church, so I suppose it's all right in a private prayer, isn't it?" she interjected, lifting her head for a moment. "Gracious heavenly Father, I thank Thee for the White Way of Delight and the Lake of Shining Waters and Bonny and the Snow Queen. I'm really extremely grateful for them. And that's all the blessings I can think of just now to thank Thee for. As for the things I want, they're so numerous that it would take a great deal of time to name them all, so I will only mention the two most important. Please let me stay at Green Gables; and please let me be good-looking when I grow up. I remain,

"Yours respectfully,
"ANNE SHIRLEY.

"There, did I do it all right?" she asked eagerly, getting up. "I could have made it much more flowery if I'd had a little more time to think it over."

Poor Marilla was only preserved from complete collapse by re-membering that it was not irreverence, but simply spiritual ignorance on the part of Anne that was responsible for this extraordinary petition. She tucked the child up in bed, mentally vowing that she should be taught a prayer the very next day, and was leaving the room with the light when Anne called her back.

"I've just thought of it now. I should have said 'Amen' in place of 'yours respectfully,' shouldn't I?—the way the ministers do. I'd forgotten it, but I felt a prayer should be finished off in some way, so I put in the other. Do you suppose it will make any difference?"

"I—I don't suppose it will," said Marilla. "Go to sleep now like a good child. Good night."

"I can say good night tonight with a clear conscience," said Anne, cuddling luxuriously down among her pillows.

Marilla retreated to the kitchen, set the candle firmly on the table, and glared at Matthew.

"Matthew Cuthbert, it's about time somebody adopted that child and taught her something. She's next door to a perfect heathen. Will you believe that she never said a prayer in her life till tonight? I'll send to the manse tomorrow and borrow the Peep of Day series, that's what I'll do. And she shall go to Sunday-school just as soon as I can get some suitable clothes made for her. I foresee that I shall have my hands full. Well, well, we can't get through this world without our share of trouble. I've had a pretty easy life of it so far, but my time has come at last and I suppose I'll just have to make the best of it."

CHAPTER 8

ANNE'S BRINGING-UP IS BEGUN

FOR REASONS best known to herself, Marilla did not tell Anne that she was to stay at Green Gables until the next afternoon. During the forenoon she kept the child busy with various tasks and watched over her with a keen eye while she did them. By noon she had concluded that Anne was smart and obedient, willing to work and quick to learn; her most serious shortcoming seemed to be a tendency to fall into day-dreams in the middle of a task and forget all about it until such times as she was sharply recalled to earth by a reprimand or a catastrophe.

When Anne had finished the dinner dishes she suddenly confronted Marilla with the air and expression of one desparately determined to learn the worst. Her thin little body trembled from head to foot; her face flushed and her eyes dilated until they were almost black; she clasped her hands tightly and said in an imploring voice:

"Oh, please, Miss Cuthbert, won't you tell me if you are going to send me away or not? I've tried to be patient all the morning, but I really feel that I cannot bear not knowing any longer. It's a dreadful feeling. Please tell me."

"You haven't scalded the dish-cloth in clean hot water as I told you to do," said Marilla immovably. "Just go and do it before you ask any more questions, Anne."

Anne went and attended to the dish-cloth. Then she returned to Marilla and fastened imploring eyes on the latter's face.

"Well," said Marilla, unable to find any excuse for deferring her explanation longer, "I suppose I might as well tell you. Matthew and I have decided to keep you—that is, if you will try to be a good girl and show yourself grateful. Why, child, whatever is the matter?"

"I'm crying," said Anne in a tone of bewilderment. "I can't think why. I'm glad as glad can be. Oh, *glad* doesn't seem the right word at all. I was glad about the White Way and the cherry blossoms—but this! Oh, it's something more than glad. I'm so happy. I'll try to be so good. It will be up-hill work, I expect, for Mrs. Thomas often told me I was desperately wicked. However, I'll do my very best. But can you tell me why I'm crying?"

"I suppose it's because you're all excited and worked up," said Marilla disapprovingly. "Sit down on that chair and try to calm yourself. I'm afraid you both cry and laugh far too easily. Yes, you can stay here and we will try to do right by you. You must go to school; but it's only a fortnight till vacation so it isn't worth while for you to start before it opens again in September."

"What am I to call you?" asked Anne. "Shall I always say Miss Cuthbert? Can I call you Aunt Marilla?"

"No; you'll call me just plain Marilla. I'm not used to being called Miss Cuthbert and it would make me nervous."

"It sounds awfully disrespectful to say just Marilla," protested Anne.

"I guess there'll be nothing disrespectful in it if you're careful and speak respectfully. Everybody, young and old, in Avonlea calls me Marilla except the minister. He says Miss Cuthbert—when he thinks of it."

"I'd love to call you Aunt Marilla," said Anne wistfully. "I've never had an aunt or any relation at all—not even a grandmother. It would make me feel as if I really belonged to you. Can't I call you Aunt Marilla?"

"No. I'm not your aunt and I don't believe in calling people names that don't belong to them."

"But we could imagine you were my aunt."

"I couldn't," said Marilla grimly.

"Do you never imagine things different from what they really are?" asked Anne wide-eyed.

"No."

"Oh!" Anne drew a long breath. "Oh, Miss—Marilla, how much you miss!"

"I don't believe in imagining things different from what they really are," retorted Marilla. "When the Lord puts us in certain circumstances He doesn't mean for us to imagine them away. And that reminds me. Go into the sitting-room, Anne—be sure your feet are clean and don't let any flies in—and bring me out the illustrated card that's on the mantelpiece. The Lord's Prayer is on it and you'll devote your spare time this afternoon to learning it off by heart. There's to be no more of such praying as I heard last night."

"I suppose I was very awkward," said Anne apologetically, "but then, you see, I'd never had any practice. You couldn't really expect a person to pray very well the first time she tried, could you? I thought out a splendid prayer after I went to bed, just as I promised you I would. It was nearly as long as the minister's and so poetical. But would you believe it? I couldn't remember one word when I woke up this morning. And I'm afraid I'll never be able to think out another one as good. Somehow, things are never so good when they're thought out a second time. Have you ever noticed that?"

"Here is something for you to notice, Anne. When I tell you to do a thing I want you to obey me at once and not stand stock-still and discourse about it. Just you go and do as I bid you."

Anne promptly departed for the sitting-room across the hall; she failed to return; after waiting ten minutes Marilla laid down her knitting and marched after her with a grim expression. She found Anne standing motionless before a picture hanging on the wall between the two windows, with her hands clasped behind her, her face uplifted, and her eyes astar with dreams. The white and green light strained through apple-trees and clustering vines outside fell over the rapt little figure with half-unearthly radiance.

"Anne, whatever are you thinking of?" demanded Marilla sharply.

Anne came back to earth with a start.

"That," she said, pointing to the picture—a rather vivid chromo entitled, "Christ Blessing Little Children"—"and I was just imagining I was one of them—that I was the little girl in the blue dress, standing off by herself in the corner as if she didn't belong to anybody, like me. She looks lonely and sad, don't you think? I guess she hadn't any father or mother of her own. But she wanted to be blessed, too, so she just crept shyly up on the outside of the crowd, hoping nobody would notice her—except Him. I'm sure I know just how she felt. Her heart must have beat and her hands must have got cold, like mine did when I asked you if I could stay. She was afraid He mightn't notice her. But it's likely He did, don't you think? I've been trying to imagine it all out—her edging a little nearer all the time until she was quite close to Him; and then He would look at her and put His hand on her hair and oh, such a thrill of joy as would run over her! But I wish the artist hadn't painted Him so sorrowful-looking. All His pictures are like that, if you've noticed. But I don't believe He could really have looked so sad or the children would have been afraid of Him."

"Anne," said Marilla, wondering why she had not broken into this speech long before, "you shouldn't talk that way. It's irreverent—positively irreverent."

Anne's eyes marvelled.

"Why, I felt just as reverent as could be. I'm sure I didn't mean to be irreverent."

"Well, I don't suppose you did—but it doesn't sound right to talk so familiarly about such things. And another thing, Anne, when I send you after something you're to bring it at once and not fall into mooning and imagining before pictures. Remember that. Take that card and come right to the kitchen. Now, sit down in the corner and learn that prayer off by heart."

Anne set the card up against the jugful of apple blossoms she had brought in to decorate the dinner table—Marilla had eyed that decoration askance, but had said nothing—propped her chin on her hands, and fell to studying it intently for several silent minutes.

"I like this," she announced at length. "It's beautiful. I've heard it before—I heard the superintendent of the asylum Sunday-school say it over once. But I didn't like it then. He had such a cracked voice and he prayed it so mournfully. I really felt sure he thought praying was a disagreeable duty. This isn't poetry, but it makes me feel just the same way poetry does. 'Our Father who art in heaven, hallowed be Thy name.' That is just like a line of music. Oh, I'm so glad you thought of making me learn this, Miss—Marilla.''

"Well, learn it and hold your tongue," said Marilla shortly.

Anne tipped the vase of apple blossoms near enough to bestow a soft kiss on a pink-cupped bud, and then studied diligently for some moments longer.

"Marilla," she demanded presently, "do you think that I shall ever have a bosom friend in Avonlea?"

"A—a what kind of a friend?"

"A bosom friend—an intimate friend, you know—a really kindred spirit to whom I can confide my inmost soul. I've dreamed of meeting her all my life. I never really supposed I would, but so many of my loveliest dreams have come true all at once that perhaps this one will, too. Do you think it's possible?"

"Diana Barry lives over at Orchard Slope and she's about your age. She's a very nice little girl, and perhaps she will be a playmate for you when she comes home. She's visiting her aunt over at Carmody just now. You'll have to be careful how you behave yourself, though. Mrs. Barry is a very particular woman. She won't let Diana play with any little girl who isn't nice and good."

Anne looked at Marilla through the apple blossoms, her eyes aglow with interest.

"What is Diana like? Her hair isn't red is it? Oh, I hope not. It's bad enough to have red hair myself, but I positively couldn't endure it in a bosom friend."

"Diana is a very pretty little girl. She has black eyes and hair and rosy cheeks. And she is good and smart, which is better than being pretty."

Marilla was as fond of morals as the Duchess in Wonderland, and was firmly convinced that one should be tacked on to every remark made to a child who was being brought up.

But Anne waved the moral inconsequently aside and seized only on the delightful possibilities before it.

"Oh, I'm so glad she's pretty. Next to being beautiful oneself— and that's impossible in my case—it would be best to have a beautiful bosom friend. When I lived with Mrs. Thomas she had a bookcase in her sitting room with glass doors. There weren't any books in it; Mrs. Thomas kept her best china and her preserves there—when she had any preserves to keep. One of the doors was broken. Mr. Thomas smashed it one night when he was slightly intoxicated. But the other was whole and I used to pretend that my reflection in it was another little girl who lived in it. I called her Katie Maurice, and we were very intimate. I used to talk to her by the hour, especially on Sunday, and tell her everything. Katie was the comfort and consolation of my life. We used to pretend that the bookcase was enchanted and that if I only knew the spell I could open the door and step right into the room where Katie Maurice lived, instead of into Mrs. Thomas' shelves of preserves and china. And then Katie Maurice would have taken me by the hand and led me out into a wonderful place, all flowers and sunshine and fairies, and we would have lived there happy for ever after. When I went to live with Mrs. Hammond it just broke my heart to leave Katie Maurice. She felt it dreadfully, too, I know she did, for she was crying when she kissed me good-bye through the bookcase door. There was no bookcase at Mrs. Hammond's. But just up the river a little way from the house there was a long green little valley, and the loveliest echo lived there. It echoed back every word you said, even if you didn't talk a bit loud. So I imagined that it was a little girl called Violetta and we were great friends and I loved her almost as well as I loved Katie Maurice—not quite, but almost, you know. The night before I went to the asylum I said good-bye to Violetta, and oh, her good-bye came back to me in such sad, sad tones. I had become so attached to her that I hadn't the heart to imagine a bosom friend at the asylum, even if there had been any scope for imagination there.''

''I think it's just as well there wasn't,'' said Marilla drily. ''I don't approve of such goings-on. You seem to half believe your own imaginations. It will be well for you to have a real live friend to put such nonsense out of your head. But don't let Mrs. Barry hear you talking about your Katie Maurices and your Violettas or she'll think you tell stories.''

''Oh, I won't. I couldn't talk of them to everybody—their memories are too sacred for that. But I thought I'd like to have you know about them. Oh, look, here's a big bee just tumbled out of an apple blossom. Just think what a lovely place to live—in an apple blossom! Fancy going to sleep in it when the wind was rocking it. If I wasn't a human girl I think I'd like to be a bee and live among the flowers.''

''Yesterday you wanted to be a sea-gull,'' sniffed Marilla. ''I think you are very fickle-minded. I told you to learn that prayer and not talk. But it seems impossible for you to stop talking if you've got anybody that will listen to you. So go up to your room and learn it.''

"Oh, I know it pretty nearly all now—all but just the last line."

"Well, never mind, do as I tell you. Go to your room and finish learning it well, and stay there until I call you down to help me get tea."

"Can I take the apple blossoms with me for company?" pleaded Anne.

"No; you don't want your room cluttered up with flowers. You should have left them on the tree in the first place."

"I did feel a little that way, too," said Anne. "I kind of felt I shouldn't shorten their lovely lives by picking them—I wouldn't want to be picked if I were an apple blossom. But the temptation was *irresistible*. What do you do when you meet with an irresistible temptation?"

"Anne, did you hear me tell you to go to your room?"

Anne sighed, retreated to the east gable, and sat down in a chair by the window.

"There—I know this prayer. I learned that last sentence coming upstairs. Now I'm going to imagine things into this room so that they'll always stay imagined. The floor is covered with a white velvet carpet with pink roses all over it and there are pink silk curtains at the windows. The walls are hung with gold and silver brocade tapestry. The furniture is mahogany. I never saw any mahogany, but it does sound *so* luxurious. This is a couch all heaped with gorgeous silken cushions, pink and blue and crimson and gold, and I am reclining gracefully on it. I can see my reflection in that splendid big mirror hanging on the wall. I am tall and regal, clad in a gown of trailing white lace, with a pearl cross on my breast and pearls in my hair. My hair is of midnight darkness and my skin is a clear ivory pallor. My name is the Lady Cordelia Fitzgerald. No, it isn't—I can't make *that* seem real."

She danced up to the little looking-glass and peered into it. Her pointed freckled face and solemn gray eyes peered back at her.

"You're only Anne of Green Gables," she said earnestly, "and I see you, just as you are looking now, whenever I try to imagine I'm the Lady Cordelia. But it's a million times nicer to be Anne of Green Gables than Anne of nowhere in particular, isn't it?"

She bent forward, kissed her reflection affectionately, and betook herself to the open window.

"Dear Snow Queen, good afternoon. And good afternoon, dear birches down in the hollow. And good afternoon, dear gray house up on the hill. I wonder if Diana is to be my bosom friend. I hope she

will, and I shall love her very much. But I must never quite forget Katie Maurice and Violetta. They would feel so hurt if I did and I'd hate to hurt anybody's feelings, even a little bookcase girl's or a little echo girl's. I must be careful to remember them and send them a kiss every day.''

Anne blew a couple of airy kisses from her fingertips past the cherry blossoms and then, with her chin in her hands, drifted luxuriously out on a sea of daydreams.

CHAPTER 9

MRS. RACHEL LYNDE IS PROPERLY HORRIFIED

ANNE HAD been a fortnight at Green Gables before Mrs. Lynde arrived to inspect her. Mrs. Rachel, to do her justice, was not to blame for this. A severe and unseasonable attack of grippe had confined that good lady to her house ever since the occasion of her last visit to Green Gables. Mrs. Rachel was not often sick and had a well-defined contempt for people who were; but grippe, she asserted, was like no other illness on earth and could only be interpreted as one of the special visitations of Providence. As soon as her doctor allowed her to put her foot out-of-doors she hurried up to Green Gables, bursting with curiosity to see Matthew's and Marilla's orphan, concerning whom all sorts of stories and suppositions had gone abroad in Avonlea.

Anne had made good use of every waking moment of that fortnight. Already she was acquainted with every tree and shrub about the place. She had discovered that a lane opened out below the apple orchard and ran up through a belt of woodland; and she had explored it to its furthest end in all its delicious vagaries of brook and bridge, fir coppice and wild cherry arch, corners thick with fern, and branching byways of maple and mountain ash.

She had made friends with the spring down in the hollow—that wonderful deep, clear icy-cold spring; it was set about with smooth red sandstones and rimmed in by great palm-like clumps of water fern; and beyond it was a log bridge over the brook.

That bridge led Anne's dancing feet up over a wooded hill beyond, where perpetual twilight reigned under the straight, tick-growing firs and spruces; the only flowers there were myriads of delicate "June bells," those shyest and sweetest of woodland blooms, and a few pale, aerial starflowers, like the spirits of last year's blossoms. Gossamers glimmered like threads of silver among the trees and the fir boughs and tassels seemed to utter friendly speech.

All these raptured voyages of exploration were made in the odd half-hours which she was allowed for play, and Anne talked Matthew and Marilla half-deaf over her discoveries. Not that Matthew complained, to be sure; he listened to it all with a wordless smile of enjoyment on his face; Marilla permitted the "chatter" until she found herself becoming too interested in it, whereupon she always promptly quenched Anne by a curt command to hold her tongue.

Anne was out in the orchard when Mrs. Rachel came, wandering at her own sweet will through the lush, tremulous grasses splashed with ruddy evening sunshine; so that good lady had an excellent chance to talk her illness fully over, describing every ache and pulse-beat with such evident enjoyment that Marilla thought even grippe must bring its compensations. When details were exhausted Mrs. Rachel introduced the real reason of her call.

"I've been hearing some surprising things about you and Matthew."

"I don't suppose you are any more surprised than I am myself," said Marilla. "I'm getting over my surprise now."

"It was too bad there was such a mistake," said Mrs. Rachel sympathetically. "Couldn't you have sent her back?"

"I suppose we could, but we decided not to. Matthew took a fancy to her. And I must say I like her myself—although I admit she has her faults. The house seems a different place already. She's a real bright little thing."

Marilla said more than she had intended to say when she began, for she read disapproval in Mrs. Rachel's expression.

"It's a great responsibility you've taken on yourself," said that lady gloomily, "especially when you've never had any experience with children. You don't know much about her or her real disposition, I suppose, and there's no guessing how a child like that will turn out. But I don't want to discourage you I'm sure, Marilla."

"I'm not feeling discouraged," was Marilla's dry response. "When I make up my mind to do a thing it stays made up. I suppose you'd like to see Anne. I'll call her in."

Anne came running in presently, her face sparkling with the delight of her orchard rovings; but, abashed at finding herself in the unexpected presence of a stranger, she halted confusedly inside the door. She certainly was an odd-looking little creature in the short tight wincey dress she had worn from the asylum, below which her thin legs seemed ungracefully long. Her freckles were more numerous and obtrusive than ever; the wind had ruffled her hatless hair into over-brilliant disorder; it had never looked redder than at that moment.

"Well, they didn't pick you for your looks, that's sure and certain," was Mrs. Rachel Lynde's emphatic comment. Mrs. Rachel was one of those delightful and popular people who pride themselves on speaking their mind without fear or favour. "She's terrible skinny and homely, Marilla. Come here, child, and let me have a look at you. Lawful heart, did anyone ever see such freckles? And hair as red as carrots! Come here, child, I say."

Anne "came there," but not exactly as Mrs. Rachel expected. With one bound she crossed the kitchen floor and stood before Mrs. Rachel, her face scarlet with anger, her lips quivering, and her whole slender form trembling from head to foot.

"I hate you," she cried in a choked voice, stamping her foot on the floor. "I hate you—I hate you—I hate you—" a louder stamp with each assertion of hatred. "How dare you call me skinny and ugly? How dare you say I'm freckled and redheaded? You are a rude, impolite, unfeeling woman!"

"Anne!" exclaimed Marilla in consternation.

But Anne continued to face Mrs. Rachel undauntedly, head up, eyes blazing, hands clenched, passionate indignation exhaling from her like an atmosphere.

"How dare you say such things about me?" she repeated vehemently. "How would you like to have such things said about you? How would you like to be told that you are fat and clumsy and probably hadn't a spark of imagination in you? I don't care if I do hurt your feelings by saying so! I hope I hurt them. You have hurt mine worse than they were ever hurt before even by Mrs. Thomas' intoxicated husband. And I'll *never* forgive you for it, never, never!"

Stamp! Stamp!

"Did anybody ever see such a temper!" exclaimed the horrified Mrs. Rachel.

"Anne, go up to your room and stay there until I come up," said

Marilla, recovering her powers of speech with difficulty.

Anne, bursting into tears, rushed to the hall door, slammed it until the tins on the porch wall outside rattled in sympathy, and fled through the hall and up the stairs like a whirlwind. A subdued slam above told that the door of the east gable had been shut with equal vehemence.

"Well, I don't envy you your job bringing *that* up, Marilla," said Mrs. Rachel with unspeakable solemnity.

Marilla opened her lips to say she knew not what of apology or deprecation. What she did say was a surprise to herself then and ever afterwards.

"You shouldn't have twitted her about her looks, Rachel."

"Marilla Cuthbert, you don't mean to say that you are upholding her in such a terrible display of temper as we've just seen?" demanded Mrs. Rachel indignantly.

"No," said Marilla slowly, "I'm not trying to excuse her. She's been very naughty and I'll have to give her a talking to about it. But we must make allowances for her. She's never been taught what is right. And you *were* too hard on her, Rachel."

Marilla could not help tacking on that last sentence, although she was again surprised at herself for doing it. Mrs. Rachel got up with an air of offended dignity.

"Well, I see that I'll have to be very careful what I say after this, Marilla, since the fine feelings of orphans, brought from goodness knows where, have to be considered before anything else. On, no, I'm not vexed—don't worry yourself. I'm too sorry for you to leave any room for anger in my mind. You'll have your own troubles with that child. But if you'll take my advice—which I suppose you won't do, although I've brought up ten children and buried two—you'll do that 'talking to' you mention with a fair-sized birch switch. I should think *that* would be the most effective language for that kind of a child. Her temper matches her hair I guess. Well, good evening, Marilla. I hope you'll come down to see me often as usual. But you can't expect me to visit here again in a hurry, if I'm liable to be flown at and insulted in such a fashion. It's something new in *my* experience."

Whereat Mrs. Rachel swept out and away—if a fat woman who always waddled *could* be said to sweep away—and Marilla with a very solemn face betook herself to the east gable.

On the way upstairs she pondered uneasily as to what she ought to do. She felt no little dismay over the scene that had just been enacted.

How unfortunate that Anne should have displayed such temper before Mrs. Rachel Lynde, of all people! Then Marilla suddenly became aware of an uncomfortable and rebuking consciousness that she felt more humiliation over this than sorrow over the discovery of such a serious defect in Anne's disposition. And how was she to punish her? The amiable suggestion of the birch switch—to the efficiency of which all of Mrs. Rachel's own children could have borne smarting testimony—did not appeal to Marilla. She did not believe she could whip a child. No, some other method of punishment must be found to bring Anne to a proper realization of the enormity of her offence.

Marilla found Anne face downward on her bed, crying bitterly, quite oblivious of muddy boots on a clean counterpane.

"Anne," she said, not ungently.

No answer.

"Anne," with greater severity, "get off that bed this minute and listen to what I have to say to you."

Anne squirmed off the bed and sat rigidly on a chair beside it, her face swollen and tear-stained and her eyes fixed stubbornly on the floor.

"This is a nice way for you to behave, Anne! Aren't you ashamed of yourself?"

"She hadn't any right to call me ugly and redheaded," retorted Anne, evasive and defiant.

"You hadn't any right to fly into such a fury and talk the way you did to her, Anne. I was ashamed of you—thoroughly ashamed of you. I wanted you to behave nicely to Mrs. Lynde, and instead of that you have disgraced me. I'm sure I don't know why you should lose your temper like that just because Mrs. Lynde said you were red-haired and homely. You say it yourself often enough."

"Oh, but there's such a difference between saying a thing yourself and hearing other people say it," wailed Anne. "You may know a thing is so, but you can't help hoping other people don't quite think it is. I suppose you think I have an awful temper, but I couldn't help it. When she said those things something just rose right up in me and choked me. I *had* to fly out at her."

"Well, you made a fine exhibition of yourself I must say. Mrs. Lynde will have a nice story to tell about you everywhere—and she'll tell it, too. It was a dreadful thing for you to lose your temper like that, Anne."

"Just imagine how you would feel if somebody told you to your face that you were skinny and ugly," pleaded Anne tearfully.

An old remembrance suddenly rose up before Marilla. She had been a very small child when she had heard one aunt say of her to another, "What a pity she is such a dark, homely little thing." Marilla was every day of fifty before the sting had gone out of that memory.

"I don't say that I think Mrs. Lynde was exactly right in saying what she did to you, Anne," she admitted in a softer tone. "Rachel is too outspoken. But that is no excuse for such behavior on your part. She was a stranger and an elderly person and my visitor—all three very good reasons why you should have been respectful to her. You were rude and saucy and"—Marilla had a saving inspiration of punishment—"you must go to her and tell her you are very sorry for your bad temper and ask her to forgive you."

"I can never do that," said Anne determinedly and darkly. "You can punish me in any way you like, Marilla. You can shut me up in a dark, damp dungeon inhabited by snakes and toads and feed me only on bread and water and I shall not complain. But I cannot ask Mrs. Lynde to forgive me."

"We're not in the habit of shutting people up in dark, damp dungeons," said Marilla drily, "especially as they're rather scarce in Avonlea. But apologize to Mrs. Lynde you must and shall and you'll stay here in your room until you can tell me you're willing to do it."

"I shall have to stay here for ever then," said Anne mournfully, "because I can't tell Mrs. Lynde I'm sorry I said those things to her. How can I? I'm *not* sorry. I'm sorry I've vexed you; but I'm *glad* I told her just what I did. It was a great satisfaction. I can't say I'm sorry when I'm not, can I? I can't even *imagine* I'm sorry."

"Perhaps your imagination will be in better working order by the morning," said Marilla, rising to depart. "You'll have the night to think over your conduct in and come to a better frame of mind. You said you would try to be a very good girl if we kept you at Green Gables, but I must say it hasn't seemed very much like it this evening."

Leaving this Parthian shaft to rankle in Anne's stormy bosom, Marilla descended to the kitchen, grievously troubled in mind and vexed in soul. She was as angry with herself as with Anne, because, whenever she recalled Mrs. Rachel's dumfounded countenance her lips twitched with amusement and she felt a most reprehensible desire to laugh.

CHAPTER 10

ANNE'S APOLOGY

MARILLA SAID nothing to Matthew about the affair that evening; but when Anne proved still refractory the next morning an explanation had to be made to account for her absence from the breakfast table. Marilla told Matthew the whole story, taking pains to impress him with a due sense of the enormity of Anne's behaviour.

"It's a good thing Rachel Lynde got a calling down; she's a meddlesome old gossip," was Matthew's consolatory rejoinder.

"Matthew Cuthbert, I'm astonished at you. You know that Anne's behaviour was dreadful, and yet you take her part! I suppose you'll be saying next thing that she oughtn't to be punished at all."

"Well now—no—not exactly," said Matthew uneasily. "I reckon she ought to be punished a little. But don't be too hard on her, Marilla. Recollect she hasn't ever had any one to teach her right. You're—you're going to give her something to eat, aren't you?"

"When did you ever hear of me starving people into good behaviour?" demanded Marilla indignantly. "She'll have her meals regular, and I'll carry them up to her myself. But she'll stay up there until she's willing to apologize to Mrs. Lynde, and that's final, Matthew."

Breakfast, dinner, and supper were very silent meals—for Anne still remained obdurate. After each meal Marilla carried a well-filled tray to the east gable and brought it down later on not noticeably depleted. Matthew eyed its last descent with a troubled eye. Had Anne eaten anything at all?

When Marilla went out that evening to bring the cows from the back pasture, Matthew, who had been hanging about the barns and watching, slipped into the house with the air of a burglar and crept upstairs. As a general thing Matthew gravitated between the kitchen and the little bedroom off the hall where he slept; once in a while he ventured uncomfortably into the parlour or sitting-room when the minister came to tea. But he had never been upstairs in his own house since the spring he helped Marilla paper the spare bedroom, and that was four years ago.

He tiptoed along the hall and stood for several minutes outside the door of the east gable before he summoned courage to tap on it with his fingers and then open the door to peep in.

Anne was sitting on the yellow chair by the window, gazing mournfully out into the garden. Very small and unhappy she looked, and Matthew's heart smote him. He softly closed the door and tiptoed over to her.

"Anne," he whispered, as if afraid of being overheard," how are you making it, Anne?"

Anne smiled wanly.

"Pretty well. I imagine a good deal, and that helps to pass the time. Of course, it's rather lonesome. But then, I may as well get used to that."

Anne smiled again, bravely facing the long years of solitary imprisonment before her.

Matthew recollected that he must say what he had come to say without loss of time, lest Marilla return prematurely.

"Well now, Anne, don't you think you'd better do it and have it over with?" he whispered. "It'll have to be done sooner or later, you know, for Marilla's a dreadful determined woman—dreadful determined, Anne. Do it right off, I say, and have it over."

"Do you mean apologize to Mrs. Lynde?"

"Yes—apologize—that's the very word," said Matthew eagerly. "Just smooth it over so to speak. That's what I was trying to get at."

"I suppose I could do it to oblige you," said Anne thoughtfully. "It would be true enough to say I am sorry, because I *am* sorry now. I wasn't a bit sorry last night. I was mad clear through, and I stayed mad all night. I know I did because I woke up three times and I was just furious every time. But this morning it was all over. I wasn't in a temper any more—and it left a dreadful sort of goneness, too. I felt so ashamed of myself. But I just couldn't think of going and telling Mrs. Lynde so. It would be so humiliating. I made up my mind I'd stay shut up here for ever rather than do that. But still—I'd do anything for you—if you really want me to—"

"Well now, of course I do. It's terrible lonesome downstairs without you. Just go and smooth it over—that's a good girl."

"Very well," said Anne resignedly. "I'll tell Marilla as soon as she comes in that I've repented."

"That's right—that's right, Anne. But don't tell Marilla I said anything about it. She might think I was putting my oar in and I promised not to do that."

"Wild horses won't drag the secret from me," promised Anne solemnly. "How would wild horses drag a secret from a person anyhow?"

But Matthew was gone, scared at his own success. He fled hastily to the remotest corner of the horse pasture lest Marilla should suspect what he had been up to. Marilla herself, upon her return to the house, was agreeably surprised to hear a plaintive voice calling, "Marilla," over the banisters.

"Well?" she said, going into the hall.

"I'm sorry I lost my temper and said rude things, and I'm willing to go and tell Mrs. Lynde so."

"Very well." Marilla's crispness gave no sign of her relief. She had been wondering what under the canopy she should do if Anne did not give in. "I'll take you down after milking."

Accordingly, after milking, behold Marilla and Anne walking down the lane, the former erect and triumphant, the latter drooping and dejected. But half-way down Anne's dejection vanished as if by enchantment. She lifted her head and stepped lightly along, her eyes fixed on the sunset sky and an air of subdued exhilaration about her. Marilla beheld the change disapprovingly. This was no meek penitent such as it behooved her to take into the presence of the offended Mrs. Lynde.

"What are you thinking of, Anne?" she asked sharply.

"I'm imagining out what I must say to Mrs. Lynde," answered Anne dreamily.

This was satisfactory—or should have been so. But Marilla could not rid herself of the notion that something in her scheme of punishment was going askew. Anne had no business to look so rapt and radiant.

Rapt and radiant Anne continued until they were in the very presence of Mrs. Lynde, who was sitting knitting by her kitchen window. Then the radiance vanished. Mournful penitence appeared on every feature. Before a word was spoken Anne suddenly went down on her knees before the astonished Mrs. Rachel and held out her hands beseechingly.

"Oh, Mrs. Lynde, I am so extremely sorry," she said with a quiver in her voice. "I could never express all my sorrow, no, not if I used up a whole dictionary. You must just imagine it. I behaved terribly to you—and I've disgraced the dear friends, Matthew and Marilla, who have let me stay at Green Gables although I'm not a boy. I'm a dreadfully wicked and ungrateful girl, and I deserve to be punished and cast out by respectable people for ever. It was very wicked of me to fly into a temper because you told me the truth. It *was* the truth; every word you said was true. My hair is red and I'm freckled and skinny and ugly. What I said to you was true, too, but I shouldn't have said it. Oh, Mrs. Lynde, please, please, forgive me. If you refuse it will be a lifelong sorrow to me. You wouldn't like to inflict a lifelong sorrow on a poor little orphan girl, would you, even if she had a dreadful temper? Oh, I am sure you wouldn't. Please say you forgive me, Mrs. Lynde.''

Anne clasped her hands together, bowed her head, and waited for the word of judgment.

There was no mistaking her sincerity—it breathed in every tone of her voice. Both Marilla and Mrs. Lynde recognized its unmistakable ring. But the former understood in dismay that Anne was actually enjoying her valley of humiliation—was revelling in the thoroughness of her abasement. Where was the wholesome punishment upon which she, Marilla, had plumed herself? Anne had turned it into a species of positive pleasure.

Good Mrs. Lynde, not being overburdened with perception, did not see this. She only perceived that Anne had made a very thorough apology and all resentment vanished from her kindly, if somewhat officious, heart.

"There, there, get up child," she said heartily. "Of course I forgive you. I guess I was a little too hard on you, anyway. But I'm such an outspoken person. You just mustn't mind me, that's what. It can't be denied your hair is terrible red; but I knew a girl once—went to school with her, in fact—whose hair was every mite as red as yours when she was young, but when she grew up it darkened to a real handsome auburn. I wouldn't be a mite surprised if yours did, too—not a mite.''

"Oh, Mrs. Lynde!" Anne drew a long breath as she rose to her feet. "You have given me a hope. I shall always feel that you are a benefactor. Oh, I could endure anything if I only thought my hair would be a handsome auburn when I grew up. It would be so much easier to be good if one's hair was a handsome auburn, don't you think? And now may I go out into your garden and sit on that bench under the apple trees while you and Marilla are talking? There is so much more scope for imagination out there.''

"Laws, yes, run along, child. And you can pick a bouquet of them white June lilies over in the corner if you like.''

As the door closed behind Anne Mrs. Lynde got briskly up to light a lamp.

"She's a real odd little thing. Take this chair, Marilla; it's easier than the one you've got; I just keep that for the hired boy to sit on. Yes, she certainly is an odd child, but there is something kind of taking about her after all. I don't feel so surprised at you and Matthew keeping her as I did—nor so sorry for you, either. She may turn out all right. Of course, she has a queer way of expressing herself—a little too—well, too kind of forcible, you know; but she'll likely get over that now that she's come to live among civilized folks. And then, her temper's pretty quick, I guess; but there's one comfort, a child that has a quick temper, just blaze up and cool down, ain't never likely to be sly or deceitful. Preserve me from a sly child, that's what. On the whole, Marilla, I kind of like her."

When Marilla went home Anne came out of the fragrant twilight of the orchard with a sheaf of white narcissi in her hands.

"I apologized pretty well, didn't I?" she said proudly as they went down the lane. "I thought since I had to do it I might as well do it thoroughly."

"You did it thoroughly, all right enough," was Marilla's comment. Marilla was dismayed at finding herself inclined to laugh over the recollection. She had also an uneasy feeling that she ought to scold Anne for apologizing so well; but then that was ridiculous! She compromised with her conscience by saying severely:

"I hope you won't have occasion to make many more such apologies. I hope you'll try to control you temper now, Anne."

"That wouldn't be so hard if people wouldn't twit me about my looks," said Anne with a sigh. "I don't get cross about other things; but I'm *so* tired of being twitted about my hair and it just makes me boil right over. Do you suppose my hair will really be a handsome auburn when I grow up?"

"You shouldn't think so much about your looks, Anne. I'm afraid you are a very vain little girl."

"How can I be vain when I know I'm homely?" protested Anne. "I love pretty things; and I hate to look in the glass and see something that isn't pretty. It makes me feel so sorrowful—just as I feel when I look at any ugly thing. I pity it because it isn't beautiful."

"Handsome is as handsome does," quoted Marilla.

"I've had that said to me before, but I have my doubts about it," remarked skeptical Anne, sniffing at her narcissi. "Oh, aren't these flowers sweet! It was lovely of Mrs. Lynde to give them to me. I have no hard feelings against Mrs. Lynde now. It gives you a lovely, comfortable feeling to apologize and be forgiven, doesn't it? Aren't the stars bright tonight? If you could live in a star, which one would you pick? I'd like that lovely clear big one away over there above that dark hill."

"Anne, do hold your tongue," said Marilla, thoroughly worn out trying to follow the gyrations of Anne's thoughts.

Anne said no more until they turned into their own lane. A little gypsy wind came down it to meet them, laden with the spicy perfume of young dew-wet ferns. Far up in the shadows a cheerful light gleamed out through the trees from the kitchen at Green Gables. Anne suddenly came close to Marilla and slipped her hand into the older woman's hard palm.

"It's lovely to be going home and know it's home," she said. "I love Green Gables already, and I never loved any place before. No place ever seemed like home. Oh, Marilla, I'm so happy. I could pray right now and not find it a bit hard."

Something warm and pleasant welled up in Marilla's heart at touch of that thin little hand in her own—a throb of the maternity she had missed, perhaps. Its very unaccustomedness and sweetness disturbed her. She hastened to restore her sensations to their normal calm by inculcating a moral.

"If you'll be a good girl you'll always be happy, Anne. And you should never find it hard to say your prayers."

"Saying one's prayers isn't exactly the same thing as praying," said Anne meditatively. "But I'm going to imagine that I'm the wind that is blowing up there in those tree-tops. When I get tired of the trees I'll imagine I'm gently waving down here in the ferns—and then I'll fly over to Mrs. Lynde's garden and set the flowers dancing—and then I'll go with one great swoop over the clover field—and then I'll blow over the Lake of Shining Waters and ripple it all up into little sparkling waves. Oh, there's so much scope for imagination in a wind! So I'll not talk any more just now, Marilla."

"Thank be to goodness for that," breathed Marilla in devout relief.

CHAPTER 11

ANNE'S IMPRESSIONS OF SUNDAY-SCHOOL

"WELL, HOW do you like them?" said Marilla.

Anne was standing in the gable-room, looking solemnly at three new dresses spread out on the bed. One was of snuffy colored gingham which Marilla had been tempted to buy from a peddler the preceding summer because it looked so serviceable; one was of black-and-white checked sateen which she had picked up at a bargain counter in the winter; and one was a stiff print of an ugly blue shade which she had purchased that week at a Carmody store.

She had made them herself, and they were all made alike—plain skirts fulled tightly to plain waists, with sleeves as plain as waist and skirt and tight as sleeves could be.

"I'll imagine that I like them," said Anne soberly.

"I don't want you to imagine it," said Marilla, offended. "Oh, I can see you don't like the dresses! What is the matter with them? Aren't they neat and clean and new?"

"Yes."

"Then why don't you like them?"

"They're—they're not—pretty," Anne said reluctantly.

"Pretty!" Marilla sniffed. "I didn't trouble my head about getting pretty dresses for you. I don't believe in pampering vanity, Anne, I'll tell you that right off. Those dresses are good, sensible, serviceable dresses, without any frills or furbelows about them, and they're all you'll get this summer. The brown gingham and the blue print will do you for school when you begin to go. The sateen is for church and Sunday school. I'll expect you to keep them neat and clean and not to tear them. I should think you'd be grateful to get most anything after those skimpy wincey things you've been wearing."

"Oh, I *am* grateful," protested Anne. "But I'd be ever so much gratefuller if—if you'd made just one of them with puffed sleeves. Puffed sleeves are so fashionable now. It would give me such a thrill, Marilla, just to wear a dress with puffed sleeves."

"Well, you'll have to do without your thrill. I hadn't any material to waste on puffed sleeves. I think they are ridiculous-looking things anyhow. I prefer the plain, sensible ones."

"But I'd rather look ridiculous when everybody else does than plain and sensible all by myself," persisted Anne mournfully.

"Trust you for that! Well, hang those dresses carefully up in your closet, and then sit down and learn the Sunday school lesson. I got a quarterly from Mr. Bell for you and you'll go to Sunday school tomorrow," said Marilla, disappearing downstairs in high dudgeon.

Anne clasped her hands and looked at the dresses.

"I did hope there would be a white one with puffed sleeves," she whispered disconsolately. "I prayed for one, but I didn't much expect it on that account. I didn't suppose God would have time to bother about a ittle orphan girl's dress. I knew I'd just have to depend on Marilla for it. Well, fortunately I can imagine that one of them is of snow-white muslin with lovely lace frills and three-puffed sleeves.''

The next morning warnings of a sick headache prevented Marilla from going to Sunday school with Anne.

''You'll have to go down and call for Mrs. Lynde, Anne,'' she said. ''She'll see that you get into the right class. Now, mind you behave yourself properly. Stay to preaching afterwards and ask Mrs. Lynde to show you our pew. Here's a cent for collection. Don't stare at people and don't fidget. I shall expect you to tell me the text when you come home.''

Anne started off irreproachably, arrayed in the stiff black-and-white sateen, which, while decent as regards length and certainly not open to the charge of skimpiness, contrived to emphasize every corner and angle of her thin figure. Her hat was a little, flat, glossy, new sailor, the extreme plainness of which had likewise much disappointed Anne, who had permitted herself secret visions of ribbon and flowers. The latter, however, were supplied before Anne reached the main road, for, being confronted halfway down the lane with a golden frenzy of wind-stirred buttercups and a glory of wild roses, Anne promptly and liberally garlanded her hat with a heavy wreath of them. Whatever other people might have thought of the result it satisfied Anne, and she tripped gaily down the road, holding her ruddy head with its decoration of pink and yellow very proudly.

When she reached Mrs. Lynde's house she found that lady gone. Nothing daunted Anne proceeded onward to the church alone. In the porch she found a crowd of little girls, all more or less gaily attired in whites and blues and pinks, and all staring with curious eyes at this stranger in their midst, with her extraordinary head adornment. Avonlea little girls had already heard queer stories about Anne; Mrs. Lynde said she had an awful temper; Jerry Buote, the hired boy at Green Gables, said she talked all the time to herself or to the trees and flowers like a crazy girl. They looked at her and whispered to each other behind their quarterlies. Nobody made any friendly advances, then or later on when the opening exercises were over and Anne found herself in Miss Rogerson's class.

Miss Rogerson was a middle-aged lady who had taught a Sunday school class for twenty years. Her method of teaching was to ask the printed questions from the quarterly and look sternly over its edge at

THEY LOOKED AT HER AND WHISPERED TO EACH OTHER.

the particular little girl she thought ought to answer the quesion. She looked often at Anne, and Anne, thanks to Marilla's drilling, answered promptly; but it may be questioned if she understood very much about either question or answer.

She did not think she liked Miss Rogerson, and she felt very miserable; every other little girl in the class had puffed sleeves. Anne felt that life was really not worth living without puffed sleeves.

"Well, how did you like Sunday school?" Marilla wanted to know when Anne came home. Her wreath having faded, Anne had discarded it in the lane, so Marilla was spared the knowledge of that for a time.

"I didn't like it a bit. It was horrid."

"Anne Shirley!" said Marilla rebukingly.

Anne sat down on the rocker with a long sigh, kissed one of Bonny's leaves, and waved her hand to a blossoming fuchsia.

"They might have been lonesome while I was away," she explained. "And now about the Sunday school. I behaved well, just as you told me. Mrs. Lynde was gone, but I went right on myself. I went into the church, with a lot of other little girls, and I sat in the corner of a pew by the window while the opening exercises went on. Mr. Bell made an awfully long prayer. I would have been dreadfully tired before he got through if I hadn't been sitting by that window. But it looked right out on the Lake of Shining Waters, so I just gazed at that and imagined all sorts of splendid things."

"You shouldn't have done anything of the sort. You should have listened to Mr. Bell."

"But he wasn't talking to me," protested Anne. "He was talking to God and he didn't seem to be very much interested in it, either. I think he thought God was too far off to make it worth while. I said a little prayer myself, though. There was a long row of white birches hanging over the lake and the sunshine fell down through them, 'way, 'way down, deep into the water. Oh, Marilla, it was like a beautiful dream! It gave me a thrill and I just said, 'Thank you for it, God,' two or three times."

"Not out loud, I hope," said Marilla anxiously.

"Oh, no, just under my breath. Well, Mr. Bell did get through at last and they told me to go into the classroom with Miss Rogerson's class. There were nine other girls in it. They all had puffed sleeves. I tried to imagine mine were puffed, too, but I couldn't. Why couldn't I? It was as easy as could be to imagine they were puffed when I was alone in the east gable, but it was awfully hard there among the others who had really truly puffs.''

"You shouldn't have been thinking about your sleeves in Sunday school. You should have been attending to the lesson. I hope you knew it."

"Oh, yes; and I answered a lot of questions. Miss Rogerson asked ever so many. I don't think it was fair for her to do all the asking. There were lots I wanted to ask her, but I didn't like to because I didn't think she was a kindred spirit. Then all the other little girls recited a paraphrase. She asked me if I knew any. I told her I didn't, but I could recite, 'The Dog at His Master's Grave' if she liked. That's in the Third Royal Reader. It isn't a really truly religious piece of poetry, but it's so sad and melancholy that it might as well be. She said it wouldn't do and she told me to learn the nineteenth paraphrase for next Sunday. I read it over in church afterwards and it's splendid. There are two lines in particular that just thrill me.

> *Quick as the slaughtered squadrons fell*
> *In Midian's evil day.*

I don't know what 'squadrons' means nor 'Midian,' either, but it sounds *so* tragical. I can hardly wait until next Sunday to recite it. I'll practise it all the week. After Sunday school I asked Miss Rogerson—because Mrs. Lynde was too far away—to show me your pew. I sat just as still as I could and the text was Revelations, third chapter, second and third verses. It was a very long text. If I was a minister I'd pick the short, snappy ones. The sermon was awfully long, too. I suppose the minister had to match it to the text. I didn't think he was a bit interesting. The trouble with him seems to be that he hasn't enough imagination. I didn't listen to him very much. I just let my thoughts run and I thought of the most surprising things.''

Marilla felt helplessly that all this should be sternly reproved, but she was hampered by the undeniable fact that some of the things Anne had said, especially about the minister's sermons and Mr. Bell's prayers, were what she herself had really thought deep down in her heart for years, but had never given expression to. It almost seemed to her that those secret, unuttered, critical thoughts had suddenly taken visible and accusing shape and form in the person of this outspoken morsel of neglected humanity.

CHAPTER 12

A SOLEMN VOW AND PROMISE

I T WAS not until the next Friday that Marilla heard the story of the flower-wreathed hat. She came home from Mrs. Lynde's and called Anne to account.

"Anne, Mrs. Rachel says you went to church last Sunday with your hat rigged out ridiculous with roses and buttercups. What on earth put you up to such a caper? A pretty-looking object you must have been!"

"Oh. I know pink and yellow aren't becoming to me," began Anne.

"Becoming fiddlesticks! It was putting flowers on your hat at all, no matter what color they were, that was ridiculous. You are the most aggravating child!"

"I don't see why it's any more ridiculous to wear flowers on your hat than on your dress," protested Anne. "Lots of little girls there had bouquets pinned on their dresses. What was the difference?"

Marilla was not to be drawn from the safe concrete into dubious paths of the abstract.

"Don't answer me back like that, Anne. It was very silly of you to do such a thing. Never let me catch you at such a trick again. Mrs. Rachel says she thought she would sink through the floor when she saw you come in all rigged out like that. She couldn't get near enough to tell you to take them off till it was too late. She says people talked about it something dreadful. Of course they would think I had no better sense than to let you go decked out like that."

"Oh, I'm so sorry," said Anne, tears welling into her eyes. "I never thought you'd mind. The roses and buttercups were so sweet and pretty I thought they'd look lovely on my hat. Lots of the little girls had artificial flowers on their hats. I'm afraid I'm going to be a dreadful trial to you. Maybe you'd better send me back to the asylum. That would be terrible; I don't think I could endure it; most likely I would go into consumption; I'm so thin as it is, you see. But that would be better than being a trial to you."

"Nonsense," said Marilla, vexed at herself for having made the child cry. "I don't want to send you back to the asylum, I'm sure. All I want is that you should behave like other little girls and not make yourself ridiculous. Don't cry any more. I've got some news for you. Diana Barry came home this afternoon. I'm going up to see if I can borrow a skirt pattern from Mrs. Barry, and if you like you can come with me and get acquainted with Diana.''

Anne rose to her feet, with clasped hands, the tears still glistening on her cheeks; the dish-towel she had been hemming slipped unheeded to the floor.

"Oh, Marilla, I'm frightened—now that it has come I'm actually frightened. What if she shouldn't like me! It would be the most tragical disappointment of my life.''

"Now, don't get into a fluster. And I do wish you wouldn't use such long words. It sounds so funny in a little girl. I guess Diana'll like you well enough. It's her mother you've got to reckon with. If she doesn't like you it won't matter how much Diana does. If she had heard about your outburst to Mrs. Lynde and going to church with buttercups round your hat I don't know what she'll think of you. You must be polite and well-behaved, and don't make any of your startling speeches. For pity's sake, if the child isn't actually trembling!''

Anne *was* trembling. Her face was pale and tense.

"Oh, Marilla, you'd be excited, too, if you were going to meet a little girl you hoped would be your bosom friend and whose mother mightn't like you,'' she said as she hastened to get her hat.

They went over to Orchard Slope by the short cut across the brook and up the firry hill grove. Mrs. Barry came to the kitchen door in answer to Marilla's knock. She was a tall, black-eyed, black-haired woman, with a very resolute mouth. She had the reputation of being very strict with her children.

"How do you do, Marilla?'' she said cordially. "Come in. And this is the little girl you have adopted, I suppose?''

"Yes, this is Anne Shirley,'' said Marilla.

"Spelled with an *e*,'' gasped Anne, who, tremulous and excited as she was, was determined there should be no misunderstanding on that important point.

Mrs. Barry, not hearing or not comprehending, merely shook hands and said kindly:

"How are you?''

"I am well in body although considerably rumpled in spirit, thank you, ma'am,'' said Anne gravely. Then aside to Marilla in an audible whisper, "There wasn't anything startling in that, was there, Marilla?''

Diana was sitting on the sofa, reading a book which was dropped when the callers entered. She was a very pretty little girl, with her mother's black eyes and hair, and rosy cheeks, and the merry expression which was her inheritance from her father.

"This is my little girl, Diana," said Mrs. Barry. "Diana, you might take Anne out into the garden and show her your flowers. It will be better for you than straining your eyes over that book. She reads entirely to much—" this to Marilla as the little girls went out—"and I can't prevent her, for her father aids and abets her. She's always poring over a book. I'm glad she has the prospect of a playmate—perhaps it will take her more out-of-doors."

Outside in the garden, which was full of mellow sunset light streaming through the dark old firs to the west of it, stood Anne and Diana, gazing bashfully at one another over a clump of gorgeous tiger lilies.

The Barry garden was a bowery wilderness of flowers which would have delighted Anne's heart at any time less fraught with destiny. It was encircled by huge old willows and tall firs, beneath which flourished flowers that loved the shade. Prim, right-angled paths, neatly bordered with clam-shells, intersected it like moist red ribbons and in the beds between old-fashioned flowers ran riot. There were rosy bleeding-hearts and great splendid crimson peonies; white, fragrant narcissi and thorny, sweet Scotch roses; pink and blue and white columbines and lilac-tinted Bouncing Bets; clumps of southern-wood and ribbon grass and mint; purple Adam-and-Eve, daffodils, and masses of sweet clover white with its delicate, fragrant, feathery sprays; scarlet lightning that shot its fiery lances over prim white musk-flowers; a garden it was where sunshine lingered and bees hummed, and winds, beguiled into loitering, purred and rustled.

"Oh, Diana," said Anne at last, clasping her hands and speaking almost in a whisper, "do you think—oh, do you think you can like me a little—enough to be my bosom friend?"

Diana laughed. Diana always laughed before she spoke.

"Why, I guess so," she said frankly. "I'm awfully glad you've come to live at Green Gables. It will be jolly to have somebody to play with. There isn't any other girl who lives near enough to play with, and I've no sisters big enough."

"Will you swear to be my friend for ever and ever?" demanded Anne eagerly.

Diana looked shocked.

"Why, it's dreadfully wicked to swear," she said rebukingly.

"Oh no, not my kind of swearing. There are two kinds, you know."

"I never heard of but one kind," said Diana doubtfully.

"There really is another. Oh, it isn't wicked at all. It just means vowing and promising solemnly."

"Well, I don't mind doing that," agreed Diana, relieved. "How do you do it?"

"We must join hands—so," said Anne gravely. "It ought to be over running water. We'll just imagine this path is running water. I'll repeat the oath first. I solemnly swear to be faithful to my bosom friend, Diana Barry, as long as the sun and moon shall endure. Now you say it and put my name in."

Diana repeated the "oath" with a laugh fore and aft. Then she said:

"You're a queer girl, Anne. I heard before that you were queer. But I believe I'm going to like you real well."

When Marilla and Anne went home Diana went with them as far as the log bridge. The two little girls walked with their arms about each other. At the brook they parted with many promises to spend the next afternoon together.

"Well, did you find Diana a kindred spirit?" asked Marilla as they went up throught the garden of Green Gables.

"Oh, yes," sighed Anne, blissfully unconscious of any sarcasm on Marilla's part. "Oh, Marilla, I'm the happiest girl on Prince Edward Island this very moment. I assure you I'll say my prayers with a right good-will tonight. Diana and I are going to build a playhouse in Mr. William Bell's birch grove tomorrow. Can I have those broken pieces of china that are out in the wood-shed? Diana's birthday is in February and mine is in March. Don't you think that is a very strange coincidence? Diana is going to lend me a book to read. She says it's perfectly splendid and tremenjusly exciting. She's going to show me a place back in the woods where rice lilies grow. Don't you think Diana has got very soulful eyes? I wish I had soulful eyes. Diana is going to teach me to sing a song called 'Nelly in the Hazel Dell.' She's going to give me a picture to put up in my room; it's a perfectly beautiful picture, she says—a lovely lady in a pale blue silk dress. A sewing-maching agent gave it to her. I wish I had something to give Diana. I'm an inch taller than Diana, but she is ever so much fatter; she says she'd like to be thin because it's so much more graceful, but I'm afraid she only said it to soothe my feelings. We're going to the shore some day to gather shells. We have agreed to call the spring down by the log bridge the Dryad's Bubble. Isn't that a perfectly elegant name? I read a story once about a spring called that. A dryad is a sort of grown-up fairy, I think."

"Well, all I hope is you won't talk Diana to death," said Marilla.

"But remember this in all your planning, Anne. You're not going to play all the time nor most of it. You'll have your work to do and it'll have to be done first."

Anne's cup of happiness was full, and Matthew caused it to overflow. He had just got home from a trip to the store at Carmody, and he sheepishly produced a small parcel from his pocket and handed it to Anne, with a deprecatory look at Marilla.

"I heard you say you liked chocolate sweeties, so I got you some," he said.

"Humph," sniffed Marilla. "It'll ruin her teeth and stomach. There, there, child, don't look so dismal. You can eat those, since Matthew has gone and got them. He'd better have brought you some peppermints. They're wholesomer. Don't sicken yourself eating them all at once now."

"Oh, no, indeed, I won't," said Anne eagerly. "I'll just eat one tonight, Marilla. And I can give Diana half of them, can't I? The other half will taste twice as sweet to me if I give some to her. It's delightful to think I have something to give her."

"I will say it for the child," said Marilla when Anne had gone to her gable, "she isn't stingy. I'm glad, for of all faults I detest stinginess in a child. Dear me, it's only three weeks since she came, and it seems as if she'd been here always. I can't imagine the place without her. Now, don't be looking I-told-you-so, Matthew. That's bad enough in a woman, but isn't to be endured in a man. I'm perfectly willing to own up that I'm glad I consented to keep the child and that I'm getting fond of her, but don't you rub it in, Matthew Cuthbert."

CHAPTER 13

THE DELIGHTS OF ANTICIPATION

"IT'S TIME Anne was in to do her sewing," said Marilla, glancing at the clock and then out into the yellow August afternoon where everything drowsed in the heat. "She stayed playing with Diana more than half and hour more'n I gave her leave to; and now she's perched out there on the woodpile talking to Matthew, nineteen to the dozen, when she knows perfectly well that she ought to be at her work. And of course he's listening to her like a perfect ninny. I never saw such an infatuated man. The more she talks and the odder the things she says, the more he's delighted evidently. Anne Shirley, you come right in here this minute, do you hear me!''

A series of staccato taps on the west window brought Anne flying in from the yard, eyes shining, cheeks faintly flushed with pink, unbraided hair streaming behind her in a torrent of brightness.

"Oh, Marilla," she exclaimed breathlessly, "there's going to be a Sunday-school picnic next week—in Mr. Harmon Andrews' field, right near the Lake of Shining Waters. And Mrs. Superintendent Bell and Mrs. Rachel Lynde are going to make ice-cream—think of it, Marilla—*ice-cream!* And oh, Marilla, can I go to it?"

"Just look at the clock, if you please, Anne. What time did I tell you to come in?"

"Two o'clock—but isn't it splendid about the picnic, Marilla? Please can I go? Oh, I've never been to a picnic—I've dreamed of picnics, but I've never—"

"Yes, I told you to come at two o'clock. And it's a quarter to three. I'd like to know why you didn't obey me, Anne."

"Why, I meant to, Marilla, as much as could be. But you have no idea how fascinating Idlewild is. And then, of course, I had to tell Matthew about the picnic. Matthew is such a sympathetic listener. Please can I go?"

"You'll have to learn to resist the fascination of Idle-whatever-you-call-it. When I tell you to come in at a certain time I mean that time and not half an hour later. And you needn't stop to discourse with sympathetic listeners on your way, either. As for the picnic, of course you can go. You're a Sunday-school scholar, and it's not likely I'd refuse to let you go when all the other little girls are going."

"But—but," faltered Anne, "Diana says that everybody must take a basket of things to eat. I can't cook, as you know, Marilla, and—and—I don't mind going to a picnic without puffed sleeves so much, but I'd feel terribly humiliated if I had to go without a basket. It's been preying on my mind ever since Diana told me."

"Well, it needn't prey any longer. I'll bake you a basket."

"Oh, you dear good Marilla. Oh, you are so kind to me. Oh, I'm so much obliged to you."

Getting through with her "ohs" Anne cast herself into Marilla's arms and rapturously kissed her sallow cheek. It was the first time in her whole life that childish lips had voluntarily touched Marilla's face. Again that sudden sensation of startling sweetness thrilled her. She was secretly vastly pleased at Anne's impulsive caress, which was probably the reason why she said brusquely:

"There, there, never mind your kissing nonsense. I'd sooner see you doing strictly as you're told. As for cooking, I mean to begin giving you lessons in that some of these days. But you're so feather-brained, Anne, I've been waiting to see if you'd sober down a little and learn to be steady before I begin. You've got to keep your wits about you in cooking and not stop in the middle of things to let your thoughts rove over all creation. Now, get out your patchwork and have your square done before tea-time."

"I do *not* like patchwork," said Anne dolefully, hunting out her workbasket and sitting down before a little heap of red and white diamonds with a sigh. "I think some kinds of sewing would be nice; but there's no scope for imagination in patchwork. It's just one little seam after another and you never seem to be getting anywhere. But of course I'd rather be Anne of Green Gables sewing patchwork than Anne of any other place with nothing to do but play. I wish time went as quick sewing patches as it does when I'm playing with Diana, though. Oh, we do have such elegant times, Marilla. I have to furnish most of the imagination, but I'm well able to do that. Diana is simply perfect in every other way. You know that little piece of land across the brook that runs up between our farm and Mr. Barry's. It belongs to Mr. William Bell, and right in the corner there is a little ring of white birch trees—the most romantic spot, Marilla. Diana and I have our playhouse there. We call it Idlewild. Isn't that a poetical name? I assure you it took me some time to think it out. I stayed awake nearly a whole night before I invented it. Then, just as I was dropping off to sleep, it came like an inspiration. Diana was *enraptured* when she heard it. We have got our house fixed up elegantly. You must come and see it Marilla—won't you? We have great big stones, all covered with moss, for seats, and boards from tree to tree for shelves. And we have all our dishes on them. Of course, they're broken but it's the easiest thing in the world to imagine that they are whole. There's a piece of a plate with a spray of red and yellow ivy on it that is especially beautiful. We keep it in the parlor and we have the fairy glass there, too. The fairy glass is as lovely as a dream. Diana found it out in the woods behind their chicken house. It's all full of rainbows—just little young rainbows that haven't grown big yet—and Diana's mother told her it was broken off a hanging lamp they once had. But it's nicer to imagine the fairies lost it one night when they had a ball, so we call it the fairy glass. Matthew is going to make us a table. Oh, we have named that little round pool over in Mr. Barry's field Willowmere. I got that name out of the book Diana lent me. That was a thrilling book, Marilla. The heroine had five lovers. I'd be satisfied with one, wouldn't you? She was very handsome and she went through great tribulations. She could faint as easy as anything. I'd love to be able to faint, wouldn't you, Marilla? It's so romantic. But I'm really very healthy for all I'm so thin. I believe I'm getting fatter, though. Don't you think I am? I look at my elbows every morning when I get up to see if any dimples are coming. Diana is having a new dress made with elbow sleeves. She is going to wear it to the picnic. Oh, I do hope it will be fine next Wednesday. I don't feel that I could endure the disappointment if anything happened to prevent me from getting to the picnic. I suppose I'd live through it, but I'm certain it would be a lifelong sorrow. It wouldn't matter if I got to a hundred picnics in after years; they wouldn't make up for missing this one. They're going to have boats on the Lake of Shining Waters—and ice-cream as I told you. I have never tasted ice-cream. Diana tried to explain what it was like, but I guess ice-cream is one of those things that are beyond imagination."

"Anne, you have talked even on for ten minutes by the clock," said Marilla. "Now, just for curiosity's sake, see if you can hold your tongue for the same length of time."

Anne held her tongue as desired. But for the rest of the week she talked picnic and thought picnic and dreamed picnic. On Saturday it rained and she worked herself up into such a frantic state lest it should keep on raining until and over Wednesday, that Marilla made her sew an extra patchwork square by way of steadying her nerves.

On Sunday Anne confided to Marilla on the way home from church that she grew actually cold all over with excitement when the minister announced the picnic from the pulpit.

"Such a thrill as went up and down my back, Marilla! I don't think I'd ever really believed until then that there was honestly going to be a picnic. I couldn't help fearing I'd only imagined it. But when a minster says a thing in the pulpit you just have to believe it."

"You set your heart too much on things, Anne," said Marilla with a sigh. "I'm afraid there'll be a great many disappointments in store for you through life."

"Oh, Marilla, looking forward to things is half the pleasure of them," exclaimed Anne. "You mayn't get the things themselves; but nothing can prevent you from having the fun of looking forward to them. Mrs. Lynde says, 'Blessed are they who expect nothing for they shall not be disappointed.' But I think it would be worse to expect nothing than to be disappointed.''

Marilla wore her amethyst brooch to church that day as usual. Marilla always wore her amethyst brooch to church. She would have thought it rather sacrilegious to leave it off—as bad as forgetting her Bible or her collection dime. That amethyst brooch was Marilla's most treasured possession. A sea-faring uncle had given it to her mother who in turn had bequeathed it to Marilla. It was an old-fashioned oval, containing a braid of her mother's hair, surrounded by a border of very fine amethysts. Marilla knew too little about precious stones to realize how fine the amethysts actually were; but she thought them very beautiful and was always pleasantly conscious of their violet shimmer at her throat, above her good brown satin dress, even although she could not see it.

Anne had been smitten with delighted admiration when she first saw that brooch.

"Oh, Marilla, it's a perfectly elegant brooch. I don't know how you can pay attention to the sermon or the prayers when you have it on. *I* couldn't. I know. I think amethysts are just sweet. They are what I used to think diamonds were like. Long ago, before I had seen a diamond, I read about them and I tried to imagine what they would be like. I thought they would be lovely glimmering purple stones. When I saw a real diamond in a lady's ring one day I was so disappointed I cried. Of course, it was very lovely but it wasn't my idea of a diamond. Will you let me hold the brooch for one minute, Marilla? Do you think amethysts can be the souls of good violets?''

CHAPTER 14

ANNE'S CONFESSION

ON THE Monday evening before the picnic Marilla came down from her room with a troubled face.

"Anne," she said to that small personage, who was shelling peas by the spotless table and singing "Nelly of the Hazel Dell" with a vigour and expression that did credit to Diana's teaching, "did you see anything of my amethyst brooch? I though I stuck it in my pincushion when I came home from church yesterday evening, but I can't find it anywhere.

"I—I saw it this afternoon when you were away at the Aid Society," said Anne, a little slowly. "I was passing your door when I saw it on the cushion, so I went in to look at it."

"Did you touch it?" said Marilla sternly.

"Y-e-e-s," admitted Anne, "I took it up and I pinned it on my breast just to see how it would look."

"You had not business to do anything of the sort. It's very wrong in a little girl to meddle. You shouldn't have gone into my room in the first place and you shouldn't have touched a brooch that didn't belong to you in the second. Where did you put it?"

"Oh, I put it back on the bureau. I hadn't it on a minute. Truly, I didn't mean to meddle, Marilla. I didn't think about its being wrong to go in and try on the brooch; but I see now that it was and I'll never do it again. That's one good thing about me. I never do the same naughty thing twice."

"You didn't put it back," said Marilla. "That brooch isn't anywhere on the bureau. You've taken it out or something, Anne."

"I *did* put it back," said Anne quickly—pertly, Marilla thought. "I don't just remember whether I stuck it on the pincushion or laid it in the china tray. But I'm perfectly certain I put it back."

"I'll go and have another look," said Marilla, determining to be just. "If you put that brooch back it's there still. If it isn't I'll know you didn't, that's all!"

Marilla went to her room and made a thorough search, not only over the bureau but in every other place she thought the brooch might possibly be. It was not to be found and she returned to the kitchen.

"Anne, the brooch is gone. By your own admission you were the last person to handle it. Now, what have you done with it? Tell me the truth at once. Did you take it out and lose it?"

"No, I didn't," said Anne solemnly, meeting Marilla's angry gaze squarely. "I never took the brooch out of your room and that is the truth, if I was to be led to the block for it—although I'm not very certain what a block is. So there, Marilla."

Anne's "so there" was only intended to emphasize her assertion, but Marilla took it as a display of defiance.

"I believe you are telling me a falsehood, Anne," she said sharply. "I know you are. There now, don't say anything more unless you are prepared to tell the whole truth. Go to your room and stay there until you are ready to confess."

"Will I take the peas with me?" said Anne meekly.

"No, I'll finish shelling them myself. Do as I bid you."

When Anne had gone Marilla went about her evening tasks in a very disturbed state of mind. She was worried about her valuable brooch. What if Anne had lost it? And how wicked of the child to deny having taken it, when anybody could see she must have! With such an innocent face, too!

"I don't know what I wouldn't sooner have had happen," thought Marilla, as she nervously shelled the peas. "Of course, I don't suppose she meant to steal it or anything like that. She's just taken it to play with or help along that imagination of hers. She must have taken it, that's clear, for there hasn't been a soul in that room since she was in it, by her own story, until I went up tonight. And the brooch is gone, there's nothing surer. I suppose she has lost it and is afraid to own up for fear she'll be punished. It's a dreadful thing to think she tells falsehoods. It's a far worse thing than her fit of temper. It's a fearful responsibility to have a child in your house you can't trust. Slyness and untruthfulness—that's what she has displayed. I declare I feel worse about that than about the brooch. If she'd only have told the truth about it I wouldn't mind so much."

Marilla went to her room at intervals all through the evening and searched for the brooch, without finding it. A bed-time visit to the east gable produced no result. Anne persisted in denying that she knew anything about the brooch but Marilla was only the more firmly convinced that she did.

She told Matthew the story the next morning. Matthew was confounded and puzzled; he could not so quickly lose faith in Anne but he had to admit that circumstances were against her.

"You're sure it hasn't fell down behind the bureau?" was the only suggestion he could offer.

"I've moved the bureau and I've taken out the drawers and I've looked in every crack and cranny," was Marilla's positive answer. "The brooch is gone and that child has taken it and lied about it. That's the plain, ugly truth, Matthew Cuthbert, and we might as well look it in the face."

"Well now, what are you going to do about it?" Matthew asked forlornly, feeling secretly thankful that Marilla and not he had to deal with the situation. He felt no desire to put his oar in this time.

"She'll stay in her room until she confesses," said Marilla grimly, remembering the success of this method in the former case.

"Then we'll see. Perhaps we'll be able to find the brooch if she'll only tell where she took it; but in any case she'll have to be severely punished, Matthew."

"Well now, you'll have to punish her," said Matthew, reaching for his hat. "I've nothing to do with it, remember. You warned me off yourself."

Marilla felt deserted by everyone. She could not even go to Mrs. Lynde for advice. She went up to the east gable with a very serious face and left it with a face more serious still. Anne steadfastly refused to confess. She persisted in asserting that she had not taken the brooch. The child had evidently been crying and Marilla felt a pang of pity which she sternly repressed. By night she was, as she expressed it, "beat out."

"You'll stay in this room until you confess, Anne. You can make up your mind to that," she said firmly.

"But the picnic is tomorrow, Marilla," cried Anne. "You won't keep me from going to that, will you? Then I'll stay here as long as you like afterwards *cheerfully*. But I *must* go to the picnic."

"You'll not go to picnics nor anywhere else until you've confessed, Anne."

"Oh, Marilla," gasped Anne.

But Marilla had gone out and shut the door.

Wednesday morning dawned as bright and fair as if expressly made to order for the picnic. Birds sang around Green Gables; the Madonna lilies in the garden sent out whiffs of perfume that entered in on viewless winds at every door and window, and wandered through halls and rooms like spirits of benediction. The birches in the hollow waved joyful hands as if watching for Anne's usual morning greeting from the east gable. But Anne was not at her window. When Marilla took her breakfast up to her she found the child sitting primly on her bed, pale and resolute, with tight-shut lips and gleaming eyes.

"Marilla, I'm ready to confess."

"Ah!" Marilla laid down her tray. Once again her method had succeeded; but her success was very bitter to her. "Let me hear what you have to say then, Anne."

"I took the amethyst brooch," said Anne, as if repeating a lesson she had learned. "I took it just as you said. I didn't mean to take it when I went in. But it did look so beautiful, Marilla, when I pinned it on my breast that I was overcome by an irresistible temptation. I imagined how perfectly thrilling it would be to take it to Idlewild and play I was the Lady Cordelia Fitzgerald. It would be so much easier to imagine I was Lady Cordelia if I had a real amethyst brooch on. Diana and I made necklaces of roseberries but what are roseberries compared to amethysts? So I took the brooch. I thought I could put it back before you came home. I went all the way around by the road to lengthen out the time. When I was going over the bridge across the Lake of Shining Waters I took the brooch off to have another look at it. Oh, how it did shine in the sunlight! And then, when I was leaning over the bridge, it just slipped through my fingers—so—and went down—down—down, all purply-sparkling, and sank forevermore beneath the Lake of Shining Waters. And that's the best I can do at confessing, Marilla.''

Marilla felt hot anger surge up into her heart again. This child had taken and lost her treasured amethyst brooch and now sat there calmly reciting the details thereof without the least apparent compunction or repentance.

"Anne, this is terrible," she said, trying to speak calmly. "You are the very wickedest girl I ever heard of."

"Yes, I suppose I am," agreed Anne tranquilly. "And I know I'll have to be punished. It'll be your duty to punish me, Marilla. Won't you please get it over right off because I'd like to go the picnic with nothing on my mind."

"Picnic, indeed! You'll go to no picnic today, Anne Shirley. That shall be your punishment. And it isn't half severe enough either for what you've done!"

"Not go to the picnic!" Anne sprang to her feet and clutched Marilla's hand. "But you *promised* me I might! Oh, Marilla, I must go to the picnic. That was why I confessed. Punish me any way you like but that. Oh, Marilla, please, please, let me go to the picnic. Think of the ice-cream! For anything you know I may never have a chance to taste ice-cream again."

Marilla disengaged Anne's clinging hands stonily.

"You needn't plead, Anne. You are not going to the picnic and that's final. No, not a word."

Anne realized that Marilla was not to be moved. She clasped her hands together, gave a piercing shriek, and then flung herself face downwards on the bed, crying and writhing in an utter abandonment of disappointment and despair.

"For land's sake!" gasped Marilla, hastening from the room. "I believe the child is crazy. No child in her senses would behave as she does. If she isn't she's utterly bad. Oh dear, I'm afraid Rachel was right from the first. But I've put my hand to the plough and I won't look back."

That was a dismal morning. Marilla worked fiercely and scrubbed the porch and the dairy shelves when she could find nothing else to do. Neither the shelves nor the porch needed it—but Marilla did. Then she went out and raked the yard.

When dinner was ready she went to the stairs and called Anne. A tear-stained face appeared, looking tragically over the banisters.

"Come down to your dinner, Anne."

"I don't want any dinner, Marilla," said Anne sobbingly. "I couldn't eat anything. My heart is broken. You'll feel remorse of conscience some day, I expect, for breaking it, Marilla, but I forgive you. Remember when the time comes that I forgive you. But please don't ask me to eat anything, especially boiled pork and greens. Boiled pork and greens are so unromantic when one is in affliction."

Exasperated Marilla returned to the kitchen and poured out her tale of woe to Matthew, who, between his sense of justice and his unlawful sympathy with Anne, was a miserable man.

"Well now, she shouldn't have taken the brooch, Marilla, or told stories about it," he admitted, mournfully surveying his plateful of unromantic pork and greens as if he, like Anne, thought it a food unsuited to crises of feeling, "but she's such a little thing—such an interesting little thing. Don't you think it's pretty rough not to let her go to the picnic when she's so set on it?"

"Matthew Cuthbert, I'm amazed at you. I think I've let her off entirely too easy. And she doesn't appear to realize how wicked she's been at all—that's what worries me most. If she'd really felt sorry it wouldn't be so bad. And you don't seem to realize it, neither; you're making excuses for her all the time to yourself—I can see that."

"Well now, she's such a little thing," feebly reiterated Matthew. "And there should be allowances made, Marilla. You know she's never had any bringing up."

"Well, she's having it now," retorted Marilla.

The retort silenced Matthew if it did not convince him. That dinner was a very dismal meal. The only cheerful thing about it was Jerry Buote, the hired boy, and Marilla resented his cheerfulness as a personal insult.

When her dishes were washed and her bread sponge set and her hens fed Marilla remembered that she had noticed a small rent in her best black lace shawl when she had taken it off on Monday afternoon on returning from the Ladies' Aid. She would go and mend it.

The shawl was in a box in her trunk. As Marilla lifted it out, the sunlight, falling through the vines that clustered thickly about the window, struck upon something caught in the shawl—something that glittered and sparkled in facets of violet light. Marilla snatched at it with a gasp. It was the amethyst brooch, hanging to a thread of the lace by its catch!

"Dear life and heart," said Marilla blankly, "what does this mean? Here's my brooch safe and sound that I thought was at the bottom of Barry's pond. Whatever did that girl mean by saying she took it and lost it? I declare I believe Green Gables is bewitched. I remember now that when I took off my shawl Monday afternoon I laid it on the bureau for a minute. I suppose the brooch got caught in it somehow. Well!"

Marilla betook herself to the east gable, brooch in hand. Anne had cried herself out and was sitting dejectedly by the window.

"Anne Shirley," said Marilla solemnly, "I've just found my brooch hanging to my black lace shawl. Now I want to know what that rigmarole you told me this morning meant."

"Why, you said you'd keep me here until I confessed," returned Anne wearily, "and so I decided to confess because I was bound to get to the picnic. I thought out a confession last night after I went to bed and made it as interesting as I could. And I said it over and over so that I wouldn't forget it. But you wouldn't let me go to the picnic after all, so all my trouble was wasted."

Marilla had to laugh in spite of herself. But her conscience pricked her.

"Anne, you do beat all! But I was wrong—I see that now. I shouldn't have doubted your word when I'd never known you to tell a story. Of course, it wasn't right for you to confess to a thing you hadn't done—it was very wrong to do so. But I drove you to it. So if you'll forgive me, Anne, I'll forgive you and we'll start square again. And now get yourself ready for the picnic."

Anne flew up like a rocket.

"Oh, Marilla, isn't it too late?"

"No, it's only two o'clock. They won't be more than well gathered yet and it'll be an hour before they have tea. Wash your face and comb your hair and put on your gingham. I'll fill a basket for you. There's plenty of stuff baked in the house. And I'll get Jerry to hitch up the sorrel and drive you down to the picnic ground."

"Oh, Marilla," exclaimed Anne, flying to the washstand. "Five minutes ago I was so miserable I was wishing I'd never been born and now I wouldn't change places with an angel!"

That night a thoroughly happy, completely tired out Anne returned to Green Gables in a state of beatification impossible to describe.

"Oh, Marilla, I've had a perfectly scrumptious time. Scrumptious is a new word I learned today. I heard Mary Alice Bell use it. Isn't it very expressive? Everything was lovely. We had a splendid tea and then Mr. Harmon Andrews took us all for a row on the Lake of Shining Waters—six of us at a time. And Jane Andrews fell overboard. She was leaning out to pick water lilies and if Mr. Andrews hadn't caught her by her sash just in the nick of time she'd have fallen in and prob'ly been drowned. I wish it had been me. It would have been such a romantic experience to have been nearly drowned. It would be such a thrilling tale to tell. And we had the ice-cream. Words fail me to describe that ice-cream. Marilla, I assure you it was sublime."

That evening Marilla told the whole story to Matthew over her stocking basket.

"I'm willing to own up that I made a mistake," she concluded candidly, "but I've learned a lesson. I have to laugh when I think of Anne's 'confession,' although I suppose I shouldn't for it really was a falsehood. But it doesn't seem as bad as the other would have been, somehow, and anyhow I'm responsible for it. That child is hard to understand in some respects. But I believe she'll turn out all right yet. And there's one thing certain, no house will ever be dull that she's in."

CHAPTER 15

A TEMPEST IN THE SCHOOL TEAPOT

"WHAT A splendid day!" said Anne, drawing a long breath. "Isn't it good just to be alive on a day like this? I pity the people who aren't born yet for missing it. They may have good days, of course, but they can never have this one. And it's splendider still to have such a lovely way to go to school by, isn't it?"

"It's a lot nicer than going round by the road; that is so dusty and hot," said Diana practically, peeping into her dinner basket and mentally calculating if the three juicy, toothsome, raspberry tarts reposing there were divided among ten girls how many bites each girl would have.

The little girls of Avonlea school always pooled their lunches, and to eat three raspberry tarts all alone or even to share them only with one's chum would have forever and ever branded as "awful mean" the girl who did it. And yet, when tarts were divided among ten girls you just got enough to tantalize you.

The way Anne and Diana went to school *was* a pretty one. Anne thought those walks to and from school with Diana couldn't be improved upon even by imagination. Going around by the main road would have been so unromantic; but to go by Lover's Lane and Willowmere and Violet Vale and the Birch Path was romantic, if ever anything was.

Lover's Lane opened out below the orchard at Green Gables and stretched far up into the woods to the end of the Cuthbert farm. It was the way by which the cows were taken to the back pasture and the wood hauled home in winter. Anne had named it Lover's Lane before she had been a month at Green Gables.

"Not that lovers ever really walk there," she explained to Marilla, "but Diana and I are reading a perfectly magnificent book and there's a Lover's Lane in it. So we want to have one, too. And it's a very pretty name, don't you think? So romantic! We can imagine the lovers into it, you know. I like that lane because you can think out loud there without people calling you crazy."

Anne, starting out alone in the morning, went down Lover's Lane as far as the brook. Here Diana met her, and the two little girls went on up the lane under the leafy arch of maples—"maples are such sociable trees," said Anne; "they're always rustling and whispering to you,"—until they came to a rustic bridge. Then they left the lane and walked through Mr. Barry's back field and past Willowmere. Beyond Willowmere came Violet Vale—a little green dimple in the shadow of Mr. Andrew Bell's big woods. "Of course there are no violets there now," Anne told Marilla, "but Diana says there are millions of them in spring. Oh, Marilla, can't you just imagine you see them? It actually takes away my breath. I named it Violet Vale. Diana says she never saw the beat of me for hitting on fancy names for places. It's nice to be clever at something, isn't it? But Diana named the Birch Path. She wanted to, so I let her; but I'm sure I could have found something more poetical than plain Birch Path. Anybody can think of a name like that. But the Birch Path is one of the prettiest places in the world, Marilla.''

It was. Other people besides Anne thought so when they stumbled on it. It was a little narrow, twisting path, winding down over a long hill straight through Mr. Bell's woods, where the light came down sifted through so many emerald screens that it was as flawless as the heart of a diamond. It was fringed in all its length with slim young birches, white-stemmed and lissom boughed; ferns and starflowers and wild lilies-of-the-valley and scarlet tufts of pigeon berries grew thickly along it; and always there was a delightful spiciness in the air and music of bird calls and the murmur and laugh of wood winds in the trees overhead. Now and then you might see a rabbit skipping across the road if you were quiet—which, with Anne and Diana, happened about once in a blue moon. Down in the valley the path came out to the main road and then it was just up the spruce hill to the school.

The Avonlea school was a whitewashed building low in the eaves and wide in the windows, furnished inside with comfortable substantial old-fashioned desks that opened and shut, and were carved all over their lids with the initials and hieroglyphics of three generations of school-children. The schoolhouse was set back from the road and behind it was a dusky fir wood and a brook where all the children put their bottles of milk in the morning to keep cool and sweet until dinner hour.

Marilla had seen Anne start off to school on the first day of September with many secret misgivings. Anne was such an odd girl. How would she get on with the other children? And how on earth would she ever manage to hold her tongue during school hours?

Things went better than Marilla feared, however. Anne came home that evening in high spirits.

''I think I'm going to like school here,'' she announced. ''I don't think much of the master, though. He's all the time curling his moustache and making eyes at Prissy Andrews. Prissy is grown-up, you know. She's sixteen and she's studying for the entrance examination into Queen's Academy at Charlottetown next year. Tillie Boulter says that the master is *dead gone* on her. She's got a beautiful complexion and curly brown hair and she does it up so elegantly. She sits in the long seat at the back and he sits there, too, most of the time—to explain her lessons, he says. But Ruby Gillis says she saw him writing something on her slate and when Prissy read it she blushed as red as a beet and giggled; and Ruby Gillis says she doesn't believe it had anything to do with the lesson.''

"Anne Shirley, don't let me hear you talking about your teacher in that way again," said Marilla sharply. "You don't go to school to criticize the master. I guess he can teach *you* something and it's your business to learn. And I want you to understand right off that you are not to come home telling tales about him. That is something I won't encourage. I hope you were a good girl."

"Indeed I was," said Anne comfortably. "It wasn't so hard as you might imagine, either. I sit with Diana. Our seat is right by the window and we can look down to the Lake of Shining Waters. There are a lot of nice girls in school and we had scrumptious fun playing at dinner time. It's so nice to have a lot of little girls to play with. But of course I like Diana best and always will. I *adore* Diana. I'm dreadfully far behind the others. They're all in the fifth book and I'm only in the fourth. I feel that it's kind of a disgrace. But there's not one of them has such an imagination as I have and I soon found that out. We had reading and geography and Canadian History and dictation today. Mr. Phillips said my spelling was disgraceful and he held up my slate so that everybody could see it, all marked over. I felt so mortified, Marilla; he might have been politer to a stranger, I think. Ruby Gillis gave me an apple and Sophia Sloane lent me a lovely pink card with 'May I see you home?' on it. I'm to give it back to her tomorrow. And Tillie Boulter let me wear her bead ring all the afternoon. Can I have some of those pearl beads off the old pincushion in the garret to make myself a ring? And oh Marilla, Jane Andrews told me that Minnie MacPherson told her that she heard Prissy Andrews tell Sara Gillis that I had a very pretty nose. Marilla, that is the first compliment I have ever had in my life and you can't imagine what a strange feeling it gave me. Marilla, have I really a pretty nose? I know you'll tell me the truth."

"Your nose is well enough," said Marilla shortly. Secretly she thought Anne's nose was a remarkably pretty one; but she had no intention of telling her so.

That was three weeks ago and all had gone smoothly so far. And now, this crisp September morning, Anne and Diana were tripping blithely down the Birch Path, two of the happiest little girls in Avonlea.

"I guess Gilbert Blythe will be in school today," said Diana. "He's been visiting his cousins over in New Brunswick all summer and he only came home Saturday night. He's *aw'fly* handsome, Anne. And he teases the girls something terrible. He just torments our lives out."

Diana's voice indicated that she rather liked having her life tormented out than not.

"Gilbert Blythe?" said Anne. "Isn't it his name that's written up on the porch wall with Julia Bell's and a big 'Take Notice' over them?"

"Yes," said Diana, tossing her head, "but I'm sure he doesn't like Julia Bell so very much. I've heard him say he studied the multiplication table by her freckles."

"Oh, don't speak about freckles to me," implored Anne. "It isn't delicate when I've got so many. But I do think that writing take-notices up on the wall about the boys and girls is the silliest ever. I should just like to see anybody dare to write my name up with a boy's. Not, of course," she hastened to add, "that anybody would."

Anne sighed. She didn't want her name written up. But it was a little humiliating to know that there was no danger of it.

"Nonsense," said Diana, whose black eyes and glossy tresses had played such havoc with the hearts af Avonlea schoolboys that her name figured on the porch walls in half a dozen take-notices. "It's only meant as a joke. And don't you be too sure your name won't ever be written up. Charlie Sloane is *dead gone* on you. He told his mother—his *mother* mind you—that you were the smartest girl in school. That's better than being good-looking."

"No, it isn't," said Anne, feminine to the core. "I'd rather be pretty than clever. And I hate Charlie Sloane. I can't bear a boy with goggle eyes. If anyone wrote my name up with his I'd *never* get over it, Diana Barry. But it *is* nice to keep head of your class."

"You'll have Gilbert in your class after this," said Diana, "and he's used to being head of his class, I can tell you. He's only in the fourth book although he's nearly fourteen. Four years ago his father was sick and had to go out to Alberta for his health and Gilbert went with him. They were there three years and Gil didn't go to school hardly any until they came back. you won't find it so easy to keep head after this, Anne."

"I'm glad," said Anne quickly. "I couldn't really feel proud of keeping head of little boys and girls of just nine or ten. I got up yesterday spelling 'ebullition.' Josie Pye was head and, mind you, she peeped in her book. Mr. Phillips didn't see her—he was looking at Prissy Andrews—but I did. I just swept her a look of freezing scorn and she got as red as a beet and spelled it wrong after all."

"Those Pye girls are cheats all round," said Diana indignantly, as they climbed the fence of the main road. "Gertie Pye actually went and put her milk bottle in my place in the brook yesterday. Did you ever? I don't speak to her now.''

When Mr. Phillips was in the back of the room hearing Prissy Andrews' Latin Diana whispered to Anne,

''That's Gilbert Blythe sitting right across the aisle from you, Anne. Just look at him and see if you don't think he's handsome.''

Anne looked accordingly. She had a good chance to do so, for the said Gilbert Blythe was absorbed in stealthily pinning the long yellow braid of Ruby Gillis, who sat in front of him, to the back of her seat. He was a tall boy, with curly brown hair, roguish hazel eyes and a mouth twisted into a teasing smile. Presently Ruby Gillis started up to take a sum to the master; she fell back into her seat with a little shriek, believing that her hair was pulled out by the roots. Everybody looked at her and Mr. Phillips glared so sternly that Ruby began to cry. Gilbert had whisked the pin out of sight and was studying his history with the soberest face in the world; but when the commotion subsided he looked at Anne and winked with inexpressible drollery.

''I think your Gilbert Blythe *is* handsome,'' confided Anne to Diana, ''but I think he's very bold. It isn't good manners to wink at a strange girl.''

But it was not until the afternoon that things really began to happen.

Mr. Phillips was back in the corner explaining a problem in algebra to Prissy Andrews and the rest of the scholars were doing pretty much as they pleased, eating green apples, whispering, drawing pictures on their slates, and driving crickets, harnessed to strings, up and down the aisle. Gilbert Blythe was trying to make Anne Shirley look at him and failing utterly, because Anne was at that moment totally oblivious, not only of the very existence of Gilbert Blythe, but of every other scholar in Avonlea school and of Avonlea school itself. With her chin propped on her hands and her eyes fixed on the blue glimpse of the Lake of Shining Waters that the west window afforded, she was far away in a gorgeous dreamland, hearing and seeing nothing save her own wonderful visions.

Gilbert Blythe wasn't used to putting himself out to make a girl look at him and meeting with failure. She *should* look at him, that red-haired Shirley girl with the little pointed chin and the big eyes that weren't like the eyes of any other girl in Avonlea school.

Gilbert reached across the aisle, picked up the end of Anne's long red braid, held it out at arm's length and said in a piercing whisper,

"Carrots! Carrots!"

Then Anne looked at him with a vengeance!

She did more than look. She sprang to her feet, her bright fancies fallen into cureless ruin. She flashed one indignant glance at Gilbert from eyes whose angry sparkle was swiftly quenched in equally angry tears.

"You mean, hateful boy!" she exclaimed passionately. "How dare you!"

And then—Thwack! Anne had brough her slate down on Gilbert's head and cracked it—slate, not head—clear across.

Avonlea school always enjoyed a scene. This was an especially enjoyable one. Everybody said, "Oh" in horrified delight. Diana gasped. Ruby Gillis, who was inclined to be hysterical, began to cry. Tommy Sloane let his team of crickets escape him altogether while he stared open-mouthed at the tableau.

Mr. Phillips stalked down the aisle and laid his hand heavily on Anne's shoulder.

"Anne Shirley, what does this mean?" he said angrily.

Anne returned no answer. It was asking too much of flesh and blood to expect her to tell before the whole school that she had been called "carrots." Gilbert it was who spoke up stoutly.

"It was my fault, Mr. Phillips. I teased her."

Mr. Phillips paid no heed to Gilbert.

"I am sorry to see a pupil of mine displaying such a temper and such a vindictive spirit," he said in a solemn tone, as if the mere fact of being a pupil of his ought to root out all evil passions from the hearts of small imperfect mortals. "Anne, go and stand on the platform in front of the blackboard for the rest of the afternoon."

Anne would have infinitely preferred a whipping to this punishment, under which her sensitive spirit quivered as from a whiplash. With a white, set face she obeyed. Mr. Phillips took a chalk crayon and wrote on the blackboard above her head.

"Ann Shirley has a very bad temper. Ann Shirley must learn to control her temper," and then read it aloud so that even the primer class, who couldn't read writing, should understand it.

Anne stood there the rest of the afternoon with that legend above her. She did not cry or hang her head. Anger was still too hot in her heart for that and it sustained her amid all her agony of humiliation. With resentful eyes and passion-red cheeks she confronted alike Diana's sympathetic gaze and Charlie Sloane's indignant nods and Josie Pye's malicious smiles. As for Gilbert Blythe, she would not even look at him. She would *never* look at him again! She would never speak to him!!

When school was dismissed Anne marched out with her red head held high. Gilbert Blythe tried to intercept her at the porch door.

"I'm awful sorry I made fun of your hair, Anne," he whispered contritely, "Honest I am. Don't be mad for keeps, now."

Anne swept by disdainfully, without look or sign of hearing. "Oh, how could you, Anne? breathed Diana as they went down the road, half reproachfully, half admiringly. Diana felt that *she* could never have resisted Gilbert's plea.

"I shall never forgive Gilbert Blythe," said Anne firmly. "And Mr. Phillips spelled my name without an *e*, too. The iron has entered into my soul, Diana."

Diana hadn't the least idea what Anne meant but she understood it was something terrible.

"You mustn't mind Gilbert making fun of your hair," she said soothingly. "Why, he makes fun of all the girls. He laughs at mine because it's so black. He's called me a crow a dozen times; and I never heard him apologize for anything before, either."

"There's a great deal of difference between being called a crow and being called carrots," said Anne with dignity. "Gilbert Blythe has hurt my feelings *excruciatingly,* Diana."

It is possible the matter might have blown over without more excruciation if nothing else had happened. But when things begin to happen they are apt to keep on.

Avonlea scholars often spent noon hour picking gum in Mr. Bell's spruce grove over the hill and across his big pasture field. From there they could keep an eye on Eben Wright's house where the master boarded. When they saw Mr. Phillips emerging therefrom they ran for the schoolhouse; but the distance being about three times longer than Mr. Wright's lane they were very apt to arrive there, breathless and gasping, some three minutes too late.

On the following day Mr. Phillips was seized with one of his spasmodic fits of reform and announced, before going home to dinner, that he should expect to find all the scholars in their seats when he returned. Anyone who came in late would be punished.

All the boys and some of the girls went to Mr. Bell's spruce grove as usual, fully intending to stay only long enough to "pick a chew." But spruce groves are seductive and yellow nuts of gum beguiling; they picked and loitered and strayed; and as usual the first thing that recalled them to a sense of the flight of time was Jimmy Glover

THWACK! ANNE BROUGHT HER SLATE DOWN ON GILBERT'S HEAD.

shouting from the top of a patriarchal old spruce, "Master's coming."

The girls, who were on the ground, started first and managed to reach the schoolhouse in time but without a second to spare. The boys, who had to wriggle hastily down from the tress, were later; and Anne, who had not been picking gum at all but was wandering happily in the far end of the grove, waist deep among the bracken, singing softly to herself, with a wreath of rice lilies on her hair as if she were some wild divinity of the shadowy places, was latest of all. Anne could run like a deer, however; run she did with the impish result that she overtook the boys at the door and was swept into the schoolhouse among them just as Mr. Phillips was in the act of hanging up his hat.

Mr. Phillips' brief reforming energy was over; he didn't want the bother of punishing a dozen pupils; but it was necessary to do someting to save his word, so he looked about for a scapegoat and found it in Anne, who had dropped into her seat, gasping for breath, with her forgotten lily wreath hanging askew over one ear and giving her a particularly rakish and dishevelled appearance.

"Anne Shirley, since you seem to be so fond of the boys' company we shall indulge your taste for it this afternoon," he said sarcastically. "Take those flowers out of your hair and sit with Gilbert Blythe." The other boys snickered. Diana, turning pale with pity, plucked the wreath from Anne's hair and squeezed her hand. Anne stared at the master as if turned to stone.

"Did you hear what I said, Anne?" queried Mr. Phillips sternly.

"Yes, sir," said Anne slowly, "but I didn't suppose you really meant it."

"I assure you I did,"—still with the sarcastic inflection which all the children, and Anne especially, hated. It flicked on the raw. "Obey me at once."

For a moment Anne looked as if she meant to disobey. Then, realizing that there was no help for it, she rose haughtily, stepped across the aisle, sat down beside Gilbert Blythe, and buried her face in her arms on the desk. Ruby Gillis, who got a glimpse of it as it went down, told the others going home from school that she'd "acksually never seen anything like it—it was so white, with awful little red spots in it."

To Anne, this was as the end of all things. It was bad enough to be singled out for punishment from among a dozen equally guilty ones; it was worse still to be sent to sit with a boy; but that that boy should be Gilbert Blythe was heaping insult on injury to a degree utterly unbearable. Anne felt that she could *not* bear it and it would be of no use to try. Her whole being seethed with shame and anger and humiliation.

At first the other scholars looked and whispered and giggled and nudged. But as Anne never lifted her head and as Gilbert worked fractions as if his whole soul was absorbed in them and them only, they soon returned to their own tasks and Anne was forgotten. When Mr. Phillips called the history class out Anne should have gone; but Anne did not move, and Mr. Phillips, who had been writing some verse "To Priscilla" before he called the class, was thinking about an obstinate rhyme still and never missed her. Once, when nobody was looking, Gilbert took from his desk a little pink candy heart with a gold motto on it, "You are sweet," and slipped it under the curve of Anne's arm. Whereupon Anne arose, took the pink heart gingerly between the tips of her fingers, dropped it on the floor, ground it to powder beneath her heel, and resumed her position without deigning to bestow a glance on Gilbert.

When school went out Anne marched to her desk, ostenatiously took out everything therein, books and writing tablet, pen and ink, testament and arithmetic, and piled them neatly on her crack slate.

"What are you taking all those things home for, Anne?" Diana wanted to know, as soon as they were out on the road. She had not dared to ask the question before.

"I am not coming back to school any more," said Anne.

Diana gasped and stared at Anne to see if she meant it.

"Will Marilla let you stay home?" she asked.

"She'll have to," said Anne. "I'll *never* go to school to that man again."

"Oh, Anne!" Diana looked as if she were ready to cry. "I do think you're mean. What shall I do? Mr. Phillips will make me sit with that horrid Gertie Pye—I know he will because she is sitting alone. Do come back, Anne."

"I'd do almost anything in the world for you, Diana," said Anne sadly. "I'd let myself be torn limb from limb if it would do you any good. But I can't do this, so please don't ask it. You harrow up my very soul."

"Just think of all the fun you will miss," mourned Diana. "We are going to build the loveliest new house down by the brook; and we'll be playing ball next week and you've never played ball, Anne. It's tremendously exciting. And we're going to learn a new song—

Jane Andrews is practising it up now; and Alice Andrews is going to bring a new Pansy book next week and we're all going to read it out loud, chapter about, down by the brook. And you know you are so fond of reading out loud, Anne.''

Nothing moved Anne in the least. Her mind was made up. She would not go to school to Mr. Phillips again; she told Marilla so when she got home.

"Nonsense," said Marilla.

"It isn't nonsence at all," said Anne, gazing at Marilla with solemn, reproachful eyes. "Don't you understand, Marilla? I've been insulted."

"Insulted fiddlesticks! You'll go to school tomorrow as usual."

"Oh, no." Anne shook her head gently. "I'm not going back, Marilla. I'll learn my lessons at home and I'll be as good as I can be and hold my tongue all the time if it's possible at all. But I will not go back to school I assure you."

Marilla saw something remarkably like unyielding stubbornness looking out of Anne's small face. She understood that she would have trouble in overcoming it; but she resolved wisely to say nothing more just then.

"I'll run down and see Rachel about it this evening," she thought. "There's no use reasoning with Anne now. She's too worked up and I've an idea she can be awful stubborn if she takes the notion. Far as I can make out from her story, Mr. Phillips has been carrying matters with a rather high hand. But it would never do to say so to her. I'll just talk it over with Rachel. She's sent ten children to school and she ought to know something about it. She'll have heard the whole story, too, by this time."

Marilla found Mrs. Lynde knitting quilts as industriously and cheerfully as usual.

"I suppose you know what I've come about," she said, a little shamefacedly.

Mrs. Rachel nodded.

"About Anne's fuss in school, I reckon," she said. "Tillie Boulter was in on her way home from school and told me about it."

"I don't know what to do with her," said Marilla. "She declares she won't go back to school. I never saw a child so worked up. I've been expecting trouble ever since she started to school. I knew things were going too smooth to last. She's so high-strung. What would you advise, Rachel?"

"Well, since you've asked my advice, Marilla," said Mrs. Lynde amiably—Mrs. Lynde dearly loved to be asked for advice—"I'd just humor her a little at first, that's what I'd do. It's my belief that Mr. Phillips was in the wrong. Of course, it doesn't do to say so to the children, you know. And of course he did right to punish her yesterday for giving way to temper. But today it was different. The others who were late should have been punished as well as Anne, that's what. And I don't believe in making the girls sit with the boys for punishment. It isn't modest. Tille Boulter was real indignant. She took Anne's part right through and said all the scholars did, too. Anne seems real popular among them, somehow. I never thought she'd take with them so well.''

''Then you really think I'd better let her stay home,'' said Marilla in amazement.

''Yes. That is, I wouldn't say school to her again until she said it herself. Depend upon it, Marilla, she'll cool off in a week or so and be ready enough to go back of her own accord, that's what, while, if you were to make her go back right off, dear knows what freak or tantrum she'd take next and make more trouble than ever. The less fuss made the better, in my opinion. She won't miss much by not going to school, as far as *that* goes. Mr. Phillips isn't any good at all as a teacher. The order he keeps is scandalous, that's what, and he neglects the young fry and puts all his time on those big scholars he's getting ready for Queen's. He'd never have got the school for another year if his uncle hadn't been a trustee—*the* trustee, for he just leads the other two around by the nose, that's what. I declare, I don't know what education in this Island is coming to.''

Mrs. Rachel shook her head, as much as to say if she were only at the head of the educational system of the Province things would be much better managed.

Marilla took Mrs. Rachel's advice and not another word was said to Anne about going back to school. She learned her lessons at home, did her chores, and played with Diana in the chilly purple autumn twilights; but when she met Gilbert Blythe on the road or encountered him in Sunday-school she passed him by with an icy contempt that was no whit thawed by his evident desire to appease her. Even Diana's efforts as a peacemaker were of no avail. Anne had evidently made up her mind to hate Gilbert Blythe to the end of life.

As much as she hated Gilbert, however, did she love Diana, with all the love of her passionate little heart, equally intense in its likes and dislikes. One evening Marilla, coming in from the orchard with a basket of apples, found Anne sitting alone by the east window in the twilight, crying bitterly.

''Whatever's the matter now, Anne?'' she asked.

"It's about Diana," sobbed Anne luxuriously. "I love Diana so, Marilla. I cannot ever live without her. But I know very well when we grow up that Diana will get married and go away and leave me. And oh, what shall I do? I hate her husband—I just hate him furiously. I've been imagining it all out—the wedding and everything—Diana dressed in snowy garments, with a veil, and looking beautiful and regal as a queen; and me the bridesmaid, with a lovely dress, too, and puffed sleeves, but with a breaking heart hid beneath my smiling face. And then bidding Diana good-by-e-e—" Here Anne broke down entirely and wept with increasing bitterness.

Marilla turned quickly away to hide her twitching face; but it was no use; she collapsed on the nearest chair and burst into such a hearty and unusual peal of laughter that Matthew, crossing the yard outside, halted in amazement. When had he heard Marilla laugh like that before?

"Well, Anne Shirley," said Marilla as soon as she could speak, "if you must borrow trouble, for pity's sake borrow it handier home. I should think you had an imagination, sure enough."

CHAPTER 16

DIANA IS INVITED TO TEA WITH TRAGIC RESULTS

OCTOBER WAS a beautiful month at Green Gables, when the birches in the hollow turned as golden as sunshine and the maples behind the orchard were royal crimson and the wild cherry-trees along the lane put on the loveliest shades of dark red and bronzy green, while the fields sunned themselves in aftermaths.

Anne revelled in the world of color about her.

"Oh, Marilla," she exclaimed one Saturday morning, coming dancing in with her arms full of gorgeous boughs. "I'm so glad I live in a world where there are Octobers. It would be terrible if we just skipped from September to November, wouldn't it? Look at these maple branches. Don't they give you a thrill—several thrills? I'm going to decorate my room with them."

"Messy things," said Marilla, whose aesthetic sense was not

noticeably developed. "You clutter up your room entirely too much with out-of-doors stuff, Anne. Bedrooms were made to sleep in."

"Oh, and dream in too, Marilla. And you know one can dream so much better in a room where there are pretty things. I'm going to put these boughs in the old blue jug and set them on my table."

"Mind you don't drop leaves all over the stairs then. I'm going to a meeting of the Aid Society at Carmody this afternoon, Anne, and I won't likely be home before dark. You'll have to get Matthew and Jerry their supper, so mind you don't forget to put the tea to draw until you sit down at the table as you did last time."

"It was dreadful of me to forget," said Anne apologetically, "but that was the afternoon I was trying to think of a name for Violet Vale and it crowded other things out. Matthew was so good. He never scolded a bit. He put the tea down himself and said we could wait awhile as well as not. And I told him a lovely fairy story while we were waiting, so he didn't find the time long at all. It was a beautiful fairy story, Marilla. I forgot the end of it, so I made up an end for it myself and Matthew said he couldn't tell where the join came in."

"Matthew would think it all right, Anne, if you took a notion to get up and have dinner in the middle of the night. But you keep your wits about you this time. And—I don't really know if I'm doing right—it may make you more addle-pated than ever—but you can ask Diana to come over and spend the afternoon with you and have tea here."

"Oh, Marilla!" Anne clasped her hands. "How perfectly lovely! You *are* able to imagine things after all or else you'd never have understood how I've longed for that very thing. It will seem so nice and grown-uppish. No fear of my forgetting to put the tea to draw when I have company. Oh, Marilla, can I use the rosebud spray tea-set?"

"No, indeed! The rosebud tea-set! Well, what next? You know I never use that except for the minister or the Aids. You'll put down the old brown tea-set. But you can open the little yellow crock of cherry preserves. It's time it was being used anyhow—I believe it's beginning to work. And you can cut some fruit-cake and have some of the cookies and snaps."

"I can just imagine myself sitting down at the head of the table and pouring out the tea," said Anne, shutting her eyes ecstatically. "And asking Diana if she takes sugar! I know she doesn't but of course I'll ask her just as if I didn't know. And then pressing her to take another piece of fruit-cake and another helping of preserves.

Oh, Marilla, it's a wonderful sensation just to think of it. Can I take her into the spare room to lay off her hat when she comes? And then into the parlor to sit?''

"No. The sitting-room will do for you and your company. But there's a bottle half full of raspberry cordial that was left over from the church social the other night. It's on the second shelf of the sitting-room closet and you and Diana can have it if you like, and a cooky to eat with it along in the afternoon, for I daresay Matthew'll be late coming in to tea since he's hauling potatoes to the vessel.''

Anne flew down to the hollow, past the Dryad's Bubble and up the spruce path to Orchard Slope, to ask Diana to tea. As a result, just after Marilla had driven off to Carmody, Diana came over, dressed in her second best dress and looking exactly as it is proper to look when asked out to tea. At other times she was wont to run into the kitchen without knocking; but now she knocked primly at the front door. And when Anne, dressed in *her* second best, as primly opened it, both little girls shook hands as gravely as if they had never met before. This unnatural solemnity lasted until after Diana had been taken to the east gable to lay off her hat and then had sat for ten minutes in the sitting-room, toes in position.

"How is your mother?'' inquired Anne politely, just as if she had not seen Mrs. Barry picking apples that morning in excellent health and spirits.

"She is very well, thank you. I suppose Mr. Cuthbert is hauling potatoes to the *Lily Sands* this afternoon, is he?'' said Diana, who had ridden down to Mr. Harmon Andrews' that morning in Matthew's cart.

"Yes. Our potato crop is very good this year. I hope your father's potato crop is good, too.''

"It is fairly good, thank you. Have you picked many of your apples yet?''

"Oh, ever so many,'' said Anne, forgetting to be dignified and jumping up quickly. "Let's go out to the orchard and get some of the Red Sweetings, Diana. Marilla says we can have all that are left on the tree. Marilla is a very generous woman. She said we could have fruit-cake and cherry preserves for tea. But it isn't good manners to tell your company what you are going to give them to eat, so I won't tell you what she said we could have to drink. Only it begins with an *r* and a *c* and it's a bright red color. I love bright red drinks, don't you? They taste twice as good as any other color.''

The orchard, with its great sweeping boughs that bent to the ground with fruit, proved so delightful that the little girls spent most of the afternoon in it, sitting in a grassy corner where the frost had spared the green and the mellow autumn sunshine lingered warmly, eating apples and talking as hard as they could. Diana had much to tell Anne of what went on in school. She had to sit with Gertie Pye and she hated it; Gertie squeaked her pencil all the time and it just made her—Diana's—blood run cold; Ruby Gillis had charmed all her warts away, true's you live, with a magic pebble that old Mary Joe from the Creek gave her. You had to rub the warts with the pebble and then throw it away over your left shoulder at the time of the new moon and the warts would all go. Charlie Sloane's name was written up with Em White's on the porch wall and Em White was *awful mad* about it; Sam Boulter had "sassed" Mr. Phillips in class and Mr. Phillips whipped him and Sam's father came to the school and dared Mr. Phillips to lay a hand on one of his children again; and Mattie Andrews had a new red hood and a blue crossover with tassels on it and the airs she put on about it were perfectly sickening; and Lizzie Wright didn't speak to Mamie Wilson because Mamie Wilson's grown-up sister had cut out Lizzie Wright's grown-up sister with her beau; and everybody missed Anne so and wished she'd come to school again; and Gilbert Blythe—

But Anne didn't want to hear about Gilbert Blythe. She jumped up hurriedly and said suppose they go in and have some raspberry cordial.

Anne looked on the second shelf of the room pantry but there was no bottle of raspberry cordial there. Search revealed it away back on the top shelf. Anne put it on a tray and set it on the table with a tumbler.

"Now, please help yourself, Diana," she said politely. "I don't believe I'll have any just now. I don't feel as if I wanted any after all those apples."

Diana poured herself out a tumblerful, looked at its bright red hue admiringly, and then sipped it daintily.

"That's awfully nice raspberry cordial, Anne," she said. "I didn't know raspberry cordial was so nice."

"I'm real glad you like it. Take as much as you want. I'm going to run out and stir the fire up. There are so many responsibilities on a person's mind when they're keeping house, isn't there?"

When Anne came back from the kitchen Diana was drinking her second glassful of cordial; and, being entreated thereto by Anne, she offered no particular objection to the drinking of a third. The tumblerfuls were generous ones and the raspberry cordial was certainly very nice.

"The nicest I ever drank," said Diana. "It's ever so much nicer than Mrs. Lynde's although she brags of hers so much. It doesn't taste a bit like hers."

"I should think Marilla's raspberry cordial would prob'ly be much nicer than Mrs. Lynde's," said Anne loyally. "Marilla is a famous cook. She is trying to teach me to cook but I assure you, Diana, it is uphill work. There's so little scope for imagination in cookery. You have to go by rules. The last time I made a cake I forgot to put the flour in. I was thinking the loveliest story about you and me, Diana. I thought you were desperately ill with smallpox and everybody deserted you, but I went boldly to your bedside and nursed you back to life; and then I took the smallpox and died and I was buried under those poplar trees in the graveyard and you planted a rosebush by my grave and watered it with your tears; and you never, never forgot the friend of your youth who sacrificed her life for you. Oh, it was a pathetic tale, Diana. The tears just rained down over my cheeks while I mixed the cake. But I forgot the flour and the cake was a dismal failure. Flour is so essential to cakes, you know. Marilla was very cross and I don't wonder. I'm a great trial to her. She was terribly mortified about the pudding sauce last week. We had a plum pudding for dinner on Tuesday and there was half the pudding and a pitcherful of sauce left over. Marilla said there was enough for another dinner and told me to set it on the pantry shelf and cover it. I meant to cover it just as much as could be, Diana, but when I carried it in I was imagining I was a nun—of course I'm a Protestant but I imagined I was a Catholic—taking the veil to bury a broken heart in cloistered seclusion; and I forgot all about covering the pudding sauce. I thought of it next morning and ran to the pantry. Diana, fancy if you can my extreme horror at finding a mouse drowned in that pudding sauce! I lifted the mouse out with a spoon and threw it in the yard and then I washed the spoon in three waters. Marilla was out milking and I fully intended to ask her when she came in if I'd give the sauce to the pigs; but when she did come in I was imagining that I was a frost fairy going through the woods turning the trees red and yellow, whichever they wanted to be, so I never thought about the pudding sauce again and Marilla sent me out to pick apples. Well, Mr. and Mrs. Chester Ross from Spencervale came here that morning. You know they are very stylish people, especially Mrs. Chester Ross. When Marlla called me in dinner was ready and everybody was at the table. I tried to be as polite and dignified as I could be, for I wanted Mrs. Chester Ross to think I was a ladylike little girl even if I wasn't pretty. Everything went right until I saw Marilla coming with the plum pudding in one hand and the pitcher of pudding sauce, *warmed up,* in the other. Diana, that was a terrible moment. I remembered everything and I just stood up in my place and shrieked out, 'Marilla, you mustn't use that pudding sauce. There was a mouse drowned in it. I forgot to tell you before.' Oh, Diana, I shall never forget that awful moment if I live to be a hundred. Mrs. Chester Ross just *looked* at me and I thought I would sink through the floor with mortification. She is such a perfect housekeeper and fancy what she must have thought of us. Marilla turned red as fire but she never said a word—then. She just carried that sauce and pudding out and brought in some strawberry preserves. She even offered me some, but I couldn't swallow a mouthful. It was like heaping coals of fire on my head. After Mrs. Chester Ross went away Marilla gave me a dreadful scolding. Why, Diana, what it the matter?''

Diana had stood up very unsteadily; then she sat down again, putting her hands to her head.

"I'm—I'm awful sick," she said, a little thickly. "I—I—must go right home."

"Oh, you mustn't dream of going home without your tea," cried Anne in distress. "I'll get it right off—I'll go and put the tea down this very minute."

"I must go home," repeated Diana, stupidly but determinedly.

"Let me get you a lunch anyhow," implored Anne. "Let me give you a bit of fruit-cake and some of the cherry preserves. Lie down on the sofa for a little while and you'll be better. Where do you feel bad?"

"I must go home," said Diana, and that was all she would say. In vain Anne pleaded.

"I never heard of company going home without tea," she mourned. "Oh, Diana, do you suppose that it's possible you're really taking the smallpox? If you are I'll go and nurse you, you can depend on that. I'll never foresake you. But I do wish you'd stay till after tea. Where do you feel bad?"

"I'm awful dizzy," said Diana.

And indeed, she walked very dizzily. Anne, with tears of disappointment in her eyes, got Diana's hat and went with her as far as the Barry yard fence. Then she wept all the way back to Green Gables, where she sorrowfully put the remainder of the raspberry cordial back into the pantry and got tea for Matthew and Jerry, with all the zest gone out of the performance.

The next day was Sunday and as the rain poured down in torrents from dawn till dusk Anne did not stir abroad from Green Gables. Monday afternoon Marilla sent her down to Mrs. Lynde's on an errand. In a very short space of time Anne came flying back up the lane, with tears rolling down her cheeks. Into the kitchen she dashed and flung herself downward on the sofa in an agony.

"Whatever has gone wrong now, Anne?" queried Marilla in doubt and dismay. "I do hope you haven't gone and been saucy to Mrs. Lynde again."

No answer from Anne save more tears and stormier sobs!

"Anne Shirley, when I ask you a question I want to be answered. Sit right up this very minute and tell me what you are crying about."

Anne sat up, tragedy personified.

"Mrs. Lynde was up to see Mrs. Barry today and Mrs. Barry was in an awful state," she wailed. "She says that I set Diana *drunk* Saturday and sent her home in a disgraceful condition. And she says I must be a thoroughly bad, wicked little girl and she's never, never going to let Diana play with me again. Oh, Marilla, I'm just overcome with woe."

Marilla stared in blank amazement.

"Set Diana drunk!" she said when she found her voice. "Anne, are you or Mrs. Barry crazy? What on earth did you give her?"

"Not a thing but raspberry cordial," sobbed Anne. "I never thought raspberry cordial would set people drunk, Marilla,—not even if they drank three big tumblerfuls as Diana did. Oh, it sounds so—so—like Mrs. Thomas' husband! But I didn't mean to set her drunk."

"Drunk fiddlesticks!" said Marilla, marching to the sitting-room pantry. There on the shelf was a bottle which she at once recognized as one containing some of her three year old homemade currant wine for which she was celebrated in Avonlea, although certain of the stricter sort, Mrs. Barry among them, disapproved strongly of it. And at the same time Marilla recollected that she had put the bottle of raspberry cordial down in the cellar instead of in the pantry as she had told Anne.

She went back to the kitchen with the wine bottle in her hand. Her face was twitching in spite of herself.

"Anne, you certainly have a genius for getting into trouble. You went and gave Diana currant wine instead of raspberry cordial.

Didn't you know the difference yourself?''

"I never tasted it," said Anne. "I thought it was the cordial. I meant to be so—so—hospitable. Diana got awfully sick and had to go home. Mrs. Barry told Mrs. Lynde she was simply dead drunk. She just laughed silly like when her mother aksed what was the matter and went to sleep and slept for hours. Her mother smelled her breath and knew she was drunk. She had a fearful headache all day yesterday. Mrs. Barry is so indignant. She will never believe but what I did it on purpose.''

"I should think she would better punish Diana for being so greedy as to drink three glassfuls of anything," said Marilla shortly. "Why, three of those big glasses would have made her sick even if it had only been cordial. Well, this story will be a nice handle for those folks who are so down on me for making currant wine, although I haven't made any for three years ever since I found out that the minister didn't approve. I just kept that bottle for sickness. There, there, child, don't cry. I can't see as you were to blame although I'm sorry it happened so.''

"I must cry," said Anne. "My heart is broken. The stars in their courses fight against me, Marilla. Diana and I are parted forever. Oh, Marilla, I little dreamed of this when first we swore our vows of friendship.''

"Don't be foolish, Anne. Mrs. Barry will think better of it when she finds you're not really to blame. I suppose she thinks you've done it for a silly joke or something of that sort. You'd best go up this evening and tell her how it was.''

"My courage fails me at the thought of facing Diana's injured mother," sighed Anne. "I wish you'd go, Marilla. You're so much more dignified than I am. Likely she'd listen to you quicker than to me.''

"Well, I will," said Marilla, reflecting that it would probably be the wiser course. "Don't cry any more, Anne. It will be all right.''

Marilla had changed her mind about its being all right by the time she got back from Orchard Slope. Anne was watching for her coming and flew to the porch door to meet her.

"Oh, Marilla, I know by your face that it's been no use," she said sorrowfully. "Mrs. Barry won't forgive me?''

"Mrs. Barry, indeed!" snapped Marilla. "Of all the unreasonable women I ever saw she's the worst. I told her it was all a mistake and you weren't to blame, but she just simply didn't believe me. And she rubbed it well in about my currant wine and how I'd always said it couldn't have the least effect on anybody. I just told her plainly that

currant wine wasn't meant to be drunk three tumblerfuls at a time and
that if a child I had to do with was so greedy I'd sober her up with a
right good spanking.''

Marilla whisked into the kitchen, grievously disturbed, leaving a
very much distracted little soul in the porch behind her. Presently
Anne stepped out bare-headed into the chill autumn dusk; very
determinedly and steadily she took her way down through the sere
clover field over the log bridge and up through the spruce grove,
lighted by a pale little moon hanging low over the western woods.
Mrs. Barry, coming to the door in answer to a timid knock, found a
white-lipped, eager-eyed suppliant on the doorstep.

Her face hardened. Mrs. Barry was a woman of strong prejudices
and dislikes, and her anger was of the cold, sullen sort which is
always hardest to overcome. To do her justice, she really believed
Anne had made Diana drunk out of sheer malice prepense, and she
was honestly anxious to preserve her little daughter from the con-
tamination of further intimacy with such a child.

"What do you want?" she said stiffly.

Anne clasped her hands.

"Oh, Mrs. Barry, please forgive me. I did not mean to—to—
intoxicate Diana. How could I? Just imagine if you were a poor little
orphan girl that kind people had adopted and you had just one bosom
friend in all the world. Do you think you would intoxicate her on
purpose? I thought it was only raspberry cordial. I was firmly convinced it was raspberry cordial. Oh, please don't say that you won't
let Diana play with me any more. If you do you will cover my life
with a dark cloud of woe.''

This speech, which would have softened good Mrs. Lynde's heart
in a twinkling, had no effect on Mrs. Barry except to irritate her still
more. She was suspicious of Anne's big words and dramatic gestures
and imagined that the child was making fun of her.

"I don't think you are a fit little girl for Diana to associate with.
You'd better go home and behave yourself.''

Anne's lip quivered.

"Won't you let me see Diana just once to say farewell?" she
implored.

"Diana has gone over to Carmody with her father," said Mrs.
Barry, going in and shutting the door.

Anne went back to Green Gables calm with despair.

"My last hope is gone," she told Marilla. "I went up and saw
Mrs. Barry myself and she treated me very insultingly. Marilla, I do
not think she is a well-bred woman. There is nothing more to do

except pray and I haven't much hope that that'll do much good because, Marilla, I do not believe that God Himself can do very much with such an obstinate person as Mrs. Barry.''

''Anne, you shouldn't say such things,'' rebuked Marilla, striving to overcome that unholy tendency to laughter which she was dismayed to find growing upon her. And indeed, when she told the whole story to Matthew that night, she did laugh heartily over Anne's tribulations.

But when she slipped into the east gable before going to bed and found that Anne had cried herself to sleep an unaccustomed softness crept into her face.

''Pour little soul,'' she murmured, lifting a loose curl of hair from the child's tear-stained face. Then she bent down and kissed the flushed cheek on the pillow.

CHAPTER 17

A NEW INTEREST IN LIFE

THE NEXT afternoon Anne, bending over her patchwork at the kitchen window, happened to glance out and beheld Diana down by the Dryad's Bubble beckoning mysteriously. In a trice Anne was out of the house and flying down to the hollow, astonishment and hope struggling in her expressive eyes. But the hope faded when she saw Diana's dejected countenance.

''Your mother hasn't relented?'' she gasped.

Diana shook her head mournfully.

''No; and oh, Anne, she says I'm never to play with you again. I've cried and cried and I told her it wasn't your fault, but it wasn't any use. I had ever such a time coaxing her to let me come down and say good-bye to you. She said I was only to stay ten minutes and she's timing me by the clock.''

''Ten minutes isn't very long to say an eternal farewell in,'' said Anne tearfully. ''Oh, Diana, will you promise faithfully never to forget me, the friend of your youth, no matter what dearer friends may caress thee?''

''Indeed I will,'' sobbed Diana, ''and I'll never have another bosom friend—I don't want to have. I couldn't love anybody as I love you."

"Oh, Diana," cried Anne, clasping her hands, "do you *love* me?"

"Why, of course I do. Didn't you know that?"

"No." Anne drew a long breath. "I thought you *liked* me of course, but I never hoped you *loved* me. Why, Diana, I didn't think anybody could love me. Nobody ever has loved me since I can remember. Oh, this is wonderful! It's a ray of light which will forever shine on the darkness of a path severed from thee, Diana. Oh, just say it once again."

"I love you devotedly, Anne," said Diana stanchly, "and I always will, you may be sure of that."

"And I will always love thee, Diana," said Anne, solemnly extending her hand. "In the years to come thy memory will shine like a star over my lonely life, as that last story we read together says. Diana, wilt thou give me a lock of thy jet-black tresses in parting to treasure forevermore?"

"Have you got anything to cut it with?" queried Diana, wiping away the tears which Anne's affecting accents had caused to flow afresh, and returning to practicalities.

"Yes. I've got my patchwork scissors in my apron pocket fortunately," said Anne. She solemnly clipped one of Diana's curls. "Fare thee well, my beloved friend. Henceforth we must be as strangers living side by side. But my heart will ever be faithful to thee."

Anne stood and watched Diana out of sight, mournfully waving her hand to the latter whenever she turned to look back. Then she returned to the house, not a little consoled for the time being by this romantic parting.

"It is all over," she informed Marilla. "I shall never have another friend. I'm really worse off than ever before, for I haven't Katie Maurice and Violetta now. And even if I had it wouldn't be the same. Somehow, little dream girls are not satisfying after a real friend. Diana and I had such an affecting farewell down by the spring. It well be sacred in my memory forever. I used the most pathetic language I could think of and said 'thou' and 'thee.' 'Thou' and 'thee' seem so much more romantic than 'you.' Diana gave me a lock of her hair and I'm going to sew it up in a little bag and wear it around my neck all my life. Please see that it is buried with me, for I don't believe I'll live very long. Perhaps when she sees me lying cold and dead before her Mrs. Barry may feel remorse for what she has done and will let Diana come to my funeral.''

''I don't think there is much fear of your dying of grief as long as you can talk, Anne,'' said Marilla unsympathetically.

The following Monday Anne surprised Marilla by coming down from her room with her basket of books on her arm and her lips primmed up into a line of determination.

''I'm going back to school,'' she announced. ''That is all there is left in life for me, now that my friend has been ruthlessly torn from me. In school I can look at her and muse over days departed.''

''You'd better muse over your lessons and sums,'' said Marilla, concealing her delight at this development of the situation. ''If you're going back to school I hope we'll hear no more of breaking slates over people's heads and such carryings-on. Behave yourself and do just what your teacher tells you.''

''I'll try to be a model pupil,'' agreed Anne dolefully. ''There won't be much fun in it, I expect. Mr. Phillips said Minnie Andrews was a model pupil and there isn't a spark of imagination or life in her. She is just dull and poky and never seems to have a good time. But I feel so depressed that perhpas it will come easy to me now. I'm going round by the road. I couldn't bear to go by the Birch Path all alone. I should weep bitter tears if I did.''

Anne was welcomed back to school with open arms. Her imagination had been sorely missed in games, her voice in the singing, and her dramatic ability in the perusal aloud of books at dinner hour. Ruby Gillis smuggled three plums over to her during testament reading; Ella May Macpherson gave her an enormous yellow pansy cut from the covers of a floral catalogue—a species of desk decoration much prized in Avonlea school. Sophia Sloane offered to teach her a perfectly elegant new pattern of knit lace, *so* nice for trimming aprons. Katie Boulter gave her a perfume bottle to keep slate-water in and Julia Bell copied carefully on a piece of pale pink paper, scalloped on the edges, the following effusion:

TO ANNE
When twilight drops her curtain down
And pins it with a star
Remember that you have a friend
Though she may wander far.

"It's so nice to be appreciated," sighed Anne rapturously to Marilla that night.

The girls were not the only scholars who "appreciated" her. When Anne went to her seat after dinner hour—she had been told by Mr. Phillips to sit with the model Minnie Andrews—she found on her desk a big luscious "strawberry apple." Anne caught it up all ready to take a bite, when she remembered that the only place in Avonlea where strawberry apples grew was in the old Blythe orchard on the other side of the Lake of Shining Waters. Anne dropped the apple as if it were a red-hot coal and ostentatiously wiped her fingers on her handkerchief. The apple lay untouched on her desk until the next morning, when little Timothy Andrews, who swept the school and kindled the fire, annexed it as one of his perquisites. Charlie Sloane's slate pencil, gorgeously bedizened with striped red and yellow paper, costing two cents where ordinary pencils cost only one, which he sent up to her after dinner hour, met with a more favorable reception. Anne was graciously pleased to accept it and rewarded the donor with a smile which exalted that infatuated youth straightway into the seventh heaven of delight and caused him to make such fearful errors in his dictation that Mr. Phillips kept him after to rewrite it.

But as,

> *The Caesar's pageant shorn of Brutus' bust*
> *Did but of Rome's best son remind her more*

so the marked absence of any tribute or recognition from Diana Barry, who was sitting with Gertie Pye, embittered Anne's little triumph.

"Diana might just have smiled at me once, I think," she mourned to Marilla that night. But the next morning a note, most fearfully and wonderfully twisted and folded, and a small parcel, were passed across to Anne.

"Dear Anne," ran the former, "Mother says I'm not to play with you or talk to you even in school. It isn't my fault and don't be cross at me, because I love you as much as ever. I miss you awfully to tell all my secrets to and I don't like Gertie Pye one bit. I made you one of the new bookmarkers out of red tissue paper. They are awfully fashionable now and only three girls in school know how to make them. When you look at it remember

"Your true friend,
"DIANA BARRY"

Anne read the note, kissed the bookmark, and despatched a prompt reply back to the other side of the school.

"MY OWN DARLING DIANA:—

"Of course I am not cross at you because you have to obey your mother. Our spirits can commune. I shall keep your lovely present forever. Minnie Andrews is a very nice little girl—although she has no imagination—but after having been Diana's busum friend I cannot be Minnie's. Please excuse mistakes because my spelling isn't very good yet, although much improoved.

"Yours until death us do part,
"ANNE or CORDELIA SHIRLEY.

"P.S. I shall sleep with your letter under my pillow tonight.

"A. or C.S."

Marilla pessimistically expected more trouble since Anne had again begun to go to school. But none developed. Perhaps Anne caught something of the "model" spirit from Minnie Andrews; at least she got on very well with Mr. Phillips thenceforth. She flung herself into her studies heart and soul, determined not to to be outdone in any class by Gilbert Blythe. The rivalry between them was soon apparent; it was entirely good-natured on Gilbert's side; but it is much to be feared that the same thing cannot be said of Anne, who had certainly an unpraiseworthy tenacity for holding grudges. She was as intense in her hatreds as in her loves. She would not stoop to admit that she meant to rival Gilbert in his school work, because that would have been to acknowledge his existence which Anne persistently ignored; but the rivalry was there and honors fluctuated between them. Now Gilbert was head of the spelling class; now Anne, with a toss of her long red braids, spelled him down. One morning Gilbert had all his sums done correctly and had his name written on the blackboard on the roll of honour; the next morning Anne, having wrestled wildly with decimals the entire evening before, would be first. One awful day they were ties and their names were written up together. It was almost as bad as a "take-notice" and Anne's mortification was as evident as Gilbert's satisfaction. When the written examinations at the end of each month were held the suspense was terrible. The first month Gilbert came out three marks ahead. The second Anne beat him by five. But her triumph was marred by the fact that Gilbert congratulated her heartily before the whole school. It would have been ever so much sweeter to her if he had felt the sting of his defeat.

Mr. Phillips might not be a very good teacher; but a pupil so inflexibly determined on learning as Anne was could hardly escape making progress under any kind of a teacher. By the end of the term Anne and Gilbert were both promoted into the fifth class and allowed to begin studying the elements of "the branches"—by which Latin, geometry, French and algebra were meant. In geometry Anne met her Waterloo.

"It's perfectly awful stuff, Marilla," she groaned. "I'm sure I'll never be able to make head or tail of it. There is no scope for imagination in it at all. Mr. Phillips says I'm the worst dunce he ever saw at it. And Gil—I mean some of the others are so smart at it. It is extremely mortifying, Marilla. Even Diana gets along better than I do. But I don't mind being beaten by Diana. Even although we meet as strangers now I still love her with an *inextinguishable* love. It makes me very sad at times to think about her. But really, Marilla, one can't stay sad very long in such an interesting world, can one?"

CHAPTER 18

ANNE TO THE RESCUE

ALL THINGS great are wound up with all things little. At first glance it might not seem that the decision of a certain Canadian Premier to include Prince Edward Island in a political tour could have much or anything to do with the fortunes of little Anne Shirley at Green Gables. But it had.

It was in January the Premier came, to address his loyal supporters and such of his non-supporters as chose to be present at the monster mass meeting held in Charlottetown. Most of the Avonlea people were on the Premier's side of politics; hence, on the night of the meeting nearly all the men and a goodly proportion of the women had gone to town, thirty miles away. Mrs. Rachel Lynde had gone too. Mrs. Rachel Lynde was a red-hot politician and couldn't have believed that the political rally could be carried through without her, although she was on the opposite side of politics. So she went to town and took her husband—Thomas would be useful in looking after the horse—and Marilla Cuthbert with her. Marilla had a sneaking interest in politics herself, and as she thought it might be her only chance to see a real live Premier, she promptly took it, leaving Anne and Matthew to keep house until her return the following day.

Hence, while Marilla and Mrs. Rachel were enjoying themselves hugely at the mass meeting, Anne and Matthew had the cheerful kitchen at Green Gables all to themselves. A bright fire was glowing in the old-fashioned Waterloo stove and blue-white frost crystals were shining on the window-panes. Matthew nodded over a *Farmers' Advocate* on the sofa and Anne at the table studied her lessons with grim determination, despite sundry wistful glances at the clock shelf, where lay a new book that Jane Andrews had lent her that day. Jane had assured her that it was warranted to produce any number of thrills, or words to that effect, and Anne's fingers tingled to reach out for it. But that would mean Gilbert Bythe's triumph on the morrow. Anne turned her back on the clock shelf and tried to imagine it wasn't there.

"Matthew, did you ever study geometry when you went to school?"

"Well now, no, I didn't," said Matthew, coming out of his doze with a start.

"I wish you had," sighed Anne, "because then you'd be able to sympathize with me. You can't sympathize properly if you've never studied it. It is casting a cloud over my whole life. I'm such a dunce at it, Matthew."

"Well now, I dunno," said Matthew soothingly. "I guess you're all right at anything. Mr. Phillips told me last week in Blair's store at Carmody that you was the smartest scholar in school and was making rapid progress. 'Rapid progress' was his very words. There's them as runs down Teddy Phillips and says he ain't much of a teacher; but I guess he's all right."

Matthew would have thought any one who praised Anne was "all right."

"I'm sure I'd get on better with geometry if only he wouldn't change the letters," complained Anne. "I learn the proposition off by heart, and then he draws it on the blackboard and puts different letters from what are in the book and I get all mixed up. I don't think a teacher should take such a mean advantage, do you? We're studying agriculture now and I've found out at last what makes the roads red. It's a great comfort. I wonder how Marilla and Mrs. Lynde are enjoying themselves. Mrs. Lynde says Canada is going to the dogs the way things are being run at Ottawa, and that it's an awful warning to the electors. She says if women were allowed to vote we would soon see a blessed change. What way do you vote, Matthew?"

"Conservative," said Matthew promptly. To vote Conservative was part of Matthew's religion.

"Then I'm Conservative too," said Anne decidely. "I'm glad, because Gil—because some of the boys in school are Grits. I guess Mr. Phillips is a Grit too, because Prissy Andrews' father is one, and Ruby Gillis says that when a man is courting he always has to agree with the girl's mother in religion and her father in politics. Is that true, Matthew?"

"Well now, I dunno," said Matthew.

"Did you ever go courting, Matthew?"

"Well, now, no, I dunno's I ever did," said Matthew, who had certainly never thought of such a thing in his whole existence.

Anne reflected with her chin in her hands.

"It must be rather interesting, don't you think, Matthew? Ruby Gillis says when she grows up she's going to have ever so many beaus on the string and have them all crazy about her; but I think that would be too exciting. I'd rather have just one in his right mind. But Ruby Gillis knows a great deal about such matters because she has so many big sisters, and Mrs. Lynde says the Gillis girls have gone off like hot cakes. Mr. Phillips goes up to see Prissy Andrews nearly every evening. He says it is to help her with her lessons, but Miranda Sloane is studying for Queen's, too, and I should think she needed help a lot more than Prissy because she's ever so much stupider, but he never goes to help her in the evenings at all. There are a great many things in this world that I can't understand very well, Matthew."

"Well now, I dunno as I comprehend them all myself," acknowledged Matthew.

"Well, I suppose I must finish up my lessons. I won't allow myself to open that new book Jane lent me until I'm through. But it's a terrible temptation, Matthew. Even when I turn my back on it I can see it there just as plain. Jane said she cried herself sick over it. I love a book that makes me cry. But I think I'll carry that book into the sitting-room and lock it in the jam closet and give you the key. And you must *not* give it to me, Matthew, until my lessons are done, not even if I implore you on my bended knees. It's all very well to say resist temptation, but it's ever so much easier to resist it if you can't get the key. And then shall I run down the cellar and get some russets, Matthew? Wouldn't you like some russets?''

''Well now, I dunno but what I would,'' said Matthew, who never ate russets but knew Anne's weakness for them.

Just as Anne emerged triumphantly from the cellar with her plateful of russets came the sound of flying footsteps on the icy board walk outside and the next moment the kitchen door was flung open and in rushed Diana Barry, white-faced and breathless, with a shawl wrapped hastily around her head. Anne promptly let go of her candle and plate in her surprise, and plate, candle, and apples crashed together down the cellar ladder and were found at the bottom embedded in melted grease, the next day, by Marilla, who gathered them up and thanked mercy the house hadn't been set on fire.

''Whatever is the matter, Diana?'' cried Anne. ''Has your mother relented at last?''

''Oh, Anne, do come quick,'' implored Diana nervously. ''Minnie May is awful sick—she's got croup, Young Mary Joe says—and father and mother are away to town and there's nobody to go for the doctor. Minnie May is awful bad and Young Mary Joe doesn't know what to do—and oh, Anne, I'm so scared!''

Matthew, without a word, reached out for cap and coat, slipped past Diana and away into the darkness of the yard.

''He's gone to harness the sorrel mare to go to Carmody for the doctor,'' said Anne, who was hurrying on hood and jacket. ''I know it as well as if he'd said so. Matthew and I are such kindred spirits I can read his thoughts without words at all.''

''I don't believe he'll find the doctor at Carmody,'' sobbed Diana. ''I know that Doctor Blair went to town and I guess Doctor Spencer would go too. Young Mary Joe never saw anybody with croup and Mrs. Lynde is away. Oh, Anne!''

''Don't cry, Di,'' said Anne cheerily. ''I know exactly what to do for croup. You forget that Mrs. Hammond had twins three times. When you look after three pairs of twins you naturally get a lot of experience. They all had croup regularly. Just wait till I get the ipecac bottle—you mayn't have any at your house. Come on now.''

The two litle girls hastened out hand in hand and hurried through Lovers' Lane and across the crusted field beyond, for the snow was too deep to go by the shorter wood way. Anne, although sincerely sorry for Minnie May, was far from being insensible to the romance of the situation and to the sweetness of once more sharing that romance with a kindred spirit.

The night was clear and frosty, all ebony of shadow and silver of snowy slope; big stars were shining over the silent fields; here and there the dark pointed firs stood up with snow powdering their branches and the wind whistling through them. Anne thought it was truly delightful to go skimming through all this mystery and loveliness with your bosom friend who had been so long estranged.

Minnie May, aged three, was really very sick. She lay on the kitchen sofa, feverish and restless, while her hoarse breathing could be heard all over the house. Young Mary Joe, a buxom, broad-faced French girl from the Creek, whom Mrs. Barry had engaged to stay with the children during her absence, was helpless and bewildered, quite incapable of thinking what to do, or doing it if she thought of it.

Anne went to work with skill and promptness.

"Minnie may has croup all right; she's pretty bad, but I've seen them worse. First we must have lots of hot water. I declare, Diana, there isn't more than a cupful in the kettle! There, I've filled it up, and, Mary Joe, you may put some wood in the stove. I don't want to hurt your feelings, but it seems to me you might have thought of this before if you'd any imagination. Now, I'll undress Minnie May and put her to bed, and you try to find some soft flannel cloths, Diana. I'm going to give her a dose of ipecac first of all.''

Minnie May did not take kindly to the ipecac, but Anne had not brought up three pairs of twins for nothing. Down that ipecac went, not only once, but many times during the long, anxious night when the two little girls worked patiently over the suffering Minnie May, and Young Mary Joe, honestly anxious to do all she could, kept on a roaring fire and heated more water than would have been needed for a hospital of croupy babies.

It was three o'clock when Matthew came with the doctor, for he had been obliged to go all the way to Spencervale for one. But the pressing need for assistance was past. Minnie May was much better and was sleeping soundly.

"I was awfully near giving up in despair," explained Anne. "She got worse and worse until she was sicker than ever the Hammond twins were, even the last pair. I actually thought she was going to choke to death. I gave her every drop of ipecac in that bottle, and when the last dose went down I said to myself—not to Diana or Young Mary Joe, because I didn't want to worry them any more than they were worried, but I had to say it to myself just to relieve my feelings—'This is the last lingering hope and I fear 'tis a vain one.' But in about three minutes she coughed up the phlegm and began to get better right away. You must just imagine my relief, doctor, because I can't express it in words. You know there are some things that cannot be expressed in words.''

"Yes, I know," nodded the doctor. He looked at Anne as if he were thinking some things about her that couldn't be expressed in words. Later on, however, he expressed them to Mr. and Mrs. Barry.

"That little red-headed girl they have over at Cuthbert's is as smart as they make 'em. I tell you she saved that baby's life, for it would have been too late by the time I got here. She seems to have a skill and presence of mind perfectly wonderful in a child of her age. I never saw anything like the eyes of her when she was explaining the case out to me."

Anne had gone home in the wonderful, white-frosted winter morning, heavy-eyed from loss of sleep, but still talking unweariedly to Matthew as they crossed the long white field and walked under the glittering fairy arch of the Lovers' Lane maples.

"Oh, Matthew, isn't it a wonderful morning? The world looks like something God had just imagined for His own pleasure, doesn't it? Those trees look as if I could blow them away with a breath—pouf! I'm so glad I live in a world where there are white frosts, aren't you? And I'm so glad Mrs. Hammond had three pairs of twins after all. If she hadn't I mightn't have known what to do for Minnie May. I'm real sorry I was ever cross with Mrs. Hammond for having twins. But, oh, Matthew, I'm so sleepy. I can't go to school. I just know I couldn't keep my eyes open and I'd be so stupid. But I hate to stay home for Gil—some of the others will get head of the class, and it's so hard to get up again—although of course the harder it is the more satisfaction you have when you do get up, haven't you?''

"Well now, I guess you'll manage all right," said Matthew, looking at Anne's white little face and the dark shadows under her eyes. "You just go right to bed and have a good sleep. I'll do all the chores.''

Anne accordingly went to bed and slept so long and soundly that it was well on in the white and rosy winter afternoon when she awoke and descended to the kitchen where Marilla, who had arrived home in the meantime, was sitting knitting.

"Oh, did you see the Premier?" exclaimed Anne at once. "What did he look like, Marilla?"

"Well, he never got to be Premier on account of his looks," said Marilla. "Such a nose as that man had! But he can speak. I was proud of being a Conservative. Rachel Lynde, of course, being a Liberal, had no use for him. Your dinner is in the oven, Anne; and you can get yourself some blue plum preserve out of the pantry. I guess you're hungry. Matthew has been telling me about last night. I must say it was fortunate you knew what to do. I wouldn't have had any idea myself, for I never saw a case of croup. There now, never mind talking till you've had your dinner. I can tell by the look of you that you're just full up with speeches, but they'll keep."

Marilla had something to tell Anne, but she did not tell it just then, for she knew if she did Anne's consequent excitement would lift her clear out of the region of such material matters as appetite or dinner. Not until Anne had finished her saucer of blue plums did Marilla say:

"Mrs. Barry was here this afternoon, Anne. She wanted to see you, but I wouldn't wake you up. She says you saved Minnie May's life, and she is very sorry she acted as she did in that affair of the currant wine. She says she knows now you didn't mean to set Diana drunk, and she hopes you'll forgive her and be good friends with Diana again. You're to go over this evening if you like, for Diana can't stir outside the door on account of a bad cold she caught last night. Now, Anne Shirley, for pity's sake don't fly clean up into the air."

The warning seemed not unnecessary, so uplifted and aerial was Anne's expression and attitude as she sprang to her feet, her face irradiated with the flame of her spirit.

"Oh, Marilla, can I go right now—without washing my dishes? I'll wash them when I come back, but I cannot tie myself down to anything so unromantic as dish-washing at this thrilling moment."

"Yes, yes, run along," said Marilla indulgently. "Anne Shirley—are you crazy? Come back this instant and put something on you. I might as well call to the wind. She's gone without a cap or wrap. Look at her tearing through the orchard with her hair streaming. It'll be a mercy if she doesn't catch her death of cold."

Anne came dancing home in the purple winter twilight across the snowy places. Afar in the southwest was the great shimmering, pearl-like sparkle of an evening star in a sky that was pale golden and ethereal rose over gleaming white spaces and dark glens of spruce. The tinkles of sleigh-bells among the snowy hills came like elfin chimes through the frosty air, but their music was not sweeter than the song in Anne's heart and on her lips.

"You see before you a perfectly happy person, Marilla," she announced. "I'm perfectly happy—yes, in spite of my red hair. Just at present I have a soul above red hair. Mrs. Barry kissed me and cried and said she was so sorry and she could never repay me. I felt fearfuly embarrassed, Marilla, but I just said as politely as I could, 'I have no hard feelings for you, Mrs. Barry. I assure you once for all that I did not mean to intoxicate Diana and henceforth I shall cover the past with the mantle of oblivion.' That was a pretty dignified way of speaking, wasn't it, Marilla? I felt that I was heaping coals of fire on Mrs. Barry's head. And Diana and I had a lovely afternoon. Diana showed me a new fancy crochet stitch her aunt over at Carmody taught her. Not a soul in Avonlea knows it but us, and we pledged a solemn vow never to reveal it to any one else. Diana gave me a beautiful card with a wreath of roses on it and a verse of poetry:

> *If you love me as I love you*
> *Nothing but death can part us two.*

And that is true, Marilla. We're going to ask Mr. Phillips to let us sit together in school again, and Gertie Pye can go with Minnie Andrews. We had an elegant tea. Mrs. Barry had the very best china set out, Marilla, just as if I was real company. I can't tell you what a thrill it gave me. Nobody ever used their very best china on my account before. And we had fruit-cake and pound-cake and doughnuts and two kinds of preserves, Marilla. And Mrs. Barry asked me if I took tea and said, 'Pa, why don't you pass the biscuits to Anne?' It must be lovely to be grown up, Marilla, when just being treated as if you were is so nice."

"I don't know about that," said Marilla with a brief sigh.

"Well, anyway, when I am grown up," said Anne decidely, "I'm always going to talk to little girls as if they were, too, and I'll never laugh when they use big words. I know from sorrowful experience how that hurts one's feelings. After tea Diana and I made taffy. The taffy wasn't very good, I suppose because neither Diana nor I had ever made any before. Diana left me to stir it while she buttered the plates and I forgot and let it burn; and then when we set it out on the platform to cool the cat walked over one plate and that had to be thrown away. But the making of it was splendid fun. Then when I came home Mrs. Barry asked me to come over as often as I could and Diana stood at the window and threw kisses to me all the way down to Lovers' Lane. I assure you, Marilla, that I feel like praying tonight and I'm going to think out a special brand new prayer in honor of the occasion.''

CHAPTER 19

A CONCERT, A CATASTROPHE, AND A CONFESSION

''MARILLA, CAN I go over to see Diana just for a minute?'' asked Anne, running breathlessly down from the east gable one February evening.

''I don't see what you want to be traipsing about after dark for,'' said Marilla shortly. ''You and Diana walked home from school together and then stood down there in the snow for half an hour more, your tongues going the whole blessed time, clickety-clack. So I don't think you're very badly off to see her again.''

''But she wants to see me,'' pleaded Anne. ''She has something very important to tell me.''

''How do you know she has?''

''Because she just signalled to me from her window. We have arranged a way to signal with our candles and cardboard. We set the candle on the windowsill and make flashes by passing the cardboard back and forth. So many flashes mean a certain thing. It was my idea, Marilla.''

''I'll warrant you it was,'' said Marilla emphatically. ''And the next thing you'll be setting fire to the curtains with your signalling nonsense.''

''Oh, we're very careful, Marilla. And it's so interesting. Two flashes mean, 'Are you there?' Three means 'yes' and four 'no.' Five mean, 'Come over as soon as possible because I have something important to reveal.' Diana has just signalled five flashes, and I'm really suffering to know what it is.''

"Well, you needn't suffer any longer," said Marilla sarcastically. "You can go, but you're to be back here in just ten minutes, remember that."

Anne did remember it and was back in the stipulated time, although probably no mortal will ever know just what it cost her to confine the discussion of Diana's important communication within the limits of ten minutes. But at least she had made good use of them.

"Oh, Marilla, what do you think? You know tomorrow is Diana's birthday. Well, her mother told her she could ask me to go home with her from school and stay all night with her. And her cousins are coming over from Newbridge in a big pung sleigh to go to the Debating Club concert at the hall tomorrow night. And they are going to take Diana and me to the concert—if you'll let me go, that is. You will, won't you, Marilla? Oh, I feel so excited."

"You can calm down then, because you're not going. You're better at home in your own bed, and as for that Club concert, it's all nonsense, and little girls should not be allowed to go out to such places at all."

"I'm sure the Debating Club is a most respectable affair," pleaded Anne.

"I'm not saying it isn't. But you're not going to begin gadding about to concerts and staying out all hours of the night. Pretty doings for children. I'm surprised at Mrs. Barry's letting Diana go."

"But it's such a very special occasion," mourned Anne, on the verge of tears. "Diana has only one birthday in a year. It isn't as if birthdays were common things, Marilla. Prissy Andrews is going to recite 'Curfew Must Not Ring To-night.' That is such a good moral piece, Marilla, I'm sure it would do me lots of good to hear it. And the choir are going to sing four lovely pathetic songs that are pretty near as good as hymns. And oh, Marilla, the minister is going to take part; yes, indeed, he is; he's going to give an address. That will be just about the same thing as a sermon. Please, mayn't I go, Marilla?"

"You heard what I said, Anne, didn't you? Take off your boots now and go to bed. It's past eight."

"There's just one more thing, Marilla," said Anne, with the air of producing the last shot in her locker. "Mrs. Barry told Diana that we might sleep in the spare-room bed. Think of the honor of your little Anne being put in the spare-room bed."

"It's an honor you'll have to get along without. Go to bed, Anne, and don't let me hear another word out of you."

When Anne, with tears rolling over her cheeks, had gone sorrowfully upstairs, Matthew, who had been apparently sound asleep on the lounge during the whole dialogue, opened his eyes and said decidedly:

"Well now, Marilla, I think you ought to let Anne go."

"I don't then," retorted Marilla. "Who's bringing this child up, Matthew, you or me?"

"Well now, you," admitted Matthew.

"Don't interfere then."

"Well now, I ain't interfering. It ain't interfering to have your own opinion. And my opinion is that you ought to let Anne go."

"You'd think I ought to let Anne go to the moon if she took the notion, I've no doubt," was Marilla's amiable rejoinder. "I might have let her spend the night with Diana, if that was all. But I don't approve of this concert plan. She'd go there and catch cold like as not, and have her head filled up with nonsense and excitement. It would unsettle her for a week. I understand that child's disposition and what's good for it better than you, Matthew."

"I think you ought to let Anne go," repeated Matthew firmly. Argument was not his strong point, but holding fast to his opinion certainly was. Marilla gave a gasp of helplessness and took refuge in silence. The next morning, when Anne was washing the breakfast dishes in the pantry, Matthew paused on his way out to the barn to say to Marilla again:

"I think you ought to let Anne go, Marilla.

For a moment Marilla looked things not lawful to be uttered. Then she yielded to the inevitable and said tartly:

"Very well, she can go, since nothing else'll please you."

Anne flew out of the pantry, dripping dish-cloth in hand.

"Oh, Marilla, Marilla, say those blessed words again."

"I guess once is enough to say them. This is Matthew's doings and I wash my hands of it. If you catch pneumonia sleeping in a strange bed or coming out of that hot hall in the middle of the night, don't blame me, blame Matthew. Anne Shirley, you're dripping greasy water all over the floor. I never saw such a careless child."

"Oh, I know I'm a great trial to you, Marilla," said Anne repentantly. "I make so many mistakes. But then just think of all the mistakes I don't make, although I might. I'll get some sand and scrub up the spots before I go to school. Oh, Marilla, my heart was just set on going to that concert. I never was to a concert in my life, and when the other girls talk about them in school I feel so out of it. You didn't know just how I felt about it, but you see Matthew did. Matthew understands me, and it's so nice to be understood, Marilla.''

Anne was too excited to do herself justice as to lessons that morning in school. Gilbert Blythe spelled her down in class and left her clear out of sight in mental arithmetic. Anne's consequent humiliation was less than it might have been, however, in view of the concert and the spare-room bed. She and Diana talked so constantly about it all day that with a stricter teacher than Mr. Phillips dire disgrace must inevitably have been their portion.

Anne felt that she could not have borne it if she had not been going to the concert, for nothing else was discussed that day in school. The Avonlea Debating Club, which met fortnightly all winter, had had several smaller free entertainments; but this was to be a big affair, admission ten cents, in aid of the library. The Avonlea young people had been practising for weeks, and all the scholars were especially interested in it by reason of older brothers and sisters who were going to take part. Everybody in school over nine years of age expected to go, except Carrie Sloane, whose father shared Marilla's opinions about small girls going out to night concerts. Carrie Sloane cried into her grammar all the afternoon and felt that life was not worth living.

For Anne the real excitement began with the dismissal of school and increased therefrom in crescendo until it reached to a crash of positive ecstasy in the concert itself. They had a ''perfectly elegant tea;'' and then came the delicious occupation of dressing in Diana's little room upstairs. Diana did Anne's front hair in the new pompadour style and Anne tied Diana's bows with the especial knack she possessed; and they experimented with at least half a dozen different ways of arranging their back hair. At last they were ready, cheeks scarlet and eyes glowing with excitement.

True, Anne could not help a little pang when she contrasted her plain black tam and shapeless, tight-sleeved home-made gray cloth coat with Diana's jaunty fur cap and smart little jacket. But she remembered in time that she had an imagination and could use it.

Then Diana's cousins, the Murrays from Newbridge, came; they all crowded into the big pung sleigh, among straw and furry robes. Anne revelled in the drive to the hall, slipping along over the satin-smooth roads with the snow crisping under the runners. There was a magnificent sunset, and the snowy hills and deep blue water of the St. Lawrence Gulf seemed to rim in the splendor like a huge bowl of pearl and sapphire brimmed with wine and fire. Tinkles of sleigh-bells and distant laughter, that seemed like the mirth of wood elves, came from every quarter.

"Oh, Diana," breathed Anne, squeezing Diana's mittened hand under the fur robe, "isn't it all like a beautiful dream? Do I really look the same as usual? I feel so different that it seems to me it must show in my looks."

"You look awfully nice," said Diana, who having just received a compliment from one of her cousins, felt that she ought to pass it on. "You've got the loveliest color."

The program that night was a series of "thrills" for at least one listener in the audience, and, as Anne assured Diana, every succeeding thrill was thrillier than the last. When Prissy Andrews, attired in a new pink silk waist with a string of pearls about her smooth white throat and real carnations in her hair—rumor whispered that the master had sent all the way to town for them for her—"climbed the slimy ladder, dark without one ray of light," Anne shivered in luxurious sympathy; when the choir sang "Far Above the Gentle Daisies" Anne gazed at the ceiling as if it were frescoed with angels; when Sam Sloane proceeded to explain and illustate "How Sockery Set a Hen" Anne laughed until people sitting near her laughed too, more out of sympathy with her than with amusement at a selection that was rather threadbare even in Avonlea; and when Mr. Phillips gave Mark Antony's oration over the dead body of Caesar in the most heart-stirring tones—looking at Prissy Andrews at the end of every sentence—Anne felt that she could rise and mutiny on the spot if but one roman citizen led the way.

Only one number on the program failed to interest her. When Gilbert Blythe recited "Bingen on the Rhine" Anne picked up Rhoda Murray's library book and read it until he had finished, when she sat rigidly stiff and motionless while Diana clapped her hands until they tingled.

It was eleven when they got home, sated with dissipation, but with the exceeding sweet pleasure of talking it all over still to come. Everybody seemed asleep and the house was dark and silent. Anne and Diana tiptoed into the parlor, a long narrow room out of which the spare room opened. It was pleasantly warm and dimly lighted by the embers of a fire in the grate.

"Let's undress here," said Diana. "It's so nice and warm."

"Hasn't it been a delightful time?" sighed Anne rapturously "It must be splendid to get up and recite there. Do you suppose we will ever be asked to do it, Diana?"

"Yes, of course, some day. They're always wanting the big scholars to recite. Gilbert Bythe does often and he's only two years older than us. Oh, Anne, how could you pretend not to listen to him? When he came to the line,

There's another, not a sister

he looked right down at you.''

"Diana," said Anne with dignity, "you are my bosom friend, but I cannot allow even you to speak to me of that person. Are you ready for bed? Let's run a race and see who'll get to the bed first.''

The suggestion appealed to Diana. The two little white-clad figures flew down the long room, through the spare-room door, and bounded on the bed at the same moment. And then—something—moved beneath them, there was a gasp and a cry—and somebody said in muffled accents:

"Merciful goodness!''

Anne and Diana were never able to tell just how they got off that bed and out of the room. They only knew that after one frantic rush they found themselves tiptoeing shiveringly upstairs.

"Oh, who was it—*what* was it?'' whispered Anne, her teeth chattering with cold and fright.

"It was Aunt Josephine," said Diana, gasping with laughter. "Oh, Anne, it was Aunt Josephine, however she came to be there. Oh, and I know she will be furious. It's dreadful—it's really dreadful—but did you ever know anything so funny, Anne?''

"Who is your Aunt Josephine?''

"She's father's aunt and she lives in Charlottetown. She's awfully old—seventy anyhow—and I don't believe she was *ever* a little girl. We were expecting her out for a visit, but not so soon. She's awfully prim and proper and she'll scold dreadfully about this, I know. Well, we'll have to sleep with Minnie May—and you can't think how she kicks.''

Miss Josephine Barry did not appear at the early breakfast the next morning. Mrs. Barry smiled kindly at the two little girls.

"Did you have a good time last night? I tried to stay awake until you came home, for I wanted to tell you Aunt Josephine had come and that you would have to go upstairs after all, but I was so tired I fell alseep. I hope you didn't disturb your aunt, Diana.''

Diana preserved a discreet silence, but she and Anne exchanged furtive smiles of guilty amusement across the table. Anne hurried home after breakfast and so remained in blissful ignorance of the disturbance which presently resulted in the Barry household until the late afternoon, when she went down to Mrs. Lynde's on an errand for Marilla.

"So you and Diana nearly frightened poor old Miss Barry to death last night?" said Mrs. Lynde severely, but with a twinkle in her eye. "Mrs. Barry was here a few minutes ago on her way to Carmody. She's feeling real worried over it. Old Miss Barry was in a terrible temper when she got up this morning—and Josephine Barry's temper is no joke, I can tell you that. She wouldn't speak to Diana at all."

"It wasn't Diana's fault," said Anne contritely. "It was mine. I suggested racing to see who would get into bed first."

"I knew it!" said Mrs. Lynde with the exultation of a correct guesser. "I knew the idea came out of your head. Well, it's made a nice lot of trouble, that's what. Old Miss Barry came out to stay for a month, but she declared she won't stay another day and is going right back to town tomorrow, Sunday and all as it is. She'd have gone today if they could have taken her. She had promised to pay for a quarter's music lessons for Diana, but now she is determined to do nothing at all for such a tomboy. Oh, I guess they had a lively time of it there this morning. The Barrys must feel cut up. Old Miss Barry is rich and they'd like to keep on the good side of her. Of course, Mrs. Barry didn't say just that to me, but I'm a pretty good judge of human nature, that's what."

"I'm such an unlucky girl," mourned Anne. "I'm always getting into scrapes myself and getting my best friends—people I'd shed my heart's blood for—into them, too. Can you tell me why it is so, Mrs. Lynde?"

"It's because you're too heedless and impulsive, child, that's what. You never stop to think—whatever comes into your head to say or do you say or do it without a moment's reflection."

"Oh, but that's the best of it," protested Anne. "Something just flashes into your mind, so exciting, and you must out with it. If you stop to think it over you spoil it all. Haven't you never felt that yourself, Mrs.Lynde?"

No, Mrs. Lynde had not. She shook her head sagely.

"You must learn to think a little, Anne, that's what. The proverb you need to go by is 'look before you leap'—especially into spare-room beds."

Mrs. Lynde laughed comfortably over her mild joke, but Anne remained pensive. She saw nothing to laugh at in the situation, which to her eyes appeared very serious. When she left Mrs. Lynde's she took her way across the crusted fields to Orchard Slope. Diana met her at the kitchen door.

"Your Aunt Josephine was very cross about it, wasn't she?" whispered Anne.

"Yes," answered Diana, stifling a giggle with an apprehensive glance over her shoulder at the closed sitting-room door. "She was fairly dancing with rage, Anne. Oh, how she scolded. She said I was the worst-behaved girl she ever saw and that my parents ought to be ashamed of the way they had brought me up. She says she won't stay and I'm sure I don't care. But father and mother do."

"Why didn't you tell them it was my fault?" demanded Anne.

"It's likely I'd do such a thing, isn't it?" said Diana with just scorn. "I'm no telltale, Anne Shirely, and anyhow I was just as much to blame as you."

"Well, I'm going in to tell her myself," said Anne resolutely. Diana stared.

"Anne Shirely, you'd never! why—she'll eat you alive!"

"Don't frighten me any more than I am frightened," implored Anne. "I'd rather walk up to a cannon's mouth. But I've got to do it, Diana. It was my fault and I've got to confess. I've had practice in confessing fortunately."

"Well, she's in the room," said Diana. "You can go in if you want to. I wouldn't dare. And I don't believe you'll do a bit of good."

With this encouragement Anne bearded the lion in its den—that is to say, walked resolutely up to the sitting-room door and knocked faintly. A sharp "Come in" followed.

Miss Josephine Barry, thin, prim and rigid, was knitting fiercely by the fire, her wrath quite unappeased and her eyes snapping through her gold-rimmed glasses. She wheeled around in her chair expecting to see Diana, and beheld a white-faced girl whose great eyes were brimmed up with a mixture of desperate courage and shrinking terror.

"Who are you?" demanded Miss Josephine Barry without ceremony.

"I'm Anne of Green Gables," said the small visitor tremulously, clasping her hands with her characteristic gesture, "and I've come to confess, if you please."

"Confess what?"

"That it was all my fault about jumping into bed on you last night. I suggested it. Diana would never have thought of such a thing, I am sure. Diana is a very lady-like girl, Miss Barry. So you must see how unjust it is to blame her."

"Oh, I must, hey? I rather think Diana did her share of the

jumping at least. Such carryings-on in a respectable house!''

''But we were only in fun,'' persisted Anne. ''I think you ought to forgive us, Miss Barry, now that we've apologized. And anyhow, please forgive Diana and let her have her music lessons. Diana's heart is set on her music lessons, Miss Barry, and I know too well what it is to set your heart on a thing and not get it. If you must be cross with anyone, be cross with me. I've been so used in my early days to having people cross at me that I can endure it much better than Diana can.''

Much of the snap had gone out of the old lady's eyes by this time and was replaced by a twinkle of amused interest. But she still said severely:

''I don't think it is any excuse for you that you were only in fun. Little girls never indulged in that kind of fun when I was young. You don't know what it is to be awakened out of a sound sleep, after a long and arduous journey, by two great girls coming bounce down on you.''

''I don't *know*, but I can *imagine*,'' said Anne eagerly. ''I'm sure it must have been very disturbing. But then, there is our side of it too. Have you any imagination, Miss Barry? If you have, just put yourself in our place. We didn't know there was anybody in that bed and you nearly scared us to death. It was simply awful the way we felt. And then we couldn't sleep in the spare room after being promised. I suppose you are used to sleeping in spare rooms. But just imagine what you would feel like if you were a little orphan girl who had never had such an honor.''

All the snap had gone by this time. Miss Barry actually laughed— a sound which caused Diana, waiting in speechless anxiety in the kitchen outside, to give a great gasp of relief.

''I'm afraid my imagination is a little rusty—it's so long since I used it,'' she said. ''I dare say your claim to sympathy is just as strong as mine. It all depends on the way we look at it. Sit down here and tell me about yourself.''

''I am very sorry I can't,'' said Anne firmly. ''I would like to, because you seem like an interesting lady, and you might even be a kindred spirit although you don't look very much like it. But it is my duty to go home to Miss Marilla Cuthbert. Miss Marilla Cuthbert is a very kind lady who has taken me to bring up properly. She is doing her best, but it is very discouraging work. You must not blame her because I jumped on the bed. But before I go I do wish you would tell me if you will forgive Diana and stay just a long as you meant to in Avonlea.''

"I think perhaps I will if you will come over and talk to me occasionally," said Miss Barry.

That evening Miss Barry gave Diana a silver bangle bracelet and told the senior members of the household that she had unpacked her valise.

"I've made up my mind to stay simply for the sake of getting better acquainted with that Anne-girl," she said frankly. "She amuses me, and at my time of life an amusing person is a rarity."

Marilla's only comment when she heard the story was, "I told you so." This was for Matthew's benefit.

Miss Barry stayed her month out and over. She was a more agreeable guest than usual, for Anne kept her in good humor. They became firm friends.

When Miss Barry went away she said:

"Remember, you Anne-girl, when you come to town you're to visit me and I'll put you in my very sparest spare-room bed to sleep."

"Miss Barry was a kindred spirit, after all," Anne confided to Marilla. "You wouldn't think so to look at her, but she is. You don't find it right out at first, as in Matthew's case, but after a while you come to see it. Kindred spirits are not so scarce as I used to think. It's splendid to find out there are so many of them in the world."

CHAPTER 20

A GOOD IMAGINATION GONE WRONG

SPRING HAD come once more to Green Gables—the beautiful, capricious, reluctant Canadian spring, lingering along through April and May in a succession of sweet, fresh, chilly days, with pink sunsets and miracles of resurrection and growth. The maples in Lovers' Lane were red-budded and little curly ferns pushed up around the Dryad's Bubble. Away up in the barrens, behind Mr. Silas Sloane's place, the Mayflowers blossomed out, pink and white stars of sweetness under their brown leaves. All the school girls and boys had one golden afternoon gathering them, coming home in the clear, echoing twilight with arms and baskets full of flowery spoil.

"I'm so sorry for people who live in lands where there are no

Mayflowers,'' said Anne. ''Diana says perhaps they have something better, but there couldn't be anything better than Mayflowers, could there, Marilla? And Diana says if they don't know what they are like they don't miss them. But I think that is the saddest thing of all. I think it would be *tragic*, Marilla, not to know what Mayflowers are like and *not* to miss them. Do you know what I think Mayflowers are, Marilla? I think they must be the soul of the flowers that died last summer and this is their heaven. But we had a splendid time today, Marilla. We had our lunch down in a big mossy hollow by an old well—such a *romantic* spot. Charlie Sloane dared Arty Gillis to jump over it, and Arty did because he wouldn't take a dare. Nobody would in school. It is very *fashionable* to dare. Mr. Phillips gave all the Mayflowers he found to Prissy Andrews and I heard him say 'sweets to the sweet.' He got that out of a book, I know; but it shows he has some imagination. I was offered some Mayflowers too, but I rejected them with scorn. I can't tell you the person's name because I have vowed never to let it cross my lips. We made wreaths of the Mayflowers and put them on our hats; and when the time came to go home we marched in procession down the road, two by two, with our bouquets and wreaths, singing 'My Home on the Hill.' Oh, it was so thrilling, Marilla. All Mr. Silas Sloane's folks rushed out to see us and everybody we met on the road stopped and stared after us. We made a real sensation.''

''Not much wonder! Such silly doings!'' was Marilla's response.

After the Mayflowers came the violets, and Violet Vale was empurpled with them. Anne walked through it on her way to school with reverent steps and worshipping eyes, as if she trod on holy ground.

''Somehow,'' she told Diana, ''when I'm going through here I don't really care whether Gil—whether anybody gets ahead of me in class or not. But when I'm up in school it's all different and I care as much as ever. There's such a lot of different Annes in me. I sometimes think that is why I'm such a troublesome person. If I was just the one Anne it would be ever so much more comfortable, but then it wouldn't be half so interesting.''

One June evening, when the orchards were pink-blossomed again, when the frogs were singing silverly sweet in the marshes about the head of the Lake of Shining Waters, and the air as full of the savor of clover fields and balsamic fir woods, Anne was sitting by her gable window. She had been studying her lessons, but it had grown too dark to see the book, so she had fallen into wide-eyed reverie, looking out past the boughs of the Snow Queen, once more bestarred with its tufts of blossom.

In all essential respects the little gable chamber was unchanged. The walls were as white, the pincushion as hard, the chairs as stiffly and yellowly upright as ever. Yet the whole character of the room was altered. It was full of a new vital, pulsing personality that seemed to pervade it and to be quite independent of schoolgirl books and dresses and ribbons, and even of the cracked blue jug full of apple blossoms on the table. It was as if all the dreams, sleeping and waking, of its vivid occupant had taken a visible although immaterial form and had tapestried the bare room with splendid filmy tissues of rainbow and moonshine. Presently Marilla came briskly in with some of Anne's freshly ironed school aprons. She hung them over a chair and sat down with a short sigh. She had had one of her headaches that afternoon, and although the pain had gone she felt weak and "tuckered out," as she expressed it. Anne looked at her with eyes limpid with sympathy.

"I do truly wish I could have had the headache in your place, Marilla. I would have endured it joyfully for your sake."

"I guess you did your part in attending to the work and letting me rest," said Marilla. "You seem to have got on fairly well and made fewer mistakes than usual. Of course it wasn't exactly necessary to starch Matthew's handkerchiefs! And most people when they put a pie in the oven to warm up for dinner take it out and eat it when it gets hot instead of leaving it to be burned to a crisp. But that doesn't seem to be your way evidently."

Headaches always left Marilla somewhat sarcastic.

"Oh, I'm so sorry," said Anne penitently. "I never thought about that pie from the moment I put it in the oven till now, although I felt *instinctively* that there was something missing on the dinner table. I was firmly resolved, when you left me in charge this morning, not to imagine anything, but keep my thoughts on facts. I did pretty well until I put the pie in, and then an irresistible temptation came to me to imagine I was an enchanted princess shut up in a lonely tower with a handsome knight riding to my rescue on a coal-black steed. So that is how I came to forget the pie. I didn't know I starched the hand-kerchiefs. All the time I was ironing I was trying to think of a name for a new island Diana and I have discovered up the brook. It's the most ravishing spot, Marilla. There are two maple trees on it and the brook flows right around it. At last it struck me that it would be splendid to call it Victoria Island because we found it on the Queen's

birthday. Both Diana and I are very loyal. But I'm very sorry about
that pie and the handkerchiefs. I wanted to be extra good today
because it's an anniversary. Do you remember what happened this
day last year, Marilla?''

"No, I can't think of anything special."

"Oh, Marilla, it was the day I came to Green Gables. I shall never
forget it. It was the turning point in my life. Of course it wouldn't
seem so important to you. I've been here for a year and I've been so
happy. Of course, I've had my troubles, but one can live down
troubles. Are you sorry you kept me, Marilla?''

"No, I can't say I'm sorry," said Marilla, who sometimes
wondered how she could have lived before Anne came to Green
Gables, ''no, not exactly sorry. If you've finished your lessons,
Anne, I want you to run over and ask Mrs. Barry if she'll lend me
Diana's apron pattern.''

"Oh—it's—too dark," cried Anne.

"Too dark? Why, it's only twilight. And goodness knows you've
gone over enough after dark.''

"I'll go over early in the morning," said Anne eagerly. "I'll get
up at sunrise and go over, Marilla.''

"What has got into your head now, Anne Shirley? I want that
pattern to cut out your new apron this evening. Go at once and be
smart, too.''

"I'll have to go around by the road, then," said Anne, taking up
her hat reluctantly.

"Go by the road and waste half an hour! I'd like to catch you!''

"I can't go through the Haunted Wood, Marilla," cried Anne
desperately.

Marilla stared.

"The Haunted Wood! Are you crazy? What under the canopy is
the Haunted Wood?''

"The spruce wood over the brook," said Anne in a whisper.

"Fiddlesticks! There is no such thing as a haunted wood anywhere. Who has been telling you such stuff?''

"Nobody," confessed Anne. "Diana and I just imagined the
wood was haunted. All the places around here are so—so—*commonplace*. We just got this up for our own amusement. We began it
in April. A haunted wood is so very romantic, Marilla. We chose the
spruce grove because it's so gloomy. Oh, we have imagined the most
harrowing things. There's a white lady walks along the brook just
about this time of the night and wrings her hands and utters wailing
cries. She appears when there is to be a death in the family. And the

ghost of a little murdered child haunts the corner up by Idlewild; it creeps up behind you and lays its cold fingers on your hand—so. Oh, Marilla, it gives me a shudder to think of it. And there's a headless man stalks up and down the path and skeletons glower at you between the boughs. Oh, Marilla, I wouldn't go through the Haunted Wood after dark now for anything. I'd be sure that white things would reach out from behind the trees and grab me."

"Did ever any one hear the like!" ejaculated Marilla, who had listened in dumb amazement. "Anne Shirley, do you mean to tell me you believe all that wicked nonsense of your own imagination?"

"Not believe *exactly*" faltered Anne. "At least, I don't believe it in daylight. But after dark, Marilla, it's different. That is when ghosts walk."

"There are no such things as ghosts, Anne."

"Oh, but there are, Marilla," cried Anne eagerly. "I know people who have seen them. And they are respectable people. Charlie Sloane says that his grandmother saw his grandfather driving home the cows one night after he'd been buried for a year. You know Charlie Sloane's grandmother wouldn't tell a story for anything. She's a very religious woman. And Mrs. Thomas' father was pursued home one night by a lamb of fire with its head cut off hanging by a strip of skin. He said he knew it was the spirit of his brother and that it was warning he would die within nine days. He didn't, but he died two years after, so you see it was really true. And Ruby Gillis says—"

"Anne Shirley," interrupted Marilla firmly, "I never want to hear you talking in this fashion again. I've had my doubts about that imagination of yours right along, and if this is going to be the outcome of it, I won't countenance any such doings. You'll go right over to Barry's, and you'll go through that spruce grove, just for a lesson and a warning to you. And never let me hear a word out of your head about haunted woods again."

Anne might plead and cry as she liked—and did, for her terror was very real. Her imagination had run away with her and she held the spruce grove in mortal dread after nightfall. But Marilla was inexorable. She marched the shrinking ghostseer down to the spring and ordered her to proceed straightway over the bridge and into the dusky retreats of wailing ladies and headless spectres beyond.

"Oh, Marilla, how can you be so cruel?" sobbed Anne. "What would you feel like if a white thing did snatch me up and carry me off?"

"I'll risk it," said Marilla unfeelingly. "You know I always mean what I say. I'll cure you of imagining ghosts into places. March, now.''

Anne marched. That is, she stumbled over the bridge and went shuddering up the horrible dim path beyond. Anne never forgot that walk. Bitterly did she repent the license she had given to her imagination. The goblins of her fancy lurked in every shadow about her, reaching out their cold, fleshless hands to grasp the terrified small girl who had called them into being. A white strip of birch bark blowing up from the hollow over the brown floor of the grove made her heart stand still. The long-drawn wail of two old boughs rubbing against each other brought out the perspiration in beads on her forehead. The swoop of bats in the darkness over her was as the wings of unearthly creatures. When she reached Mr. William Bell's field she fled across it as if pursued by an army of white things, and arrived at the Barry kitchen door so out of breath that she could hardly gasp out her request for the apron pattern. Diana was away so that she had no excuse to linger. The dreadful return journey had to be faced. Anne went back over it with shut eyes, preferring to take the risk of dashing her brains out among the boughs to that of seeing a white thing. When she finally tumbled over the log bridge she drew one long shivering breath of relief.

"Well, so nothing caught you?" said Marilla unsympathetically.

"Oh, Mar—Marilla," chattered Anne, "I'll b-b-be cont-t-tented with c-c-commonplace places after this."

CHAPTER 21

A NEW DEPARTURE IN FLAVORINGS

"DEAR ME, there is nothing but meetings and partings in this world, as Mrs. Lynde says," remarked Anne plaintively, putting her slate and books down on the kitchen table on the last day of June and wiping her red eyes with a very damp handkerchief. "Wasn't it fortunate, Marilla, that I took an extra handkerchief to school today? I had a presentiment that it would be needed."

"I never thought you were so fond of Mr. Phillips that you'd require two handkerchiefs to dry your tears just because he was going away," said Marilla.

"I don't think I was crying because I was really so very fond of him," reflected Anne. "I just cried because all the others did. It was Ruby Gillis started it. Ruby Gillis has always declared she hated Mr. Phillips, but just as soon as he got up to make his farewell speech she burst into tears. Then all the girls began to cry, one after the other. I tried to hold out, Marilla. I tried to remember the time Mr. Phillips made me sit with Gil—with a boy; and the time he spelled my name without an *e* on the blackboard; and how he said I was the worst dunce he ever saw at geometry and laughed at my spelling; and all the times he had been so horrid and sarcastic; but somehow I couldn't, Marilla, and I just had to cry too. Jane Andrews has been talking for a month about how glad she'd be when Mr. Phillips went away and she declared she'd never shed a tear. Well, she was worse than any of us and had to borrow a handkerchief from her brother—of course the boys didn't cry—because she hadn't brought one of her own, not expecting to need it. Oh, Marilla, it was heartrending. Mr. Phillips made such a beautiful farewell speech beginning, 'The time has come for us to part.' It was very affecting. And he had tears in hs eyes too, Marilla. Oh, I felt dreadfully sorry and remorseful for all the times I'd talked in school and drawn pictures of him on my slate and made fun of him and Prissy. I can tell you I wished I'd been a model pupil like Minnie Andrews. *She* hadn't anything on her conscience. The girls cried all the way home from school. Carrie Sloane kept saying every few minutes, 'The time has come for us to part,' and that would start us off again whenever we were in any danger of cheering up. I do feel dreadfully sad, Marilla. But one can't feel quite in the depths of despair with two months vacation before them, can they, Marilla? And besides, we met the new minister and his wife coming from the station. For all I was feeling so bad about Mr. Phillips going away I couldn't help taking a little interest in a new minister, could I? His wife is very pretty. Not exactly regally lovely, of course—it wouldn't do, I suppose, for a minister to have a regally lovely wife, because it might set a bad example. Mrs. Lynde says the minister's wife over at Newbridge sets a very bad example because she dresses so fashionably. Our new minister's wife was dressed in blue muslin with lovely puffed sleeves and a hat trimmed with roses. Jane Andrews said she thought puffed sleeves were too worldly for a minister's wife, but I didn't make any such uncharitable remark, Marilla, because I know what it is to long for puffed sleeves. Besides, she's only been a minister's wife for a little while, so one should make allowances, shouldn't they? They are going to board with Mrs. Lynde until the manse is ready."

If Marilla, in going down to Mrs. Lynde's that evening, was actuated by any motive save her avowed one of returning the quilting-frames she had borrowed the preceding winter, it was an amiable weakness shared by most of the Avonlea people. Many a thing Mrs. Lynde had lent, sometimes never expecting to see it again, came home that night in charge of the borrowers thereof. A new minister, and moreover a minister with a wife, was a lawful object of curiosity in a quiet little country settlement where sensations were few and far between.

Old Mr. Bentley, the minister whom Anne had found lacking in imagination, had been pastor of Avonlea for eighteen years. He was a widower when he came, and a widower he remained, despite the fact that gossip regularly married him to this, that or the other one, every year of his sojourn. In the preceding February he had resigned his charge and departed amid the regrets of his people, most of whom had the affection born of long intercourse for their good old minister in spite of his shortcomings as an orator. Since then the Avonlea church had enjoyed a variety of religious dissipation in listening to the many and various candidates and "supplies" who came Sunday after Sunday to preach on trial. These stood or fell by the judgment of the fathers and mothers in Israel; but a certain small, red-haired girl who sat meekly in the corner of the old Cuthbert pew also had her opinions about them and discussed the same in full with Matthew, Marilla always declining from principle to criticize ministers in any shape or form.

"I don't think Mr. Smith would have done, Matthew," was Anne's final summing up. "Mrs. Lynde says his delivery was so poor, but I think his worst fault was just like Mr. Bentley's—he had no imagination. And Mr. Terry had too much; he let it run away with him just as I did mine in the matter of the Haunted Wood. Besides, Mrs. Lynde says his theology wasn't sound. Mr. Gresham was a very good man and a very religious man, but he told too many funny stories and made the people laugh in church; he was undignified, and you must have some dignity about a minister, mustn't you, Matthew? I thought Mr. Marshall was decidedly attractive; but Mrs. Lynde says he isn't married, or even engaged, because she made special inquiries about him, and she says it would never do to have a young unmarried minister in Avonlea, because he might marry in the congregation and that would make trouble. Mrs. Lynde is a very far-seeing woman, isn't she, Matthew? I'm very glad they've called Mr. Allan. I liked him because his sermon was interesting and he prayed as if he meant it and not just as if he did it because he was in the habit of it. Mrs. Lynde says he isn't perfect, but she says she supposes we couldn't expect a perfect minister for seven hundred and fifty dollars a year, and anyhow his theology is sound because she questioned him thoroughly on all the points of doctrine. And she knows his wife's people and they are most respectable and the women are all good housekeepers. Mrs. Lynde says that sound doctrine in the man and good housekeeping in the woman make an ideal combination for a minister's family.''

The new minister and his wife were a young, pleasant-faced couple, still in their honeymoon, and full of all good and beautiful enthusiasms for their chosen life-work. Avonlea opened its heart to them from the start. Old and young liked the frank, cheerful young man with his high ideals, and the bright, gentle little lady who assumed the mistress-ship of the manse. With Mrs. Allan Anne fell promptly and whole-heartedly in love. She had discovered another kindred spirit.

''Mrs. Allan is perfectly lovely,'' she announced one Sunday afternoon. ''She's taken our class and she's a splendid teacher. She said right away she didn't think it was fair for the teacher to ask all the questions, and you know, Marilla, that is exactly what I've always thought. She said we could ask her any question we liked, and I asked ever so many. I'm good at asking questions, Marilla.''

''I believe you,'' was Marilla's emphatic comment.

''Nobody else asked any except Ruby Gillis, and she asked if there was to be a Sunday school picnic this summer. I didn't think that was a very proper question to ask because it hadn't any connection with the lesson—the lesson was about Daniel in the lion's den—but Mrs. Allan just smiled and said she thought there would be. Mrs. Allan has a lovely smile; she has such *exquisite* dimples in her cheeks. I wish I had dimples in my cheeks, Marilla. I'm not half so skinny as I was when I came here, but I have no dimples yet. If I had perhaps I could influence people for good. Mrs. Allan said we ought always to try to influence other people for good. She talked so nice about everything. I never knew before that religion was such a cheerful thing. I always thought it was kind of melancholy, but Mrs. Allan's isn't, and I'd like to be a Christian if I could be one like her. I wouldn't want to be one like Mr. Superintendent Bell.''

''It's very naughty of you to speak so about Mr. Bell,'' said Marilla severely. ''Mr. Bell is a real good man.''

''Oh, of course he's good,'' agreed Anne, ''but he doesn't seem to get any comfort out of it. If I could be good I'd dance and sing all day because I was glad of it. I suppose Mrs. Allan is too old to dance and sing and of course it wouldn't be dignified in a minister's wife. But I can just feel she's glad she's a Christian and that she'd be one even if she could get to heaven without it."

"I suppose we must have Mr. and Mrs. Allan up to tea some day soon," said Marilla reflectively. "They've been most everywhere but here. Let me see. Next Wednesday would be a good time to have them. But don't say a word to Matthew about it, for if he knew they were coming he'd find some excuse to be away that day. He'd got so used to Mr. Bentley he didn't mind him, but he's going to find it hard to get acquainted with a new minister, and a new minister's wife will frighten him to death."

"I'll be as secret as the dead," assured Anne. "But oh, Marilla, will you let me make a cake for the occasion? I'd love to do something for Mrs. Allan, and you know I can make a pretty good cake by this time."

"You can make a layer cake," promised Marilla.

Monday and Tuesday great preparations went on at Green Gables. Having the minister and his wife to tea was a serious and important undertaking, and Marilla was determined not to be eclipsed by any of the Avonlea housekeepers. Anne was wild with excitement and delight. She talked it all over with Diana Tuesday night in the twilight, as they sat on the big red stones by the Dryad's Bubble and made rainbows in the water with little twigs dipped in fir balsam.

"Everything is ready, Diana, except my cake which I'm to make in the morning, and the baking-powder biscuits which Marilla will make just before tea-time. I assure you, Diana, that Marilla and I have had a busy two days of it. It's such a responsibility having a minister's family to tea. I never went through such an experience before. You should just see our pantry. It's a sight to behold. We're going to to have jellied chicken and cold tongue. We're to have two kinds of jelly, red and yellow, and whipped cream and lemon pie, and cherry pie, and three kinds of cookies, and fruitcake, and Marilla's famous yellow plum reserves that she keeps especially for ministers, and pound cake and layer cake, and biscuits as aforesaid; and new bread and old both, in case the minister is dyspeptic and can't eat new. Mrs. Lynde says ministers are mostly dyspeptic, but I don't think Mr. Allan has been a minister long enough for it to have had a bad effect on him. I just grow cold when I think of my layer cake. Oh, Diana, what if it shouldn't be good! I dreamed last night that I was chased all around by a fearful goblin with a big layer cake for a head."

"It'll be good, all right," assured Diana, who was a very comfortable sort of friend. "I'm sure that piece of the one you made that we had for lunch in Idlewild two weeks ago was perfectly elegant."

"Yes; but cakes have such a terrible habit of turning out bad just when you especially want them to be good," sighed Anne, setting a particularly well-balsamed twig afloat. "However, I suppose I shall just have to trust to Providence and be careful to put in the flour. Oh, look, Diana, what a lovely rainbow! Do you suppose the dryad will come out after we go away and take it for a scarf?"

"You know there is no such thing as a dryad," said Diana. Diana's mother had found out about the Haunted Wood and had been decidedly angry over it. As a result Diana had abstained from any further imitative flights of imagination and did not think it prudent to cultivate a spirit of belief even in harmless dryads.

"But it's so easy to imagine there is," said Anne. "Every night, before I go to bed, I look out of my window and wonder if the dryad is really sitting here, combing her locks with the spring for a mirror. Sometimes I look for her footprints in the dew in the morning. Oh, Diana, don't give up your faith in the dryad!"

Wednesday morning came. Anne got up at sunrise because she was too excited to sleep. She had caught a severe cold in the head by reason of her dabbling in the spring on the preceding evening; but nothing short of absolute pneumonia could have quenched her interest in culinary matters that morning. After breakfast she proceeded to make her cake. When she finally shut the oven door upon it she drew a long breath.

"I'm sure I haven't forgotten anything this time, Marilla. But do you think it will rise? Just suppose perhaps the baking-powder isn't good? I used it out of the new can. And Mrs. Lynde says you can never be sure of getting good baking-powder nowadays when everything is so adulterated. Mrs. Lynde says the Government ought to take the matter up, but she says we'll never see the day when a Tory Government will do it. Marilla, what if that cake doesn't rise?"

"We'll have plenty without it," was Marilla's unimpassioned way of looking at the subject.

The cake did rise, however, and came out of the oven as light and feathery as golden foam. Anne, flushed with delight, clapped it together with layers of ruby jelly and, in imagination, saw Mrs. Allan eating it and possibly asking for another piece!

"You'll be using the best tea set, of course, Marilla," she said. "Can I fix up the table with ferns and wild roses?"

"I think that's all nonsense," sniffed Marilla. "In my opinion it's the eatables that matter and not flummery decorations."

"Mrs. Barry had *her* table decorated," said Anne, who was not entirely guiltless of the wisdom of the serpent, "and the minister paid her an elegant compliment. He said it was a feast for the eye as well as the palate."

"Well, do as you like," said Marilla, who was quite determined not to be surpassed by Mrs. Barry or anybody else. "Only mind you leave enough room for the dishes and the food."

Anne laid herself out to decorate in a manner and after a fashion that should leave Mrs. Barry's nowhere. Having abundance of roses and ferns and a very artistic taste of her own, she made that tea table such a thing of beauty that when the minister and his wife sat down to it they exclaimed in chorus over its loveliness.

"It's Anne's doings," said Marilla, grimly just; and Anne felt that Mrs. Allan's approving smile was almost too much happiness for this world.

Matthew was there, having been inveigled into the party only goodness and Anne knew how. He had been in such a state of shyness and nervousness that Marilla had given him up in despair, but Anne took him in hand so successfully that he now sat at the table in his best clothes and white collar and talked to the minister not uninterestingly. He never said a word to Mrs. Allan, but that perhaps was not to be expected.

All went merry as a marriage bell until Anne's layer cake was passed. Mrs. Allan, having already been helped to a bewildering variety, declined it. But Marilla, seeing the disappointment on Anne's face, said smilingly:

"Oh, you must take a piece of this, Mrs. Allan. Anne made it on purpose for you."

"In that case I must sample it," laughed Mrs. Allan, helping herself to a plump triangle, as did also the minister and Marilla.

Mrs. Allan took a mouthful of hers and a most peculiar expression crossed her face; not a word did she say, however, but steadily ate away at it. Marilla saw the expression and hastened to taste the cake.

"Anne Shirley!" she exclaimed, "what on earth did you put into that cake?"

"Nothing but what the recipe said, Marilla," cried Anne with a look of anguish. "Oh, isn't it all right?"

"All right! It's simply horrible. Mrs. Allan, don't try to eat it. Anne, taste it yourself. What flavoring did you use?"

"Vanilla," said Anne, her face scarlet with mortification after tasting the cake. "Only vanilla. Oh, Marilla, it must have been the baking powder. I had my suspicions of that bak—"

"Baking-powder fiddlesticks! Go and bring me the bottle of vanilla you used."

Anne fled to the pantry and returned with a small bottle partially filled with a brown liquid and labelled yellowly, "Best Vanilla."

Marilla took it, uncorked, it smelled it.

"Mercy on us, Anne, you've flavored that cake with *anodyne liniment*. I broke the liniment bottle last week and poured what was left into an old empty vanilla bottle. I suppose it's partly my fault—I should have warned you—but for pity's sake why couldn't you have smelled it?"

Anne dissolved into tears under this double disgrace.

"I couldn't—I had such a cold!" and with this she fairly fled to the gable chamber, where she cast herself on the bed and wept as one who refuses to be comforted.

Presently a light step sounded on the stairs and somebody entered the room.

"Oh, Marilla," sobbed Anne without looking up, "I'm disgaced for ever. I shall never be able to live this down. It will get out—things always do get out in Avonlea. Diana will ask me how my cake turned out and I shall have to tell her the truth. I shall always be pointed at as the girl who flavored a cake with anodyne liniment. Gil—the boys in school will never get over laughing at it. Oh, Marilla, if you have a spark of Christian pity don't tell me that I must go down and wash the dishes after this. I'll wash them when the minister and his wife are gone, but I cannot ever look Mrs. Allan in the face again. Perhaps she'll think I tried to poison her. Mrs. Lynde says she knows an orphan girl who tried to poison her benefactor. But the liniment isn't poisonous. It's meant to be taken internally—although not in cakes. Won't you tell Mrs. Allan so, Marilla?"

"Suppose you jump up and tell her so yourself," said a merry voice.

Anne flew up, to find Mrs. Allan standing by her bed, surveying her with laughing eyes.

"My dear little girl, you mustn't cry like this," she said, genuinely disturbed by Anne's tragic face. "Why, it's all a funny mistake that anybody might make."

"Oh, no, it takes me to make such a mistake," said Anne forlornly. "And I wanted to have that cake so nice for you, Mrs. Allan."

"Yes, I know, dear. And I assure you I appreciate your kindness and thoughtfulness just as much as if it had turned out all right. Now, you mustn't cry any more, but come down with me and show me your flower garden. Miss Cuthbert tells me you have a little plot all your own. I want to see it, for I'm very much interested in flowers."

Anne permitted herself to be led down and comforted, reflecting that it was really providential that Mrs. Allan was a kindred spirit. Nothing more was said about the liniment cake, and when the guests went away Anne found that she had enjoyed the evening more than could have been expected, considering that terrible incident. Nevertheless she sighed deeply.

"Marilla, isn't it nice to think that tomorrow is a new day with no mistakes in it yet?"

"I'll warrant you'll make plenty in it," said Marilla. "I never saw your beat for making mistakes, Anne."

"Yes, and well I know it," admitted Anne mournfully. "But have you ever noticed one encouraging thing about me, Marilla? I never make the same mistake twice."

"I don't know as that's much benefit when you're always making new ones."

"Oh, don't you see, Marilla? There *must* be a limit to the mistakes one person can make, and when I get to the end of them, then I'll be through with them. That's a very comforting thought."

"Well, you'd better go and give that cake to the pigs," said Marilla. "It isn't fit for any human to eat, not even Jerry Buote."

CHAPTER 22

ANNE IS INVITED OUT TO TEA

AND WHAT are your eyes popping out of your head about now?" asked Marilla, when Anne had just come in from a run to the post office. "Have you discovered another kindred spirit?"

Excitement hung around Anne like a garment, shone in her eyes, kindled in every feature. She had come dancing up the lane, like a wind-blown sprite, through the mellow sunshine and lazy shadows of the August evening.

"No, Marilla, but oh, what do you think? I am invited to tea at the manse tomorrow afternoon! Mrs. Allan left the letter for me at the post-office. Just look at it, Marilla. 'Miss Anne Shirley, Green Gables.' That is the first time I was ever called 'Miss.' Such a thrill as it gave me! I shall cherish it for ever among my choicest treasures."

"Mrs. Allan told me she meant to have all the members of her Sunday school class to tea in turn," said Marilla, regarding the wonderful event very coolly. "You needn't get in such a fever over it. Do learn to take things calmly, child."

For Anne to take things calmly would have been to change her nature. All "spirit and fire and dew," as she was, the pleasures and pains of life came to her with trebled intensity. Marilla felt this and was vaguely troubled over it, realizing that the ups and downs of existence would probably bear hardly on this impulsive soul and not sufficiently understanding that the equally great capacity for delight might more than compensate. Therefore Marilla conceived it to be her duty to drill Anne into a tranquil uniformity of disposition as impossible and alien to her as to a dancing sunbeam in one of the brook shallows. She did not make much headway, as she sorrowfully admitted to herself. The downfall of some dear hope or plan punged Anne into "deeps of affliction." The fulfilment thereof exalted her to dizzy realms of delight. Marilla had almost begun to despair of ever fashioning this waif of the world into her model little girl of demure manners and prim deportment. Neither would she have believed that she really liked Anne much better as she was.

Anne went to bed that night speechless with misery because Matthew had said the wind was round northeast and he feared it would be a rainy day tomorrow. The rustle of the poplar leaves about the house worried her, it sounded so like pattering raindrops, and the dull, faraway roar of the gulf, to which she listened delightedly at other times, loving its strange, sonorous, haunting rhythm, now seemed like a prophecy of storm and disaster to a small maiden who particularly wanted a fine day. Anne thought that the morning would never come.

But all things have an end, even nights before the day on which you are invited to take tea at the manse. The morning, in spite of

Matthew's predictions, was fine and Anne's spirits soared to their highest.

"Oh, Marilla, there is something in me today that makes me just love everybody I see," she exclaimed as she washed the breakfast dishes. "You don't know how good I feel! Wouldn't it be nice if it could last? I believe I could be a model child if I were just invited out to tea every day. But oh, Marilla, it's a solemn occasion, too. I feel so anxious. What if I shouldn't behave properly? You know I never had tea at a mance before, and I'm not sure that I know all the rules of etiquette, although I've been studying the rules given in the Etiquette Department of the *Family Herald* ever since I came here. I'm so afraid I'll do something silly or forget to do something I should do. Would it be good manners to take a second helping of anything if you wanted to *very* much?"

"The trouble with you, Anne, is that you're thinking too much about yourself. You should just think of Mrs. Allan and what would be nicest and most agreeable for her," said Marilla, hitting for once in her life on a very sound and pithy piece of advice. Anne instantly realized this.

"You are right, Marilla. I'll try not to think about myself at all."

Anne evidently got through her visit without any serious breach of "etiquette" for she came home through the twilight, under a great, high-sprung sky gloried over with trails of saffron and rosy cloud, in a beatified state of mind and told Marilla all about it happily, sitting on the big red sandstone slab at the kitchen door with her tired curly head in Marilla's gingham lap.

A cool wind was blowing down over the long harvest fields from the rims of firry western hills and whistling through the poplars. One clear star hung above the orchard and the fireflies were flitting over in Lovers' Lane, in and out among the ferns and rustling boughs. Anne watched them as she talked and somehow felt that wind and stars and fireflies were all tangled up together into something unutterably sweet and enchanting.

"Oh, Marilla, I've had a most *fascinating* time. I feel that I have not lived in vain and I shall always feel like that even if I should never be invited to tea at a manse again. When I got there Mrs. Allan met me at the door. She was dressed in the sweetest dress of pale pink organdy, with dozens of frills and elbow sleeves, and she looked just like a seraph. I really think I'd like to be a minister's wife when I grow up, Marilla. A minister mightn't mind my red hair because he wouldn't be thinking of such worldly things. But then of course one would have to be naturally good and I'll never be that, so I suppose there's no use in thinking about it. Some people are naturally good, you know, and others are not. I'm one of the others. Mrs. Lynde says I'm full of original sin. No matter how hard I try to be good I can never make such a success of it as those who are naturally good. It's a good deal like geometry, I expect. But don't you think the trying so hard ought to count for something? Mrs. Allan is one of the naturally good people. I love her passionately. You know there are some people, like Matthew and Mrs. Allan, that you can love right off without any trouble. And there are others, like Mrs. Lynde, that you have to try very hard to love. You know you *ought* to love them because they know so much and are such active workers in the church, but you have to keep reminding yourself of it all the time or else you forget. There was another little girl at the manse to tea, from the White Sands Sunday school. Her name was Lauretta Bradley, and she was a very nice little girl. Not exactly a kindred spirit, you know, but still very nice. We had an elegant tea, and I think I kept all the rules of etiquette pretty well. After tea Mrs. Allan played and sang and she got Lauretta and me to sing, too. Mrs. Allan says I have a good voice and she says I must sing in the Sunday school choir after this. You can't think how I was thrilled at the mere thought. I've longed so to sing in the Sunday school choir, as Diana does, but I feared it was an honor I could never aspire to. Lauretta had to go home early because there is a big concert in the White Sands hotel tonight and her sister is to recite at it. Lauretta says that the Americans at the hotel give a concert every fortnight in aid of the Charlottetown hospital, and they ask lots of the White Sands people to recite. Lauretta said she expected to be asked herself some day. I just gazed in awe at her. After she had gone Mrs. Allan and I had a heart to heart talk. I told her everything—about Mrs. Thomas and the twins and Katie Maurice and Violetta and coming to Green Gables and my troubles over geometry. And would you believe it, Marilla? Mrs. Allan told me she was a dunce at geometry, too. You don't know how that encouraged me. Mrs. Lynde came to the manse just before I left, and what do you think, Marilla? The trustees have hired a new teacher and it's a lady. Her name is Miss Muriel Stacy. Isn't that a romantic name? Mrs. Lynde says they've never had a female teacher in Avonlea before and she thinks it is a dangerous innovation. But I think it will be splendid to have a lady teacher, and I really don't see how I'm going to live through the two weeks before school begins, I'm so impatient to see her.

CHAPTER 23

ANNE COMES TO GRIEF IN AN AFFAIR OF HONOR

ANNE HAD to live through more than two weeks, as it happened. Almost a month having elapsed since the liniment cake episode, it was high time for her to get into fresh trouble of some sort, little mistakes, such as absent-mindedly emptying a pan of skim milk into a basket of yarn balls in the pantry instead of into the pigs' bucket, and walking clean over the edge of the log bridge into the brook while wrapped in imaginative reverie, not really being worth counting.

A week after the tea at the manse Diana Barry gave a party.

"Small and select," Anne assured Marilla. "Just the girls in our class."

They had a very good time and nothing untoward happened until after tea, when they found themselves in the Barry garden, a little tired of all their games and ripe for any enticing form of mischief which might present itself. This presently took the form of "daring."

Daring was the fashionable amusement among the Avonlea small fry just then. It had begun among the boys, but soon spread to the girls, and all the silly things that were done in Avonlea that summer because the doers thereof were "dared" to do them would fill a book by themselves.

First of all Carrie Sloane dared Ruby Gillis to climb to a certain point in the huge old willow tree before the front door; which Ruby Gillis, albeit in mortal dread of the fat green caterpillars with which said tree was infested and with the fear of her mother before her eyes if she should tear her new muslin dress, nimbly did, to the discomfiture of the aforesaid Carrie Sloane.

Then Josie Pye dared Jane Andrews to hop on her left leg around the garden without stopping once or putting her right foot to the ground; which Jane Andrews gamely tried to do, but gave out at the third corner and had to confess herself defeated.

Josie's triumph being rather more pronounced than good taste permitted, Anne Shirley dared her to walk along the top of the board fence which bounded the garden to the east. Now, to "walk" board fences requires more skill and steadiness of head and heel than one might suppose who has never tried it. But Josie Pye, if deficient in some qualities that make for popularity, had at least a natural and inborn gift, duly cultivated, for walking board fences. Josie walked the Barry fence with an airy unconcern which seemed to imply that a little thing like that wasn't worth a "dare." Reluctant admiration greeted her exploit, for most of the other girls could appreciate it, having suffered many things themselves in their efforts to walk fences. Josie descended from her perch, flushed with victory, and darted a defiant glance at Anne.

Anne tossed her red braids.

"I don't think it's such a very wonderful thing to walk a little, low, board fence," she said. "I knew a girl in Marysville who could walk the ridge-pole of a roof."

"I don't believe it," said Josie flatly. "I don't believe anybody could walk a ridge-pole. *You* couldn't anyhow."

"Couldn't I?" cried Anne rashly.

"Then I dare you to do it," said Josie defiantly. "I dare you to climb up there and walk the ridge-pole of Mr. Barry's kitchen roof."

Anne turned pale, but there was clearly only one thing to be done. She walked towards the house, where a ladder was leaning against the kitchen roof. All the fifth-class girls said, "Oh!" partly in excitement, partly in dismay.

Don't you do it, Anne," entreated Diana. "You'll fall off and be killed. Never mind Josie Pye. It isn't fair to dare anybody to do anything so dangerous."

"I must do it. My honor is at stake," said Anne solemnly. "I shall walk that ridge-pole, Diana, or perish in the attempt. If I am killed you are to have my pearl bead ring."

Anne climbed the ladder amid breathless silence, gained the ridge-pole, balanced herself uprightly on that precarious footing, and started to walk along it, dizzily conscious that she was uncomfortably high up in the world and that walking ridge-poles was not a thing in which your imagination helped you out much. Nevertheless, she managed to take several steps before the catastrophe came. Then she swayed, lost her balance, stumbled, staggered and fell, sliding down over the sun-baked roof and crashing off it through the tangle of Virginia creeper beneath—all before the dismayed circle below could give a simultaneous, terrified shriek.

If Anne had tumbled off the roof on the side up which she ascended, Diana would probably have fallen heir to the pearl bead ring then and there. Fortunately she fell on the other side, where the roof extended down over the porch so nearly to the ground that a fall therefrom was a much less serious thing. Nevertheless, when Diana and the other girls had rushed frantically around the house—except

Ruby Gillis, who remained as if rooted to the ground and went into hysterics—they found Anne lying all white and limp among the wreck and ruin of the Virginia creeper.

"Anne, are you killed?" shrieked Diana, throwing herself on her knees beside her friend. "Oh, Anne, dear Anne, speak just one word to me and tell me if you're killed."

To the immense relief of all the girls, and especially of Josie Pye, who, in spite of lack of imagination, had been seized with horrible visions of a future branded as the girl who was the cause of Anne Shirley's early and tragic death, Anne sat dizzily up and answered uncertainly:

"No, Diana, I am not killed, but I think I am rendered unconscious."

"Where?" sobbed Carrie Sloane. "Oh, where, Anne?"

Before Anne could answer, Mrs. Barry appeared on the scene. At sight of her Anne tried to scramble to her feet, but sank back again with a sharp little cry of pain.

"What's the matter? Where have you hurt yourself?" demanded Mrs. Barry.

"My ankle," gasped Anne. "Oh, Diana, please find your father and ask him to take me home. I know I can never walk there. And I'm sure I couldn't hop so far on one foot when Jane couldn't even hop around the garden."

Marilla was out in the orchard picking a panful of summer apples when she saw Mr. Barry coming over the log bridge and up the slope, with Mrs. Barry beside him and a whole procession of little girls trailing after him. In his arms he carried Anne, whose head lay limply against his shoulder.

At that moment Marilla had a revelation. In the sudden stab of fear that pierced to her very heart she realized what Anne had come to mean to her. She would have admitted that she liked Anne—nay, that she was very fond of Anne. But now she knew as she hurried wildly down the slope that Anne was dearer to her than anything on earth.

"Mr. Barry, what has happened to her?" she gasped, more white and shaken than the self-contained, sensible Marilla had been for many years.

Anne herself answered, lifting her head.

"Don't be frightened, Marilla. I was walking the ridge-pole and I fell off. I expect I have sprained my ankle. But, Marilla, I might have broken my neck. Let us look on the bright side of things."

"I might have known you'd go and do something of the sort when

"I SHALL WALK THAT RIDGE-POLE, OR PERISH IN THE ATTEMPT."

I let you go to that party,'' said Marilla, sharp and shrewish in her very relief. "Bring her in here, Mr. Barry, and lay her on the sofa. Mercy me, the child has gone and fainted!''

It was quite true. Overcome by the pain of her injury, Anne had one more of her wishes granted to her. She had fainted dead away.

Matthew, hastily summoned from the harvest field, was straightway despatched for the doctor, who in due time came, to discover that the injury was more serious than they had supposed. Anne's ankle was broken.

That night, when Marilla went up the the east gable, where a white-faced girl was lying, a plaintive voice greeted her from the bed.

"Aren't you very sorry for me, Marilla?''

"It was your own fault,'' said Marilla, twitching down the blind and lighting a lamp.

"And that is just why you should be sorry for me,'' said Anne, "because the thought that it *is* all my own fault is what makes it so hard. If I could blame it on anybody I would feel so much better. But what would you have done, Marilla, if you had been dared to walk a ridge-pole?''

" I'd have stayed on good firm ground and let them dare away. Such absurdity!'' said Marilla.

Anne sighed.

"But you have such strength of mind, Marilla. I haven't. I just felt that I couldn't bear Josie Pye's scorn. She would have crowed over me all my life. And I think I have been punished so much that you needn't be very cross with me, Marilla. It's not a bit nice to faint, after all. And the doctor hurt me dreadfully when he was setting my ankle. I won't be able to go around for six or seven weeks and I'll miss the new lady teacher. She won't be new anymore by the time I'm able to go to school. And Gil—everbody will get ahead of me in class. Oh, I am an afflicted mortal. But I'll try to bear it all bravely if only you won't be cross with me, Marilla.''

"There, there, I'm not cross,'' said Marilla. "You're an unlucky child, there's no doubt about that; but, as you say, you'll have the suffering of it. Here now, try and eat some supper.''

"Isn't it fortunate I've got such an imagination?'' said Anne. "It will help me through splendidly, I expect. What do people who haven't any imagination do when they break their bones, do you suppose, Marilla?''

Anne had good reason to bless her imagination many a time and oft during the tedious seven weeks that followed. But she was not solely dependent on it. She had many visitors and not a day passed without one or more of the schoolgirls dropping in to bring her flowers and books and tell her all the happenings in the juvenile world of Avonlea.

"Everybody has been so good and kind, Marilla," sighed Anne happily, on the day when she could first limp across the floor. "It isn't very pleasant to be laid up, but there *is* a bright side to it, Marilla. You find out how many friends you have. Why, even Superintendent Bell came to see me, and he's really a very fine man. Not a kindred spirit, of course; but still I like him and I'm awfully sorry I ever criticized his prayers. I believe now he really does mean them, only he has got into the habit of saying them as if he didn't. He could get over that if he'd take a little trouble. I gave him a good broad hint. I told him how hard I tried to make my own little private prayers interesting. He told me all about the time he broke his ankle when he was a boy. It does seem so strange to think of Superintendent Bell ever being a boy. Even my imagination has its limits for I can't imagine *that*. When I try to imagine him as a boy I see him with gray whiskers and spectacles, just as he looks in Sunday school, only small. Now, it's so easy to imagine Mrs. Allan as a little girl. Mrs. Allan has been to see me fourteen times. Isn't that something to be proud of, Marilla? When a minister's wife has so many claims on her time! She is such a cheerful person to have visit you, too. She never tells you it's your own fault and she hopes you'll be a better girl on account of it. Mrs. Lynde always told me that when she came to see me; and she said it in a kind of way that made me feel she might hope I'd be a better girl, but didn't really believe I would. Even Josie Pye came to see me. I received her as politely as I could, because I think she was sorry she dared me to walk a ridge-pole. If I had been killed she would have had to carry a dark burden of remorse all her life. Diana has been a faithful friend. She's been over every day to cheer my lonely pillow. But oh, I shall be so glad when I can go to school for I've heard such exciting things about the new teacher. The girls all think she is perfectly sweet. Diana says she has the loveliest fair curly hair and such fascinating eyes. She dresses beautifully, and her sleeve puffs are bigger than anybody else's in Avonlea. Every other Friday afternoon she has recitations and everybody has to say a piece or take part in a dialogue. Oh, it's just glorious to think of it. Josie Pye says she hates it, but that is just because Josie has so little imagination. Diana and Ruby Gillis and Jane Andrews are preparing a dialogue, called 'A Morning Visit,' for next Friday. And the Friday afternoons they don't have recitations Miss Stacy takes them all to the woods for a 'field' day and they study ferns and flowers and birds. And they have physical culture exercises every morning and evening. Mrs. Lynde says she never heard of such goings-on and it all comes of having a lady teacher. But I think it must be splendid and I believe I shall find that Miss Stacy is a kindred spirit.''

"There's one thing plain to be seen, Anne," said Marilla, "and that is that your fall off the Barry roof hasn't injured your tongue at all.''

CHAPTER 24

MISS STACY AND HER PUPILS GET UP A CONCERT

IT WAS October again when Anne was ready to go back to school—a glorious October, all red and gold, with mellow mornings when the valleys were filled with delicate mists as if the spirit of autumn had poured them in for the sun to drain—amethyst, pearl, silver rose, and smoke-blue. The dews were so heavy that the fields glistened like cloth of silver and there were such heaps of rustling leaves in the hollows of many-stemmed woods to run crisply through. The Birch Path was a canopy of yellow and the ferns were sear and brown all along it. There was a tang in the very air that inspired the hearts of small maidens tripping, unlike snails, swiftly and willingly to school; and it *was* jolly to be back again at the little brown desk beside Diana, with Ruby Gillis nodding across the aisle and Carrie Sloane sending up notes and Julie Bell passing a "chew" of gum down from the back seat. Anne drew a long breath of happiness as she sharpened her pencil and arranged her picture cards in her desk. Life was certainly very interesting.

In the new teacher she found another true and helpful friend. Miss Stacy was a bright, sympathetic young woman with the happy gift of winning and holding the affections of her pupils and bringing out the best that was in them mentally and morally. Anne expanded like a flower under this wholesome influence and carried home to the admiring Matthew and the critical Marilla glowing accounts of school work and aims.

"I love Miss Stacy with my whole heart, Marilla. She is so ladylike and she has such a sweet voice. When she pronounces my name I feel *instinctively* that she's spelling it with an *e*. We had recitations this afternoon. I just wish you could have been there to hear me recite 'Mary, Queen of Scots.' I just put my whole soul into it. Ruby Gillis told me coming home that the way I said the line, 'Now for my father's arm, she said, my woman's heart farewell,' just made her blood run cold.''

''Well now, you might recite for me some of these days, out in the barn,'' suggested Matthew.

''Of course I will,'' said Anne meditatively, ''but I won't be able to do it so well, I know. It won't be so exciting as it is when you have a whole schoolful before you hanging breathlessly on your words. I know I won't be able to make your blood run cold.''

''Mrs. Lynde says it made *her* blood run cold to see the boys climbing to the very tops of those big trees on Bell's hill after crows' nests last Friday,'' said Marilla. ''I wonder at Miss Stacy for encouraging it.''

''But we wanted a crow's nest for nature study,'' explained Anne. ''That was on our field afternoon. Field afternoons are splendid, Marilla. And Miss Stacy explains everything so beautifully. We have to write compositions on our field afternoons and I write the best ones.''

''It's very vain of you to say so then. You'd better let your teacher say it.''

''But she *did* say it, Marilla. And indeed I'm not vain about it. How can I be, when I'm such a dunce at geometry? Although I'm really beginning to see through it a little, too. Miss Stacy makes it so clear. Still, I'll never be good at it and I assure you it is a humbling reflection. But I love writing compositions. Mostly Miss Stacy lets us choose our own subjects; but next week we are to write a composition on some remarkable person. It's hard to choose among so many remarkable people who have lived. Mustn't it be splendid to be remarkable and have compositions written about you after you're dead? Oh, I would dearly love to be remarkable. I think when I grow up I'll be a trained nurse and go with the Red Crosses to the field of battle as a messenger of mercy. That is, if I don't go out as a foreign missionary. That would be very romantic, but one would have to be very good to be a missionary, and that would be a stumbling-block. We have physical culture exercises every day, too. They make you graceful and promote digestion.''

''Promote fiddlesticks!'' said Marilla, who honestly thought it was all nonsense.

But all the field afternoons and recitation Fridays and physical culture contortions paled before a project which Miss Stacy brought forward in November. This was that the scholars of Avonlea school should get up a concert and hold it in the hall on Christmas night, for the laudable purpose of helping to pay for a schoolhouse flag. The pupils one and all taking graciously to this plan, the preparations for a program were begun at once. And of all the excited performers-elect none was so excited as Anne Shirley, who threw herself into the undertaking heart and soul, hampered as she was by Marilla's disapproval. Marilla thought it all rank foolishness.

"It's just filling your heads up with nonsense and taking time that ought to be put on your lessons," she grumbled. "I don't approve of children's getting up concerts and racing about to practices. It makes them vain and forward and fond of gadding."

"But think of the worthy object," pleaded Anne. "A flag will cultivate a spirit of patriotism, Marilla."

"Fudge! There's precious little patriotism in the thoughts of any of you. All you want is a good time."

"Well, when you can combine patriotism and fun, isn't it all right? Of course it's real nice to be getting up a concert. We're going to have six choruses and Diana is to sing a solo. I'm in two dialogues—'The Society fo the Suppression of Gossip' and 'The Fairy Queen.' The boys are going to have a dialogue, too. And I'm to have two recitations, Marilla. I just tremble when I think of it, but it's a nice thrilly kind of tremble. And we're to have a tableau at the last—'Faith, Hope and Charity.' Diana and Ruby and I are to be in it, all draped in white with flowing hair. I'm to be Hope, with my hands clasped—so—and my eyes uplifted. I'm going to practise my recitations in the garret. Don't be alarmed if you hear me groaning. I have to groan heartrendingly in one of them, and it's really hard to get up a good artistic groan, Marilla. Josie Pye is sulky because she didn't get the part she wanted in the dialogue. She wanted to be the fairy queen. That would have been ridiculous, for who ever heard of a fairy queen as fat as Josie? Fairy queens must be slender. Jane Andrews is to be the queen and I am to be one of her maids of honor. Josie says she thinks a red-haired fairy is just as ridiculous as a fat one, but I do not let myself mind what Josie says. I'm to have a wreath of white roses on my hair and Ruby Gillis is going to lend me her slippers because I haven't any of my own. It's necessary for fairies to have slippers, you know. You couldn't imagine a fairy wearing boots, could you? Especially with copper toes? We are going to decorate the hall with creeping spruce and fir mottoes with pink tissue-paper roses in them. And we are all to march in two by two after the audience is seated, while Emma White plays a march on the organ. Oh, Marilla, I know you aren't so enthusiastic about it as I am, but don't you hope your little Anne will distinguish herself?''

"All I hope is that you'll behave yourself. I'll be heartily glad when all this fuss is over and you'll be able to settle down. You are simply good for nothing just now with your head stuffed full of dialogues and groans and tableaus. As for your tongue, it's a marvel it's not clean worn out.''

Anne sighed and betook herself to the back yard, over which a young new moon was shining through the leafless poplar boughs from an apple-green western sky, and where Matthew was splitting wood. Anne perched herself on a block and talked the concert over with him, sure of an appreciative and sympathetic listener in this instance at least.

"Well now, I reckon it's going to be a pretty good concert. And I expect you'll do your part fine,'' he said, smiling down into her eager, vivacious little face. Anne smiled back at him. Those two were the best of friends and Matthew thanked his stars many a time and oft that he had nothing to do with bringing her up. That was Marilla's exclusive duty; if it had been his he would have been worried over frequent conflicts between inclination and said duty. As it was, he was free to "spoil Anne"—Marilla's phrasing—as much as he liked. But it was not such a bad arrangement after all; a little "appreciation" sometimes does quite as much good as all the conscientious "bringing up" in the world.

CHAPTER 25

MATTHEW INSISTS ON PUFFED SLEEVES

MATTHEW WAS having a bad ten minutes of it. He had come into the kitchen, in the twilight of a cold, gray December evening, and had sat down in the wood-box corner to take off his heavy boots, unconscious of the fact that Anne and a bevy of her schoolmates were having a practice of "The Fairy Queen" in the sitting-room. Presently they came trooping through the hall and out into the kitchen, laughing and chattering gaily. The did not see Matthew, who shrank bashfully back into the shadows beyond the wood-box with a boot in one hand and a bootjack in the other, and he watched them shyly for the aforesaid ten minutes as they put on caps and jackets and talked about the dialogue and the concert. Anne stood among them, bright-eyed and animated as they; but Matthew suddenly became conscious that there was something about her different from her mates. And what worried Matthew was that the difference impressed him as being something that should not exist. Anne had a brighter face, and bigger, starrier eyes, and more delicate features than the others; even shy, unobservant Matthew had learned to take note of these things; but the difference that disturbed him did not consist in any of these respects. Then in what did it consist?

Matthew was haunted by this question long after the girls had gone, arm in arm, down the long, hard-frozen lane and Anne had betaken herself to her books. He could not refer it to Marilla, who, he felt, would be quite sure to sniff scornfully and remark that the only difference she saw between Anne and the other girls was that they sometimes kept their tongues quiet while Anne never did. This, Matthew felt, would be no great help.

He had recourse to his pipe that evening to help him study it out, much to Marilla's disgust. After two hours of smoking and hard reflection Matthew arrived at a solution of his problem. Anne was not dressed like the other girls!

The more Matthew thought about the matter the more he was convinced that Anne never had been dressed like the other girls— never since she had come to Green Gables. Marilla kept her clothed in plain, dark dresses, all made after the same unvarying pattern. If Matthew knew there was such a thing as fashion in dress it is as much as he did; but he was quite sure that Anne's sleeves did not look at all like the sleeves the other girls wore. He recalled the cluster of little girls he had seen around her that evening—all gay in waists of red and blue and pink and white—and he wondered why Marilla always kept her so plainly and soberly gowned.

Of course, it must be all right. Marilla knew best and Marilla was bringing her up. Probably some wise, inscrutable motive was to be served thereby. But surely it would do not harm to let the child have one pretty dress—something like Diana Barry always wore. Matthew decided that he would give her one; that surely could not be objected to as an unwarranted putting in of his oar. Christmas was only a fortnight off. A nice new dress would be the very thing for a present. Matthew, with a sigh of satisfaction, put away his pipe and went to bed, while Marilla opened all the doors and aired the house.

The very next evening Matthew betook himself to Carmody to buy the dress, determined to get the worst over and have done with it. It would be, he felt assured, no trifling ordeal. There were some things Matthew could buy and prove himself no mean bargainer; but he knew he would be at the mercy of shopkeepers when it came to buying a girl's dress.

After much cogitation Matthew resolved to go to Samuel Lawson's store instead of William Blair's. To be sure, the Cuthberts always had gone to William Blair's; it was almost as much a matter of conscience with them as to attend the Presbyterian church and vote Conservative. But William Blair's two daughters frequently waited on customers there and Matthew held them in absolute dread. He could contrive to deal with them when he knew exactly what he wanted and could point it out; but in such a matter as this, requiring explanation and consultation, Matthew felt that he must be sure of a man behind the counter. So he would go to Lawson's where Samuel or his son would wait on him.

Alas! Matthew did not know that Samuel, in the recent expansion of his business, had set up a lady clerk also; she was a niece of his wife's and a very dashing young person indeed, with a huge, drooping pompadour, big, rolling brown eyes, and a most extensive and bewildering smile. She was dressed with exceeding smartness and wore several bangle bracelets that glittered and rattled and tinkled with every movement of her hands. Matthew was covered with confusion at finding her there at all; and those bangles completely wrecked his wits at one fell swoop.

"What can I do for you this evening, Mr. Cuthbert?" Miss Lucilla Harris inquired, briskly and ingratiatingly, tapping the counter with both hands.

"Have you any—any—well now, say any garden rakes?" stammered Matthew.

Miss Harris looked somewhat surprised, as well she might, to hear a man inquiring for garden rakes in the middle of December.

"I believe we have one or two left over," she said, "but they're upstairs in the lumber room. I'll go and see."

During her absence Matthew collected his scattered senses for another effort.

When Miss Harris returned with the rake and cheerfully inquired: "Anything else tonight, Mr. Cuthbert?" Matthew took his courage in both hands and replied: "Well now, since you suggest it, I might as well—take—that is—look at—buy some—some hayseed."

Miss Harris had heard Matthew Cuthbert called odd. She now concluded that he was entirely crazy.

"We only keep hayseed in the spring," she explained loftily. "We've none on hand just now."

"Oh, certainly—certainly—just as you say," stammered unhappy Matthew, seizing the rake and making for the door. At the threshold he recollected that he had not paid for it and he turned miserably back. While Miss Harris was counting out his change he rallied his powers for a final desperate attempt.

"Well now—if it isn't too much trouble—I might as well—that is—I'd like to look at—at—some sugar."

"White or brown?" queried Miss Harris patiently.

"Oh—well now—brown," said Matthew feebly.

"There's a barrel of it over there," said Miss Harris, shaking her bangles at it. "It's the only kind we have."

"I'll—I'll take twenty pounds of it," said Matthew, with beads of perspiration standing on his forehead.

Matthew had driven halfway home before he was his own man again. It had been a gruesome experience, but it served him right, he thought, for committing the heresy of going to a strange store. When he reached home he hid the rake in the toolhouse, but the sugar he carried in to Marilla.

"Brown sugar!" exclaimed Marilla. "Whatever possessed you to get so much? You know I never use it except for the hired man's porridge or black fruit-cake. Jerry's gone and I've made my cake long ago. It's not good sugar, either—it's coarse and dark—William Blair doesn't ususally keep sugar like that."

"I—I thought it might come in handy sometime," said Matthew, making good his escape.

When Matthew came to think the matter over he decided that a woman was required to cope with the situation. Marilla was out of the question. Matthew felt sure she would throw cold water on his project at once. Remained only Mrs. Lynde; for of no other woman in Avonlea would Matthew have dared to ask advice. To Mrs. Lynde he went accordingly, and that good lady promptly took the matter out of the harassed man's hands.

"Pick out a dress for you to give Anne? To be sure I will. I'm going to Carmody tomorrow and I'll attend to it. Have you something particular in mind? No? Well, I'll just go by my own judgment then.

I believe a nice rich brown would just suit Anne, and William Blair has some new gloria in that's real pretty. Perhaps you'd like me to make it up for her, too, seeing that if Marilla was to make it Anne would probably get wind of it before the time and spoil the surprise? Well, I'll do it. No, it isn't a mite of trouble. I like sewing. I'll make it to fit my niece, Jenny Gillis, for she and Anne are as like as two peas as far as figure goes.''

"Well now, I'm much obliged,'' said Matthew, "and—and—I dunno—but I'd like—I think they make the sleeves different nowadays to what they used to be. If it wouldn't be asking too much I—I'd like them made in the new way.''

"Puffs? Of course. You needn't worry a speck more about it, Matthew. I'll make it up in the very latest fashion,'' said Mrs. Lynde. To herself she added when Matthew had gone:

"It'll be a real satisfaction to see that poor child wearing something decent for once. The way Marilla dresses her is positively ridiculous, that's what, and I've ached to tell her so plainly a dozen times. I've held my tongue though, for I can see Marilla doesn't want advice and she thinks she knows more about bringing children up than I do for all she's an old maid. But that's always the way. Folks that has brought up children know that there's no hard and fast method in the world that'll suit every child. But them as never have think it's all as plain and easy as Rule of Three—just set your three terms down so fashion, and the sum'll work out correct. But flesh and blood don't come under the head of arithmetic and that's where Marilla Cuthbert makes her mistake. I suppose she's trying to cultivate a spirit of humility in Anne by dressing her as she does; but it's more likely to cultivate envy and discontent. I'm sure the child must feel the difference between her clothes and the other girls'. But to think of Matthew taking notice of it! That man is waking up after being asleep for over sixty years.''

Marilla knew all the following fortnight that Matthew had something on his mind, but what it was she could not guess, until Christmas Eve, when Mrs. Lynde brought up the new dress. Marilla behaved pretty well on the whole, although it is very likely she distrusted Mrs. Lynde's diplomatic explanation that she had made the dress because Matthew was afraid Anne would find out about it too soon if Marilla made it.

"So this is what Matthew has been looking so mysterious over and grinning about to himself for two weeks, is it?'' she said a little stiffly but tolerantly. "I knew he was up to some foolishness. Well, I must

say I don't think Anne needed any more dresses. I made her three
good, warm, serviceable ones this fall, and anything more is sheer
extravagance. There's enough material in those sleeves alone to
make a waist, I declare there is. You'll just pamper Anne's vanity,
Matthew, and she's as vain as a peacock now. Well, I hope she'll be
satisfied at last, for I know she's been hankering after those silly
sleeves ever since they came in, although she never said a word after
the first. The puffs have been getting bigger and more ridiculous
right along; they're as big as balloons now. Next year anybody who
wears them will have to go through a door sideways.''

Christmas morning broke on a beautiful white world. It had been a
very mild December and people had looked forward to a green
Christmas; but just enough snow fell softly in the night to transfigure
Avonlea. Anne peeped out from her frosted gable window with
delighted eyes. The firs in the Haunted Wood were all feathery and
wonderful; the birches and wild cherry-trees were outlined in pearl;
the ploughed fields were stretches of snowy dimples; and there was a
crisp tang in the air that was glorious. Anne ran downstairs singing
until her voice reechoed through Green Gables.

''Merry Christmas, Marilla! Merry Christmas, Matthew! Isn't it a
lovely Christmas? I'm so glad it's white. Any other kind of Christmas doesn't seem real, does it? I don't like green Christmases.
They're *not* green—they're just nasty faded browns and grays. What
makes people call them green? Why—why—Matthew, is that for
me? Oh, Matthew!''

Matthew had sheepishly unfolded the dress from its paper swa-
things and held it out with a deprecatory glance at Marilla, who
feigned to be contemptuously filling the teapot, but nevertheless
watched the scene out of the corner of her eye with a rather interested
air.

Anne took the dress and looked at it in reverent silence. Oh, how
pretty it was—a lovely soft brown gloria with all the gloss of silk; a
skirt with dainty frills and shirrings; a waist elaborately pintucked in
the most fashionable way, and a little ruffle of filmy lace at the neck.
But the sleeves—they were the crowning glory! Long elbow cuffs,
and above them two beautiful puffs divided by rows of shirring and
bows of brown silk ribbon.

''That's a Christmas present for you, Anne,'' said Matthew shyly.
''Why—why Anne, don't you like it? Well now—well now.''

For Anne's eyes had suddenly filled with tears.

''*Like* it! Oh, Matthew!'' Anne laid the dress over a chair and
clasped her hands. ''Matthew, it's perfectly exquisite. Oh, I can

never thank you enough. Look at those sleeves! Oh, it seems to me this must be a happy dream.''

"Well, well, let us have breakfast," interrupted Marilla. "I must say, Anne, I don't think you needed the dress; but since Matthew has got it for you, see that you take good care of it. There's a hair ribbon Mrs. Lynde left for you. It's brown to match the dress. Come now, sit in."

"I don't see how I'm going to eat breakfast," said Anne rapturously. "Breakfast seems so commonplace at such an exciting moment. I'd rather feast my eyes on that dress. I'm so glad that puffed sleeves are still fashionable. It did seem to me that I'd never get over it if they went out before I had a dress with them. I'd never have felt quite satisfied, you see. It was lovely of Mrs. Lynde to give me the ribbon, too. I feel that I ought to be a very good girl indeed. It's at times like this I'm sorry I'm not a model little girl; and I always resolve that I will be in future. But somehow it's hard to carry out your resolutions when irresistible temptations come. Still, I really will make an extra effort after this.''

When the commonplace breakfast was over Diana appeared, crossing the white log bridge in the hollow, a gay little figure in her crimson ulster. Anne flew down the slope to meet her.

"Merry Christmas, Diana! And oh, it's a wonderful Christmas. I've something splendid to show you. Matthew has given me the loveliest dress, with *such* sleeves. I couldn't even imagine any nicer.''

"I've got something more for you," said Diana breathlessly. "Here—this box. Aunt Josephine sent us out a big box with ever so many things in it—and this is for you. I'd have brought it over last night, but it didn't come until after dark, and I never feel very comfortable coming through the Haunted Wood in the dark now.''

Anne opened the box and peeped in. First a card with "For the Anne-girl and Merry Christmas," written on it; and then, a pair of the daintiest little kid slippers, with beaded toes and satin bows and glistening buckles.

"Oh," said Anne, "Diana, this is too much. I must be dreaming.''

"*I* call it providential," said Diana. "You won't have to borrow Ruby's slippers now, and that's a blessing, for they're two sizes too big for you, and it would be awful to hear a fairy shuffling. Josie Pye would be delighted. Mind you, Rob Wright went home with Gertie Pye from the practice night before last. Did you ever hear anything equal to that?''

All the Avonlea scholars were in a fever of excitement that day, for the hall had to be decorated and a last grand rehearsal held.

The concert came off in the evening and was a pronounced success. The little hall was crowded; all the performers did excellently well, but Anne was the bright particular star of the occasion, as even envy, in the shape of Josie Pye, dared not deny.

"Oh, hasn't it been a brilliant evening?" sighed Anne, when it was all over and she and Diana were walking home together under a dark, starry sky.

"Everything went off very well," said Diana practically. "I guess we have made as much as ten dollars. Mind you, Mr. Allan is going to send an account of it to the Charlottetown papers."

"Oh, Diana, will we really see our names in print? It makes me thrill to think of it. Your solo was perfectly elegant, Diana. I felt prouder than you did when it was encored. I just said to myself, 'It is my dear bosom friend who is so honored.' "

"Well, your recitations just brought down the house, Anne. That sad one was simply splendid."

"Oh, I was so nervous, Diana. When Mr. Allan called out my name I really cannot tell how I ever got up on that platform. I felt as if a million eyes were looking at me and through me, and for one dreadful moment I was sure I couldn't begin at all. Then I thought of my lovely puffed sleeves and took courage. I knew that I must live up to those sleeves, Diana. So I started in, and my voice seemed to be coming from ever so far away. I just felt like a parrot. It's providential that I practiced those recitations so often up in the garret, or I'd never have been able to get through. Did I groan all right?"

"Yes, indeed, you groaned lovely," assured Diana.'

"I saw old Mrs. Sloane wiping away tears when I sat down. It was splendid to think I had touched somebody's heart. It's so romantic to take part in a concert, isn't it? Oh, it's been a very memorable occasion indeed."

"Wasn't the boys' dialogue fine?" said Diana. "Gilbert Blythe was just splendid. Anne, I do think it's awful mean the way you treat Gil. Wait till I tell you. When you ran off the platform after the fairy dialogue one of your roses fell out of your hair. I saw Gil pick it up and put it in his breast-pocket. There now. You're so romantic that I'm sure you ought to be pleased at that."

"It's nothing to me what that person does," said Anne loftily. "I simply never waste a thought on him, Diana."

That night Marilla and Matthew, who had been out to a concert for the first time in twenty years, sat for awhile by the kitchen fire after Anne had gone to bed.

"Well now, I guess our Anne did as well as any of them," said Matthew proudly.

"Yes, she did," admitted Marilla. "She's a bright child, Matthew. And she looked real nice, too. I've been kind of opposed to this concert scheme, but I suppose there's no real harm in it after all. Anyhow, I was proud of Anne tonight, although I'm not going to tell her so."

"Well now, I was proud of her and I did tell her so 'fore she went upstairs," said Matthew. "We must see what we can do for her some of these days, Marilla. I guess she'll need something more than Avonlea school by and by."

"There's time enough to think of that," said Marilla. "She's only thirteen in March. Though tonight it struck me she was growing quite a big girl. Mrs. Lynde made that dress a mite too long, and it makes Anne look so tall. She's quick to learn and I guess the best thing we can do for her will be to send her to Queen's after a spell. But nothing need be said about that for a year or two yet."

"Well now, it'll do no harm to be thinking it over off and on," said Matthew. "Things like that are all the better for lots of thinking over."

CHAPTER 26

THE STORY CLUB IS FORMED

JUNIOR AVONLEA found it hard to settle down to humdrum existence again. To Anne in particular things seemed fearfully flat, stale, and unprofitable after the goblet of excitement she had been sipping for weeks. Could she go back to the former quiet pleasures of those far-away days before the concert? At first, as she told Diana, she did not really think she could.

"I'm positively certain, Diana, that life can never be quite the same again as it was in those olden days," she said mournfully, as if referring to a period of at least fifty years back. "Perhaps after a while I'll get used to it, but I'm afraid concerts spoil people for everyday life. I suppose that is why Marilla disapproves of them. Marilla is such a sensible woman. It must be a great deal better to be sensible;

but still, I don't believe I'd really like to be a sensible person, because they are so unromantic. Mrs. Lynde says there is no danger of my ever being one, but you can never tell. I feel just now that I may grow up to be sensible yet. But perhaps that is only because I'm tired. I simply couldn't sleep last night for ever so long. I just lay awake and imagined the concert over and over again. That's one splendid thing about such affairs—it's so lovely to look back to them.''

Eventually, however, Avonlea school skipped back into its old groove and took up its old interests. To be sure, the concert left traces. Ruby Gillis and Emma White, who had quarrelled over a point of precedence in their platform seats, no longer sat at the same desk, and a promising friendship of three years was broken up. Josie Pye and Julia Bell did not ''speak'' for three months, because Josie Pye had told Bessie Wright that Julia Bell's bow when she got up to recite made her think of a chicken jerking up its head, and Bessie told Julia. None of the Sloanes would have any dealings with the Bells, because the Bells had declared that the Sloanes had too much to do in the program, and the Sloanes had retorted that the Bells were not capable of doing the little they had to do properly. Finally, Charlie Sloane fought Moody Spurgeon MacPherson, because Moody Spurgeon had said that Anne Shirley put on airs about her recitations, and Moody Spurgeon was ''licked;'' consequently Moody Spurgeon's sister, Ella May, would not ''speak'' to Anne Shirley all the rest of the winter. With the exception of these trifling frictions, work in Miss Stacy's little kingdom went on with regularity and smoothness.

The winter weeks slipped by. It was an unusually mild winter, with so little snow that Anne and Diana could go to school nearly every day by way of the Birch Path. On Anne's birthday they were tripping lightly down it, keeping eyes and ears alert amid all their chatter, for Miss Stacy had told them that they must soon write a composition on ''A Winter's Walk in the Woods,'' and it behooved them to be observant.

''Just think, Diana, I'm thirteen years old today,'' remarked Anne in an awed voice. ''I can scarcely realize that I'm in my teens. When I woke this morning it seemed to me that everything must be different. You've been thirteen for a month, so I suppose it doesn't seem such a novelty to you as it does to me. It makes life seem so much more interesting. In two more years I'll be really grown up. It's a great comfort to think that I'll be able to use big words then without being laughed at.''

"Ruby Gillis says she means to have a beau as soon as she's fifteen," said Diana.

"Ruby Gillis thinks of nothing but beaus," said Anne disdainfully. "She's actually delighted when any one writes her name up in a take-notice for all she pretends to be so mad. But I'm afraid that is an uncharitable speech. Mrs. Allan says we should never make uncharitable speeches; but they do slip out so often before you think, don't they? I simply can't talk about Josie Pye without making an uncharitable speech, so I never mention her at all. You may have noticed that. I'm trying to be as much like Mrs. Allan as I possibly can, for I think she's perfect. Mr. Allan thinks so too. Mrs. Lynde says he just worships the ground she treads on and she doesn't really think it right for a minister to set his affections so much on a mortal being. But then, Diana, even ministers are human and have their besetting sins just like everybody else. I had such an interesting talk with Mrs. Allan about besetting sins last Sunday afternoon. There are just a few things it's proper to talk about on Sundays and that is one of them. My besetting sin is imagining too much and forgetting my duties. I'm striving very hard to overcome it and now that I'm really thirteen perhaps I'll get on better."

"In four more years we'll be able to put our hair up," said Diana. "Alice Bell is only sixteen and she is wearing hers up, but I think that's ridiculous. I shall wait until I'm seventeen."

"If I had Alice Bell's crooked nose," said Anne decidely, "I wouldn't—but there! I won't say what I was going to because it was extremely uncharitable. Besides, I was comparing it with my own nose and that's vanity. I'm afraid I think too much about my nose ever since I heard that compliment about it long ago. It really is a great comfort to me. Oh, Diana, look, there's a rabbit. That's something to remember for our woods composition. I really think the woods are just as lovely in winter as in summer. They're so white and still, as if they were asleep and dreaming pretty dreams."

"I won't mind writing that composition when its time comes," sighed Diana. "I can manage to write about the woods, but the one we're to hand in Monday is terrible. The idea of Miss Stacy telling us to write a story out of our own heads!"

"Why it's as easy as a wink," said Anne.

"It's easy for you because you have an imagination," retorted Diana, "but what would you do if you had been born without one? I suppose you have your composition all done?"

Anne nodded, trying hard not to look virtuously complacent and failing miserably.

"I wrote it last Monday evening. It's called 'The Jealous Rival; or, in Death Not Divided.' I read it to Marilla and she said it was stuff and nonsense. Then I read it to Matthew and he said it was fine. That is the kind of critic I like. It's a sad, sweet story. I just cried like a child while I was writing it. It's about two beautiful maidens called Cordelia Montmorency and Geraldine Seymour who live in the same village and were devotedly attached to each other. Cordelia was a regal brunette with a coronet of midnight hair and duskly flashing eyes. Geraldine was a queenly blonde with hair like spun gold and velvety purple eyes.''

"I never saw anybody with purple eyes,'' said Diana dubiously.

"Neither did I. I just imagined them. I wanted something out of the common. Geraldine had an alabaster brow, too. I've found out what an alabaster brow is. That is one of the advantages of being thirteen. You know so much more than you did when you were only twelve.''

"Well, what became of Cordelia and Geraldine?'' asked Diana, who was beginning to feel rather interested in their fate.

"They grow in beauty side by side until they were sixteen. Then Bertram DeVere came to their native village and fell in love with the fair Geraldine. He saved her life when her horse ran away with her in a carriage, and she fainted in his arms and he carried her home three miles; because, you understand, the carriage was all smashed up. I found it rather hard to imagine the proposal because I had no experience to go by. I asked Ruby Gillis if she knew anything about how men proposed because I thought she'd likely be an authority on the subject, having so many sisters married. Ruby told me she was hid in the hall pantry when Malcolm Andrews proposed to her sister Susan. She said Malcolm told Susan that his dad had given him the farm in his own name and then said, 'What do you say, darling pet, if we get hitched this fall?' And Susan said, 'Yes—no—I don't know—let me see,'—and there they were, engaged as quick as that. But I didn't think that sort of a proposal was a very romantic one, so in the end I had to imagine it out as well as I could. I made it very flowery and poetical and Bertram went on his knees, although Ruby Gillis says it isn't done nowadays. Geraldine accepted him in a speech a page long. I can tell you I took a lot of trouble with that speech. I rewrote it five times and I look upon it as my masterpiece. Bertram gave her a diamond ring and a ruby necklace and told her they would go to Europe for a wedding tour, for he was immensely wealthy. But then, alas, shadows began to darken over their path.

Cordelia was secretly in love with Bertram herself and when Geraldine told her about the engagement she was simply furious, especially when she saw the necklace and the diamond ring. All her affection for Geraldine turned to bitter hate and she vowed that she should never marry Bertram. But she pretended to be Geraldine's friend the same as ever. One evening they were standing on the bridge over a rushing turbulent stream and Cordelia, thinking they were alone, pushed Geraldine over the brink with a wild, mocking 'Ha, ha, ha.' But Bertram saw it all and he at once plunged into the current, exclaiming, 'I will save thee, my peerless Geraldine.' But alas, he had forgotten he couldn't swim and they were both drowned, clasped in each other's arms. Their bodies were washed ashore soon afterwards. They were buried in the one grave and their funeral was most imposing, Diana. It's so much more romantic to end a story up with a funeral than a wedding. As for Cordelia, she went insane with remorse and was shut up in a lunatic asylum. I thought that was a poetical retribution for her crime.''

''How perfectly lovely!'' sighed Diana, who belonged to Matthew's school of critics. ''I don't see how you can make up such thrilling things out of your own head, Anne. I wish my imagination was as good as yours.''

''It would be if you'd only cultivate it,'' said Anne cheeringly. ''I've just thought of a plan, Diana. Let you and I have a story club all our own and write stories for practice. I'll help you along until you can do them by yourself. You ought to cultivate your imagination, you know. Miss Stacy says so. Only we must take the right way. I told her about the Haunted Wood, but she said we went the wrong way about it in that.''

This was how the story club came into existence. It was limited to Diana and Anne at first, but soon it was extended to include Jane Andrews and Ruby Gillis and one or two others who felt that their imaginations needed cultivating. No boys were allowed in it—although Ruby Gillis opined that their admission would make it more exciting—and each member had to produce one story a week.

''It's extremely interesting,'' Anne told Marilla. ''Each girl has to read her story out loud and then we talk it over. We are going to keep them all sacredly and have them to read to our descendants. We each write under a nom-de-plume. Mine is Rosamond Montmorency. All the girls do pretty well. Ruby Gillis is rather sentimental. She puts too much love-making into her stories and you know too much is worse than too little. Jane never puts any because she says it makes her feel so silly when she has to read it out loud. Jane's stories are extremely sensible. Then Diana puts too many murders into hers. She says most of the time she doesn't know what to do with the people so she kills them off to get rid of them. I mostly always have to tell them what to write about, but that isn't hard for I've millions of ideas.''

''I think this story-writing business is the foolishest yet,'' scoffed Marilla. ''You'll get a pack of nonsense into your heads and waste time that should be put on your lessons. Reading stories is bad enough but writing them is worse.''

''But we're so careful to put a moral into them all, Marilla,'' explained Anne. ''I insist upon that. All the good people are rewarded and all the bad ones are suitably punished. I'm sure that must have a wholesome effect. The moral is the great thing. Mr. Allan says so. I read one of my stories to him and Mrs. Allan and they both agreed that the moral was excellent. Only they laughed in the wrong places. I like it better when people cry. Jane and Ruby almost always cry when I come to the pathetic parts. Diana wrote her Aunt Joesphine about our club and her Aunt Josephine wrote back that we were to send her some of our stories. So we copied out four of our very best and sent them. Miss Josephine Barry wrote back that she had never read anything so amusing in her life. That kind of puzzled us because the stories were all very pathetic and almost everybody died. But I'm glad Miss Barry liked them. It shows our club is doing some good in the world. Mrs. Allan says that ought to be our object in everything. I do really try to make it my object but I forget so often when I'm having fun. I hope I shall be a little like Mrs. Allan when I grow up. Do you think there is any prospect of it, Marilla?''

''I shouldn't say there was a great deal,'' was Marilla's encouraging answer. ''I'm sure Mrs. Allan was never such a silly, forgetful little girl as you are.''

''No; but she wasn't always so good as she is now either,'' said Anne seriously. ''She told me so herself—that is, she said she was a dreadful mischief when she was a girl and was always getting into scrapes. I felt so encouraged when I heard that. Is it very wicked of me, Marilla, to feel encouraged when I hear that other people have been bad and mischievous? Mrs. Lynde says it is. Mrs. Lynde says she always feels shocked when she hears of any one ever having been naughty, no matter how small they were. Mrs. Lynde says she once heard a minister confess that when he was a boy he stole a strawberry tart out of his aunt's pantry and she never had any respect for that minister again. Now, I wouldn't have felt that way. I'd have thought that it was real noble of him to confess it, and I'd have thought what an encouraging thing it would be for small boys nowadays who do naughty things and are sorry for them to know that perhaps they may grow up to be ministers in spite of it. That's how I'd feel, Marilla.''

''The way I feel at present, Anne,'' said Marilla, ''is that it's high time you had those dishes washed. You've taken half an hour longer than you should with all your chattering. Learn to work first and talk afterwards.''

CHAPTER 27

VANITY AND VEXATION OF SPIRIT

MARILLA, WALKING home one late April evening from an Aid meeting, realized that the winter was over and gone with the thrill of delight that spring never fails to bring to the oldest and saddest as well as to the youngest and merriest. Marilla was not given to the subjective analysis of her thoughts and feelings. She probably imagined that she was thinking about the Aids and their missionary box and the new carpet for the vestry-room, but under these reflections was a harmonious consciousness of red fields smoking into pale-purply mists in the declining sun, of long, sharp-pointed fir shadows falling over the meadow beyond the brook, of still crimson-budded maples around a mirror-like wood-pool, of a wakening in the world and a stir of hidden pulses under the gray sod. The spring was abroad in the land and Marilla's sober, middle-aged step was lighter and swifter because of its deep, primal gladness.

Her eyes dwelt affectionately on Green Gables, peering through its network of trees and reflecting the sunlight back from its windows in several little coruscations of glory. Marilla, as she picked her steps along the damp lane, thought that it was really a satisfaction to know that she was going home to a briskly snapping wood fire and a table nicely spread for tea, instead of to the cold comfort of old Aid meeting evenings before Anne had come to Green Gables.

Consequently, when Marilla entered her kitchen and found the fire black out, with no sign of Anne anywhere, she felt justly disappointed and irritated. She had told Anne to be sure and have tea ready at five o'clock, but now she must hurry to take off her second-best dress and prepare the meal herself against Matthew's return from ploughing.

"I'll settle Miss Anne when she comes home," said Marilla grimly, as she shaved up kindlings with a carving knife and more vim than was strictly necessary. Matthew had come in and was waiting patiently for his tea in his corner. "She's gadding off somewhere with Diana, writing stories or practising dialogues or some such tomfoolery, and never thinking once about the time or her duties. She's just got to be pulled up short and sudden on this sort of thing. I don't care if Mrs. Allan does say she's the brightest and sweetest child she ever knew. She may be bright and sweet enough, but her head is full of nonsense and there's never any knowing what shape it'll break out in next. Just as soon as she grows out of one freak she takes up with another. But there! Here I am saying the very thing I was so riled with Rachel Lynde for saying at the Aid today. I was real glad when Mrs. Allan spoke up for Anne, for if she hadn't I know I'd have said something too sharp to Rachel before everybody. Anne's got plenty of faults, goodness knows, and far be it from me to deny it. But I'm bringing her up and not Rachel Lynde, who'd pick faults in the Angel Gabriel himself if he lived in Avonlea. Just the same, Anne has no business to leave the house like this when I told her she was to stay home this afternoon and look after things. I must say, with all her faults, I never found her disobedient or untrustworthy before and I'm real sorry to find her so now."

"Well now, I dunno," said Matthew, who, being patient and wise, and above all, hungry, had deemed it best to let Marilla talk her wrath out unhindered, having learned by experience that she got through with whatever work was on hand much quicker if not delayed by untimely argument. "Perhaps you're judging her too hasty, Marilla. Don't call her untrustworthy until you're sure she has disobeyed you. Mebbe it can all be explained—Anne's a great hand at explaining."

"She's not here when I told her to stay," retorted Marilla. "I reckon she'll find it hard to explain *that* to my satisfaction. Of course I knew you'd take her part, Matthew. But I'm bringing her up, not you."

It was dark when supper was ready, and still no sign of Anne, coming hurriedly over the log bridge or up Lovers' Lane, breathless and repentant with a sense of neglected duties. Marilla washed and put away the dishes grimly. Then, wanting a candle to light her down cellar, she went up to the east gable for the one that generally stood on Anne's table. Lighting it, she turned around to see Anne herself lying on the bed, face downward among the pillows.

"Mercy on us," said astonished Marilla, "have you been asleep, Anne?"

"No," was the muffled reply.

"Are you sick then?" demanded Marilla anxiously, going over to the bed.

Anne cowered deeper into her pillows as if desirous of hiding herself for ever from mortal eyes.

"No. But please, Marilla, go away and don't look at me. I'm in the depths of despair and I don't care who gets head in class or writes the best composition or sings in the Sunday school choir any more. Little things like that are of no importance now because I don't suppose I'll ever be able to go anywhere again. My career is closed. Please, Marilla, go away and don't look at me."

"Did any one ever hear the like?" the mystified Marilla wanted to know. "Anne Shirley, whatever is the matter with you? What have you done? Get right up this minute and tell me. This minute, I say. There now, what is it?"

Anne had slid to the floor in despairing obedience.

"Look at my hair, Marilla," she whispered.

Accordingly, Marilla lifted her candle and looked scrutinizingly at Anne's hair, flowing in heavy masses down her back. It certainly had a very strange appearance.

"Anne Shirley, what have you done to your hair? Why, its *green!*"

Green it might be called, if it were any earthly color—a queer, dull, bronzy green, with streaks here and there of the original red to heighten the ghastly effect. Never in all her life had Marilla seen anything so grotesque as Anne's hair at that moment.

"Yes, it's green," moaned Anne. "I thought nothing could be as bad as red hair. But now I know it's ten times worse to have green hair. Oh, Marilla, you little know how utterly wretched I am."

"I little know how you got into this fix, but I mean to find out," said Marilla. "Come right down to the kitchen—it's too cold up here—and tell me just what you've done. I've been expecting something queer for some time. You haven't got into any scrape for over two months, and I was sure another one was due. Now, then, what did you do to your hair?''

''I dyed it.''

''Dyed it! Dyed your hair! Anne Shirley, didn't you know it was a wicked thing to do?''

''Yes, I knew it was a little wicked,'' admitted Anne. ''But I thought it was worth while to be a little wicked to get rid of red hair. I counted the cost, Marilla. Besides, I meant to be extra good in other ways to make up for it.''

''Well,'' said Marilla sarcastically, ''if I'd decided it was worth while to dye my hair I'd have dyed it a decent color at least. I wouldn't have dyed it green.''

''But I didn't mean to dye it green, Marilla,'' protested Anne dejectedly. ''If I was wicked I meant to be wicked to some purpose. He said it would turn my hair a beautiful raven black—he positively assured me that it would. How could I doubt his word, Marilla? I know what it feels like to have your word doubted. And Mrs. Allan says we should never suspect any one of not telling us the truth unless we have proof that they're not. I have proof now—green hair is proof enough for anybody. But I hadn't then and I believed every word he said *implicitly*.''

''Who said? Who are you talking about?''

''The pedlar that was here this afternoon. I bought the dye from him.''

''Anne Shirley, how often have I told you never to let one of those Italians in the house! I don't believe in encouraging them to come around at all.''

''Oh, I didn't let him in the house. I remembered what you told me, and I went out, carefully shut the door, and looked at his things on the step. Besides, he wasn't an Italian—he was a German Jew. He had a big box full of very interesting things and he told me he was working hard to make enough money to bring his wife and children out from Germany. He spoke so feelingly about them that it touched my heart. I wanted to buy something from him to help him in such a worthy object. Then all at once I saw the bottle of hair dye. The pedlar said it was warranted to dye any hair a beautiful raven black and wouldn't wash off. In a trice I saw myself with beautiful raven black hair and the temptation was irresistible. But the price of the bottle was seventy-five cents and I had only fifty cents left out of my chicken money. I think the pedlar had a very kind heart, for he said that, seeing it was me, he'd sell it for fifty cents and that was just giving it away. So I bought it, and as soon as he had gone I came up here and applied it with an old hair-brush as the directions said. I used up the whole bottle, and oh, Marilla, when I saw the dreadful color it turned my hair I repented of being wicked, I can tell you. And I've been repenting ever since.''

"Well, I hope you'll repent to good purpose," said Marilla severely, "and that you've got your eyes opened to where your vanity has led you, Anne. Goodness knows what's to be done. I suppose the first thing is to give your hair a good washing and see if that will do any good.''

Accordingly, Anne washed her hair, scrubbing it vigorously with soap and water, but for all the difference it made she might as well have been scouring its original red. The pedlar had certainly spoken the truth when he declared that the dye wouldn't wash off, however his veracity might be impeached in other respects.

"Oh, Marilla, what shall I do?" questioned Anne in tears. "I can never live this down. People have pretty well forgotten my other mistakes—the liniment cake and setting up Diana drunk and flying into a temper with Mrs. Lynde. But they'll never forget this. They will think I am not respectable. Oh, Marilla, 'what a tangled web we weave when first we practise to deceive.' That is poetry, but it is true. And oh, how Josie Pye will laugh! Marilla, I *cannot* face Josie Pye. I am the unhappiest girl in Prince Edward Island.''

Anne's unhappiness continued for a week. During that time she went nowhere and shampooed her hair every day. Diana alone of outsiders knew the fatal secret, but she promised solemnly never to tell, and it may be stated here and now that she kept her word. At the end of the week Marilla said decidedly:

"It's no use, Anne. That is fast dye if ever there was any. Your hair must be cut off; there is no other way. You can't go out with it looking like that.''

Anne's lips quivered, but she realized the bitter truth of Marilla's remarks. With a dismal sigh she went for the scissors.

"Please cut it off at once, Marilla, and have it over. Oh, I feel that my heart is broken. This is such an unromantic affliction. The girls in books lose their hair in fevers or sell it to get money for some good deed, and I'm sure I wouldn't mind losing my hair in some such fashion half so much. But there is nothing comforting in having your hair cut off because you've dyed it a dreadful color, is there? I'm going to weep all the time you're cutting it off, if it won't interfere. It seems such a tragic thing.''

Anne wept then, but later on, when she went upstairs and looked in the glass, she was calm with despair. Marilla had done her work thoroughly and it had been necessary to shingle the hair as closely as possible. The result was not becoming, to state the case as mildly as may be. Anne promptly turned her glass to the wall.

"I'll never, never look at myself again until my hair grows," she exclaimed passionately.

Then she suddenly righted the glass.

"Yes, I will, too. I'd do penance for being wicked that way. I'll look at myself every time I come to my room and see how ugly I am. And I won't try to imagine it away, either. I never thought I was vain about my hair, of all things, but now I know I was, in spite of its being red, because it was so long and thick and curly. I expect something will happen to my nose next.''

Anne's clipped head made a sensation in school on the following Monday, but to her relief nobody guessed the real reason for it, not even Josie Pye, who, however, did not fail to inform Anne that she looked like a perfect scarecrow.

"I didn't say anything when Josie said that to me,'' Anne confided that evening to Marilla, who was lying on the sofa after one of her headaches, "because I thought it was part of my punishment and I ought to bear it patiently. It's hard to be told you look like a scarecrow and I wanted to say something back. But I didn't. I just swept her one scornful look and then I forgave her. It makes you feel very virtuous when you forgive people, doesn't it? I mean to devote all my energies to being good after this and I shall never try to be beautiful again. Of course it's better to be good. I know it is, but it's sometimes so hard to believe a thing even when you know it. I do really want to be good, Marilla, like you and Mrs. Allan and Miss Stacy, and grow up to be a credit to you. Diana says when my hair begins to grow to tie a black velvet ribbon around my head with a bow at one side. She says she thinks it will be very becoming. I will call it a snood—that sounds so romantic. But am I talking too much, Marilla? Does it hurt your head?''

"My head is better now. It was terrible bad this afternoon, though. These headaches of mine are getting worse and worse. I'll have to see a doctor about them. As for your chatter, I don't know that I mind it—I've got so used to it.''

Which was Marilla's way of saying that she liked to hear it.

CHAPTER 28

AN UNFORTUNATE LILY MAID

"OF COURSE you must be Elaine, Anne," said Diana. "I could never have the courage to float down there."

"Nor I," said Ruby Gillis with a shiver. "I don't mind floating down when there's two or three of us in the flat and we can sit up. It's fun then. But to lie down and pretend I was dead—I just couldn't. I'd die really of fright."

"Of course it would be romantic," conceded Jane Andrews. "But I know I couldn't keep still. I'd be popping up ever minute or so to see where I was and if I wasn't drifting too far out. And you know, Anne, that would spoil the effect."

"But it's so ridiculous to have a red-headed Elaine," mourned Anne. "I'm not afraid to float down and I'd *love* to be Elaine. But it's ridiculous just the same. Ruby ought to be Elaine because she is so fair and has such lovely long golden hair—Elaine had 'all her bright hair streaming down,' you know. And Elaine was the lily maid. Now, a red-haired person cannot be a lily maid."

"Your complexion is just as fair as Ruby's," said Diana earnestly, "and your hair is ever so much darker than it used to be before you cut it."

"Oh, do you really think so?" exclaimed Anne, flushing sensitively with delight. "I've sometimes thought it was myself—but I never dared to ask anyone for fear she would tell me it wasn't. Do you think it could be called auburn now, Diana?"

"Yes, and I think it is real pretty," said Diana, looking admiringly at the short, silky curls that clustered over Anne's head and were held in place by a very jaunty black velvet ribbon and bow.

They were standing on the bank of the pond, below Orchard Slope, where a little headland fringed with birches ran out from the bank; at its tip was a small wooden platform built out into the water for the convenience of fishermen and duck hunters. Ruby and Jane were spending the midsummer afternoon with Diana, and Anne had come over to play with them.

Anne and Diana had spent most of their playtime that summer on and about the pond. Idlewild was a thing of the past, Mr. Bell having ruthlessly cut down the little circle of trees in his back pasture in the spring. Anne had sat among the stumps and wept, not without an eye to the romance of it; but she was speedily consoled, for, after all, as she and Diana said, big girls of thirteen, going on fourteen, were too old for such childish amusements as playhouses, and there were more fascinating sports to be found about the pond. It was splendid to fish for trout over the bridge and the two girls learned to row themselves about in the little flat-bottomed dory Mr. Barry kept for duck shooting.

It was Anne's idea that they dramatize Elaine. They had studied Tennyson's poem in school the preceding winter, the Superintendent of Education having prescribed it in the English course for the Prince Edward Island schools. They had analyzed and parsed it and torn it to pieces in general until it was a wonder there was any meaning at all left in it for them, but at least the fair lily maid and Lancelot and Guinevere and King Arthur had become very real people to them, and Anne was devoured by secret regret that she had not been born in Camelot. Those days, she said, were so much more romantic than the present.

Anne's plan was hailed with enthusiasm. The girls had discovered that if the flat were pushed off from the landing-place it would drift down with the current under the bridge and finally strand itself on another headland lower down which ran out at a curve in the pond. They had often gone down like this and nothing could be more convenient for playing Elaine.

"Well, I'll be Elaine," said Anne, yielding reluctantly, for, although she would have been delighted to play the principal character, yet her artistic sense demanded fitness for it and this, she felt, her limitations made impossible. "Ruby, you must be King Arthur and Jane will be Guinevere and Diana must be Lancelot. But first you must be the brothers and the father. We can't have the old dumb servitor because there isn't room for two in the flat when one is lying down. We must pall the barge all its length in blackest samite. That old black shawl of your mother's will be just the thing, Diana."

The black shawl having been procured, Anne spread it over the flat and then lay down on the bottom, with closed eyes and hands folded over her breast.

"Oh, she does look really dead," whispered Ruby Gillis nervously, watching the still, white little face under the flickering shadows of the birches. "It makes me feel frightened, girls. Do you suppose it's really right to act like this? Mrs. Lynde says that all play-acting is abominably wicked."

"Ruby, you shouldn't talk about Mrs. Lynde," said Anne severely. "It spoils the effect because this is hundreds of years before Mrs. Lynde was born. Jane, you arrange this. It's silly for Elaine to be talking when she's dead."

Jane rose to the occasion. Cloth of gold for coverlet there was none, but an old piano scarf of yellow Japanese crêpe was an excellent substitute. A white lily was not obtainable just then, but the effect of a tall blue iris placed in one of Anne's folded hands was all that could be desired.

"Now, she's all ready," said Jane. "We must kiss her quiet brows and, Diana, you say, 'Sister, farewell for ever,' and Ruby, you say, 'Farewell, sweet sister,' both of you as sorrowfully as you possibly can. Anne, for goodness sake smile a little. You know Elaine 'lay as though she smiled.' That's better. Now push the flat off."

The flat was accordingly pushed off, scraping roughly over an old embedded stake in the process. Diana and Jane and Ruby only waited long enough to see it caught in the current and headed for the bridge before scampering up through the woods, across the road, and down to the lower headland where, as Lancelot and Guinevere and the King, they were to be in readiness to receive the lily maid.

For a few minutes Anne, drifting slowly down, enjoyed the romance of her situation to the full. Then something happened not at all romantic. The flat began to leak. In a very few moments it was necessary for Elaine to scramble to her feet, pick up her cloth of gold coverlet and pall of blackest samite and gaze blankly at a big crack in the bottom of her barge through which the water was literally pouring. That sharp stake at the landing had torn off the strip of batting nailed on the flat. Anne did not know this, but it did not take her long to realize that she was in a dangerous plight. At this rate the flat would fill and sink long before it could drift to the lower headland. Where were the oars? Left behind at the landing!

Anne gave one gasping little scream which nobody ever heard; she was white to the lips, but she did not lose her self-possession. There was one chance—just one.

"I was horribly frightened," she told Mrs. Allan the next day, "and it seemed like years while the flat was drifting down to the bridge and the water rising in it every moment. I prayed, Mrs. Allan, most earnestly, but I didn't shut my eyes to pray, for I knew the only way God could save me was to let the flat float close enought to one of the bridge piles for me to climb up on it. You know the piles are just old tree trunks and there are lots of knots and old branch stubs on them. It was proper to pray, but I had to do my part by watching out and right well I knew it. I just said, 'Dear God, please take the flat close to a pile and I'll do the rest,' over and over again. Under such circumstances you don't think much about making a flowery prayer. But mine was answered, for the flat bumped right into a pile for a minute and I flung the scarf and the shawl over my shoulder and scrambled up on a big providential stub. And there I was, Mrs. Allan, clinging to that slippery old pile with no way of getting up or down. It was a very unromantic position, but I didn't think about that at the time. You don't think much about romance when you have just escaped from a watery grave. I said a grateful prayer at once and then I gave all my attention to holding on tight, for I knew I should probably have to depend on human aid to get back to dry land.''

The flat drifted under the bridge and then promptly sank in midstream. Ruby, Jane, and Diana, already awaiting it on the lower headland, saw it disappear before their very eyes and had not a doubt but that Anne had gone down with it. For a moment they stood still, white as sheets, frozen with horror at the tragedy; then, shrieking at the tops of their voices, they started on a frantic run up through the woods, never pausing as they crossed the main road to glance the way of the bridge. Anne, clinging desperately to her precarious foothold, saw their flying forms and heard their shrieks. Help would soon come, but meanwhile her position was a very uncomfortable one.

The minutes passed by, each seeming an hour to the unfortunate lily maid. Why didn't somebody come? Where had the girls gone? Suppose they had fainted, one and all! Suppose nobody ever came! Suppose she grew so tired and cramped that she could hold on no longer! Anne looked at the wicked green depths below her, wavering with long, oily shadows, and shivered. Her imagination began to suggest all manner of gruesome possibilities to her.

Then, just as she thought she really could not endure the ache in her arms and wrists another moment, Gilbert Blythe came rowing under the bridge in Harmon Andrews' dory!

Gilbert glanced up and, much to his amazement, beheld a little white scornful face looking down upon him with big, frightened but also scornful gray eyes.

''Anne Shirley! How on earth did you get there?'' he exclaimed.

Without waiting for an answer he pulled close to the pile and extended his hand. There was no help for it; Anne, clinging to Gilbert Blythe's hand, scrambled down into the dory, where she sat, drabbled and furious, in the stern with her arms full of dripping shawl

HE PULLED CLOSE TO THE PILE AND EXTENDED HIS HAND.

and wet crêpe. It was certainly extremely difficult to be dignified under the circumstances!

"What has happened, Anne?" asked Gilbert, taking up his oars.

"We were playing Elaine," explained Anne frigidly, without even looking at her rescuer, "and I had to drift down to Camelot in the barge—I mean the flat. The flat began to leak and I climbed out on the pile. The girls went for help. Will you be kind enough to row me to the landing?"

Gilbert obligingly rowed to the landing and Anne, disdaining assistance, sprang nimbly on shore.

"I'm very much obliged to you," she said haughtily as she turned away. But Gilbert had also sprung from the boat and now laid a detaining hand on her arm.

"Anne," he said hurriedly, "look here. Can't we be good friends? I'm awfully sorry I made fun of your hair that time. I didn't mean to vex you and I only meant it for a joke. Besides, it's so long ago. I think your hair is awfully pretty now—honest I do. Let's be friends."

For a moment Anne hesitated. She had an odd, newly awakened consciousness under all her outraged dignity that the half-shy, half-eager expression in Gilbert's hazel eyes was something that was very good to see. Her heart gave a quick, queer little beat. But the bitterness of her old grievance promptly stiffened up her wavering determination. That scene of two years before flashed back into her recollection as vividly as if it had taken place yesterday. Gilbert had called her "carrots" and had brought about her disgrace before the whole school. Her resentment, which to other and older people might be as laughable as its cause, was in no whit allayed and softened by time seemingly. She hated Gilbert Blythe! She would never forgive him!

"No," she said coldly, "I shall never be friends with you, Gilbert Blythe; and I don't want to be!"

"All right!" Gilbert sprang into his skiff with an angry color in his cheeks. "I'll never ask you to be friends again, Anne Shirley. And I don't care either!"

He pulled away with swift defiant strokes, and Anne went up the steep, ferny little path under the maples. She held her head very high, but she was conscious of an odd feeling of regret. She almost wished she had answered Gilbert differently. Of course, he had insulted her terribly, but still—! Altogether, Anne rather thought it would be a relief to sit down and have a good cry. She was really quite unstrung, for the reaction from her fright and cramped clinging was making itself felt.

Half-way up the path she met Jane and Diana rushing back to the pond in a state narrowly removed from positive frenzy. They had found nobody at Orchard Slope, both Mr. and Mrs. Barry being away. Here Ruby Gillis had succumbed to hysterics, and was left to recover from them as best she might, while Jane and Diana flew through the Haunted Wood and across the brook to Green Gables. There they had found nobody either, for Marilla had gone to Carmody and Matthew was making hay in the back field.

"Oh, Anne," gasped Diana, fairly falling on the former's neck and weeping with relief and delight, "Oh, Anne—we thought—you were—drowned—and we felt like murderers—because we had made—you be—Elaine. And Ruby is in hysterics—oh, Anne, how did you escape?"

"I climbed up on one of the piles," explained Anne wearily, "and Gilbert Blythe came along in Mr. Andrews' dory and brought me to land."

"Oh, Anne, how splendid of him! Why, it's so romantic!" said Jane, finding breath enough for utterance at last. "Of course you'll speak to him after this."

"Of course I won't," flashed Anne with a momentary return of her old spirit. "And I don't want ever to hear the word romantic again, Jane Andrews. I'm awfully sorry you were so frightened, girls. It is all my fault. I feel sure I was born under an unlucky star. Everything I do gets me or my dearest friends into a scrape. We've gone and lost your father's flat, Diana, and I have a presentiment that we'll not be allowed to row on the pond any more."

Anne's presentiment proved more trustworthy than presentiments are apt to do. Great was the consternation in the Barry and Cuthbert households when the events of the afternoon became known.

"Will you *ever* have any sense, Anne?" groaned Marilla.

"Oh, yes, I think I will, Marilla," returned Anne optimistically. A good cry, indulged in the grateful solitude of the east gable, had soothed her nerves and restored her to her wonted cheerfulness. "I think my prospects of becoming sensible are brighter now than ever."

"I don't see how," said Marilla.

"Well," explained Anne, "I've learned a new and valuable lesson today. Ever since I came to Green Gables I've been making mistakes, and each mistake has helped to cure me of some great shortcoming. The affair of the amethyst brooch cured me of meddling with things that didn't belong to me. The Haunted Wood mistake cured me of letting my imagination run away with me. The liniment cake mistake cured me of carelessness in cooking. Dyeing my hair cured me of vanity. I never think about my hair and nose now—at least, very seldom. And today's mistake is going to cure me of being too romantic. I have come to the conclusion that it is no use trying to be romantic in Avonlea. It was probably easy enough in towered Camelot hundreds of years ago, but romance is not appreciated now. I feel quite sure that you will soon see a great improvement in me in this respect, Marilla.''

''I'm sure I hope so,'' said Marilla skeptically.

But Matthew, who had been sitting mutely in his corner, laid a hand on Anne's shoulder when Marilla had gone out.

''Don't give up all your romance, Anne,'' he whispered shyly, ''a little of it is a good thing—not too much, of course—but keep a little of it, Anne, keep a little of it.''

―――――――――― CHAPTER 29 ――――――――――

AN EPOCH IN ANNE'S LIFE

ANNE WAS bringing the cows home from the back pasture by way of Lovers' Lane. It was a September evening and all the gaps and clearings in the woods were brimmed up with ruby sunset light. Here and there the lane was splashed with it, but for the most part it was already quite shadowy beneath the maples, and the spaces under the firs were filled with a clear violet dusk like airy wine. The winds were out in their tops, and there is no sweeter music on earth than that which the wind makes in the fir-trees at evening.

The cows swung placidly down the lane, and Anne followed them dreamily, repeating aloud the battle canto from ''Marmion''— which had also been part of their English course the preceding winter and which Miss Stacy had made them learn off by heart—and exulting in its rushing lines and the clash of spears in its imagery. When she came to the lines:

The stubborn spearsmen still made good
Their dark impenetrable wood,

she stopped in ecstasy to shut her eyes that she might the better fancy
herself one of that heroic ring. When she opened them again it was to
behold Diana coming through the gate that led into the Barry field
and looking so important that Anne instantly divined there was news
to be told. But betray too eager curiosity she would not.

"Isn't this evening just like a purple dream, Diana? It makes me so
glad to be alive. In the mornings I always think the mornings are best;
but when evening comes I think it's lovelier still."

"It's a very fine evening," said Diana, "but oh, I have such news,
Anne. Guess. You can have three guesses."

"Charlotte Gillis is going to be married in the church after all and
Mrs. Allan wants us to decorate it," cried Anne.

"No. Charlotte's beau won't agree to that, because nobody ever
has been married in the church yet, and he thinks it would seem too
much like a funeral. It's too mean, because it would be such fun.
Guess again."

"Jane's mother is going to let her have a birthday party?"

Diana shook her head, her black eyes dancing with merriment.

"I can't think what it can be," said Anne in despair, "unless it's
that Moody Spurgeon MacPherson saw you home from prayer-meeting last night. Did he?"

"I should think not," exclaimed Diana indignantly. "I wouldn't
be likely to boast of it if he did, the horrid creature! I knew you
couldn't guess it. Mother had a letter from Aunt Josephine today,
and Aunt Josephine wants you and me to go to town next Tuesday
and stop with her for the Exhibition. There!"

"Oh, Diana," whispered Anne, finding it necessary to lean up
against a maple-tree for support, "do you really mean it? But I'm
afraid Marilla won't let me go. She will say that she can't encourage
gadding about. That was what she said last week when Jane invited
me to go with them in their double-seated buggy to the American
concert at the White Sands Hotel. I wanted to go, but Marilla said I'd
better be home learning my lessons and so would Jane. I was bitterly
disappoined, Diana. I felt so heart-broken that I wouldn't say my
prayers when I went to bed. But I repented of that and got up in the
middle of the night and said them."

"I'll tell you," said Diana, "we'll get mother to ask Marilla.
She'll be more likely to let you go then; and if she does we'll have the

time of our lives, Anne. I've never been to an Exhibition, and it's so aggravating to hear the other girls talking about their trips. Jane and Ruby have been twice, and they're going this year again.''

"I'm not going to think about it at all until I know whether I can go or not," said Anne resolutely. "If I did and then was disappointed, it would be more than I could bear. But in case I do go I'm very glad my new coat will be ready by that time. Marilla didn't think I needed a new coat. She said my old one would do very well for another winter and that I ought to be satisfied with having a new dress. The dress is very pretty, Diana—navy blue and made so fashionably. Marilla always makes my dresses fashionably now, because she says she doesn't intend to have Matthew going to Mrs. Lynde to make them. I'm so glad. It is ever so much easier to be good if your clothes are fashionable. At least, it is easier for me. I suppose it doesn't make such a difference to naturally good people. But Matthew said I must have a new coat, so Marilla bought a lovely piece of blue broadcloth, and it's being made by a real dressmaker over at Carmody. It's to be done Saturday night, and I'm trying not to imagine myself walking up the church aisle on Sunday in my new suit and cap, because I'm afraid it isn't right to imagine such things. But it just slips into my mind in spite of me. My cap is so pretty. Matthew bought it for me the day we were over at Carmody. It is one of those little blue velvet ones that are all the rage, with gold cord and tassels. Your new hat is elegant, Diana, and so becoming. When I saw you come into church last Sunday my heart swelled with pride to think you were my dearest friend. Do you suppose it's wrong for us to think so much about clothes? Marilla says it is very sinful. But it *is* such an interesting subject, isn't it?''

Marilla agreed to let Anne go to town, and it was arranged that Mr. Barry should take the girls in on the following Tuesday. As Charlottetown was thirty miles away and Mr. Barry wished to go and return the same day, it was necessary to make a very early start. But Anne counted it all joy, and was up before sunrise on Tuesday morning. A glance from her window assured her that the day would be fine, for the eastern sky behind the firs of the Haunted Wood was all silvery and cloudless. Through the gap in the trees a light was shining in the western gable of Orchard Slope, a token that Diana was also up.

Anne was dressed by the time Matthew had the fire on and had the breakfast ready when Marilla came down, but for her own part was much too excited to eat. After breakfast the jaunty new cap and jacket were donned, and Anne hastened over the brook and up through the firs to Orchard Slope. Mr. Barry and Diana were waiting for her, and they were soon on the road.

It was a long drive, but Anne and Diana enjoyed every minute of it. It was delightful to rattle along over the moist roads in the early red sunlight that was creeping across the shorn harvest fields. The air was fresh and crisp, and little smoke-blue mists curled throught the valleys and floated off from the hills. Sometimes the road went through the woods where maples were beginning to hang out scarlet banners; sometimes it crossed rivers on bridges that made Anne's flesh cringe with the old, half-delightful fear; sometimes it wound along a harbor shore and passed by a little cluster of weather-gray fishing huts; again it mounted to hills whence a far sweep of curving upland or misty blue sky could be seen; but wherever it went there was much of interest to discuss. It was almost noon when they reached town and found their way to "Beechwood." It was quite a fine old mansion, set back from the street in a seclusion of green elms and branching beeches. Miss Barry met them at the door with a twinkle in her sharp black eyes.

"So you've come to see me at last, you Anne-girl." she said. "Mercy, child, how you have grown! You're taller than I am, I declare. And you're ever so much better-looking than you used to be, too. But I dare say you know that without being told."

"Indeed I didn't," said Anne radiantly. "I know I'm not so freckled as I used to be, so I've much to be thankful for, but I really hadn't dared to hope there was any other improvement. I'm so glad you think there is, Miss Barry."

Miss Barry's house was furnished with "great magnificence," as Anne told Marilla afterwards. The two little country girls were rather abashed by the splendor of the parlor where Miss Barry left them when she went to see about dinner.

"Isn't it just like a palace?" whispered Diana. "I never was in Aunt Josephine's house before, and I'd no idea it was so grand. I just wish Julia Bell could see this—she puts on such airs about her mother's parlor."

"Velvet carpet," sighed Anne luxuriously, "*and* silk curtains! I've dreamed of such things, Diana. But do you know I don't believe I feel very comfortable with them after all. There are so many things in this room and all so splendid that there is no scope for imagination. That is one consolation when you are poor—there are so many more things you can imagine about."

Their sojourn in town was something that Anne and Diana dated from for years. From first to last it was crowded with delights.

On Wednesday Miss Barry took them to the Exhibition grounds and kept them there all day.

"It was splendid," Anne related to Marilla later on. "I never imagined anything so interesting. I don't really know which department was the most interesting. I think I liked the horses and the flowers and the fancy work best. Josie Pye took first prize for knitted lace. I was real glad she did. And I was glad that I felt glad, for it shows I'm improving, don't you think, Marilla, when I can rejoice in Josie's success? Mr. Harmon Andrews took second prize for Gravenstein apples and Mr. Bell took first prize for a pig. Diana said she thought it was ridiculous for a Sunday-school superintendent to take a prize in pigs, but I don't see why. Do you? She said she would always think of it after this when he was praying so solemnly. Clara Louise MacPherson took a prize for painting, and Mrs. Lynde got first prize for home-made butter and cheese. So Avonlea was pretty well represented, wasn't it? Mrs. Lynde was there that day, and I never knew how much I really liked her until I saw her familiar face among all those strangers. There were thousands of people there, Marilla. It made me feel dreadfully insignificant. And Miss Barry took us up to the grand stand to see the horse-races. Mrs. Lynde wouldn't go; she said horse-racing was an abomination, and she being a church-member, thought it her bounden duty to set a good example by staying away. But there were so many there I don't believe Mrs. Lynde's absence would ever be noticed. I don't think, though, that I ought to go very often to horse-races, because they *are* awfully fascinating. Diana got so excited that she offered to bet me ten cents that the red horse would win. I didn't believe he would, but I refused to bet, because I wanted to tell Mrs. Allan all about everything, and I felt sure it wouldn't do to tell her that. It's always wrong to do anything you can't tell the minister's wife. It's as good as an extra conscience to have a minister's wife for your friend. And I was very glad I didn't bet, because the red horse *did* win, and I would have lost ten cents. So you see that virture was its own reward. We saw a man go up in a balloon. I'd love to go up in a balloon, Marilla; it would be simply thrilling; and we saw a man selling fortunes. You paid him ten cents and a little bird picked out your fortune for you. Miss Barry gave Diana and me ten cents each to have our fortunes told. Mine was that I would marry a dark-complected man who was very wealthy, and I would go across water to live. I looked carefully at all the dark men I saw after that, but I didn't care much for any of them, and anyhow I suppose it's too early to be looking out for him yet. Oh, it was a never-to-be-forgotten day, Marilla. I was so tired I couldn't sleep at night. Miss Barry put us in the spare room, according to promise. It was an elegant room, Marilla, but somehow sleeping in a spare room isn't what I used to think it was. That's the worst part of growing up, and I'm beginning to realize it. The things you wanted so much when you were a child don't seem half so wonderful to you when you get them.''

Thursday the girls had a drive in the park, and in the evening Miss Barry took them to a concert in the Academy of Music, where a noted prima donna was to sing. To Anne the evening was a glittering vision of delight.

"Oh, Marilla, it was beyond description. I was so excited I couldn't even talk, so you may know what it was like. I just sat in enraptured silence. Madame Selitsky was perfectly beautiful, and wore white satin and diamonds. But when she began to sing I never thought about anything else. Oh, I can't tell you how I felt. But it seemed to me that it could never be hard to be good any more. I felt like I do when I look up to the stars. Tears came into my eyes, but, oh, they were such happy tears. I was so sorry when it was all over, and I told Miss Barry I didn't see how I was ever to return to common life again. She said she thought if we went over to the restaurant across the street and had an ice-cream it might help me. That sounded so prosaic; but to my surprise I found it true. The ice-cream was so delicious, Marilla, and it was so lovely and dissipated to be sitting there eating it at eleven o'clock at night. Diana said she believed she was born for city life. Miss Barry asked me what my opinion was, but I said I would have to think it over very seriously before I could tell her what I really thought. So I thought it over after I went to bed. That is the best time to think things out. And I came to the conclusion, Marilla, that I wasn't born for city life and that I was glad of it. It's nice to be eating ice-cream at brilliant restaurants at eleven o'clock at night once in awhile; but as a regular thing I'd rather be in the east gable at eleven, sound asleep, but kind of knowing even in my sleep that the stars were shining outside and that the wind was blowing in the firs across the brook. I told Miss Barry so at breakfast the next morning and she laughed. Miss Barry generally laughed at anything I said, even when I said the most solemn things. I don't think I liked it, Marilla, because I wasn't trying to be funny. But she is a most hospitable lady and treated us royally.''

Friday brought going-home time, and Mr. Barry drove in for the girls.

"Well, I hope you've enjoyed yourselves," said Miss Barry, as she bade them good-bye.

"Indeed we have," said Diana.

"And you, Anne-girl?"

"I've enjoyed every minute of the time," said Anne, throwing her arms impulsively about the old woman's neck and kissing her wrinkled cheek. Diana would never have dared to do such a thing, and felt rather aghast at Anne's freedom. But Miss Barry was pleased, and she stood on her veranda and watched the buggy out of sight. Then she went back into her big house with a sigh. It seemed very lonely, lacking those fresh young lives. Miss Barry was a rather selfish old lady, if the truth must be told, and had never cared much for anybody but herself. She valued people as they were of service to her or amused her. Anne had amused her, and consequently stood high in the old lady's good graces. But Miss Barry found herself thinking less about Anne's quaint speeches than of her fresh enthusiasms, her transparent emotions, her little winning ways, and the sweetness of her eyes and lips.

"I thought Marilla Cuthbert was an old fool when I heard she'd adopted a girl out of an orphan asylum," she said to herself, "but I guess she didn't make much of a mistake after all. If I'd a child like Anne in the house all the time I'd be a better and happier woman."

Anne and Diana found the drive home as pleasant as the drive in—pleasanter, indeed, since there was the delightful consciousness of home waiting at the end of it. It was sunset when they passed through White Sands and turned into the shore road. Beyond, the Avonlea hills came out darkly against the saffron sky. Behind them the moon was rising out of the sea that grew all radiant and transfigured in her light. Every little cove along the curving road was a marvel of dancing ripples. The waves broke with a soft swish on the rocks below them, and the tang of the sea was in the strong, fresh air.

"Oh, but it's good to be alive and to be going home," breathed Anne.

When she crossed the log bridge over the brook the kitchen light of Green Gables winked her a friendly welcome back, and through the open door shone the hearth fire, sending out its warm red glow athwart the chilly autumn night. Anne ran blithely up the hill and into the kitchen, where a hot supper was waiting on the table.

"So, you've got back?" said Marilla, folding up her knitting.

"Yes, and, oh, it's so good to be back," said Anne joyously. "I could kiss everything, even to the clock. Marilla, a broiled chicken! You don't mean to say you cooked that for me!"

"Yes, I did," said Marilla. "I thought you'd be hungry after such a drive and need something real appetizing. Hurry and take off your things, and we'll have supper as soon as Matthew comes in. I'm glad you've got back, I must say. It's been fearful lonesome here without you, and I never put in four longer days."

After supper Anne sat before the fire between Matthew and Marilla, and gave them a full account of her visit.

"I've had a splendid time," she concluded happily, "and I feel that it marks an epoch in my life. But the best of it all was the coming home."

CHAPTER 30

THE QUEEN'S CLASS IS ORGANIZED

MARILLA LAID her knitting on her lap and leaned back in her chair. Her eyes were tired, and she thought vaguely that she must see about having her glasses changed the next time she went to town, for her eyes had grown tired very often of late.

It was nearly dark, for the full November twilight had fallen around Green Gables, and the only light in the kitchen came from the dancing red flames in the stove.

Anne was curled up Turk-fashion on the hearth-rug, gazing into that joyous glow where the sunshine of a hundred summers was being distilled from the maple cord-wood. She had been reading, but her book had slipped to the floor, and now she was dreaming, with a smile on her parted lips. Glittering castles in Spain were shaping themselves out of the mists and rainbows of her lively fancy; adventures wonderful and enthralling were happening to her in cloud-land—adventures that always turned out triumphantly and never involved her in scrapes like those of actual life.

Marilla looked at her with a tenderness that would never have been suffered to reveal itself in any clearer light than that soft mingling of fireshine and shadow. The lesson of a love that should display itself easily in spoken word and open look was one Marilla could never learn. But she had learned to love this slim, gray-eyed girl with an affection all the deeper and stronger from its very undemonstrativeness. Her love made her afraid of being unduly indulgent, indeed. She had an uneasy feeling that it was rather sinful to set one's heart so intensely on any human creature as she had set hers on Anne, and perhaps she performed a sort of unconscious penance for this by being stricter and more critical than if the girl had been less dear to her. Certainly Anne herself had no idea how Marilla loved her. She sometimes thought wistfully that Marilla was very hard to please and distinctly lacking in sympathy and understanding. But she always checked the thought reproachfully, remembering what she owed to Marilla.

"Anne," said Marilla abruptly, "Miss Stacy was here this afternoon when you were out with Diana.

Anne came back from her other world with a start and a sigh.

"Was she? Oh, I'm so sorry I wasn't in. Why didn't you call me, Marilla? Diana and I were only over in the Haunted Wood. It's lovely in the woods now. All the little wood things—the ferns and the satin leaves and the crackerberries—have gone to sleep, just as if somebody had tucked them away until spring under a blanket of leaves. I think it was a little gray fairy with a rainbow scarf that came tiptoeing along the last moonlight night and did it. Diana wouldn't say much about that, though. Diana has never forgotten the scolding her mother gave her about imagining ghosts into the Haunted Wood. It had a very bad effect on Diana's imagination. It blighted it. Mrs. Lynde says Myrtle Bell is a blighted being. I asked Ruby Gillis why Myrtle was blighted, and Ruby said she guessed it was because her young man had gone back on her. Ruby Gillis thinks of nothing but young men, and the older she gets the worse she is. Young men are all very well in their place, but it doesn't do to drag them into everything, does it? Diana and I are thinking seriously of promising each other that we will never marry but be nice old maids and live together forever. Diana hasn't quite made up her mind though, because she thinks perhaps it would be nobler to marry some wild, dashing, wicked young man and reform him. Diana and I talk a great deal about serious subjects now, you now. We feel that we are so much older than we used to be that it isn't becoming to talk of childish matters. It's such a solemn thing to be almost fourteen, Marilla. Miss Stacy took all us girls who are in our teens down to the brook last Wednesday, and talked to us about it. She said we couldn't be too careful what habits we formed and what ideals we acquired in our teens, because by the time we were twenty our characters would be developed and the foundation laid for our whole future life. And she said if the foundation was shaky we could never build anything really worth while on it. Diana and I talked the matter over coming home from school. We felt extremely solemn, Marilla. And we decided that we would try to be very careful indeed and form respectable habits and learn all we could and be as sensible as possible, so that by the time we were twenty our characters would be properly developed. It's perfectly appalling to think of being twenty, Marilla. It sounds so fearfully old and grown up. But why was Miss Stacy here this afternoon?''

''That is what I want to tell you, Anne, if you'll ever give me a chance to get a a word in edgewise. She was talking about you.''

''About me?'' Anne looked rather scared. Then she flushed and exclaimed:

''Oh, I know what she was saying. I meant to tell you, Marilla, honestly I did, but I forgot. Miss Stacy caught me reading 'Ben Hur' in school yesterday afternoon when I should have been studying my Canadian history. Jane Andrews lent it to me. I was reading it at dinner hour, and I had just got to the chariot-race when school went in. I was simply wild to know how it turned out—although I felt sure 'Ben Hur' must win, because it wouldn't be poetical justice if he didn't—so I spread the history open on my desk lid and then tucked 'Ben-Hur' between the desk and my knee. It just looked as if I were studying Canadian history, you know, while all the while I was revelling in 'Ben Hur.' I was so interested in it that I never noticed Miss Stacy coming down the aisle until all at once I just looked up and there she was looking down at me, so reproachful like. I can't tell you how ashamed I felt, Marilla, especially when I heard Josie Pye giggling. Miss Stacy took 'Ben Hur' away, but she never said a word then. She kept me in at recess and talked to me. She said I had done very wrong in two respects. First, I was wasting the time I ought to have put on my studies; and secondly I was deceiving my teacher in trying to make it appear I was reading a history when it was a story-book instead. I had never realized until that moment, Marilla, that what I was doing was deceitful. I was shocked. I cried bitterly, and asked Miss Stacy to forgive me and I'd never do such a thing again; and I offered to do penance by never so much as looking at 'Ben Hur' for a whole week, not even to see how the chariot-race turned out. But Miss Stacy said she wouldn't require that, and she forgave me freely. So I think it wasn't very kind of her to come up here to you about it after all."

"Miss Stacy never mentioned such a thing to me, Anne, and it's only your guilty conscience that's the matter with you. You have no business to be taking storybooks to school. You read too many novels, anyhow. When I was a girl I wasn't so much as allowed to look at a novel."

"Oh, how can you call 'Ben Hur' a novel when it's really such a religious book?" protested Anne. "Of course it's a little too exciting to be proper reading for Sunday, and I only read it on weekdays. And I never read *any* book now unless either Miss Stacy or Mrs. Allan thinks it is a proper book for a girl of thirteen and three-quarters to read. Miss Stacy made me promise that. She found me reading a book one day called, 'The Lurid Mystery of the Haunted Hall.' It was one Ruby Gillis had lent me, and oh, Marilla, it was so fascinating and creepy. It just curdled the blood in my veins. But Miss Stacy said it was a very silly, unwholesome book, and she asked me not to read any more of it or any like it. It's really wonderful, Marilla, what you can do when you're truly anxious to please a certain person."

"Well, I guess I'll light the lamp and get to work," said Marilla. "I see plainly that you don't want to hear what Miss Stacy had to say. You're more interested in the sound of your own tongue than in anything else."

"Oh, indeed, Marilla, I do want to hear it," cried Anne contritely. "I won't say another word—not one. I know I talk too much, but I am really trying to overcome it, and although I say far too much, yet if you only knew how many things I want to say and don't, you'd give me some credit for it. Please tell me, Marilla."

"Well, Miss Stacy wants to organize a class among her advanced students who mean to study for the entrance examination into Queen's. She intends to give them extra lessons for an hour after school. And she came to ask Matthew and me if we would like to have you join it. What do you think about it yourself, Anne? Would you like to go to Queen's and pass for a teacher?"

"Oh, Marilla!" Anne straightened to her knees and clasped her hands. "It's been the dream of my life—that is, for the last six months, ever since Ruby and Jane began to talk of studying for the entrance. But I didn't say anything about it, because I supposed it would be perfectly useless. I'd love to be a teacher. But won't it be dreadfully expensive? Mr. Andrews says it cost him one hundred and fifty dollars to put Prissy through, and Prissy wasn't a dunce in geometry."

"I guess you needn't worry about that part of it. When Matthew and I took you to bring up we resolved we would do the best we could for you and give you a good education. I believe in a girl being fitted to earn her own living whether she ever has to or not. You'll always have a home at Green Gables as long as Matthew and I are here, but nobody knows what is going to happen in this uncertain world, and it's just as well to be prepared. So you can join the Queen's class if you like, Anne."

"Oh, Marilla, thank you." Anne flung her arms about Marilla's waist and looked up earnestly into her face. "I'm extremely grateful to you and Matthew. And I'll study as hard as I can and do my very best to be a credit to you. I warn you not to expect much in geometry, but I think I can hold my own in anything else if I work hard."

"I dare say you'll get along well enough. Miss Stacy says you are bright and diligent." Not for worlds would Marilla have told Anne just what Miss Stacy had said about her; that would have been to pamper vanity. "You needn't rush to any extreme of killing yourself over your books. There is no hurry. You won't be ready to try the entrance for a year and a half yet. But it's well to begin in time and be thoroughly grounded, Miss Stacy says."

"I shall take more interest than ever in my studies now," said Anne blissfully, "because I have a purpose in life. Mr. Allan says everybody should have a purpose in life and pursue it faithfully. Only he says we must first make sure that it is a worthy purpose. I would call it a worthy purpose to want to be a teacher like Miss Stacy, wouldn't you, Marilla? I think it's a very noble profession."

The Queen's class was organized in due time. Gilbert Blythe, Anne Shirley, Ruby Gillis, Jane Andrews, Josie Pye, Charlie Sloane, and Moody Spurgeon MacPherson joined it. Diana Barry did not, as her parents did not intend to send her to Queen's. This seemed nothing short of a calamity to Anne. Never, since the night on which Minnie May had had the croup, had she and Diana been separated in anything. On the evening when the Queen's class first remained in school for the extra lessons and Anne saw Diana go slowly out with the others, to walk home alone through the Birch Path and Violet Vale, it was all the former could do to keep her seat and refrain from rushing impulsively after her chum. A lump came into her throat, and she hastily retired behind the pages of her uplifted Latin grammar to hide the tears in her eyes. Not for worlds would Anne have had Gilbert Blythe or Josie Pye see those tears.

"But, oh, Marilla, I really felt that I had tasted the bitterness of death, as Mr. Allan said in his sermon last Sunday, when I saw Diana go out alone," she said mournfully that night. "I thought how splendid it would have been if Diana had only been going to study for the Entrance, too. But we can't have things perfect in this imperfect world, as Mrs. Lynde says. Mrs. Lynde isn't exactly a comforting person sometimes, but there's no doubt she says a great many very true things. And I think the Queen's class is going to be extremely interesting. Jane and Ruby are just going to study to be teachers. That is the height of their ambition. Ruby says she will only teach for two years after she gets through, and then she intends to be married. Jane says she will devote her life to teaching, and never, never marry, because you are paid a salary for teaching, but a husband won't pay you anything, and growls if you ask for a share in the egg and butter money. I expect Jane speaks from mournful experience, for Mrs. Lynde says that her father is a perfect old crank, and meaner than second skimmings. Josie Pye says she is just going to college for education's sake, because she won't have to earn her own living; she says of course it is diferent with orphans who are living on charity— *they* have to hustle. Moody Spurgeon is going to be a minister. Mrs. Lynde says he couldn't be anything else with a name like that to live up to. I hope it isn't wicked of me, Marilla, but really the thought of Moody Spurgeon being a minister makes me laugh. He's such a funny-looking boy with that big fat face, and his little blue eyes, and his ears sticking out like flaps. But perhaps he will be more intellectual-looking when he grows up. Charlie Sloane says he's going to go into politics and be a member of Parliament, but Mrs. Lynde says he'll never succeed at that, because the Sloanes are all honest people, and it's only rascals that get on in politics nowadays.''

"What is Gilbert Blythe going to be?'' queried Marilla, seeing that Anne was opening her Caesar.

"I don't happen to know what Gilbert Blythe's ambition in life is—if he has any,'' said Anne scornfully.

There was open rivalry between Gilbert and Anne now. Previously the rivalry ahd been rather one-sided, but there was no longer any doubt that Gilbert was as determined to be first in class as Anne was. He was a foeman worthy of her steel. The other members of the class tacitly acknowledged their superiority, and never dreamed of trying to compete with them.

Since the day by the pond when she had refused to listen to his plea for forgiveness, Gilbert, save for the aforesaid determined rivalry, had evinced no recognition whatever of the existence of Anne Shirley. He talked and jested with the other girls, exchanged books and puzzles with them, discussed lessons and plans, sometimes walked home with one or the other of them from prayer meeting or Debating Club. But Anne Shirley he simply ignored, and Anne found out that it is not pleasant to be ignored. It was in vain that she told herself with a toss of her head that she did not care. Deep down in her wayward, feminine little heart she knew that she did care, and that if she had that chance of the Lake of Shining Waters again she would answer very differently. All at once, as it seemed, and to her secret dismay, she found that the old resentment she had cherished against him was gone—gone just when she most needed its sustaining power. It was in vain that she recalled every incident and emotion of that memorable occasion and tried to feel the old satisfying anger. That day by the pond had witnessed its last spasmodic flicker. Anne realized that she had forgiven and forgotten without knowing it. But it was too late.

And at least neither Gilbert nor anybody else, not even Diana, should ever suspect how sorry she was and how much she wished she hadn't been so proud and horrid! She determined to "shroud her feelings in deepest oblivion," and it may be stated here and now that she did it, so successfully that Gilbert, who possibly was not quite so indifferent as he seemed, could not console himself with any belief that Anne felt his retaliatory scorn. The only poor comfort he had was that she snubbed Charlie Sloane, unmercifully, continually and undeservedly.

Otherwise the winter passed away in a round of pleasant duties and studies. For Anne the days slipped by like golden beads on the necklace of the year. She was happy, eager, interested; there were lessons to be learned and honors to be won; delightful books to read; new pieces to be practised for the Sunday school choir; pleasant Saturday afternoons at the manse with Mrs. Allan; and then, almost before Anne realized it, spring had come again to Green Gables. And all the world was abloom once more.

Studies palled just a wee bit then; the Queen's class, left behind in school while the others scattered to green lanes and leafy wood-cuts and meadow byways, looked wistfully out of the windows and discovered that Latin verbs and French exercises had somehow lost the tang and zest they had possessed in the crisp winter months. Even Anne and Gilbert lagged and grew indifferent. Teacher and taught were alike glad when the term was ended and the glad vacation days stretched rosily before them.

"But you've done good work this past year," Miss Stacy told them on the last evening, "and you deserve a good, jolly vacation.

Have the best time you can in the out-of-door world and lay in a good stock of health and vitality and ambition to carry you through next year. It will be the tug of war, you know—the last year before the Entrance.''

"Are you going to be back next year, Miss Stacy?'' asked Josie Pye.

Josie Pye never scrupled to ask questions; in this instance the rest of the class felt grateful to her; none of them would have dared to ask it of Miss Stacy, but all wanted to, for there had been alarming rumors running at large through the school for some time that Miss Stacy was not coming back the next year—that she had been offered a position in the graded school of her own home district and meant to accept. The Queen's class listened in breathless suspense for her answer.

"Yes, I think I will,'' said Miss Stacy. "I thought of taking another school, but I have decided to come back to Avonlea. To tell the truth, I've grown so interested in my pupils here that I found I couldn't leave them. So I'll stay and see you through.''

"Hurrah!'' said Moody Spurgeon. Moody Spurgeon had never been so carried away by his feelings before, and he blushed uncomfortably every time he thought about it for a week.

"Oh, I'm so glad,'' said Anne with shining eyes. "Dear Miss Stacy, it would be perfectly dreadful if you didn't come back. I don't believe I could have the heart to go on with my studies at all if another teacher came here.''

When Anne got home that night she stacked all her text-books away in an old trunk in the attic, locked it, and threw the key into the blanket box.

"I'm not even going to look at a school book in vacation,'' she told Marilla. "I've studied as hard all the term as I possibly could and I've pored over that geometry until I know every proposition in the first book off by heart, even when the letters *are* changed. I just feel tired of everything sensible and I'm going to let my imagination run riot for the summer. Oh, you needn't be alarmed, Marilla. I'll only let it run riot within reasonable limits. But I want to have a real good jolly time this summer, for maybe it's the last summer I'll be a little girl. Mrs. Lynde says that if I keep stretching out next year as I've done this I'll have to put on longer skirts. She says I'm all running to legs and eyes. And when I put on longer skirts I shall feel that I have to live up to them and be very dignified. It won't even do to believe in fairies then, I'm afraid; so I'm going to believe in them with all my whole heart this summer. I think we're going to have a very gay vacation. Ruby Gillis is going to have a birthday party soon and there's the Sunday school picnic and the missionary concert next month. And Mr. Barry says that some evening he'll take Diana and me over to the White Sands Hotel and have dinner there. They have dinner there in the evening, you know. Jane Andrews was over once last summer and she says it was a dazzling sight to see the electric lights and the flowers and all the lady guests in such beautiful dresses. Jane says it was her first glimpse into high life and she'll never forget it to her dying day."

Mrs. Lynde came up the next afternoon to find out why Marilla had not been at the Aid meeting on Thursday. When Marilla was not at Aid meeting people knew there was something wrong at Green Gables.

"Matthew had a bad spell with his heart Thursday," Marilla explained, "and I didn't feel like leaving him. Oh, yes, he's all right again, now, but he takes them spells oftener than he used to and I'm anxious about him. The doctor says he must be careful to avoid excitement. That's easy enough, for Matthew doesn't go about looking for excitement by any means and never did, but he's not to do any very heavy work either and you might as well tell Matthew not to breathe as not to work. Come and lay off your things, Rachel. You'll stay to tea?"

"Well, seeing you're so pressing, perhaps I might as well stay," said Mrs. Rachel, who had not the slightest intention of doing anything else.

Mrs. Rachel and Marilla sat comfortably in the parlor while Anne got the tea and made hot biscuits that were light and white enough to defy even Mrs. Rachel's criticism.

"I must say Anne has turned out a real smart girl," admitted Mrs. Rachel, as Marilla accompanied her to the end of the lane at sunset. "She must be a great help to you."

"She is," said Marilla, "and she's real steady and reliable now. I used to be afraid she'd never get over her feather-brained ways, but she has and I wouldn't be afraid to trust her in anything now."

"I never would have thought she'd have turned out so well that first day I was here three years ago," said Mrs. Rachel. "Lawful heart, shall I ever forget that tantrum of hers! When I went home that night I says to Thomas, says I, 'Mark my words, Thomas, Marilla Cuthbert'll live to rue the step she's took.' But I was mistaken and I'm real glad of it. I ain't one of those kind of people, Marilla, as can never be brought to own up that they've made a mistake. No, that never was my way, thank goodness. I did make a mistake in judging Anne, but it weren't no wonder, for an odder, unexpecteder witch of a child there never was in this world, that's what. There was no ciphering her out by the rules that worked with other children. It's nothing short of wonderful how she's improved these three years, but especially in looks. She's a real pretty girl got to be, though I can't say I'm overly partial to that pale, big-eyed style myself. I like more snap and color, like Diana Barry has or Ruby Gillis. Ruby Gillis' looks are real showy. But somehow—I don't know how it is but when Anne and them are together, though she ain't half as handsome, she makes them look kind of common and overdone— something like them white June lilies she calls narcissus alongside of the big, red peonies, that's what.''

CHAPTER 31

WHERE THE BROOK AND RIVER MEET

ANNE HAD her ''good'' summer and enjoyed it whole-heartedly. She and Diana fairly lived outdoors, revelling in all the delights that Lovers' Lane and the Dryad's Bubble and Willowmere and Victoria Island afforded. Marilla offered no objections to Anne's gipsyings. The Spencervale doctor who had come the night Minnie May had the croup met Anne at the house of a patient one afternoon early in vacation, looked her over sharply, screwed up his mouth, shook his head, and sent a message to Marilla Cuthbert by another person. It was:

''Keep that red-headed girl of yours in the open air all summer and don't let her read books until she gets more spring into her step.''

This message frightened Marilla wholesomely. She read Anne's death warrant by consumption in it unless it was scrupulously obeyed. As a result, Anne had the golden summer of her life as far as freedom and frolic went. She walked, rowed, berried and dreamed to her heart's content; and when September came she was bright-eyed and alert, with a step that would have satisfied the Spencervale doctor and a heart full of ambition and zest once more.

"I feel just like studying with might and main," she declared as she brought her books down from the attic. "Oh, you good old friends, I'm glad to see your honest faces once more—yes, even you, geometry. I've had a perfectly beautiful summer, Marilla, and now I'm rejoicing as a strong man to run a race, as Mr. Allan said last Sunday. Doesn't Mr. Allan preach magnificent sermons? Mrs. Lynde says he is improving every day and the first thing we know some city church will gobble him up and then we'll be left and have to turn to and break in another green preacher. But I don't see the use of meeting trouble half-way, do you, Marilla? I think it would be better just to enjoy Mr. Allan while we have him. If I were a man I think I'd be a minister. They can have such an influence for good, if their theology is sound; and it must be thrilling to preach splendid sermons and stir your hearers' hearts. Why can't women be ministers, Marilla? I asked Mrs. Lynde that and she was shocked and said it would be a scandalous thing. She said there might be female ministers in the States and she believed there was, but thank goodness we hadn't got to that stage in Canada yet and she hoped we never would. But I don't see why. I think women would make splendid ministers. When there is a social to be got up or a church tea or anything else to raise money the women have to turn to and do the work. I'm sure Mrs. Lynde can pray ever bit as well as Superintendent Bell and I've no doubt she could preach too with a little practice."

"Yes, I believe she could," said Marilla drily. "She does plenty of unofficial preaching as it is. Nobody has much of a chance to go wrong in Avonlea with Rachel to oversee them."

"Marilla," said Anne in a burst of confidence, "I want to tell you something and ask you what you think about it. It has worried me terribly—on Sunday afternoons, that is, when I think specially about such matters. I do really want to be good; and when I'm with you or Mrs. Allan or Miss Stacy I want it more than ever and I want to do just what would please you and what you would approve of. But mostly when I'm with Mrs. Lynde I feel desperately wicked and as if I wanted to go and do the very thing she tells me I oughtn't to do. I feel irresistibly tempted to do it. Now, what do you think is the reason I feel like that? Do you think it's because I'm really bad and unregenerate?"

Marilla looked dubious for a moment. Then she laughed.

"If you are I guess I am too, Anne, for Rachel often has that very effect on me. I sometimes think she'd have more of an influence for good, as you say youself, if she didn't keep nagging people to do right. There should have been a special commandment against nagging. But there, I shouldn't talk so. Rachel is a good Christian woman and she means well. There isn't a kinder soul in Avonlea and she never shirks her share of work."

"I'm very glad you feel the same," said Anne decidedly. "It's so encouraging. I shan't worry so much over that after this. But I dare say there'll be other things to worry me. They keep coming up new all the time—things to perplex you, you know. You settle one question and there's another right after. There are so many things to be thought over and decided when you're beginning to grow up. It keeps me busy all the time thinking them over and deciding what is right. It's a serious thing to grow up, isn't it, Marilla? But when I have such good friends as you and Matthew and Mrs. Allan and Miss Stacy I ought to grow up successfully, and I'm sure it will be my own fault if I don't. I feel it's a great responsibility because I have only the one chance. If I don't grow up right I can't go back and begin all over again. I've grown two inches this summer, Marilla. Mr. Gillis measured me at Ruby's party. I'm so glad you made my new dresses longer. That dark green one is so pretty and it was sweet of you to put on the flounce. Of course I know it wasn't really necessary, but flounces are so stylish this fall and Josie Pye has flounces on all her dresses. I know I'll be able to study better because of mine. I shall have such a comfortable feeling deep down in my mind about that flounce."

"It's worth something to have that," admitted Marilla.

Miss Stacy came back to Avonlea school and found all her pupils eager for work once more. Especially did the Queen's class gird up their loins for the fray, for at the end of the coming year, dimly shadowing their pathway already, loomed up that fateful thing known as "the Entrance," at the thought of which one and all felt their hearts sink into their very shoes. Suppose they did not pass! That thought was doomed to haunt Anne through the waking hours of that winter, Sunday afternoons inclusive, to the almost entire exclusion of moral and theological problems. When Anne had bad dreams she found herself staring miserably at pass lists of the Entrance exams, where Gilbert Blythe's name was blazoned at the top and in which she did not appear at all.

But it was a jolly, busy, happy swift-flying winter. School work was as interesting, class rivalry as absorbing, as of yore. New worlds of thought, feeling, and ambition, fresh, fascinating fields of unexplored knowledge seemed to be opening out before Anne's eager eyes.

Hills peeped o' er hill and Alps on Alps arose.

Much of all this was due to Miss Stacy's tactful, careful, broadminded guidance. She led her class to think and explore and discover for themselves and encouraged straying from the old beaten paths to a degree that quite shocked Mrs. Lynde and the school trustees, who viewed all innovations on established methods rather dubiously.

Apart from her studies Anne expanded socially, for Marilla, mindful of the Spencervale doctor's dictum, no longer vetoed occasional outings. The Debating Club flourished and gave several concerts; there were one or two parties almost verging on grown-up affairs; there were sleigh drives and skating frolics galore.

Between times Anne grew, shooting up so rapidly that Marilla was astonished one day, when they were standing side by side, to find the girl was taller than herself.

"Why, Anne, how you've grown!" she said, almost unbelievingly. A sigh followed on the words. Marilla felt a queer regret over Anne's inches. The child she had learned to love had vanished somehow and here was this tall, serious-eyed girl of fifteen, with the thoughtful brows and the proudly poised little head, in her place. Marilla loved the girl as much as she had loved the child, but she was conscious of a queer sorrowful sense of loss. And that night when Anne had gone to prayer-meeting with Diana, Marilla sat alone in the wintry twilight and indulged in the weakness of a cry. Matthew, coming in with a lantern, caught her at it and gazed at her in such consternation that Marilla had to laugh through her tears.

"I was thinking about Anne," she explained. "She's got to be such a big girl—and she'll probably be away from us next winter. I'll miss her terrible."

"She'll be able to come home often," comforted Matthew, to whom Anne was as yet and always would be the little, eager girl he had brought home from Bright River on that June evening four years before. "The branch railroad will be built to Carmody by that time."

"It won't be the same thing as having her all the time," sighed Marilla gloomily, determined to enjoy her luxury of grief uncomforted. "But there—men can't understand these things!"

There were other changes in Anne no less real than the physical change. For one thing, she became much quieter. Perhaps she thought all the more and dreamed as much as ever, but she certainly talked less. Marilla noticed and commented on this also.

"You don't chatter half as much as you used to, Anne, nor use half as many big words. What has come over you?"

Anne colored and laughed a little, as she dropped her book and looked dreamily out of the window, where big fat red buds were bursting out on the creeper in response to the lure of the spring sunshine.

"I don't know—I don't want to talk as much," she said, denting her chin thoughtfully with her forefinger. "It's nicer to think dear, pretty thoughts and keep them in one's heart, like treasures. I don't like to have them laughed at or wondered over. And somethow I don't want to use big words any more. It's almost a pity, isn't it, now that I'm really growing big enough to say them if I did want to. It's fun to be almost grown up in some ways, but it's not the kind of fun I expected, Marilla. There's so much to learn and do and think that there isn't time for big words. Besides, Miss Stacy says the short ones are much stronger and better. She makes us write all our essays as simply as possible. It was hard at first. I was so used to crowding in all the fine big words I could think of—and I thought of any number of them. But I've got used to it now and I see it's so much better."

"What has become of your story club? I haven't heard you speak of it for a long time."

"The story club isn't in existence any longer. We hadn't time for it—and anyhow I think we had got tired of it. It was silly to be writing about love and murder and elopements and mysteries. Miss Stacy sometimes has us write a story for training in composition, but she won't let us write anything but what might happen in Avonlea in our own lives, and she criticizes it very sharply and makes us criticize our own too. I never thought my compositions had so many faults until I began to look for them myself. I felt so ashamed I wanted to give up altogether, but Miss Stacy said I could learn to write well if I only trained myself to be my own severest critic. And so I am trying to."

"You've only two more months before the Entrance," said Marilla. "Do you think you'll be able to get through?"

Anne shivered.

"I don't know. Sometimes I think I'll be all right—and then I get horribly afraid. We've studied hard and Miss Stacy has drilled us thoroughly, but we mayn't get through for all that. We've each got a stumbling-block. Mine is geometry of course, and Jane's is Latin and Ruby's and Charlie's is algebra and Josie's is arithmetic. Moody Spurgeon says he feels it in his bones that he is going to fail in English history. Miss Stacy is going to give us examinations in June just as hard as we'll have at the Entrance and mark us just as strictly, so we'll have some idea. I wish it was all over, Marilla. It haunts me. Sometimes I wake up in the night and wonder what I'll do if I don't pass.''

''Why, go to school next year and try again,'' Marilla said unconcernedly.

''Oh, I don't believe I'd have the heart for it. It would be such a disgrace to fail, especially if Gil—if the others passed. And I get so nervous in an examination that I'm likely to make a mess of it. I wish I had nerves like Jane Andrews. Nothing rattles her.''

Anne sighed and, dragging her eyes from the witcheries of the spring world, the beckoning day of breeze and blue, and the green things upspringing in the garden, buried herself resolutely in her book. There would be other springs, but if she did not succeed in passing the Entrance Anne felt convinced that she would never recover sufficiently to enjoy them.

CHAPTER 32

THE PASS LIST IS OUT

WITH THE end of June came the close of the term and the close of Miss Stacy's rule in Avonlea school. Anne and Diana walked home that evening feeling very sober indeed. Red eyes and damp handkerchiefs bore convincing testimony to the fact that Miss Stacy's farewell words must have been quite as touching as Mr. Phillips' had been under similar circumstances three years before. Diana looked back at the schoolhouse from the foot of the spruce hill and sighed deeply.

''It does seem as if it was the end of everything, doesn't it?'' she said dismally.

"You oughtn't to feel half as badly as I do," said Anne, hunting vainly for a dry spot on her handkerchief. "You'll be back again next winter, but I suppose I've left the dear old school for ever—if I have good luck, that is."

"It won't be a bit the same. Miss Stacy won't be there, nor you nor Jane nor Ruby probably. I shall have to sit all alone, for I couldn't bear to have another deskmate after you. Oh, we have had jolly times, haven't we, Anne? It's dreadful to think they're all over."

Two big tears rolled down by Diana's nose.

"If you would stop crying I could," said Anne imploringly. "Just as soon as I put away my hanky I see you brimming up and that starts me off again. As Mrs. Lynde says, 'If you can't be cheerful, be as cheerful as you can.' After all, I dare say I'll be back next year. This is one of the times I *know* I'm not going to pass. They're getting alarmingly frequent."

"Why, you came out splendidly in the exams Miss Stacy gave."

"Yes, but those exams didn't make me nervous. When I think of the real thing you can't imagine what a horrid cold fluttery feeling comes round my heart. And then my number is thirteen and Josie Pye says it's so unlucky. I am *not* superstitious and I know it can make no difference. But still I wish it wasn't thirteen."

"I do wish I were going in with you," said Diana. "Wouldn't we have a perfectly elegant time? But I suppose you'll have to cram in the evenings."

"No; Miss Stacy has made us promise not to open a book at all. She says it would only tire and confuse us and we are to go out walking and not think about the exams at all and go to bed early. It's good advice, but I expect it will be hard to follow; good advice is apt to be, I think. Prissy Andrews told me that she sat up half the night every night of her Entrance week and crammed for dear life; and I had determined to sit up *at least* as long as she did. It was so kind of your Aunt Josephine to ask me to stay at Beechwood while I'm in town."

"You'll write to me while you're in, won't you?"

"I'll write Tuesday night and tell you how the first day goes," promised Anne.

"I'll be haunting the post-office Wednesday," vowed Diana.

Anne went to town the following Monday and on Wednesday Diana haunted the post-office, as agreed, and got her letter.

"Dearest Diana," wrote Anne, "here it is Tuesday night and I'm writing this in the library at Beechwood. Last night I was horribly lonesome all alone in my room and wished so much you were with me. I couldn't 'cram' because I'd promised Miss Stacy not to, but it was as hard to keep from opening my history as it used to be to keep from reading a story before my lessons were learned.

"This morning Miss Stacy came for me and we went to the Academy, calling for Jane and Ruby and Josie on our way. Ruby asked me to feel her hands and they were as cold as ice. Josie said I looked as if I hadn't slept a wink and she didn't believe I was strong enough to stand the grind of the teacher's course even if I did get through. There are times and seasons even yet when I don't feel that I've made any great headway in learning to like Josie Pye!

"When we reached the Academy there were scores of students there from all over the Island. The first person we saw was Moody Spurgeon sitting on the steps and muttering away to himself. Jane asked him what on earth he was doing and he said he was repeating the multiplication table over and over to steady his nerves and for pity's sake not to interrupt him, because if he stopped for a moment he got frightened and forgot everything he ever knew, but the multiplication table kept all his facts firmly in their proper place!

"When we were assigned to our rooms Miss Stacy had to leave us. Jane and I sat together and Jane was so composed that I envied her. No need of the multiplication table for good, steady, sensible Jane! I wondered if I looked as I felt and if they could hear my heart thumping clear across the room. Then a man came in and began distributing the English examination sheets. My hands grew cold then and my head fairly whirled around as I picked it up. Just one awful moment,—Diana, I felt exactly as I did four years ago when I asked Marilla if I might stay at Green Gables—and then everything cleared up in my mind and my heart began beating again—I forgot to say that it had stopped altogether!—for I knew I could do something with *that* paper anyhow.

"At noon we went home for dinner and then back again for history in the afternoon. The history was a pretty hard paper and I got dreadfully mixed up in the dates. Still, I think I did fairly well today. But oh, Diana, tomorrow the geometry exam comes off and when I think of it it takes every bit of determination I possess to keep from opening my Euclid. If I thought the multiplication table would help me any I would recite it from now till tomorrow morning.

"I went down to see the other girls this evening. On my way I met Moody Spurgeon wandering distractedly around. He said he knew he had failed in history and he was born to be a disappointment to his parents and he was going home on the morning train; and it would be easier to be a carpenter than a minister, anyhow. I cheered him up and persuaded him to stay to the end because it would be unfair to Miss Stacy if he didn't. Sometimes I have wished I was born a boy, but when I see Moody Spurgeon I'm always glad I'm a girl and not his sister.

"Ruby was in hysterics when I reached their boarding house; she had just discovered a fearful mistake she had made in her English paper. When she recovered we went uptown and had an ice-cream. How we wished you had been with us.

"Oh, Diana, if only the geometry examination were over! But there, as Mrs. Lynde would say, the sun will go on rising and setting whether I fail in geometry or not. That is true but not especially comforting. I think I'd rather it *didn't* go on if I failed!

"Yours devotedly,

"ANNE."

The geometry examination and all the others were over in due time and Anne arrived home Friday evening, rather tired but with an air of chastened triumph about her. Diana was over at Green Gables when she arrived and they met as if they had been parted for years.

"You old darling, it's perfectly splendid to see you back again. It seems like an age since you went to town and oh, Anne, how did you get along?"

"Pretty well, I think, in everything but the geometry. I don't know whether I passed in it or not and I have a creepy, crawly presentiment that I didn't. Oh, how good it is to be back! Green Gables is the dearest, loveliest spot in the world."

"How did the others do?"

"The girls say they know they didn't pass, but I think they did pretty well. Josie says the geometry was so easy a child of ten could do it! Moody Spurgeon still thinks he failed in history and Charlie says he failed in algebra. But we don't really know anything about it and won't until the pass list is out. That won't be for a fortnight. Fancy living a fortnight in such suspense! I wish I could go to sleep and never wake up until it is over."

Diana knew it would be useless to ask how Gilbert Blythe had fared, so she merely said:"

"Oh, you'll pass all right Don't worry."

"I'd rather not pass at all than not come out pretty well up on the list," flashed Anne, by which she meant—and Diana knew she meant—that success would be incomplete and bitter if she did not come out ahead of Gilbert Blythe.

With this end in view Anne had strained every nerve during the examinations. So had Gilbert. They had met and passed each other on the street a dozen times without any sign of recognition and every time Anne had held her head a little higher and wished a little more earnestly that she had made friends with Gilbert when he asked her, and vowed a little more determinedly to surpass him in the examination. She knew that all Avonlea junior was wondering which would come out first; she even knew that Jimmy Glover and Ned Wright had a bet on the question and that Josie Pye had said there was no doubt in the world that Gilbert would be first; and she felt that her humiliation would be unbearable if she failed.

But she had another and nobler motive for wishing to do well. She wanted to "pass high" for the sake of Matthew and Marilla—especially Matthew. Matthew had declared to her his conviction that she "would beat the whole Island." That, Anne felt, was something it would be foolish to hope for even in the wildest dreams. But she did hope fervently that she would be among the first ten at least, so that she might see Matthew's kindly brown eyes gleam with pride in her achievement. That, she felt, would be a sweet reward indeed for all her hard work and patient grubbing among unimaginative equations and conjugations.

At the end of the fortnight Anne took to "haunting" the post office also, in the distracted company of Jane, Ruby and Josie, opening the Charlottetown dailies with shaking hands and cold, sinkaway feelings as bad as any experienced during the Entrance week. Charlie and Gilbert were not above doing this too, but Moody Spurgeon stayed resolutely away.

"I haven't got the grit to go there and look at a paper in cold blood," he told Anne. "I'm just going to wait until somebody comes and tells me suddenly whether I've passed or not."

When three weeks had gone by without the pass list appearing Anne began to feel that she really couldn't stand the strain much longer. Her appetite failed and her interest in Avonlea doings languished. Mrs. Lynde wanted to know what else you could expect with a Tory superintendent of education at the head of affairs, and Matthew, noting Anne's paleness and indifference and the lagging steps that bore her home from the post office every afternoon, began seriously to wonder if he hadn't better vote Grit at the next election.

But one evening the news came. Anne was sitting at her open window, for the time forgetful of the woes of examinations and the cares of the world, as she drank in the beauty of the summer dusk, sweet-scented with flower-breaths from the garden below and sibilant and rustling from the stir of poplars. The eastern sky above the firs was flushed faintly pink from the reflection of the west, and Anne was wondering dreamily if the spirit of color looked like that, when she saw Diana come flying down through the firs, over the log bridge, and up the slope, with a fluttering newspaper in her hand.

Anne sprang to her feet, knowing at once what that paper contained. The pass list was out! Her head whirled and her heart beat until it hurt her. She could not move a step. It seemed an hour to her before Diana came rushing along the hall and burst into the room without even knocking, so great was her excitement.

"Anne, you've passed," she cried, "passed the *very first*—you and Gilbert both—you're ties—but your name is first. Oh, I'm so proud!"

Diana flung the paper on the table and herself on Anne's bed, utterly breathless and incapable of further speech. Anne lighted the lamp, oversetting the match-safe and using up half a dozen matches before her shaking hands could accomplish the task. Then she snatched up the paper. Yes, she had passed—there was her name at the very top of a list of two hundred! That moment was worth living for.

"You did just splendidly, Anne," puffed Diana, recovering sufficiently to sit up and speak, for Anne, starry-eyed and rapt, had not uttered a word. "Father brought the paper home from Bright River not ten minutes ago—it came out on the afternoon train, you know, and won't be here till tomorrow by mail—and when I saw the pass list I just rushed over like a wild thing. You've all passed, every one of you, Moody Spurgeon and all, although he's conditioned in history. Jane and Ruby did pretty well—they're half-way up—and so did Charlie. Josie just scraped through with three marks to spare, but you'll see she'll put on as many airs as if she'd led. Won't Miss Stacy be delighted? Oh, Anne, what does it feel like to see your name at the head of a pass list like that? If it were me I know I'd go crazy with joy. I am pretty near crazy as it is, but you're as calm and cool as a spring evening."

"I'm just dazzled inside," said Anne. "I want to say a hundred things, and I can't find words to say them in. I never dreamed of this—yes, I did, too, just once! I let myself think *once*, 'What if I should come out first?' quakingly, you know, for it seemed so vain and presumptuous to think I could lead the Island. Excuse me a minute, Diana. I must run right out to the field to tell Matthew. Then we'll go up the road and tell the good news to the others.''

They hurried to the hayfield below the barn where Matthew was coiling hay, and, as luck would have it, Mrs. Lynde was talking to Marilla at the lane fence.

"Oh, Matthew,'' exclaimed Anne, "I've passed and I'm first— or one of the first! I'm not vain, but I'm thankful.''

"Well now, I always said it,'' said Matthew, gazing at the pass list delightedly. "I knew you could beat them all easy.''

"You've done pretty well, I must say, Anne,'' said Marilla, trying to hide her extreme pride in Anne from Mrs. Rachel's critical eye. But that good soul said heartily:

"I just guess she has done well, and far be it from me to be backward in saying it. You're a credit to your friends, Anne, that's what, and we're all proud of you.''

That night Anne, who had wound up a delightful evening by a serious little talk with Mrs. Allan at the manse, knelt sweetly by her open window in a great sheen of moonshine and murmured a prayer of gratitude and aspiration that came straight from her heart. There was in it thankfulness for the past and reverent petition for the future; and when she slept on her white pillow her dreams were as fair and bright and beautiful as maidenhood might desire.

CHAPTER 33

THE HOTEL CONCERT

PUT ON your white organdy, by all means, Anne,'' advised Diana decidely.

They were together in the east gable chamber; outside it was only twilight—a lovely yellowish-green twilight with a clear blue cloudless sky. A big round moon, slowly deepening from her pallid lustre into burnished silver, hung over the Haunted Wood; the air was full of sweet summer sounds—sleepy birds twittering, freakish breezes, far-away voices and laughter. But in Anne's room the blind was drawn and the lamp lighted, for an important toilet was being made.

The east gable was a very different place from what it had been on that night four years before, when Anne had felt its bareness penetrate to the marrow of her spirit with its inhospitable chill. Changes had crept in, Marilla conniving at them resignedly, until it was as sweet and dainty a nest as a young girl could desire.

The velvet carpet with the pink roses and the pink silk curtains of Anne's early visions had certainly never materialized; but her dreams had kept pace with her growth, and it is not probable she lamented them. The floor was covered with a pretty matting, and the curtains that softened the high window and fluttered in the vagrant breezes were of pale green art muslin. The walls, hung not with gold and silver brocade tapestry, but with a dainty apple-blossom paper, were adorned with a few good pictures given Anne by Mrs. Allan. Miss Stacy's photograph occupied the place of honor, and Anne made a sentimental point of keeping fresh flowers on the bracket under it. Tonight a spike of white lilies faintly perfumed the room like the dream of a fragrance. There was no "mahogany furniture," but there was a white-painted bookcase filled with books, a cushioned wicker rocker, a toilet-table befrilled with white muslin, a quaint, gilt-framed mirror with chubby pink cupids and purple grapes painted over its arched top, that used to hang in the spare room, and a low white bed.

Anne was dressing for a concert at the White Sands Hotel. The guests had got it up in aid of the Charlottetown hospital, and had hunted out all the available amateur talent in the surrounding districts to help it along. Bertha Sampson and Pearl Clay of the White Sands Baptist choir had been asked to sing a duet; Milton Clark of Newbridge was to give a violin solo; Winnie Adella Blair of Carmody was to sing a Scotch ballad; and Laura Spencer of Spencervale and Anne Shirley of Avonlea were to recite.

As Anne would have said at one time, it was "an epoch in her life," and she was deliciously athrill with the excitement of it. Matthew was in the seventh heaven of gratified pride over the honor conferred on his Anne, and Marilla was not far behind, although she would have died rather than admit it, and said she didn't think it was very proper for a lot of young folks to be gadding over to the hotel without any responsible person with them.

Anne and Diana were to drive over with Jane Andrews and her brother Billy in their double-seated buggy; and several other Avonlea girls and boys were going, too. There was a party of visitors expected out from town, and after the concert a supper was to be given to the performers.

"Do you really think the organdy will be best?" queried Anne anxiously. "I don't think it's as pretty as my blue-flowered muslin—and it certainly isn't so fashionable."

"But it suits you ever so much better," said Diana. "It's so soft and frilly and clinging. The muslin is stiff, and makes you look too dressed up. But the organdy seems as if it grew on you."

Anne sighed and yielded. Diana was beginning to have a reputation for notable taste in dressing, and her advice on such subjects was much sought after. She was looking very pretty herself on this particular night in a dress of the lovely wild-rose pink, from which Anne was for ever debarred; but she was not to take any part in the concert, so her appearance was of minor importance. All her pains were bestowed upon Anne, who, she vowed, must, for the credit of Avonlea, be dressed and combed and adorned to the queen's taste.

"Pull out that frill a little more—so; here, let me tie your sash; now for your slippers. I'm going to braid your hair in two thick braids, and tie them half-way up with big white bows—no, don't pull out a single curl over your forehead—just have the soft part. There is no way you do your hair suits you so well, Anne, and Mrs. Allan says you look like a Madonna when you part it so. I shall fasten this little white house rose just behind your ear. There was just one on my bush, and I saved it for you."

"Shall I put my pearl beads on?" asked Anne. "Matthew brought me a string from town last week, and I know he'd like to see them on me."

Diana pursed up her lips, put her black head on one side critically, and finally pronounced in favor of the beads, which were thereupon tied around Anne's slim milk-white throat.

"There's something so stylish about you, Anne," said Diana, with unenvious admiration. "You hold your head with such an air. I suppose it's your figure. I am just a dumpling. I've always been afraid of it, and now I know it is so. Well, I suppose I shall just have to resign myself to it."

"But you have such dimples," said Anne, smiling affectionately into the pretty, vivacious face so near her own. "Lovely dimples, like little dents in cream. I have given up all hope of dimples. My dimple-dream will never come true; but so many of my dreams have that I mustn't complain. Am I all ready now?"

"All ready," assured Diana, as Marilla appeared in the doorway, a gaunt figure with grayer hair than of yore and no fewer angles, but with a much softer face. "Come right in and look at our elocutionist, Marilla. Doesn't she look lovely?"

Marilla emitted a sound between a sniff and a grunt.

"She looks neat and proper. I like that way of fixing her hair. But I expect she'll ruin that dress driving over there in the dust and dew with it, and it looks most too thin for these damp nights. Organdy's the most unserviceable stuff in the world anyhow, and I told Matthew so when he got it. But there is no use in saying anything to Matthew nowadays. Time was when he would take my advice, but now he just buys things for Anne regardless, and the clerks at Carmody know they can palm anything off on him. Just let them tell him a thing is pretty and fashionable, and Matthew plunks his money down for it. Mind you keep your skirt clear of the wheel, Anne, and put your warm jacket on."

Then Marilla stalked downstairs, thinking proudly how sweet Anne looked, with that

One moonbeam from the forehead to the crown

and regretting that she could not go to the concert herself to hear her girl recite.

"I wonder if it *is* too damp for my dress," said Anne anxiously.

"Not a bit of it," said Diana, pulling up the window blind. "It's a perfect night, and there won't be any dew. Look at the moonlight."

"I'm so glad my window looks east into the sunrising," said Anne, going over to Diana. "It's so splendid to see the morning coming up over those long hills and glowing through those sharp fir tops. It's new every morning, and I feel as if I washed my very soul in that bath of earliest sunshine. Oh, Diana, I love this little room so dearly. I don't know how I'll get along without it when I go to town next month."

"Don't speak of your going away tonight," begged Diana. "I don't want to think of it, it makes me so miserable, and I do want to have a good time this evening. What are you going to recite, Anne? And are you nervous?"

"Not a bit. I've recited so often in public I don't mind at all now. I've decided to give 'The Maiden's Vow.' It's so pathetic. Laura Spencer is going to give a comic recitation, but I'd rather make people cry than laugh."

"THERE'S SOMETHING SO STYLISH ABOUT YOU, ANNE,"
SAID DIANA.

"What will you recite if they encore you?"

"They won't dream of encoring me," scoffed Anne, who was not without her own secret hopes that they would, and already visioned herself telling Matthew all about it at the next morning's breakfast table. "There are Billy and Jane now—I hear the wheels. Come on."

Billy Andrews insisted that Anne should ride on the front seat with him, so she unwillingly climbed up. She would have much preferred to sit back with the girls, where she could have laughed and chattered to her heart's content. There was not much of either laughter or chatter in Billy. He was a big, fat, stolid youth of twenty, with a round, expressionless face, and a painful lack of conversational gifts. But he admired Anne immensely, and was puffed up with pride over the prospect of driving to White Sands with that slim, upright figure beside him.

Anne, by dint of talking over her shoulder to the girls and occasionally passing a sop of civility to Billy—who grinned and chuckled and never could think of any reply until it was too late—contrived to enjoy the drive in spite of all. It was a night for enjoyment. The road was full of buggies, all bound for the hotel, and laughter, silver-clear, echoed and re-echoed along it. When they reached the hotel it was a blaze of light from top to bottom. They were met by the ladies of the concert committee, one of whom took Anne off to the performers' dressing room, which was filled with the members of a Charlottetown Symphony Club, among whom Anne felt suddenly shy and frightened and countrified. Her dress, which, in the east gable, had seemed so dainty and pretty, now seemed simple and plain—too simple and plain, she thought, among all the silks and laces that glistened and rustled around her. What were her pearl beads compared to the diamonds of the big, handsome lady near her? And how poor her one wee white rose must look beside all the hothouse flowers the others wore! Anne laid her hat and jacket away, and shrank miserably into a corner. She wished herself back in the white room at Green Gables.

It was still worse on the platform of the big concert hall of the hotel, where she presently found herself. The electric lights dazzled her eyes, the perfume and hum bewildered her. She wished she were sitting down in the audience with Diana and Jane, who seemed to be having a splendid time away at the back. She was wedged in between a stout lady in pink silk and a tall, scornful looking girl in a white lace dress. The stout lady occasionally turned her head squarely around and surveyed Anne through her eyeglasses until Anne, acutely sensitive of being so scrutinized, felt that she must scream aloud; and the white lace girl kept talking audibly to her next neighbor about the "country bumpkins" and "rustic belles" in the audience, languidly anticipating "such fun" from the displays of local talent on the programme. Anne believed that she would hate that white lace girl to the end of life.

Unfortunately for Anne, a professional elocutionist was staying at the hotel and had consented to recite. She was a lithe, dark-eyed woman in a wonderful gown of shimmering gray stuff like woven moonbeams, with gems on her neck and in her dark hair. She had a marvellously flexible voice and wonderful power of expression; the audience went wild over her selection. Anne, forgetting all about herself and her troubles for the time, listened with rapt and shining eyes; but when the recitation ended she suddenly put her hands over her face. She could never get up and recite after that—never. Had she ever thought she could recite? Oh, if she were only back at Green Gables!

At this unpropitious moment her name was called. Somehow, Anne—who did not notice the rather guilty little start of surprise the white lace girl gave, and would not have understood the subtle compliment if she had—got on her feet, and moved dizzily out to the front. She was so pale that Diana and Jane, down in the audience, clasped each other's hands in nervous sympathy.

Anne was the victim of an overwhelming attack of stage fright. Often as she had recited in public, she had never before faced such an audience as this, and the sight of it paralyzed her energies completely. Everything was so strange, so brilliant, so bewildering—the rows of ladies in evening dress, the critical faces, the whole atmosphere of wealth and culture about her. Very different this from the plain benches at the Debating Club, filled with the homely, smypathetic faces of friends and neighbors. These people, she thought, would be merciless critics. Perhaps, like the white lace girl, they anticipated amusement from her "rustic" efforts. She felt hopelessly, helplessly ashamed and miserable. Her knees trembled, her heart fluttered, a horrible faintness came over her; not a word could she utter, and the next moment she would have fled from the platform despite the humiliation which, she felt, must ever after be her portion if she did so.

But suddenly, as her dilated, frightened eyes gazed out over the audience, she saw Gilbert Blythe away at the back of the room, bending forward with a smile on his face—a smile which seemed to Anne at once triumphant and taunting. In reality it was nothing of the kind. Gilbert was merely smiling with appreciation of the whole affair in general and of the effect produced by Anne's slender white form and spiritual face against a background of palms in particular. Josie Pye, whom he had driven over, sat beside him, and her face certainly was both triumphant and taunting. But Anne did not see Josie, and would not have cared if she had. She drew a long breath and flung her head up proudly, courage and determination tingling over her like an electric shock. She *would not* fail before Gilbert Blythe—he should never be able to laugh at her, never, never! Her fright and nervousness vanished; and she began her recitation, her clear, sweet voice reaching to the farthest corner of the room without a tremor or a break. Self-possession was fully restored to her, and in the reaction from that horrible moment of powerlessness she recited as she had never done before. When she finished there were bursts of honest applause. Anne, stepping back to her seat, blushing with shyness and delight, found her hand vigorously clasped and shaken by the stout lady in pink silk.

"My dear, you did splendidly," she puffed. "I've been crying like a baby, actually I have. There, they're encoring you—they're bound to have you back!"

"Oh, I can't go," said Anne confusedly. "But yet—I must, or Matthew will be disappointed. He said they would encore me."

"Then don't disappoint Matthew," said the pink lady, laughing.

Smiling, blushiing, limpid-eyed, Anne tripped back and gave a quaint, funny little selection that captivated her audience still further. The rest of the evening was quite a little triumph for her.

When the concert was over, the stout, pink lady—who was the wife of an American millionaire—took her under her wing, and introduced her to everybody; and everybody was very nice to her. The professional elocutionist, Mrs. Evans, came and chatted with her, telling her that she had a charming voice and "interpreted" her selections beautifully. Even the white lace girl paid her a languid little compliment. They had supper in the big, beautifully decorated dining room; Diana and Jane were invited to partake of this, also, since they had come with Anne, but Billy was nowhere to be found, having decamped in mortal fear of some such invitation. He was in waiting for them, with the team, however, when it was all over, and the three girls came merrily out into the calm, white moonshine radiance. Anne breathed deeply, and looked into the clear sky beyond the dark boughs of the firs.

Oh, it was good to be out again in the purity and silence of the night! How great and still and wonderful everything was, with the murmur of the sea sounding through it and the darkling cliffs beyond like grim giants guarding enchanted coasts.

"Hasn't it been a perfectly splendid time?" sighed Jane, as they drove away. "I just wish I was a rich American and could spend my summer at a hotel and wear jewels and low-necked dresses and have ice-cream and chicken salad every blessed day. I'm sure it would be ever so much more fun than teaching school. Anne, your recitations was simply great, although I thought at first you were never going to begin. I think it was better than Mrs. Evans'."

"Oh, no don't say things like that, Jane," said Anne quickly, "because it sounds silly. It couldn't be better than Mrs. Evans', you know, for she is a professional, and I'm only a schoolgirl, with a little knack of reciting. I'm quite satisfied if the people just liked mine pretty well."

"I've a compliment for you, Anne," said Diana. "At least I think it must be a compliment because of the tone he said it in. Part of it was anyhow. There was an American sitting behind Jane and me— such a romantic-looking man, with coal-black hair and eyes. Josie Pye says he is a distinguished artist, and that her mother's cousin in Boston is married to a man that used to go to school with him. Well, we heard him say—didn't we, Jane?—'Who is that girl on the platform with the splendid Titian hair? She has a face I should like to paint.' There now, Anne. But what does Titian hair mean?"

"Being interpreted it means plain red, I guess," laughed Anne. "Titian was a very famous artist who liked to paint red-haired women."

"*Did* you see all the diamonds those ladies wore?" sighed Jane. "They were simply dazzling. Wouldn't you just love to be rich, girls?"

"We *are* rich," said Anne stanchly. "Why, we have sixteen years to our credit, and we're happy as queens, and we've all got imaginations, more or less. Look at that sea, girls—all silver and shadow and vision of things not seen. We couldn't enjoy its loveliness any more if we had millions of dollars and ropes of diamonds. You wouldn't change into any of those women if you could. Would you want to be that white lace girl and wear a sour look all your life, as if you'd been born turning up your nose at the world? Or the pink lady, kind and nice as she is, so stout and short that you'd really no figure at all? Or even Mrs. Evans, with that sad, sad look in her eyes? She must have been dreadfully unhappy sometime to have such a look. You *know* you wouldn't, Jane Andrews!''

"I *don't* know—exactly,'' said Jane unconvinced. "I think diamonds would comfort a person for a good deal.''

"Well, I don't want to be any one but myself, even if I go uncomforted by diamonds all my life,'' declared Anne. "I'm quite content to be Anne of Green Gables, with my string of pearl beads. I know Matthew gave me as much love with them as ever went with Madame the Pink Lady's jewels.''

CHAPTER 34

A QUEEN'S GIRL

THE NEXT three weeks were busy ones at Green Gables, for Anne was getting ready to go to Queen's, and there was much sewing to be done, and many things to be talked over and arranged. Anne's outift was ample and pretty, for Matthew saw to that, and Marilla for once made no objections whatever to anything he purchased or suggested. More—one evening she went up to the east gable with her arms full of a delicate pale green material.

"Anne, here's something for a nice light dress for you. I don't suppose you really need it; you've plenty of pretty waists; but I thought maybe you'd like something real dressy to wear if you were asked out anywhere of an evening in town, to a party or anything like that. I hear that Jane and Ruby and Josie have got 'evening dresses,' as they call them, and I don't mean you shall be behind them. I got Mrs. Allan to help me pick it in town last week; and we'll get Emily Gillis to make it up for you. Emily has got taste, and her fits aren't to be equalled.''

"Oh, Marilla, it's just lovely,'' said Anne. "Thank you so much. I don't believe you ought to be so kind to me—it's making it harder every day for me to go away.''

The green dress was made up with as many tucks and frills and shirrings as Emily's taste permitted. Anne put it on one evening for Matthew's and Marilla's benefit, and recited "The Maiden's Vow" for them in the kitchen. As Marilla watched the bright, animated face and graceful motions her thoughts went back to the evening Anne had arrived at Green Gables, and memory recalled a vivid picture of the odd, frightened child in her preposterous yellowish-brown wincey dress, the heartbreak looking out of her tearful eyes. Something in the memory brought tears to Marilla's eyes.

"I declare, my recitation has made you cry, Marilla," said Anne gaily, stooping over Marilla's chair to drop a butterfly kiss on that lady's cheek. "Now, I call that a positive triumph."

"No, I wasn't crying over your piece," said Marilla, who would have scorned to be betrayed into such weakness by any "poetry stuff." "I just couldn't help thinking of the little girl you used to be, Anne. And I was wishing you could have stayed a little girl, even with all your queer ways. You've grown up now and you're going away; and you look so tall and stylish and so—so—different altogether in that dress—as if you didn't belong in Avonlea at all—and I just got lonesome thinking it all over."

"Marilla!" Anne sat down on Marilla's gingham lap, took Marilla's lined face between her hands, and looked gravely and tenderly into Marilla's eyes. "I'm not a bit changed—not really. I'm only just pruned down and branched out. The real *me*—back here—is just the same. It won't make a bit of difference where I go or how much I change outwardly; at heart I shall always be your little Anne, who will love you and Matthew and dear Green Gables more and better every day of her life."

Anne laid her fresh young cheek against Marilla's faded one, and reached out a hand to pat Matthew's shoulder. Marilla would have given much just then to have possessed Anne's power of putting her feelings into words; but nature and habit had willed it otherwise, and she could only put her arms close about her girl and hold her tenderly to her heart, wishing that she need never let her go.

Matthew, with a suspicious moisture in his eyes, got up and went out-of-doors. Under the stars of the blue summer night he walked agitatedly across the yard to the gate under the poplars.

"Well now, I guess she ain't been much spoiled," he muttered, proudly. "I guess my putting in my oar occasional never did much harm after all. She's smart and pretty, and loving, too, which is better than all the rest. She's been a blessing to us, and there never was a luckier mistake than what Mrs. Spencer made—if it *was* luck. I don't believe it was any such thing. It was Providence, because the Almighty saw we needed her, I reckon.''

The day finally came when Anne must go to town. She and Matthew drove in one fine September morning, after a tearful parting with Diana and an untearful, practical one—on Marilla's side at least—with Marilla. But when Anne had gone Diana dried her tears and went to a beach picnic at White Sands with some of her Carmody cousins, where she contrived to enjoy herself tolerably well; while Marilla plunged fiercely into unnecessary work and kept at it all day long with the bitterest kind of a heartache—the ache that burns and gnaws and cannot wash itself away in ready tears. But that night when Marilla went to bed, acutely and miserably conscious that the little gable room at the end of the hall was untenanted by any vivid young life and unstirred by any soft breathing, she buried her face in her pillow, and wept for her girl in a passion of sobs that appalled her when she grew calm enough to reflect how very wicked it must be to take on so about a sinful fellow creature.

Anne and the rest of the Avonlea scholars reached town just in time to hurry off to the Academy. That first day passed pleasantly enough in a whirl of excitement, meeting all the new students, learning to know the professors by sight and being assorted and organized into classes. Anne intended taking up the Second Year work, being advised to do so by Miss Stacy; Gilbert Blythe elected to do the same. This meant getting a First Class teacher's license in one year instead of two, if they were successful; but it also meant much more and harder work. Jane, Ruby, Josie, Charlie, and Moody Spurgeon, not being troubled with the stirrings of ambition, were content to take up the Second Class work. Anne was conscious of a pang of loneliness when she found herself in a room with fifty other students, not one of whom she knew, except the tall, brown-haired boy across the room; and knowing him in the fashion she did, did not help her much, as she reflected pessimistically. Yet she was undeniably glad that they were in the same class; the old rivalry could still be carried on, and Anne would hardly have known what to do if it had been lacking.

''I wouldn't feel comfortable without it,'' she thought. ''Gilbert looks awfully determined. I suppose he's making up his mind, here and now, to win the medal. What a splendid chin he has! I never noticed it before. I do wish Jane and Ruby had gone in for First Class, too. I suppose I won't feel so much like a cat in a strange garret when I get acquainted, though. I wonder which of the girls here are going to be my friends. It's really an interesting speculation. Of course I promised Diana that no Queen's girl, no matter how much I liked her, should ever be as dear to me as she is; but I've lots of second-best affections to bestow. I like the look of that girl with the brown eyes and the crimson waist. She looks vivid and red-rosy; and there's that pale, fair one gazing out of the window. She has lovely hair, and looks as if she knew a thing or two about dreams. I'd like to know them both—know them well—well enough to walk with my arm about their waists, and call them nicknames. But just now I don't know them and they don't know me, and probably don't want to know me particularly. Oh, it's lonesome!''

It was lonesomer still when Anne found herself alone in her hall bedroom that night at twilight. She was not to board with the other girls, who all had relatives in town to take pity on them. Miss Josephine Barry would have liked to board her, but Beechwood was so far from the Academy that it was out of the question; so Miss Barry hunted up a boarding-house, assuring Matthew and Marilla that it was the very place for Anne.

"The lady who keeps it is a reduced gentlewoman," explained Miss Barry. "Her husband was a British officer, and she is very careful what sort of boarders she takes. Anne will not meet with any objectionable persons under her roof. The table is good, and the house is near the Academy, in a quiet neighborhood.''

All this might be quite true, and, indeed, proved to be so, but it did not materially help Anne in the first agony of homesickness that seized upon her. She looked dismally about her narrow little room, with its dull-papered, pictureless walls, its small iron bedstead and empty bookcase; and a horrible choke came into her throat as she thought of her own white room at Green Gables, where she would have the pleasant consciousness of a great green still outdoors, of sweet peas growing in the garden, and moonlight falling on the orchard, of the brook below the slope and the spruce boughs tossing in the night wind beyond it, of a vast starry sky, and the light from Diana's window shining out through the gap in the trees. Here there was nothing of this; Anne knew that outside of her window was a hard street, with a network of telephone wires shutting out the sky, the tramp of alien feet, and a thousand lights gleaming on stranger faces. She knew that she was going to cry, and fought against it.

"I *won't* cry. It's silly—and weak—there's the third tear splashing down by my nose. There are more coming! I must think of something funny to stop them. But there's nothing funny except what is connected with Avonlea, and that only makes things worse—four—five—I'm going home next Friday, but that seems a hundred years away. Oh, Matthew is nearly home by now—and Marilla is at the gate, looking down the lane for him—six—seven—eight—oh, there's no use in counting them! They're coming in a flood presently. I can't cheer up—I don't *want* to cheer up. It's nicer to be miserable!"

The flood of tears would have come, no doubt, had not Josie Pye appeared at that moment. In the joy of seeing a familiar face Anne forgot that there had never been much love lost between her and Josie. As a part of Avonlea life even a Pye was welcome.

"I'm so glad you came up," Anne said sincerely.

"You've been crying," remarked Josie, with aggravating pity. "I suppose you're homesick—some people have so little self-control in that respect. I've no intention of being homesick, I can tell you. Town's too jolly after that poky old Avonlea. I wonder how I ever existed there so long. You shouldn't cry, Anne; it isn't becoming, for your nose and eyes get red, and then you seem *all* red. I'd a perfectly scrumptious time in the Academy today. Our French professor is simply a duck. His moustache would give you kerwollops of the heart. Have you anything eatable around, Anne? I'm literally starving. Ah, I guessed likely Marilla'd load you up with cake. That's why I called round. Otherwise I'd have gone to the park to hear the band play with Frank Stockley. He boards same place as I do, and he's a sport. He noticed you in class today, and asked me who the red-headed girl was. I told him you were an orphan that the Cuthberts had adopted, and nobody knew very much about what you'd been before that."

Anne was wondering if, after all, solitude and tears were not more satisfactory than Josie Pye's companionship when Jane and Ruby appeared, each with an inch of Queen's color ribbon—purple and scarlet—pinned proudly to her coat. As Josie was not "speaking" to Jane just then she had to subside into comparative harmlessness.

"Well," said Jane with a sigh, "I feel as if I'd lived many moons since the morning. I ought to be home studying my Virgil—that horrid old professor gave us twenty lines to start in on tomorrow. But I simply couldn't settle down to study tonight. Anne, methinks I see the traces of tears. If you've been crying *do* own up. It will restore my self-respect, for I was shedding tears freely before Ruby came along. I don't mind being a goose so much if somebody else is goosey, too. Cake? You'll give me a teeny piece, won't you? Thank you. It has the real Avonlea flavor.''

Ruby, perceiving the Queen's calendar lying on the table, wanted to know if Anne meant to try for the gold medal.

Anne blushed and admitted she was thinking of it.

"Oh, that reminds me," said Josie, "Queen's is to get one of the Avery scholarships after all. The word came today. Frank Stockley told me—his uncle is one of the board of governors, you know. It will be announced in the Academy tomorrow.''

An Avery scholarship! Anne felt her heart beat more quickly, and the horizons of her amibiton shifted and broadened as if by magic. Before Josie had told the news Anne's highest pinnacle of aspiration had been a teacher's provincial license, Class First, at the end of the year, and perhaps the medal! But now in one moment Anne saw herself winning the Avery scholarship, taking an Arts course at Redmond College, and graduating in a gown and mortar-board, all before the echo of Josie's words had died away. For the Avery scholarship was in English, and Anne felt that here her foot was on her native heath.

A wealthy manufacturer of New Brunswick had died and left part of his fortune to endow a large number of scholarships to be distributed among the various high schools and academies of the Maritime Provinces, according to their respective standings. There had been much doubt whether one would be allotted to Queen's, but the matter was settled at last, and at the end of the year the graduate who made the highest mark in English and English Literature would win the scholarship—two hundred and fifty dollars a year for four years at Redmond College. No wonder that Anne went to bed that night with tingling cheeks!

"I'll win that scholarship if hard work can do it," she resolved. "Wouldn't Matthew be proud if I got to be a B.A.? Oh, it's delightful to have ambitions. I'm so glad I have such a lot. And there never seems to be any end to them—that's the best of it. Just as soon as you attain to one ambition you see another one glittering higher up still. It does make life so interesting.''

CHAPTER 35

THE WINTER AT QUEEN'S

ANNE'S HOMESICKNESS wore off, greatly helped in the wearing by her weekend visits home. As long as the open weather lasted the Avonlea students went out to Carmody on the new branch railway every Friday night. Diana and several other Avonlea young folks were generally on hand to meet them and they all walked over to Avonlea in a merry party. Anne thought those Friday evening gipsyings over the autumnal hills in the crisp golden air, with the homelights of Avonlea twinkling beyond, were the best and dearest hours in the whole week.

Gilbert Blythe nearly always walked with Ruby Gillis and carried her satchel for her. Ruby was a very handsome young lady, now thinking herself quite as grown up as she really was; she wore her skirts as long as her mother would let her and did her hair up in town, though she had to take it down when she went home. She had large, bright blue eyes, a brilliant complexion, and a plump showy figure. She laughed a great deal, was cheerful and good-tempered, and enjoyed the pleasant things of life frankly.

"But I shouldn't think she was the sort of girl Gilbert would like," whispered Jane to Anne. Anne did not think so either, but she would not have said so for the Avery scholarship. She could not help thinking, too, that it would be very pleasant to have such a friend as Gilbert to jest and chatter with and exchange ideas about books and studies and ambitions. Gilbert had ambitions, she knew, and Ruby Gillis did not seem the sort of person with whom such could be profitably discussed.

There was no silly sentiment in Anne's ideas concerning Gilbert. Boys were to her, when she thought about them at all, merely possible good comrades. If she and Gilbert had been friends she would not have cared how many other friends he had nor with whom he walked. She had a genius for friendship; girlfriends she had in plenty, but she had a vague consciousness that masculine friendship might also be a good thing to round out one's conceptions of companionship and furnish broader standpoints of judgment and comparison. Not that Anne could have put her feelings on the matter into just such clear definition. But she thought that if Gilbert had ever walked home with her from the train, over the crisp fields and along the ferny byways, they might have had many and merry and interesting conversations about the new world that was opening around them and their hopes and ambitions therein. Gilbert was a clever young fellow, with his own thoughts about things and a determination to get the best out of life and put the best into it. Ruby Gillis told Jane Andrews that she didn't understand half the things Gilbert Blythe said; he talked just like Anne Shirley did when she had a thoughtful fit on and for her part she didn't think it any fun to be bothering about books and that sort of thing when you didn't have to. Frank Stockley had lots more dash and go, but then he wasn't half as good-looking as Gilbert and she really couldn't decide which she liked best!

In the Academy Anne gradually drew a little circle of friends about her, thoughtful, imaginative, ambitious students like herself. With the "rose-red" girl, Stella Maynard, and the "dream girl," Priscilla Grant, she soon became intimate, finding the latter pale spiritual-looking maiden to be full to the brim of mischief and pranks and fun, while the vivid, black-eyed Stella had a heartful of wistful dreams and fancies, as aerial and rainbow-like as Anne's own.

After the Christmas holidays the Avonlea students gave up going home on Fridays and settled down to hard work. By this time all the Queen's scholars had gravitated into their own places in the ranks and the various classes had assumed distinct and settled shadings of individuality. Certain facts had become generally accepted. It was admitted that the medal contestants had practically narrowed down to three—Gilbert Blythe, Anne Shirley, and Lewis Wilson; the Avery scholarship was more doubtful, any one of a certain six being a possible winner. The bronze medal for mathematics was considered as good as won by a fat, funny little up-country boy with a bumpy forehead and a patched coat.

Ruby Gillis was the handsomest girl of the year at the Academy; in the Second Year classes Stella Maynard carried off the palm for beauty, with a small but critical minority in favor of Anne Shirley. Ethel Marr was admitted by all competent judges to have the most stylish modes of hair-dressing, and Jane Andrews—plain, plodding, conscientious Jane—carried off the honors in the domestic science course. Even Josie Pye attained a certain preeminence as the sharpest-tongued young lady in attendance at Queen's. So it may be fairly stated that Miss Stacy's old pupils held their own in the wider arena of the academical course.

Anne worked hard and steadily. Her rivalry with Gilbert was as intense as it had ever been in Avonlea school, although it was not

known in the class at large, but somehow the bitterness had gone out
of it. Anne no longer wished to win for the sake of defeating Gilbert;
rather, for the proud consciousness of a well-won victory over a
worthy foeman. It would be worth while to win, but she no longer
thought life would be insupportable if she did not.

In spite of lessons the students found opportunities for pleasant
times. Anne spent many of her spare hours at Beechwood and
generally ate her Sunday dinners there and went to church with Miss
Barry. The latter was, as she admitted, growing old, but her black
eyes were not dim nor the vigor of her tongue in the least abated. But
she never sharpened the latter on Anne, who continued to be a prime
favorite with the critical old lady.

"That Anne-girl improves all the time," she said. "I get tired of
other girls—there is such a provoking and eternal sameness about
them. Anne has as many shades as a rainbow and every shade is the
prettiest while it lasts. I don't know that she is as amusing as she was
when she was a child, but she makes me love her and I like people
who make me love them. It saves me so much trouble in making
myself love them."

Then, almost before anybody realized it, spring had come; out in
Avonlea the Mayflowers were peeping pinkly out on the sere barrens
where snow-wreaths lingered; and the "mist of green" was on the
woods and in the valleys. But in Charlottetown harassed Queen's
students thought and talked only of examinations.

"It doesn't seem possible that the term is nearly over," said Anne.
"Why, last fall it seemed so long to look forward to—a whole winter
of studies and classes. And here we are, with the exams looming up
next week. Girls, sometimes I feel as if those exams meant everything, but when I look at the big buds swelling on those chestnut trees
and the misty blue air at the end of the streets they don't seem half so
important.'

Jane and Ruby and Josie, who had dropped in, did not take this
view of it. To them the coming examinations were constantly very
important indeed—far more important than chestnut buds or May-
time hazes. It was all very well for Anne, who was sure of passing at
least, to have her moments of belittling them, but when your whole
future depended on them—as the girls truly thought theirs did—you
could not regard them philosphically.

"I've lost seven pounds in the last two weeks," sighed Jane. "It's
no use to say don't worry. I *will* worry. Worrying helps you some—it
seems as if you were doing something when you're worrying. It

would be dreadful if I failed to get my license after going to Queen's all winter and spending so much money."

"*I* don't care," said Josie Pye. "If I don't pass this year I'm coming back next. My father can afford to send me. Anne, Frank Stockely says that Professor Tremaine said Gilbert Blythe was sure to get the medal and that Emily Clay would likely win the Avery scholarship."

"That may make me feel badly tomorrow, Josie," laughed Anne, "but just now I honestly feel that as long as I know the violets are coming out all purple down in the hollow below Green Gables and that little ferns are poking their heads up in Lovers' Lane, it's not a great deal of difference whether I begin to understand what is meant by the 'joy of the strife.' Next to trying and winning, the best thing is trying and failing. Girls, don't talk about exams! Look at that arch of pale green sky over those houses and picture to yourselves what it must look like over the purply-dark beechwoods back of Avonlea."

"What are you going to wear for commencement, Jane?" asked Ruby practically.

Jane and Josie both answered at once and the chatter drifted into a side eddy of fashions. But Anne, with her elbows on the window sill, her soft cheek laid against her clasped hands, and her eyes filled with visions, looked out unheedingly across city roof and spire to that glorious dome of sunset sky and wove her dreams of a possible future from the golden tissue of youth's own optimism. All the Beyond was hers with its possibilities lurking rosily in the oncoming years—each year a rose of promise to be woven into an immortal chaplet.

CHAPTER 36

THE GLORY AND THE DREAM

ON THE morning when the final results of all the examinations were to be posted on the bulletin board at Queen's, Anne and Jane walked down the street together. Jane was smiling and happy; examinations were over and she was comfortably sure she had made a pass at least; further considerations troubled Jane not at all; she had no soaring ambitions and consequently was not affected with the unrest attendant thereon. For we pay a price for everything we get or take in this world; and although ambitions are well worth having, they are not to be cheaply won, but exact their dues of work and self-denial, anxiety and discouragement. Anne was pale and quiet; in ten more minutes she would know who had won the medal and who the Avery. Beyond those ten minutes there did not seem, just then, to be anything worth being called Time.

"Of course you'll win one of them anyhow," said Jane, who couldn't understand how the faculty could be so unfair as to order it otherwise.

"I have no hope of the Avery," said Anne. "Everybody says Emily Clay will win it. And I'm not going to march up to that bulletin board and look at it before everybody. I haven't the moral courage. I'm going straight to the girls' dressing-room. You must read the announcements and then come and tell me, Jane. And I implore you in the name of our old friendship to do it as quickly as possible. If I have failed just say so, without trying to break it gently; and whatever you do *don't* sympathize with me. Promise me this, Jane."

Jane promised solemnly; but, as it happened, there was no necessity for such a promise. When they went up the entrance steps of Queen's they found the hall full of boys who were carrying Gilbert Blythe around on their shoulders and yelling at the tops of their voices, "Hurrah for Blythe, Medallist!"

For a moment Anne felt one sickening pang of defeat and disappointment. So she had failed and Gilbert had won! Well, Matthew would be sorry—he had been so sure she would win.

And then!

Somebody called out:

"Three cheers for Miss Shirley, winner of the Avery!"

"Oh, Anne," gasped Jane, as they fled to the girls' dressing-room amid hearty cheers. "Oh, Anne, I'm so proud! Isn't it splendid?"

And then the girls were around them and Anne was the centre of a laughing, congratulating group. Her shoulders were thumped and her hands shaken vigorously. She was pushed and pulled and hugged and among it all she managed to whisper to Jane:

"Oh, won't Matthew and Marilla be pleased! I must write the news home right away."

Commencement was the next important happening. The exercises were held in the big assembly hall of the Academy. Addresses were given, essays read, songs sung, the public award of diplomas, prizes and medals made.

Matthew and Marilla were there, with eyes and ears for only one student on the platform—a tall girl in pale green, with faintly flushed cheeks and starry eyes, who read the best essay and was pointed out and whispered about as the Avery winner.

"Reckon you're glad we kept her, Marilla?" whispered Matthew, speaking for the first time since he had entered the hall, when Anne had finished her essay.

"It's not the first time I've been glad," retorted Marilla. "You do like to rub things in, Matthew Cuthbert."

Miss Barry, who was sitting behind them, leaned forward and poked Marilla in the back with her parasol.

"Aren't you proud of that Anne-girl? I am," she said.

Anne went home to Avonlea with Matthew and Marilla that evening. She had not been home since April and she felt that she could not wait another day. The apple-blossoms were out and the world was fresh and young. Diana was at Green Gables to meet her. In her own white room, where Marilla had set a flowering house rose on the window sill, Anne looked about her and drew a long breath of happiness.

"Oh, Diana, it's so good to be back again. It's so good to see those pointed firs coming out against the pink sky—and that white orchard and the old Snow Queen. Isn't the breath of the mint delicious? And that tea rose—why, it's *good* to see you again, Diana!"

"I thought you liked that Stella Maynard better than me," said Diana reproachfully. "Josie Pye told me you did. Josie said you were *infatuated* with her."

Anne lauged and pelted Diana with the faded "June lilies" of her bouquet.

"Stella Maynard is the dearest girl in the world except one and you are that one, Diana," she said. "I love you more than ever—and I've so many things to tell you. But just now I feel as if it were joy enough to sit here and look at you. I'm tired, I think—tired of being studious and ambitious. I mean to spend at least two hours tomorrow lying out in the orchard grass, thinking of absolutely nothing."

"You've done splendidly, Anne. I suppose you won't be teaching now that you've won the Avery?"

"No. I'm going to Redmond in September. Doesn't it seem wonderful? I'll have a brand-new stock of ambition laid in by that time after three glorious, golden months of vacation. Jane and Ruby are going to teach. Isn't it splendid to think we all got through even to Moody Spurgeon and Josie Pye?"

"The Newbridge trustees have offered Jane their school already," said Diana. "Gilbert Blythe is going to teach, too. He has to. His father can't afford to send him to college next year, after all, so he means to earn his own way through. I expect he'll get the school here if Miss Ames decides to leave."

Anne felt a queer little sensation of dismayed surprise. She had not known this; she had expected Gilbert would be going to Redmond also. What would she do without their inspiring rivalry? Would not work, even at a co-educational college with a real degree in prospect, be rather flat without her friend the enemy?

The next morning at breakfast it suddenly struck Anne that Matthew was not looking well. Surely he was much grayer than he had been a year before.

"Marilla," she said hesitatingly when he had gone out, "is Matthew quite well?"

"No, he isn't," said Marilla in a troubled tone. "He's had some real bad spells with his heart this spring and he won't spare himself a mite. I've been real worried about him, but he's some better this while back and we've got a good hired man, so I'm hoping he'll kind of rest and pick up. Maybe he will now you're home. You always cheer him up."

Anne leaned across the table and took Marilla's face in her hands.

"You are not looking as well yourself as I'd like to see you, Marilla. You look tired. I'm afraid you've been working too hard. You must take a rest, now that I'm home. I'm just going to take this one day off to visit all the dear old spots and hunt up my old dreams, and then it well be your turn to be lazy while I do the work."

Marilla smiled affectionately at her girl.

"It's not the work—it's my head. I've a pain so often now—behind my eyes. Doctor Spencer's been fussing with glasses, but they don't do me any good. There is a distinguished oculist coming to the Island the last of June and the doctor says I must see him. I guess I'll have to. I can't read or sew with any comfort now. Well, Anne, you've done real well at Queen's I must say. To take First Class License in one year and win the Avery scholarship—well, well, Mrs. Lynde says pride goes before a fall and she doesn't believe in the higher education of women at all; she says it unfits them for woman's true sphere. I don't believe a word of it. Speaking of Rachel reminds me—did you hear anything about the Abbey Bank lately, Anne?"

"I heard that it was shaky," answered Anne. "Why?"

"That is what Rachel said. She was up here one day last week and said there was some talk about it. Matthew felt real worried. All we have saved is in that bank—every penny. I wanted Matthew to put it in the Savings Bank in the first place, but old Mr. Abbey was a great friend of father's and he'd always banked with him. Matthew said any bank with him at the head of it was good enough for anybody.''

''I think he has only been its nominal head for many years,'' said Anne. ''He is a very old man; his nephews are really at the head of the institution.''

''Well, when Rachel told us that, I wanted Matthew to draw our money right out and he said he'd think of it. But Mr. Russell told him yesterday that the bank was all right.''

Anne had her good day in the companionship of the outdoor world. She never forgot that day; it was so bright and golden and fair, so free from shadow and so lavish of blossom. Anne spent some of its rich hours in the orchard; she went to the Dryad's Bubble and Willowmere and Violet Vale; she called at the manse and had a satisfying talk with Mrs. Allan; and finally in the evening she went with Matthew for the cows, through Lovers' Lane to the back pasture. The woods were all gloried through with sunset and the warm splendor of it streamed down through the hill gaps in the west. Matthew walked slowly with bent head; Anne, tall and erect, suited her springing step to his.

''You've been working too hard today, Matthew,'' she said reproachfully. ''Why won't you take things easier?''

''Well now, I can't seem to,'' said Matthew, as he opened the yard gate to let the cows through. ''It's only that I'm getting old, Anne, and keep forgetting it. Well, well, I've always worked pretty hard and I'd rather drop in harness.''

''If I had been the boy you sent for,' said Anne wistfully, ''I'd be able to help you so much now and spare you in a hundred ways. I could find it in my heart to wish I had been, just for that.''

''Well, no, I'd rather have you than a dozen boys, Anne,'' said Matthew patting her hand. ''Just mind you that—rather than a dozen boys. Well now, I guess it wasn't a boy that took the Avery scholarship, was it? It was a girl—my girl—my girl that I'm proud of.''

He smiled his shy smile at her as he went into the yard. Anne took the memory of it with her when she went to her room that night and sat for a long while at her open window, thinking of the past and dreaming of the future. Outside the Snow Queen was mistily white in the moonshine; the frogs were singing in the marsh beyond Orchard Slope. Anne always remembered the silvery, peaceful beauty and fragrant calm of that night. It was the last night before sorrow touched her life; and no life is ever quite the same again once that cold, sanctifying touch has been laid upon it.

CHAPTER 37

THE REAPER WHOSE NAME IS DEATH

"MATTHEW—MATTHEW—What is the matter? Matthew, are you sick?"

It was Marilla who spoke, alarm in every jerky word. Anne came through the hall, her hands full of white narcissus,—it was long before Anne could love the sight or odor of white narcissus again,— in time to hear her and to see Matthew standing in the porch doorway, a folded paper in his hand, and his face strangely drawn and gray. Anne dropped her flowers and sprang across the kitchen to him at the same moment as Marilla. They were both too late; before they could reach him Matthew had fallen across the threshold.

"He's fainted," gasped Marilla. "Anne, run for Martin—quick, quick! He's at the barn."

Martin, the hired man, who had just driven home from the post-office, started at once for the doctor, calling at Orchard Slope on his way to send Mr. and Mrs. Barry over. Mrs. Lynde, who was there on an errand, came too. They found Anne and Marilla distractedly trying to restore Matthew to consciousness.

Mrs. Lynde pushed them gently aside, tried his pulse, and then laid her ear over his heart. She looked at their anxious faces sorrowfully and the tears came into her eyes.

"Oh, Marilla," she said gravely. "I don't think—we can do anything for him."

"Mrs. Lynde, you don't think—you can't think Matthew is— is—" Anne could not say the dreadful word; she turned sick and pallid.

"Child, yes, I'm afraid of it. Look at his face. When you've seen that look as often as I have you'll know what it means."

Anne looked at the still face and there beheld the seal of the Great Presence.

When the doctor came he said that death had been instantaneous and probably painless, caused in all likelihood by some sudden shock. The secret of the shock was discovered to be in the paper Matthew had held and which Martin had brought from the office that morning. It contained an account of the failure of the Abbey Bank.

The news spread quickly through Avonlea, and all day friends and neighbors thronged Green Gables and came and went on errands of kindness for the dead and living. For the first time shy, quiet Matthew Cuthbert was a person of central importance; the white majesty of death had fallen on him and set him apart as one crowned.

When the calm night came softly down over Green Gables the old house was hushed and tranquil. In the parlor lay Matthew Cuthbert in his coffin, his long gray hair framing his placid face on which there was a little kindly smile as if he but slept, dreaming pleasant dreams. There were flowers about him—sweet old-fashioned flowers which his mother had planted in the homestead garden in her bridal days and for which Matthew had always had a secret, wordless love. Anne had gathered them and brought them to him, her anguished, tearless eyes burning in her white face. It was the last thing she could do for him.

The Barrys and Mrs. Lynde stayed with them that night. Diana, going to the east gable, where Anne was standing at her window, said gently:

"Anne dear, would you like to have me sleep with you tonight?"

"Thank you, Diana." Anne looked earnestly into her friend's face. "I think you won't misunderstand me when I say that I want to be alone. I'm not afraid. I haven't been alone one minute since it happened—and I want to be. I want to be quite silent and quiet and try to realize it. I *can't* realize it. Half the time it seems to me that Matthew can't be dead; and the other half it seems as if he must have been dead for a long time and I've had this horrible dull ache ever since."

Diana did not quite understand. Marilla's impassioned grief, breaking all the bounds of natural reserve and lifelong habit in its stormy rush, she could comprehend better than Anne's tearless agony. But she went away kindly, leaving Anne alone to keep her first vigil with sorrow.

Anne hoped that tears would come in solitude. It seemed to her a terrible thing that she could not shed a tear for Matthew, whom she had loved so much and who had been so kind to her, Matthew, who had walked with her last evening at sunset and was now lying in the dim room below with that awful peace on his brow. But no tears came at first, even when she knelt by her window in the darkness and prayed, looking up to the stars beyond the hills—no tears, only the same horrible dull ache of misery that kept on aching until she fell asleep, worn out with the day's pain and excitement.

In the night she awakened, with the stillness and the darkness about her, and the recollection of the day came over her like a wave of sorrow. She could see Matthew's face smiling at her as he had smiled when they parted at the gate that last evening—she could hear his voice saying, "My girl—my girl that I'm proud of." Then the tears came and Anne wept her heart out. Marilla heard her and crept in to comfort her.

"There—there—don't cry so, dearie. It can't bring him back. It—it—isn't right to cry so. I knew that today, but I couldn't help it then. He'd always been such a good, kind brother to me—but God knows best."

"Oh, just let me cry, Marilla," sobbed Anne. "The tears don't hurt me like that ache did. Stay here for a little while with me and keep your arm round me—so. I couldn't have Diana stay, she's good and kind and sweet—but it's not her sorrow—she's outside of it and she couldn't come close enough to my heart to help me. It's our sorrow—yours and mine. Oh, Marilla, what will we do without him?"

"We've got each other, Anne. I don't know what I'd do if you weren't here—if you'd never come. Oh, Anne, I know I've been kind of strict and harsh with you maybe—but you mustn't think I didn't love you as well as Matthew did, for all that. I want to tell you now when I can. It's never been easy for me to say things out of my heart, but at times like this it's easier. I love you as dear as if you were my own flesh and blood and you've been my joy and comfort ever since you came to Green Gables.

Two days afterwards they carried Matthew Cuthbert over his homestead threshold and away from the fields he had tilled and the orchards he had loved and the trees he had planted; and then Avonlea settled back to its usual placidity and even at Green Gables affairs slipped into their old groove and work was done and duties fulfilled with regularity as before, although always with the aching sense of "loss in all familiar things." Anne, new to grief, thought it almost sad that it could be so—that they *could* go on in the old way without Matthew. She felt something like shame and remorse when she discovered that the sunrises behind the firs and the pale pink buds opening in the garden gave her the old inrush of gladness when she saw them—that Diana's visits were pleasant to her and that Diana's merry words and ways moved her to laughter and smiles—that, in brief, the beautiful world of blossom and love and friendship had lost none of its power to please her fancy and thrill her heart, that life still called to her with many insistent voices.

"It seems like disloyalty to Matthew, somehow, to find pleasure in these things now that he has gone," she said wistfully to Mrs. Allan one evening when they were together in the manse garden. "I miss him so much—all the time—and yet, Mrs. Allan, the world and life seem very beautiful and interesting to me for all. Today Diana said something funny and I found myself laughing. I thought when it happened I could never laugh again. And it somehow seems as if I oughtn't to."

"When Matthew was here he liked to hear you laugh and he liked to know that you found pleasure in the pleasant things around you," said Mrs. Allan gently. "He is just away now; and he likes to know it is just the same. I am sure we should not shut our hearts against the healing influences that nature offers us. But I understand your feeling. I think we all experience the same thing. We resent the thought that anything can please us when someone we love is no longer here to share the pleasure with us, and we almost feel as if we were unfaithful to our sorrow when we find our interest in life returning to us."

"I was down to the graveyard to plant a rosebush on Matthew's grave this afternoon," said Anne dreamily. "I took a slip of the little white Scotch rosebush his mother brought out from Scotland long ago; Matthew always liked those roses the best—they were so small and sweet on their thorny stems. It made me feel glad that I could plant it by his grave—as if I were doing something that must please him in taking it there to be near him. I hope he has roses like them in heaven. Perhaps the souls of all those little white roses that he has loved so many summers were all there to meet him. I must go home now. Marilla is all alone and she gets lonely at twilight."

"She will be lonelier still, I fear, when you go away again to college," said Mrs. Allan.

Anne did not reply; she said good night and went slowly back to Green Gables. Marilla was sitting on the front door steps and Anne sat down beside her. The door was open behind them, held back by a big pink conch shell with hints of sea sunsets in its smooth inner convolutions.

Anne gathered some sprays of pale yellow honeysuckle and put them in her hair. She liked the delicious hint of fragrance, as of some aerial benediction, above her every time she moved.

"Doctor Spencer was here while you were away," Marilla said. "He says that the specialist will be in town tomorrow and he insists that I must go in and have my eyes examined. I suppose I'd better go and have it over. I'll be more than thankful if the man can give me the right kind of glasses to suit my eyes. You won't mind staying here alone while I'm away, will you? Martin will have to drive me in and there's ironing and baking to do."

"I shall be all right. Diana will come over for company for me. I shall attend to the ironing and baking beautifully—you needn't fear that I'll starch the handkerchiefs or flavor the cake with liniment."

Marilla laughed.

"What a girl you were for making mistakes in them days, Anne. You were always getting into scrapes. I did use to think you were possessed. Do you mind the time you dyed your hair?"

"Yes, indeed. I shall never forget it," smiled Anne, touching the heavy braid of hair that was wound about her shapely head. "I laugh a little now sometimes when I think what a worry my hair used to be to me—but I don't laught *much*, because it was a very real trouble then. I did suffer terribly over my hair and my freckles. My freckles are really gone; and people are nice enough to tell me my hair is auburn now—all but Josie Pye. She informed me yesterday that she really thought it was redder than ever, or at least my black dress made it look redder, and she asked me if people who had red hair ever got used to having it. Marilla, I've almost decided to give up trying to like Josie Pye. I've made what I would once have called a heroic effort to like her, but Josie Pye won't *be* liked."

"Josie is a Pye," said Marilla sharply, "so she can't help being disagreeable. I suppose people of that kind serve some useful purpose in society, but I must say I don't know what it is any more than I know the use of thistles. Is Josie going to teach?"

"No, she is going back to Queen's next year. So are Moody Spurgeon and Charlie Sloane. Jane and Ruby are going to teach and they have both got schools—Jane at Newbridge and Ruby at some place up west."

"Gilbert Blythe is going to teach too, isn't he?"

"Yes"—briefly.

"What a nice-looking young fellow he is," said Marilla absently. "I saw him in church last Sunday and he seemed so tall and manly. He looks a lot like his father did at the same age. John Blythe was a nice boy. We used to be real good friends, he and I. People called him my beau."

Anne looked up with swift interest.

"Oh, Marilla—and what happened?—why didn't you—"

"We had a quarrel. I wouldn't forgive him when he asked me to. I meant to, after awhile—but I was sulky and angry and I wanted to punish him first. He never came back—the Blythes were all mighty independent. But I always felt—rather sorry. I've always kind of wished I'd forgiven him when I had the chance."

"So you've had a bit of romance in your life, too," said Anne softly.

"Yes, I suppose you might call it that. You wouldn't think so to look at me, would you? But you never can tell about people from their outsides. Everybody has forgot about me and John. I'd forgotten myself. But it all came back to me when I saw Gilbert last Sunday."

CHAPTER 38

THE BEND IN THE ROAD

MARILLA WENT to town the next day and returned in the evening. Anne had gone over to Orchard Slope with Diana and came back to find Marilla in the kitchen, sitting by the table with her head leaning on her hand. Something in her dejected attitude struck a chill to Anne's heart. She had never seen Marilla sit limply inert like that.

"Are you very tired, Marilla?"

"Yes—no—I don't know," said Marilla wearily, looking up. "I suppose I am tired but I haven't thought about it. It's not that."

"Did you see the oculist? What did he say?" asked Anne anxiously.

"Yes, I saw him. He examined my eyes. He says that if I give up all reading and sewing entirely and any kind of work that strains the eyes, and if I'm careful not to cry, and if I wear the glasses he's given me he thinks my eyes may not get any worse and my headaches will be cured. But if I don't he says I'll certainly be stone blind in six months. Blind! Anne, just think of it!"

For a minute Anne, after her first quick exclamation of dismay, was silent. It seemed to her that she could *not* speak. Then she said bravely, but with a catch in her voice:

"Marilla, *don't* think of it. You know he has given you hope. If you are careful you won't lose your sight altogether; and if his glasses cure your headaches it will be a great thing."

"I don't call it much hope," said Marilla bitterly. "What am I to live for if I can't read or sew or do anything like that? I might as well be blind—or dead. And as for crying, I can't help that when I get lonesome. But there, it's no good talking about it. If you'll get me a cup of tea I'll be thankful. I'm about done out. Don't say anything about this to any one for a spell yet, anyway. I can't bear that folks should come here to question and sympathize and talk about it."

When Marilla had eaten her lunch Anne persuaded her to go to bed. Then Anne went herself to the east gable and sat down by her window in the darkness alone with her tears and her heaviness of heart. How sadly things had changed since she had sat there the night after coming home! Then she had been full of hope and joy and the future had looked rosy with promise. Anne felt as if she had lived years since then, but before she went to bed there was a smile on her lips and peace in her heart. She had looked her duty courageously in the face and found it a friend—as duty ever is when we meet it frankly.

One afternoon a few days later Marilla came slowly in from the yard where she had been talking to a caller—a man whom Anne knew by sight as John Sadler from Carmody. Anne wondered what he could have been saying to bring that look to Marilla's face.

"What did Mr. Sadler want, Marilla?"

Marilla sat down by the window and looked at Anne. There were tears in her eyes in defiance of the oculist's prohibition and her voice broke as she said:

"He heard that I was going to sell Green Gables and he wants to buy it."

"Buy it! Buy Green Gables?" Anne wondered if she had heard aright. "Oh, Marilla, you don't mean to sell Green Gables!"

"Anne, I don't know what else is to be done. I've thought it all over. If my eyes were strong I could stay here and make out to look after things and manage, with a good hired man. But as it is I can't. I may lose my sight altogether; and anyway I'll not be fit to run things. Oh, I never thought I'd live to see the day when I'd have to sell my home. But things would only go behind worse and worse all the time, till nobody would want to buy it. Every cent of our money went in that bank; and there's some notes Matthew gave last fall to pay. Mrs.

Lynde advises me to sell the farm and board somewhere—with her I suppose. It won't bring much—it's small and the buildings are old. But it'll be enough for me to live on I reckon. I'm thankful you're provided for with that scholarship, Anne. I'm sorry you won't have a home to come to in your vacations, that's all, but I suppose you'll manage somehow.''

Marilla broke down and wept bitterly.

"You mustn't sell Green Gables," said Anne resolutely.

"Oh, Anne, I wish I didn't have to. But you can see for yourself. I can't stay here alone. I'd go crazy with trouble and loneliness. And my sight would go—I know it would.''

"You won't have to stay here alone, Marilla. I'll be with you. I'm not going to Redmond.''

"Not going to Redmond!'' Marilla lifted her worn face from her hands and looked at Anne. "Why, what do you mean?''

"Just what I say. I'm not going to take the scholarship. I decided so the night after you came home from town. You surely don't think I could leave you alone in your trouble, Marilla, after all you've done for me. I've been thinking and planning. Let me tell you my plans. Mr. Barry wants to rent the farm for next year. So you won't have any bother over that. And I'm going to teach. I've applied for the school here—but I don't expect to get it for I understand the trustees have promised it to Gilbert Blythe. But I can have the Carmody school— Mr. Blair told me so last night at the store. Of course that won't be quite as nice or convenient as if I had the Avonlea school. But I can board home and drive myself over to Carmody and back, in the warm weather at least. And even in winter I can come home Fridays. We'll keep a horse for that. Oh, I have it all planned out, Marilla. And I'll read to you and keep you cheered up. You shan't be dull or lonesome. And we'll be real cosy and happy here together, you and I.''

Marilla had listened like a woman in a dream.

"Oh, Anne, I could get on real well if you were here, I know. But I can't let you sacrifice yourself so for me. It would be terrible.''

"Nonsense!'' Anne laughed merrily. "There is no sacrifice. Nothing could be worse than giving up Green Gables—nothing could hurt me more. We must keep the dear old place. My mind is quite made up, Marilla. I'm *not* going to Redmond; and I *am* going to stay here and teach. Don't you worry about me a bit.''

"But your ambitions—and—''

"I'm just as ambitious as ever. Only, I've changed the object of my ambitions. I'm going to be a good teacher—and I'm going to save your eyesight. Besides, I mean to study at home here and take a little college course all by myself. Oh, I've dozens of plans, Marilla. I've been thinking them out for a week. I shall give life here my best, and I believe it will give its best to me in return. When I left Queen's my future seemed to stretch out before me like a straight road. I thought I could see along it for many a milestone. Now there is a bend in it. I don't know what lies around the bend, but I'm going to believe that the best does. It has a fascination of its own, that bend, Marilla. I wonder how the road beyond it goes—what there is of green glory and soft, checkered light and shadows—what new landscapes—what new beauties—what curves and hills and valleys further on.''

''I don't feel as if I ought to let you give it up,'' said Marilla, referring to the scholarship.

''But you can't prevent me. I'm sixteen and a half, 'obstinate as a mule,' as Mrs. Lynde once told me,'' laughed Anne. ''Oh, Marilla, don't you go pitying me. I don't like to be pitied, and there is no need for it. I'm heart glad over the very thought of staying at dear Green Gables. Nobody could love it as you and I do—so we must keep it.''

''You blessed girl!'' said Marilla, yeilding. ''I feel as if you'd given me new life. I guess I ought to stick out and make you go to college—but I know I can't, so I ain't going to try. I'll make it up to you though, Anne.''

When it became noised abroad in Avonlea that Anne Shirley had given up the idea of going to college and intended to stay home and teach there was a good deal of discussion over it. Most of the good folks, not knowing about Marilla's eyes, thought she was foolish. Mrs. Allan did not. She told Anne so in approving words that brought tears of pleasure to the girl's eyes. Neither did good Mrs. Lynde. She came up one evening and found Anne and Marilla sitting at the front door in the warm, scented summer dusk. They liked to sit there when the twilight came down and the white moths flew about in the garden and the odor of mint filled the dewy air.

Mrs. Rachel deposited her substantial person upon the stone bench by the door, behind which grew a row of tall pink and yellow hollyhocks, with a long breath of mingled weariness and relief.

''I declare I'm glad to sit down. I've been on my feet all day, and two hundred pounds is a good bit for two feet to carry round. It's a great blessing not to be fat, Marilla. I hope you appreciate it. Well, Anne, I hear you've given up your notion of going to college. I was real glad to hear it. You've got as much education now as a woman can be comfortable with. I don't believe in girls going to college and cramming their heads full of Latin and Greek and all that nonsense.''

"But I'm going to study Latin and Greek just the same, Mrs. Lynde,'' said Anne laughing. "I'm going to take my Arts course right here at Green Gables, and study everything that I would at college.''

Mrs. Lynde lifted her hands in holy horror.

"Anne Shirley, you'll kill yourself.''

"Not a bit of it. I shall thrive on it. Oh, I'm not going to overdo things. As 'Josiah Allen's wife' says, I shall be 'mejum.' But I'll have lots of spare time in the long winter evenings, and I've no vocation for fancy work. I'm going to teach over at Carmody, you know.''

"I don't know it. I guess you're going to teach right here in Avonlea. The trustees have decided to give you the school.''

"Mrs. Lynde!'' cried Anne, springing to her feet in her surprise. "Why, I thought they had promised it to Gilbert Blythe!''

"So they did. But as soon as Gilbert heard that you had applied for it he went to them—they had a business meeting at the school last night, you know—and told them that he withdrew his application, and suggested that they accept yours. He said he was going to teach at White Sands. Of course he gave up the school just to oblige you, because he knew how much you wanted to stay with Marilla, and I must say I think it was real kind and thoughtful in him, that's what. Real self-sacrificing, too, for he'll have his board to pay at White Sands, and everybody knows he's got to earn his own way through college. So the trustees decided to take you. I was tickled to death when Thomas came home and told me.''

"I don't feel that I ought to take it,'' murmured Anne. "I mean—I don't think I ought to let Gilbert make such a sacrifice for—for me.''

"I guess you can't prevent him now. He's signed papers with the White Sands trustees. So it wouldn't do him any good now if you were to refuse. Of course you'll take the school. You'll get along all right, now that there are no Pyes going. Josie was the last of them, and a good thing she was, that's what. There's been some Pye or other going to Avonlea school for the last twenty years, and I guess their mission in life was to keep school-teachers reminded that earth isn't their home. Bless my heart! What does all that winking and blinking at the Barry gable mean?''

"Diana is signalling for me to go over,'' laughed Anne. "You know we keep up the old custom. Excuse me while I run over and see what she wants.''

Anne ran down the clover slope like a deer, and disappeared in the firry shadows of the Haunted Wood. Mrs. Lynde looked after her indulgently.

"There's a good deal of the child about her yet in some ways."

"There's a good deal more of the woman about her in others," retorted Marilla, with a momentary return of her old crispness.

But crispness was no longer Marilla's distinguishing characteristic. As Mrs. Lynde told her Thomas that night.

"Marilla Cuthbert has got *mellow*. That's what."

Anne went to the little Avonlea graveyard the next evening to put fresh flowers on Matthew's grave and water the Scotch rosebush. She lingered there until dusk, liking the peace and calm of the little place, with its poplars whose rustle was like low, friendly speech, and its whispering grasses growing at will among the graves. When she finally left it and walked down the long hill that sloped to the Lake of Shining Waters it was past sunset and all Avonlea lay before her in a dreamlike afterlight—"a haunt of ancient peace." There was a freshness in the air as of a wind that had blown over honey-sweet fields of clover. Home lights twinkled out here and there among the homestead trees. Beyond lay the sea, misty and purple, with its haunting, unceasing murmur. The west was a glory of soft mingled hues, and the pond reflected them all in still softer shadings. The beauty of it all thrilled Anne's heart, and she gratefully opened the gates of her soul to it.

"Dear old world," she murmured, "you are very lovely, and I am glad to be alive in you."

Halfway down the hill a tall lad came whistling out of a gate before the Blythe homestead. It was Gilbert, and the whistle died on his lips as he recognized Anne. He lifted his cap courteously, but he would have passed on in silence, if Anne had not stopped and held out her hand.

"Gilbert," she said, with scarlet cheeks, "I want to thank you for giving up the school for me. It was very good of you—and I want you to know that I appreciate it."

Gilbert took the offered hand eagerly.

"It wasn't particularly good of me at all, Anne. I was pleased to be able to do you some small service. Are we going to be friends after this? Have you really forgiven me my old fault?"

Anne laughed and tried unsuccessfully to withdraw her hand.

"I forgave you that day by the pond landing, although I didn't know it. What a stubborn little goose I was. I've been—I may as well make a complete confession—I've been sorry ever since."

"COME, I'M GOING TO WALK WITH YOU."

"We are going to be the best of friends," said Gilbert, jubilantly. "We were born to be good friends, Anne. You've thwarted destiny long enough. I know we can help each other in many ways. You are going to keep up with your studies, aren't you? So am I. Come, I'm going to walk home with you."

Marilla looked curiously at Anne when the latter entered the kitchen.

"Who was that came up the lane with you, Anne?"

"Gilbert Blythe," answered Anne, vexed to find herself blushing. "I met him on Barry's hill."

"I didn't think you and Gilbert Blythe were such good friends that you'd stand for half an hour at the gate talking to him," said Marilla, with a dry smile.

"We haven't been—we've been good enemies. But we have decided that it will be much more sensible to be good friends in future. Were we really there half an hour? It seemed just a few minutes. But, you see, we have five years' lost conversations to catch up with, Marilla."

Anne sat long at her window that night companioned by a glad content. The wind purred softly in the cherry boughs, and the mint breaths came up to her. The stars twinkled over the pointed firs in the hollow and Diana's light gleamed through the old gap.

Anne's horizons had closed in since the night she had sat there after coming home from Queen's; but if the path set before her feet was to be narrow she knew that flowers of quiet happiness would bloom along it. The joys of sincere work and worthy aspirations and congenial friendship were to be hers; nothing could rob her of her birthright of fancy or her ideal world of dreams. And there was always the bend in the road!

" 'God's in his heaven, all's right with the world,' " whispered Anne softly.

Anne of Avonlea

CHAPTER 1

AN IRATE NEIGHBOR

A TALL, slim girl, "half-past sixteen," with serious gray eyes and hair which her friends called auburn, had sat down on the broad red sandstone doorstep of a Prince Edward Island farmhouse one ripe afternoon in August, firmly resolved to construe so many lines of Virgil.

But an August afternoon, with blue hazes scarfing the harvest slopes, little winds whispering elfishly in the poplars, and a dancing splendour of red poppies outflaming against the dark coppice of young firs in a corner of the cherry orchard, was fitter for dreams than dead languages. The Virgil soon slipped unheeded to the ground, and Anne, her chin propped on her clasped hands, and her eyes on the splendid mass of fluffy clouds that were heaping up just over Mr. J. A. Harrison's house like a great white mountain, was far away in a delicious world where a certain schoolteacher was doing a wonderful work shaping the destinies of future statesmen, and inspiring youthful minds and hearts with high and lofty ambitions.

To be sure, if you came down to harsh facts . . . which, it must be confessed, Anne seldom did until she had to . . . it did not seem likely that there was much promising material for celebrities in Avonlea school; but you could never tell what might happen if a teacher used her influence for good. Anne had certain rose-tinted ideals of what a teacher might accomplish if she only went the right way about it; and she was in the midst of a delightful scene, forty years hence, with a famous personage . . . just exactly what he was to be famous for was left in convenient haziness, but Anne thought it would be rather nice to have him a college president or a Canadian premier . . . bowing low over her wrinkled hand and assuring her that it was she who had first kindled his ambition, and that all his success in life was due to the lessons she had instilled so long ago in Avonlea school. This pleasant vision was shattered by a most unpleasant interruption.

A demure little Jersey cow came scuttling down the land and five seconds later Mr. Harrison arrived . . . if "arrived" be not too mild a term to describe the manner of his irruption into the yard.

He bounced over the fence without waiting to open the gate, and angrily confronted astonished Anne, who had risen to her feet and stood looking at him in some bewilderment. Mr. Harrison was their new right-hand neighbor and she had never met him before, although she had seen him once or twice.

In early April, before Anne had come home from Queen's, Mr. Robert Bell, whose farm adjoined the Cuthbert place on the west, had sold out and moved to Charlottetown. His farm had been bought by a certain Mr. J. A. Harrison, whose name, and the fact that he was a New Brunswick man, were all that was known about him. But before he had been a month in Avonlea he had won the reputation of being an odd person . . . "a crank," Mrs. Rachel Lynde said. Mrs. Rachel was an outspoken lady, as those of you who may have already made her acquaintance will remember. Mr. Harrison was certainly different from other people . . . and that is the essential characteristic of a crank, as everybody knows.

In the first place he kept house for himself and had publicly stated that he wanted no fools of women around his diggings. Feminine Avonlea took its revenge by the gruesome tales it related about his housekeeping and cooking. He had hired little John Henry Carter of White Sands and John Henry started the stories. For one thing, there was never any stated time for meals in the Harrison establishment. Mr. Harrison "got a bite" when he felt hungry, and if John Henry were around at the time, he came in for a share, but if he were not, he had to wait until Mr. Harrison's next hungry spell. John Henry mournfully averred that he would have starved to death if it wasn't that he got home on Sundays and got a good filling up, and that his mother always gave him a basket of "grub" to take back with him on Monday mornings.

As for washing dishes, Mr. Harrison never made any pretence of doing it unless a rainy Sunday came. Then he went to work and washed them all at once in the rainwater hogshead, and left them to drain dry.

Again, Mr. Harrison was "close." When he was asked to subscribe to the Rev. Mr. Allan's salary he said he'd wait and see how many dollars' worth of good he got out of his preaching first . . . *he* didn't believe in buying a pig in a poke. And when Mrs. Lynde went to ask for a contribution to missions . . . and incidentally to see the inside of the house . . . he told her there more heathens among the old woman gossips in Avonlea than anywhere else he knew of, and he'd cheerfully contribute to a mission for Christianizing them if she'd undertake it. Mrs. Rachel got herself away and said it was a mercy poor Mrs. Robert Bell was safe in her grave, for it would have broken her heart to see the state of her house in which she used to take so much pride.

"Why, she scrubbed the kitchen floor every second day," Mrs. Lynde told Marilla Cuthbert indignantly, "and if you could see it now! I had to hold up my skirts as I walked across it."

Finally, Mr. Harrison kept a parrot called Ginger. Nobody in Avonlea had ever kept a parrot before; consequently that proceeding was considered barely respectable. And such a parrot! If you took John Henry Carter's word for it, never was such an unholy bird. It swore terribly. Mrs. Carter would have taken John Henry away at once if she had been sure she could get another place for him. Besides, Ginger had bitten a piece right out of the back of John Henry's neck one day when he had stooped down too near the cage. Mrs. Carter showed everybody the mark when the luckless John Henry went home on Sundays.

All these things flashed through Anne's mind as Mr. Harrison stood, quite speechless with wrath apparently, before her. In his most amiable mood Mr. Harrison could not have been considered a handsome man; he was short and fat and bald; and now, with his round face purple with rage and his prominent blue eyes almost sticking out of his head, Anne thought he was really the ugliest person she had ever seen.

All at once Mr. Harrison found his voice.

"I'm not going to put up with this," he spluttered, "not a day longer, do you hear, miss. Bless my soul, this is the third time, miss . . . the third time! Patience has ceased to be a virtue, miss. I warned your aunt the last time not to let it occur again . . . and she's let it . . . she's done it . . . what does she mean by it, that is what I want to know. That is what I'm here about, miss.''

"Will you explain what the trouble is?'' asked Anne, in her most dignified manner. She had been practising it considerably of late to have it in good working order when school began; but it had no apparent effect on the irate J. A. Harrison.

"Trouble, is it? Bless my soul, trouble enough, I should think. The trouble is, miss, that I found that Jersey cow of your aunt's in my oats again, not half an hour ago. The third time, mark you. I found her in last Tuesday and I found her in yesterday. I came here and told your aunt not to let it occur again. She *has* let it occur again. Where's your aunt, miss? I just want to see her for a minute and give her a piece of my mind . . . a piece of J. A. Harrison's mind, miss.''

"If you mean Miss Marilla Cuthbert, she is *not* my aunt, and she has gone down to East Grafton to see a distant relative of hers who is very ill, '' said Anne, with due increase of dignity at every word. "I am very sorry that my cow should have broken into your oats . . . she *is* my cow and not Miss Cuthbert's . . . Matthew gave her to me three years ago when she was a little calf and he bought her from Mr. Bell.''

"Sorry, miss! Sorry isn't going to help matters any. You'd better go and look at the havoc that animal has made in my oats . . . trampled them from center to circumference, miss.''

"I am very sorry,'' repeated Anne firmly, "but perhaps if you kept your fences in better repair Dolly might not have broken in. It is your part of the line fence that separates your oatfield from our pasture and I noticed the other day that it was not in very good condition.''

"My fence is all right,'' snapped Mr. Harrison, angrier than ever at this carrying of the war into the enemy's country. "The jail fence couldn't keep a demon of a cow like that out. And I can tell you, you red-headed snippet, that if the cow is yours, as you say, you'd better be employed in watching her out of other people's grain than in sitting round reading yellow-covered novels,'' . . . with a scathing glance at the innocent tan-colored Virgil by Anne's feet.

Something at that moment was red besides Anne's hair . . . which had always been a tender point with her.

"I'd rather have red hair than none at all, except a little fringe round my ears,'' she flashed.

The shot told, for Mr. Harrison was really very sensitive about his bald head. His anger choked him up again and he could only glare speechlessly at Anne, who recovered her temper and followed up her advantage.

"I can make allowance for you, Mr. Harrison, because I have an imagination. I can easily imagine how very trying it must be to find a cow in your oats and I shall not cherish any hard feelings against you for the things you've said. I promise you that Dolly shall never break into your oats again. I give you my word of honor on *that* point."

"Well, mind you she doesn't," muttered Mr. Harrison in a somewhat subdued tone; but he stamped off angrily enough and Anne heard him growling to himself until he was out of earshot.

Grievously disturbed in mind, Anne marched across the yard and shut the naughty Jersey up in the milking pen.

"She can't possibly get out of that unless she tears the fence down," she reflected. "She looks pretty quiet now. I daresay she has sickened herself on those oats. I wish I'd sold her to Mr. Shearer when he wanted her last week, but I thought it was just as well to wait until we had the auction of the stock and let them all go together. I believe it is true about Mr. Harrison being a crank. Certainly there's nothing of the kindred spirit about *him*."

Anne had always a weather eye open for kindred spirits.

Marilla Cuthbert was driving into the yard as Anne returned from the house, and the latter flew to get tea ready. They discussed the matter at the tea table.

"I'll be glad when the auction is over," said Marilla. "It is too much responsibility having so much stock about the place and nobody but that unreliable Martin to look after them. He has never come back yet and he promised that he would certainly be back last night if I'd give him the day off to go to his aunt's funeral. I don't know how many aunts he has got, I am sure. That's the fourth that's died since he hired here a year ago. I'll be more than thankful when the crop is in and Mr. Barry takes over the farm. We'll have to keep Dolly shut up in the pen till Martin comes, for she must be put in the back pasture and the fences there have to be fixed. I declare, it is a world of trouble, as Rachel says. Here's poor Mary Keith dying and what is to become of those two children of hers is more than I know. She has a brother in British Columbia and she has written to him about them, but she hasn't heard from him yet."

"What are the children like? How old are they?"

"Six past . . . they're twins."

"Oh, I've always been especially interested in twins ever since

Mrs. Hammond had so many,'' said Anne eagerly. ''Are they pretty?''

''Goodness, you couldn't tell . . . they were too dirty. Davy had been out making mud pies and Dora went out to call him in. Davy pushed her headfirst into the biggest pie and then, because she cried, he got into it himself and wallowed in it to show her it was nothing to cry about. Mary said Dora was really a very good child but that Davy was full of mischief. He has never had any bringing up you might say. His father died when he was a baby and Mary has been sick almost ever since.''

''I'm always sorry for children that have had no bringing up,'' said Anne soberly. ''You know *I* hadn't any till you took me in hand. I hope their uncle will look after them. Just what relation is Mrs. Keith to you?''

''Mary? None in the world. It was her husband . . . he was our third cousin. There's Mrs. Lynde coming through the yard. I thought she'd be up to hear about Mary.''

''Don't tell her about Mr. Harrison and the cow,'' implored Anne.

Marilla promised; but the promise was quite unnecessary, for Mrs. Lynde was no sooner fairly seated than she said,

''I saw Mr. Harrison chasing your Jersey out of his oats today when I was coming home from Carmody. I thought he looked pretty mad. Did he make much of a rumpus?''

Anne and Marilla furtively exchanged amused smiles. Few things in Avonlea ever escaped Mrs. Lynde. It was only that morning Anne had said,

''If you went to your own room at midnight, locked the door, pulled down the blind, and *sneezed,* Mrs. Lynde would ask you the next day how your cold was!''

''I believe he did,'' admitted Marilla. ''I was away. He gave Anne a piece of his mind.''

''I think he is a very disagreeable man,'' said Anne, with a resentful toss of her ruddy head.

''You never said a truer word,'' said Mrs. Rachel solemnly. ''I knew there'd be trouble when Robert Bell sold his place to a New Brunswick man, that's what. I don't know what Avonlea is coming to, with so many strange people rushing into it. It'll soon not be safe to go to sleep in our beds.''

''Why, what other strangers are coming in?'' asked Marilla.

''Haven't you heard? Well, there's a family of Donnells, for one thing. They've rented Peter Sloane's old house. Peter has hired the man to run his mill. They belong down east and nobody knows anything about them. Then that shiftless Timothy Cotton family are going to move up form White Sands and they'll simply be a burden on the public. He is in consumption . . . when he isn't stealing . . . and his wife is a slack-twisted creature that can't turn her hand to a thing. She washes her dishes *sitting down*. Mrs. George Pye has taken her husband's orphan nephew, Anthony Pye. He'll be going to school to you, Anne, so you may expect trouble, that's what. And you'll have another strange pupil, too. Paul Irving is coming from the States to live with his grandmother. You remember his father, Marilla . . . Stephen Irving, him that jilted Lavendar Lewis over at Grafton?''

"I don't think he jilted her. There was a quarrel . . . I suppose there was blame on both sides.''

"Well, anyway, he didn't marry her, and she's been as queer as possible ever since, they say . . . living all by herself in that little stone house she calls Echo Lodge. Stephen went off to the States and went into business with his uncle and married a Yankee. He's never been home since, though his mother has been up to see him once or twice. His wife died two years ago and he's sending the boy home to his mother for a spell. He's ten years old and I don't know if he'll be a very desirable pupil. You can never tell about those Yankees.''

Mrs. Lynde looked upon all people who had the misfortune to be born or brought up elsewhere than in Prince Edward Island with a decided can-any-good-thing-come-out-of-Nazareth air. They *might* be good people of course; but you were on the safe side in doubting it. She had a special prejudice against "Yankees.'' Her husband had been cheated out of ten dollars by an employer for whom he had once worked in Boston and neither angels nor principalities nor powers could have convinced Mrs. Rachel that the whole United States was not responsible for it.

"Avonlea school won't be the worse for a little new blood,'' said Marilla drily, "and if this boy is anything like his father he'll be all right. Steve Irving was the nicest boy that was ever raised in these parts, though some people did call him proud. I should think Mrs. Irving would be very glad to have the child. She has been very lonesome since her husband died.''

"Oh, the boy may be well enough, but he'll be different from Avonlea children,'' said Mrs. Rachel, as if that clinched the matter. Mrs. Rachel's opinions concerning any person, place, or thing, were always warranted to wear. "What's this I hear about your going to start up a Village Improvement Society, Anne?''

"I was just talking it over with some of the girls and boys at the last Debating Club," said Anne, flushing. "They thought it would be rather nice . . . and so do Mr. and Mrs. Allan. Lots of villages have them now."

"Well, you'll get into no end of hot water if you do. Better leave it alone, Anne, that's what. People don't like being improved."

"Oh, we are not going to try to improve the *people*. It is Avonlea itself. There are lots of things which might be done to make it prettier. For instance, if we could coax Mr. Levi Boulter to pull down that dreadful old house on his upper farm wouldn't that be an improvement?''

"It certainly would," admitted Mrs. Rachel. "That old ruin has been an eyesore to the settlement for years. But if you Improvers can coax Levi Boulter to do anything for the public that he isn't to be paid for doing, may I be there to see and hear the process, that's what. I don't want to discourage you, Anne, for there may be something in your idea, though I suppose you did get it out of some rubbishy Yankee magazine; but you'll have your hands full with your school and I advise you as a friend not to bother with your improvements, that's what. But there, I know you'll go ahead with it if you've set your mind on it. You were always one to carry a thing through somehow."

Something about the firm outlines of Anne's lips told that Mrs. Rachel was not far astray in this estimate. Anne's heart was bent on forming the Improvement Society. Gilbert Blythe, who was to teach in White Sands but would always be home from Friday night to Monday morning, was enthusiastic about it; and most of the other young folks were willing to go in for anything that meant occasional meetings and consequently some "fun." As for what the "improvements" were to be, nobody had any very clear idea except Anne and Gilbert. They had talked them over and planned them out until an ideal Avonlea existed in their minds, if nowhere else.

Mrs. Rachel had still another item of news.

"They've given the Carmody school to a Priscilla Grant. Didn't you go to Queen's with a girl of that name, Anne?''

"Yes, indeed. Priscilla to teach at Carmody! How perfectly lovely!'' exclaimed Anne, her gray eyes lighting up until they looked like evening stars, causing Mrs. Lynde to wonder anew if she would ever get it settled to her satisfaction whether Anne Shirley were really a pretty girl or not.

CHAPTER 2

SELLING IN HASTE AND REPENTING AT LEISURE

ANNE DROVE over to Carmody on a shopping expedition the next afternoon and took Diana Barry with her. Diana was, of course, a pledged member of the Improvement Society, and the two girls talked about little else all the way to Carmody and back.

"The very first thing we ought to do when we get started is to have that hall painted," said Diana, as they drove past the Avonlea hall, a rather shabby building set down in a wooded hollow, with spruce trees hooding it about on all sides. "It's a disgraceful looking place and we must attend to it even before we try to get Mr. Levi Boulter to pull his house down. Father says we'll never succeed in doing *that* . . . Levi Boulter is too mean to spend the time it would take."

"Perhaps he'll let the boys take it down if they promise to haul the boards and split them up for him for kindling wood," said Anne hopefully. "We must do our best and be content to go slowly at first. We can't expect to improve everything all at once. We'll have to educate public sentiment first, of course."

Diana wasn't exactly sure what educating public sentiment meant; but it sounded fine and she felt rather proud that she was going to belong to a society with such an aim in view.

"I thought of something last night that we could do, Anne. You know that three-cornered piece of ground where the roads from Carmody and Newbridge and White Sands meet? It's all grown over with young spruce; but wouldn't it be nice to have them all cleared out, and just leave the two or three birch trees that are on it?"

"Splendid," agreed Anne gaily. "And have a rustic seat put under the birches. And when spring comes we'll have a flower-bed made in the middle of it and plant geraniums."

"Yes; only we'll have to devise some way of getting old Mrs. Hiram Sloane to keep her cow off the road, or she'll eat our geraniums up," laughed Diana. "I begin to see what you mean by educating public sentiment, Anne. There's the old Boulter house now. Did you ever see such a rookery? And perched right close to the road too. An old house with its windows gone always makes me think of something dead with its eyes picked out."

"I think an old, deserted house is such a sad sight," said Anne dreamily. "It always seems to me to be thinking about its past and mourning for its old-time joys. Marilla says that a large family was raised in that old house long ago, and that it was a real pretty place, with a lovely garden and roses climbing all over it. It was full of little children and laughter and songs; and now it is empty, and nothing ever wanders through it but the wind. How lonely and sorrowful it must feel! Perhaps they all come back on moonlit nights . . . the ghosts of the little children of long ago and the roses and the songs . . . and for a little while the old house can dream it is young and joyous again.''

Diana shook her head.

''I never imagine things like that about places now, Anne. Don't you remember how cross mother and Marilla were when we imagined ghosts into the Haunted Wood? To this day I can't go through that bush comfortably after dark and if I began imagining such things about the old Boulter house I'd be frightened to pass it too. Besides, those children aren't dead. They're all grown up and doing well . . . and one of them is a butcher. And flowers and songs couldn't have ghosts anyhow.''

Anne smothered a little sigh. She loved Diana dearly and they had always been good comrades. But she had long ago learned that when she wandered into the realm of fancy she must go alone. The way to it was by an enchanted path where not even her dearest might follow her.

A thunder-shower came up while the girls were at Carmody; it did not last long, however, and the drive home, through lanes where the raindrops sparkled on the boughs and little leafy valleys where the drenched ferns gave out spicy odors, was delightful. But just as they turned into the Cuthbert lane Anne saw something that spoiled the beauty of the landscape for her.

Before them on the right extended Mr. Harrison's broad, gray-green field of late oats, wet and luxuriant; and there, standing squarely in the middle of it, up to her sleek sides in the lush growth, and blinking at them calmly over the intervening tassels, was a Jersey cow!

Anne dropped the reins and stood up with a tightening of the lips that boded no good to the predatory quadruped. Not a word said she, but she climbed nimbly down over the wheels, and whisked across the fence before Diana understood what had happened.

''Anne, come back,'' shrieked the latter, as soon as she found her voice. ''You'll ruin your dress in that wet grain . . . ruin it. She doesn't hear me! Well, she'll never get that cow out by herself. I must go and help her, of course.''

Anne was charging through the grain like a mad thing. Diana hopped briskly down, tied the horse securely to a post, turned the skirt of her pretty gingham dress over her shoulders, mounted the fence, and started in pursuit of her frantic friend. She could run faster than Anne, who was hampered by her clinging and drenched skirt, and soon overtook her. Behind them they left a trail that would break Mr. Harrison's heart when he should see it.

''Anne, for mercy's sake, stop,'' panted poor Diana. ''I'm right out of breath and you are wet to the skin.''

''I must . . . get . . . that cow . . . out . . . before . . . Mr. Harrison . . . sees her,'' gasped Anne. ''I don't . . . care . . . if I'm . . . drowned . . . if we . . . can . . . only . . . do that.''

But the Jersey cow appeared to see no good reason for being hustled out of her luscious browsing ground. No sooner had the two breathless girls got near her than she turned and bolted squarely for the opposite corner of the field.

''Head her off,'' screamed Anne. ''Run, Diana, run.''

Diana did run. Anne tried to, and the wicked Jersey went around the field as if she were possessed. Privately, Diana thought she was. It was fully ten minutes before they headed her off and drove her through the corner gap into the Cuthbert lane.

There is no denying that Anne was in anything but an angelic temper at that precise moment. Nor did it soothe her in the least to behold a buggy halted just outside the lane, wherein sat Mr. Shearer of Carmody and his son, both of whom wore a broad smile.

''I guess you'd better have sold me that cow when I wanted to buy her last week, Anne,'' chuckled Mr. Shearer.

''I'll sell her to you now, if you want her,'' said her flushed and dishevelled owner. ''You may have her this very minute.''

''Done. I'll give you twenty for her as I offered before, and Jim can drive her right over to Carmody. She'll go to town with the rest of the shipment this evening. Mr. Reed of Brighton wants a Jersey cow.''

Five minutes later Jim Shearer and the Jersey cow were marching up the road, and impulsive Anne was driving along the Green Gables lane with her twenty dollars.

''What will Marilla say?'' asked Diana.

''Oh, she won't care. Dolly was my own cow and it isn't likely she'd bring more than twenty dollars at the auction. But oh dear, if Mr. Harrison sees that grain he will know she has been in again, and after my giving him my word of honor that I'd never let it happen! Well, it has taught me a lesson not to give my word of honor about cows. A cow that could jump over or break through our milk-pen fence couldn't be trusted anywhere.''

Marilla had gone down to Mrs. Lynde's, and when she returned knew all about Dolly's sale and transfer, for Mrs. Lynde had seen most of the transaction from her window and guessed the rest.

''I suppose it's just as well she's gone, though you *do* do things in a dreadful headlong fashion, Anne. I don't see how she got out of the pen, though. She must have broken some of the boards off.''

''I didn't think of looking,'' said Anne, ''but I'll go and see now. Martin has never come back yet. Perhaps some more of his aunts have died. I think it's something like Mr. Peter Sloane and the octogenarians. The other evening Mrs. Sloane was reading a newspaper and she said to Mr. Sloane, 'I see here that another octogenarian has just died. What *is* an octogenarian, Peter?' And Mr. Sloane said he didn't know, but they must be very sickly creatures, for you never heard tell of them but they were dying. That's the way with Martin's aunts.''

''Martin's just like all the rest of those French,'' said Marilla in disgust. ''You can't depend on them for a day.''

Marilla was looking over Anne's Carmody purchases when she heard a shrill shriek in the barnyard. A minute later Anne dashed into the kitchen, wringing her hands.

''Anne Shirley, what's the matter now?''

''Oh, Marilla, whatever shall I do? This is terrible. And it's all my fault. Oh, will I *ever* learn to stop and reflect a little before doing reckless things? Mrs. Lynde always told me I would do something dreadful some day, and now I've done it!''

''Anne, you are the most exasperating girl! *What* is it you've done?''

''Sold Mr. Harrison's Jersey cow . . . the one he bought from Mr. Bell . . . to Mr. Shearer! Dolly is out in the milking pen this very minute.''

''Anne Shirley, are you dreaming?''

''I only wish I were. There's no dream about it, though it's very like a nightmare. And Mr. Harrison's cow is in Charlottetown by this time. Oh, Marilla, I thought I'd finished getting into scrapes, and here

I am in the very worst one I ever was in in my life. What can I do?''

"Do? There's nothing to do, child, except to go and see Mr. Harrison about it. We can offer him our Jersey in exchange if he doesn't want to take the money. She is just as good as his.''

"I'm sure he'll be awfully cross and disagreeable about it, though,'' moaned Anne.

"I daresay he will. He seems to be an irritable sort of man. I'll go and explain to him if you like.''

"No, indeed, I'm not as mean as that,'' exclaimed Anne. "This is all my fault and I'm certainly not going to let you take my punishment. I'll go myself and I'll go at once. The sooner it's over the better, for it will be terribly humiliating.''

Poor Anne got her hat and her twenty dollars and was passing out when she happened to glance through the open pantry door. On the table reposed a nut cake which she had baked that morning . . . a particularly toothsome concoction iced with pink icing and adorned with walnuts. Anne had intended it for Friday evening, when the youth of Avonlea were to meet at Green Gables to organize the Improvement Society. But what were they compared to the justly offended Mr. Harrison? Anne thought that cake ought to soften the heart of any man, especially one who had to do his own cooking, and she promptly popped it into a box. She would take it to Mr. Harrison as a peace offering.

"That is, if he gives me a chance to say anything at all,'' she thought ruefully, as she climbed the lane fence and started on a short cut across the fields, golden in the light of the dreamy August evening. "I know now just how people feel who are being led to execution.''

CHAPTER 3

MR. HARRISON AT HOME

MR. HARRISON'S house was an old-fashioned, low eaved, white-washed structure, set against a thick spruce grove.

Mr. Harrison himself was sitting on his vine-shaded veranda, in his shirt sleeves, enjoying his evening pipe. When he realized who was coming up the path he sprang suddenly to his feet, bolted into the house, and shut the door. This was merely the uncomfortable result of his surprise, mingled with a good deal of shame over his outburst of temper the day before. But it nearly swept the remnant of her courage from Anne's heart.

"If he's so cross now what will he be when he hears what I've done," she reflected miserably, as she rapped at the door.

But Mr. Harrison opened it, smiling sheepishly, and invited her to enter in a tone quite mild and friendly, if somewhat nervous. He had laid aside his pipe and donned his coat; he offered Anne a very dusty chair very politely, and her reception would have passed off pleasantly enough if it had not been for that tell-tale of a parrot who was peering through the bars of his cage with wicked golden eyes. No sooner had Anne seated herself than Ginger exclaimed,

"Bless my soul, what's that red-headed snippet coming here for?"

It would be hard to say whose face was the redder, Mr. Harrison's or Anne's.

"Don't you mind that parrot," said Mr. Harrison, casting a furious glance at Ginger. "He's . . . he's always talking nonsense. I got him from my brother who was a sailor. Sailors don't always use the choicest language, and parrots are very imitative birds."

"So I should think," said poor Anne, the remembrance of her errand quelling her resentment. She couldn't afford to snub Mr. Harrison under the circumstances, that was certain. When you had just sold a man's Jersey cow offhand, without his knowledge or consent, you must not mind if his parrot repeated uncomplimentary things. Nevertheless, the "red-headed snippet" was not quite so meek as she might otherwise have been.

"I've come to confess something to you, Mr. Harrison," she said resolutely. "It's . . . it's about . . . that Jersey cow."

"Bless my soul," exclaimed Mr. Harrison nervously, "has she gone and broken into my oats again? Well, never mind . . . never mind if she has. It's no difference . . . none at all. I . . . I was too hasty yesterday, that's a fact. Never mind if she has."

"Oh, if it were only that," sighed Anne. "But it's ten times worse. I don't . . ."

"Bless my soul, do you mean to say she's got into my wheat?"

"No . . . no . . . not the wheat. But . . ."

"Then it's the cabbages! She's broken into my cabbages that I was raising for Exhibition, hey?"

"It's *not* the cabbages, Mr. Harrison. I'll tell you everything . . . that is what I came for—but please don't interrupt me. It makes me so nervous. Just let me tell my story and don't say anything till I get through—and then no doubt you'll say plenty," Anne concluded, but in thought only.

"I won't say another word," said Mr. Harrison, and he didn't. But Ginger was not bound by any contract of silence and kept ejaculating, "Red-headed snippet" at intervals until Anne felt quite wild.

"I shut my Jersey cow up in our pen yesterday. This morning I went to Carmody and when I came back I saw a Jersey cow in your oats. Diana and I chased her out and you can't imagine what a hard time we had. I was so dreadfully wet and tired and vexed—and Mr. Shearer came by that very minute and offered to buy the cow. I sold her to him on the spot for twenty dollars. It was wrong of me. I should have waited and consulted Marilla, of course. But I'm dreadfully given to doing things without thinking—everybody who knows me will tell you that. Mr. Shearer took the cow right away to ship her on the afternoon train."

"Red-headed snippet," quoth Ginger in a tone of profound contempt.

At this point Mr. Harrison arose and, with an expression that would have struck terror into any bird but a parrot, carried Ginger's cage into an adjoining room and shut the door. Ginger shrieked, swore, and otherwise conducted himself in keeping with his reputation, but finding himself left alone, relapsed into sulky silence.

"Excuse me and go on," said Mr. Harrison, sitting down again. "My brother the sailor never taught that bird any manners."

"I went home and after tea I went out to the milking pen. Mr. Harrison" . . . Anne leaned forward, clasping her hands with her old childish gesture, while her big gray eyes gazed imploringly into Mr. Harrison's embarrassed face . . . "I found my cow still shut up in the pen. It was *your* cow I had sold to Mr. Shearer."

"Bless my soul," exclaimed Mr. Harrison, in blank amazement at this unlooked-for conclusion. "What a *very* extraordinary thing!"

"Oh, it isn't in the least extraordinary that I should be getting myself and other people into scrapes," said Anne mournfully. "I'm noted for that. You might suppose I'd have grown out of it by this time . . . I'll be seventeen next March . . . but it seems that I haven't. Mr. Harrison, is it too much to hope that you'll forgive me? I'm afraid it's too late to get your cow back, but here is the money for her . . . or you can have mine in exchange if you'd rather. She's a very good cow. And I can't express how sorry I am for it all."

"Tut, tut," said Mr. Harrison briskly, "don't say another word about it, miss. It's of no consequence . . . no consequence whatever. Accidents will happen. I'm too hasty myself sometimes, miss . . . far too hasty. But I can't help speaking out just what I think and folks must take me as they find me. If that cow had been in my cabbages now . . . but never mind, she wasn't, so it's all right. I think I'd rather have your cow in exchange, since you want to be rid of her."

"Oh, thank you, Mr. Harrison. I'm so glad you are not vexed. I was afraid you would be."

"And I suppose you were scared to death to come here and tell me, after the fuss I made yesterday, hey? But you mustn't mind me. I'm a terrible outspoken old fellow, that's all . . . awful apt to tell the truth, no matter if it is a bit plain."

"So is Mrs. Lynde," said Anne, before she could prevent herself.

"Who? Mrs. Lynde? Don't you tell me I'm like that old gossip," said Mr. Harrison irritably. "I'm not . . . not a bit. What have you got in that box?"

"A cake," said Anne archly. In her relief at Mr. Harrison's unexpected amiability her spirits soared upward feather-light. "I brought it over for you . . . I thought perhaps you didn't have cake very often."

"I don't, that's a fact, and I'm mighty fond of it, too. I'm much obliged to you. It looks good on top. I hope it's good all the way through."

"It is," said Anne, gaily confident. "I have made cakes in my time that were *not,* as Mrs. Allan could tell you, but this one is all right. I made it for the Improvement Society, but I can make another for them."

"Well, I'll tell you what, miss, you must help me eat it. I'll put the kettle on and we'll have a cup of tea. How will that do?"

"Will you let me make the tea?" said Anne dubiously.

Mr. Harrison chuckled.

"I see you haven't much confidence in my ability to make tea. You're wrong . . . I can brew up as good a jorum of tea as ever you drank. But go ahead yourself. Fortunately it rained last Sunday, so there's plenty clean dishes."

Anne hopped briskly up and went to work. She washed the teapot in several waters before she put the tea to steep. Then she swept the stove and set the table, bringing the dishes out of the pantry. The state of that pantry horrified Anne, but she wisely said nothing. Mr. Harrison told her where to find the bread and butter and a can of peaches. Anne adorned the table with a bouquet from the garden and shut her eyes to the stains on the tablecloth. Soon the tea was ready and Anne found herself sitting opposite Mr. Harrison at his own table, pouring his tea for him, and chatting freely to him about her school and friends and plans. She could hardly believe the evidence of her senses.

Mr. Harrison had brought Ginger back, averring that the poor bird would be lonesome; and Anne, feeling that she could forgive everybody and everything, offered him a walnut. But Ginger's feeling had been grievously hurt and he rejected all overtures of friendship. He sat moodily on his perch and ruffled his feathers up until he looked like a mere ball of green and gold.

"Why do you call him Ginger?" asked Anne, who liked appropriate names and thought Ginger accorded not at all with such gorgeous plumage.

"My brother the sailor named him. Maybe it had some reference to his temper. I think a lot of that bird though . . . you'd be surprised if you knew how much. He has his faults of course. That bird has cost me a good deal one way and another. Some people object to his swearing habits but he can't be broken of them. I've tried . . . other people have tried. Some folks have prejudices against parrots. Silly, ain't it? I like them myself. Ginger's a lot of company to me. Nothing would induce me to give that bird up . . . nothing in the world, miss."

Mr. Harrison flung the last sentence at Anne as explosively as if he suspected her of some latent design of persuading him to give Ginger up. Anne, however, was beginning to like the queer, fussy, fidgety little man, and before the meal was over they were quite good friends. Mr. Harrison found out about the Improvement Society and was disposed to approve of it.

"That's right. Go ahead. There's lots of room for improvement in this settlement . . . and in the people too.''

"Oh, I don't know," flashed Anne. To herself, or to her particular cronies, she might admit that there were some small imperfections, easily removable, in Avonlea and its inhabitants. But to hear a practical outsider like Mr. Harrison saying it was an entirely different thing. "I think Avonlea is a lovely place; and the people in it are very nice, too.''

"I guess you've got a spice of temper," commented Mr. Harrison, surveying the flushed cheeks and indignant eyes opposite him. "It goes with hair like yours, I reckon. Avonlea is a pretty decent place or I wouldn't have located here; but I suppose even you will admit that it has *some* faults?''

"I like it all the better for them," said loyal Anne. "I don't like places or people either that haven't any faults. Mrs. Milton White says she never met a perfect person, but she's heard enough about one . . . her husband's first wife. Don't you think it must be very uncomfortable to be married to a man whose first wife was perfect?''

"It would be more uncomfortable to be married to the perfect wife," declared Mr. Harrison, with a sudden and inexplicable warmth.

When tea was over Anne insisted on washing the dishes, although Mr. Harrison assured her that there were enough in the house to do for weeks yet. She would dearly have loved to sweep the floor also, but no broom was visible and she did not like to ask where it was for fear there wasn't one at all.

"You might run across and talk to me once in a while," suggested Mr. Harrison when she was leaving. "'Tisn't far and folks ought to be neighborly. I'm kind of interested in that society of yours. Seems to me there'll be some fun in it. Who are you going to tackle first?''

"We are not going to meddle with *people* . . . it is only *places* we mean to improve," said Anne, in a dignified tone. She rather suspected that Mr. Harrison was making fun of the project.

When she had gone Mr. Harrison watched her from the window . . . a lithe, girlish shape, tripping light-heartedly across the fields in the sunset afterglow.

"I'm a crusty, lonesome, crabbed old chap," he said aloud, "but there's something about that little girl makes me feel young again . . . and it's such a pleasant sensation I'd like to have it repeated once in a while.''

"Red-headed snippet," croaked Ginger mockingly.

Mr. Harrison shook his fist at the parrot.

"You ornery bird," he muttered, "I almost wish I'd wrung your neck when my brother the sailor brought you home. Will you never be done getting me into trouble?"

Anne ran home blithely and recounted her adventures to Marilla, who had been not a little alarmed by her long absence and was on the point of starting out to look for her.

"It's a pretty good world, after all, isn't it, Marilla?" concluded Anne happily. "Mrs. Lynde was complaining the other day that it wasn't much of a world. She said whenever you looked forward to anything pleasant you were sure to be more or less disappointed . . . that nothing ever came up to your expectations. Well, perhaps that is true. But there is a good side to it too. The bad things don't always come up to your expectations either . . . they nearly always turn out ever so much better than you think. I looked forward to a dreadfully unpleasant experience when I went over to Mr. Harrison's tonight; and instead he was quite kind and I had almost a nice time. I think we're going to be real good friends if we make plenty of allowances for each other, and everything has turned out for the best. But all the same, Marilla, I shall certainly never again sell a cow before making sure to whom she belongs. And I do *not* like parrots!"

CHAPTER 4

DIFFERENT OPINIONS

ONE EVENING at sunset, Jane Andrews, Gilbert Blythe, and Anne Shirley were lingering by a fence in the shadow of gently swaying spruce boughs, where a wood cut known as the Birch Path joined the main road. Jane had been up to spend the afternoon with Anne, who walked part of the way home with her; at the fence they met Gilbert, and all three were now talking about the fateful morrow; for that morrow was the first of September and the schools would open. Jane would go to Newbridge and Gilbert to White Sands.

"You both have the advantage of me," sighed Anne. "You're going to teach children who don't know you, but I have to teach my own old schoolmates, and Mrs. Lynde says she's afraid they won't respect me as they would a stranger unless I'm very cross from the first. But I don't believe a teacher should be cross. Oh, it seems to me such a responsibility!''

"I guess we'll get on all right," said Jane comfortably. Jane was not troubled by any aspirations to be an influence for good. She meant to earn her salary fairly, please the trustees, and get her name on the School Inspector's roll of honor. Further ambitions Jane had none. "The main thing will be to keep order and a teacher has to be a little cross to do that. If my pupils won't do as I tell them I shall punish them."

"How?"

"Give them a good whipping, of course."

"Oh, Jane, you wouldn't," cried Anne, shocked. "Jane, you *couldn't!*"

"Indeed, I could and would, if they deserved it," said Jane decidedly.

"I could *never* whip a child," said Anne with equal decision. "I don't believe in it *at all*. Miss Stacy never whipped any of us and she had perfect order; and Mr. Phillips was always whipping and he had no order at all. No, if I can't get along without whipping I shall not try to teach school. There are better ways of managing. I shall try to win my pupils' affections and then they will *want* to do what I tell them."

"But suppose they don't?" said practical Jane.

"I wouldn't whip them anyhow. I'm sure it wouldn't do any good. Oh, don't whip your pupils, Jane dear, no matter what they do."

"What do you think about it, Gilbert?" demanded Jane. "Don't you think there are some children who really need a whipping now and then?"

"Don't you think it's a cruel, barbarous thing to whip a child . . . *any* child?" exclaimed Anne, her face flushing with earnestness.

"Well," said Gilbert slowly, torn between his real convictions and his wish to measure up to Anne's ideal, "there's something to be said on both sides. I don't belive in whipping children *much*. I think, as you say, Anne, that there are better ways of managing as a rule, and the corporal punishment should be a last resort. But on the other hand, as Jane says, I believe there is an occasional child who can't be influenced in any other way and who, in short, needs a whipping and would be improved by it. Corporal punishment as a last resort is to be my rule."

Gilbert, having tried to please both sides, succeeded, as is usual and eminently right, in pleasing neither. Jane tossed her head.

"I'll whip my pupils when they're naughty. It's the shortest and easiest way of convincing them."

Anne gave Gilbert a disappointed glance.

"I shall never whip a child," she repeated firmly. "I feel sure it isn't either right or necessary."

"Suppose a boy sauced you back when you told him to do something?" said Jane.

"I'd keep him in after school and talk kindly and firmly to him," said Anne. "There is some good in every person if you can find it. It is a teacher's duty to find and develop it. That is what our School Management professor at Queen's told us, you know. Do you suppose you could find any good in a child by whipping him? It's far more important to influence the children aright than it is even to teach them the three R's, Professor Rennie says."

"But the Inspector examines them in the three R's, mind you, and he won't give you a good report if they don't come up to his standard," protested Jane.

"I'd rather have my pupils love me and look back to me in after years as a real helper than be on the roll of honor," asserted Anne decidedly.

"Wouldn't you punish children at all, when they misbehaved?" asked Gilbert.

"Oh, yes, I suppose I shall have to, although I know I'll hate to do it. But you can keep them in at recess or stand them on the floor or give them lines to write."

"I suppose you won't punish the girls by making them sit with the boys?" said Jane slyly.

Gilbert and Anne looked at each other and smiled rather foolishly. Once upon a time, Anne had been made to sit with Gilbert for punishment and sad and bitter had been the consequences thereof.

"Well, time will tell which is the best way," said Jane philosophically as they parted.

Anne went back to Green Gables by way of the Birch Path, shadowy, rustling, fern-scented, through Violet Vale and past Willowmere, where dark and light kissed each other under the firs, and down through Lover's Lane . . . spots she and Diana had so named long ago. She walked slowly, enjoying the sweetness of wood and field and the starry summer twilight, and thinking soberly about the new duties she was to take up on the morrow. When she reached the yard at Green Gables Mrs. Lynde's loud, decided tones floated out through the open kitchen window.

"Mrs. Lynde has come to give me good advice about tomorrow," thought Anne with a grimace, "but I don't believe I'll go in. Her advice is much like pepper, I think . . . excellent in small quantities but rather scorching in her doses. I'll run over and have a chat with Mr. Harrison instead."

This was not the first time Anne had run over and chatted with Mr. Harrison since the notable affair of the Jersey cow. She had been there several evenings and Mr. Harrison and she were very good friends, although there were times and seasons when Anne found the outspokenness on which he prided himself rather trying. Ginger still continued to regard her with suspicion, and never failed to greet her sarcastically as "red-headed snippet." Mr. Harrison had tried vainly to break him of the habit by jumping excitedly up whenever he saw Anne coming and exclaiming,

"Bless my soul, here's that pretty little girl again," or something equally flattering. But Ginger saw through the scheme and scorned it. Anne was never to know how many compliments Mr. Harrison paid her behind her back. He certainly never paid her any to her face.

"Well, I suppose you've been back in the woods laying in a supply of switches for tomorrow?" was his greeting as Anne came up the veranda steps.

"No, indeed," said Anne indignantly. She was an excellent target for teasing because she always took things so seriously. "I shall never have a switch in my school, Mr. Harrison. Of course, I shall have to have a pointer, but I shall use it for pointing *only*."

"So you mean to strap them instead? Well, I don't know but you're right. A switch stings more at the time but the strap smarts longer, that's a fact."

"I shall not use anything of the sort. I'm not going to whip my pupils."

"Bless my soul," exclaimed Mr. Harrison in genuine astonishment, "how do you lay out to keep order then?"

"I shall govern by affection, Mr. Harrison."

"It won't do," said Mr. Harrison, "won't do at all, Anne. 'Spare the rod and spoil the child.' When I went to school the master whipped me regular every day because he said if I wasn't in mischief just then I was plotting it."

"Methods have changed since your schooldays, Mr. Harrison."

"But human nature hasn't. Mark my words, you'll never manage the young fry unless you keep a rod in a pickle for them. The thing is impossible."

"Well, I'm going to try my way first," said Anne, who had a fairly strong will of her own and was apt to cling very tenaciously to her theories.

"You're pretty stubborn, I reckon," was Mr. Harrison's way of putting it. "Well, well, we'll see. Some day when you get riled up . . . and people with hair like yours are desperate apt to get riled . . . you'll forget all your pretty little notions and give some of them a whaling. You're too young to be teaching anyhow . . . far too young and childish."

Altogether, Anne went to bed that night in a rather pessimistic mood. She slept poorly and was so pale and tragic at breakfast next morning that Marilla was alarmed and insisted on making her take a cup of scorching ginger tea. Anne sipped it patiently, although she could not imaging what good ginger tea would do. Had it been some magic brew, potent to confer age and experience, Anne would have swallowed a quart of it without flinching.

"Marilla, what if I fail!'

"You'll hardly fail completely in one day and there's many more days coming," said Marilla. "The trouble with you, Anne, is that you'll expect to teach those children everything and reform all their faults right off, and if you can't you'll think you've failed."

CHAPTER 5

A FULL-FLEDGED SCHOOLMA'AM

WHEN ANNE reached the school that morning . . . for the first time in her life she had traversed the Birch Path deaf and blind to its beauties . . . all was quiet and still. The preceding teacher had trained the children to be in their places at her arrival, and when Anne entered the schoolroom she was confronted by prim rows of "shining morning faces" and bright, inquisitive eyes. She hung up her hat and faced her pupils, hoping that she did not look as frightened and foolish as she felt and that they would not perceive how she was trembling.

She had sat up until nearly twelve the preceding night composing a speech she meant to make to her pupils upon opening the school. She had revised and improved it painstakingly, and then she had learned it off by heart. It was a very good speech and had some very fine ideas in it, especially about mutual help and earnest striving after knowledge. The only trouble was that she could not now remember a word of it.

After what seemed to her a year . . . about ten seconds in reality . . . she said faintly,

"Take your Testaments, please," and sank breathlessly into her chair under cover of the rustle and clatter of desk lids that followed. While the children read their verses Anne marshalled her shaky wits into order and looked over the array of little pilgrims to the Grown-up Land.

Most of them were, of course, quite well known to her. Her own classmates had passed out in the preceding year but the rest had all gone to school with her, excepting the primer class and ten newcomers to Avonlea. Anne secretly felt more interest in these ten than in those whose possibilities were already fairly well mapped out to her. To be sure, they might be just as commonplace as the rest; but on the other hand there *might* be a genius among them. It was a thrilling idea.

Sitting by himself at a corner desk was Anthony Pye. He had a dark, sullen little face, and was staring at Anne with a hostile expression in his black eyes. Anne instantly made up her mind that she would win that boy's affection and discomfit the Pyes utterly.

In the other corner another strange boy was sitting with Arty Sloane . . . a jolly looking little chap, with a snub nose, freckled face, and big, light blue eyes, fringed with whitish lashes . . . probably the Donnell boy; and if resemblance went for anything, his sister was sitting across the aisle with Mary Bell. Anne wondered what sort of mother the child had, to send her to school dressed as she was. She wore a faded pink silk dress, trimmed with a great deal of cotton lace, soiled white kid slippers, and silk stockings. Her sandy hair was tortured into innumerable kinky and unnatural curls, surmounted by a flamboyant bow of pink ribbon bigger than her head. Judging from her expression she was very well satisfied with herself.

A pale little thing, with smooth ripples of fine, silky, fawn-colored hair flowing over her shoulders, must, Anne thought, be Annetta Bell, whose parents had formerly lived in the Newbridge school district, but, by reason of hauling their house fifty yards north of its old site were now in Avonlea. Three pallid little girls crowded into one seat were certainly Cottons; and there was no doubt that the small beauty with the long brown curls and hazel eyes, who was casting coquettish looks at Jack Gillis over the edge of her Testament, was Prillie Rogerson, whose father had recently married a second wife and brought Prillie home from her grandmother's in Grafton. A tall, awkward girl in a back seat, who seemed to have too many feet and hands, Anne could not place at all, but later on discovered that her name was Barbara Shaw and that she had come to live with an Avonlea aunt. She was also able to find that if Barbara ever managed to walk down the aisle without falling over her own or somebody else's feet the Avonlea scholars wrote the unusual fact up on the porch wall to commemorate it.

But when Anne's eyes met those of the boy at the front desk facing her own, a queer little thrill went over her, as if she had found her genius. She knew this must be Paul Irving and that Mrs. Rachel Lynde had been right for once when she prophesied that he would be unlike the Avonlea children. More than that, Anne realized that he was unlike other children anywhere, and that there was a soul subtly akin to her own gazing at her out of the very dark blue eyes that were watching her so intently.

She knew Paul was ten but he looked no more than eight. He had the most beautiful little face she had ever seen in a child . . . features of exquisite delicacy and refinement, framed in a halo of chestnut curls. His mouth was delicious, being full without pouting, the crimson lips just softly touching and curving into finely finished little corners that narrowly escaped being dimpled. He had a sober, grave, meditative expression, as if his spirit was much older than his body; but when Anne smiled softly at him it vanished in a sudden answering smile, which seemed an illumination of his whole being, as if some lamp had suddenly kindled into flame inside of him, irradiating him from top to toe. Best of all, it was involuntary, born of no external effort or motive, but simply the outflashing of a hidden personality, rare and fine and sweet. With that quick interchange of smiles Anne and Paul were fast friends for ever before a word had passed between them.

The day went by like a dream. Anne could never clearly recall it afterwards. It almost seemed as if it were not she who was teaching but somebody else. She heard classes and worked sums and set copies mechanically. The children behaved quite well; only two cases of discipline occurred. Morley Andrews was caught driving a pair of trained crickets in the aisle. Anne stood Morley on the platform for an hour and . . . which Morley felt much more keenly . . . confiscated his crickets. She put them in a box and on the way from school set them free in Violet Vale; but Morley believed, then and ever afterwards, that she took them home and kept them for her own private amusement.

The other culprit was Anthony Pye, who poured the last drops of water from his slate bottle down the back of Aurelia Clay's neck. Anne kept Anthony in at recess and talked to him about what was expected of gentlemen, admonishing him that they never poured water down ladies' necks. She wanted all her boys to be gentlemen, she said. Her little lecture was quite kind and touching; but unfortunately, Anthony remained absolutely untouched. He listened to her in silence, with the same sullen expression, and whistled scornfully as he went out. Anne sighed; and then cheered herself up by remembering that winning a Pye's affections, like the building of Rome, wasn't the work of a day. In fact, it was doubtful whether some of the Pyes had any affections to win; but Anne hoped better things of Anthony, who looked as if he might be a rather nice boy if one ever got behind his sullenness.

When school was dismissed and the children had gone Anne dropped wearily into her chair. Her head ached and she felt woefully discouraged. There was no real reason for discouragement, since nothing very dreadful had occurred; but Anne was very tired and inclined to believe that she would never learn to like teaching. And how terrible it would be to be doing something you didn't like every day for . . . well, say forty years. Anne was of two minds whether to have her cry out then and there, or wait till she was safely in her own white room at home. Before she could decide there was a click of heels and a silken swish on the porch floor, and Anne found herself confronted by a lady whose appearance made her recall a recent criticism of Mr. Harrison's on an overdressed female he had seen in a Charlottetown store. "She looked like a head-on collision between a fashion plate and a nightmare."

The newcomer was gorgeously arrayed in a pale blue summer silk, puffed, frilled, and shirred wherever puff, frill, or shirring could possibly be placed. Her head was surmounted by a huge white chiffon hat, bedecked with three long but rather stringy ostrich feathers. A veil of pink chiffon, lavishly sprinkled with huge black dots, hung like a flounce from the hat brim to her shoulders and floated off in two airy streamers behind her. She wore all the jewelry that could be crowded on one small woman, and a very strong odor of perfume attended her.

"I am Mrs. Don*nell* . . . Mrs. H. B. Don*nell*," announced this vision, "and I have come in to see you about something Clarice Almira told me when she came home to dinner today. It annoyed me *excessively*."

"I'm sorry," faltered Anne, vainly trying to recollect any incident of the morning connected with the Donnell children.

"Clarice Almira told me that you pronounced our name *Don*nell. Now, Miss Shirley, the correct pronunciation of our name is Don*nell* . . . accent on the last syllable. I *hope* you'll remember this in future."

"I'll try to," gasped Anne, choking back a wild desire to laugh. "I know by experience that it's very unpleasant to have one's name *spelled* wrong and I suppose it must be even worse to have it pronounced wrong."

"Certainly it is. And Clarice Almira also informed me that you call my son Jacob."

"He told me his name was Jacob," protested Anne.

"I might have expected that," said Mrs. H. B. Don*nell*, in a tone which implied that gratitude in children was not to be looked for in this degenerate age. "That boy has such plebeian tastes, Miss Shirley. When he was born I wanted to call him St. Clair . . . it sounds *so* aristocratic, doesn't it? But his father insisted he should be called Jacob after his uncle. I yielded, because Uncle Jacob was a rich old bachelor. And what do you think, Miss Shirley? When our innocent boy was five years old Uncle Jacob actually went and got married and now he has three boys of his own. Did you ever hear of such ingratitude? The moment the invitation to the wedding . . . for he had the impertinence to send us an invitation, Miss Shirley . . . came to the house I said, 'No more Jacobs for me, thank you.' From that day I called my son St. Clair and St. Clair I am determined he shall be called. His father obstinately continues to call him Jacob, and the boy himself has a perfectly unaccountable preference for the vulgar name. But St. Clair he is and St. Clair he shall remain. You will kindly remember this, Miss Shirley, will you not? *Thank* you. I told Clarice Almira that I was sure it was only a misunderstanding and that a word would set it right. Don*nell* . . . accent on last syllable . . . and St. Clair . . . on *no* account Jacob. You'll remember? *Thank* you.''

When Mrs. H. B. Don*nell* had skimmed away Anne locked the school door and went home. At the foot of the hill she found Paul Irving by the Birch Path. He held out to her a cluster of the dainty little wild orchids which Avonlea children called ''rice lilies.''

''Please, teacher, I found these in Mr. Wright's field,'' he said shyly, ''and I came back to give them to you because I thought you were the kind of lady that would like them, and because . . . '' he lifted his big, beautiful eyes . . . ''I like you, teacher.''

''You darling,'' said Anne, taking the fragrant spikes. As if Paul's words had been a spell of magic, discouragement and weariness passed from her spirit, and hope upwelled in her heart like a dancing fountain. She went through the Birch Path light-footedly, attended by the sweetness of her orchids as by a benendiction.

''Well, how did you get along?'' Marilla wanted to know.

''Ask me that a month later and I may be able to tell you. I can't now . . . I don't know myself . . . I'm too near it. My thoughts feel as if they had been all stirred up until they were thick and muddy. The only thing I feel really sure of having accomplished today is that I taught Cliffie Wright that A is A. He never knew it before. Isn't it something to have started a soul along a path that may end in Shakespeare and Paradise Lost?''

Mrs. Lynde came up later on with more encouragement. That good lady had waylaid the schoolchildren at her gate and demanded of them how they liked their new teacher.

''And every one of them said they liked you splendid, Anne, except Anthony Pye. I must admit he didn't. He said you 'weren't any good, just like all girl teachers.' There's the Pye leaven for you. But never mind.''

''I'm not going to mind,'' said Anne quietly, ''and I'm going to make Anthony Pye like me yet. Patience and kindness will surely win him.''

''Well, you can never tell about a Pye,'' said Mrs. Rachel cautiously. ''They go by contraries, like dreams, often as not. As for that *Don*nell woman, she'll get no Don*nell*ing from me, I can assure you. The name is *Don*nell and always has been. The woman is crazy, that's what. She has a pug dog she calls Queenie and it has its meals at the table along with the family, eating off a china plate. I'd be afraid of a judgment if I was her. Thomas says Donnell himself is a sensible, hard-working man, but he hadn't much gumption when he picked out a wife, that's what.''

CHAPTER 6

ALL SORTS AND CONDITIONS OF MEN...
AND WOMEN

A SEPTEMBER day on Prince Edward Island hills; a crisp wind blowing up over the sand dunes from the sea; a long red road, winding through fields and woods, now looping itself about a corner of thick set spruces, now threading a plantation of young maples with great feathery sheets of ferns beneath them, now dipping down into a hollow where a brook flashed out of the woods and into them again, now basking in open sunshine between ribbons of golden rod and smoke-blue asters; air athrill with the pipings of myriads of crickets, those glad little pensioners of the summer hills; a plump brown pony ambling along the road; two girls behind him, full to the lips with the simple, priceless joy of youth and life.

"Oh, this is a day left over from Eden, isn't it, Diana?" . . . and Anne sighed for sheer happiness. "The air has magic in it. Look at the purple in the cup of that harvest valley, Diana. And oh, do smell the dying fir! It's coming up from that little sunny hollow where Mr. Eben Wright has been cutting fence poles. Bliss is it on such a day to be alive; but to smell dying fir is very heaven. That's two thirds Wordsworth and one third Anne Shirley. It doesn't seem possible that there should be dying fir in heaven, does it? And yet it doesn't seem to me that heaven would be quite perfect if you couldn't get a whiff of dead fir as you went through its woods. Perhaps we'll have the odor there without the death. Yes, I think that will be the way. That delicious aroma must be the souls of the firs . . . and of course it will be just souls in heaven.''

"Trees haven't souls," said practical Diana, "but the smell of dead fir is certainly lovely. I'm going to make a cushion and fill it with fir needles. You'd better make one too, Anne.''

''I think I shall . . . and use it for my naps. I'd be certain to dream I was a dryad or a wood-nymph then. But just this minute I'm well content to be Anne Shirley, Avonlea schoolma'am, driving over a road like this on such a sweet, friendly day.''

''It's a lovely day but we have anything but a lovely task before us,'' sighed Diana. ''Why on earth did you offer to canvass this road, Anne? Almost all the cranks in Avonlea live along it, and we'll probably be treated as if we were begging for ourselves. It's the very worst road of all.''

''That is why I chose it. Of course Gilbert and Fred would have taken this road if we had asked them. But you see, Diana, I feel myself responsible for the A.V.I.S., since I was the first to suggest it, and it seems to me that I ought to do the most disagreeable things. I'm sorry on your account; but you needn't say a word at the cranky places. I'll do all the talking . . . Mrs. Lynde would say I was well able to. Mrs. Lynde doesn't know whether to approve of our enterprise or not. She inclines to, when she remembers that Mr. and Mrs. Allan are in favor of it; but the fact that village improvement societies first originated in the States is a count against it. So she is halting between two opinions and only success will justify us in Mrs. Lynde's eyes. Priscilla is going to write a paper for our next Improvement meeting, and I expect it will be good, for her aunt is such a clever writer and no doubt it runs in the family. I shall never forget the thrill it gave me when I found out that Mrs. Charlotte E. Morgan was Priscilla's aunt. It seemed so wonderful that I was a friend of the girl whose aunt wrote 'Edgewood Days' and 'The Rosebud Garden.' ''

''Where does Mrs. Morgan live?''

''In Toronto. And Priscilla says she is coming to the Island for a visit next summer, and if it is possible Priscilla is going to arrange to have us meet her. That seems almost too good to be true—but it's something pleasant to imagine after you go to bed.''

The Avonlea Village Improvement Society was an organized fact. Gilbert Blythe was president, Fred Wright vice-president, Anne Shirley secretary, and Diana Barry treasurer. The ''Improvers,'' as they were promptly christened, were to meet once a fortnight at the homes of the members. It was admitted that they could not expect to affect many improvements so late in the season; but they meant to plan the next summer's campaign, collect and discuss ideas, write and read papers, and, as Anne said, educate public sentiment generally.

There was some disapproval, of course, and . . . which the Improvers felt much more keenly . . . a good deal of ridicule. Mr. Elisha Wright was reported to have said that a more appropriate name for the organization would be Courting Club. Mrs. Hiram Sloane declared she had heard the Improvers meant to plough up all the roadsides and set them out with geraniums. Mr. Levi Boulter warned his neighbors that the Improvers would insist that everybody pull down his house and rebuild it after plans approved by the society. Mr. James Spencer sent them word that he wished they would kindly shovel down the church hill. Eben Wright told Anne that he wished the Improvers could induce old Josiah Sloane to keep his whiskers trimmed. Mr. Lawrence Bell said he would whitewash his barns if nothing else would please them but he would *not* hang lace curtains in his cowstable windows. Mr. Major Spencer asked Clifton Sloane, an Improver who drove the milk to the Carmody cheese factory, if it was true that everybody would have to have his milk-stand hand-painted next summer and keep an embroidered centerpiece on it.

In spite of . . . or perhaps, human nature being what it is, because of . . . this, the Society went gamely to work at the only improvement they could hope to bring about that fall. At the second meeting, in the Barry parlor, Oliver Sloane moved that they start a subscription to re-shingle and paint the hall; Julia Bell seconded it, with an uneasy feeling that she was doing something not exactly ladylike. Gilbert put the motion, it was carried unanimously, and Anne gravely recorded it in her minutes. The next thing was to appoint a committee, and Gertie Pye, determined not to let Julia Bell carry off all the laurels, boldly moved that Miss Jane Andrews be chairman of said committee. This motion being also duly seconded and carried, Jane returned the compliment by appointing Gertie on the committee, along with Gilbert, Anne, Diana, and Fred Wright. The committee chose their routes in private conclave. Anne and Diana were told off for the Newbridge road, Gilbert and Fred for the White Sands road, and Jane and Gertie for the Carmody road.

"Because," explained Gilbert to Anne, as they walked home together through the Haunted Wood, "the Pyes all live along that road and they won't give a cent unless one of themselves canvasses them."

The next Saturday Anne and Diana started out. They drove to the end of the road and canvassed homeward, calling first on the "Andrews girls."

"If Catherine is alone we may get something," said Diana, "but if Eliza is there we won't."

Eliza was there . . . very much so . . . and looked even grimmer than usual. Miss Eliza was one of those people who give you the impression that life is indeed a vale of tears, and that a smile, never to speak of a laugh, is a waste of nervous energy truly reprehensible. The Andrews girls had been ''girls'' for fifty odd years and seemed likely to remain girls to the end of their earthly pilgrimage. Catherine, it was said, had not entirely given up hope, but Eliza, who was born a pessimist, had never had any. They lived in a little brown house built in a sunny corner scooped out of Mark Andrews' beech woods. Eliza complained that it was terrible hot in summer, but Catherine was wont to say it was lovely and warm in winter.

Eliza was sewing patchwork, not because it was needed but simply as a protest against the frivolous lace Catherine was crocheting. Eliza listened with a frown and Catherine with a smile, as the girls explained their errand. To be sure, whenever Catherine caught Eliza's eye she discarded the smile in guilty confusion; but it crept back the next moment.

''If I had money to waste,'' said Eliza grimly, ''I'd burn it up and have the fun of seeing a blaze maybe; but I wouldn't give it to that hall, not a cent. It's no benefit to the settlement . . . just a place for young folks to meet and carry on when they's better be home in their beds.''

''Oh, Eliza, young folks must have some amusement,'' protested Catherine.

''I don't see the necessity. We didn't gad about to halls and places when we were young, Catherine Andrews. This world is getting worse every day.''

''I think it's getting better,'' said Catherine firmly.

''You think!'' Miss Eliza's voice expressed the utmost contempt. ''It doesn't signify what you think, Catherine Andrews. Facts is facts.''

''Well, I always like to look on the bright side, Eliza.''

''There isn't any bright side.''

''Oh, indeed there is,'' cried Anne, who couldn't endure such heresy in silence. ''Why, there are ever so many bright sides, Miss Andrews. It's really a beautiful world.''

''You won't have such a high opinion of it when you've lived as long in it as I have,'' retorted Miss Eliza sourly, ''and you won't be so enthusiastic about improving it either. How is your mother, Diana? Dear me, but she has failed of late. She looks terrible run down. And how long is it before Marilla expects to be stone blind, Anne?''

''The doctor thinks her eyes will not get any worse if she is very careful,'' faltered Anne.

Eliza shook her head.

"Doctors always talk like that just to keep people cheered up. I wouldn't have much hope if I was her. It's best to be prepared for the worst."

"But oughtn't we to be prepared for the best too?" pleaded Anne. "It's just as likely to happen as the worst."

"Not in my experience, and I've fifty-seven years to set against your sixteen," retorted Eliza. "Going, are you? Well, I hope this new society of yours will be able to keep Avonlea from running any further down hill but I haven't much hope of it."

Anne and Diana got themselves thankfully out, and drove away as fast as the fat pony could go. As they rounded the curve below the beech wood a plump figure came speeding over Mr. Andrews' pasture, waving to them excitedly. It was Catherine Andrews and she was so out of breath that she could hardly speak, but she thrust a couple of quarters into Anne's hand.

"That's my contribution to painting the hall," she gasped. "I'd like to give you a dollar but I don't dare take more from my egg money for Eliza would find it out if I did. I'm real interested in your society and I believe you're going to do a lot of good. I'm an optimist. I *have* to be, living with Eliza. I must hurry back before she misses me . . . she thinks I'm feeding the hens. I hope you'll have good luck canvassing, and don't be cast down over what Eliza said. The world *is* getting better . . . it certainly is."

The next house was Daniel Blair's.

"Now, it all depends on whether his wife is home or not," said Diana, as they jolted along a deep-rutted lane. "If she is we won't get a cent. Everybody says Dan Blair doesn't dare have his hair cut without asking her permission; and it's certain she's very close, to state it moderately. She says she has to be just before she's generous. But Mrs. Lynde says she's so much 'before' that generosity never catches up with her at all."

Anne related their experience at the Blair place to Marilla that evening.

"We tied the horse and then rapped at the kitchen door. Nobody came but the door was open and we could hear somebody in the pantry, going on dreadfully. We couldn't make out the words but Diana says she knows they were swearing by the sound of them. I can't believe that of Mr. Blair, for he is always so quiet and meek; but at least he had great provocation, for Marilla, when that poor man came to the door, red as a beet, with perspiration streaming down his face, he had on one of his wife's big gingham aprons. 'I can't get this

durned thing off,' he said, 'for the strings are tied in a hard knot and I
can't bust 'em, so you'll have to excuse me, ladies.' We begged him
not to mention it and went in and sat down. Mr. Blair sat down too;
he twisted the apron around to his back and rolled it up, but he did
look so ashamed and worried that I felt sorry for him, and Diana said
she feared we had called at an inconvenient time. 'Oh, not at all,'
said Mr. Blair, trying to smile . . . you know he is always very
polite . . . 'I'm a little busy . . . getting ready to bake a cake as it
were. My wife got a telegram today that her sister from Montreal is
coming tonight and she's gone to the train to meet her and left orders
for me to make a cake for tea. She writ out the recipe and told me
what to do but I've clean forgot half the directions already. And it
says, "flavor according to taste." What does that mean? How can
you tell? And what if my taste doesn't happen to be other people's
taste? Would a tablespoon of vanilla be enough for a small layer
cake?'

"I felt sorrier than ever for the poor man. He didn't seem to be in
his proper sphere at all. I had heard of henpecked husbands and now I
felt that I saw one. It was on my lips to say, 'Mr. Blair, if you'll give
us a subscription for the hall I'll mix up your cake for you.' But I
suddenly thought it wouldn't be neighborly to drive too sharp a
bargain with a fellow creature in distress. So I offered to mix the cake
for him without any conditions at all. He just jumped at my offer. He
said he'd been used to making his own bread before he was married
but he feared cake was beyond him, and yet he hated to disappoint his
wife. He got me another apron, and Diana beat the eggs and I mixed
the cake. Mr. Blair ran about and got us the materials. He had
forgotten all about his apron and when he ran it streamed out
behind him and Diana said she thought she would die to see it.
He said he could bake the cake all right . . . he was used to
that . . . and then he asked for our list and put down four dollars. So
you see we were rewarded. But even if he hadn't given a cent I'd
always feel that we had done a truly Christian act in helping him."

Theodore White's was the next stopping place. Neither Anne nor
Diana had ever been there before, and they had only a very slight
acquaintance with Mrs. Theodore, who was not given to hospitality.
Should they go the back or front door? While they held a whispered
consultation Mrs. Theodore appeared at the front door with an
armful of newspapers. Deliberately she laid them down one by one
on the porch floor and the porch steps, and then down the path to the
very feet of her mystified callers.

"Will you please wipe your feet carefully on the grass and then walk on these papers?" she said anxiously. "I've just swept the house all over and I can't have any more dust tracked in. The path's been real muddy since the rain yesterday."

"Don't you dare laugh," warned Anne in a whisper, as they marched along the newspapers. "And I implore you, Diana, not to look at me, no matter what she says, or I shall not be able to keep a sober face."

The papers extended across the hall and into a prim, fleckless parlor. Anne and Diana sat down gingerly on the nearest chairs and explained their errand. Mrs. White heard them politely, interrupting only twice, once to chase out an adventurous fly, and once to pick up a tiny wisp of grass that had fallen on the carpet from Anne's dress. Anne felt wretchedly guilty; but Mrs. White subscribed two dollars and paid the money down . . . "to prevent us from having to go back for it," Diana said when they got away. Mrs. White had the newspapers gathered up before they had their horse untied and as they drove out of the yard they saw her busily wielding a broom in the hall.

"I've always heard that Mrs. Theodore White was the neatest woman alive and I'll believe it after this," said Diana, giving way to her suppressed laughter as soon as it was safe.

"I'm glad she has no children," said Anne solemnly. "It would be dreadful beyond words for them if she had."

At the Spencers' Mrs. Isabella Spencer make them miserable by saying something ill-natured about everyone in Aveonlea. Mr. Thomas Boulter refused to give anything because the hall, when it had been built, twenty years before, hadn't been built on the site he recommended. Mrs. Esther Bell, who was the picture of health, took half an hour to detail all her aches and pains, and sadly put down fifty cents because she wouldn't be there that time next year to do it . . . no, she would be in her grave.

Their worst reception, however, was at Simon Fletcher's. When they drove into the yard they saw two faces peering at them through the porch window. But although they rapped and waited patiently and persistently nobody came to the door. Two decidedly ruffled and indignant girls drove away from Simon Fletcher's. Even Anne admitted that she was beginning to feel discouraged. But the tide turned after that. Several Sloane homesteads came next, where they got liberal subscriptions, and from that to the end they fared well, with only an occasional snub. Their last place of call was at Robert

Dickson's by the pond bridge. They stayed to tea here, although they were nearly home, rather than risk offending Mrs. Dickson, who had the reputation of being a very "touchy" woman.

While they were there old Mrs. James White called in.

"I've just been down to Lorenzo's," she announced. "He's the proudest man in Avonlea this minute. What do you think? There's a brand new boy there . . . and after seven girls that's quite an event, I can tell you."

Anne pricked up her ears, and when they drove away she said,

"I'm going straight to Lorenzo White's."

"But he lives on the White Sands road and it's quite a distance out of our way," protested Diana. "Gilbert and Fred will canvass him."

"They are not going around until next Saturday and it will be too late by then," said Anne firmly. "The novelty will be worn off. Lorenzo White is dreadfully mean but he will subscribe to *anything* just now. We mustn't let such a golden opportunity slip, Diana."

The result justified Anne's foresight. Mr. White met them in the yard, beaming like the sun upon an Easter day. When Anne asked for a subscription he agreed enthusiastically.

"Certain, certain. Just put me down for a dollar more than the highest subscription you've got."

"That will be five dollars . . . Mr. Daniel Blair put down four," said Anne, half afraid. But Lorenzo did not flinch.

"Five it is . . . and here's the money on the spot. Now, I want you to come into the house. There's something in there worth seeing . . . something very few people have seen as yet. Just come in and pass *your* opinion."

"What will we say if the baby isn't pretty?" whispered Diana in trepidation as they followed the excited Lorenzo into the house.

"Oh, there will certainly be something else nice to say about it," said Anne easily. "There always is about a baby."

The baby *was* pretty, however, and Mr. White felt that he got his five dollars' worth out of the girls' honest delight over the plump little newcomer. But that was the first, last, and only time that Lorenzo White ever subscribed to anything.

Anne, tired as she was, made one more effort for the public weal that night, slipping over the field to interview Mr. Harrison, who was as usual smoking his pipe on the veranda with Ginger beside him. Strictly speaking he was on the Carmody road; but Jane and Gertie, who were not acquainted with him save by doubtful report, had nervously begged Anne to canvass him.

Mr. Harrison, however, flatly refused to subscribe a cent, and all Anne's wiles were in vain.

"But I thought you approved of our society, Mr. Harrison," she mourned.

"So I do . . . so I do . . . but my approval doesn't go as deep as my pocket, Anne."

"A few more experiences such as I have had today would make me as much of a pessimist as Miss Eliza Andrews," Anne told her reflection in the east gable mirror at bedtime.

CHAPTER 7

THE POINTING OF DUTY

ANNE LEANED back in her chair one mild October evening and sighed. She was sitting at a table covered with text books and exercises, but the closely written sheets of paper before her had no apparent connection with studies or school work.

"What is the matter?" asked Gilbert, who had arrived at the open kitchen door just in time to hear the sigh.

Anne colored, and thrust her writing out of sight under some school compositions.

"Nothing very dreadful. I was just trying to write out some of my thoughts, as Professor Hamilton advised me, but I couldn't get them to please me. They seem so stiff and foolish directly they're written down on white paper with black ink. Fancies are like shadows . . . you can't cage them, they're such wayward, dancing things. But perhaps I'll learn the secret some day if I keep trying. I haven't a great many spare moments, you know. By the time I finish correcting school exercises and compositions, I don't always feel like writing any of my own."

"You are getting on splendidly in school, Anne. All the children like you," said Gilbert, sitting down on the stone step.

"No, not all. Anthony Pye doesn't and *won't* like me. What is worse, he doesn't respect me . . . no, he doesn't. He simply holds me in contempt and I don't mind confessing to you that it worries me miserably. It isn't that he is so very bad . . . he is only rather mischievous, but no worse than some of the others. He seldom disobeys me; but he obeys with a scornful air of toleration as if it wasn't worth while disputing the point or he would . . . and it has a bad effect on the others. I've tried every way to win him but I'm beginning to fear I never shall. I want to, for he's rather a cute little lad, if he *is* a Pye, and I could like him if he'd let me.''

''Probably it's merely the effect of what he hears at home.''

''Not altogether. Anthony is an independent little chap and makes up his own mind about things. He has always gone to men before and he says girl teachers are no good. Well, we'll see what patience and kindness will do. I like overcoming difficulties and teaching is really very interesting work. Paul Irving makes up for all that is lacking in the others. That child is a perfect darling, Gilbert, and a genius into the bargain. I'm persuaded the world will hear of him some day,'' concluded Anne in a tone of conviction.

''I like teaching, too,'' said Gilbert. ''It's good training, for one thing. Why, Anne, I've learned more in the weeks I've been teaching the young ideas of White Sands than I learned in all the years I went to school myself. We all seem to be getting on pretty well. The Newbridge people like Jane, I hear; and I think White Sands is tolerably satisfied with your humble servant . . . all except Mr. Andrew Spencer. I met Mrs. Peter Blewett on my way home last night and she told me she thought it her duty to inform me that Mr. Spencer didn't approve of my methods.''

''Have you ever noticed,'' asked Anne reflectively, ''that when people say it is their duty to tell you a certain thing you may prepare for something disagreeable? Why is it that they never seem to think it a duty to tell you the pleasant things they hear about you? Mrs. H. B. Don*nell* called at the school again yesterday and told me she thought it *her* duty to inform that Mrs. Harmon Andrews didn't approve of my reading fairy tales to the children, and that Mr. Rogerson thought Prillie wasn't coming on fast enough in arithmetic. If Prillie would spend less time making eyes at the boys over her slate she might do better. I feel quite sure that Jack Gillis works her class sums for her, though I've never been able to catch him red-handed.''

''Have you succeeded in reconciling Mrs. Don*nell's* hopeful son to his saintly name?''

''Yes,'' laughed Anne, ''but it was really a difficult task. At first, when I called him 'St. Clair' he would not take the least notice until

I'd spoken two or three times; and then, when the other boys nudged him, he would look up with such an aggrieved air, as if I'd called him John or Charlie and he couldn't be expected to know I meant him. So I kept him in after school one night and talked kindly to him. I told him his mother wished me to call him St. Clair and I couldn't go against her wishes. He saw it when it was all explained out . . . he's really a very reasonable little fellow . . . and he said *I* could call him St. Clair but that he'd 'lick the stuffing' out of any of the boys that tried it. Of course, I had to rebuke him again for using such shocking language. Since then *I* call him St. Clair and the boys call him Jake and all goes smoothly. He informs me that he means to be a carpenter, but Mrs. Don*nell* says I am to make a college professor out of him."

The mention of college gave a new direction to Gilbert's thoughts, and they talked for a time of their plans and wishes . . . gravely, earnestly, hopefully, as youth loves to talk, while the future is yet an untrodden path full of wonderful possibilities.

Gilbert had finally made up his mind that he was going to be a doctor.

"It's a splendid profession," he said enthusiastically. "A fellow has to fight something all through life . . . didn't somebody once define man as a fighting animal? . . . and I want to fight disease and pain and ignorance . . . which are all members one of another. I want to do my share of honest, real work in the world, Anne . . . add a little to the sum of human knowledge that all the good men have been accumulating since it began. The folks who lived before me have done so much for me that I want to show my gratitude by doing something for the folks who will live after me. It seems to me that is the only way a fellow can get square with his obligations to the race."

"I'd like to add some beauty to life," said Anne dreamily. "I don't exactly want to make people *know* more . . . though I know that *is* the noblest ambition . . . but I'd love to make them have a pleasanter time because of me . . . to have some little joy or happy thought that would never have existed if I hadn't been born."

"I think you're fulfilling that ambition every day," said Gilbert admiringly.

And he was right. Anne was one of the children of light by birthright. After she had passed through a life with a smile or word thrown across it like a gleam of sunshine the owner of that life saw it, for the time being at least, as hopeful and lovely and of good report.

Finally Gilbert rose regretfully.

"Well, I must run up to MacPhersons'. Moody Spurgeon came home from Queen's today for Sunday and he was to bring me out a book Professor Boyd is lending me."

"And I must get Marilla's tea. She went to see Mrs. Keith this evening and she will soon be back."

Anne had tea ready when Marilla came home; the fire was cracking cheerily, a vase of frost-bleached ferns and ruby-red maple leaves adorned the table, and delectable odors of ham and toast pervaded the air. But Marilla sank into her chair with a deep sigh.

"Are your eyes troubling you? Does your head ache?" queried Anne anxiously.

"No. I'm only tired . . . and worried. It's about Mary and those children. Mary is worse . . . she can't last much longer. And as for the twins, *I* don't know what is to become of them."

"Hasn't their uncle been heard from?"

"Yes, Mary had a letter from him. He's working in a lumber camp and 'shacking it,' whatever that means. Anyway, he says he can't possibly take the children till the spring. He expects to be married then and will have a home to take them to; but he says she must get some of the neighbors to keep them for the winter. She says she can't bear to ask any of them. Mary never got on any too well with the East Grafton people and that's a fact. And the long and short of it is, Anne, that I'm sure Mary wants me to take those children . . . she didn't say so but she *looked* it."

"Oh!" Anne clasped her hands, all athrill with excitement. "And of course you will, Marilla, won't you?"

"I haven't made up my mind," said Marilla rather tartly. "I don't rush into things in your headlong way, Anne. Third cousinship is a pretty slim claim. And it will be a fearful responsibility to have two children of six years to look after . . . twins, at that."

Marilla had an idea that twins were just twice as bad as single children.

"Twins are very interesting . . . at least one pair of them," said Anne. "It's only when there are two or three pairs that it gets monotonous. And I think it would be real nice for you to have something to amuse you when I'm away in school."

"I don't reckon there'd be much amusement in it . . . more worry and bother than anything else, I should say. It wouldn't be so risky if they were even as old as you were when I took you. I wouldn't mind Dora so much . . . she seems good and quiet. But that Davy is a limb."

Anne was fond of children and her heart yearned over the Keith twins. The remembrance of her own neglected childhood was very vivid with her still. She knew that Marilla's only vulnerable point was her stern devotion to what she believed to be her duty, and Anne skilfully marshalled her arguments along this line.

"If Davy is naughty it's all the more reason why he should have good training, isn't it, Marilla? If we don't take them we don't know who will, nor what kind of influences may surround them. Suppose Mrs. Keith's next door neighbors, the Sprotts, were to take them. Mrs. Lynde says Henry Sprott is the most profane man that ever lived and you can't believe a word his children say. Wouldn't it be dreadful to have the twins learn anything like that? Or suppose they went to the Wiggins'. Mrs. Lynde says that Mr. Wiggins sells everything off the place that can be sold and brings his family up on skim milk. You wouldn't like our relations to be starved, even if they were only third cousins, would you? It seems to me, Marilla, that it is our duty to take them."

"I suppose it is," assented Marilla gloomily. "I daresay I'll tell Mary I'll take them. You needn't look so delighted, Anne. It will mean a good deal of extra work for you. I can't sew a stitch on account of my eyes, so you'll have to see to the making and mending of their clothes. And you don't like sewing."

"I hate it," said Anne calmly, "but if you are willing to take those children from a sense of duty surely I can do their sewing from a sense of duty. It does people good to have to do things they don't like . . . in moderation."

CHAPTER 8

MARILLA ADOPTS TWINS

MRS. RACHEL LYNDE was siting at her kitchen window, knitting a quilt, just as she had been sitting one evening several years previously when Matthew Cuthbert had driven down over the hill with what Mrs. Rachel called "his imported orphan." But that had been in springtime; and this was late autumn, and all the woods were

leafless and the fields sere and brown. The sun was just setting with a
great deal of purple and golden pomp behind the dark woods west of
Avonlea when a buggy drawn by a comfortable brown nag came
down the hill. Mrs. Rachel peered at it eagerly.

"There's Marilla getting home from the funeral," she said to her
husband, who was lying on the kitchen lounge. Thomas Lynde lay
more on the lounge nowadays than he had been used to do, but Mrs.
Rachel, who was so sharp at noticing anything beyond her own
household, had not as yet noticed this. "And she's got the twins with
her, . . . yes, there's Davy leaning over the dashboard grabbing at
the pony's tail and Marilla jerking him back. Dora's sitting up on the
seat as prim as you please. She always looks as if she'd just been
starched and ironed. Well, poor Marilla is going to have her hands
full this winter and no mistake. Still, I don't see that she could do
anything less than take them, under the circumstances, and she'll
have Anne to help her. Anne's tickled to death over the whole
business, and she has a real knacky way with children, I must say.
Dear me, it doesn't seem a day since poor Matthew brought Anne
herself home and everybody laughed at the idea of Marilla bringing
up a child. And now she has adopted twins. You're never safe from
being surprised till you're dead."

The fat pony jogged over the bridge in Lynde's Hollow and along
the Green Gables lane. Marilla's face was rather grim. It was ten
miles from East Grafton and Davy Keith seemed to be possessed
with a passion for perpetual motion. It was beyond Marilla's power
to make him sit still and she had been in an agony the whole way lest he
fall over the back of the wagon and break his neck, or tumble over the
dashboard under the pony's heels. In despair she finally threatened to
whip him soundly when she got him home. Whereupon Davy
climbed into her lap, regardless of the reins, flung his chubby arms
about her neck and gave her a bear-like hug.

"I don't believe you mean it," he said, smacking her wrinkled
cheek affectionately. "You don't *look* like a lady who'd whip a little
boy just 'cause he couldn't keep still. Didn't you find it awful hard to
keep still when you was only's old as me?"

"No, I always kept still when I was told," said Marilla, tying to
speak sternly, albeit she felt her heart waxing soft within her under
Davy's impulsive caresses.

"Well, I s'pose that was 'cause you was a girl," said Davy,
squirming back to his place after another hug. "You *was* a girl once,
I s'pose, though it's awful funny to think of it. Dora can sit still . . .
but there ain't much fun in it *I* don't think. Seems to me it must be

slow to be a girl. Here, Dora, let me liven you up a bit.''

Davy's method of ''livening up'' was to grasp Dora's curls in his fingers and give them a tug. Dora shrieked and then cried.

''How can you be such a naughty boy and your poor mother just laid in her grave this very day?'' demanded Marilla despairingly.

''But she was glad to die,'' said Davy confidentially. ''I know, 'cause she told me so. She was awful tired of being sick. We'd a long talk the night before she died. She told me you was going to take me and Dora for the winter and I was to be a good boy. I'm going to be good, but can't you be good running round just as well as sitting still? And she said I was always to be kind to Dora and stand up for her, and I'm going to.''

''Do you call pulling her hair being kind to her?''

''Well, I ain't going to let anybody else pull it,'' said Davy, doubling up his fists and frowning. ''They'd just better try it. I didn't hurt her much . . . she just cried 'cause she's a girl. I'm glad I'm a boy but I'm sorry I'm a twin. When Jimmy Sprott's sister conterdicks him he just says, 'I'm oldern you, so of course I know better,' and that settles *her*. But I can't tell Dora that, and she just goes on thinking diffrunt from me. You might let me drive the gee-gee for a spell, since I'm a man.''

Altogether, Marilla was a thankful woman when she drove into her own yard, where the wind of the autumn night was dancing with the brown leaves. Anne was at the gate to meet them and lift the twins out. Dora submitted calmly to be kissed, but Davy responded to Anne's welcome with one of his hearty hugs and the cheerful announcement, ''I'm Mr. Davy Keith.''

At the supper table Dora behaved like a little lady, but Davy's manners left much to be desired.

''I'm so hungry I ain't got time to eat p'litely,'' he said when Marilla reproved him. ''Dora ain't half as hungry as I am. Look at all the ex'cise I took on the road here. That cake's awful nice and plummy. We haven't had any cake at home for ever'n ever so long, 'cause mother was too sick to make it and Mrs. Sprott said it was as much as she could do to bake our bread for us. And Mrs. Wiggins never puts any plums in *her* cakes. Catch her! Can I have another piece?''

Marilla would have refused but Anne cut a generous second slice. However, she reminded Davy that he ought to say ''Thank you'' for it. Davy merely grinned at her and took a huge bite. When he had finished the slice he said,

''If you'll give me *another* piece I'll say thank you for *it*.''

"No, you have had plenty of cake," said Marilla in a tone which Anne knew and Davy was to learn to be final.

Davy winked at Anne, and then, leaning over the table, snatched Dora's first piece of cake, from which she had just taken one dainty little bite, out of her very fingers and, opening his mouth to the fullest extent, crammed the whole slice in. Dora's lip trembled and Marilla was speechless with horror. Anne promptly exclaimed, with her best "schoolma'am" air,

"Oh, Davy, gentlemen don't do things like that."

"I know they don't," said Davy, as soon as he could speak, "but I ain't a gemplum."

"But don't you want to be?" said shocked Anne.

"Course I do. But you can't be a gemplum till you grow up."

"Oh, indeed you can," Anne hastened to say, thinking she saw a chance to sow good seed betimes. "You can begin to be a gentleman when you are a little boy. And gentlemen *never* snatch things from ladies . . . or forget to say thank you . . . or pull anybody's hair."

"They don't have much fun, that's a fact," said Davy frankly. "I guess I'll wait till I'm grown up to be one."

Marilla, with a resigned air, had cut another piece of cake for Dora. She did not feel able to cope with Davy just then. It had been a hard day for her, what with the funeral and the long drive. At that moment she looked forward to the future with a pessimism that would have done credit to Eliza Andrews herself.

The twins were not noticeably alike, although both were fair. Dora had long sleek curls that never got out of order. Davy had a crop of fuzzy little yellow ringlets all over his round head. Dora's hazel eyes were gentle and mild; Davy's were as rouguish and dancing as an elf's. Dora's nose was straight, Davy's was a positive snub; Dora had a "prunes and prisms" mouth, Davy's was all smiles; and besides, he had a dimple in one cheek and none in the other, which gave him a dear, comical, lop-sided look when he laughed. Mirth and mischief lurked in every corner of his little face.

"They'd better go to bed," said Marilla, who thought it was the easiest way to dispose of them. "Dora will sleep with me and you can put Davy in the west gable. You're not afraid to sleep alone, are you, Davy?"

"No, but I ain't going to bed for ever so long yet," said Davy comfortably.

"Oh, yes, you are." That was all the much-tried Marilla said, but something in her tone squelched even Davy. He trotted obediently upstairs with Anne.

"When I'm grown up the very first thing I'm going to do is stay up *all* night just to see what it would be like," he told her confidentially.

In after years Marilla never thought of that first week of the twins' sojourn at Green Gables without a shiver. Not that it really was so much worse than the weeks that followed it; but it seemed so by reason of its novelty. There was seldom a waking minute of any day when Davy was not in mischief or devising it; but his first notable exploit occurred two days after his arrival, on Sunday morning . . . a fine, warm day, as hazy and mild as September. Anne dressed him for church while Marilla attended to Dora. Davy at first objected strongly to having his face washed.

"Marilla washed it yesterday . . . and Mrs. Wiggins scoured me with hard soap the day of the funeral. That's enough for one week. I don't see the good of being so awful clean. It's lots more comfable being dirty."

"Paul Irving washes his face every day of his own accord," said Anne astutely.

Davy had been an inmate of Green Gables for little over forty-eight hours; but he already worshipped Anne and hated Paul Irving, whom he had heard Anne praising enthusiastically the day after his arrival. If Paul Irving washed his face every day, that settled it. He, Davy Keith, would do it too, if it killed him. The same consideration induced him to submit meekly to the other details of his toilet, and he was really a handsome little lad when all was done. Anne felt an almost maternal pride in him as she led him into the old Cuthbert pew.

Davy behaved quite well at first, being occupied in casting covert glances at all the small boys within view and wondering which was Paul Irving. The first two hymns and the Scripture reading passed off uneventfully. Mr. Allan was praying when the sensation came.

Lauretta White was sitting in front of Davy, her head slightly bent and her fair hair hanging in two long braids, between which a tempting expanse of white neck showed, encased in a loose lace frill. Lauretta was a fat, placid-looking child of eight, who had conducted herself irreproachably in church from the very first day her mother carried her there, an infant of six months.

Davy thrust his hand into his pocket and produced . . . a caterpillar, a furry, squirming caterpillar. Marilla saw and clutched at him but she was too late. Davy dropped the caterpillar down Lauretta's neck.

Right into the middle of Mr. Allan's prayer burst a series of piercing shrieks. The minister stopped appalled and opened his eyes. Every head in the congregation flew up. Lauretta White was dancing up and down in her pew, clutching frantically at the back of her dress.

"Ow . . . mommer . . . mommer . . . ow . . . take it off . . . ow . . . get it out . . . ow . . . that bad boy put it down my neck . . . ow . . . mommer . . . it's going further down . . . ow . . . ow . . ."

Mrs. White rose and with a set face carried the hysterical, writhing Lauretta out of church. Her shrieks died away in the distance and Mr. Allan proceeded with the service. But everybody felt it was a failure that day. For the first time in her life Marilla took no notice of the text and Anne sat with scarlet cheeks of mortification.

When they got home Marilla put Davy to bed and made him stay there for the rest of the day. She would not give him any dinner but allowed him a plain tea of bread and milk. Anne carried it to him and sat sorrowfully by him while he ate it with an unrepentant relish. But Anne's mournful eyes troubled him.

"I s'pose," he said reflectively, "that Paul Irving wouldn't have dropped a caterpillar down a girl's neck in church, would he?"

"Indeed he wouldn't," said Anne sadly.

"Well, I'm kind of sorry I did it, then," conceded Davy. "But it was such a jolly big caterpillar . . . I picked him up on the church steps just as we went in. It seemed a pity to waste him. And say, wasn't it fun to hear that girl yell?"

Tuesday afternoon the Aid Society met at Green Gables. Anne hurried home from school, for she knew that Marilla would need all the assistance she could give. Dora, neat and proper, in her nicely starched white dress and black sash, was sitting with the members of the Aid in the parlor speaking demurely when spoken to, keeping silence when not, and in every way comporting herself as a model child. Davy, blissfully dirty, was making mud pies in the barnyard.

"I told him he might," said Marilla wearily. "I thought it would keep him out of worse mischief. He can only get dirty at that. We'll have our teas over before we call him to his. Dora can have hers with us, but I would never dare to let Davy sit down at the table with all the Aids here."

When Anne went to call the Aids to tea she found that Dora was not in the parlor. Mrs. Jasper Bell said Davy had come to the front door and called her out. A hasty consultation with Marilla in the pantry resulted in a decision to let both children have their teas together later on.

Tea was half over when the dining room was invaded by a forlorn figure. Marilla and Anne stared in dismay, the Aids in amazement.

Could that be Dora . . . that sobbing nondescript in a drenched, dripping dress and hair from which the water was streaming on Marilla's new coin-spot rug?

"Dora, what has happened to you?" cried Anne, with a guilty glance at Mrs. Jasper Bell, whose family was said to be the only one in the world in which accidents never occurred.

"Davy made me walk the pigpen fence," wailed Dora. "I didn't want to but he called me a fraid-cat. And I fell off into the pigpen and my dress got all dirty and the pig runned right over me. My dress was just awful but Davy said if I'd stand under the pump he'd wash it clean, and I did and he pumped water all over me but my dress ain't a bit cleaner and my pretty sash and shoes is all spoiled."

Anne did the honors of the table alone for the rest of the meal while Marilla went upstairs and redressed Dora in her old clothes. Davy was caught and sent to bed without any supper. Anne went to his room at twilight and talked to him seriously . . . a method in which she had great faith, not altogether unjustified by results. She told him she felt very badly over his conduct.

"I feel sorry now myself," admitted Davy, "but the trouble is I never feel sorry for doing things till after I've did them. Dora wouldn't help me make pies 'cause she was afraid of messing her clo'es and that made me hopping mad. I s'pose Paul Irving wouldn't have made *his* sister walk a pigpen fence if he knew she'd fall in?"

"No, he would never dream of such a thing. Paul is a perfect little gentleman."

Davy screwed his eyes tight shut and seemed to meditate on this for a time. Then he crawled up and put his arms about Anne's neck, snuggling his flushed little face down on her shoulder.

"Anne, don't you like me a little bit, even if I ain't a good boy like Paul?"

"Indeed I do," said Anne sincerly. Somehow, it was impossible to help liking Davy. "But I'd like you better still if you weren't so naughty."

"I . . . did something else today," went on Davy in a muffled voice. "I'm sorry now but I'm awful scared to tell you. You won't be very cross, will you? And you won't tell Marilla, will you?"

"I don't know, Davy. Perhaps I ought to tell her. But I think I can promise you I won't if you promise me that you will never do it again, whatever it is."

"No, I never will. Anyhow, it's not likely I'd find any more of them this year. I found this one on the cellar steps."

"Davy, what is it you've done?"

"I put a toad in Marilla's bed. You can go and take it out if you like. But say, Anne, wouldn't it be fun to leave it there?"

"Davy Keith!" Anne sprang from Davy's clinging arms and flew across the hall to Marilla's room. The bed was slightly rumpled. She threw back the blankets in nervous haste and there in very truth was the toad, blinking at her from under a pillow.

"How can I carry that awful thing out?" moaned Anne with a shudder. The fire shovel suggested itself to her and she crept down to get it while Marilla was busy in the pantry. Anne had her own troubles carrying that toad downstairs, for it hopped off the shovel three times and once she thought she had lost it in the hall. When she finally deposited it in the cherry orchard she drew a long breath of relief.

"If Marilla knew she'd never feel safe getting into bed again in her life. I'm so glad that little sinner repented in time. There's Diana signalling to me from her window. I'm glad . . . I really feel the need of some diversion, for what with Anthony Pye in school and Davy Keith at home my nerves have had about all they can endure for one day."

CHAPTER 9

A QUESTION OF COLOR

"THAT OLD nuisance of a Rachel Lynde was here again today, pestering me for a subscription towards buying a carpet for the vestry room," said Mr. Harrison wrathfully. "I detest that woman more than anybody I know. She can put a whole sermon, text, comment, and application, into six words, and throw it at you like a brick."

Anne, who was perched on the edge of the veranda, enjoying the charm of a mild west wind blowing across a newly ploughed field on a gray November twilight and piping a quaint little melody among the twisted firs below the garden, turned her dreamy face over her shoulder.

"The trouble is, you and Mrs. Lynde don't understand one another," she explained. "That is always what is wrong when people don't like each other. I didn't like Mrs. Lynde at first either; but as soon as I came to understand her I learned to."

"Mrs. Lynde may be an acquired taste with some folks; but I didn't keep on eating bananas because I was told I'd learn to like them if I did," growled Mr. Harrison. "And as for understanding her, I understand that she is a confirmed busybody and I told her so."

"Oh, that must have hurt her feelings very much," said Anne reproachfully. "How could you say such a thing? *I* said some dreadful things to Mrs. Lynde long ago but it was when I had lost my temper. I couldn't say them *deliberately*."

"It was the truth and I believe in telling the truth to everybody."

"But you don't tell the whole truth," objected Anne. "You only tell the disagreeable part of the truth. Now, you've told me a dozen times that my hair was red, but you've never once told me that I had a nice nose."

"I daresay you know it without any telling," chuckled Mr. Harrison.

"I know I have red hair too . . . although it's *much* darker than it used to be . . . so there's no need of telling me that either."

"Well, well, I'll try and not mention it again since you're so sensitive. You must excuse me, Anne. I've got a habit of being outspoken and folks mustn't mind it."

"But they can't help minding it. And I don't think it's any help that it's your habit. What would you think of a person who went about sticking pins and needles into people and saying, 'Excuse me, you mustn't mind it . . . it's just a habit I've got.' You'd think he was crazy, wouldn't you? And as for Mrs. Lynde being a busybody, perhaps she is. But did you tell her she had a very kind heart and always helped the poor, and never said a word when Timothy Cotton stole a crock of butter out of her dairy and told his wife he'd bought it from her? Mrs. Cotton cast it up to her the next time they met that it tasted of turnips and Mrs. Lynde just said she was sorry it had turned out so poorly."

"I suppose she has some good qualities," conceded Mr. Harrison grudgingly. "Most folks have. I have some myself, though you might never suspect it. But anyhow I ain't going to give anything to that carpet. Folks are everlasting begging for money here, it seems to me. How's your project of painting the hall coming on?"

"Splendidly. We had a meeting of the A.V.I.S. last Friday night and found that we had plenty of money subscribed to paint the hall and shingle the roof too. *Most* people gave very liberally, Mr. Harrison."

Anne was a sweet-souled lass, but she could instill some venom into innocent italics when occasion required.

"What color are you going to have it?"

We have decided on a very pretty green. The roof will be dark red, of course. Mr. Roger Pye is going to get the paint in town today."

"Who's got the job?"

"Mr. Joshua Pye of Carmody. He has nearly finished the shingling. We had to give him the contract, for every one of the Pyes . . . and there are four families, you know . . . said they wouldn't give a cent unless Joshua got it. They had subscribed twelve dollars between them and we thought that was too much to lose, although some people think we shouldn't have given in to the Pyes. Mrs. Lynde says they try to run everything."

"The main question is will this Joshua do his work well. If he does I don't see that it matters whether his name is Pye or Pudding."

"He has the reputation of being a good workman, though they say he's a very peculiar man. He hardly ever talks."

"He's peculiar enough all right then," said Mr. Harrison drily. "Or at least, folks here will call him so. I never was much of a talker till I came to Avonlea and then I had to begin in self-defence or Mrs. Lynde would have said I was dumb and started a subscription to have me taught sign language. You're not going yet, Anne?"

"I must. I have some sewing to do for Dora this evening. Besides, Davy is probably breaking Marilla's heart with some new mischief by this time. This morning the first thing he said was, 'Where does the dark go, Anne? I want to know.' I told him it went around to the other side of the world but after breakfast he declared it didn't . . . that it went down the well. Marilla says she caught him hanging over the well-box four times today, trying to reach down to the dark."

"He's a limb," declared Mr. Harrison. "He came over here yesterday and pulled six feathers out of Ginger's tail before I could get in from the barn. The poor bird has been moping ever since. Those children must be a sight of trouble to you folks."

"Everything that's worth having is some trouble," said Anne, secretly resolving to forgive Davy's next offence, whatever it might be, since he had avenged her on Ginger.

Mr. Roger Pye brought the hall paint home that night and Mr. Joshua Pye, a surly, taciturn man, began painting the next day. He was not disturbed in his task. The hall was situated on what was called "the lower road." In late autumn this road was always muddy and wet, and people going to Carmody travelled by the longer "upper" road. The hall was so closely surrounded by fir woods that it was invisible unless you were near it. Mr. Joshua Pye painted away in the solitude and independence that was so dear to his unsociable heart.

Friday afternoon he finished his job and went home to Carmody. Soon after his departure Mrs. Rachel Lynde drove by, having braved the mud of the lower road out of curiosity to see what the hall looked like in its new coat of paint. When she rounded the spruce curve she saw.

The sight affected Mrs. Lynde oddly. She dropped the reins, held up her hands, and said "Gracious Providence!" She stared as if she could not believe her eyes. Then she laughed almost hysterically.

"There must be some mistake . . . there *must*. I knew those Pyes would make a mess of things."

Mrs. Lynde drove home, meeting several people on the road and stopping to tell them about the hall. The news flew like wildfire. Gilbert Blythe, poring over a text book at home, heard it from his father's hired boy at sunset, and rushed breathlessly to Green Gables, joined on the way by Fred Wright. They found Diana Barry, Jane Andrews, and Anne Shirley, despair personified, at the yard gate of Green Gables, under the big leafless willows.

"It isn't true surely, Anne?" exclaimed Gilbert.

"It *is* true," answered Anne, looking like the muse of tragedy. "Mrs. Lynde called on her way from Carmody to tell me. Oh, it is simply dreadful! *What* is the use of trying to improve anything?"

"What is dreadful?" asked Oliver Sloane, arriving at this moment with a bandbox he had brought from town for Marilla.

"Haven't you heard?" said Jane wrathfully. "Well, it's simply this . . . Joshua Pye *has gone and painted the hall blue instead of green* . . . a deep, brilliant blue, the shade they use for painting carts and wheelbarrows. And Mrs. Lynde says it is the most hideous color for a building, especially when combined with a red roof, that she ever saw or imagined. You could simply have knocked me down with a feather when I heard it. It's heart-breaking, after all the trouble we've had."

"How on earth could such a mistake have happened?" wailed Diana.

The blame of this unmerciful disaster was eventually narrowed down to the Pyes. The Improvers had decided to use Morton-Harris paints and Morton-Harris paint cans were numbered according to a color card. A purchaser chose his shade on the card and ordered by the accompanying number. Number 147 was the shade of green desired and when Mr. Roger Pye sent word to the Improvers by his son, John Andrew, that he was going to town and would get their paint for them, the Improvers told John Andrew to tell his father to

get 147. John Andrew always averred that he did so, but Mr. Roger
Pye as stanchly declared that John Andrew told him 157; and there
the matter stands to this day.

That night there was blank dismay in every Avonlea house where
an Improver lived. The gloom at Green Gables was so intense that it
quenched even Davy. Anne wept and would not be comforted.

"I *must* cry, even if I am almost seventeen, Marilla," she sobbed.
"It's so mortifying. And it sounds the death knell of our society.
We'll simply be laughed out of existence."

In life, as in dreams, however, things often go by contraries. The
Avonlea people did not laugh; they were too angry. *Their* money had
gone to paint the hall and consequently *they* felt themselves bitterly
aggrieved by the mistake. Public indignation centered on the Pyes.
Roger Pye and John Andrew had bungled the matter between them;
and as for Joshua Pye, he must be a born fool not to suspect there was
something wrong when he opened the cans and saw the color of the
paint. Joshua Pye, when thus animadverted upon, retorted that the
Avonlea taste in colors was no business of his, whatever his private
opinion of it might be; he had been hired to paint the hall, not to talk
about it; and he meant to have his money for it.

The Improvers paid him his money in bitterness of spirit, after
consulting Mr. Peter Sloane, who was a magistrate.

"You'll have to pay it," Peter told them. "You can't hold him
responsible for the mistake, since he claims he was never told what
the color was supposed to be but just given the cans and told to go
ahead. But it's a burning shame and that hall certainly does look
awful."

The luckless Improvers expected that Avonlea would be more
prejudiced than ever against them; but instead, public sympathy
veered around in their favor. People thought the eager, enthusiastic
little band who had worked so hard for their object had been badly
used. Mrs. Lynde told them to keep on and show the Pyes that there
really were people in the world who could do things without making
a muddle of them. Mr. Major Spencer sent them word that he would
clean out all the stumps along the road front of his farm and seed it
down with grass at his own expense; and Mrs. Hiram Sloane called at
the school one day and beckoned Anne mysteriously out into the
porch to tell her that if the "Sassiety" wanted to make a geranium
bed at the cross roads in the spring they needn't be afraid of her cow,
for she would see that the marauding animal was kept within safe
bounds. Even Mr. Harrison chuckled, if he chuckled at all, in

private, and was all sympathy outwardly.

"Never mind, Anne. Most paints fade uglier every year but that blue is as ugly as it can be to begin with, so it's bound to fade prettier. And the roof is shingled and painted all right. Folks will be able to sit in the hall after this without being leaked on. You've accomplished so much anyhow."

"But Avonlea's blue hall will be a byword in all the neighboring settlements from this time time out," said Anne bitterly.

And it must be confessed that it was.

CHAPTER 10

DAVY IN SEARCH OF A SENSATION

ANNE, WALKING home from school through the Birch Path one November afternoon, felt convinced afresh that life was a very wonderful thing. The day had been a good day; all had gone well in her little kingdom. St. Clair Donnell had *not* fought any of the other boys over the question of his name; Prillie Rogerson's face had been so puffed up from the effects of toothache that she did not once try to coquette with the boys in her vicinity. Barbara Shaw had met with only *one* accident . . . spilling a dipper of water over the floor . . . and Anthony Pye had not been in school at all.

"What a nice month this November has been!" said Anne, who had never quite got over her childish habit of talking to herself. "November is usually such a disagreeable month . . . as if the year had suddenly found out that she was growing old and could do nothing but weep and fret over it. This year is growing old gracefully . . . just like a stately old lady who knows she can be charming even with gray hair and wrinkles. We've had lovely days and delicious twilights. This last fortnight has been so peaceful, and even Davy has been almost well-behaved. I really think he is improving a great deal. How quiet the woods are today . . . not a murmur except that soft wind purring in the treetops! It sounds like surf on a faraway shore. How dear the woods are! You beautiful trees! I love every one of you as a friend."

Anne paused to throw her arm about a slim young birch and kiss its cream-white trunk. Diana, rounding a curve in the path, saw her and laughed.

"Anne Shirley, you're only pretending to be grown up. I believe when you're alone you're as much a little girl as you ever were."

"Well, one can't get over the habit of being a little girl all at once," said Anne gaily. "You see, I was little for fourteen years and I've only been grownuppish for scarcely three. I'm sure I shall always feel like a child in the woods. These walks home from school are almost the only time I have for dreaming . . . except the half hour or so before I go to sleep. I'm so busy with teaching and studying and helping Marilla with the twins that I haven't another moment for imagining things. You don't know what splendid adventures I have for a little while after I go to bed in the east gable every night. I always imagine I'm something very brilliant and triumphant and splendid . . . a great prima donna or a Red Cross nurse or a queen. Last night I was a queen. It's really splendid to imagine you are a queen. You have all the fun of it without any of the inconveniences and you can stop being a queen whenever you want to, which you couldn't in real life. But here in the woods I like best to imagine quite different things . . . I'm a dryad living in an old pine, or a little brown wood-elf hiding under a crinkled leaf. That white birch you caught me kissing is a sister of mine. The only difference is, she's a tree and I'm a girl, but that's no real difference. Where are you going, Diana?"

"Down to the Dicksons'. I promised to help Alberta cut out her new dress. Can't you walk down in the evening, Anne, and come home with me?"

"I might . . . since Fred Wright is away in town," said Anne with a rather too innocent face.

Diana blushed, tossed her head, and walked on. She did not look offended, however.

Anne fully intended to go down to the Dicksons' that evening, but she did not. When she arrived at Green Gables she found a state of affairs which banished every other thought from her mind. Marilla met her in the yard . . . a wild-eyed Marilla.

"Anne, Dora is lost!"

"Dora! Lost!" Anne looked at Davy, who was swinging on the yard gate, and detected merriment in his eyes. "Davy, do you know where she is?"

"No, I don't," said Davy stoutly. "I haven't seen her since dinner time, cross my heart."

"I've been away ever since one o'clock," said Marilla. "Thomas Lynde took sick all of a sudden and Rachel sent up for me to go at once. When I left here Dora was playing with her doll in the kitchen and Davy was making mud pies behind the barn. I only got home half an hour ago . . . and no Dora to be seen. Davy declares he never saw her since I left."

"Neither I did," avowed Davy solemnly.

"She must be somewhere around," said Anne. "She would never wander far away alone . . . you know how timid she is. Perhaps she has fallen asleep in one of the rooms."

Marilla shook her head.

"I've hunted the whole house through. But she may be in some of the buildings."

A thorough search followed. Every corner of house, yard, and outbuildings was ransacked by those two distracted people. Anne roved the orchards and the Haunted Wood, calling Dora's name. Marilla took a candle and explored the cellar. Davy accompanied each of them in turn, and was fertile in thinking of places where Dora could possibly be. Finally they met again in the yard.

"It's a most mysterious thing," groaned Marilla.

"Where can she be?" said Anne miserably.

"Maybe she's tumbled into the well," suggested Davy cheerfully.

Anne and Marilla looked fearfully into each other's eyes. The thought had been with them both through their entire search but neither had dared to put it into words.

"She . . . she might have," whispered Marilla.

Anne, feeling faint and sick, went to the well box and peered over. The bucket sat on the shelf inside. Far down below was a tiny glimmer of still water. The Cuthbert well was the deepest in Avonlea. If Dora . . . but Anne could not face the idea. She shuddered and turned away.

"Run across for Mr. Harrison," said Marilla, wringing her hands.

"Mr. Harrison and John Henry are both away . . . they went to town today. I'll go for Mr. Barry."

Mr. Barry came back with Anne, carrying a coil of rope to which was attached a claw-like instrument that had been the business end of a grubbing fork. Marilla and Anne stood by, cold and shaken with horror and dread, while Mr. Barry dragged the well, and Davy, astride the gate, watched the group with a face indicative of huge enjoyment.

Finally Mr. Barry shook his head, with a relieved air.

"She can't be down there. It's a mighty curious thing where she could have got to, though. Look here, young man, are you sure you've no idea where your sister is?"

"I've told you a dozen times that I haven't," said Davy, with an injured air. "Maybe a tramp come and stole her."

"Nonsense," said Marilla sharply, relieved from her horrible fear of the well. "Anne, do you suppose she could have strayed over to Mr. Harrison's? She has always been talking about his parrot ever since that time you took her over."

"I can't believe Dora would venture so far alone but I'll go over and see," said Anne.

Nobody was looking at Davy just then or it would have been seen that a very decided change came over his face. He quietly slipped off the gate and ran, as fast as his fat legs could carry him, to the barn.

Anne hastened across the fields to the Harrison establishement in no very hopeful frame of mind. The house was locked, the window shades were down, and there was no sign of anything living about the place. She stood on the veranda and called Dora loudly.

Ginger, in the kitchen behind her, shrieked and swore with sudden fierceness; but between his outbursts Anne heard a plaintive cry from the little building in the yard which served Mr. Harrison as a toolhouse. Anne flew to the door, unhasped it, and caught up a small mortal with a tear-stained face who was sitting forlornly on an upturned nail keg.

"Oh, Dora, Dora, what a fright you have given us! How came you to be here?"

"Davy and I come over to see Ginger," sobbed Dora, "but we couldn't see him after all, only Davy made him swear by kicking the door. And then Davy brought me here and run out and shut the door; and I couldn't get out. I cried and cried, I was so frightened, and oh, I'm so hungry and cold; and I thought you'd never come, Anne."

"Davy?" But Anne could say no more. She carried Dora home with a heavy heart. Her joy at finding the child safe and sound was drowned out in the pain caused by Davy's behavior. The freak of shutting Dora up might easily have been pardoned. But Davy had told falsehoods . . . downright cold-blooded falsehoods about it. That was the ugly fact and Anne could not shut her eyes to it. She could have sat down and cried with sheer disappointment. She had grown to love Davy dearly . . . how dearly she had not known until this minute . . . and it hurt her unbearably to discover that he was guilty of deliberate falsehood.

Marilla listened to Anne's tale in a silence that boded no good Davy-ward; Mr. Barry laughed and advised that Davy be summarily dealt with. When he had gone home Anne soothed and warmed the sobbing, shivering Dora, got her her supper and put her to bed. Then she returned to the kitchen, just as Marilla came grimly in, leading, or rather pulling, the reluctant, cobwebby Davy, whom she had just found hidden away in the darkest corner of the stable.

She jerked him to the mat on the middle of the floor and then went and sat down by the east window. Anne was sitting limply by the west window. Between them stood the culprit. His back was towards Marilla and it was a meek, subdued, frightened back; but his face was towards Anne and although it was a little shamefaced there was a gleam of comradeship in Davy's eyes, as if he knew he had done wrong and was going to be punished for it, but could count on a laugh over it all with Anne later on.

But no half hidden smile answered him in Anne's gray eyes, as there might have done had it been only a question of mischief. There was something else . . . something ugly and repulsive.

"How could you behave so, Davy?" she asked sorrowfully.

Davy squirmed uncomfortably.

"I just did it for fun. Things had been so awful quiet here for so long that I thought it would be fun to give you folks a big scare. It was, too."

In spite of fear and a little remorse Davy grinned over the recollection.

"But you told a falsehood about it, Davy," said Anne, more sorrowfully than ever.

Davy looked puzzled.

"What's a falsehood? Do you mean a whopper?"

"I mean a story that was not true."

"Course I did," said Davy frankly. "If I hadn't you wouldn't have been scared. I *had* to tell it."

Anne was feeling the reaction from her fright and exertions. Davy's impenitent attitude gave the finishing touch. Two big tears brimmed up in her eyes.

"Oh, Davy, how could you?" she said, with a quiver in her voice. "Don't you know how wrong it was?"

Davy was aghast. Anne crying . . . he had made Anne cry! A flood of real remorse rolled like a wave over his warm little heart and engulfed it. He rushed to Anne, hurled himself into her lap, flung his arms around her neck, and burst into tears.

"I didn't know it was wrong to tell whoppers," he sobbed. "How did you expect me to know it was wrong? All Mr. Sprott's children told them *regular* every day, and cross their hearts too. I s'pose Paul Irving never tells whoppers and here I've been trying awful hard to be as good as him, but now I s'pose you'll never love me again. But I think you might have told me it was wrong. I'm awful sorry I've made you cry, Anne, and I'll never tell a whopper again."

Davy buried his face in Anne's shoulder and cried stormily. Anne, in a sudden glad flash of understanding, held him tight and looked over his curly thatch at Marilla.

"He didn't know it was wrong to tell falsehoods, Marilla. I think we must forgive him for that part of it this time if he will promise never to say what isn't true again."

"I never will, now that I know it's bad," asseverated Davy between sobs. "If you ever catch me telling a whopper again you can . . . " Davy groped mentally for a suitable penance . . . "you can skin me alive, Anne."

"Don't say 'whopper,' Davy . . . say 'falsehood,' " said the schoolma'am.

"Why?" queried Davy, settling comfortably down and looking up with a tear-stained, investigating face. "Why ain't whopper as good as falsehood? I want to know. It's just as big a word."

"It's slang; and it's wrong for little boys to use slang."

"There's an awful lot of things it's wrong to do," said Davy with a sigh. "I never s'posed there was so many. I'm sorry it's wrong to tell whop . . . falsehoods, 'cause it's awful handy, but since it is I'm never going to tell anymore. What are you going to do to me for telling them this time? I want to know." Anne looked beeeechingly at Marilla.

"I don't want to be too hard on the child," said Marilla. "I daresay nobody ever did tell him it was wrong to tell lies, and those Sprott children were no fit companions for him. Poor Mary was too sick to train him properly and I presume you couldn't expect a six year old child to know things like that by instinct. I suppose we'll just have to assume he doesn't know *anything* right and begin at the beginning. But he'll have to be punished for shutting Dora up, and I can't think of any way except to send him to bed without his supper and we've done that so often. Can't you suggest something else, Anne? I should think you ought to be able to, with that imagination you're always talking of."

"But punishments are so horrid and I like to imagine only pleasant things,'' said Anne, cuddling Davy. ''There are so many unpleasant things in the world already that there is no use in imagining any more.''

In the end Davy was sent to bed, as usual, there to remain until noon next day. He evidently did some thinking, for when Anne went up to her room a little later she head him calling her name softly. Going in, she found him sitting up in bed, with his elbows on his knees and his chin propped on his hands.

''Anne,'' he said solemnly, ''is it wrong for everybody to tell whop . . . falsehoods? I want to know.''

''Yes, indeed.''

''Is it wrong for a grown-up person?''

''Yes.''

''Then,'' said Davy decidedly, ''Marilla is bad, for *she* tells them. And she's worse'n me, for I didn't know it was wrong but she does.''

''Davy Keith, Marilla never told a story in her life,'' said Anne indignantly.

''She did so. She told me last Tuesday that something dreadful would happen to me if I didn't say my prayers every night. And I haven't said them for over a week, just to see what *would* happen . . . and nothing has,'' concluded Davy in an aggrieved tone.

Anne choked back a mad desire to laugh with the conviction that it would be fatal, and then earnestly set about saving Marilla's reputation.

''Why, Davy Keith,'' she said solemnly,'' something dreadful *has* happened to you this very day.''

Davy looked skeptical.

''I s'pose you mean being sent to bed without any supper,'' he said scornfully, ''but *that* isn't dreadful. Course, I don't like it, but I've been sent to bed so much since I come here that I'm getting used to it. And you don't save anything by making me go without supper either, for I always eat twice as much for breakfast.''

''I don't mean your being sent to bed. I mean the fact that you told a falsehood today. And, Davy,'' . . . Anne leaned over the foot-board of the bed and shook her fingers impressively at the culprit . . . ''For a boy to tell what isn't true is almost the worst thing that *could* happen to him . . . almost the very worst. So you see Marilla told you the truth.''

''But I thought the something bad would be exciting,'' protested Davy in an injured tone.

''Marilla isn't to blame for what you thought. Bad things aren't always exciting. They've very often just nasty and stupid.''

"It was awful funny to see Marilla and you looking down the well, though,'' said Davy, hugging his knees.

Anne kept a sober face until she got downstairs and then she collapsed on the sitting room lounge and laughed until her sides ached.

"I wish you'd tell me the joke,'' said Marilla, a little grimly. "I haven't seen much to laugh at today.''

"You'll laugh when you hear this,'' assured Anne. And Marilla did laugh, which showed how much her education had advanced since the adoption of Anne. But she sighed immediately afterwards.

"I suppose I shouldn't have told him that, although I heard a minister say it to a child once. But he did aggravate me so. It was that night you were at the Carmody concert and I was putting him to bed. He said he didn't see the good of praying until he got big enough to be of some importance to God. Anne, I do not know what we are going to do with that child. I never saw his beat. I'm feeling clean discouraged.''

"Oh, don't say that, Marilla. Remember how bad I was when I came here.''

"Anne, you never were bad . . . never. I see that now, when I've learned what real badness is. You were always getting into terrible scrapes, I'll admit, but your motive was always good. Davy is just bad from sheer love of it.''

"Oh, no, I don't think it is real badness with him either,'' pleaded Anne. "It's just mischief. And it is rather quiet for him here, you know. He has no other boys to play with and his mind has to have something to occupy it. Dora is so prim and proper she is no good for a boy's playmate. I really think it would be better to let them go to school, Marilla.''

"No,'' said Marilla resolutely, "my father always said that no child should be cooped up in the four walls of a school until it was seven years old, and Mr. Allan says that same thing. The twins can have a few lessons at home but go to school they shan't till they're seven.''

"Well, we must try to reform Davy at home then,'' said Anne cheerfully. "With all his faults he's really a dear little chap. I can't help loving him. Marilla, it may be a dreadful thing to say, but honestly, I like Davy better than Dora, for all she's so good.''

"I don't know but that I do, myself,'' confessed Marilla, "and it isn't fair, for Dora isn't a bit of trouble. There couldn't be a better child and you'd hardly know she was in the house.''

"Dora is too good," said Anne. "She'd behave just as well if there wasn't a soul to tell her what to do. She was born already brought up, so she doesn't need us; and I think," concluded Anne, hitting on a very vital truth, "that we always love best the people who need us. Davy needs us badly."

"He certainly needs something," agreed Marilla. "Rachel Lynde would say it was a good spanking."

CHAPTER 11

FACTS AND FANCIES

"TEACHING IS really very interesting work," wrote Anne to a Queen's Academy chum. "Jane says she thinks it is monotonous but I don't find it so. Something funny is almost sure to happen every day, and the children say such amusing things. Jane says she punishes her pupils when they make funny speeches, which is probably why she finds teaching monotonous. This afternoon little Jimmy Andrews was trying to spell 'speckled' and couldn't manage it. 'Well,' he said finally, 'I can't spell it but I know what it means.'

"'What?' I asked.

"'St. Clair Donnell's face, miss.'

"St. Clair is certainly very much freckled, although I try to prevent the others from commenting on it . . . for *I* was freckled once and well do I remember it. But I don't think St. Clair minds. It was because Jimmy called him 'St. Clair' that St. Clair pounded him on the way home from school. I heard of the pounding, but not officially, so I don't think I'll take any notice of it.

"Yesterday I was trying to teach Lottie Wright to do addition. I said, 'If you had three candies in one hand and two in the other, how many would you have altogether?' 'A mouthful,' said Lottie. And in the nature study class, when I asked them to give me a good reason why toads shouldn't be killed, Benjie Sloane gravely answered, 'Because it would rain the next day.'

"It's so hard not to laugh, Stella. I have to save up all my amusement until I get home, and Marilla says it makes her nervous to hear wild shrieks of mirth proceeding from the east gable without any apparent cause. She says a man in Grafton went insane once and that was how it began.

"Did you know that Thomas à Becket was canonized as a *snake?* Rose Bell says he was . . . also that William Tyndale *wrote* the New Testament. Claude White says a 'glacier' is a man who puts in window frames!

"I think the most difficult thing in teaching, as well as the most interesting, is to get the children to tell you their real thoughts about things. One stormy day last week I gathered them around me at dinner hour and tried to get them to talk to me just as if I were one of themselves. I asked them to tell me the things they most wanted. Some of the answers were commonplace enough . . . dolls, ponies, and skates. Others were decidedly original. Hester Boulter wanted 'to wear her Sunday dress every day and eat in the sitting room.' Hannah Bell wanted 'to be good without having to take any trouble about it.' Marjory White, aged ten, wanted to be a *widow*. Questioned why, she gravely said that if you weren't married people called you an old maid, and if you were your husband bossed you; but if you were a widow there'd be no danger of either. The most remarkable wish was Sally Bell's. She wanted a 'honeymoon.' I asked her if she knew what it was and she said she thought it was an extra nice kind of bicycle because her cousin in Montreal went on a honeymoon when he was married and he had always had the very latest in bicycles!

"Another day I asked them all to tell me the naughtiest thing they had ever done. I couldn't get the older ones to do so, but the third class answered quite freely. Eliza Bell had 'set fire to her aunt's carded rolls.' Asked if she meant to do it she said, 'not altogether.' She just tried a little end to see how it would burn and the whole bundle blazed up in a jiffy. Emerson Gillis had spent ten cents for candy when he should have put it in his missionary box. Annetta Bell's worst crime was 'eating some blueberries that grew in the graveyard.' Willie White had 'slid down the sheephouse roof a lot of times with his Sunday trousers on.' 'But I was punished for it 'cause I had to wear patched pants to Sunday School all summer, and when you're punished for a thing you don't have to repent of it,' declared Willie.

"I wish you could see some of their compositions . . . so much do I wish it that I'll send you copies of some written recently. Last week I told the fourth class I wanted them to write me letters about anything they pleased, adding by way of suggestion that they might tell me of some place they had visited or some interesting thing or person they had seen. They were to write the letters on real note paper, seal them in an envelope, and address them to me, all without any assistance from other people. Last Friday morning I found a pile of letters on my desk and that evening I realized afresh that teaching has its pleasures as well as its pains. Those compositions would atone for much. Here is Ned Clay's, address, spelling, and grammar as originally penned.

" 'Miss teacher ShiRley
" 'Green gabels.
" 'p.e. Island can

" 'birds

" 'Dear teacher I think I will write you a composition about birds. birds is very useful animals. my cat catches birds. His name is William but pa calls him tom. he is oll striped and he got one of his ears froz of last winter. only for that he would be a good-looking cat. My unkle has acopted a cat. it come to his house one day and woudent go away and unkle says it has forgot more than most people ever knowed. he lets it sleep on his rocking chare and my aunt says he thinks more of it than he does of his children. that is not right. we ought to be kind to cats and given them new milk but we ought not to be better to them than to our children. this is oll I can think of so no more at present from

" 'edward blake ClaY.'

"St. Clair Donnell's is, as usual, short and to the point. St. Clair never wastes words. I do not think he chose his subject or added the postscript out of malice aforethought. It is just that he has not a great deal of tact or imagination.

" 'Dear Miss Shirley
" 'You told us to describe something strange we have seen. I will describe the Avonlea Hall. It has two doors, an inside one and an outside one. It has six windows and a chimney. It has two ends and two sides. It is painted blue. That is what makes it strange. It is built on the lower Carmody road. It is the third most important building in Avonlea. The others are the church and the

blacksmith shop. They hold debating clubs and lectures in it and concerts.

" 'Your truly,
"Jacob Donnell.

" 'P.S. The hall is a very bright blue.'

"Annette Bell's letter was quite long, which surprised me, for writing essays is not Annetta's forte, and hers are generally as brief as St. Clair's. Annetta is a quiet little puss and a model of good behavior, but there isn't a shadow of originality in her. Here is her letter;—

" 'Dearest teacher,

" 'I think I will write you a letter to tell you how much I love you. I love you with my whole heart and soul and mind . . . with all there is of me to love . . . and I want to serve you for ever. It would be my highest privilege. That is why I try so hard to be good in school and learn my lessuns.

" 'You are so beautiful, my teacher. Your voice is like music and your eyes are like pansies when the dew is on them. You are like a tall stately queen. Your hair is like rippling gold. Anthony Pye says it is red, but you needn't pay any attention to Anthony.

" 'I have only known you for a few months but I cannot realize that there was ever a time when I did not know you . . . when you had not come into my life to bless and hallow it. I will always look back to this year as the most wonderful in my life because it brought you to me. Besides, it's the year we moved to Avonlea from new-bridge. My love for you has made my life very rich and it has kept me from much of harm and evil. I owe this all to you, my sweetest teacher.

" 'I shall never forget how sweet you looked the last time I saw you in that black dress with flowers in your hair. I shall see you like that forever, even when we are both old and gray. You will always be young and fair to me, dearest teacher. I am thinking of you all the time . . . in the morning and at the noontide and at the twilight. I love you when you laugh and when you sigh . . . even when you look disdainful. I never saw you look cross though Anthony Pye says you always look so but I don't wonder you look cross at him for he deserves it. I love you in every dress . . you seem more adorable in each new dress than the last.

" 'Dearest teacher, good night. The sun has set and the stars are shining . . . stars that are as bright and beautiful as your eyes. I kiss your hands and face, my sweet. May God watch over you and protect you from all harm.

" 'Your afecksionate pupil
" 'Annetta Bell.'

"This extraordinary letter puzzled me not a little. I knew Annetta couldn't have composed it any more than she could fly. When I went to school the next day I took her for a walk down to the brook at recess and asked her to tell me the truth about the letter. Annetta cried and 'fessed up freely. She said she had never written a letter and she didn't know how to, or what to say, but there was a bundle of love letters in her mother's top bureau drawer which had been written to her by an old 'beau.'

" 'It wasn't father,' sobbed Annetta, 'it was someone who was studying for a minister, and so he could write lovely letters, but ma didn't marry him after all. She said she couldn't make out what he was driving at half the time. But I thought the letters were sweet and that I'd just copy things out of them here and there to write you. I put "teacher" where he put "lady" and I put in something of my own when I could think of it and I changed some words. I put "dress" in place of "mood." I didn't know just what a "mood" was but I s'posed it was something to wear. I didn't s'pose you'd know the difference. I don't see how you found out it wasn't all mine. You must be awful clever, teacher.'

"I told Annetta it was very wrong to copy another person's letter and pass it off as her own. But I'm afraid that all Annetta repented of was being found out.

" 'And I *do* love you, teacher,' she sobbed. 'It was all true, even if the minister wrote it first. I do love you with all my heart.'

"It's very difficult to scold anybody properly under such circumstances.

"Here is Barbara Shaw's letter. I can't reproduce the blots of the original.

" 'Dear teacher,

" 'You said we might write about a visit. I never visited but once. It was at my Aunt Mary's last winter. My Aunt Mary is a very particular woman and a great housekeeper. The first night I was there we were at tea. I knocked over a jug and broke it. Aunt Mary said she had had that jug ever since she was married and nobody had ever broken it before. When we got up I stepped on her dress and all the gathers tore out of the skirt. The next morning when I got up I hit the pitcher against the basin and cracked them both and I upset a cup of tea on the tablecloth at breakfast. When I was helping Aunt Mary with the dinner dishes I dropped a china plate and it smashed. That evening I fell downstairs and sprained my ankle and had to stay in bed for a week. I heard Aunt Mary tell Uncle Joseph it was a mercy or I'd have broken everything in the house. When I got better it was time to go home. I don't like visiting very much. I like going to school better, especially since I came to Avonlea.

" 'Yours respectfully,
" 'Barbara Shaw.'

"Willie White's began,

" 'Respected Miss,

" 'I want to tell you about my Very Brave Aunt. She lives in Ontario and one day she went out to the barn and saw a dog in the yard. The dog had no business there so she got a stick and whacked him hard and drove him into the barn and shut him up. Pretty soon a man came looking for an imaginary lion' (Query;—Did Willie mean a menagerie lion?) 'that had run away from a circus. And it turned out that the dog was a lion and my Very Brave Aunt had druv him into the barn with a stick. It is a wonder she was not et up but she was very brave. Emerson Gillis says if she thought it was a dog she wasn't any braver than if it really was a dog. But Emerson is jealous because he hasn't got a Brave Aunt himself, nothing but uncles.'

"I have kept the best for the last. You laugh at me because I think Paul is a genius but I am sure his letter will convince you that he is a very uncommon child. Paul lives away down near the shore with his grandmother and he has no playmates . . . no *real* playmates. You remember our School Management professor told us that we must not have 'favorites' among our pupils, but I can't help loving Paul Irving the best of all mine. I don't think it does any harm, though, for everybody loves Paul, even Mrs. Lynde, who says she could never have believed she'd get so fond of a Yankee. The other boys in school like him too. There is nothing weak or girlish about him in spite of his dreams and fancies. He is very manly and can hold his own in all games. He fought St. Clair Donnell recently because St. Clair said the Union Jack was away ahead of the Stars and Stripes as a flag. The result was a drawn battle and a mutual agreement to respect each other's patriotism henceforth. St. Clair says he can hit the *hardest* but Paul can hit the *oftenest*.

"Paul's Letter.

    " 'My dear teacher,

        " 'You told us we might write you about some interesting people we knew. I think the most interesting people I know are my rock people and I mean to tell you about them. I have never told anybody about them except grandma and father but I would like to have you know about them because you understand things. There are a great many people who do *not* understand things so there is no use use in telling them.

    " 'My rock people live at the shore. I used to visit them almost every evening before the winter came. Now I can't go till spring, but they will be there, for people like that never change . . . that is the splendid thing about them. Nora was the first one of them I got acquainted with and so I think I love her the best. She lives in Andrews' Cove and she has black hair and black eyes, and she knows all about the mermaids and the water kelpies. You ought to hear the stories she can tell. Then there are the Twin Sailors. They don't live anywhere, they sail all the time, but they often come ashore to talk to me. They are a pair of jolly tars and they have seen everything in the world . . . and more than what is in the world. Do you know what happened to the youngest Twin Sailor once? He was sailing and he sailed right into a moonglade. A moonglade is the tack the full moon makes on the water when it is rising from the sea, you know, teacher. Well, the youngest Twin Sailor sailed along the moonglade till he came right up to the moon, and there was a little golden door in the moon and he opened it and sailed right through. He had some wonderful adventures in the moon but it would make this letter too long to tell them.

    " 'Then there is the Golden Lady of the cave. One day I found a big cave down on the shore and I went away in and after a while I found the Golden Lady. She has golden hair right down to her feet and her dress is all glittering and glistening like gold that is alive. And she has a golden harp and plays on it all day long . . . you can hear the music any time along shore if you listen carefully but most people would think it was only the wind among the rocks. I've never told Nora about the Golden Lady. I was afraid it might hurt her feelings. It even hurt her feelings if I talked too long with the Twin Sailors.

    " 'I always met the Twin Sailors at the Striped Rocks. The youngest Twin Sailor is very good-tempered but the oldest Twin Sailor can look dreadfully fierce at times. I have my suspicions about that oldest Twin. I believe he'd be a pirate if he dared. There's really something very mysterious about him. He swore once and I told him if he ever did it again he needn't come ashore to talk to me because I'd promised grandmother I'd never associate with anybody that swore. He was pretty well scared, I can tell you, and he said if I would forgive him he would take me to the sunset. So the next evening when I was sitting on the Striped Rocks the oldest Twin came sailing over the sea in an enchanted boat and I got in her. The boat was all pearly and rainbowy, like the inside of the mussel shells, and her sail was like moonshine. Well, we sailed right across to the sunset. Think of that, teacher, I've been in the sunset. And what do you suppose it is? The sunset is a land all flowers, like a great garden, and the clouds are beds of flowers. We sailed into a great harbor, all the color of gold, and I stepped right out of the boat on a big meadow all covered with buttercups as big as roses. I stayed there for ever so long. It seemed nearly a year but the Oldest Twin says it was only a few minutes. You see, in the sunset land the time is ever so much longer than it is here.

" 'Your loving pupil,

" 'Paul Irving.

" 'P.S. Of course, this letter isn't really true, teacher.

P.I.' "

CHAPTER 12

A JONAH DAY

IT REALLY began the night before with a restless, wakeful vigil of grumbling toothache. When Anne arose in the dull, bitter winter morning she felt that life was flat, stale, and unprofitable.

She went to school in no angelic mood. Her cheek was swollen and her face ached. The schoolroom was cold and smoky, for the fire refused to burn and the chidren were huddled about it in shivering groups. Anne sent them to their seats with a sharper tone than she had ever used before. Anthony Pye strutted to his with his usual impertinent swagger and she saw him whisper something to his seat-mate and then glance at her with a grin.

Never, so it seemed to Anne, had there been so many squeaky pencils as there were that morning; and when Barbara Shaw came up to the desk with a sum she tripped over the coal scuttle with disastrous results. The coal rolled to every part of the room, her slate was broken into fragments, and when she picked herself up, her face, stained with coal dust, sent the boys into roars of laughter.

Anne turned from the second reader class which she was hearing.

"Really, Barbara," she said icily, "if you cannot move without falling over something you'd better remain in your seat. It is positively disgraceful for a girl of your age to be so awkward."

Poor Barbara stumbled back to her desk, her tears combining with the coal dust to produce an effect truly grotesque. Never before had her beloved, sympathetic teacher spoken to her in such a tone or fashion, and Barbara was heart-broken. Anne herself felt a prick of conscience but it only served to increase her mental irritation, and the second reader class remember that lesson yet, as well as the unmerciful infliction of arithmetic that followed. Just as Anne was snapping the sums out St. Clair Donnell arrived breathlessly.

"You are half an hour late, St. Clair," Anne reminded him frigidly. "Why is this?"

"Please, miss, I had to help ma make a pudding for dinner 'cause we're expecting company and Clarice Almira's sick," was St. Clair's answer, given in a perfectly respectful voice but nevertheless provocative of great mirth among his mates.

"Take your seat and work out the six problems on page eighty-four of your arithmetic for punishment," said Anne. St. Clair looked rather amazed at her tone but he went meekly to his desk and took out his slate. Then he steathily passed a small parcel to Joe Sloane across the aisle. Anne caught him in the act and jumped to a fatal conclusion about that parcel.

Old Mrs. Hiram Sloane had lately taken to making and selling "nut cakes" by way of adding to her scanty income. The cakes were specially tempting to small boys and for several weeks Anne had had not a little trouble in regard to them. On their way to school the boys would invest their spare cash at Mrs. Hiram's, bring the cakes along with them to school, and, if possible, eat them and treat their mates during school hours. Anne had warned them that if they brought any more cakes to school they would be confiscated; and yet here was St. Clair Donnell coolly passing a parcel of them, wrapped up in the blue and white striped paper Mrs. Hiram used, under her very eyes.

"Joseph," said Anne quietly, "bring that parcel here."

Joe, startled and abashed, obeyed. He was a fat urchin who always blushed and stuttered when he was frightened. Never did anybody look more guilty than poor Joe at that moment.

"Throw it into the fire," said Anne.

Joe looked very blank.

"P . . . p . . . p . . . lease, m . . . m . . . miss," he began.

"Do as I tell you, Joseph, without any words about it."

"B . . . b . . . but m . . . m . . . miss . . . th . . . th . . . they're . . ." gasped Joe in desperation.

"Joseph, are you going to obey me or are you *not*?" said Anne.

A bolder and more self-possessed lad than Joe Sloane would have been overawed by her tone and the dangerous flash of her eyes. This was a new Anne whom none of her pupils had ever seen before. Joe, with an agonized glance at St. Clair, went to the stove, opened the big, square front door, and threw the blue and white parcel in, before St. Clair, who had sprung to his feet, could utter a word. Then he dodged back just in time.

For a few moments the terrified occupants of Avonlea school did not know whether it as an earthquake or a volcanic explosion that had occurred. The innocent looking parcel which Anne had rashly supposed to contain Mrs.Hiram's nut cakes really held an assortment of firecrackers and pin-wheels for which Warren Sloane had sent to town by St. Clair Donnell's father the day before, intending to have a birthday celebration that evening. The crackers went off in a thunderclap of noise and the pin-wheels bursting out of the door spun madly around the room, hissing and spluttering. Anne dropped into her chair white with dismay and all the girls climbed shrieking upon their desks. Joe Sloane stood as one transfixed in the midst of the commotion and St. Clair, helpless with laughter, rocked to and fro in the aisle. Prillie Rogerson fainted and Annetta Bell went into hysterics.

It seemed a long time, although it was really only a few minutes, before the last pin-wheel subsided. Anne, recovering herself, sprang to open doors and windows and let out the gas and smoke which filled the room. Then she helped the girls carry the unconscious Prillie into the porch, where Barbara Shaw, in an agony of desire to be useful, poured a pailful of half frozen water over Prillie's face and shoulders before anyone could stop her.

It was a full hour before quiet was restored . . . but it was a quiet that might be felt. Everybody realized that even the explosion had not cleared the teacher's mental atmosphere. Nobody, except Anthony Pye, dared whisper a word. Ned Clay accidentally squeaked his pencil while working a sum, caught Anne's eye and wished the floor would open and swallow him up. The geography class were whisked through a continent with a speed that made them dizzy. The grammar class were parsed and analyzed within an inch of their lives. Chester Sloane, spelling "odoriferous" with two f's, was made to feel that he could never live down the disgrace of it, either in this world or that which is to come.

Anne knew that she had made herself ridiculous and that the incident would be laughed over that night at a score of tea-tables, but the knowledge only angered her further. In a calmer mood she could have carried off the situation with a laugh but now that was impossible; so she ignored it in icy disdain.

When Anne returned to the school after dinner all the children were as usual in their seats and every face was bent studiously over a desk except Anthony Pye's. He peered across his book at Anne, his black eyes sparkling with curiosity and mockery. Anne twitched open the drawer of her desk in search of chalk and under her very hand a lively mouse sprang out of the drawer, scampered over the desk, and leaped to the floor.

Anne screamed and sprang back, as if it had been a snake, and Anthony Pye laughed aloud.

Then a silence fell . . . a very creepy, uncomfortable silence. Annetta Bell was of two minds whether to go into hysterics again or not, especially as she didn't know just where the mouse had gone. But she decided not to. Who could take any comfort out of hysterics with a teacher so white faced and so blazing eyed standing before one?

"Who put that mouse in my desk?" said Anne. Her voice was quite low but it made a shiver go up and down Paul Irving's spine. Joe Sloane caught her eye, felt responsible from the crown of his head to the sole of his feet, but stuttered out wildly,

"N . . . n . . . not m . . . m . . . me t . . . t . . . teacher, n . . . n . . . not m . . . m . . . me."

Anne paid no attention to the wretched Joseph. She looked at Anthony Pye, and Anthony Pye looked back, unabashed and unashamed.

"Anthony, was it you?"

"Yes, it was," said Anthony insolently.

Anne took her pointer from her desk. It was a long, heavy hardwood pointer.

"Come here, Anthony."

It was far from being the most severe punishment Anthony Pye had ever undergone. Anne, even the stormy-souled Anne she was at that moment, could not have punished any child cruelly. But the pointer nipped keenly and finally Anthony's bravado failed him; he winced and the tears came to his eyes.

Anne, conscience-stricken, dropped the pointer and told Anthony to go to his seat. She sat down at her desk feeling ashamed, repentant, and bitterly mortified. Her quick anger was gone and she would have given much to have been able to seek relief in tears. So all her boasts had come to this . . . she had actually whipped one of her pupils. How Jane would triumph! And how Mr. Harrison would chuckle! But worse than this, bitterist thought of all, she had lost her last chance of winning Anthony Pye. Never would he like her now.

Anne, by what somebody has called "a Herculaneum effort," kept back her tears until she got home that night. Then she shut herself in the east gable room and wept all her shame and remorse and disappointment into her pillows . . . wept so long that Marilla grew alarmed, invaded the room, and insisted on knowing what the trouble was.

"The trouble is, I've got things the matter with my conscience," sobbed Anne. "Oh, this has been such a Jonah day, Marilla. I'm so ashamed of myself. I lost my temper and whipped Anthony Pye."

"I'm glad to hear it," said Marilla with decision. "It's what you should have done long ago."

Oh, no, no, Marilla. And I don't see how I can ever look those children in the face again. I feel that I have humiliated myself to the very dust. You don't know how cross and hateful and horrid I was. I can't forget the expression in Paul Irving's eyes . . . he looked so surprised and dispappointed. Oh, Marilla, I *have* tried so hard to be patient and to win Anthony's liking . . . and now it has all gone for nothing."

Marilla passed her hard work-worn hand over the girl's glossy, tumbled hair with a wonderful tenderness. When Anne's sobs grew quieter she said, very gently for her,

"You take things too much to heart, Anne. We all make mistakes . . . but people forget them. And Jonah days come to everybody. As for Anthony Pye, why need you care if he does dislike you? He is the only one."

"I can't help it. I want everybody to love me and it hurts me so when anybody doesn't. And Anthony never will now. Oh, I just made an idiot of myself today, Marilla. I'll tell you the whole story."

Marilla listened to the whole story, and if she smiled at certain parts of it Anne never knew. When the tale was ended she said briskly,

"Well, never mind. This day's done and there's a new one coming tomorrow, with no mistakes in it yet, as you used to say yourself. Just come downstairs and have your supper. You'll see if a good cup of tea and those plum puffs I made today won't hearten you up."

"Plum puffs won't minister to a mind diseased," said Anne disconsolately; but Marilla thought it a good sign that she had recovered sufficiently to adapt a quotation.

The cheerful supper table, with the twins' bright faces, and Marilla's matchless plum puffs . . . of which Davy ate four . . . did "hearten her up" considerably after all. She had a good sleep that night and awakened in the morning to find herself and the world transformed. It had snowed softly and thickly all through the hours of darkness and the beautiful whiteness, glittering in the frosty sunshine, looked like a mantle of charity cast over all the mistakes and humiliations of the past.

> *"Every morn is a fresh beginning,*
> *Every morn is the world made new,"*

sang Anne, as she dressed.

Owing to the snow she had to go around by the road to school and she thought it was certainly an impish coincidence that Anthony Pye should come ploughing along just as she left the Green Gables lane. She felt as guilty as if their positions were reversed; but to her unspeakable astonishment Anthony not only lifted his cap . . . which he had never done before . . . but said easily,

"Kind of bad walking, ain't it? Can I take those books for you, teacher?"

Anne surrendered her books and wondered if she could possibly be awake. Anthony walked on in silence to the school, but when Anne took her books she smiled down at him . . . not the stereotyped "kind" smile she had so persistently assumed for his benefit but a sudden outflashing of good comradeship. Anthony smiled . . . no, if the truth must be told, Anthony *grinned* back. A grin is not generally supposed to be a respectful thing; yet Anne suddenly felt that if she had not yet won Anthony's liking she had, somehow or other, won his respect.

Mrs. Rachel Lynde came up the next Saturday and confirmed this.

"Well, Anne, I guess you've won over Anthony Pye, that's what. He says he believes you are some good after all, even if you are a girl. Says that whipping you gave him was 'just as good as a man's.' "

"I never expected to win him by whipping him, though," said Anne, a little mournfully, feeling that her ideals had played her false somewhere. "It doesn't seem right. I'm *sure* my theory of kindness *can't* be wrong."

"No, but the Pyes are an exception to every known rule, that's what," declared Mrs. Rachel with conviction.

Mr. Harrison said "Thought you'd come to it," when he heard it, and Jane rubbed it in rather unmercifully.

CHAPTER 13

A GOLDEN PICNIC

ANNE, ON her way to Orchard Slope, met Diana, bound for Green Gables, just where the mossy old log bridge spanned the brook below the Haunted Wood, and they sat down by the margin of the Dryad's Bubble, where tiny ferns were unrolling like curly-headed green pixy folk wakening up from a nap.

"I was just on my way over to invite you to help me celebrate my birthday on Saturday," said Anne.

"Your birthday? But your birthday was in March!"

"That wasn't my fault," laughed Anne. "If my parents had consulted me it would never had happened then. I should have chosen to be born in spring, of course. It must be delightful to come into the world with the mayflowers and violets. You would always feel that you were their foster sister. But since I didn't, the next best thing is to celebrate my birthday in the spring. Priscilla is coming over Saturday and Jane will be home. We'll all four start off to the woods and spend a golden day making the acquaintance of the spring. We none of us really know her yet, but we'll meet her back there as we never can anywhere else. I want to explore all those fields and lonely places anyhow. I have a conviction that there are scores of beautiful nooks there that have never really been *seen* although they may have been *looked* at. We'll make friends with wind and sky and sun, and bring home the spring in our hearts.''

"It *sounds* awfully nice," said Diana, with some inward distrust of Anne's magic of words. "But won't it be very damp in some places yet?''

"Oh, we'll wear rubbers," was Anne's concession to practicalities. "And I want you to come over early Saturday morning and help me prepare lunch. I'm going to have the daintiest things possible . . . things that will match the spring, you understand . . . little jelly tarts and lady fingers, and drop cookies frosted with pink and yellow icing, and buttercup cake. And we must have sandwiches too, though they're *not* very poetical.''

Saturday proved an ideal day for a picnic . . . a day of breeze and blue, warm, sunny, with a little rollicking wind blowing across meadow and orchard. Over every sunlit upland and field was a delicate, flower-starred green.

Mr. Harrison, harrowing at the back of his farm and feeling some of the spring witch-work even in his sober, middle-aged blood, saw four girls, basket laden, tripping across the end of his field where it joined a fringing woodland of birch and fir. Their blithe voices and laughter echoed down to him.

"It's so easy to be happy on a day like this, isn't it?" Anne was saying, with true Anneish philosophy. "Let's try to make this a really golden day, girls, a day to which we can always look back with delight. We're to seek for beauty and refuse to see anything else. 'Begone, dull care!' Jane, you are thinking of something that went wrong in school yesterday.''

"How do you know?" gasped Jane, amazed.

"Oh, I know the expression . . . I've felt it often enough on my own face. But put it out of your mind, there's a dear. It will keep till Monday . . . or if it doesn't so much the better. Oh, girls, girls, see that patch of violets! There's something for memory's picture gallery. When I'm eighty years old . . . if I ever am . . . I shall shut my eyes and see those violets just as I see them now. That's the first good gift our day has given us.''

"If a kiss could be seen I think it would look like a violet," said Priscilla.

Anne glowed.

"I'm so glad you *spoke* that thought, Priscilla, instead of just thinking it and keeping it to yourself. This world would be a much more interesting place . . . although it *is* very interesting anyhow . . . if people spoke out their real thoughts."

"It would be too hot to hold some folks," quoth Jane sagely.

"I suppose it might be, but that would be their own faults for thinking nasty things. Anyhow, we can tell all our thoughts today because we are going to have nothing but beautiful thoughts. Everybody can say just what comes into her head. *That* is conversation. Here's a little path I never saw before. Let's explore it."

The path was a winding one, so narrow that the girls walked in single file and even then the fir bough brushed their faces. Under the firs were velvety cushions of moss, and further on, where the trees were smaller and fewer, the ground was rich in a variety of green growing things.

"What a lot of elephant's ears," exclaimed Diana. "I'm going to pick a big bunch, they're so pretty."

"How did such graceful feathery things ever come to have such a dreadful name?" asked Priscilla.

"Because the person who first named them either had no imagination at all or else far too much," said Anne. "Oh, girls, look at that!"

"That" was a shallow woodland pool in the center of a little open glade where the path ended. Later on in the season it would be dried up and its place filled with a rank growth of ferns; but now it was a glimmering placid sheet, round as a saucer and clear as crystal. A ring of slender young birches encircled it and little ferns fringed its margin.

"*How* sweet!" said Jane.

"Let us dance around it like wood-nymphs," cried Anne, dropping her basket and extending her hands.

But the dance was not a success for the ground was boggy and Jane's rubbers came off.

"You can't be a wood-nymph if you have to wear rubbers," was her decision.

"Well, we must name this place before we leave it," said Anne, yielding to the indisputable logic of facts. "Everybody suggest a name and we'll draw lots. Diana?"

"Birch Pool," suggested Diana promptly.

"Crystal Lake," said Jane.

Anne, standing behind them, implored Priscilla with her eyes not to perpetrate another such name and Priscilla rose to the occasion with "Glimmerglass." Anne's selection was "The Fairies' Mirror."

The names were written on strips of birch bark with a pencil Schoolma'am Jane produced from her pocket, and placed in Anne's hat. Then Priscilla shut her eyes and drew one. "Crystal Lake," read Jane triumphantly. Crystal Lake it was, and if Anne thought that chance had played the pool a shabby trick she did not say so.

Pushing through the undergrowth beyond, the girls came out to the young green seclusion of Mr. Silas Sloane's back pasture. Across it they found the entrance to a lane striking up through the woods and voted to explore it also. It rewarded their quest with a succession of pretty surprises. First, skirting Mr. Sloane's pasture, came an archway of wild cherry trees all in bloom. The girls swung their hats on their arms and wreathed their hair with the creamy, fluffy blossoms. Then the lane turned at right angles and plunged into a spruce wood so thick and dark that they walked in a gloom as of twilight, with not a glimpse of sky or sunlight to be seen.

"This is where the bad wood elves dwell," whispered Anne. "They are impish and malicious but they can't harm us, because they are not allowed to do evil in the spring. There was one peeping at us around that old twisted fir; and didn't you see a group of them on that big freckly toadstool we just passed? The good fairies always dwell in the sunshiny places."

"I wish there really were fairies," said Jane. "Wouldn't it be nice to have three wishes granted you . . . or even only one? What would you wish for, girls, if you could have a wish granted? I'd wish to be rich and beautiful and clever."

"I'd wish to be tall and slender," said Diana.

"I would wish to be famous," said Priscilla.

Anne thought of her hair and then dismissed the thought as unworthy.

"I'd wish it might be spring all the time and in everybody's heart and all our lives," she said.

"But that," said Priscilla, "would be just wishing this world were like heaven."

"Only like a part of heaven. In the other parts there would be summer and autumn . . . yes, and a bit of winter, too. I think I want glittering snowy fields and white frosts in heaven sometimes. Don't you, Jane?"

"I . . . I don't know," said Jane uncomfortably. Jane was a good girl, a member of the church, who tried conscientiously to live up to her profession and believed everything she had been taught. But she never thought about heaven any more than she could help, for all that.

"Minnie May asked me the other day if we would wear our best dresses every day in heaven," laughed Diana.

"And didn't you tell her we would?" asked Anne.

"Mercy, no! I told her we wouldn't be thinking of dresses at all there."

"Oh, I think we will . . . a *little*," said Anne earnestly. "There'll be plenty of time in all eternity for it without neglecting more important things. I believe we'll all wear beautiful dresses . . . or I suppose *raiment* would be a more suitable way of speaking. I shall want to wear pink for a few centuries at first . . . it would take me that long to get tired of it, I feel sure. I do love pink so and I can never wear it in *this* world."

"Past the spruces the lane dipped down into a sunny little open where a log bridge spanned a brook; and then came the glory of a sunlit beechwood where the air was like transparent golden wine, and the leaves fresh and green, and the wood floor a mosaic of tremulous sunshine. Then more wild cherries, and a little valley of lissome firs, and then a hill so steep that the girls lost their breath climbing it; but when they reached the top and came out into the open the prettiest surprise of all awaited them.

Beyond were the "back fields" of the farms that ran out to the upper Carmody road. Just before them, hemmed in by beeches and firs but open to the south, was a little corner and in it a garden . . . or what had once been a garden. A tumbledown stone dyke, overgrown with mosses and grass, surrounded it. Along the eastern side ran a row of garden cherry trees, white as a snowdrift. There were traces of old paths still and a double line of rosebushes through the middle; but all the rest of the space was a sheet of yellow and white narcissi, in their airiest, most lavish, wind-swayed bloom above the lush green grasses.

"Oh, how perfectly lovely!" three of the girls cried. Anne only gazed in eloquent silence.

"How in the world does it happen that there ever was a garden back here?" said Priscilla in amazement.

"It must be Hester Gray's garden," said Diana. "I've heard mother speak of it but I never saw it before, and I wouldn't have supposed that it could be in existence still. You've heard the story, Anne?"

"No, but the name seems familiar to me."

"Oh, you've seen it in the graveyard. She is buried down there in the poplar corner. You know the little brown stone with the opening gates carved on it and 'Sacred to the memory of Hester Gray, aged twenty-two.' Jordan Gray is buried right beside her but there's no stone to him. It's a wonder Marilla never told you about it, Anne. To be sure, it happened thirty years ago and everybody has forgotten."

"Well, if there's a story we must have it," said Anne. "Let's sit right down here among the narcissi and Diana will tell it. Why, girls, there are hundreds of them . . . they've spread over everything. It looks as if the garden were carpeted with moonshine and sunshine combined. This is a discovery worth making. To think that I've lived within a mile of this place for six years and have never seen it before! Now, Diana."

"Long ago," began Diana, "this farm belonged to old Mr. David Gray. He didn't live on it . . . he lived where Silas Sloane lives now. He had one son, Jordan, and he went up to Boston one winter to work and while he was there he fell in love with a girl named Hester Murray. She was working in a store and she hated it. She'd been brought up in the country and she always wanted to get back. When Jordan asked her to marry him she said she would if he'd take her away to some quiet spot where she'd see nothing but fields and trees. So he brought her to Avonlea. Mrs. Lynde said he was taking a fearful risk in marrying a Yankee, and it's certain that Hester was very delicate and a very poor housekeeper; but mother says she was very pretty and sweet and Jordan just worshipped the ground she walked on. Well, Mr. Gray gave Jordan this farm and he built a little house back here and Jordan and Hester lived in it for four years. She never went out much and hardly anybody went to see her except mother and Mrs. Lynde. Jordan made her this garden and she was crazy about it and spent most of her time in it. She wasn't much of a housekeeper but she had a knack with flowers. And then she got sick. Mother says she thinks she was in consumption before she ever came here. She never really laid up but just grew weaker and weaker all the time. Jordan wouldn't have anybody to wait on her. He did it all himself and mother says he was as tender and gentle as a woman. Every day he'd wrap her in a shawl and carry her out to the garden and she'd lie there on a bench quite happy. They say she used to make Jordan kneel down by her every night and morning and pray with her that she might die out in the garden when the time came. And her prayer was answered. One day Jordan carried her out to the bench and then he picked all the roses that were out and heaped them over her; and she just smiled up at him . . . and closed her eyes . . . and that," concluded Diana softly, "was the end."

"Oh, what a dear story," sighed Anne, wiping away her tears.

"What became of Jordan?" asked Priscilla.

"He sold the farm after Hester died and went back to Boston. Mr. Jabez Sloane bought the farm and hauled the little house out to the road. Jordan died about ten years after and he was brought home and buried beside Hester."

"I can't understand how she could have wanted to live back here, away from everything," said Jane.

"Oh, I can easily understand *that*," said Anne thoughtfully. "I wouldn't want it myself for a steady thing, because, although I love the fields and woods, I love people too. But I can understand it in Hester. She was tired to death of the noise of the big city and the crowds of people always coming and going and caring nothing for her. She just wanted to escape from it all to some still, green, friendly place where she could rest. And she got just what she wanted, which is something very few people do, I believe. She had four beautiful years before she died . . . four years of perfect happiness, so I think she was to be envied more than pitied. And then to shut your eyes and fall asleep among roses, with the one you loved best on earth smiling down at you . . . oh, I think it was beautiful!"

"She set out those cherry trees over there," said Diana. "She told mother she'd never live to eat their fruit, but she wanted to think that something she had planted would go on living and helping to make the world beautiful after she was dead."

"I'm so glad we came this way," said Anne, the shining eyed. "This is my adopted birthday, you know, and this garden and its story is the birthday gift it has given me. Did your mother ever tell you what Hester Gray looked like, Diana?"

"No . . . only just that she was pretty."

"I'm rather glad of that, because I can imagine what she looked like, without being hampered by facts. I think she was very slight and small, with softly curling dark hair and big, sweet, timid brown eyes, and a little wistful, pale face."

The girls left their baskets in Hester's garden and spent the rest of the afternoon rambling in the woods and fields surrounding it, discovering many pretty nooks and lanes. When they got hungry they had lunch in the prettiest spot of all . . . on the steep bank of a gurgling brook where white birches shot up out of long feathery grasses. The girls sat down by the roots and did full justice to Anne's dainties, even the unpoetical sandwiches being greatly appreciated by hearty, unspoiled appetites sharpened by all the fresh air and exercise they had enjoyed. Anne had brought glasses and lemonade for her guests, but for her own part drank cold brook water from a cup fashioned out of birch bark. The cup leaked, and the water tasted of earth, as brook water is apt to do in spring; but Anne thought it more appropriate to the occasion than lemonade.

"Look, do you see that poem?" she said suddenly, pointing.

"Where?" Jane and Diana stared, as if expecting to see Runic rhymes on the birch trees.

"There . . . down in the brook . . . that old green, mossy log with the water flowing over it in those smooth ripples that look as if they'd been combed, and that single shaft of sunshine falling right athwart it, far down into the pool. Oh, it's the most beautiful poem I ever saw."

"I should rather call it a picture," said Jane. "A poem is lines and verses."

"Oh dear me, no." Anne shook her head with its fluffy wild cherry coronal positively. "The lines and verses are only the outward garments of the poem and are no more really it than your ruffles and flounces are *you*, Jane. The real poem is the soul within them . . . and that beautiful bit is the soul of an unwritten poem. It is not every day one sees a soul . . . even of a poem."

"I wonder what a soul . . . a person's soul . . . would look like," said Priscilla dreamily.

"Like that, I should think," answered Anne, pointing to a radiance of sifted sunlight streaming through a birch tree. "Only with shape and features of course. I like to fancy souls as being made of light. And some are all shot through with rosy stains and quivers . . . and some have a soft glitter like moonlight on the sea . . . and some are pale and transparent like mist at dawn."

"I read somewhere once that souls were like flowers," said Priscilla.

"Then your soul is a golden narcissus," said Anne, "and Diana's is like a red, red rose. Jane's is an apple blossom, pink and wholesome and sweet."

"And your own is a white violet, with purple streaks in its heart," finished Priscilla.

Jane whispered to Diana that she really could not understand what they were talking about. Could she?

The girls went home by the light of a calm golden sunset, their baskets filled with narcissus blossoms from Hester's garden, some of which Anne carried to the cemetery next day and laid upon Hester's grave. Minstrel robins were whistling in the firs and the frogs were singing in the marshes. All the basins among the hills were brimmed with topaz and emerald light.

"Well, we have had a lovely time after all," said Diana, as if she had hardly expected to have it when she set out.

"It has been a truly golden day," said Priscilla.

"I'm really awfully fond of the woods myself," said Jane.

Anne said nothing. She was looking afar into the western sky and thinking of little Hester Gray.

CHAPTER 14

A DANGER AVERTED

ANNE, WALKING home from the postoffice one Friday evening, was joined by Mrs. Lynde, who was as usual cumbered with all the cares of church and state.

"I've just been down to Timothy Cotton's to see if I could get Alice Louise to help me for a few days," she said. "I had her last week, for, though she's too slow to stop quick, she's better than nobody. But she's sick and can't come. Timothy's sitting there, too, coughing and complaining. He's been dying for ten years and he'll go on dying for ten years more. That kind can't even die and have done with it . . . they can't stick to anything, even to being sick, long enough to finish it. They're a terrible shiftless family and what is to become of them I don't know, but perhaps Providence does."

Mrs. Lynde sighed as if she rather doubted the extent of Providential knowledge on the subject.

"Marilla was in about her eyes again Tuesday, wasn't she? What did the specialist think of them?" she continued.

"He was much pleased," said Anne brightly. "He says there is a great improvement in them and he thinks the danger of her losing her sight completely is past. But he says she'll never be able to read much or do any fine hand-work again. How are your preparations for your bazaar coming on?"

The Ladies' Aid Society was preparing for a fair and supper, and Mrs. Lynde was the head and front of the enterprise."

"Pretty well . . . and that reminds me. Mrs. Allan thinks it would be nice to fix up a booth like an old time kitchen and serve a supper of baked beans, doughnuts, pie, and so on. We're collecting old-fashioned fixings everywhere. Mrs. Simon Fletcher is going to lend us her mother's braided rugs and Mrs. Levi Boulter some old chairs and Aunt Mary Shaw will lend us her cupboard with the glass doors. I suppose Marilla will let us have her brass candlesticks? And we want all the old dishes we can get. Mrs. Allan is specially set on having a real blue willow ware platter if we can find one. But nobody seems to have one. Do you know where we could get one?"

"Miss Josephine Barry has one. I'll write and ask her if she'll lend it for the occasion," said Anne.

"Well, I wish you would. I guess we'll have the supper in about a fortnight's time. Uncle Abe Andrews is prophesying rain and storms for about that time; and that's a pretty sure sign we'll have fine weather."

The said "Uncle Abe," it may be mentioned, was at least like other prophets in that he had small honor in his own country. He was, in fact, considered in the light of a standing joke, for few of his weather predictions were ever fulfilled. Mr. Elisha Wright, who labored under the impression that he was a local wit, used to say that nobody in Avonlea ever thought of looking in the Charlottetown dailies for weather probabilities. No; they just asked Uncle Abe what it was going to be tomorrow and expected the opposite. Nothing daunted, Uncle Abe kept on prophesying.

"We want to have the fair over before the election comes off," continued Mrs. Lynde, "for the candidates will be sure to come and spend lots of money. The Tories are bribing right and left, so they might as well be given a chance to spend their money honestly for once."

Anne was a red-hot Conservative, out of loyalty to Matthew's memory, but she said nothing. She knew better than to get Mrs. Lynde started on politics.

She had a letter for Marilla, postmarked from a town in British Columbia.

"It's probably from the children's uncle," she said excitedly, when she got home. "Oh, Marilla, I wonder what he says about them."

"The best plan might be to open it and see," said Marilla curtly. A close observer might have thought that she was excited also, but she would rather have died than show it.

Anne tore open the letter and glanced over the somewhat untidy and poorly written contents.

"He says he can't take the children this spring . . . he's been sick most of the winter and his wedding is put off. He wants to know if we can keep them till the fall and he'll try and take them then. We will, of course, won't we, Marilla?"

"I don't see that there is anything else for us to do," said Marilla rather grimly, although she felt a secret relief. "Anyhow they're not so much trouble as they were . . . or else we've got used to them. Davy has improved a great deal."

"His *manners* are certainly much better," said Anne cautiously, as if she were not prepared to say as much for his morals.

Anne had come home from school the previous evening, to find Marilla away at an Aid meeting, Dora asleep on the kitchen sofa, and Davy in the sitting room closet, blissfully absorbing the contents of a jar of Marilla's famous yellow plum preserves . . . "company jam," Davy called it . . . which he had been forbidden to touch. He looked very guilty when Anne pounced on him and whisked him out of the closet.

"Davy Keith, don't you know that it is very wrong of you to be eating that jam, when you were told never to meddle with anything in *that* closet?"

"Yes, I knew it was wrong," admitted Davy uncomfortably, "but plum jam is awful nice, Anne. I just peeped in and it looked so good I thought I'd take just a weeny taste. I stuck my finger in . . . " Anne groaned . . . "and licked it clean. And it was so much gooder than I'd ever thought that I got a spoon and just *sailed in*."

Anne gave him such a serious lecture on the sin of stealing plum jam that Davy became conscience stricken and promised with repentant kisses never to do it again.

"Anyhow, there'll be plenty of jam in heaven, that's one comfort," he said complacently.

Anne nipped a smile in the bud.

"Perhaps there will . . . if we want it," she said, "but what makes you think so?"

"Why, it's in the catechism," said Davy.

"Oh, no, there is nothing like *that* in the catechism, Davy."

"But I tell you there is," persisted Davy. "It was in that question Marilla taught me last Sunday. 'Why should we love God?' It says, 'Because He makes preserves, and redeems us.' Preserves is just a holy way of saying jam."

"I must get a drink of water," said Anne hastily. When she came back it cost her some time and trouble to explain to Davy that a certain comma in the said catechism question made a great deal of difference in the meaning.

"Well, I thought it was too good to be true," he said at last, with a sigh of disappointed conviction. "And besides, I didn't see when He'd find time to make jam if it's one endless Sabbath day, as the hymn says. I don't believe I want to go to heaven. Won't there ever be any Saturdays in heaven, Anne?"

"Yes, Saturdays, and every other kind of beautiful days. And every day in heaven will be more beautiful than the one before it, Davy," assured Anne, who was rather glad that Marilla was not by to be shocked. Marilla, it is needless to say, was bringing the twins up in the good old ways of theology and discouraged all fanciful speculations thereupon. Davy and Dora were taught a hymn, a catechism question, and two Bible verses every Sunday. Dora learned meekly and recited like a little machine, with perhaps as much understanding or interst as if she were one. Davy, on the contrary, had a lively curiosity, and frequently asked questions which made Marilla tremble for his fate.

"Chester Sloane says we'll do nothing all the time in heaven but walk around in white dresses and play on harps; and he says he hopes he won't have to go till he's an old man, 'cause maybe he'll like it better then. And he thinks it will be horrid to wear dresses and I think so too. Why can't men angels wear trousers, Anne? Chester Sloane is interested in those things, 'cause they're going to make a minister of him. He's *got* to be a minister 'cause his grandmother left the money to send him to college and he can't have it unless he is a minister. She thought a minister was such a 'spectable thing to have in a family. Chester says he doesn't mind much . . . though he'd rather be a blacksmith . . . but he's bound to have all the fun he can before he begins to be a minister, 'cause he doesn't espect to have much afterwards. *I* ain't going to be a minister. I'm going to be a storekeeper, like Mr. Blair, and keep heaps of candy and bananas. But I'd rather like going to your kind of a heaven if they'd let me play a mouth organ instead of a harp. Do you s'pose they would?"

"Yes, I think they would if you wanted it," was all Anne could trust herself to say.

The A.V.I.S. met at Mr. Haron Andrews' that evening and a full attendance had been requested, since important business was to be discussed. The A.V.I.S. was in a flourishing condition, and had already accomplished wonders. Early in the spring Mr. Major Spencer had redeemed his promise and had stumped, graded, and seeded down all the road front of his farm. A dozen other men, some prompted by a determination not to let a Spencer get ahead of them, others goaded into action by Improvers in their own households, had followed his example. The result was that there were long strips of smooth velvet turf where once had been unsightly undergrowth or brush. The farm fronts that had not been done looked so badly by contrast that their owners were secretly shamed into resolving to see what they could do another spring. The triangle of ground at the cross roads had also been cleared and seeded down, and Anne's bed of geraniums, unharmed by any marauding cow, was already set out in the center.

Altogether, the Improvers thought that they were getting on beautifully, even if Mr. Levi Boulter, tactfully approached by a carefully selected committee in regard to the old house on his upper farm, did bluntly tell them that he wasn't going to have it meddled with.

At this especial meeting they intended to draw up a petition to the school trustees, humbly praying that a fence be put around the school grounds; and a plan was also to be discussed for planting a few ornamental trees by the church, if the funds of the society would permit of it . . . , for, as Anne said, there was no use in starting another subscription as long as the hall remained blue. The members were assembled in the Andrews' parlor and Jane was already on her feet to move the appointment of a committee which should find out and report on the price of said trees, when Gertie Pye swept in, pompadoured and frilled within an inch of her life. Gertie had a habit of being late . . . "to make her entrance more effective," spiteful people said. Gertie's entrance in this instance was certainly effective, for she paused dramatically on the middle of the floor, threw up her hands, rolled her eyes, and exclaimed,

"I've just heard something perfectly awful. What *do* you think? Mr. Judson Parker *is going to rent all the road fence of his farm to a patent medicine company to paint advertisements on.*"

For once in her life Gertie Pye made all the sensation she desired. If she had thrown a bomb among the complacent Improvers she could hardly have made more.

"It *can't* be true," said Anne blankly.

"That's just what *I* said when I heard it first, don't you know," said Gertie, who was enjoying herself hugely. "*I* said it couldn't be true . . . that Judson Parker wouldn't have the *heart* to do it, don't you know. But father met him this afternoon and asked him about it and he said it *was* true. Just fancy! His farm is side-on to the Newbridge road and how perfectly awful it will look to see advertisements of pills and plasters all along it, don't you know?"

The Improvers *did* know, all too well. Even the least imaginative among them could picture the grotesque effect of half a mile of board fence adorned with such advertisements. All thought of church and school grounds vanished before this new danger. Parliamentary rules and regulations were forgotten, and Anne, in despair, gave up trying to keep minutes at all. Everybody talked at once and fearful was the hubbub.

"Oh, let us keep calm," implored Anne, who was the most excited of them all, "and try to think of some way of preventing him."

"I don't know how you're going to prevent him," exclaimed Jane bitterly. "Everybody knows what Judson Parker is. He'd do *any-thing* for money. He hasn't a *spark* of public spirit or *any* sense of the beautiful."

The prospect looked rather unpromising. Judson Parker and his sister were the only Parkers in Avonlea, so that no leverage could be exerted by family connections. Martha Parker was a lady of all too certain age who disapproved of young people in general and the Improvers in particular. Judson was a jovial, smooth-spoken man, so uniformly good-natured and bland that it was surprising how few friends he had. Perhaps he had got the better in too many business transactions . . . which seldom makes for popularity. He was reputed to be very "sharp" and it was the general opinion that he "hadn't much principle."

"If Judson Parker has a chance to 'turn an honest penny,' as he says himself, he'll never lose it," declared Fred Wright.

"Is there *nobody* who has any influence over him?" asked Anne despairingly.

"He goes to see Louisa Spencer at White Sands," suggested Carrie Sloane. "Perhaps she could coax him not to rent his fences."

"Not she," said Gilbert emphatically. "I know Louisa Spencer well. She doesn't 'believe' in Village Improvement Societies, but she *does* believe in dollars and cents. She'd be more likely to urge Judson on than to dissuade him."

"The only thing to do is to appoint a committee to wait on him and protest," said Julia Bell, "and you must send girls, for he'd hardly be civil to boys . . . but *I* won't go, so nobody need nominate me."

"Better send Anne alone," said Oliver Sloane. "She can talk Judson over if anybody can."

Anne protested. She was willing to go and do the talking; but she must have others with her "for moral support." Diana and Jane were therefore appointed to support her morally and the Improvers broke up, buzzing like angry bees with indignation. Anne was so worried that she didn't sleep until nearly morning, and then she dreamed that the trustees had put a fence around the school and painted "Try Purple Pills" all over it.

The committee waited on Judson Parker the next afternoon. Anne pleaded eloquently against his nefarious design and Jane and Diana supported her morally and valiantly. Judson was sleek, suave, flattering; paid them several compliments of the delicacy of sunflowers; felt real bad to refuse such charming young ladies . . . but business was business; couldn't afford to let sentiment stand in the way these hard times.

"But I'll tell you what I *will* do," he said, with a twinkle in his light, full eyes. "I'll tell the agent he must use only handsome, tasty colors . . . red and yellow and so on. I'll tell him he musn't paint the ads. *blue* on any account."

The vanquished committee retired, thinking things not lawful to be uttered.

"We have done all we can do and must simply trust the rest to Providence," said Jane, with an unconscious imitation of Mrs. Lynde's tone and manner.

"I wonder if Mr. Allan could do anything," reflected Diana.

Anne shook her head.

"No, it's no use to worry Mr. Allan, especially now when the baby's so sick. Judson would slip away from him as smoothly as from us, although he *has* taken to going to church quite regularly just now. That is simply because Louisa Spencer's father is an elder and very particular about such things."

"Judson Parker is the only man in Avonlea who would dream of renting his fences," said Jane indignantly. "Even Levi Boulter or Lorenzo White would never stoop to that, tight fisted as they are. They would have too much respect for public opinion."

Public opinion was certainly down on Judson Parker when the facts became known, but that did not help matters much. Judson chuckled to himself and defied it, and the Improvers were trying to reconcile themselves to the prospect of seeing the prettiest part of the Newbridge road defaced by advertisements, when Anne rose quietly at the president's call for reports of committees on the occasion of the next meeting of the Society, and announced that Mr. Judson Parker had instructed her to inform the Society that he was *not* going to rent his fences to the Patent Medicine Company.

Jane and Diana stared as if they found it hard to believe their ears. Parliamentary etiquette, which was generally very strictly enforced in the A.V.I.S., forbade them giving instant vent to their curiosity, but after the Society adjourned Anne was besieged for explanations. Anne had no explanation to give. Judson Parker had overtaken her on the road the preceding evening and told her that he had decided to humor the A.V.I.S. in its peculiar prejudice against patent medicine advertisements. That was all Anne would say, then or ever afterwards, and it was the simple truth; but when Jane Andrews, on her way home, confided to Oliver Sloane her firm belief that there was more behind Judson Parker's mysterious change of heart than Anne Shirley had revealed, she spoke the truth also.

Anne had been down to old Mrs. Irving's on the shore road the preceding evening and had come home by a short cut which led her first over the low-lying shore fields, and then through the beech wood below Robert Dickson's, by a little footpath that ran out to the main road just above the Lake of Shining Waters . . . known to unimaginative people as Barry's pond.

Two men were sitting in their buggies, reined off to the side of the road, just at the entrance of the path. One was Judson Parker; the other was Jerry Corcoran, a Newbridge man against whom, as Mrs. Lynde would have told you in eloquent italics, nothing shady had ever been *proved*. He was an agent for agricultural implements and a prominent personage in matters political. He had a finger . . . some people said *all* his fingers . . . in every political pie that was cooked; and as Canada was on the eve of a general election Jerry Corcoran had been a busy man for many weeks, canvassing the county in the interests of his party's candidate. Just as Anne emerged from under the overhanging beech boughs she heard Corcoran say,

"If you'll vote for Amesbury, Parker . . .well, I've a note for that pair of harrows you've got in the spring. I suppose you wouldn't object to having it back, eh?"

"We . . . ll, since you put it in that way," drawled Judson with a grin, "I reckon I might as well do it. A man must look out for his own interests in these hard times."

Both saw Anne at this moment and conversation abruptly ceased. Anne bowed frostily and walked on, with her chin slightly more tilted than usual. Soon Judson Parker overtook her.

"Have a lift, Anne?" he inquired genially.

"Thank you, no," said Anne politely, but with a fine, needle-like disdain in her voice that pierced even Judson Parker's none too sensitive consciousness. His face reddened and he twitched his reins angrily; but the next second prudential considerations checked him.

He looked uneasily at Anne, as she walked steadily on, glancing neither to the right nor to the left. Had she heard Corcoran's unmistakable offer and his own too plain acceptance of it? Confound Corcoran! If he couldn't put his meaning into less dangerous phrases he'd get into trouble some of these long-come-shorts. And confound red-headed school-ma'ams with a habit of popping out of beechwoods where they had no business to be. If Anne had heard, Judson Parker, measuring her corn in his own half bushel, as the country saying went, and cheating himself thereby, as such people generally do, believed that she would tell it far and wide. Now, Judson Parker, as has been seen, was not overly regardful of public opinion; but to be known as having accepted a bribe would be a nasty thing; and if it ever reached Isaac Spencer's ears farewell for ever to all hope of winning Louisa Jane with her comfortable prospects as the heiress of a well-to-do farmer. Judson Parker knew that Mr. Spencer looked somewhat askance at him as it was; he could not afford to take any risks.

"Ahem . . . Anne, I've been wanting to see you about that little matter we were discussing the other day. I've decided not to let my fences to that company after all. A society with an aim like yours ought to be encouraged."

Anne thawed out the merest trifle.

"Thank you," she said.

"And . . . and . . . you needn't mention that little conversation of mine with Jerry."

"I have no intention of mentioning it in any case," said Anne icily, for she would have seen every fence in Avonlea painted with advertisements before she would have stooped to bargain with a man who would sell his vote.

"Just so . . . just so," agreed Judson, imagining that they understood each other beautifully. "I didn't suppose you would. Of course, I was only stringing Jerry . . . he thinks he's so all-fired cute and smart. I've no intention of voting for Amesbury. I'm going to vote for Grant as I've always done . . . you'll see that when the election comes off. I just led Jerry on to see if he would commit himself. And it's all right about the fence . . . you can tell the Improvers that."

"It takes all sorts of people to make a world, as I've often heard, but I think there are some who could be spared," Anne told her reflection in the east gable mirror that night. "I wouldn't have mentioned the disgraceful thing to a soul anyhow, so my conscience is clear on *that* score. I really don't know who or what is to be thanked for this. *I* did nothing to bring it about, and it's hard to believe that Providence ever works by means of the kind of politics men like Judson Parker and Jerry Corcoran have.''

CHAPTER 15

THE BEGINNING OF VACATION

ANNE LOCKED the schoolhouse door on a still, yellow evening, when the winds were purring in the spruces around the playground, and the shadows were long and lazy by the edge of the woods. She dropped the key into her pocket with a sigh of satisfaction. The school year was ended, she had been reengaged for the next, with many expressions of satisfaction . . . only Mr. Harmon Andrews told her she ought to use the strap oftener . . . and two delightful months of well-earned vacation beckoned her invitingly. Anne felt at peace with the world and herself as she walked down the hill with her basket of flowers in her hand. Since the earliest mayflowers Anne had never missed her weekly pilgrimage to Matthew's grave. Everybody else in Avonlea, except Marilla, had already forgotten quiet, shy, unimportant Matthew Cuthbert; but his memory was still green in Anne's heart and always would be. She could never forget the kind old man who had been the first to give her the love and sympathy her starved childhood had craved.

At the foot of the hill a boy was sitting on the fence in the shadow of the spruces . . . a boy with big, dreamy eyes and a beautiful, sensitive face. He swung down and joined Anne, smiling; but there were traces of tears on his cheeks.

"I thought I'd wait for you, teacher, because I knew you were going to the graveyard," he said, slipping his hand into hers. "I'm going there, too . . . I'm taking this bouquet of geraniums to put on Grandpa Irving's grave for grandma. And look, teacher, I'm going to put this bunch of white roses beside Grandpa's grave in memory of my little mother . . . because I can't go to her grave to put it there. But don't you think she'll know all about it, just the same?"

''Yes, I am sure she will, Paul.''

''You see, teacher, it's just three years today since my little mother died. It's such a long, long time but it hurts just as much as ever . . . and I miss her just as much as ever. Sometimes it seems to me that I just can't bear it, it hurts so.''

Paul's voice quivered and his lips trembled. He looked down at his roses, hoping that his teacher would not notice the tears in his eyes.

''And yet,'' said Anne, very softly, ''you wouldn't want it to stop hurting . . . you wouldn't want to forget your little mother even if you could.''

''No, indeed, I wouldn't . . . that's just the way I feel. You're so good at understanding, teacher. Nobody else understands so well . . . not even grandma, although she's so good to me. Father understood pretty well, but still I couldn't talk much to him about mother, because it made him feel so bad. When he put his hand over his face I always knew it was time to stop. Poor father, he must be dreadfully lonesome without me; but you see he has nobody but a housekeeper now and he thinks housekeepers are no good to bring up little boys, especially when he has to be away from home so much on business. Grandmothers are better, next to mothers. Some day, when I'm brought up, I'll go back to father and we're never going to be parted again.''

Paul had talked so much to Anne about his mother and father that she felt as if she had known them. She thought his mother must have been very like what he was himself, in temperament and disposition; and she had an idea that Stephen Irving was a rather reserved man with a deep and tender nature which he kept hidden scrupulously from the world.

''Father's not very easy to get acquainted with,'' Paul had said once. ''I never got really acquainted with him until after my little mother died. But he's splendid when you do get to know him. I love him the best in all the world, and Grandma Irving next, and then you, teacher. I'd love you next to father if it wasn't my *duty* to love Grandma Irving best, because she's doing so much for me. *You* know, teacher. I wish she would leave the lamp in my room till I go to sleep, though. She takes it right out as soon as she tucks me up because she says I mustn't be a coward. I'm *not* scared, but I'd *rather* have the light. My little mother used always to sit beside me and hold my hand till I went to sleep. I expect she spoiled me. Mothers do sometimes, you know.''

No, Anne did not know this, although she might imagine it. She

thought sadly of *her* "little mother," the mother who had thought
her so "perfectly beautiful" and who had died so long ago and was
buried beside her boyish husband in that unvisited grave far away.
Anne could not remember her mother and for this reason she almost
envied Paul.

"My birthday is next week," said Paul, as they walked up the
long red hill, basking in the June sunshine, "and father wrote me that
he is sending me something that he thinks I'll like better than
anything else he could send. I believe it has come already, for
Grandma is keeping the bookcase drawer locked and that is something new. And when I asked her why, she just looked mysterious
and said little boys mustn't be too curious. It's very exciting to have a
birthday, isn't it? I'll be eleven. You'd never think it to look at me,
would you? Grandma says I'm very small for my age and that it's all
because I don't eat enough porridge. I do my very best, but Grandma
gives such *generous* platefuls . . . there's nothing mean about Grandma, I can tell you. Ever since you and I had that talk about praying
going home from Sunday School that day, teacher . . . when you
said we ought to pray about all our difficulties . . . I've prayed
every night that God would give me enough grace to enable me to eat
every bit of my porridge in the mornings. But I've never been able to
do it yet, and whether it's because I have too little grace or too much
porridge I really can't decide. Grandma says father was brought up
on porridge, and it certainly did work in his case, for you ought to see
the shoulders he has. But sometimes," concluded Paul with a sigh
and a meditative air, "I really think porridge will be the death of
me."

Anne permitted herself a smile, since Paul was not looking at her.
All Avonlea knew that old Mrs. Irving was bringing her grandson up
in accordance with the good, old-fashioned methods of diet and
morals.

"Let us hope not, dear," she said cheerfully. "How are your rock
people coming on? Does the oldest Twin still continue to behave
himself?"

"He *has* to," said Paul emphatically. "He knows I won't associate with him if he doesn't. He is really full of wickedness, *I*
think."

"And has Nora found out about the Golden Lady yet?"

"No; but I think she suspects. I'm almost sure she watched me the
last time I went to the cave. *I* don't mind if she finds out . . . it is
only for *her* sake I don't want her to . . . so that her feelings won't

be hurt. But if she is *determined* to have her feelings hurt it can't be helped."

"If I were to go to the shore some night with you do you think I could see your rock people too?"

Paul shook his head gravely.

"No, I don't think you could see *my* rock people. I'm the only person who can see them. But you could see rock people of your own. You're one of the kind that can. We're both that kind. *You* know, teacher," he added, squeezing her hand chummily. "Isn't it splendid to be that kind, teacher?"

"Splendid," Anne agreed, gray shining eyes looking down into blue shining ones. Anne and Paul both knew

> *How fair the realm*
> *Imagination opens to the view,*

and both knew the way to that happy land. There the rose of joy bloomed immortal by dale and stream; clouds never darkened the sunny sky; sweet bells never jangled out of tune; and kindred spirits abounded. The knowledge of that land's geography . . . "east o' the sun, west o' the moon" . . . is priceless lore, not to be bought in any market place. It must be the gift of the good fairies at birth and the years can never deface it or take it away. It is better to possess it, living in a garret, than to be the inhabitant of palaces without it.

The Avonlea graveyard was as yet the grass-grown solitude it had always been. To be sure, the Improvers had an eye on it, and Priscilla Grant had read a paper on cemeteries before the last meeting of the Society. At some future time the Improvers meant to have the lichened, wayword old board fence replaced by a neat wire railing, the grass mown and the leaning monuments straightened up.

Anne put on Matthew's grave the flowers she had brought for it, and then went over to the little poplar shaded corner where Hester Gray slept. Ever since the day of the spring picnic Anne had put flowers on Hester's grave when she visited Matthew's. The evening before she had made a pilgrimage back to the deserted garden in the woods and brought therefrom some of Hester's own white roses.

"I though you would like them better than any others, dear," she said softly.

Anne was still sitting there when a shadow fell over the grass and she looked up to see Mrs. Allan. They walked home together.

Mrs. Allan's face was not the face of the girl-bride whom the minister had brought to Avonlea five years before. It had lost some of its bloom and youthful curves, and there were fine, patient lines about eyes and mouth. A tiny grave in that very cemetery accounted for some of them; and some new ones had come during the recent illness, now happily over, of her little son. But Mrs. Allan's dimples were as sweet and sudden as ever, her eyes as clear and bright and true; and what her face lacked in girlish beauty was now more than atoned for in added tenderness and strength.

"I suppose you are looking forward to your vacation, Anne?" she said, as they left the graveyard.

Anne nodded.

"Yes. . . . I could roll the word as a sweet morsel under my tongue. I think the summer is going to be lovely. For one thing, Mrs. Morgan is coming to the Island in July and Priscilla is going to bring her up. I feel one of my old 'thrills' at the mere thought."

"I hope you'll have a good time, Anne. You've worked very hard this past year and you have succeeded."

"Oh, I don't know. I've come so far short in so many things. I haven't done what I meant to do when I began to teach last fall. . . . I haven't lived up to my ideals."

"None of us ever do," said Mrs. Allan with a sigh. "But then, Anne, you know what Lowell says, 'Not failure but low aim is crime.' We must have ideals and try to live up to them, even if we never quite succeed. Life would be a sorry business without them. With them it's grand and great. Hold fast to your ideals, Anne."

"I shall try. But I have let go of most of my theories," said Anne, laughing a little. "I had the most beautiful set of theories you ever knew when I started out as a schoolma'am, but every one of them has failed me at some pinch or another."

"Even the theory on corporal punishment," teased Mrs. Allan.

"I shall never forgive myself for whipping Anthony."

"Nonsense, dear, he deserved it. And it agreed with him. You have had no trouble with him since and he has come to think there's nobody like you. Your kindness won his love after the idea that a 'girl was no good' was rooted out of his stubborn mind."

"He may have deserved it, but that is not the point. If I had calmly and deliberately decided to whip him because I thought it a just punishment for him I would not feel over it as I do. But the truth is, Mrs. Allan, that I just flew into a temper and whipped him because of that. I wasn't thinking whether it was just or unjust . . . even if he hadn't deserved it I'd have done it just the same. That is what humiliates me."

"Well, we all make mistakes, dear, so just put it behind you. We should regret our mistakes and learn from them, but never carry them forward into the future with us. There goes Gilbert Blythe on his wheel . . . home for his vacation too, I suppose. How are you and he getting on with your studies?''

''Pretty well. We plan to finish the Virgil tonight . . . there are only twenty lines to do. Then we are not going to study any more until September.''

''Do you think you will ever get to college?''

''Oh, I don't know.'' Anne looked dreamily afar to the opal-tinted horizon. ''Marilla's eyes will never be much better than they are now, although we are so thankful to think that they will not get worse. And then there are the twins . . . somehow I don't believe their uncle will ever really send for them. Perhaps college may be around the bend in the road, but I haven't got to the bend yet and I don't think much about it lest I might grow discontented.''

''Well, I should like to see you go to college, Anne; but if you never do, don't be discontented about it. We make our own lives wherever we are, after all . . . college can only help us to do it more easily. They are broad or narrow according to what we put into them, not what we get out. Life is rich and full here . . . everywhere . . . if we can only learn how to open our whole hearts to its richness and fulness.''

''I think I understand what you mean,'' said Anne thoughtfully, ''and I know I have so much to feel thankful for . . . oh, so much . . . my work, and Paul Irving, and the dear twins, and all my friends. Do you know, Mrs. Allan, I'm so thankful for friendship. It beautifies life so much.''

''True friendship is a very helpful thing indeed,'' said Mrs. Allan, ''and we should have a very high ideal of it, and never sully it by any failure in truth and sincerity. I fear the name of friendship is often degraded to a kind of intimacy that has nothing of real friendship in it.''

''Yes . . . like Gertie Pye's and Julia Bell's. They are very intimate and go everywhere together; but Gertie is always saying nasty things of Julia behind her back and everybody thinks she is jealous of her because she is so pleased when anybody criticizes Julia. I think it is desecration to call *that* friendship. If we have friends we should look only for the best in them and give them the best that is in us, don't you think? Then friendship would be the most beautiful thing in the world.''

''Friendship *is* very beautiful,'' smiled Mrs. Allan, ''but some day . . . ''

Then she paused abruptly. In the delicate, white-browed face beside her, with its candid eyes and mobile features, there was still far more of the child than of the woman. Anne's heart so far harbored only dreams of friendship and ambition, and Mrs. Allan did not wish to brush the bloom from her sweet unconsciousness. So she left her sentence for the future years to finish.

CHAPTER 16

THE SUBSTANCE OF THINGS HOPED FOR

"ANNE," SAID Davy appealingly, scrambling up on the shiny, leather-covered sofa in the Green Gables kitchen, where Anne sat, reading a letter, "Anne, I'm *awful* hungry. You've no idea."

"I'll get you a piece of bread and butter in a minute," said Anne absently. Her letter evidently contained some exciting news, for her cheeks were as pink as the roses on the big bush outside, and her eyes were as starry as only Anne's eyes could be.

"But I ain't bread and butter hungry," said Davy in a disgusted tone. "I'm plum cake hungry."

"Oh," laughed Anne, laying down her letter and putting her arm about Davy to give him a squeeze, "that's a kind of hunger that can be endured very comfortably, Davy-boy. You know it's one of Marilla's rules that you can't have anything but bread and butter between meals."

"Well, gimme a piece then . . . please."

Davy had been at last taught to say "please," but he generally tacked it on as an afterthought. He looked with approval at the generous slice Anne presently brought to him. "You always put such a nice lot of butter on it, Anne. Marilla spreads it pretty thin. It slips down a lot easier when there's plenty of butter."

The slice "slipped down" with tolerable ease, judging from its rapid disappearance. Davy slid head first off the sofa, turned a double somersault on the rug, and then sat up and announced decidedly,

"Anne, I've made up my mind about heaven. I don't want to go there."

"Why not?" asked Anne gravely.

"'Cause heaven is in Simon Fletcher's garret, and I don't like Simon Fletcher."

"Heaven in . . . Simon Fletcher's garret!" gasped Anne, too amazed even to laugh. "Davy Keith, whatever put such an extraordinary idea into your head?"

"Milty Boulter says that's where it is. It was last Sunday in Sunday School. The lesson was about Elijah and Elisha, and I up and asked Miss Rogerson where heaven was. Miss Rogerson looked awful offended. She was cross anyhow, because when she'd asked us what Elijah left Elisha when he went to heaven Milty Boulter said, 'His old clo'es,' and us fellows all laughed before we thought. I wish you could think first and do things afterwards, 'cause then you wouldn't do them. But Milty didn't mean to be disrespeckful. He just couldn't think of the name of the thing. Miss Rogerson said heaven was where God was and I wasn't to ask questions like that. Milty nudged me and said in a whisper, 'Heaven's in Uncle Simon's garret and I'll esplain about it on the road home.' So when we was coming home he esplained. Milty's a great hand at esplaining things. Even if he don't know anything about a thing he'll make up a lot of stuff and so you get it esplained all the same. His mother is Mrs. Simon's sister and he went with her to the funeral when his cousin, Jane Ellen, died. The minister said she'd gone to heaven, though Milty says she was lying right before them in the coffin. But he s'posed they carried the coffin up to the garret afterwards. Well, when Milty and his mother went upstairs after it was all over to get her bonnet he asked her where heaven was that Jane Ellen had gone to, and she pointed right to the ceiling and said, 'Up there.' Milty knew there wasn't anything but the garret over the ceiling, so that's how *he* found out. And he's been awful scared to go to his Uncle Simon's ever since."

Anne took Davy on her knee and did her best to straighten out this theological tangle also. She was much better fitted for the task than Marilla, for she remembered her own childhood and had an instinctive understanding of the curious ideas that seven year olds sometimes get about matters that are, of course, very plain and simple to grown up people. She had just succeeded in convincing Davy that heaven was *not* in Simon Fletcher's garret when Marilla came in from the garden, where she and Dora had been picking peas. Dora was an industrious little soul and never happier than when "helping" in various small tasks suited to her chubby fingers. She fed chickens, picked up chips, wiped dishes, and ran errands galore. She was neat, faithful and observant; she never had to be told how to do a thing twice and never forgot any of her little duties. Davy, on the other hand, was rather heedless and forgetful; but he had the born knack of winning love, and even yet Anne and Marilla liked him the better.

While Dora proudly shelled the peas and Davy made boats of the pods, with masts of matches and sails of paper, Anne told Marilla about the wonderful contents of her letter.

"Oh, Marilla, what do you think? I've had a letter from Priscilla and she says that Mrs. Morgan is on the Island, and that if it is fine Thursday they are going to drive up to Avonlea and will reach here about twelve. They will spend the afternoon with us and go to the hotel at White Sands in the evening, because some of Mrs. Morgan's American friends are staying there. Oh, Marilla, isn't it wonderful? I can hardly believe I'm not dreaming."

"I daresay Mrs. Morgan is a lot like other people," said Marilla drily, although she did feel a trifle excited herself. Mrs. Morgan was a famous woman and a visit from her was no commonplace occurrence. "They'll be here to dinner, then?"

"Yes; and oh, Marilla, may I cook every bit of the dinner myself? I want to feel that I can do something for the author of 'The Rosebud Garden,' if it is only to cook a dinner for her. You won't mind, will you?"

"Goodness, I'm not so fond of stewing over a hot fire in July that it would vex me very much to have someone else do it. You're quite welcome to the job."

"Oh, thank you," said Anne, as if Marilla had just conferred a tremendous favor, "I'll make out the menu this very night."

"You'd better not try to put on too much style," warned Marilla, a little alarmed by the high-flown sound of "menu." "You'll likely come to grief if you do."

"Oh, I'm not going to put on any 'style,' if you mean trying to do or have things we don't usually have on festal occasions," assured Anne. "That would be affectation, and, although I know I haven't as much sense and steadiness as a girl of seventeen and a schoolteacher ought to have, I'm not so silly as *that*. But I want to have everything as nice and dainty as possible. Davy-boy, don't leave those pea-pods on the back stairs . . . someone might slip on them. I'll have a light soup to begin with . . . you know I can make lovely cream-of-onion soup . . . and then a couple of roast fowls. I'll have the two white roosters. I have a real affection for those roosters and they've been pets ever since the gray hen hatched out just the two of them . . . little balls of yellow down. But I know they would have to be sacrificed sometime, and surely there couldn't be a worthier occasion than this. But oh, Marilla, *I* cannot kill them . . . not even for Mrs. Morgan's sake. I'll have to ask John Henry Carter to come over and do it for me.''

"I'll do it," volunteered Davy, "if Marilla'll hold them by the legs, 'cause I guess it'd take both my hands to manage the axe. It's awfully jolly fun to see them hopping about after their heads are cut off.''

"Then I'll have peas and beans and creamed potatoes and a lettuce salad, for vegetables," resumed Anne, "and for dessert, lemon pie with whipped cream, and coffee and cheese and lady fingers. I'll make the pies and lady fingers tomorrow and do up my white muslin dress. And I must tell Diana tonight, for she'll want to do up hers. Mrs. Morgan's heroines are nearly always dressed in white muslin, and Diana and I have always resolved that that was what we would wear if we ever met her. It will be such a delicate compliment, don't you think? Davy, dear, you mustn't poke pea-pods into the cracks of the floor. I must ask Mr. and Mrs. Allan and Miss Stacy to dinner, too, for they're all very anxious to meet Mrs. Morgan. It's so fortunate she's coming while Miss Stacy is here. Davy dear, don't sail the pea-pods in the water bucket . . . go out to the trough. Oh, I do hope it will be fine Thursday, and I think it will, for Uncle Abe said last night when he called at Mr. Harrison's, that it was going to rain most of this week.''

"That's a good sign," agreed Marilla.

Anne ran across to Orchard Slope that evening to tell the news to Diana, who was also very much excited over it, and they discussed the matter in the hammock swung under the big willow in the Barry garden.

"Oh, Anne, mayn't I help you cook the dinner?" implored Diana. "You know I can make splendid lettuce salad.''

"Indeed you may," said Anne unselfishly. "And I shall want you to help me decorate too. I mean to have the parlor simply a *bower* of blossoms . . . and the dining table is to be adorned with wild roses. Oh, I do hope everything will go smoothly. Mrs. Morgan's heroines *never* get into scrapes or are taken at a disadvantage, and they are always so self-possessed and such good housekeepers. They seem to be *born* good housekeepers. You remember that *Gerturde* in 'Edgewood Days' kept house for her father when she was only eight years old. When I was eight years old I hardly knew how to do a thing except bring up children. Mrs. Morgan must be an authority on girls when she has written so much about them, and I do want her to have a good opinion of us. I've imagined it all out a dozen different ways . . . what she'll look like, and what she'll say, and what I'll say. And I'm so anxious about my nose. There are seven freckles on it, as you can see. They came at the A.V.I.S. picnic, when I went around in the sun without my hat. I suppose it's ungrateful of me to worry over them, when I should be thankful they're not spread all over my face as they once were; but I do wish they hadn't come . . . all Mrs. Morgan's heroines have such perfect complexions. I can't recall a freckled one among them.''

''Yours are not very noticeable,'' comforted Diana. ''Try a little lemon juice on them tonight.''

The next day Anne made her pies and lady fingers, did up her muslin dress, and swept and dusted every room in the house . . . a quite unnecessary proceeding, for Green Gables was, as usual, in the apple pie order dear to Marilla's heart. But Anne felt that a fleck of dust would be a desecration in a house that was to be honored by a visit from Charlotte E. Morgan. She even cleaned out the ''catch-all'' closet under the stairs, although there was not the remotest possibility of Mrs. Morgan's seeing its interior.

''But I want to *feel* that it is in perfect order, even if she isn't to see it,'' Anne told Marilla. ''You know, in her book, 'Golden Keys,' she makes her two heroines *Alice* and *Louisa* take for their motto that verse of Longfellow's,

> *In the elder days of art*
> *Builders wrought with greatest care*
> *Each minute and unseen part,*
> *For the gods see everywhere,*

and so they always kept their cellar stairs scrubbed and never forgot to sweep under the beds. I should have a guilty conscience if I thought this closet was in disorder when Mrs. Morgan was in the house. Ever since we read 'Golden Keys,' last April, Diana and I have taken that verse for our motto too.''

That night John Henry Carter and Davy between them contrived to execute the two white roosters, and Anne dressed them, the usually distasteful task quite glorified in her eyes by the destination of the plump birds.

''I don't like picking fowls,'' she told Marilla, ''but isn't it fortunate we don't have to put our souls into what our hands may be doing? I've been picking chickens with my hands but in imagination I've been roaming the Milky Way.''

"I thought you'd scattered more feathers over the floor than usual,'' remarked Marilla.

Then Anne put Davy to bed and made him promise that he would behave perfectly the next day.

"If I'm as good as good can be all day tomorrow will you let me be just as bad as I like all the next day?'' asked Davy.

"I couldn't do that,'' said Anne discreetly, "but I'll take you and Dora for a row in the flat right to the bottom of the pond, and we'll go ashore on the sandhills and have a picnic.''

"It's a bargain,'' said Davy. "I'll be good, you bet. I meant to go over to Mr. Harrison's and fire peas from my new popgun at Ginger but another day'll do as well. I espect it will be just like Sunday, but a picnic at the shore'll make up for *that*.''

CHAPTER 17

A CHAPTER OF ACCIDENTS

ANNE WOKE three times in the night and made pilgrimages to her window to make sure that Uncle Abe's prediction was not coming true. Finally the morning dawned pearly and lustrous in a sky full of silver sheen and radiance, and the wonderful day had arrived.

Diana appeared soon after breakfast, with a basket of flowers over one arm and *her* muslin dress over the other . . . for it would not do to don it until all the dinner preparations were completed. Meanwhile she wore her afternoon pink print and a lawn apron fearfully and wonderfully ruffled and frilled; and very neat and pretty and rosy she was.

"You look simply sweet,'' said Anne admiringly.

Diana sighed.

"But I've had to let out every one of my dresses *again*. I weigh four pounds more than I did in July. Anne, *where* will this end? Mrs. Morgan's heroines are all tall and slender.''

"Well, let's forget our troubles and think of our mercies," said Anne gaily. "Mrs. Allan says that whenever we think of anything that is a trial to us we should also think of something nice that we can set over against it. If you are slightly too plump you've got the dearest dimples; and if I have a freckled nose the *shape* of it is all right. Do you think the lemon juice did any good?"

"Yes, I really think it did," said Diana critically; and, much elated, Anne led the way to the garden, which was full of airy shadows and wavering golden lights.

"We'll decorate the parlor first. We have plenty of time, for Priscilla said they'd be here about twelve or half past at the latest, so we'll have dinner at one."

There may have been two happier and more exited girls somewhere in Canada or the United States at that moment, but I doubt it. Every snip of the scissors, as rose and peony and bluebell fell, seemed to chirp, "Mrs. Morgan is coming today." Anne wondered how Mr. Harrison *could* go on placidly mowing hay in the field across the lane, just as if nothing were going to happen.

The parlor at Green Gables was a rather severe and gloomy apartment, with rigid horsehair furniture, stiff lace curtains, and white antimacassars that were always laid at a perfectly correct angle, except at such times as they clung to unfortunate people's buttons. Even Anne had never been able to infuse much grace into it, for Marilla would not permit any alterations. But it is wonderful what flowers can accomplish if you give them a fair chance; when Anne and Diana finished with the room you would not have recognized it.

A great blue bowlful of snowballs overflowed on the polished table. The shining black mantel piece was heaped with roses and ferns. Every shelf of the what-not held a sheaf of bluebells; the dark corners on either side of the grate were lighted up with jars full of glowing crimson peonies, and the grate itself was aflame with yellow poppies. All this splendor and color, mingled with the sunshine falling through the honeysuckle vines at the windows in a leafy riot of dancing shadows over walls and floor, made of the usually dismal little room the veritable "bower" of Anne's imagination, and even extorted a tribute of admiration from Marilla, who came in to criticize and remained to praise.

"Now, we must set the table," said Anne, in the tone of a priestess about to perform some sacred rite in honor of a divinity. "We'll have a big vaseful of wild roses in the center and one single rose in front of everybody's plate—and a special bouquet of rosebuds only by Mrs. Morgan's—an allusion to 'The Rosebud Garden' you know.''

The table was set in the sitting room, with Marilla's finest linen and the best china, glass, and silver. You may be perfectly certain that every article placed on it was polished or scoured to the highest possible perfection of gloss and glitter.

Then the girls tripped out to the kitchen, which was filled with appetizing odors emanating from the oven, where the chickens were already sizzling splendidly. Anne prepared the potatoes and Diana got the peas and beans ready. Then, while Diana shut herself into the pantry to compound the lettuce salad, Anne, whose cheeks were already beginning to glow crimson, as much with excitment as from the heat of the fire, prepared the bread sauce for the chickens, minced her onions for the soup, and finally whipped the cream for her lemon pies.

And what about Davy all this time? Was he redeeming his promise to be good? He was, indeed. To be sure, he insisted on remaining in the kitchen, for his curiosity wanted to see all that went on. But as he sat quietly in a corner, busily engaged in untying the knots in a piece of herring net he had brought home from his last trip to the shore, nobody objected to this.

At half past eleven the lettuce salad was made, the golden circles of the pies were heaped with whipped cream, and everything was sizzling and bubbling that ought to sizzle and bubble.

''We'd better go and dress now,'' said Anne, ''for they may be here by twelve. We must have dinner at sharp one, for the soup must be served as soon as it's done.''

Serious indeed were the toilet rites presently performed in the east gable. Anne peers anxiously at her nose and rejoiced to see that its freckles were not at all prominent, thanks either to the lemon juice or to the unusual flush on her cheeks. When they were ready they looked quite as sweet and trim and girlish as ever did any of ''Mrs. Morgan's heroines.''

''I do hope I'll be able to say something once in a while, and not sit like a mute,'' said Diana anxiously. ''All Mrs. Morgan's heroines converse so beautifully. But I'm afraid I'll be tongue-tied and stupid. And I'll be sure to say 'I seen.' I haven't often said it since Miss Stacy taught here; but in moments of excitment it's sure to pop out. Anne, if I were to say 'I seen' before Mrs. Morgan I'd die of mortification. And it would be almost as bad to have nothing to say.''

"I'm nervous about a good many things," said Anne, "but I don't think there is much fear that I won't be able to *talk*."

And, to do her justice, there wasn't.

Anne shrouded her muslin glories in a big apron and went down to concoct her soup. Marilla had dressed herself and the twins, and looked more excited than she had ever been known to look before. At half past twelve the Allans and Miss Stacy came. Everything was going well but Anne was beginning to feel nervous. It was surely time for Priscilla and Mrs. Morgan to arrive. She made frequent trips to the gate and looked as anxiously down the lane as ever her namesake in the Bluebeard story peered from the tower casement.

"Suppose they don't come at all?" she said piteously.

"Don't suppose it. It would be too mean," said Diana, who, however, was beginning to have uncomfortable misgivings on the subject.

"Anne," said Marilla, coming out from the parlor, "Miss Stacy wants to see Miss Barry's willoware platter."

Anne hastened to the sitting room closet to get the platter. She had, in accordance with her promise to Mrs. Lynde, written to Miss Barry of Charlottetown, asking for the loan of it. Miss Barry was an old friend of Anne's, and she promptly sent the platter out, with a letter exhorting Anne to be very careful of it, for she had paid twenty dollars for it. The platter had served its purpose at the Aid bazaar and had then been returned to the Green Gables closet, for Anne would not trust anybody but herself to take it back to town.

She carried the platter carefully to the front door where her guests were enjoying the cool breeze that blew up from the brook. It was examined and admired; then, just as Anne had taken it back into her own hands, a terrific crash and clatter sounded from the kitchen pantry. Marilla, Diana, and Anne fled out, the latter pausing only long enough to set the precious platter hastily down on the second step of the stairs.

When they reached the pantry a truly harrowing spectacle met their eyes . . . a guilty-looking small boy scrambling down from the table, with his clean print blouse liberally plastered with yellow filling, and on the table the shattered remnants of what had been two brave, becreamed lemon pies.

Davy had finished ravelling out his herring net and had wound the twine into a ball. Then he had gone into the pantry to put it up on the shelf above the table, where he already kept a score or so of similar balls, which, so far as could be discovered, served no useful purpose save to yield the joy of possession. Davy had to climb on the table and reach over to the shelf at a dangerous angle . . . something he had been forbidden by Marilla to do, as he had come to grief once before in the experiment. The result in this instance was disastrous. Davy slipped and came sprawling squarely down on the lemon pies. His clean blouse was ruined for that time and the pies for all time. It is, however, an ill wind that blows nobody good, and the pig was eventually the gainer by Davy's mischance.

"Davy Keith," said Marilla, shaking him by the shoulder, "didn't I forbid you to climb up on that table again? Didn't I?"

"I forgot," whimpered Davy. "You've told me not to do such an awful lot of things that I can't remember them all."

"Well, you march upstairs and stay there till after dinner. Perhaps you'll get them sorted out in your memory by that time. No, Anne, never you mind interceding for him. I'm not punishing him because he spoiled your pies . . . that was an accident. I'm punishing him for his disobedience. Go, Davy, I say,"

"Ain't I to have any dinner?" wailed Davy.

"You can come down after dinner is over and have yours in the kitchen."

"Oh, all right," said Davy, somewhat comforted. "I know Anne'll save some nice bones for me, won't you, Anne? 'Cause you know I didn't mean to fall on the pies. Say, Anne, since they *are* spoiled can't I take some of the pieces upstairs with me?"

"No, no lemon pie for you, Master Davy," said Marilla, pushing him towards the hall.

"What shall we do for dessert?" asked Anne, looking regretfully at the wreck and ruin.

"Get out a crock of strawberry preserves," said Marilla consolingly. "There's plenty of whipped cream left in the bowl for it."

One o'clock came . . . but no Priscilla or Mrs. Morgan. Anne was in an agony. Everything was done to a turn and the soup was just what soup should be, but couldn't be depended on to remain so for any length of time.

"I don't believe they're coming after all," said Marilla crossly.

Anne and Diana sought comfort in each other's eyes.

At half past one Marilla again emerged from the parlor.

"Girls, we *must* have dinner. Everybody is hungry and it's no use waiting any longer. Priscilla and Mrs. Morgan are not coming, that's plain, and nothing is being improved by waiting."

Anne and Diana set about lifting the dinner, with all the zest gone out of the performance.

"I don't believe I'll be able to eat a mouthful," Diana said dolefully.

"Nor I. But I hope everything will be nice for Miss Stacy's and Mr. and Mrs. Allan's sakes," said Anne listlessly.

When Diana dished the peas she tasted them and a very peculiar expression crossed her face.

"Anne, did *you* put sugar in these peas?"

"Yes," said Anne, mashing the potatoes with the air of one expected to do her duty. "I put a spoonful of sugar in. We always do. Don't you like it?"

"But *I* put a spoonful in too, when I set them on the stove," said Diana.

Anne dropped her masher and tasted the peas also. Then she made a grimace.

"How awful! I never dreamed you had put sugar in, because I knew your mother never does. I happened to think of it, for a wonder . . . I'm always forgetting it . . . so I popped a spoonful in."

"It's a case of too many cooks, I guess," said Marilla, who had listened to this dialogue with a rather guilty expression. "I didn't think you'd remember about the sugar, Anne, for I'm perfectly certain you never did before . . . so *I* put in a spoonful."

The guests in the parlor heard peal after peal of laughter from the kitchen, but they never knew what the fun was about. There were no green peas on the dinner table that day, however.

"Well," said Anne, sobering down again with a sigh of recollection, "we have the salad anyhow and I don't think anything has happened to the beans. Let's carry the things in and get it over."

It cannot be said that that dinner was a notable success socially. The Allans and Miss Stacy exerted themselves to save the situation and Marilla's customary placidity was not noticeably ruffled. But Anne and Diana, between their disappointment and the reaction from their excitement of the forenoon, could neither talk nor eat. Anne tried heroically to bear her part in the conversation for the sake of her guests; but all the sparkle had been quenched in her for the time being, and, in spite of her love for the Allans and Miss Stacy, she couldn't help thinking how nice it would be when everybody had gone home and she could bury her weariness and disappointment in the pillows of the east gable.

There is an old proverb that really seems at times to be inspired . . . "it never rains but it pours." The measure of that day's tribulations was not yet full. Just as Mr. Allan had finished returning thanks there arose a strange, ominous sound on the stairs, as of some hard, heavy object bounding from step to step, finishing up with a grand smash at the bottom. Everybody ran out into the hall. Anne gave a shriek of dismay.

At the bottom of the stairs lay a big pink conch shell amid the fragments of what had been Miss Barry's platter; and at the top of the stairs knelt a terrified Davy, gazing down with wide-open eyes at the havoc.

"Davy," said Marilla ominously, "did you throw that conch down *on purpose*?"

"No, I never did," whimpered Davy. "I was just kneeling here, quiet as quiet, to watch you folks through the bannisters, and my foot struck that old thing and pushed it off . . . and I'm awful hungry . . . and I do wish you'd lick a fellow and have done with it, instead of always sending him upstairs to miss all the fun."

"Don't blame Davy," said Anne, gathering up the fragments with trembling finges. "It was my fault. I set that platter there and forgot all about it. I am properly punished for my carelessness; but oh, what will Miss Barry say?"

"Well, you know she only bought it, so it isn't the same as if it was an heirloom," said Diana, trying to console.

The guests went away soon after, feeling that it was the most tactful thing to do, and Anne and Diana washed the dishes, talking less than they had ever been known to do before. Then Diana went home with a headache and Anne went with another to the east gable, where she stayed until Marilla came home from the post office at sunset, with a letter from Priscilla, written the day before. Mrs. Morgan had sprained her ankle so severely that she could not leave her room.

"And oh, Anne dear," wrote Priscilla, "I'm so sorry, but I'm afraid we won't get up to Green Gables at all now, for by the time Aunty's ankle is well she will have to go back to Toronto. She has to be there by a certain date."

"Well," sighed Anne, laying the letter down on the red sandstone step of the back porch, where she was sitting, while the twilight rained down out of a dappled sky, "I always thought it was too good to be true that Mrs. Morgan should really come. But there . . . that speech sounds as pessimistic as Miss Eliza Andrews and I'm ashamed of making it. After all, it was *not* too good to be true . . . things just as good and far better are coming true for me all the time. And I suppose the events of today have a funny side too. Perhaps when Diana and I are old and gray we shall be able to laugh over them.

But I feel that I can't expect to do it before then, for it has truly been a bitter disappointment.''

"You'll probably have a good many more and worse disappointments than that before you get through life," said Marilla, who honestly thought she was making a comforting speech. "It seems to me, Anne, that you are never going to outgrow your fashion of setting your heart so on things and then crashing down into despair because you don't get them."

"I know I'm too much inclined that way," agreed Anne ruefully. "When I think something nice is going to happen I seem to fly right up on the wings of anticipation; and then the first thing I realize I drop down to earth with a thud. But really, Marilla, the flying part *is* glorious as long as it lasts . . . it's like soaring through a sunset. I think it almost pays for the thud.''

"Well, maybe it does," admitted Marilla. "I'd rather walk calmly along and do without both flying and thud. But everybody has her own way of living . . . I used to think there was only one right way . . . but since I've had you and the twins to bring up I don't feel so sure of it. What are you going to do about Miss Barry's platter?''

"Pay her back the twenty dollars she paid for it, I suppose. I'm so thankful it wasn't a cherished heirloom because then no money could replace it.''

"Maybe you could find one like it somewhere and buy it for her.''

"I'm afraid not. Platters as old as that are very scarce. Mrs. Lynde couldn't find one anywhere for the supper. I only wish I could, for of course Miss Barry would just as soon have one platter as another, if both were equally old and genuine. Marilla, look at that big star over Mr. Harrison's maple grove, with all that holy hush of silvery sky about it. It gives me a feeling that is like a prayer. After all, when one can see stars and skies like that, little disappointments and accidents can't matter so much, can they?''

"Where's Davy?" said Marilla, with an indifferent glance at the star.

"In bed. I've promised to take him and Dora to the shore for a picnic tomorrow. Of course, the original agreement was that he must be good. But he *tried* to be good . . . and I hadn't the heart to disappoint him.''

"You'll drown yourself or the twins, rowing about the pond in that flat," grumbled Marilla. "I've lived here for sixty years and I've never been on the pond yet.''

"Well, it's never too late to mend," said Anne roguishly. "Suppose you come with us tomorrow. We'll shut Green Gables up and spend the whole day at the shore, daffing the world aside."

"No, thank you," said Marilla, with indignant emphasis. "I'd be a nice sight, wouldn't I, rowing down the pond in a flat? I think I hear Rachel pronouncing on it. There's Mr. Harrison driving away somewhere. Do you suppose there is any truth in the gossip that Mr. Harrison is going to see Isabella Andrews?"

"No, I'm sure there isn't. He just called there one evening on business with Mrs. Harmon Andrews and Mrs. Lynde saw him and said she knew he was courting because he had a white collar on. I don't believe Mr. Harrison will ever marry. He seems to have a prejudice against marriage."

"Well, you can never tell about those old bachelors. And if he had a white collar on I'd agree with Rachel that it looks suspicious, for I'm sure he never was seen with one before."

"I think he only put it on because he wanted to conclude a business deal with Harmon Andrews," said Anne. "I've heard him say that's the only time a man needs to be particular about his appearance, because if he looks prosperous the party of the second part won't be so likely to try to cheat him. I really feel sorry for Mr. Harrison; I don't believe he feels satisfied with his life. It must be very lonely to have no one to care about except a parrot, don't you think? But I notice Mr. Harrison doesn't like to be pitied. Nobody does, I imagine."

"There's Gilbert coming up the lane," said Marilla. "If he wants you to go for a row on the pond mind you put on your coat and rubbers. There's a heavy dew tonight."

CHAPTER 18

AN ADVENTURE ON THE TORY ROAD

"ANNE," SAID Davy, sitting up in bed and propping his chin on his hands, "Anne, where is sleep? People go to sleep every night, and of course I know it's the place where I do the things I dream, but I want to know *where* it is and how I get there and back without knowing anything about it . . . and in my nighty too. Where is it?''

Anne was kneeling at the west gable window watching the sunset sky that was like a great flower with petals of crocus and a heart of fiery yellow. She turned her head at Davy's question and answered dreamily,

> "Over the mountains of the moon,
> Down the valley of the shadow.''

Paul Irving would have known the meaning of this, or made a meaning out of it for himself, if he didn't; but practical Davy, who, as Anne often despairingly remarked, hadn't a particle of imagination, was only puzzled and disgusted.

"Anne, I believe you're just talking nonsense.''

"Of course I was, dear boy. Don't you know that it is only very foolish folk who talk sense all the time?''

"Well, I think you might give a sensible answer when I ask a sensible question,'' said Davy in an injured tone.

"Oh, you are too little to understand,'' said Anne. But she felt rather ashamed of saying it; for had she not, in keen remembrance of many similar snubs administered in her own early years, solemnly vowed that she would never tell any child it was too little to understand? Yet here she was doing it . . . so wide sometimes is the gulf between theory and practice.

"Well, I'm doing my best to grow,'' said Davy, "but it's a thing you can't hurry much. If Marilla wasn't so stingy with her jam I believe I'd grow a lot faster.''

"Marilla is not stingy, Davy,'' said Anne severely. "It is very ungrateful of you to say such a thing.''

"There's another word that means the same thing and sounds a lot better, but I don't just remember it,'' said Davy, frowning intently. "I heard Marilla say she was it, herself, the other day.''

"If you mean *economical*, it's a *very* different thing from being stingy. It is an excellent trait in a person if she is economical. If Marilla had been stingy she wouldn't have taken you and Dora when your mother died. Would you have liked to live with Mrs. Wiggins?''

"You just bet I wouldn't!'' Davy was emphatic on that point. "Nor I don't want to go out to Uncle Richard neither. I'd far rather live here, even if Marilla is that long-tailed word when it comes to jam, 'cause *you're* here, Anne. Say, Anne, won't you tell me a story 'fore I go to sleep? I don't want a fairy story. They're all right for girls, I s'pose, but I want something exciting . . . lots of killing and shooting in it, and a house on fire, and in'trusting things like that.''

Fortunately for Anne, Marilla called out at this moment from her room.

''Anne, Diana's signaling at a great rate. You'd better see what she wants.''

Anne ran to the east gable and saw flashes of light coming through the twilight from Diana's window in groups of five, which meant, according to their old childish code, ''Come over at once for I have something important to reveal.'' Anne threw her white shawl over her head and hastened through the Haunted Wood and across Mr. Bell's pasture corner to Orchard Slope.

''I've good news for you, Anne,'' said Diana. ''Mother and I have just got home from Carmody, and I saw Mary Sentner from Spencervale in Mr. Blair's store. She says the old Copp girls on the Tory Road have a willow-ware platter and she thinks it's exactly like the one we had at the supper. She says they'll likely sell it, for Martha Copp has never been known to keep anything she *could* sell; but if they won't there's a platter at Wesley Keyson's at Spencervale and she knows they'd sell it, but she isn't sure it's just the same kind as Aunt Josephine's.''

''I'll go right over to Spencervale after it tomorrow,'' said Anne resolutely, ''and you must come with me. It will be such a weight off my mind, for I have to go to town day after tomorrow and how can I face your Aunt Josephine without a willow-ware platter? It would be even worse than the time I had to confess about jumping on the spare room bed.''

Both girls laughed over the old memory . . . concerning which, if any of my readers are ignorant and curious, I must refer them to Anne's earlier history.

The next afternoon the girls fared forth on their platter hunting expedition. It was ten miles to Spencervale and the day was not especially pleasant for travelling. It was very warm and windless, and the dust on the road was such as might have been expected after six weeks of dry weather.''

''Oh, I do wish it would rain soon,'' sighed Anne. ''Everything is so parched up. The poor fields just seem pitiful to me and the trees seem to be stretching out their hands pleading for rain. As for my garden, it hurts me every time I go into it. I suppose I shouldn't complain about a garden when the farmers' crops are suffering so.

Mr. Harrison says his pastures are so scorched up that his poor cows can hardly get a bite to eat and he feels guilty of cruelty to animals every time he meets their eyes.''

After a wearisome drive the girls reached Spencervale and turned down the "Tory" Road . . . a green solitary highway where the strips of grass between the wheel tracks bore evidence of lack of travel. Along most of its extent it was lined with thick-set young spruces crowding down to the roadway, with here and there a break where the back field of a Spencervale farm came out to the fence or an expanse of stumps was aflame with fireweed and golden rod.

"Why is it called the Tory Road?" asked Anne.

"Mr. Allan says it is on the principle of calling a place a grove because there are no trees in it," said Diana, "for nobody lives along the road except the Copp girls and old Martin Bovyer at the further end, who is a Liberal. The Tory government ran the road through when they were in power just to show they were doing something."

Diana's father was a Liberal, for which reason she and Anne never discussed politics. Green Gables folk had always been Conservatives.

Finally the girls came to the old Copp homestead . . . a place of such exceeding external neatness that even Green Gables would have suffered by contact. The house was a very old fashioned one, situated on a slope, which fact had necessitated the building of a stone basement under one end. The house and outbuildings were all whitewashed to a condition of blinding perfection and not a weed was visible in the prim kitchen garden surrounded by its white paling.

"The shades are all down," said Diana ruefully. "I believe that nobody is home."

This proved to be the case. The girls looked at each other in perplexity.

"I don't know what to do," said Anne. "If I were sure the platter was the right kind I would not mind waiting until they came home. But if it isn't it may be too late to go to Wesley Keyson's afterwards."

Diana looked at a certain little square window over the basement.

"That is the pantry window, I feel sure," she said, "because this house is just like Uncle Charles' at Newbridge, and that is their pantry window. The shade isn't down, so if we climbed up on the roof of that little house we could look into the pantry and might be able to see the platter. Do you think it would be any harm?"

"No, I don't think so," decided Anne, after due reflection, "since our motive is not idle curiosity."

This important point of ethics being settled, Anne prepared to mount the aforesaid "little house," a construction of lathes, with a peaked room, which had in times past served as a habitation for ducks. The Copp girls had given up keeping ducks . . . "because they were such untidy birds" . . . and the house had not been in use for some years, save as an abode of correction for setting hens. Although scrupulously whitewashed it had become somewhat shaky, and Anne felt rather dubious as she scrambled up from the vantage point of a keg placed on a box.

"I'm afraid it won't bear my weight," she said as she gingerly stepped on the roof.

"Lean on the window sill," advised Diana, and Anne accordingly leaned. Much to her delight, she saw, as she peered through the pane, a willow-ware platter, exactly such as she was in quest of, on the shelf in front of the window. So much she saw before the catastrophe came. In her joy Anne forgot the precarious nature of her footing, incautiously ceased to lean on the window sill, gave an impulsive little hop of pleasure . . . and the next moment she had crashed through the roof up to her arm-pits, and there she hung, quite unable to extricate herself. Diana dashed into the duck house and, seizing her unfortunate friend by the waist, tried to draw her down.

"Ow . . . don't," shrieked poor Anne. "There are some long splinters sticking into me. See if you can put something under my feet . . . then perhaps I can draw myself up."

Diana hastily dragged in the previously mentioned keg and Anne found that it was just sufficiently high to furnish a secure resting place for her feet. But she could not release herself.

"Could I pull you out if I crawled up?" suggested Diana.

Anne shook her head hopelessly.

"No . . . the splinters hurt too badly. If you can find an axe you might chop me out, though. Oh dear, I do really begin to believe that I *was* born under an ill-omened star."

Diana searched faithfully but no axe was to be found.

"I'll have to go for help," she said, returning to the prisoner.

"No, indeed, you won't," said Anne vehemently. "If you do the story of this will get out everywhere and I shall be ashamed to show my face. No, we must just wait until the Copp girls come home and bind them to secrecy. They'll know where the axe is and get me out. I'm not uncomfortable as long as I keep perfectly still . . . not uncomfortable in *body* I mean. I wonder what the Copp girls value this house at. I shall have to pay for the damage I've done, but I wouldn't mind that if I were only sure they would understand my motive in peeping in at their pantry window. My sole comfort is that the platter is just the kind I want and if Miss Copp will only sell it to me I shall be resigned to what has happened."

"What if the Copp girls don't come home until after night . . . or till tomorrow?" suggested Diana.

"If they're not back by sunset you'll have to go for other assistance, I suppose," said Anne reluctantly, "but you mustn't go until you really have to. Oh dear, this is a dreadful predicament. I wouldn't mind my misfortunes so much if they were romantic, as Mrs. Morgan's heroines' always are, but they are always just simply ridiculous. Fancy what the Copp girls will think when they drive into their yard and see a girl's head and shoulders sticking out of the roof of one of their outhouses. Listen . . . is that a wagon? No, Diana, I believe it is thunder."

Thunder it was undoubtedly, and Diana, having made a hasty pilgrimage around the house, returned to announce that a very black cloud was rising rapidly in the northwest.

"I believe we're going to have a heavy thundershower," she exclaimed in dismay. "Oh, Anne, what will we do?"

"We must prepare for it," said Anne tranquilly. A thunderstorm seemed a trifle in comparison with what had already happened. "You'd better drive the horse and buggy into that open shed. Fortunately my parasol is in the buggy. Here . . . take my hat with you. Marilla told me I was a goose to put on my best hat to come to the Tory Road and she was right, as she always is."

Diana untied the pony and drove into the shed, just as the first heavy drops of rain fell. There she sat and watched the resulting downpour, which was so thick and heavy that she could hardly see Anne through it, holding the parasol bravely over her bare head. There was not a great deal of thunder, but for the best part of an hour the rain came merrily down. Occasionally Anne slanted back her parasol and waved an encouraging hand to her friend; but conversation at that distance and under the circumstances was quite out of the question. Finally the rain ceased, the sun came out, and Diana ventured across the puddles of the yard.

"Did you get very wet?" she asked anxiously.

"Oh, no," returned Anne cheerfully. "My head and shoulders are quite dry and my skirt is only a little damp where the rain beat through the lathes. Don't pity me, Diana, for I haven't minded it at all. I kept thinking how much good the rain will do and how glad my garden must be for it, and imagining what the flowers and buds would think when the drops began to fall. I imagined out a most interesting dialogue between the asters and the sweet peas and the wild canaries in the lilac bush and the guardian spirit of the garden. When I go home I mean to write it down. I wish I had a pencil and paper to do it now, because I daresay I'll forget the best parts before I reach home.''

Diana the faithful had a pencil and discovered a sheet of wrapping paper in the box of the buggy. Anne folded up her dripping parasol, put on her hat, spread the wrapping paper on a shingle Diana handed up, and wrote out her garden idyl under conditions that could hardly be considered as favorable to literature. Nevertheless, the result was quite pretty, and Diana was ''enraptured'' when Anne read it to her.

''Oh, Anne, it's sweet . . . just sweet. *Do* send it to the *Canadian Woman.*''

Anne shook her head.

''Oh, no, it wouldn't be suitable at all. There is no *plot* in it, you see. It's just a string of fancies. I like writing such things, but of course nothing of the sort would ever do for publication, for editors insist on plots, so Priscilla says. Oh, there's Miss Sarah Copp now. *Please*, Diana, go and explain.''

Miss Sarah Copp was a small person, garbed in shabby black, with a hat chosen less for vain adornment than for qualities that would wear well. She looked as amazed as might be expected on seeing the curious tableau in her yard, but when she heard Diana's explanation she was all sympathy. She hurriedly unlocked the back door, produced the axe, and with a few skillful blows set Anne free. The latter, somewhat tired and stiff, ducked down into the interior of her prison and thankfully emerged into liberty once more.

''Miss Copp,'' she said earnestly, ''I assure you I looked into your pantry window *only* to discover if you had a willow-ware platter. I didn't see anything else—I didn't *look* for anything else.''

''Bless you, that's all right,'' said Miss Sarah amiably. ''You needn't worry—there's no harm done. Thank goodness, we Copps keep our pantries presentable at all times and don't care who sees into them. As for that old duckhouse, I'm glad it's smashed, for maybe now Martha will agree to having it taken down. She never would before for fear it might come in handy sometime and I've had to whitewash it every spring. But you might as well argue with a post as with Martha. She went to town today—I drove her to the station. And you want to buy my platter. Well, what will you give for it?''

"Twenty dollars," said Anne, who was never meant to match business wits with a Copp, or she would not have offered her price at the start.

"Well, I'll see," said Miss Sarah cautiously. "That platter is mine fortunately or I'd never dare to sell it when Martha wasn't here. As it is, I daresay she'll raise a fuss. Martha's the boss of this establishment I can tell you. I'm getting awful tired of living under another woman's thumb. But come in, come in. You must be real tired and hungry. I'll do the best I can for you in the way of tea but I warn you not to expect anything but bread and butter and some cowcumbers. Martha locked up all the cake and cheese and preserves afore she went. She always does, because she says I'm too extravagant with them if company comes."

The girls were hungry enough to do justice to any fare, and they enjoyed Miss Sarah's excellent bread and "cowcumbers" thoroughly. When the meal was over Miss Sarah said,

"I don't know as I mind selling the platter. But it's worth twenty-five dollars. It's a very old platter."

Diana Gave Anne's foot a gentle kick under the table, meaning, "Don't agree—she'll let it go for twenty if you hold out." But Anne was not minded to take any chances in regard to that precious platter. She promptly agreed to give twenty-five and Miss Sarah looked as if she felt sorry she hadn't asked for thirty.

"Well, I guess you may have it. I want all the money I can scare up just now. The fact is—" Miss Sarah threw up her head importantly, with a proud flush on her thin cheeks—"I'm going to be married—to Luther Wallace. He wanted me twenty years ago. I liked him real well but he was poor then and father packed him off. I s'pose I shouldn't have let him go so meek but I was timid and frightened of father. Besides, I didn't know men were so skurse."

When the girls were safely away, Diana driving and Anne holding the coveted platter carefully on her lap, the green, rain-freshened solitudes of the Tory Road were enlivened by ripples of girlish laughter.

"I'll amuse your Aunt Josephine with the 'strange eventful history' of this afternoon when I go to town tomorrow. We've had a rather trying time but it's over now. I've got the platter, and that rain has laid the dust beautifully. So 'all's well that ends well.' "

"We're not home yet," said Diana rather pessimistically, "and there's no telling what may happen before we are. You're such a girl to have adventures, Anne.''

"Having adventures comes natural to some people," said Anne serenely. "You just have a gift for them or you haven't.''

CHAPTER 19

JUST A HAPPY DAY

"AFTER ALL," Anne had said to Marilla once, "I believe the nicest and sweetest days are not those on which anything very splendid or wonderful or exciting happens but just those that bring simple little pleasures, following one another softly, like pearls slipping off a string.''

Life at Green Gables was full of just such days, for Anne's adventures and misadventures, like those of other people, did not all happen at once, but were sprinkled over the year, with long stretches of harmless, happy days between, filled with work and dreams and laughter and lessons. Such a day came late in August. In the forenoon Anne and Diana rowed the delighted twins down the pond to the sandshore to pick "sweet grass" and paddle in the surf, over which the wind was harping an old lyric learned when the world was young.

In the afternoon Anne walked down to the old Irving place to see Paul. She found him stretched out on the grassy bank beside the thick fir grove that sheltered the house on the north, absorbed in a book of fairy tales. He sprang up radiantly at sight of her.

"Oh, I'm so glad you've come, teacher," he said eagerly, "because Grandma's away. You'll stay and have tea with me, won't you? It's so lonesome to have tea all by oneself. *You* know, teacher. I've had serious thoughts of asking Young Mary Joe to sit down and eat her tea with me, but I expect Grandma wouldn't approve. She says the French have to be kept in their place. And anyhow, it's difficult to talk with Young Mary Joe. She just laughs and says, 'Well, yous do beat all de kids I ever knowed.' That isn't my idea of conversation.''

"Of course I'll stay to tea," said Anne gaily. "I was dying to be asked. My mouth has been watering for some more of your grandma's delicious shortbread ever since I had tea here before.

Paul looked very sober.

"If it depended on me, teacher," he said, standing before Anne with his hands in his pockets and his beautiful little face shadowed with sudden care, "you should have shortbread with a right good will. But it depends on Mary Joe. I heard Grandma tell her before she left that she wasn't to give me any shortcake because it was too rich for little boys' stomachs. But maybe Mary Joe will cut some for you if I promise I won't eat any. Let's hope for the best."

"Yes, let us," agreed Anne, whom this cheerful philosophy suited exactly, "and if Mary Joe proves hard-hearted and won't give me any shortbread it doesn't matter in the least, so you are not to worry over that."

"You're sure you won't mind if she doesn't?" said Paul anxiously.

"Perfectly sure, dear heart."

"Then I won't worry," said Paul, with a long breath of relief, "especially as I really think Mary Joe will listen to reason. She's not a naturally unreasonable person, but she has learned by experience that it doesn't do to disobey Grandma's orders. Grandma is an excellent woman but people must do as she tells them. She was very much pleased with me this morning because I managed at last to eat all my plateful of porridge. It was a great effort but I succeeded. Grandma says she thinks she'll make a man of me yet. But, teacher, I want to ask you a very important question. You will answer it truthfully, won't you?"

"I'll try," promised Anne.

"Do you think I'm wrong in my upper story?" asked Paul, as if his very existence depended on her reply.

"Goodness, no, Paul," exclaimed Anne in amazement. "Certainly you're not. What put such an idea into your head?"

"Mary Joe . . . but she didn't know I heard her. Mrs. Peter Sloane's hired girl, Veronica, came to see Mary Joe last evening and I heard them talking in the kitchen as I was going through the hall. I heard Mary Joe say, 'Dat Paul, he is de queeres' leetle boy. He talks dat queer. I tink dere's someting wrong in his upper story.' I couldn't sleep last night for ever so long, thinking of it, and wondering if Mary Joe was right. I couldn't bear to ask Grandma about it somehow, but I made up my mind I'd ask you. I'm so glad you think I'm all right in my upper story."

"Of course you are. Mary Joe is a silly, ignorant girl, and you are never to worry about anything she says," said Anne indignantly, secretly resolving to give Mrs. Irving a discreet hint as to the advisability of restraining Mary Joe's tongue.

"Well, that's a weight off my mind," said Paul. "I'm perfectly happy now, teacher, thanks to you. It wouldn't be nice to have something wrong in your upper story, would it, teacher? I suppose the reason Mary Joe imagines I have is because I tell her what I think about things sometimes."

"It *is* a rather dangerous practice," admitted Anne, out of the depths of her own experience.

"Well, by and by I'll tell you the thoughts I told Mary Joe and you can see for yourself if there's anything queer in them," said Paul, "but I'll wait till it begins to get dark. That is the time I ache to tell people things, and when nobody else is handy I just *have* to tell Mary Joe. But after this I won't, if it makes her imagine I'm wrong in my upper story. I'll just ache and bear it."

"And if the ache gets too bad you can come up to Green Gables and tell me your thoughts," suggested Anne, with all the gravity that endeared her to children, who so dearly love to be taken seriously.

"Yes, I will. But I hope Davy won't be there when I go because he makes faces at me. I don't mind *very* much because he is such a little boy and I am quite a big one, but still it is not pleasant to have faces made at you. And Davy makes such terrible ones. Sometimes I am frightened he will never get his face straightened out again. He makes them at me in church when I ought to be thinking of sacred things. Dora likes me though, and I like her, but not so well as I did before she told Minnie May Barry that she meant to marry me when I grow up but I'm far too young to be thinking of it yet, don't you think, teacher?"

"Rather young," agreed teacher.

"Speaking of marrying, reminds me of another thing that has been troubling me of late," continued Paul. "Mrs. Lynde was down here one day last week having tea with Grandma, and Grandma made me show her my little mother's picture . . . the one father sent me for my birthday present. I didn't exactly want to show it to Mrs. Lynde. Mrs. Lynde is a good, kind woman, but she isn't the sort of person you want to show your mother's picture to. *You* know, teacher. But of course I obeyed Grandma. Mrs. Lynde said she was very pretty but kind of actressy looking, and must have been an awful lot younger than father. Then she said, 'Some of these days your pa will be marrying again likely. How will you like to have a new ma, Master Paul?' Well, the idea almost took my breath away, teacher, but I wasn't going to let Mrs. Lynde see *that*. I just looked her straight in the face . . . like this . . . and I said, 'Mrs. Lynde, father made a pretty good job of picking out my first mother and I could trust him to pick out just as good a one the second time.' And I *can* trust him, teacher. But still, I hope, if he ever does give me a new mother, he'll ask my opinion about her before it's too late. There's Mary Joe coming to call us to tea. I'll go and consult with her about the shortbread.''

As a result of the "consultation," Mary Joe cut the shortbread and added a dish of preserves to the bill of fare. Anne poured the tea and she and Paul had a very merry meal in the dim old sitting room whose windows were open to the gulf breezes, and they talked so much "nonsense" that Mary Joe was quite scandalized and told Veronica the next evening that "de school mees" was as queer as Paul. After tea Paul took Anne up to his room to show her his mother's picture, which had been the mysterious birthday present kept by Mrs. Irving in the bookcase. Paul's little low-ceilinged room was a soft whirl of ruddy light from the sun that was setting over the sea and swinging shadows from the fir trees that grew close to the square, deep-set window. From out this soft glow and glamour shone a sweet, girlish face, with tender mother eyes, that was hanging on the wall at the foot of the bed.

"That's my little mother," said Paul with loving pride. "I got Grandma to hang it there where I'd see it as soon as I opened my eyes in the morning. I never mind not having the light when I go to bed now, because it just seems as if my little mother was right here with me. Father knew just what I would like for a birthday present, although he never asked me. Isn't it wonderful how much fathers *do* know?''

"Your mother was very lovely, Paul, and you look a little like her. But her eyes and hair are darker than yours.''

"My eyes are the same color as father's," said Paul, flying about the room to heap all available cushions on the window seat, "but father's hair is gray. He has lots of it, but it is gray. You see, father is nearly fifty. That's ripe old age, isn't it? But it's only *outside* he's old. *Inside* he's just as young as anybody. Now, teacher, please sit here; and I'll sit at your feet. May I lay my head against your knee? That's the way my little mother and I used to sit. Oh, this is real splendid, I think.''

"Now, I want to hear those thoughts which Mary Joe pronounces so queer,'' said Anne, patting the mop of curls at her side. Paul never needed any coaxing to tell his thoughts . . . at least, to congenial souls.

"I thought them out in the fir grove one night," he said dreamily. "Of course I didn't *believe* them but I *thought* them. *You* know, teacher. And then I wanted to tell them to somebody and there was nobody but Mary Joe. Mary Joe was in the pantry setting bread and I sat down on the bench beside her and I said, 'Mary Joe, do you know what I think? I think the evening star is a lighthouse on the land where the fairies dwell.' And Mary Joe said, 'Well yous are de queer one. Dare ain't no such ting as fairies.' I was very much provoked. Of course, I knew there are no fairies; but that needn't prevent my thinking there is. *You* know, teacher. But I tried again quite patiently. I said, 'Well then, Mary Joe, do you know what I think? I think an angel walks over the world after the sun sets . . . a great, tall, white angel, with silvery folded wings . . . and sings the flowers and birds to sleep. children can hear him if they know how to listen.' Then Mary Joe held up her hands all over flour and said, 'Well, yous are de queer leetle boy. Yous make me feel scare.' And she really did looked scared. I went out then and whispered the rest of my thoughts to the garden. There was a little birch tree in the garden and it died. Grandma says the salt spray killed it; but I think the dryad belonging to it was a foolish dryad who wandered away to see the world and got lost. And the little tree was so lonely it died of a broken heart.''

"And when the poor, foolish little dryad gets tired of the world and comes back to her tree *her* heart will break," said Anne.

"Yes; but if dryads are foolish they must take the consequences, just as if they were real people," said Paul gravely. "Do you know what I think about the new moon, teacher? I think it is a little golden boat full of dreams.''

"And when it tips on a cloud some of them spill out and fall into your sleep.''

"Exactly, teacher. Oh, you *do* know. And I think the violets are little snips of the sky that fell down when the angels cut out holes for the stars to shine through. And the buttercups are made out of old sunshine; and I think the sweet peas will be butterflies when they go to heaven. Now, teacher, do you see anything so very queer about those thoughts?''

"No, laddie dear, they are not queer at all; they are strange and beautiful thoughts for a little boy to think, and so people who couldn't think anything of the sort themselves, if they tried for a

hundred years, think them queer. But keep on thinking them, Paul
. . . some day you are going to be a poet, I believe.''

When Anne reached home she found a very different type of
boyhood waiting to be put to bed. Davy was sulky; and when Anne
had undressed him he bounced into bed and buried his face in the
pillow.

''Davy, you have forgotten to say your prayers,'' said Anne
rebukingly.

''No, I didn't forget,'' said Davy defiantly, ''but I ain't going to
say my prayers any more. I'm going to give up trying to be good,
'cause no matter how good I am you'd like Paul Irving better. So I
might as well be bad and have the fun of it.''

''I don't like Paul Irving *better,*'' said Anne seriously. ''I like you
just as well, only in a different way.''

''But I want you to like me the same way,'' pouted Davy.

''You can't like different people the same way. You don't like
Dora and me the same way, do you?''

Davy sat up and reflected.

''No . . . o . . . o,'' he admitted at last, ''I like Dora because
she's my sister but I like you because you're *you.*''

''And I like Paul because he is Paul and Davy because he is
Davy,'' said Anne gaily.

''Well, I kind of wish I'd said my prayers then,'' said Davy,
convinced by this logic. ''But it's too much bother getting out now to
say them. I'll say them twice over in the morning, Anne. Won't that
do as well?''

No, Anne was positive it would not do as well. So Davy scrambled
out and knelt down at her knee. When he had finished his devotions
he leaned back on his little, bare, brown heels and looked up at her.

''Anne, I'm gooder than I used to be.''

''Yes, indeed you are, Davy,'' said Anne, who never hesitated to
give credit where credit was due.

''I *know* I'm gooder,'' said Davy confidently, ''and I'll tell you
how I know it. Today Marilla give me two pieces of bread and jam,
one for me and one for Dora. One was a good deal bigger than the
other and Marilla didn't say which was mine. But I give the biggest
piece to Dora. That was good of me, wasn't it?''

''Very good, and very manly, Davy.''

''Of course,'' admitted Davy, ''Dora wasn't very hungry and she
only et half her slice and then she give the rest to me. But I didn't
know she was going to do that when I give it to her, so I *was* good,
Anne.''

In the twilight Anne sauntered down to the Dryad's Bubble and saw Gilbert Blythe coming down through the dusky Haunted Wood. She had a sudden realization that Gilbert was a schoolboy no longer. And how manly he looked—the tall, frank-faced fellow, with the clear, straightforward eyes and the broad shoulders. Anne thought Gilbert was a very handsome lad, even though he didn't look at all like her ideal man. She and Diana had long ago decided what kind of a man they admired and their tastes seemed exactly similar. He must be very tall and distinguished looking, with melancholy, inscrutable eyes, and a melting, sympathetic voice. There was nothing either melancholy or inscrutable in Gilbert's physiognomy, but of course that didn't matter in friendship!

Gilbert stretched himself out on the ferns beside the Bubble and looked approvingly at Anne. If Gilbert had been asked to describe his ideal woman the description would have answered point for point to Anne, even to those seven tiny freckles whose obnoxious presence still continued to vex her soul. Gilbert was as yet little more than a boy; but a boy has his dreams as have others, and in Gilbert's future there was always a girl with big, limpid gray eyes, and a face as fine and delicate as a flower. He had made up his mind, also, that his future must be worthy of its goddess. Even in quiet Avonlea there were temptations to be met and faced. White Sands youth were a rather "fast" set, and Gilbert was popular wherever he went. But he meant to keep himself worthy of Anne's friendship and perhaps some distant day her love; and he watched over word and thought and deed as jealously as if her clear eyes were to pass in judgment on it. She held over him the unconscious influence that every girl, whose ideals are high and pure, wields over her friends; an influence which would endure as long as she was faithful to those ideals and which she would as certainly lose if she were ever false to them. In Gilbert's eyes Anne's greatest charm was the fact that she never stooped to the petty practices of so many of the Avonlea girls—the small jealousies, the little deceits and rivalries, the palpable bids for favor. Anne held herself apart from all this, not consciously or of design, but simply because anything of the sort was utterly foreign to her transparent, impulsive nature, crystal clear in its motives and aspirations.

But Gilbert did not attempt to put his thoughts into words, for he had already too good reason to know that Anne would mercilessly and frostily nip all attempts at sentiment in the bud—or laugh at him, which was ten times worse.

"You look like a real dryad under that birch tree," he said teasingly.

"I love birch trees," said Anne, laying her cheek against the creamy satin of the slim bole, with one of the pretty, caressing gestures that came so natural to her.

"Then you'll be glad to hear that Mr. Major Spencer has decided to set out a row of white birches all along the road front of his farm, by way of encouraging the A.V.I.S.," said Gilbert. "He was talking to me about it today. Major Spencer is the most progressive and public-spirited man in Avonlea. And Mr. William Bell is going to set out a spruce hedge along his road front and up his lane. Our society is getting on splendidly, Anne. It is past the experimental stage and is an accepted fact. The older folks are beginning to take an interest in it and the White Sands people are talking of starting one too. Even Elisha Wright has come around since that day the Americans from the hotel had the picnic at the shore. They praised our roadsides so highly and said they were so much prettier than in any other part of the Island. And when, in due time, the other farmers follow Mr. Spencer's good example and plant ornamental trees and hedges along their road fronts Avonlea will be the prettiest settlement in the province."

"The Aids are talking of taking up the graveyard," said Anne, "and I hope they will, because there will have to be a subscription for that, and it would be no use for the Society to try it after the hall affair. But the Aids would never have stirred in the matter if the Society hadn't put it into their thoughts unofficially. Those trees we planted on the church grounds are flourishing, and the trustees have promised me that they will fence in the school grounds next year. If they do I'll have an arbor day and every scholar shall plant a tree; and we'll have a garden in the corner by the road."

"We've succeeded in almost all our plans so far, except in getting the old Boulter house removed," said Gilbert, "and I've given *that* up in despair. Levi won't have it taken down just to vex us. There's a contrary streak in all the Boulters and it's strongly developed in him."

"Julia Bell wants to send another committee to him, but I think the better way will just be to leave him severely alone," said Anne sagely.

"And trust to Providence, as Mrs. Lynde says," smiled Gilbert. "Certainly, no more committees. They only aggravate him. Julia Bell thinks you can do anything, if you only have a committee to attempt it. Next spring, Anne, we must start an agitation for nice lawns and grounds. We'll sow good seed betimes this winter. I've a treatise here on lawns and lawn-making and I'm going to prepare a paper on the subject soon. Well, I suppose our vacation is almost over. School opens Monday. Has Ruby Gillis got the Carmody school?''

"Yes; Priscilla wrote that she had taken her own home school, so the Carmody trustees gave it to Ruby. I'm sorry Priscilla is not coming back, but since she can't I'm glad Ruby has got the school. She will be home for Saturdays and it will seem like old times, to have her and Jane and Diana and myself all together again.''

Marilla, just home from Mrs. Lynde's, was sitting on the back porch step when Anne returned to the house.

"Rachel and I have decided to have our cruise to town tomorrow,'' she said. "Mr. Lynde is feeling better this week and Rachel wants to go before he has another sick spell.''

"I intend to get up extra early tomorrow morning for I've ever so much to do,'' said Anne virtuously. "For one thing, I'm going to shift the feathers from my old bed-tick to the new one. I ought to have done it long ago but I've just kept putting it off . . . it's such a detestable task. It's a very bad habit to put off disagreeable things, and I never mean to again, or else I can't comfortably tell my pupils not to do it. That would be inconsistent. Then I want to make a cake for Mr. Harrison and finish my paper on gardens for the A.V.I.S., and write Stella, and wash and starch my muslin dress, and make Dora's new apron.''

"You won't get half done,'' said Marilla pessimistically. "I never yet planned to do a lot of things but something happened to prevent me.''

CHAPTER 20

THE WAY IT OFTEN HAPPENS

ANNE ROSE betimes the next morning and blithely greeted the fresh day, when the banners of the sunrise were shaken triumphantly across the pearly skies. Green Gables lay in a pool of sunshine, flecked with the dancing shadows of poplar and willow. Beyond the lane was Mr. Harrison's wheat-field, a great, wind-rippled expanse of pale gold. The world was so beautiful that Anne spent ten blissful minutes hanging idly over the garden gate drinking the loveliness in.

After breakfast Marilla made ready for her journey. Dora was to go with her, having been long promised this treat.

"Now, Davy, you try to be a good boy and don't bother Anne," she straitly charged him. "If you are good I'll bring you a striped candy cane from town."

For alas, Marilla had stooped to the evil habit of bribing people to be good!

"I won't be bad on purpose, but s'posen I'm bad zacksidentally?" Davy wanted to know.

"You'll have to guard against accidents," admonished Marilla. "Anne, if Mr. Shearer comes today get a nice roast and some steak. If he doesn't you'll have to kill a fowl for dinner tomorrow."

Anne nodded.

"I'm not going to bother cooking any dinner for just Davy and myself today," she said. "That cold ham bone will do for noon lunch and I'll have some steak fried for you when you come home at night."

"I'm going to help Mr. Harrison haul dulse this morning," announced Davy. "He asked me to, and I guess he'll ask me to dinner too. Mr. Harrison is an awful kind man. He's a real sociable man. I hope I'll be like him when I grow up. I mean *behave* like him . . . I don't want to *look* like him. But I guess there's no danger, for Mrs. Lynde says I'm a very handsome child. Do you s'pose it'll last, Anne? I want to know."

"I daresay it will," said Anne gravely. "You *are* a handsome boy, Davy" . . . Marilla looked volumes of disapproval . . . "but you must live up to it and be just as nice and gentlemanly as you look to be."

"And you told Minnie May Barry the other day, when you found her crying 'cause someone said she was ugly, that if she was nice and kind and loving people wouldn't mind her looks," said Davy discontentedly. "Seems to me you can't get out of being good in this world for some reason or 'nother. You just *have* to behave."

"Don't you want to be good?" asked Marilla, who had learned a great deal but had not yet learned the futility of asking such questions.

"Yes, I want to be good but not *too* good," said Davy cautiously. "You don't have to be very good to be a Sunday School superintendent. Mr. Bell's that, and he's a real bad man."

"Indeed he's not," said Marilla indignantly.

"He is . . . he says he is himself," asseverated Davy. "He said it when he prayed in Sunday School last Sunday. He said he was a vile worm and a miserable sinner and guilty of the blackest 'niquity. What did he do that was so bad, Marilla? Did he kill anybody? Or steal the collection cents? I want to know."

Fortunately Mrs. Lynde came driving up the lane at this moment and Marilla made off, feeling that she had escaped from the snare of the fowler, and wishing devoutly that Mr. Bell were not quite so highly figurative in his public petitions, especially in the hearing of small boys who were always "wanting to know."

Anne, left alone in her glory, worked with a will. The floor was swept, the beds made, the hens fed, the muslin dress washed and hung out on the line. Then Anne prepared for the transfer of feathers. She mounted to the garret and donned the first old dress that came to hand . . . a navy blue cashmere she had worn at fourteen. It was decidedly on the short side and as "skimpy" as the notable wincey Anne had worn upon the occasion of her debut at Green Gables; but at least it would not be materially injured by down and feathers. Anne completed her toilet by tying a big red and white spotted handkerchief that had belonged to Matthew over her head, and, thus accoutred, betook herself to the kitchen chamber, whither Marilla, before her departure, had helped her carry the feather bed.

A cracked mirror hung by the chamber window and in an unlucky moment Anne looked into it. There were those seven freckles on her nose, more rampant than ever, or so it seemed in the glare of the light from the unshaded window.

"Oh, I forgot to rub that lotion on last night," she thought. "I'd better run down to the pantry and do it now."

Anne had already suffered many things trying to remove those freckles. On one occastion the entire skin had peeled off her nose but the freckels remained. A few days previously she had found a recipe for a freckle lotion in a magazine and, as the ingredients were within her reach, she straightway compounded it, much to the disgust of Marilla, who thought that if Providence had placed freckles on your nose it was your bounden duty to leave them there.

Anne scurried down to the pantry, which, always dim from the big willow growing close to the window, was now almost dark by reason of the shade drawn to exclude flies. Anne caught the bottle containing the lotion from the shelf and copiously anointed her nose therewith by means of a little sponge sacred to the purpose. This important duty done, she returned to her work. Any one who has ever shifted feathers from one tick to another will not need to be told that when Anne finished she was a sight to behold. Her dress was white with down and fluff, and her front hair, escaping from the handkerchief, was adorned with a veritable halo of feathers. At this auspicious moment a knock sounded at the kitchen door.

"That must be Mr. Shearer," thought Anne. "I'm in a dreadful mess but I'll have to run down as I am, for he's always in a hurry."

Down flew Anne to the kitchen door. If ever a charitable floor did open to swallow up a miserable, befeathered damsel the Green Gables porch floor should promplty have engulfed Anne at that moment. On the doorstep were standing Priscilla Grant, golden and fair in silk attire, a short, stout, gray-haired lady in a tweed suit, and another lady, tall, stately, wonderfully gowned, with a beautiful, high-bred face and large, black-lashed violet eyes, whom Anne "instinctively felt," as she would have said in her earlier days, to be Mrs. Charlotte E. Morgan.

In the dismay of the moment one thought stood out from the confusion of Anne's mind and she grasped at it as at the proverbial straw. All Mrs. Morgan's heroines were noted for "rising to the occasion." No matter what their troubles were, they invariably rose to the occasion and showed their superiority over all ills of time, space, and quantity. Anne therefore felt it was *her* duty to rise to the occasion and she did it, so perfectly that Priscilla afterwards declared she never admired Anne Shirley more than at that moment. No matter what her outraged feelings were she did not show them. She greeted Priscilla and was introduced to her companions as calmly and composedly as if she had been arrayed in purple and fine linen. To be sure, it was somewhat of a shock to find that the lady she had instinctively felt to be Mrs. Morgan was not Mrs. Morgan at all, but an unknown Mrs. Pendexter, while the stout little gray-haired woman was Mrs. Morgan; but in the greater shock the lesser lost its power. Anne ushered her guests to the spare room and thence into the parlor, where she left them while she hastened out to help Priscilla unharness her horse.

"It's dreadful to come upon you so unexpectedly as this," apologized Priscilla, "but I did not know till last night that we were coming. Aunt Charlotte is going away Monday and she promised to spend today with a friend in town. But last night her friend telephoned to her not to come because they were quarantined for scarlet fever. So I suggested we come here instead, for I knew you were longing to see her. We called at the White Sands Hotel and brought

Mrs. Pendexter with us. She is a friend of aunt's and lives in New York and her husband is a millionaire. We can't stay very long, for Mrs. Pendexter has to be back at the hotel by five o'clock.''

Several times while they were putting away the horse Anne caught Priscilla looking at her in a furtive, puzzled way.

"She needn't stare at me so,'' Anne thought a little resentfully. "If she doesn't *know* what it is to change a feather bed she might *imagine* it.''

When Priscilla had gone to the parlor, and before Anne could escape upstairs, Diana walked into the kitchen. Anne caught her astonished friend by the arm.

"Diana Barry, who do you suppose is in that parlor at this very moment? Mrs. Charlotte E. Morgan . . . and a New York millionaire's wife . . . and here I am like *this* . . . and *not a thing in the house for dinner but a cold ham bone,* Diana!''

By this time Anne had become aware that Diana was staring at her in precisely the same bewildered fashion as Priscilla had done. It was really too much.

"Oh, Diana, don't look at me so,'' she implored. *"You,* at least, must know that the neatest person in the world couldn't empty feathers from one tick into another and remain neat in the process.''

"It . . . it . . . isn't the feathers,'' hesitated Diana. "It's . . . it's . . . your nose, Anne.''

"My nose? Oh, Diana, surely nothing has gone wrong with it!''

Anne rushed to the little looking glass over the sink. One glance revealed the fatal truth. Her nose was a brilliant scarlet!

Anne sat down on the sofa, her dauntless spirit subdued at last.

"What is the matter with it?'' asked Diana, curiosity overcoming delicacy.

"I thought I was rubbing my freckle lotion on it, but I must have used that red dye Marilla has for marking the pattern on her rugs,'' was the despairing response. "What shall I do?''

"Wash it off,'' said Diana practically.

"Perhaps it won't wash off. First I dye my hair; then I dye my nose. Marilla cut my hair off when I dyed it but that remedy would hardly be practicable in this case. Well, this is another punishment for vanity and I suppose I deserve it . . . though there's not much comfort in *that*. It is really almost enough to make one believe in ill-luck, though Mrs. Lynd says there is no such thing, because everything is foreordained.''

Fortunately the dye washed off easily and Anne, somewhat consoled, betook herself to the east gable while Diana ran home. Presently Anne came down again, clothed and in her right mind. The muslin dress she had fondly hoped to wear was bobbing merrily on the line outside, so she was forced to content herself with her black lawn. She had the fire on and the tea steeping when Diana returned; the latter wore *her* muslin, at least, and carried a covered platter in her hand.

"Mother sent you this," she said, lifting the cover and displaying a nicely carved and jointed chicken to Anne's grateful eyes.

The chicken was supplemented by light new bread, excellent butter and cheese, Marilla's fruit cake and a dish of preserved plums, floating in their golden syrup as in congealed summer sunshine. There was a big bowlful of pink-and-white asters also, by way of decoration; yet the spread seemed very meagre beside the elaborate one formerly prepared for Mrs. Morgan.

Anne's hungry guests, however, did not seem to think anything was lacking and they ate the simple viands with apparent enjoyment. But after the first few moments Anne thought no more of what was or was not on her bill of fare. Mrs. Morgan's appearance might be somewhat disappointing, as even her loyal worshippers had been forced to admit to each other; but she proved to be a delightful conversationalist. She had travelled extensively and was an excellent story teller. She had seen much of men and women, and crystallized her experiences into witty little sentences and epigrams which made her hearers feel as if they were listening to one of the people in clever books. But under all her sparkle there was a strongly felt undercurrent of true, womanly sympathy and kind heartedness which won affection as easily as her brilliancy won admiration. Nor did she monopolize the conversation. She could draw others out as skillfully and fully as she could talk herself, and Anne and Diana found themselves chattering freely to her. Mrs. Pendexter said little; she merely smiled with her lovely eyes and lips, and ate chicken and fruit cake and preserves with such exquisite grace that she conveyed the impression of dining on ambrosia and honeydew. But then, as Anne said to Diana later on, anybody so divinely beautiful as Mrs. Pendexter didn't need to talk; it was enough for her just to *look*.

After dinner they all had a walk through Lover's Lane and Violet Vale and the Birch Path, then back through the Haunted Wood to the Dryad's Bubble, where they sat down and talked for a delightful last half hour. Mrs. Morgan wanted to know how the Haunted Wood came by its name, and laughed until she cried when she heard the story and Anne's dramatic account of a certain memorable walk through it at the witching hour of twilight.

"It has indeed been a feast of reason and flow of soul, hasn't it?" said Anne, when her guests had gone and she and Diana were alone again. "I don't know which I enjoyed more . . . listening to Mrs. Morgan or gazing at Mrs. Pendexter. I believe we had a nicer time than if we'd known they were coming and been cumbered with much serving. You must stay to tea with me, Diana, and we'll talk it all over."

"Priscilla says Mrs. Pendexter's husband's sister is married to an English earl; and yet she took a second helping of the plum preserves," said Diana, as if the two facts were somehow incompatible.

"I daresay even the English earl himself wouldn't have turned up his aristocratic nose at Marilla's plum preserves," said Anne proudly.

Anne did not mention the misfortune which had befallen *her* nose when she related the day's history to Marilla that evening. But she took the bottle of freckle lotion and emptied it out of the window.

"I shall never try any beautifying messes again," she said, darkly resolute. "They may do for careful, deliberate people; but for anyone so hopelessy given over to making mistakes as I seem to be it's tempting fate to meddle with them."

—————————— CHAPTER 21 ——————————

SWEET MISS LAVENDAR

SCHOOL OPENED and Anne returned to her work, with fewer theories but considerably more experience. She had several new pupils, six and seven year olds just venturing, round-eyed, into a world of wonder. Among them were Davy and Dora. Davy sat with Milty Boulter, who had been going to school for a year and was therefore quite a man of the world. Dora had made a compact at Sunday School the previous Sunday to sit with Lily Sloane; but Lily Sloane not coming the first day, she was temporarily assigned to Mirabel Cotton, who was ten years old and therefore, in Dora's eyes, one of the "big girls."

"I think school is great fun," Davy told Marilla when he got home that night. "You said I'd find it hard to sit still and I did . . . you mostly do tell the truth, I notice . . . but you can wriggle your legs about under the desk and that helps a lot. It's splendid to have so many boys to play with. I sit with Milty Boulter and he's fine. He's longer than me but I'm wider. It's nicer to sit in the back seats but you can't sit there till your legs grow long enough to touch the floor. Milty drawed a picture of Anne on his slate and it was awful ugly and I told him if he made pictures of Anne like that I'd lick him at recess. I thought first I'd draw one of him and put horns and a tail on it, but I was afraid it would hurt his feelings, and Anne says you should never hurt anyone's feelings. It seems it's dreadful to have your feelings hurt. It's better to knock a boy down than hurt his feelings if you *must* do something. Milty said he wasn't scared of me but he'd just as soon call it somebody else to 'blige me, so he rubbed out Anne's name and printed Barbara Shaw's under it. Milty doesn't like Barbara 'cause she calls him a sweet little boy and once she patted him on his head."

Dora said primly that she liked school; but she was very quiet, even for her; and when at twilight Marilla bade her go upstairs to bed she hesitated and began to cry.

"I'm . . . I'm frightened," she sobbed. "I . . . I don't want to go upstairs alone in the dark."

"What notion have you got into your head now?" demanded Marilla. "I'm sure you've gone to bed alone all summer and never been frightened before."

Dora still continued to cry, so Anne picked her up, cuddled her sympathetically, and whispered,

"Tell Anne all about it, sweetheart. What are you frightened of?"

"Of . . . of Mirabel Cotton's uncle," sobbed Dora. "Mirabel Cotton told me all about her family today in school. Nearly everybody in her family has died . . . all her grandfathers and grandmothers and ever so many uncles and aunts. They have a habit of dying, Mirabel says. Mirabel's awful proud of having so many dead relations, and she told me what they all died of, and what they said, and how they looked in their coffins. And Mirabel says one of her uncles was seen walking around the house after he was buried. Her mother saw him. I don't mind the rest so much but I can't help thinking about that uncle."

Anne went upstairs with Dora and sat by her until she fell asleep. The next day Mirabel Cotton was kept in at recess and "gently but firmly" given to understand that when you were so unfortunate as to possess an uncle who persisted in walking about houses after he had been decently interred it was not in good taste to talk about that eccentric gentleman to your deskmate of tender years. Mirabel thought this very harsh. The Cottons had not much to boast of. How was she to keep up her prestige among her schoolmates if she were forbidden to make capital out of the family ghost?

September slipped by into a gold and crimson graciousness of October. One Friday evening Diana came over.

"I'd a letter from Ella Kimball today, Anne, and she wants us to go over to tea tomorrow afternoon to meet her cousin, Irene Trent, from town. But we can't get one of our horses to go, for they'll all be in use tomorrow, and your pony is lame . . . so I suppose we can't go."

"Why can't we walk?" suggested Anne. "If we go straight back through the woods we'll strike the West Grafton road not far from the Kimball place. I was through that way last winter and I know the road. It's no more than four miles and we won't have to walk home, for Oliver Kimball will be sure to drive us. He'll be only too glad of the excuse, for he goes to see Carrie Sloane and they say his father will hardly ever let him have a horse."

It was accordingly arranged that they should walk, and the following afternoon they set out, going by way of Lover's Lane to the back of the Cuthbert farm, where they found a road leading into the heart of acres of glimmering beech and maple woods, which were all in a wondrous glow of flame and gold, lying in a great purple stillness and peace.

"It's as if the year were kneeling to pray in a vast cathedral full of mellow stained light, isn't it?" said Anne dreamily. "It doesn't seem right to hurry through it, does it? It seems irreverent, like running in a church."

"We *must* hurry though," said Diana, glancing at her watch. "We've left ourselves little enough time as it is."

"Well, I'll walk faster but don't ask me to talk," said Anne, quickening her pace. "I just want to drink the day's loveliness in . . . I feel as if she were holding it out to my lips like a cup of airy wine and I'll take a sip at every step."

Perhaps it was because she was so absorbed in "drinking it in" that Anne took the left turning when they came to a fork in the road. She should have taken the right, but ever afterwards she counted it the most fortunate mistake of her life. They came out finally to a lonely, grassy road, with nothing in sight along it but ranks of spruce saplings.

"Why, where are we?" exclaimed Diana in bewilderment. "This isn't the West Grafton road."

"No, it's the base line road in Middle Grafton," said Anne, rather shamefacedly. "I must have taken the wrong turning back at the fork. I don't know where we are exactly, but we must be all of three miles from Kimballs' still."

"Then we can't get there by five, for it's half past four now," said Diana, with a despairing look at her watch. "We'll arrive after they have had their tea, and they'll have all the bother of getting ours over again."

"We'd better turn back and go home," suggested Anne humbly. But Diana, after consideration, vetoed this.

"No, we may as well go on and spend the evening, since we have come this far."

A few yards further on the girls came to a place where the road forked again.

"Which of these do we take?" asked Diana dubiously.

Anne shook her head.

"I don't know and we can't afford to make any more mistakes. Here is a gate and a lane leading right into the wood. There must be a house at the other side. Let us go down and inquire."

"What a romantic old lane this is," said Diana, as they walked along its twists and turns. It ran under patriarchal old firs whose branches met above, creating a perpetual gloom in which nothing except moss could grow. On either hand were brown wood floors, crossed here and there by fallen lances of sunlight. All was very still and remote, as if the world and the cares of the world were far away.

"I feel as if we were walking through an enchanted forest," said Anne in a hushed tone. "Do you suppose we'll ever find our way back to the real world again, Diana? We shall presently come to a palace with a spellbound princess in it, I think."

Around the next turn they came in sight, not indeed of a palace, but of a little house almost as surprising as a palace would have been in this province of conventional wooden farmhouses, all as much alike in general characteristics as if they had grown from the same seed. Anne stopped short in rapture and Diana exclaimed,

"Oh, I know where we are now. That is the little stone house where Miss Lavendar Lewis lives . . . Echo Lodge, she calls it, I think. I've often heard of it but I've never seen it before. Isn't it a romantic spot?"

"It's the sweetest, prettiest place I ever saw or imagined," said

Anne delightedly. "It looks like a bit out of a story book or a dream."

The house was a low-eaved structure built of undressed blocks of red Island sandstone, with a little peaked roof out of which peered two dormer windows, with quaint wooden hoods over them, and two great chimneys. The whole house was covered with a luxuriant growth of ivy, finding easy foothold on the rough stonework and turned by autumn frosts to most beautiful bronze and wine-red tints.

Before the house was an oblong garden into which the lane gate where the girls were standing opened. The house bounded it on one side; on the three others it was enclosed by an old stone dyke, so overgrown with moss and grass and ferns that it looked like a high, green bank. On the right and left the tall, dark spruces spread their palm-like branches over it; but below it was a little meadow, green with clover aftermath, sloping down to the blue loop of the Grafton River. No other house or clearing was in sight . . . nothing but hills and valleys covered with feather young firs.

"I wonder what sort of person Miss Lewis is," speculated Diana as they opened the gate into the garden. "They say she is very peculiar."

"She'll be interesting then," said Anne decidely. "Peculiar people are always that at least, whatever else they are or are not. Didn't I tell you we would come to an enchanted palace? I knew the elves hadn't woven magic over that lane for nothing."

"But Miss Lavendar Lewis is hardly a spellbound princess," laughed Diana. "She's an old maid . . . she's forty-five and quite gray, I've heard."

"Oh, that's only part of the spell," asserted Anne confidently. "At heart she's young and beautiful still . . . and if we only knew how to unloose the spell she would step forth radiant and fair again. But we don't know how . . . it's always and only the prince who knows that . . . and Miss Lavendar's prince hasn't come yet. Perhaps some fatal mischance has befallen him . . . though *that's* against the law of all fairy tales."

"I'm afraid he came long ago and went away again," said Diana. "They say she used to be engaged to Stephen Irving . . . Paul's father . . . when they were young. But they quarrelled and parted."

"Hush," warned Anne. "The door is open."

The girls paused in the porch under the tendrils of ivy and knocked at the open door. There was a patter of steps inside and a rather odd little personage presented herself . . . a girl of about fourteen, with a freckled face, a snub nose, a mouth so wide that it did really seem as if it stretched "from ear to ear," and two long braids of fair hair tied with two enormous bows of blue ribbon.

"Is Miss Lewis at home?" asked Diana.

"Yes, ma'am. Come in, ma'am . . . this way, ma'am . . . and sit down, ma'am. I'll tell Miss Lavendar you're here, ma'am. She's upstairs, ma'am."

With this the small handmaiden whisked out of sight and the girls, left alone, looked about them with delighted eyes. The interior of this wonderful little house was quite as interesting as its exterior.

The room had a low ceiling and two square, small-paned windows, curtained with muslin frills. All the furnishings were old-fashioned, but so well and daintily kept that the effect was delicious. But it must be candidly admitted that the most attractive feature, to two healthy girls who had just tramped four miles through the autumn air, was a table, set out with pale blue china and laden with delicacies, while little golden-hued ferns scattered over the cloth gave it what Anne would have termed "a festal air."

"Miss Lavendar must be expecting company to tea," she whispered. "There are six places set. But what a funny little girl she has. She looked like a messenger from pixy land. I suppose she could have told us the road, but I was curious to see Miss Lavendar. S . . . s . . . sh, she's coming."

And with that Miss Lavendar Lewis was standing in the doorway. The girls were so surprised that they forgot good manners and simply stared. They had unconsciously been expecting to see the usual type of elderly spinster as known to their experience . . . a rather angular personage, with prim gray hair and spectacles. Nothing more unlike Miss Lavendar could possibly be imagined.

She was a little lady with snow-white hair beautifully wavy and thick, and carefully arranged in becoming puffs and coils. Beneath it was an almost girlish face, pink cheeked and sweet lipped, with big soft brown eyes and dimples . . . actually dimples. She wore a very dainty gown of cream muslin with pale-hued roses on it . . . a gown which would have seemed ridiculously juvenile on most women of her age, but which suited Miss Lavendar so perfectly that you never thought about it at all.

"Charlotta the Fourth says that you wished to see me," she said, in a voice that matched her appearance.

"We wanted to ask the right road to West Grafton," said Diana. "We are invited to tea at Mr. Kimball's, but we took the wrong path coming through the woods and came out to the base line instead of the West Grafton road. Do we take the right or left turning at your gate?''

"The left," said Miss Lavendar, with a hesitating glance at her tea-table. Then she exclaimed, as if in a sudden little burst of resolution,

"But oh, won't you stay and have tea with me? Please, do. Mr. Kimball's will have tea over before you get there. And Charlotta the Fourth and I will be so glad to have you.''

Diana looked mute inquiry at Anne.

"We'd like to stay," said Anne promptly, for she had made up her mind that she wanted to know more of this surprising Miss Lavendar, "if it won't inconvenience you. But you are expecting other guests, aren't you?''

Miss Lavendar looked at her tea-table again, and blushed.

"I know you'll think me dreadfully foolish," she said. "I *am* foolish . . . and I'm ashamed of it when I'm found out, but never unless I *am* found out. I'm not expecting anybody . . . I was just pretending I was. You see, I was so lonely. I love company . . . that is, the right kind of company . . . but so few people ever come here because it is so far out of the way. Charlotta the Fourth was lonely too. So I just pretended I was going to have a tea-party. I cooked for it . . . and decorated the table for it . . . and set it with my mother's wedding china . . . and I dressed up for it.''

Diana secretly thought Miss Lavendar quite as peculiar as report had pictured her. The idea of a woman of forty-five playing at having a tea-party, just as if she were a little girl! But Anne of the shining eyes exclaimed joyfully,

"Oh, do *you* imagine things too?''

That "too" revealed a kindred spirit to Miss Lavendar.

"Yes, I do," she confessed, boldly. "Of course it's silly in anybody as old as I am. But what is the use of being an independent old maid if you can't be silly when you want to, and when it doesn't hurt anybody? A person must have some compensations. I don't believe I could live at times if I didn't pretend things. I'm not often caught at it though, and Charlotta the Fourth never tells. But I'm glad to be caught today, for you have really come and I have tea all ready for you. Will you go up to the spare room and take off your hats? It's the white door at the head of the stairs. I must run out to the kitchen and see that Charlotta the Fourth isn't letting the tea boil. Charlotta the Fourth is a very good girl but she *will* let the tea boil.''

Miss Lavendar tripped off to the kitchen on hospitable thoughts intent and the girls found their way up to the spare room, an apartment as white as its door, lighted by the ivy-hung dormer window and looking, as Anne said, like the place where happy dreams grew.

"This is quite an adventure, isn't it?" said Diana. "And isn't Miss Lavendar sweet, if she *is* a little odd? She doesn't look a bit like an old maid."

"She looks just as music sounds, I think," answered Anne.

When they went down Miss Lavendar was carrying in the teapot, and behind her, looking vastly pleased, was Charlotta the Fourth, with a plate of hot biscuits.

"Now, you must tell me your names," said Miss Lavendar. "I'm so glad you are young girls. I love young girls. It's so easy to pretend I'm a girl myself when I'm with them. I do hate" . . . with a little grimace . . . "to believe I'm old. Now, who are you . . . just for convenience' sake? Diana Barry? And Anne Shirley? May I pretend that I've known you for a hundred years and call you Anne and Diana right away?"

"You may," the girls said both together.

"Then just let's sit comfily down and eat everything," said Miss Lavendar happily. "Charlotta, you sit at the foot and help the chicken. It is so fortunate that I made the sponge cake and dough-nuts. Of course, it was foolish to do it for imaginary guests . . . I know Charlotta the Fourth thought so, didn't you, Charlotta? But you see how well it has turned out. Of course they wouldn't have been wasted, for Charlotta the Fourth and I could have eaten them through time. But sponge cake is not a thing that improves with time."

That was a merry and memorable meal; and when it was over they all went out to the garden, lying in the glamour of sunset.

"I do think you have the loveliest place here," said Diana, looking round her admiringly.

"Why do you call it Echo Lodge?" asked Anne.

"Charlotta," said Miss Lavendar, "go into the house and bring out the little tin horn that is hanging over the clock shelf."

Charlotta the Forth skipped off and returned with the horn.

"Blow it, Charlotta," commanded Miss Lavendar.

Charlotta accordingly blew, a rather raucous, strident blast. There was a moment's stillness . . . and then from the woods over the river came a multitude of fairy echoes, sweet, elusive, silvery, as if all the "horns of elfland" were blowing against the sunset. Anne and Diana exclaimed in delight.

"Now laugh, Charlotta . . . laugh loudly."

Charlotta, who would probably have obeyed if Miss Lavendar had told her to stand on her head, climbed upon the stone bench and laughed loud and heartily. Back came the echoes, as if a host of pixy people were mimicking her laughter in the purple woodlands and along the fir-fringed points."

"People always admire my echoes very much," said Miss Lavendar, as if the echoes were her personal property. "I love them myself. They are very good company . . . with a little pretending. On calm evenings Charlotta the Fourth and I often sit out here and amuse ourselves with them. Charlotta, take back the horn and hang it carefully in its place."

"Why do you call her Charlotta the Fourth?" asked Diana, who was bursting with curiosity on this point.

"Just to keep her from getting mixed up with the other Charlotta in my thoughts," said Miss Lavendar seriously. "They all look so much alike there's no telling them apart. Her name isn't really Charlotta at all. It is . . . let me see . . . what is it? I *think* it's Leonora . . . yes, it *is* Leonora. You see, it is this way. When mother died ten years ago I couldn't stay here alone . . . and I couldn't afford to pay the wages of a grown-up girl. So I got little Charlotta Bowman to come and stay with me for board and clothes. Her name really was Charlotta . . . she was Charlotta the First. She was just thirteen. She stayed with me till she was sixteen and then she went away to Boston, because she could do better there. Her sister came to stay with me then. Her name was Julietta . . . Mrs. Bowman had a weakness for fancy names I think . . . but she looked so like Charlotta that I kept calling her that all the time . . . and she didn't mind. So I just gave up trying to remember her right name. She was Charlotta the Second, and when she went away Evelina came and she was Charlotta the Third. Now I have Charlotta the Fourth; but when she is sixteen . . . she's fourteen now . . . she will want to go to Boston too, and what I shall do then I really do not know. Charlotta the Fourth is the last of the Bowman girls, and the best. The other Charlottas always let me see that they thought it silly of me to pretend things but Charlotta the Fourth never does, no matter what she may really think. I don't care what people think about me if they don't let me see it."

"Well," said Diana looking regretfully at the setting sun, "I suppose we must go if we want to get to Mr. Kimball's before dark. We've had a lovely time, Miss Lewis.''

"Won't you come again to see me?" pleaded Miss Lavendar.

Tall Anne put her arm about the little lady.

"Indeed we shall," she promised. "Now that we have discovered you we'll wear out our welcome coming to see you. Yes, we must go . . . 'we must tear ourselves away,' as Paul Irving says every time he comes to Green Gables."

"Paul Irving?" There was a subtle change in Miss Lavendar's voice. "Who is he? I didn't think there was anybody of that name in Avonlea."

Anne felt vexed at her own heedlessness. She had forgotten about Miss Lavendar's old romance when Paul's name slipped out.

"He is a little pupil of mine," she explained slowly. "He came from Boston last year to live with his grandmother, Mrs. Irving of the shore road."

"Is he Stephen Irving's son?" Miss Lavendar asked, bending over her namesake border so that her face was hidden.

"Yes."

"I'm going to give you girls a bunch of lavendar apiece," said Miss Lavendar brightly, as if she had not heard the answer to her question. "It's very sweet, don't you think? Mother always loved it. She planted these borders long ago. Father named me Lavendar because he was so fond of it. The very first time he saw mother was when he visited her home in East Grafton with her brother. He fell in love with her at first sight; and they put him in the spare room bed to sleep and the sheets were scented with lavendar and he lay awake all night and thought of her. He always loved the scent of lavendar after that . . . and that was why he gave me the name. Don't forget to come back soon, girls dear. We'll be looking for you, Charlotta the Fourth and I.''

She opened the gate under the firs for them to pass through. She looked suddenly old and tired; the glow and radiance had faded from her face; her parting smile was as sweet with ineradicable youth as ever, but when the girls looked back from the first curve in the lane they saw her sitting on the old stone bench under the silver poplar in the middle of the garden with her head leaning wearily on her hand.

"She does look lonely," said Diana softly. "We must come often to see her."

"I think her parents gave her the only right and fitting name that could possibly be given her," said Anne. "If they had been so blind as to name her Elizabeth or Nellie or Muriel she must have been called Lavendar just the same, I think. It's so suggestive of sweetness and old-fashioned graces and 'silk attire.' Now, my name just smacks of bread and butter, patchwork and chores.''

"Oh, I don't think so," said Diana. "Anne seems to me real stately and like a queen. But I'd like Kerrenhappuch if it happened to be your name. I think people make their names nice or ugly just by what they are themselves. I can't bear Josie or Gertie for names now but before I knew the Pye girls I thought them real pretty.''

"That's a lovely idea, Diana," said Anne enthusiastically. "Living so that you beautify your name, even if it wasn't beautiful to begin with . . . making it stand in people's thoughts for something so lovely and pleasant that they never think of it by itself. Thank you, Diana.''

CHAPTER 22

ODDS AND ENDS

''SO YOU had tea at the stone house with Lavendar Lewis?'' said Marilla at the breakfast table next morning. "What is she like now? It's over fifteen years since I saw her last . . . it was one Sunday in Grafton church. I suppose she has changed a great deal. Davy Keith, when you want something you can't reach, ask to have it passed and don't spread yourself over the table in that fashion. Did you ever see Paul Irving doing that when he was here to meals?''

"But Paul's arms are longer'n mine," grumbled Davy. "They've had eleven years to grow and mine've only had seven. 'Sides, I *did* ask, but you and Anne was so busy talking you didn't pay any 'tention. 'Sides, Paul's never been here to any meal except tea, and it's easier to be p'lite at tea than at breakfast. You ain't half as hungry. It's an awful long while between supper and breakfast. Now, Anne, that spoonful ain't any bigger than it was last year and *I*'m ever so much bigger.''

"Of course, I don't know what Miss Lavendar used to look like but I don't fancy somehow that she has changed a great deal," said

Anne, after she had helped Davy to maple syrup, giving him two spoonfuls to pacify him. "Her hair is snow-white but her face is fresh and almost girlish, and she has the sweetest brown eyes . . . such a pretty shade of wood-brown with little golden glints in them . . . and her voice makes you think of white satin and tinkling water and fairy bells all mixed up together."

"She was reckoned a great beauty when she was a girl," said Marilla. "I never knew her very well but I liked her as far as I did know her. Some folks thought her peculiar even then. *Davy*, if ever I catch you at such a trick again you'll be made to wait for your meals till everyone else is done, like the French."

Most conversations between Anne and Marilla in the presence of the twins, were punctuated by these rebukes Davy-ward. In this instance, Davy, sad to relate, not being able to scoop up the last drops of his syrup with his spoon, had solved the difficulty by lifting his plate in both hands and applying his small pink tongue to it. Anne looked at him with such horrified eyes that the little sinner turned red and said, half shamefacedly, half defiantly,

"There ain't any wasted that way."

"People who are different from other people are always called peculiar," said Anne. "And Miss Lavendar is certainly different, thought it's hard to say just where the difference comes in. Perhaps it is because she is one of those people who never grow old."

"One might as well grow old when all your generation do," said Marilla, rather reckless of her pronouns. "If you don't, you don't fit in anywhere. Far as I can learn Lavendar Lewis has just dropped out of everything. She's lived in that out of the way place until everybody has forgotten her. That stone house is one of the oldest on the Island. Old Mr. Lewis built it eighty years ago when he came out from England. Davy, stop joggling Dora's elbow. Oh, I saw you! You needn't try to look innocent. What does make you behave so this morning?"

"Maybe I got out of the wrong side of the bed," suggested Davy. "Milty Boulter says if you do that things are bound to go wrong with you all day. His grandmother told him. But which *is* the right side? And what are you to do when your bed's against the wall? I want to know."

"I've always wondered what went wrong between Stephen Irving and Lavendar Lewis," continued Marilla, ignoring Davy. "They were certainly engaged twenty-five years ago and then all at once it was broken off. I don't know what the trouble was but it must have been something terrible, for he went away to the States and never come home since.''

"Perhaps it was nothing very dreadful after all. I think the little things in life often make more trouble than the big things," said Anne, with one of those flashes of insight which experience could not have bettered. "Marilla, please don't say anything about my being at Miss Lavendar's to Mrs. Lynde. She'd be sure to ask a hundred questions and somehow I wouldn't like it . . . nor Miss Lavendar either if she knew, I feel sure.''

"I daresay Rachel would be curious," admitted Marilla, "though she hasn't as much time as she used to have for looking after other people's affairs. She's tied home now on account of Thomas; and she's feeling pretty down-hearted, for I think she's beginning to lose hope of his ever getting better. Rachel will be left pretty lonely if anything happens to him, with all her children settled out west, except Eliza in town; and she doesn't like her husband.''

Marilla's pronouns slandered Eliza, who was very fond of her husband.

"Rachel says if he'd only brace up and exert his will power he'd get better. But what is the use of asking a jellyfish to sit up straight?'' continued Marilla. "Thomas Lynde never had any will power to exert. His mother ruled him till he married and then Rachel carried it on. It's a wonder he dared to get sick without asking her permission. But there, I shouldn't talk so. Rachel has been a good wife to him. He's never have amounted to anything without her, that's certain. He was born to be ruled; and it's well he fell into the hands of a clever, capable manager like Rachel. He didn't mind her way. It saved him the bother of ever making up his own mind about anything. Davy, do stop squirming like an eel.''

"I've nothing else to do," protested Davy. "I can't eat any more, and it's no fun watching you and Anne eat.''

"Well, you and Dora go out and give the hens their wheat," said Marilla. "And don't you try to pull any more feathers out of the white rooster's tail either.''

"I wanted some feathers for an Injun headdress," said Davy sulkily. "Milty Boulter has a dandy one, made out of the feathers his mother give him when she killed their old white gobbler. You might let me have some. That rooster's got ever so many more'n he wants.''

"You may have the old feather duster in the garret," said Anne, "and I'll dye them green and red and yellow for you.''

"You do spoil that boy dreadfully," said Marilla, when Davy, with a radiant face, had followed prim Dora out. Marilla's education had made great strides in the past six years; but she had not yet been able to rid herself of the idea that it was very bad for a child to have too many of its wishes indulged.

"All the boys of his class have Indian headdresses, and Davy wants one too," said Anne. *I* know how it feels . . . I'll never forget how I used to long for puffed sleeves when all the other girls had them. And Davy isn't being spoiled. He is improving every day. Think what a difference there is in him since he came here a year ago."

"He certainly doesn't get into as much mischief since he began to go to school," acknowledged Marilla. "I suppose he works off the tendency with the other boys. But it's a wonder to me we haven't heard from Richard Keith before this. Never a word since last May."

"I'll be afraid to hear from him," sighed Anne, beginning to clear away the dishes. "If a letter should come I'd dread opening it, for fear it would tell us to send the twins to him."

A month later a letter did come. But it was not from Richard Keith. A friend of his wrote to say that Richard Keith had died of consumption a fortnight previously. The writer of the letter was the executor of his will and by that will the sum of two thousand dollars was left to Miss Marilla Cuthbert in trust for David and Dora Keith until they came of age or married. In the meantime the interest was to be used for their maintenance.

"It seems dreadful to be glad of anything in connection with a death," said Anne soberly. "I'm sorry for poor Mr. Keith; but I *am* glad that we can keep the twins."

"It's a very good thing about the money," said Marilla practically. "I wanted to keep them but I really didn't see how I could afford to do it, especially when they grew older. The rent of the farm doesn't do any more than keep the house and I was bound that not a cent of your money should be spent on them. You do far too much for them as it is. Dora didn't need that new hat you bought her any more than a cat needs two tails. But now the way is made clear and they are provided for."

Davy and Dora were delighted when they heard that they were to live at Green Gables "for good." The death of an uncle whom they had never seen could not weigh a moment in the balance against that. But Dora had one misgiving.

"Was Uncle Richard buried?" she whispered to Anne.

"Yes, dear, of course."

"He . . . he . . . isn't like Mirabel Cotton's uncle, is he?" in a still more agitated whisper. "He won't walk about houses after being buried, will he, Anne?"

CHAPTER 23

MISS LAVENDAR'S ROMANCE

"I THINK I'll take a walk through to Echo Lodge this evening," said Anne, one Friday afternoon in December.

"It looks like snow," said Marilla dubiously.

"It'll be there before the snow comes and I mean to stay all night. Diana can't go because she has company, and I'm sure Miss Lavendar will be looking for me tonight. It's a whole fortnight since I was there."

Anne had paid many a visit to Echo Lodge since that October day. Sometimes she and Diana drove around by the road; sometimes they walked through the woods. When Diana could not go Anne went alone. Between her and Miss Lavendar had sprung up one of those fervent, helpful friendships possible only between a woman who has kept the freshness of youth in her heart and soul, and a girl whose imagination and intuition supplied the place of experience. Anne had at last discovered a real "kindred spirit," while into the little lady's lonely, sequestered life of dreams Anne and Diana came with the wholesome joy and exhilaration of the outer existence, which Miss Lavendar, "the world forgetting, by the world forgot," had long ceased to share; they brought an atmosphere of youth and reality to the little stone house. Charlotta the Fourth always greeted them with her very widest smile . . . and Charlotta's smiles *were* fearfully wide . . . loving them for the sake of her adored mistress as well as for their own. Never had there been such "high jinks" held in the little stone house as were held there that beautiful, late-lingering autumn, when November seemed October over again, and even December aped the sunshine and hazes of summer.

But on this particular day it seemed as if December had remembered that it was time for winter and had turned suddenly dull and brooding, with a windless hush predictive of coming snow. Nevertheless, Anne keenly enjoyed her walk through the great gray maze of the beechlands; though alone she never found it lonely; her imagination peopled her path with merry companions, and with these she carried on a gay, pretended conversation that was wittier and more fascinating than conversations are apt to be in real life, where people sometimes fail most lamentably to talk up to the requirements. In a "make believe" assembly of choice spirits everybody says just the thing you want her to say and so gives you the chance to say just what *you* want to say. Attended by this invisible company, Anne traversed the woods and arrived at the fir lane just as broad, feathery flakes began to flutter down softly.

At the first bend she came upon Miss Lavendar, standing under a big, broad-branching fir. She wore a gown of warm, rich red, and her head and shoulders were wrapped in a silvery gray silk shawl.

"You look like the queen of the fir wood fairies," called Anne merrily.

"I thought you would come tonight, Anne," said Miss Lavendar, running forward. "And I'm doubly glad, for Charlotta the Fourth is away. Her mother is sick and she had to go home for the night. I should have been very lonely if you hadn't come . . . even the dreams and the echoes wouldn't have been enough company. Oh, Anne, how pretty you are," she added suddenly, looking up at the tall, slim girl with the soft rose-flush of walking on her face. "How pretty and how young! It's so delightful to be seventeen, isn't it? I do envy you," concluded Miss Lavendar candidly.

"But you are only seventeen at heart," smiled Anne.

"No, I'm old . . . or rather middle aged, which is far worse," sighed Miss Lavendar. "Sometimes I can pretend I'm not, but at other times I realize it. And I can't reconcile myself to it as most women seem to. I'm just as rebellious as I was when I discovered my first gray hair. Now, Anne, don't look as if you were trying to understand. Seventeen *can't* understand. I'm going to pretend right away that I am seventeen too, and I can do it, now that you're here. You always bring youth in your hand like a gift. We're going to have a jolly evening. Tea first . . . what do you want for tea? We'll have whatever you like. Do think of something nice and indigestible."

There were sounds of riot and mirth in the little stone house that night. What with cooking and feasting and making candy and laughing and "pretending," it is quite true that Miss Lavendar and Anne comported themselves in a fashion entirely unsuited to the dignity of a spinster of forty-five and a sedate schoolma'am. Then, when they were tired, they sat down on the rug before the grate in the parlor, lighted only by the soft fireshine and perfumed deliciously by Miss Lavendar's open rose-jar on the mantel. The wind had risen and was sighing and wailing around the eaves and the snow was thudding softly against the windows, as if a hundred storm sprites were tapping for entrance.

"I'm so glad you're here, Anne," said Miss Lavendar, nibbling at her candy. "If you weren't I should be blue . . . very blue . . . almost navy blue. Dreams and make-believes are all very well in the daytime and the sunshine, but when dark and storm come they fail to satisfy. One wants real things then. But you don't know this . . . seventeen never knows it. At seventeen dreams *do* satisfy because you think the realities are waiting for you further on. When I was seventeen, Anne, I didn't think forty-five would find me a white-haired little old maid with nothing but dreams to fill my life."

"But you aren't an old maid," said Anne, smiling into Miss Lavendar's wistful wood-brown eyes. "Old maids are *born* . . . they don't *become*."

"Some are born old maids, some achieve old maidenhood, and some have old maidenhood thrust upon them," parodied Miss Lavendar whimsically.

"You are one of those who have achieved it then," laughed Anne, "and you've done it so beautifully that if every old maid were like you they would come into the fashion, I think."

"I always like to do things as well as possible," said Miss Lavendar meditatively, "and since an old maid I had to be I was determined to be a very nice one. People say I'm odd; but it's just because I follow my own way of being an old maid and refuse to copy the traditional pattern. Anne, did anyone ever tell you anything about Stephen Irving and me?"

"Yes," said Anne candidly, "I've heard that you and he were engaged once."

"So we were . . . twenty-five years ago . . . a lifetime ago. And we were to have been married the next spring. I had my wedding dress made, although nobody but mother and Stephen ever knew *that*. We'd been engaged in a way almost all our lives, you might say. When Stephen was a little boy his mother would bring him here when she came to see my mother; and the second time he ever came . . . he was nine and I was six . . . he told me out in the garden that he had pretty well made up his mind to marry me when he grew up. I remember that I said 'Thank you;' and when he was gone I told mother very gravely that there was a great weight off my mind, because I wasn't frightened any more about having to be an old maid. How poor mother laughed!''

"And what went wrong?'' asked Anne breathlessly.

"We had just a stupid, silly, commonplace quarrel. So commonplace that, if you'll believe me, I don't even remember just how it began. I hardly know who was the more to blame for it. Stephen did really begin it, but I suppose I provoked him by some foolishness of mine. He had a rival or two, you see. I was vain and coquettish and liked to tease him a little. He was a very high-strung, sensitive fellow. Well, we parted in a temper on both sides. But I thought it would all come right; and it would have if Stephen hadn't come back too soon. Anne, my dear, I'm sorry to say'' . . . Miss Lavendar dropped her voice as if she were about to confess a predilection for murdering people, ''that I am a dreadfully sulky person. Oh, you needn't smile, . . . it's only too true. I *do* sulk; and Stephen came back before I had finished sulking. I wouldn't listen to him and I wouldn't forgive him; and so he went away for good. He was too proud to come again. And then I sulked because he didn't come. I might have sent for him perhaps, but I couldn't humble myself to do that. I was just as proud as he was . . . pride and sulkiness make a very bad combination, Anne. But I could never care for anybody else and I didn't want to. I knew I would rather be an old maid for a thousand years than marry anybody who wasn't Stephen Irving. Well, it all seems like a dream now, of course. How sympathetic you look, Anne . . . as sympathetic as only seventeen can look. But don't overdo it. I'm really a very happy, contented little person in spite of my broken heart. My heart did break, if ever a heart did, when I realized that Stephen Irving was not coming back. But, Anne, a broken heart in real life isn't half as dreadful as it is in books. It's a good deal like a bad tooth . . . though you won't think *that* a very romantic simile. It takes spells of aching and gives you a sleepless night now and then, but between times it lets you enjoy life and dreams and echoes and peanut candy as if there were nothing the matter with it. And now you're looking disappointed. You don't think I'm half as interesting a person as you did five minutes ago when you believed I was always the prey of a tragic memory bravely hidden beneath external smiles. That's the worst . . . or the best . . . of real life, Anne. It *won't* let you be miserable. It keeps on trying to make you comfortable . . . and succeeding . . . even when you're determined to be unhappy and romantic. Isn't this candy scrumptious? I've eaten far more than is good for me already but I'm going to keep recklessly on.''

After a little silence Miss Lavendar said abruptly,

"It gave me a shock to hear about Stephen's son that first day you were here, Anne. I've never been able to mention him to you since, but I've wanted to know all about him. What sort of boy is he?''

"He is the dearest, sweetest child I ever knew, Miss Lavendar . . . and he pretends things too, just as you and I do.''

"I'd like to see him," said Miss Lavendar softly, as if talking to herself. "I wonder if he looks anything like the little dream-boy who lives here with me . . . *my* little dream-boy.''

"If you would like to see Paul I'll bring him through with me sometime," said Anne.

"I *would* like it . . . but not too soon. I want to get used to the thought. There might be more pain than pleasure in it . . . if he looked too much like Stephen . . . or if he didn't look enough like him. In a month's time you may bring him.''

Accordingly, a month later Anne and Paul walked through the woods to the stone house, and met Miss Lavendar in the lane. She had not been expecting them just then and she turned very pale.

"So this is Stephen's boy," she said in a low tone, taking Paul's hand and looking at him as he stood, beautiful and boyish, in his smart little fur coat and cap. "He . . . he is very like his father.''

"Everybody says I'm a chip of the old block," remarked Paul, quite at his ease.

Anne, who had been watching the little scene, drew a relieved breath. She saw that Miss Lavendar and Paul had "taken" to each other, and that there would be no constraint or stiffness. Miss Lavendar was a very sensible person, in spite of her dreams and romance, and after that first little betrayal she tucked her feelings out of sight and entertained Paul as brightly and naturally as if he were anybody's son who had come to see her. They all had a jolly afternoon together and such a feast of fat things by way of supper as would have made old Mrs. Irving hold up her hands in horror, believing that Paul's digestion would be ruined forever.

"Come again, laddie," said Miss Lavendar, shaking hands with him at parting.

"You may kiss me if you like," said Paul gravely.

Miss Lavendar stooped and kissed him.

"How did you know I wanted to?" she whispered.

"Because you looked at me just as my little mother used to do when she wanted to kiss me. As a rule, I don't like to be kissed. Boys don't. *You* know, Miss Lewis. But I think I rather like to have you kiss me. And of course I'll come to see you again. I think I'd like to have you for a particular friend of mine, if you don't object."

"I . . . I don't think I shall object," said Miss Lavendar. She turned and went in very quickly; but a moment later she was waving a gay and smiling good-bye to them from the window.

"I like Miss Lavendar," announced Paul, as they walked through the beech woods. "I like the way she looked at me, and I like her stone house, and I like Charlotta the Fourth. I wish Grandma Irving had a Charlotta the Fourth instead of Mary Joe. I feel sure Charlotta the Fourth wouldn't think I was wrong in my upper story when I told her what I think about things. Wasn't that a splendid tea we had, teacher? Grandma says a boy shouldn't be thinking about what he gets to eat, but he can't help it sometimes when he is real hungry. *You* know, teacher. I don't think Miss Lavendar would make a boy eat porridge for breakfast if he didn't like it. She'd get things for him he did like. But of course" . . . Paul was nothing if not fair-minded . . . "that mightn't be very good for him. It's very nice for a change though, teacher. *You* know."

CHAPTER 24

A PROPHET IN HIS OWN COUNTRY

ONE MAY day Avonlea folks were mildly excited over some "Avonlea Notes," signed "Observer," which appeared in the Charlottetown *Daily Enterprise*. Gossip ascribed the authorship thereof to Charlie Sloane, partly because the said Charlie had indulged in similar literary flights in times past, and partly because one of the notes seemed to embody a sneer at Gilbert Bythe. Avonlea juvenile society persisted in regarding Gilbert Blythe and Charlie Sloane as rivals in the good graces of a certain damsel with gray eyes and an imagination.

Gossip, as ususal, was wrong. Gilbert Blythe, aided and abetted by Anne, had written the notes, putting in the one about himself as a blind. Only two of the notes have any bearing on this history.

"Rumor has it that there will be a wedding in our village ere the daisies are in bloom. A new and highly respected citizen will lead to the hymeneal altar one of our most popular ladies."

"Uncle Abe, our well-known weather prophet, predicts a violent storm of thunder and lightning for the evening of the twenty-third of May, beginning at seven o'clock sharp. The area of the storm will extend over the greater part of the Province. People travelling that evening will do well to take umbrellas and mackintoshes with them."

"Uncle Abe really has predicted a storm for sometime this spring," said Gilbert, "but do you suppose Mr. Harrison really does go to see Isabella Andrews?"

"No," said Anne, laughing, "I'm sure he only goes to play checkers with Mr. Harmon Andrews, but Mrs. Lynde says she knows Isabella Andrews must be going to get married, she's in such good spirits this spring."

Poor old Uncle Abe felt rather indignant over the notes. He suspected that "Observer" was making fun of him. He angrily denied having assigned any particular date for his storm but nobody believed him.

Life in Avonlea continued on the smooth and even tenor of its way. The "planting" was put in; the Improvers celebrated an Arbor Day. Each Improver set out, or caused to be set out, five ornamental trees. As the society now numbered forty members, this meant a total of two hundred young trees. Early oats greened over the red fields; apple orchards flung great blossoming arms about the farmhouses and the Snow Queen adorned itself as a bride for her husband. Anne liked to sleep with her window open and let the cherry fragrance blow over her face all night. She thought it very poetical. Marilla thought she was risking her life.

"Thanksgiving should be celebrated in the spring," said Anne one evening to Marilla, as they sat on the front door steps and listened to the silver-sweet chorus of the frogs. "I think it would be ever so much better than having it in November when everything is dead or asleep. Then you have to remember to be thankful; but in May one simply can't help being thankful . . . that they are alive, if for nothing else. I feel exactly as Eve must have felt in the garden of Eden before the trouble began. Is that grass in the hollow green or golden? It seems to me, Marilla, that a pearl of a day like this, when the blossoms are out and the winds don't know where to blow from next for sheer crazy delight must be pretty near as good as heaven."

Marilla looked scandalized and glanced apprehensively around to make sure the twins were not within earshot. They came around the corner of the house just then.

"Ain't it an awful nice-smelling evening?" asked Davy, sniffing delightedly as he swung a hoe in his grimy hands. He had been working in his garden. That spring Marilla, by way of turning Davy's passion for revelling in mud and clay into useful channels, had given him and Dora a small plot of ground for a garden. Both had eagerly gone to work in a characteristic fashion. Dora planted, weeded, and watered carefully, systematically, and dispassionately. As a result, her plot was already green with prim, orderly little rows of vegetables and annuals. Davy, however, worked with more zeal than discretion; he dug and hoed and raked and watered and transplanted so energetically that his seeds had no chance for their lives.

"How is your garden coming on, Davy-boy?" asked Anne.

"Kind of slow," said Davy with a sigh. "I don't know why the things don't grow better. Milty Boulter says I must have planted them in the dark of the moon and that's the whole trouble. He says you must never sow seeds or kill pork or cut your hair or do any 'portant thing in the wrong time of the moon. Is that true, Anne? I want to know."

"Maybe if you didn't pull your plants up by the roots every other day to see how they're getting on 'at the other end,' they'd do better," said Marilla sarcastically.

"I only pulled six of them up," protested Davy. "I wanted to see if there was grubs at the roots. Milty Boulter said if it wasn't the moon's fault it must be grubs. But I only found one grub. He was a great big juicy curly grub. I put him on a stone and got another stone and smashed him flat. He made a jolly sqush I tell you. I was sorry there wasn't more of them. Dora's garden was planted same time's mine and her things are growing all right. It *can't* be the moon," Davy concluded in a reflective tone.

"Marilla, look at that apple tree," said Anne. "Why, the thing is human. It is reaching out long arms to pick its own pink skirts daintily up and provoke us to admiration."

"Those Yellow Duchess trees always bear well," said Marilla complacently. "That tree'll be loaded this year. I'm real glad. . .

they're great for pies.''

But neither Marilla nor Anne nor anybody else was fated to make pies out of Yellow Duchess apples that year.

The twenty-third of May came . . . an unseasonably warm day, as none realized more keenly than Anne and her little beehive of pupils, sweltering over fractions and syntax in the Avonlea schoolroom. A hot breeze blew all the forenoon; but after noon hour it died away into a heavy stillness. At half past three Anne heard a low rumble of thunder. She promptly dismissed school at once, so that the children might get home before the storm came.

As they went out to the playground Anne perceived a certain shadow and gloom over the world in spite of the fact that the sun was still shining brightly. Annetta Bell caught her hand nervously.

"Oh, teacher, look at that awful cloud!"

Anne looked and gave an exclamation of dismay. In the northwest a mass of cloud, such as she had never in all her life beheld before, was rapidly rolling up. It was dead black, save where its curled and fringed edges showed a ghastly, livid white. There was something about it indescribably menacing as it gloomed up in the clear blue sky; now and again a bolt of lighting shot across it, followed by a savage growl. It hung so low that it almost seemed to be touching the tops of the wooded hills.

Mr. Harmon Andrews came clattering up the hill in his truck wagon, urging his team of grays to their upmost speed. He pulled them to a halt opposite the school.

"Guess Uncle Abe's hit it for once in his life, Anne," he shouted. "His storm's coming a leetle ahead of time. Did ye ever see the like of that cloud? Here, all you young ones, that are going my way, pile in, and those that ain't scoot for the post office if ye've more'n a quarter of a mile to go, and stay there till the shower's over."

Anne caught Davy and Dora by the hands and flew down the hill, along the Birch Path, and past Violet Vale and Willowmere, as fast as the twins' fat legs could go. They reached Green Gables not a moment too soon and were joined at the door by Marilla, who had been hustling her ducks and chickens under shelter. As they dashed into the kitchen the light seemed to vanish, as if blown out by some mighty breath; the awful cloud rolled over the sun and a darkness as of late twilight fell across the world. At the same moment, with a crash of thunder and a blinding glare of lightning, the hail swooped down and blotted the landscape out in one white fury.

Through all the clamor of the storm came the thud of torn branches striking the house and the sharp crack of breaking glass. In three minutes every pane in the west and north windows was broken and the hail poured in through the apertures, covering the floor with stones, the smallest of which was as big as a hen's egg. For three quarters of an hour the storm raged unabated and no one who underwent it ever forgot it. Marilla, for once in her life shaken out of her composure by sheer terror, knelt by her rocking chair in a corner of the kitchen, gasping and sobbing between the deafening thunder peals. Anne, white as paper, had dragged the sofa away from the window and sat on it with a twin on either side. Davy at the first crash had howled, "Anne, Anne, is it the Judgment Day? Anne, Anne, I never *meant* to be naughty," and then had buried his face in Anne's lap and kept it there, his little body quivering. Dora, somewhat pale but quite composed, sat with her hand clasped in Anne's, quiet and motionless. It is doubtless if an earthquake would have disturbed Dora.

Then, almost as suddenly as it began, the storm ceased. The hail stopped, the thunder rolled and muttered away to the eastward, and the sun burst out merry and radiant over a world so changed that it seemed an absurd thing to think that a scant three quarters of an hour could have effected such a transformation.

Marilla rose from her knees, weak and trembling, and dropped on her rocker. Her face was haggard and she looked ten years older.

"Have we all come out of that alive?" she asked solemnly.

"You bet we have," piped Davy cheerfully, quite his own man again. "I wasn't a bit scared either . . . only just at the first. It come on a fellow so sudden. I made up my mind quick as a wink that I wouldn't fight Teddy Sloane Monday as I'd promised; but now maybe I will. Say, Dora, was you scared?"

"Yes, I was a little scared," said Dora primly, "but I held tight to Anne's hand and said my prayers over and over again."

"Well, I'd have said my prayer too if I'd have thought of it," said Davy; "but," he added triumphantly, "you see I came through just as safe as you for all I didn't say them."

Anne got Marilla a glassful of her potent currant wine . . . *how* potent it was Anne, in her earlier days, had had all too good reason to know . . . and then they went to the door to look out on the strange scene.

Far and wide was a white carpet, knee deep, of hailstones; drifts of them were heaped up under the eaves and on the steps. When, three or four days later, those hailstones melted, the havoc they had wrought was plainly seen, for every green growing thing in field or garden was cut off. Not only was every blossom stripped from the apple trees but great boughs and branches were wrenched away. And out of the two hundred trees set out by the Improvers by far the greatest number were snapped off or torn to shreds.

"Can it possibly be the same world it was an hour ago?" asked Anne, dazedly. "It *must* have taken longer than that to play such havoc."

"The like of this has never been known in Prince Edward Island," said Marilla, "never. I remember when I was a girl there was a bad storm, but it was nothing to this. We'll hear of terrible destruction, you may be sure."

"I do hope none of the children were caught out in it," murmured Anne anxiously. As it was discovered later, none of the children had been, since all those who had any distance to go had take Mr. Andrew's excellent advice and sought refuge at the post office.

"There comes John Henry Carter," said Marilla.

John Henry came wading through the hailstones with a rather scared grin.

"Oh, ain't this awful, Miss Cuthbert? Mr. Harrison sent me over to see if yous had come out all right."

"We're none of us killed," said Marilla grimly, "and none of the buildings was struck. I hope you got off equally well."

"Yas'm. Not quite so well, ma'am. We was struck. The lightning knocked over the kitchen chimbly and come down the flue and knocked over Ginger's cage and tore a hole in the floor and went into the sullar. Yas'm."

"Was Ginger hurt?" queried Anne.

"Yas'm. He was hurt pretty bad. He was killed."

Later on Anne went over to comfort Mr. Harrison. She found him sitting by the table, stroking Ginger's gay dead body with a trembling hand.

"Poor Ginger won't call you any more names, Anne," he said mournfully.

Anne could never have imagined herself crying on Ginger's account, but the tears came into her eyes.

"He was all the company I had, Anne . . . and now he's dead. Well, well, I'm an old fool to care so much. I'll let on I don't care. I know you're going to say something sympathetic as soon as I stop talking . . . but don't. If you did I'd cry like a baby. Hasn't this been a terrible storm? I guess folks won't laugh at Uncle Abe's predictions again. Seems as if all the storms that he's been prophesying all his life that never happened came all at once. Beat all how he struck the very day though, don't it? Look at the mess we have here. I must hustle round and get some boards to patch up that hole in the floor."

Avonlea folks did nothing the next day but visit each other and compare damages. The roads were impassable for wheels by reason of the hailstones, so they walked or rode on horseback. The mail came late with ill tidings from all over the province. Houses had been struck, people killed and injured; the whole telephone and telegraph system had been disorganized, and any number of young stock exposed in the fields had perished.

Uncle Abe waded out to the blacksmith's forge early in the morning and spent the whole day there. It was Uncle Abe's hour of triumph and he enjoyed it to the full. It would be doing Uncle Abe an injustice to say that he was glad the storm had happened; but since it had to be he was very glad he had predicted it . . . to the very day, too. Uncle Abe forgot that he had ever denied setting the day. As for the trifling discrepancy in the hour, that was nothing.

Gilbert arrived at Green Gables in the evening and found Marilla and Anne busily engaged in nailing strips of oilcloth over the broken windows.

"Goodness only knows when we'll get glass for them," said Marilla. "Mr. Barry went over to Carmody this afternoon but not a pane could he get for love or money. Lawson and Blair were cleaned out by the Carmody people by ten o'clock. Was the storm bad at White Sands, Gilbert?"

"I should say so. I was caught in the school with all the children and I thought some of them would go mad with fright. Three of them fainted, and two girls took hysterics, and Tommy Blewett did nothing but shriek at the top of his voice the whole time."

"I only squealed once," said Davy proudly. "My garden was all smashed flat," he continued mournfully, "but so was Dora's," he added in a tone which indicated that there was yet balm in Gilead.

Anne came running down from the west gable.

"Oh, Gilbert, have you heard the news? Mr. Levi Boulter's old house was struck and burned to the ground. It seems to me that I'm dreadfully wicked to feel glad over *that*, when so much damage has been done. Mr. Boulter says he believes the A. V. I. S. magicked up that storm on purpose."

"Well, one thing is certain," said Gilbert, laughing, "'Observer' has made Uncle Abe's reputation as a weather prophet. 'Uncle

Abe's storm' will go down in local history. It is a most extraordinary coincidence that it should have come on the very day we selected. I actually have a half guilty feeling, as if I really had 'magicked' it up. We may as well rejoice over the house being removed, for there's not much to rejoice over where our young trees are concerned. Not ten of them have escaped."

"Ah well, we'll just have to plant them over again next spring," said Anne philosophically. "That is one good thing about this world . . . there are always sure to be more springs."

CHAPTER 25

AN AVONLEA SCANDAL

ONE BLITHE June morning, a fortnight after Uncle Abe's storm, Anne came slowly through the Green Gables yard from the garden, carrying in her hands two blighted stalks of white narcissus.

"Look, Marilla," she said sorrowfully, holding up the flowers before the eyes of a grim lady, with her hair coifed in a green gingham apron, who was going into the house with a plucked chicken, "these are the only buds the storm spared . . . and even they are imperfect. I'm so sorry . . . I wanted some for Matthew's grave. He was always so fond of June lilies."

"I kind of miss them myself," admitted Marilla, "though it doesn't seem right to lament over them when so many worse things have happened . . . all the crops destroyed as well as the fruit."

"But people have sown their oats over again," said Anne comfortingly, "and Mr. Harrison says he thinks if we have a good summer they will come out all right though late. And my annuals are all coming up again . . . but oh, nothing can replace the June lilies. Poor little Hester Gray will have none either. I went all the way back to her garden last night but there wasn't one. I'm sure she'll miss them."

"I don't think it's right for you to say such things, Anne, I really don't," said Marilla severly. "Hester Gray has been dead for thirty years and her spirit is in heaven . . . I hope."

"Yes, but I believe she loves and remembers her garden here still," said Anne. "I'm sure no matter how long I'd lived in heaven I'd like to look down and see somebody putting flowers on my grave. If I had had a garden here like Hester Gray's it would take me more than thirty years, even in heaven, to forget being homesick for it by spells."

"Well, don't let the twins hear you talking like that," was Marilla's feeble protest, as she carried her chicken into the house.

Anne pinned her narcissi on her hair and went to the lane gate, where she stood for awhile sunning herself in the June brightness before going in to attend to her Saturday morning duties. The world was growing lovely again; old Mother Nature was doing her best to remove the traces of the storm, and, though she was not to succeed fully for many a moon, she was really accomplishing wonders.

"I wish I could just be idle all day today," Anne told a bluebird, who was singing and swinging on a willow bough, "but a schoolma'am, who is also helping to bring up twins, can't indulge in laziness, birdie. How sweet you are singing, little bird. You are just putting the feelings of my heart into song ever so much better than I could myself. Why, who is coming?"

An express wagon was jolting up the lane, with two people on the front seat and a big trunk behind. When it drew near Anne recognized the driver as the son of the station agent at Bright River; but his companion was a stranger . . . a scrap of a woman who sprang nimbly down at the gate almost before the horse came to a standstill. She was a very pretty little person, evidently nearer fifty than forty, but with rosy cheeks, sparkling black eyes, and a shining black hair, surmounted by a wonderful beflowered and beplumed bonnet. In spite of having driven eight miles over a dusty road she was as neat as if she had just stepped out of the proverbial bandbox.

"Is this where Mr. James A. Harrison lives?" she inquired briskly.

"No, Mr. Harrison lives over there," said Anne, quite lost in astonishment.

"Well, I *did* think this place seemed too tidy . . . *much* too tidy for James A. to be living here, unless he has greatly changed since I knew him," chirped the little lady. "Is it true that James A. is going to be married to some woman living in this settlement?"

"No, oh no," cried Anne, flushing so guiltily that the stranger looked curiously at her, as if she half suspected her of matrimonial designs on Mr. Harrison.

"But I saw it in an Island paper," persisted the Fair Unknown. "A friend sent a marked copy to me . . . friends are always so ready to do such things. James A.'s name was written in over 'new citizen.'"

"Oh, that note was only meant as a joke," gasped Anne. "Mr. Harrison has no intention of marrying *anybody*. I assure you he hasn't."

"I'm very glad to hear it," said the rosy lady, climbing nimbly back to her seat in the wagon, "because he happens to be married already. *I* am his wife. Oh, you may well look surprised. I suppose he has been masquerading as a bachelor and breaking hearts right and left. Well, well, James A.," nodding vigorously over the fields at the long white house, "your fun is over. I am here . . . though I wouldn't have bothered coming if I hadn't thought you were up to some mischief. I suppose," turning to Anne, "that parrot of his is as profane as ever?"

"His parrot . . . is dead . . . I *think*," gasped poor Anne, who couldn't have felt sure of her own name at that precise moment.

"Dead! Everything will be all right then," cried the rosy lady jubilantly. "I can manage James A. if that bird is out of the way."

With which cryptic utterance she went joyfully on her way and Anne flew to the kitchen door to meet Marilla.

"Anne, who was that woman?"

"Marilla," said Anne solemnly, but with dancing eyes, "do I look as if I were crazy?"

"Not more so than usual," said Marilla, with no thought of being sarcastic.

"Well then, do you think I am awake?"

"Anne, what nonsense has got into you? Who was that woman, I say?"

"Marilla, if I'm not crazy and not asleep she can't be such stuff as dreams are made of . . . she must be real. Anyway, I'm sure I couldn't have imagined such a bonnet. She says she is Mr. Harrison's wife, Marilla."

Marilla stared in her turn.

"His wife! Anne Shirley! Then what has he been passing himself off as an unmarried man for?"

"I don't suppose he did, really," said Anne, trying to be just. "He never said he wasn't married. People simply took it for granted. Oh Marilla, what will Mrs. Lynde say to this?"

They found out what Mrs. Lynde had to say when she came up that evening. Mrs. Lynde wasn't surprised! Mrs. Lynde had always expected something of the sort! Mrs. Lynde had always known there was *something* about Mr. Harrison!

"To think of his deserting his wife!" she said indignantly. "It's like something you'd read of in the States, but who would expect such a thing to happen right here in Avonlea?"

"But we don't know that he deserted her," protested Anne, determined to believe her friend innocent till he was proved guilty. "We don't know the rights of it at all."

"Well, we soon will. I'm going straight over there," said Mrs. Lynde, who had never learned that there was such a word as delicacy in the dictionary. "I'm not supposed to know anything about her arrival, and Mr. Harrison was to bring some medicine for Thomas from Carmody today, so that will be a good excuse. I'll find out the whole story and come in and tell you on my way back."

Mrs. Lynde rushed in where Anne had feared to tread. Nothing would have induced the latter to go over to the Harrison place; but she had her natural and proper share of curiosity and she felt secretly glad that Mrs. Lynde was going to solve the mystery. She and Marilla waited expectantly for that good lady's return, but waited in vain. Mrs. Lynde did not revisit Green Gables that night. Davy, arriving home at nine o'clock from the Boulter place, explained why.

"I met Mrs. Lynde and some strange woman in the Hollow," he said, "and gracious, how they were talking both at once! Mrs. Lynde said to tell you she was sorry it was too late to call tonight. Anne, I'm awful hungry. We had tea at Milty's at four and I think Mrs. Boulter is real mean. She didn't give us any preserves or cake . . . and even the bread was skurce."

"Davy, when you go visiting you must never criticize anything you are given to eat," said Anne solemnly. "It is very bad manners."

"All right . . . I'll only think it," said Davy cheerfully. "Do give a fellow some supper, Anne."

Anne looked at Marilla, who followed her into the pantry and shut the door cautiously.

"You can give him some jam on his bread, Anne. I know what tea at Levi Boulter's is apt to be."

Davy took his slice of bread and jam with a sigh.

"It's a kind of disappointing world after all," he remarked. "Milty has a cat that takes fits . . . she's took a fit regular every day for three weeks. Milty says it's awful fun to watch her. I went down today on purpose to see her have one but the mean old thing wouldn't take a fit and just kept healthy as healthy, though Milty and me hung round all the afternoon and waited. But never mind'' . . . Davy brightened up as the insidious comfort of the plum jam stole into his soul . . . ''maybe I'll see her in one sometime yet. It doesn't seem likely she'd stop having them all at once when she's been so in the habit of it, does it? This jam is awful nice.''

Davy had no sorrow that plum jam could not cure.

Sunday proved so rainy that there was no stirring abroad; but by Monday everybody had heard some version of the Harrison story. The school buzzed with it and Davy came home, full of information.

''Marilla, Mr. Harrison has a new wife . . . well, not ezackly new, but they've stopped being married for quite a spell, Milty says. I always s'posed people had to keep on being married once they'd begun, but Milty says no, there's ways of stopping if you can't agree. Milty says one way is just to start off and leave your wife, and that's what Mr. Harrison did. Milty says Mr. Harrison left his wife because she throwed things at him . . . *hard* things . . . and Arty Sloane says it was because she wouldn't let him smoke, and Ned Clay says it was 'cause she never let up scolding him. I wouldn't leave *my* wife for anything like that. I'd just put my foot down and say, 'Mrs. Davy, you've just got to do what'll please *me* 'cause I'm a *man.*' *That'd* settle her pretty quick I guess. But Annetta Clay says *she* left *him* because he wouldn't scrape his boots at the door and she doesn't blame her. I'm going right over to Mr. Harrison's this minute to see what she's like.''

Davy soon returned, somewhat cast down.

''Mrs. Harrison was away . . . she's gone to Carmody with Mrs. Rachel Lynde to get new paper for the parlor. And Mr. Harrison said to tell Anne to go over and see him 'cause he wants to have a talk with her. And say, the floor is scrubbed, and Mr. Harrison is shaved, though there wasn't any preaching yesterday.''

The Harrison kitchen wore a very unfamiliar look to Anne. The floor was indeed scrubbed to a wonderful pitch of purity and so was every article of furniture in the room; the stove was polished until she could see her face in it; the walls were whitewashed and the window panes sparkled in the sunlight. By the table sat Mr. Harrison in his working clothes, which on Friday had been noted for sundry rents and tatters but which were now neatly patched and brushed. He was sprucely shaved and what little hair he had was carefully trimmed.

''Sit down, Anne, sit down,'' said Mr. Harrison, in a tone but two degrees removed from that which Avonlea people used at funerals. ''Emily's gone over to Carmody with Rachel Lynde . . .she's struck up a lifelong friendship already with Rachel Lynde. Beats all how contrary women are. Well, Anne, my easy times are over . . . all over. It's neatness and tidiness for me for the rest of my natural life, I suppose.''

Mr. Harrison did his best to speak dolefully, but an irrepressible twinkle in his eye betrayed him.

"Mr. Harrison, you are glad your wife is come back," cried Anne, shaking her finger at him. "You needn't pretend you're not, because I can see it plainly."

Mr. Harrison relaxed into a sheepish smile.

"Well . . . well . . . I'm getting used to it," he conceeded. "I can't say I was sorry to see Emily. A man really needs some protection in a community like this, where he can't play a game of checkers with a neighbor without being accused of wanting to marry that neighbor's sister and having it put in the paper."

"Nobody would have supposed you went to see Isabella Andrews if you hadn't pretended to be unmarried," said Anne severely.

"I didn't pretend I was. If anybody'd have asked me if I was married I'd have said I was. But they just took it for granted. I wasn't anxious to talk about the matter . . . I was feeling too sore over it. It would have been nuts for Mrs. Rachel Lynde if she had known my wife left me, wouldn't it now?"

"But some people say that you left her."

"She started it, Anne, she started it. I'm going to tell you the whole story, for I don't want you to think worse of me than I deserve . . . nor of Emily neither. But let's go out on the veranda. Everything is so fearful neat in here that it kind of makes me homesick. I suppose I'll get used to it after awhile but it eases me up to look at the yard. Emily hasn't had time to tidy *it* up yet."

As soon as they were comfortably seated on the veranda Mr. Harrison began his tale of woe.

"I lived in Scottsford, New Brunswick, before I came here, Anne. My sister kept house for me and she suited me fine; she was just reasonably tidy and she let me alone and spoiled me . . . so Emily says. But three years ago she died. Before she died she worried a lot about what was to become of me and finally she got me to promise I'd get married. She advised me to take Emily Scott because Emily had money of her own and was a pattern housekeeper. I said, says I, 'Emily Scott wouldn't look at me.' 'You ask her and see,' says my sister; and just to ease her mind I promised her I would . . . and I did. And Emily said she'd have me. Never was so surprised in my life, Anne . . . a smart pretty little woman like her and an old fellow like me. I tell you I thought at first I was in luck. Well, we were married and took a little wedding trip up to St. John for a fortnight and then we went home. We got home at ten o'clock at night, and I give you my word, Anne, that in half an hour that woman was at work housecleaning. Oh, I know you're thinking my house needed it . . . you've got a very expressive face, Anne; your thoughts just come out on it like print . . .but it didn't, not that bad. It had got pretty mixed up while I was keeping bachelor's hall, I admit, but I'd got a woman to come in and clean it up before I was married and there'd been considerable painting and fixing done. I tell you if you took Emily into a brand new marble palace she'd be into the scrubbing as soon as she could get an old dress on. Well, she cleaned house till one o'clock that night and at four she was up and at it again. And she kept on that way . . . far's I could see she never stopped. It was scour and sweep and dust everlasting, except on Sundays, and then she was just longing for Monday to begin again. But it was her way of amusing herself and I could have reconciled myself to it if she'd left me alone. But that she wouldn't do. She'd set out to make me over but she hadn't caught me young enough. I wasn't allowed to come into the house unless I changed my boot for slippers at the door. I darsn't smoke a pipe for my life unless I went to the barn. And I didn't use good enough grammar. Emily'd been a schoolteacher in her early life and she'd never got over it. Then she hated to see me eating with my knife. Well, there it was, pick and nag everlasting. But I s'pose, Anne, to be fair, *I* was cantankerous too. I didn't try to improve as I might have done . . . I just got cranky and disagreeable when she found fault. I told her one day she hadn't complained of my grammar when I proposed to her. It wasn't an overly tactful thing to say. A woman would forgive a man for beating her sooner than for hinting she was too much pleased to get him. Well, we bickered along like that and it wasn't exactly pleasant, but we might have got used to each other after a spell if it hadn't been for Ginger. Ginger was the rock we split on at last. Emily didn't like parrots and she couldn't stand Ginger's profane habits of speech. I was attached to the bird for my brother the sailor's sake. My brother the sailor was a pet of mine when we were little tads and he'd sent Ginger to me when he was dying. I didn't see any sense in getting worked up over his swearing. There's nothing I hate worse'n profanity in a human being, but in a parrot, that's just repeating what it's heard with no more understanding of it than I'd have of Chinese, allowances might be made. But Emily couldn't see it that way. Woman ain't logical. She tried to break Ginger of swearing but she hadn't any better success than she had in trying to make me stop saying 'I seen' and 'them things.' Seemed as if the more she tried the worse Ginger got, same as me.

"Well, things went on like this, both of us getting raspier, till the cli*max* came. Emily invited our minister and his wife to tea, and another minister and *his* wife that was visiting them. I'd promised to put Ginger away in some safe place where nobody would hear him . . . Emily wouldn't touch his cage with a ten-foot pole . . . and I meant to do it, for I didn't want the ministers to hear anything unpleasant in my house. But it slipped my mind . . . Emily was worrying me so much about clean collars and grammar that it wasn't any wonder . . . and I never thought of that poor parrot till we sat down to tea. Just as minister number one was in the very middle of saying grace, Ginger, who was on the veranda outside the dining room window, lifted up *his* voice. The gobbler had come into view in the yard and the sight of a gobbler always had an unwholesome effect on Ginger. He surpassed himself that time. You can smile, Anne, and I don't deny I've chuckled some over it since myself, but at the time I felt almost as much mortified as Emily. I went out and carried Ginger to the barn. I can't say I enjoyed that meal. I knew by the look of Emily that there was trouble brewing for Ginger and James A. When the folks went away I started for the cow pasture and on the way I did some thinking. I felt sorry for Emily and kind of fancied I hadn't been so thoughtful of her as I might; and besides, I wondered if the ministers would think that Ginger had learned his vocabulary from *me*. The long and short of it was, I decided that Ginger would have to be mercifully disposed of and when I'd druv the cows home I went in to tell Emily so. But there was no Emily and there *was* a letter on the table . . . just according to the rule in story books. Emily writ that I'd have to choose between her and Ginger; she'd gone back to her own house and there she would stay till I went and told her I'd got rid of the parrot.

"I was all riled up, Anne, and I said she might stay till doomsday if she waited for that; and I stuck to it. I packed up her belongings and sent them after her. It made an awful lot of talk . . . Scottsford was pretty near as bad as Avonlea for gossip . . . and everybody sympathized with Emily. It kept me all cross and cantankerous and I saw I'd have to get out or I'd never had any peace. I concluded I'd come to the Island. I'd been here when I was a boy and I liked it; but Emily had always said she wouldn't live in a place where folks were scared to walk out after dark for fear they'd fall off the edge. So, just to be contrary, I moved over here. And that's all there is to it. I hadn't ever heard a word from or about Emily till I come home from the back field Saturday and found her scrubbing the floor but with the first decent dinner I'd had since she left me all ready on the table. She told me to eat it first and then we'd talk . . . by which I concluded that Emily had learned some lessons about getting along with a man. So she's here and she's going to stay . . . seeing that Ginger's dead and the Island's some bigger than she thought. There's Mrs. Lynde and her now. No, don't go, Anne. Stay and get acquainted with Emily. She took quite a notion to you Saturday . . . wanted to know who that handsome red-haired girl was at the next house."

Mrs. Harrison welcomed Anne radiantly and insisted on her staying to tea.

"James A. has been telling me all about you and how kind you've been, making cakes and things for him," she said. "I want to get acquainted with all my new neighbors just as soon as possible. Mrs. Lynde is a lovely woman, isn't she? So friendly."

When Anne went home in the sweet June dusk, Mrs. Harrison went with her across the fields where fireflies were lighting their starry lamps.

"I suppose," said Mrs. Harrison confidentially, "that James A. has told you our story?"

"Yes."

"Then I needn't tell it, for James A. is a just man and he would tell the truth. The blame was far from being all on his side. I can see that now. I wasn't back in my own house an hour before I wished I hadn't been so hasty but I wouldn't give in. I seen now that I expected too much of a man. And I was real foolish to mind his bad grammar. It doesn't matter if a man does use bad grammar so long as he is a good provider and doesn't go poking round the pantry to see how much sugar you've used in a week. I feel that James A. and I are going to be real happy now. I wish I knew who 'Observer' is, so that I could thank him. I owe him a real debt of gratitude."

Anne kept her own counsel and Mrs. Harrison never knew that her gratitude found its way to its object. Anne felt rather bewildered over the far-reaching consequences of those foolish "notes." They had reconciled a man to his wife and made the reputation of a prophet.

Mrs. Lynde was in the Green Gables kitchen. She had been telling the whole story to Marilla.

"Well, and how do you like Mrs. Harrison?" she asked Anne.

"Very much. I think she's a real nice little woman."

"That's exactly what she is," said Mrs. Rachel with emphasis, "and as I've just been sayin' to Marilla, I think we ought to overlook Mr. Harrison's peculiarities for her sake and try to make her feel at home here, that's what. Well, I must get back. Thomas'll be wearying for me. I get out a little since Eliza came and he's seemed a lot better these past few days, but I never like to be long away from him. I hear Gilbert Blythe has resigned from White Sands. He'll be off to college in the fall, I suppose."

Mrs. Rachel looked sharply at Anne, but Anne was bending over a sleepy Davy nodding on the sofa and nothing was to be read in her face. She carried Davy away, her oval girlish cheek pressed against his curly yellow head. As they went up the stairs Davy flung a tired arm about Anne's neck and gave her a warm hug and a sticky kiss.

"You're awful nice, Anne. Milty Boulter wrote on his slate today and showed it to Jennie Sloane,

> *Roses red and vi'lets blue,*
> *Sugar's sweet, and so are you,*

and that 'spresses my feelings for you ezackly, Anne.''

CHAPTER 26

AROUND THE BEND

THOMAS LYNDE faded out of life as quietly and unobtrusively as he had lived it. His wife was a tender, patient, unwearied nurse. Sometimes Rachel had been a little hard on her Thomas in health, when his slowness or meekness had provoked her; but when he became ill no voice could be lower, no hand more gently skillful, no vigil more uncomplaining.

"You've been a good wife to me, Rachel," he once said simply, when she was sitting by him in the dusk, holding his thin, blanched old hand in her work-hardened one. "A good wife. I'm sorry I ain't leaving you better off; but the children will look after you. They're all smart, capable children, just like their mother. A good mother . . . a good woman. . . ."

He had fallen asleep then; and the next morning just as the white dawn was creeping up over the pointed firs in the hollow, Marilla went softly into the east gable and wakened Anne.

"Anne, Thomas Lynde is gone . . . . their hired boy just brought the word. I'm going right down to Rachel."

On the day after Thomas Lynde's funeral Marilla went about Green Gables with a strangely preoccupied air. Occasionally she looked at Anne, seemed on the point of saying something, then shook her head and buttoned up her mouth. After tea she went down to see Mrs. Rachel; and when she returned she went to the east gable, where Anne was correcting school exercises.

"How is Mrs. Lynde tonight?" asked the latter.

"She's feeling calmer and more composed," answered Marilla, sitting down on Anne's bed . . . a proceeding which betokened some unusual mental excitement, for in Marilla's code of household ethics to sit on a bed after it was made up was an unpardonable offence. "But she's very lonely. Eliza had to go home today . . . her son isn't well and she felt she couldn't stay any longer."

"When I've finished these exercises I'll run down and chat awhile with Mrs. Lynde," said Anne. "I had intended to study some Latin composition tonight but it can wait."

"I suppose Gilbert Blythe is going to college in the fall," said Marilla jerkily. "How would you like to go too, Anne?"

Anne looked up in astonishment.

"I would like it, of course, Marilla. But it isn't possible."

"I guess it can be made possible. I've always felt that you should go. I've never felt easy to think you were giving it all up on my account."

"But, Marilla, I've never been sorry for a moment that I stayed home. I've been so happy . . . Oh, these past two years have just been delightful."

"Oh yes, I know you've been contented enough. But that isn't the question exactly. You ought to go on with your education. You've saved enough to put you through one year at Redmond and the money the stock brought in will do for another year . . . and there's scholarships and things you might win."

"Yes, but I can't go, Marilla. Your eyes are better, of course; but I can't leave you alone with the twins. They need so much looking after."

"I won't be alone with them. That's what I want to discuss with you. I had a long talk with Rachel tonight. Anne, she's feeling dreadful bad over a good many things. She's not left very well off. It seems they mortgaged the farm eight years ago to give the youngest boy a start when he went west; and they've never been able to pay much more than the interest since. And then of course Thomas' illness has cost a good deal, one way and another. The farm will have to be sold and Rachel thinks there'll be hardly anything left after the bills are settled. She says she'll have to go and live with Eliza and it's breaking her heart to think of leaving Avonlea. A woman of her age doesn't make new friends and interests easy. And, Anne, as she talked about it the thought came to me that I would ask her to come and live with me, but I thought I ought to talk it over with you first before I said anything to her. If I had Rachel living with me you could go to college. How do you feel about it?''

"I feel . . . as if . . . somebody . . . had handed me . . . the moon . . . and I didn't know . . . exactly . . . what to do . . . with it,'' said Anne dazedly. ''But as for asking Mrs. Lynde to come here, that is for you to decide, Marilla. Do you think . . . are you sure . . . you would like it? Mrs. Lynde is a good woman and a kind neighbor, but . . . but . . . ''

"But she's got her faults, you mean to say? Well, she has, of course; but I think I'd rather put up with far worse faults than see Rachel go away from Avonlea. I'd miss her terrible. She's the only close friend I've got here and I'd be lost without her. We've been neighbors for forty-five years and we've never had a quarrel . . . though we came rather near it that time you flew at Mrs. Rachel for calling you homely and red-haired. Do you remember, Anne?''

"I should think I do,'' said Anne ruefully. ''People don't forget things like that. How I hated poor Mrs. Rachel at that moment!''

"And then that 'apology' you made her. Well, you were a handful, in all conscience, Anne. I did feel so puzzled and bewildered how to manage you. Matthew understood you better.''

"Matthew understood everything,'' said Anne softly, as she always spoke of him.

"Well, I think it could be managed so that Rachel and I wouldn't clash at all. It's always seemed to me that the reason two women can't get along in one house is that they try to share the same kitchen and get in each other's way. Now, if Rachel came here, she could have the north gable for her bedroom and the spare room for a kitchen as well as not, for we don't really need a spare room at all. She could put her stove there and what furniture she wanted to keep, and be real comfortable and independent. She'll have enough to live on of course . . . her children'll see to that . . . so all I'd be giving her would be house room. Yes, Anne, far as I'm concerned I'd like it.''

"Then ask her," said Anne promptly. "I'd be very sorry myself to see Mrs. Rachel go away."

"And if she comes," continued Marilla, "you can go to college as well as not. She'll be company for me and she'll do for the twins what I can't do, so there's no reason in the world why you shouldn't go."

Anne had a long meditation at her window that night. Joy and regret struggled together in her heart. She had come at last . . . suddenly and unexpectedly . . . to the bend in the road; and college *was* around it, with a hundred rainbow hopes and visions; but Anne realized as well that when she rounded that curve she must leave many sweet things behind . . . all the little simple duties and interests which had grown so dear to her in the last two years and which she had glorified into beauty and delight by the enthusiasm she had put into them. She must give up her school . . . and she loved every one of her pupils, even the stupid and naughty ones. The mere though of Paul Irving made her wonder if Redmond were such a name to conjure with after all.

"I've put out a lot of little roots these two years," Anne told the moon, "and when I'm pulled up they're going to hurt a great deal. But it's best to go, I think, and, as Marilla says, there's no good reason why I shouldn't. I must get out all my ambitions and dust them."

Anne sent in her resignation the next day; and Mrs. Rachel, after a heart to heart talk with Marilla, gratefully accepted the offer of a home at Green Gables. She elected to remain in her own house for the summer, however; the farm was not to be sold until the fall and there were many arrangements to be made.

"I certainly never thought of living as far off the road as Green Gables," sighed Mrs. Rachel to herself. "But really, Green Gables doesn't seem as out of the world as it used to . . . Anne has lots of company and the twins make it real lively. And anyhow, I'd rather live at the bottom of a well than leave Avonlea."

These two decisions being noised abroad speedily ousted the arrival of Mrs. Harrison in popular gossip. Sage heads were shaken over Marilla Cuthbert's rash step in asking Mrs. Rachel to live with her. People opined that they wouldn't get on together. They were both "too fond of their own way," and many doleful predictions were made, none of which disturbed the parties in question at all.

They had come to a clear and distinct understanding of the respective duties and rights of their new arrangements and meant to abide by them.

"I won't meddle with you nor you with me," Mrs. Rachel had said decidedly, "and as for the twins, I'll be glad to do all I can for them; but I won't undertake to answer Davy's questions, that's what. I'm not an encyclopedia, neither am I a Philadelphia lawyer. You'll miss Anne for that."

"Sometimes Anne's answers were about as queer as Davy's questions," said Marilla drily. "The twins will miss her and no mistake; but her future can't be sacrificed to Davy's thirst for information. When he asks questions I can't answer I'll just tell him children should be seen and not heard. That was how *I* was brought up, and I don't know but what it was just as good a way as all these new-fangled notions for training children."

"Well, Anne's methods seem to have worked fairly well with Davy," said Mrs. Lynde smilingly. "He is a reformed character, that's what."

"He isn't a bad little soul," conceded Marilla. "I never expected to get as fond of those children as I have. Davy gets round you somehow . . . and Dora is a lovely child, although she is . . . kind of . . . well, kind of . . ."

"Monotonous? Exactly," supplied Mrs. Rachel. "Like a book where every page is the same, that's what. Dora will make a good, reliable woman but she'll never set the pond on fire. Well, that sort of folks are comfortable to have round, even if they're not as interesting as the other kind."

Gilbert Blythe was probably the only person to whom the news of Anne's resignation brought unmixed pleasure. Her pupils looked upon it as a sheer catastrophe. Annetta Bell had hysterics when she went home. Anthony Pye fought two pitched and unprovoked battles with other boys by way of relieving his feelings. Barbara Shaw cried all night. Paul Irving defiantly told his grandmother that she needn't expect him to eat any porridge for a week.

"I can't do it, Grandma," he said, "I don't really know if I can eat *anything*. I feel as if there was a dreadful lump in my throat. I'd have cried coming home from school if Jake Donnell hadn't been watching me. I believe I will cry after I go to bed. It wouldn't show on my eyes tomorrow, would it? And it would be such a relief. But anyway, I can't eat porridge. I'm going to need all my strength of mind to bear up against this, Grandma, and I won't have any left to grapple with porridge. Oh Grandma, I don't know what I'll do when my beautiful teacher goes away. Milty Boulter says he bets Jane Andrews will get the school. I suppose Miss Andrews is very nice. But I know she won't understand things like Miss Shirley.''

Diana also took a very pessimistic view of affairs.

"It will be horribly lonesome here next winter," she mourned, one twilight when the moonlight was raining "airy silver" through the cherry boughs and filling the east gable with a soft, dream-like radiance in which the two girls sat and talked, Anne on her low rocker by the window, Diana sitting Turk-fashion on the bed. "You and Gilbert will be gone . . . and the Allans too. They are going to call Mr. Allan to Charlottetown and of course he'll accept. It's too mean. We'll be vacant all winter, I suppose, and have to listen to a long string of candidates . . . and half of them won't be any good.''

"I hope they won't call Mr. Baxter from East Grafton here, anyhow," said Anne decidedly. "He wants the call but he does preach such gloomy sermons. Mr. Bell says he's a minister of the old school, but Mrs. Lynde says there's nothing whatever the matter with him but indigestion. His wife isn't a very good cook, it seems, and Mrs. Lynde says that when a man has to eat sour bread two weeks out of three his theology is bound to get a kink in it somewhere. Mrs. Allan feels very badly about going away. She says everybody has been so kind to her since she came here as a bride that she feels as if she were leaving lifelong friends. And then, there's the baby's grave, you know. She says she doesn't see how she can go away and leave that . . . it was such a little mite of a thing and only three months old, and she says she is afraid it will miss its mother, although she knows better and wouldn't say so to Mr. Allan for anything. She says she has slipped through the birch grove back of the manse nearly every night to the graveyard and sung a little lullaby to it. She told me all about it last evening when I was up putting some of those early wild roses on Matthew's grave. I promised her that as long as I was in Avonlea I would put flowers on the baby's grave and when I was away I felt sure that . . . "

"That I would do it," supplied Diana heartily. "Of course I will. And I'll put them on Matthew's grave too, for your sake, Anne."

"Oh, thank you. I meant to ask you to if you would. And on little Hester Gray's too? Please don't forget hers. Do you know, I've thought and dreamed so much about little Hester Gray that she has become strangely real to me. I think of her, back there in her little garden in that cool, still, green corner; and I have a fancy that if I could steal back there some spring evening, just at the magic time 'twixt light and dark, and tiptoe so softly up the beech hill that my footsteps could not frighten her, I would find the garden just as it used to be, all sweet with June lilies and early roses, with the tiny house beyond it all hung with vines; and little Hester Gray would be there, with her soft eyes, and the wind ruffling her dark hair, wandering about, putting her fingertips under the chins of the lilies and whispering secrets with the roses; and I would go forward oh, so softly, and hold out my hands and say to her, 'Little Hester Gray, won't you let me be your playmate, for I love the roses too?' And we would sit down on the old bench and talk a little and dream a little, or just be beautifully silent together. And then the moon would rise and I would look around me . . . and there would be no Hester Gray and no little vine-hung house, and no roses . . . only an old waste garden starred with June lilies amid the grasses, and the wind sighing, oh, so sorrowfully in the cherry trees. And I would not know whether it had been real or if I had just imagined it all.''

Diana crawled up and got her back against the headboard of the bed. When your companion of twilight hour said such spooky things it was just as well not to be able to fancy there was anything behind you.

''I'm afraid the Improvement Society will go down when you and Gilbert are both gone,'' she remarked dolefully.

''Not a bit of fear of it,'' said Anne briskly, coming back from dreamland to the affairs of practical life. ''It is too firmly established for that, especially since the older people are becoming so enthusiastic about it. Look what they are doing this summer for their lawns and lanes. Besides, I'll be watching for hints at Redmond and I'll write a paper for it next winter and send it over. Don't take such a gloomy view of things, Diana. And don't grudge me my little hour of gladness and jubilation now. Later on, when I have to go away, I'll feel anything but glad.''

''It's all right for you to be glad . . . you're going to college and you'll have a jolly time and make heaps of lovely new friends.''

''I hope I shall make new friends,'' said Anne thoughtfully. ''The possibilities of making new friends help to make life very fascinating. But no matter how many new friends I make they'll never be as dear to me as the old ones . . . especially a certain girl with black eyes and dimples. Can you guess who she is, Diana?''

''But there'll be so many clever girls at Redmond,'' sighed Diana, ''and I'm only a stupid little country girl who says 'I seen' sometimes . . . though I really know better when I stop to think. Well, of course these past two years have really been too pleasant to last. I know *somebody* who is glad you are going to Redmond anyhow. Anne, I'm going to ask you a question . . . a serious question. Don't be vexed and do answer seriously. Do you care anything for Gilbert?''

"Ever so much as a friend and not a bit in the way you mean," said Anne calmly and decidedly; she also thought she was speaking sincerely.

Diana sighed. She wished, somehow, that Anne had answered differently.

"Don't you mean *ever* to be married, Anne?"

"Perhaps . . . some day . . . when I meet the right one," said Anne, smiling dreamily up at the moonlight.

"But how can you be sure when you do meet the right one?" persisted Diana.

"Oh, I should know him . . . *something* would tell me. You know what my ideal is, Diana."

"But people's ideals change sometimes."

"Mine won't. And I *couldn't* care for any man who didn't fulfill it."

"What if you never meet him?"

"Then I shall die an old maid," was the cheerful response. "I daresay it isn't the hardest death by any means."

"Oh, I suppose the dying would be easy enough; it's the living an old maid I shouldn't like," said Diana, with no intention of being humorous. "Although I wouldn't mind being an old maid *very* much if I could be one like Miss Lavendar. But I never could be. When I'm forty-five I'll be horribly fat. And while there might be some romance about a thin old maid there couldn't possibly be any about a fat one. Oh, mind you, Nelson Atkins proposed to Ruby Gillis three weeks ago. Ruby told me all about it. She says she never had any intention of taking him, because any one who married him will have to go in with the old folks; but Ruby says that he made such a perfectly beautiful and romantic proposal that it simply swept her off her feet. But she didn't want to do anything rash so she asked for a week to consider; and two days later she was at a meeting of the Sewing Circle at his mother's and there was a book called 'The Complete Guide To Etiquette,' lying on the parlor table. Ruby said she simply couldn't describe her feelings when in a section of it headed, 'The Deportment of Courtship And Marriage,' she found the very proposal Nelson had made, word for word. She went home and wrote him a perfectly scathing refusal; and she says his father and mother have taken turns watching him ever since for fear he'll drown himself in the river; but Ruby says they needn't be afraid; for in the Deportment of Courtship and Marriage it told how a rejected lover should behave and there's nothing about drowning in *that*. And she says Wilbur Blair is literally pining away for her but she's perfectly helpless in the matter."

Anne made an impatient movement.

"I hate to say it . . . it seems so disloyal . . . but, well, I don't like Ruby Gillis now. I liked her when we went to school and Queen's together . . . though not so well as you and Jane of course. But this last year at Carmody she seems so different . . . so . . . so."

"I know," nodded Diana. "It's the Gillis coming out in her . . . she can't help it. Mrs. Lynde says that if ever a Gillis girl thought about anything but the boys she never showed it in her walk and conversation. She talks about nothing but boys and what compliments they pay her, and how crazy they all are about her at Carmody. And the strange thing is, they *are,* too . . . " Diana admitted this somewhat resentfully. "Last night when I saw her in Mr. Blair's store she whispered to me that she'd just made a new 'mash.' I wouldn't ask her who it was, because I knew she was dying to *be* asked. Well, it's what Ruby always wanted, I suppose. You remember even when she was little she always said she meant to have dozens of beaus when she grew up and have the very gayest time she could before she settled down. She's so different from Jane, isn't she? Jane is such a nice, sensible, lady-like girl."

"Dear old Jane is a jewel," agreed Anne, "but," she added, leaning forward to bestow a tender pat on the plump, dimpled little hand hanging over her pillow, "there's nobody like my own Diana after all. Do you remember that evening we first met, Diana, and 'swore' eternal friendship in your garden? We've kept that 'oath,' I think . . . we've never had a quarrel nor even a coolness. I shall never forget the thrill that went over me the day you told me you loved me. I had had such a lonely, starved heart all through my childhood. I'm just beginning to realize how starved and lonely it really was. Nobody cared anything for me or wanted to be bothered with me. I should have been miserable if it hadn't been for that strange little dream-life of mine, wherein I imagined all the friends and love I craved. But when I came to Green Gables everything was changed. And then I met you. You don't know what your friendship meant to me. I want to thank you here and now, dear, for the warm and true affection you've always given me.''

"And always, always will," sobbed Diana. "I shall *never* love anybody . . . any *girl* . . . half as well as I love you. And if I ever do marry and have a little girl of my own I'm going to name her *Anne.*"

CHAPTER 27

AN AFTERNOON AT THE STONEHOUSE

"WHERE ARE you going, all dressed up, Anne?" Davy wanted to know. "You look bully in that dress."

Anne had come down to dinner in a new dress of pale green muslin . . . the first color she had worn since Matthew's death. It became her perfectly, bringing out all the delicate, flower-like tints of her face and the gloss and burnish of her hair.

"Davy, how many times have I told you that you mustn't use that word," she rebuked. "I'm going to Echo Lodge."

"Take me with you," entreated Davy.

"I would if I were driving. But I'm going to walk and it's too far for your eight year old legs. Besides, Paul is going with me and I fear you don't enjoy yourself in his company."

"Oh, I like Paul lots better'n I did," said Davy, beginning to make fearful inroads into his pudding. "Since I've got pretty good myself I don't mind his being gooder so much. If I can keep on I'll catch up with him someday, both in legs and goodness. 'Sides, Paul's real nice to us second primer boys in school. He won't let the other big boys meddle with us and he shows us lots of games."

"How came Paul to fall into the brook at noon hour yesterday?" asked Anne. "I met him on the playground, such a dripping figure that I sent him promptly home for dry clothes without waiting to find out what had happened."

"Well, it was partly a zacksident," explained Davy. "He stuck his head in on purpose but the rest of him fell in zacksidentally. We was all down at the brook and Prillie Rogerson got mad at Paul about something . . . she's awful mean and horrid anyway, if she *is* pretty . . . and said that his grandmother put his hair up in curl rags every night. Paul wouldn't have minded what she said, I guess, but Gracie Andrews laughed, and Paul got awful red, 'cause Gracie's his girl, you know. He's *clean gone* on her . . . brings her flowers and carries her books as far as the shore road. He got as red as a beet and said his grandmother didn't do any such thing and his hair was born curly. And then he laid down on the bank and stuck his head right into the spring to show them. Oh, it wasn't the spring we drink out of . . . '' seeing a horrified look on Marilla's face . . . ''it was the little one lower down. But the bank's awful slippy and Paul went right in. I tell you he made a bully splash. Oh, Anne, Anne, I didn't mean to say that . . . it just slipped out before I thought. He made a *splendid* splash. But he looked so funny when he crawled out, all wet and muddy. The girls laughed more'n ever, but Gracie didn't laugh. She looked sorry. Gracie's a nice girl but she's got a snub nose. When I get big enough to have a girl I won't have one with a snub nose . . . I'll pick one with a pretty nose like yours, Anne.''

''A boy who makes such a mess of syrup all over his face when he is eating his pudding will never get a girl to look at him,'' said Marilla severely.

''But I'll wash my face before I go courting,'' protested Davy, trying to improve matters by rubbing the back of his hand over the smears. ''And I'll wash behind my ears too, without being told. I remembered to this morning, Marilla. I don't forget half as often as I did. But . . . '' and Davy sighed . . . ''there's so many corners about a fellow that it's awful hard to remember them all. Well, if I can't go to Miss Lavendar's I'll go over and see Mrs. Harrison. Mrs. Harrison's an awful nice woman, I tell you. She keeps a jar of cookies in her pantry a-purpose for little boys, and she always gives me the scrapings out of a pan she's mixed up a plum cake in . A good many plums stick to the sides, you see. Mr. Harrison was always a nice man, but he's twice as nice since he got married over again. I guess getting married makes folks nicer. Why don't *you* get married, Marilla? I want to know.''

Marilla's state of single blessedness had never been a sore point with her, so she answered amiably, with an exchange of significant looks with Anne, that she supposed it was because nobody would have her.

''But maybe you never asked anybody to have you,'' protested Davy.

''Oh, Davy,'' said Dora primly, shocked into speaking without being spoken to, "it's the *men* that have to do the asking."

"I don't know why they have to do it *always,*" grumbled Davy. "Seems to me everything's put on the men in this world. Can I have some more pudding, Marilla?"

"You've had as much as was good for you," said Marilla; but she gave him a moderate second helping.

"I wish people could live on pudding. Why can't they, Marilla? I want to know."

"Because they'd soon get tired of it."

"I'd like to try that for myself," said skeptical Davy. "But I guess it's better to have pudding only on fish and company days than none at all. They never have any at Milty Boulter's. Milty says when company comes his mother gives them cheese and cuts it herself . . . one little bit apiece and one over for manners."

"If Milty Boulter talks like that about his mother at least you needn't repeat it," said Marilla severely.

"Bless my soul" . . . Davy had picked this expression up from Mr. Harrison and used it with great gusto . . . "Milty meant it as a compelment. He's awful proud of his mother 'cause folks say she could scratch a living on a rock."

"I . . . I suppose them pesky hens are in my pansy bed again," said Marilla, rising and going out hurriedly.

The slandered hens were nowhere near the pansy bed and Marilla did not even glance at it. Instead, she sat down on the cellar hatch and laughed until she was ashamed of herself.

When Anne and Paul reached the stone house that afternoon they found Miss Lavendar and Charlotta the Fourth in the garden, weeding, raking, clipping, and trimming as if for dear life. Miss Lavendar herself, all gay and sweet in the frills and laces she loved, dropped her shears and ran joyously to meet her guests, while Charlotta the Fourth grinned cheerfully.

"Welcome, Anne. I thought you'd come today. You belong to the afternoon so it brought you. Things that belong together are sure to come together. What a lot of trouble that would save some people if they only knew it. But they don't . . . and so they waste beautiful energy moving heaven and earth to bring things together that *don't* belong. And you, Paul . . . why, you've grown! You're half a head taller than when you were here before."

"Yes, I've begun to grow like pigweed in the night, as Mrs. Lynde says," said Paul, in frank delight over the fact. "Grandma says it's the porridge taking effect at last. Perhaps it is. Goodness knows . . .'' Paul sighed deeply . . . "I've eaten enough to make anyone grow. I do hope, now that I've begun, I'll keep on till I'm as tall as father. He is six feet, you know, Miss Lavendar.''

Yes, Miss Lavendar did know; the flush on her pretty cheeks deepened a little; she took Paul's hand on one side and Anne's on the other and walked to the house in silence.

"Is it a good day for the echoes, Miss Lavendar?'' queried Paul anxiously. The day of his first visit had been too windy for echoes and Paul had been much disappointed.

"Yes, just the best kind of a day,'' answered Miss Lavendar, rousing herself from her reverie. "But first we are all going in to have something to eat. I know you two folks didn't walk all the way back here through those beechwoods without getting hungry, and Charlotta the Fourth and I can eat any hour of the day . . . we have such obliging appetites. So we'll just make a raid on the pantry. Fortunately it's lovely and full. I had a presentiment that I was going to have company today and Charlotta the Fourth and I prepared.''

"I think you are one of the people who always have nice things in their pantry,'' declared Paul. "Grandma's like that too. But she doesn't approve of snacks between meals. I wonder,'' he added meditatively, "if I *ought* to eat them away from home when I know she doesn't approve.''

"Oh, I don't think she would disapprove after you have had a long walk. That makes a difference,'' said Miss Lavendar, exchanging amused glances with Anne over Paul's brown curls. "I suppose that snacks *are* extremely unwholesome. That is why we have them so often at Echo Lodge. We . . . Charlotta the Fourth and I . . . live in defiance of every known law of diet. We eat all sorts of indigestible things whenever we happen to think of it, by day or night; and we flourish like green bay trees. We are always intending to reform. When we read any article in a paper warning us against something we like we cut it out and pin it up on the kitchen wall so that we'll remember it. But we never can somehow . . . until after we've gone and eaten that very thing. Nothing has ever killed us yet; but Charlotta the Fourth has been known to have bad dreams after we had eaten doughnuts and mince pie and fruit cake before we went to bed.''

"Grandma lets me have a glass of milk and a slice of bread and butter before I go to bed; and on Sunday nights she puts jam on the bread,'' said Paul. "So I'm always glad when it's Sunday night . . . for more reasons than one. Sunday is a very long day on the shore road. Grandma says it's all too short for her and that father never found Sundays tiresome when he was a little boy. It wouldn't seem so long if I could talk to my rock people but I never do that because Grandma doesn't approve of it on Sundays. I think a good deal; but I'm afraid my thoughts are always worldly. Grandma says we should never think anything but religious thoughts on Sundays. But teacher here said once that every really beautiful thought was religious, no matter what it was about, or what day we thought it on. But I feel sure Grandma thinks that sermons and Sunday School lessons are the only things you can think truly religious thoughts about. And when it comes to a difference of opinion between Grandma and teacher I don't know what to do. In my heart'' . . . Paul laid his hand on his breast and raised very serious blue eyes to Miss Lavendar's immediately sympathetic face . . . ''I agree with teacher. But then, you see, Grandma has brought father up *her* way and made a brilliant success of him; and teacher has never brought anybody up yet, though she's helping with Davy and Dora. But you can't tell how they'll turn out till they *are* grown up. So sometimes I feel as if it might be safer to go by Grandma's opinions.''

''I think it would,'' agreed Anne solemnly. ''Anyway, I daresay that if your Grandma and I both got down to what we really do mean, under our different ways of expressing it, we'd find out we both meant the same thing. You'd better go by her way of expressing it, since it's been the result of experience. We'll have to wait until we see how the twins do turn out before we can be sure that my way is equally good.''

After lunch they went back to the garden, where Paul made the acquaintance of the echoes, to his wonder and delight, while Anne and Miss Lavendar sat on the stone bench under the poplar and talked.

''So you are going away in the fall?'' said Miss Lavendar wistfully. ''I ought to be glad for your sake, Anne . . . but I'm horribly, selfishly sorry. I shall miss you so much. Oh, sometimes I think it is of no use to make friends. They only go out of your life after awhile and leave a hurt that is worse than the emptiness before they came.''

''That sounds like something Miss Eliza Andrews might say but never Miss Lavendar,'' said Anne. *''Nothing* is worse than emptiness . . . and I'm not going out of your life. There are such things as letters and vacations. Dearest, I'm afraid you're looking a little pale and tired.''

''Oh . . . hoo . . . hoo . . . hoo,'' went Paul on the dyke, where he had been making noises diligently . . . not all of them melodious in the making, but all coming back transmuted into the very gold and silver of sound by the fairy alchemists over the river. Miss Lavendar made an impatient movement with her pretty hands.

"I'm just tired of everything . . . even of the echoes. There is nothing in my life but echoes . . . echoes of lost hopes and dreams and joys. They're beautiful and mocking. Oh Anne, it's horrid of me to talk like this when I have company. It's just that I'm getting old and it doesn't agree with me. I know I'll be fearfully cranky by the time I'm sixty. But perhaps all I need is a course of blue pills."

At this moment Charlotta the Fourth, who had disappeared after lunch, returned, and announced that the northeast corner of Mr. John Kimball's pasture was red with early strawberries, and wouldn't Miss Shirley like to go and pick some.

"Early strawberries for tea!" exclaimed Miss Lavendar. "Oh, I'm not so old as I thought . . . and I don't need a single blue pill! Girls, when you come back with your strawberries we'll have tea out here under the silver poplar. I'll have it all ready for you with home-grown cream."

Anne and Charlotta the Fourth accordingly betook themselves back to Mr. Kimball's pasture, a green remote place where the air was as soft as velvet and fragrant as a bed of violets and golden as amber.

"Oh, isn't it sweet and fresh back here?" breathed Anne. "I just feel as if I were drinking in the sunshine."

"Yes, ma'am, so do I. That's just exactly how I feel too, ma'am," agreed Charlotta the Fourth, who would have said precisely the same thing if Anne had remarked that she felt like a pelican of the wilderness. Always after Anne had visited Echo Lodge Charlotta the Fourth mounted to her little room over the kitchen and tried before her looking-glass to speak and look and move like Anne. Charlotta could never flatter herself that she quite succeeded; but practice makes perfect, as Charlotta had learned at school, and she fondly hoped that in time she might catch the trick of that dainty uplift of chin, that quick, starry outflashing of eyes, that fashion of walking as if you were a bough swaying in the wind. It seemed so easy when you watched Anne. Charlotta the Fourth admired Anne whole-heartedly. It was not that she thought her so very handsome. Diana Barry's beauty of crimson cheek and black curls was much more to Charlotta the Fourth's taste than Anne's moonshine charm of luminous gray eyes and the pale, ever-changing roses of her cheeks.

"But I'd rather look like you than be pretty," she told Anne sincerely.

Anne laughed, sipped the honey from the tribute, and cast away the sting. She was used to taking her compliments mixed. Public opinion never agreed on Anne's looks. People who had heard her called handsome met her and were disappointed. People who had heard her called plain saw her and wondered where other people's eyes were. Anne herself would never believe that she had any claim to beauty. When she looked in the glass all she saw was a little pale face with seven freckles on the nose thereof. Her mirror never revealed to her the elusive, ever-varying play of feeling that came and went over her features like a rosy illuminating flame, or the charm of dream and laughter alternating in her big eyes.

While Anne was not beautiful in any strictly defined sense of the word she possessed a certain evasive charm and distinction of appearance that left beholders with a pleasurable sense of satisfaction in that softly rounded girlhood of hers, with all its strongly felt potentialities. Those who knew Anne best felt, without realizing that they felt it, that her greatest attraction was the aura of possibility surrounding her . . . the power of future development that was in her. She seemed to walk in an atmosphere of things about to happen.

As they picked, Charlotta the Fourth confided to Anne her fears regarding Miss Lavendar. The warm-hearted little handmaiden was honestly worried over her adored mistress' condition.

"Miss Lavendar isn't well, Miss Shirley, ma'am. I'm sure she isn't, though she never complains. She hasn't seemed like herself this long while, ma'am . . . not since that day you and Paul were here together before. I feel sure she caught cold that night, ma'am. After you and him had gone she went out and walked in the garden for long after dark with nothing but a little shawl on her. There was a lot of snow on the walks and I feel sure she got a chill, ma'am. Ever since then I've noticed her acting tired and lonesome like. She don't seem to take an interest in anything, ma'am. She never pretends company's coming, nor fixes up for it, nor nothing, ma'am. It's only when you come she seems to chirk up a bit. And the worst sign of all, Miss Shirley, ma'am . . ." Charlotta the Fourth lowered her voice as if she were about to tell some exceedingly weird and awful symptom indeed . . . "is that she never gets cross now when I breaks things. Why, Miss Shirley, ma'am, yesterday I bruk her green and yaller bowl that's always stood on the bookcase. Her grandmother brought it out from England and Miss Lavendar was awful choice of it. I was dusting it just as careful, Miss Shirley, ma'am, and it slipped out, so fashion, afore I could grab holt of it, and bruk into about forty millyun pieces. I tell you I was sorry and scared. I thought Miss Lavendar would scold me awful, ma'am; and I'd ruther she had than take it the way she did. She just come in and hardly looked at it and said, 'It's no matter, Charlotta. Take up the pieces and throw them away.' Just like that, Miss Shirley, ma'am . . . 'take up the pieces and throw them away,' as if it wasn't her grandmother's bowl from England. Oh, she isn't well and I feel awful bad about it. She's got nobody to look after her but me.''

Charlotta the Fourth's eyes brimmed up with tears. Anne patted the little brown paw holding the cracked pink cup sympathetically.

"I think Miss Lavendar needs a change, Charlotta. She stays here alone too much. Can't we induce her to go away for a little trip?''

Charlotta shook her head, with its rampant bows, disconsolately.

"I don't think so, Miss Shirley, ma'am. Miss Lavendar hates visiting. She's only got three relations she ever visits and she says she just goes to see them as a family duty. Last time when she come home she said she wasn't going to visit for family duty no more. 'I've come home in love with loneliness, Charlotta,' she says to me, 'and I never want to stray from my own vine and fig-tree again. My relations try so hard to make an old lady of me and it has a bad effect on me.' Just like that Miss Shirley, ma'am. 'It has a very bad effect on me.' So I don't think it would do any good to coax her to go visiting.''

"We must see what can be done," said Anne decidedly, as she put the last possible berry in her pink cup. "Just as soon as I have my vacation I'll come through and spend a whole week with you. We'll have a picnic every day and pretend all sorts of interesting things, and see if we can't cheer Miss Lavendar up.''

"That will be the very thing, Miss Shirley, ma'am," exclaimed Charlotta the Fourth in rapture. She was glad for Miss Lavendar's sake and for her own too. With a whole week in which to study Anne constantly she would surely be able to learn how to move and behave like her.

When the girls got back to Echo Lodge they found that Miss Lavendar and Paul had carried the little square table out of the kitchen to the garden and had everything ready for tea. Nothing ever tasted so delicious as those strawberries and cream, eaten under a great blue sky all curdled over with fluffy little white clouds, and in the long shadows of the wood with its lispings and its murmurings.

After tea Anne helped Charlotta wash the dishes in the kitchen, while Miss Lavendar sat on the stone bench with Paul and heard all about his rock people. She was a good listener, this sweet Miss Lavendar, but just at the last it struck Paul that she had suddenly lost interest in the Twin Sailors.

"Miss Lavendar, why do you look at me like that?" he asked gravely.

"How do I look, Paul?"

"Just as if you were looking through me at somebody I put you in mind of," said Paul, who had such occasional flashes of uncanny insight that it wasn't quite safe to have secrets when he was about.

"You do put me in mind of somebody I knew long ago," said Miss Lavendar dreamily.

"When you were young?"

"Yes, when I was young. Do I seem very old to you, Paul?"

"Do you know, I can't make up my mind about that," said Paul confidentially. "Your hair looks old . . . I never knew a young person with white hair. But your eyes are as young as my beautiful teacher's when you laugh. I tell you what, Miss Lavendar" . . . Paul's voice and face were as solemn as a judge's . . . "I think you would make a splendid mother. You have just the right look in your eyes . . . the look my little mother always had. I think it's a pity you haven't any boys of your own."

"I have a little dream boy, Paul."

"Oh, have your really? How old is he?"

"About your age I think. He ought to be older because I dreamed him long before you were born. But I'll never let him get any older than eleven or twelve; because if I did some day he might grow up altogether and then I'd lose him."

"I know," nodded Paul. "That's the beauty of dream people . . . they stay any age you want them. You and my beautiful teacher and me are the only folks in the world that I know of that have dream people. Isn't it funny and nice we should all know each other? But I guess that kind of people always find each other out. Grandma never has dream people and Mary Joe thinks I'm wrong in the upper story because I have them. But I think it's splendid to have them. *You* know, Miss Lavendar. Tell me all about your little dream boy."

"He has blue eyes and curly hair. He steals in and wakens me with a kiss every morning. Then all day he plays here in the garden . . . and I play with him. Such games as we have. We run races and talk with the echoes; and I tell him stories. And when twilight comes . . ."

"*I* know," interrupted Paul eagerly. "He comes and sits beside you . . . *so* . . . because of course at twelve he'd be too big to climb into your lap . . . and lays his head on your shoulder . . . *so* . . . .and you put your arms about him and hold him tight, tight, and rest your cheek on his head . . . yes, that's the very way. Oh, you *do* know, Miss Lavendar."

Anne found the two of them there when she came out of the stone house, and something in Miss Lavendar's face made her hate to disturb them.

"I'm afraid we must go, Paul, if we want to get home before dark. Miss Lavendar, I'm going to invite myself to Echo Lodge for a whole week pretty soon."

"If you come for a week I'll keep you for two," threatened Miss Lavendar.

CHAPTER 28

THE PRINCE COMES BACK TO THE ENCHANTED PLACE

THE LAST of school came and went. A triumphant "semi-annual examination" was held and Anne's pupils acquitted themselves splendidly. At the close they gave her an address and a writing desk. All the girls and ladies present cried, and some of the boys had it cast up to them later on that they cried too, although they always denied it.

Mrs. Harmon Andrews, Mrs. Peter Sloane, and Mrs. William Bell walked home together and talked things over.

"I do think it is such a pity Anne is leaving when the children seem so much attached to her," sighed Mrs. Peter Sloane, who had a habit of sighing over everything and even finished off her jokes that way. "To be sure," she added hastily, "we all know we'll have a good teacher next year too."

"Jane will do her duty, I've no doubt," said Mrs. Andrews rather stiffly. "I don't suppose she'll tell the children quite so many fairy tales or spend so much time roaming about the woods with them. But she has her name on the Inspector's Roll of Honor and the Newbridge people are in a terrible state over her leaving."

"I'm real glad Anne is going to college," said Mrs. Bell. "She has always wanted it and it will be a splendid thing for her."

"Well, I don't know." Mrs. Andrews was determined not to agree fully with anybody that day. "I don't see that Anne needs any more education. She'll probably be marrying Gilbert Blythe, if his infatuation for her lasts till he gets through college, and what good will Latin and Greek do her then? If they taught you at college how to manage a man there might be some sense in her going."

Mrs. Harmon Andrews, so Avonlea gossip whispered, had never learned how to manage her "man," and as a result the Andrews household was not exactly a model of domestic happiness.

"I see that the Charlottetown call to Mr. Allan is up before the Presbytery," said Mrs. Bell. "That means we'll be losing him soon, I suppose."

"They're not going before September," said Mrs. Sloane. "It will be a great loss to the community . . . though I always did think that Mrs. Allan dressed rather too gay for a minister's wife. But we are none of us perfect. Did you notice how neat and snug Mr. Harrison looked today? I never saw such a changed man. He goes to church every Sunday and has subscribed to the salary."

"Hasn't that Paul Irving grown to be a big boy?" said Mrs. Andrews. "He was such a mite for his age when he came here. I declare I hardly knew him today. He's getting to look a lot like his father."

"He's a very smart boy," said Mrs. Bell.

"He's smart enough, but" . . . Mrs. Andrews lowered her voice . . . "I believe he tells queer stories. Gracie came home from school one day last week with the greatest rigmarole he had told her about people who lived down at the shore . . . stories there couldn't be a word of truth in, you know. I told Gracie not to believe them, and she said Paul didn't intend her to. But if he didn't what did he tell them to her for?"

"Anne says Paul is a genius," said Mrs. Sloane.

"He may be. You never know what to expect of them Americans," said Mrs. Andrews. Mrs. Andrews' only acquaintance with the word "genius" was derived from the colloquial fashion of calling any eccentric individual "a queer genius." She probably thought, with Mary Joe, that it meant a person with something wrong in his upper story.

Back in the schoolroom Anne was sitting alone at her desk, as she had sat on the first day of school two years before, her face leaning on her hand, her dewy eyes looking wistfully out of the window to the Lake of Shining Waters. Her heart was so wrung over the parting with her pupils that for the moment college had lost all its charm. She still felt the clasp of Annetta Bell's arms about her neck and heard the childish wail, "I'll *never* love any teacher as much as you, Miss Shirley, never, never."

For two years she had worked earnestly and faithfully, making many mistakes and learning from them. She had had her reward. She had taught her scholars something, but she felt that they had taught her much more . . . lessons of tenderness, self-control, innocent wisdom, lore of childish hearts. Perhaps she had not succeeded in "inspiring" any wonderful ambitions in her pupils, but she had taught them, more by her own sweet personality than by all her careful precepts, that it was good and necessary in the years that were before them to live their lives finely and graciously, holding fast to truth and courtesy and kindness, keeping aloof from all that savored of falsehood and meanness and vulgarity. They were, perhaps, all unconscious of having learned such lessons; but they would remember and practice them long after they had forgotten the capital of Afghanistan and the dates of the Wars of the Roses.

"Another chapter in my life is closed," said Anne aloud, as she locked her desk. She really felt very sad over it; but the romance in the idea of that "closed chapter" did comfort her a little.

Anne spent a fortnight at Echo Lodge early in her vacation and everybody concerned had a good time.

She took Miss Lavendar on a shopping expedition to town and persuaded her to by a new organdie dress; then came the excitement of cutting and making it together, while the happy Charlotta the Fourth basted and swept up the clippings. Miss Lavendar had complained that she could not feel much interest in anything; but the sparkle came back to her eyes over her pretty dress.

"What a foolish, frivolous person I must be," she sighed. "I'm wholesomely ashamed to think that a new dress . . . even if it is a forget-me-not organdie . . . should exhilarate me so, when a good conscience and an extra contribution to Foreign Missions couldn't do it."

Midway in her visit Anne went home to Green Gables for a day to mend the twins' stockings and settle up Davy's accumulated store of questions. In the evening she went down to the shore road to see Paul Irving. As she passed by the low, square window of the Irving sitting room she caught a glimpse of Paul on somebody's lap; but the next moment he came flying through the hall.

"Oh, Miss Shirley," he cried excitedly, "you can't think what has happened! Something so splendid. Father is here . . . just think of that! Father is here! Come right in. Father, this is my beautiful teacher. *You* know, father."

Stephen Irving came forward to meet Anne with a smile. He was a tall, handsome man of middle age, with iron-gray hair, deep-set, dark-blue eyes, and a strong, sad face, splendidly modeled about chin and brow. Just the face of a hero of romance, Anne thought with a thrill of intense satisfaction. It was so disappointing to meet someone who ought to be a hero and find him bald or stooped, or otherwise lacking in manly beauty. Anne would have thought it dreadful if the object of Miss Lavendar's romance had not looked the part.

"So this is my little son's 'beautiful teacher,' of whom I have heard so much," said Mr. Irving with a hearty handshake. "Paul's letters have been so full of you, Miss Shirley, that I feel as if I were pretty well acquainted with you already. I want to thank you for what you have done for Paul. I think your influence has been just what he needed. Mother is one of the best and dearest of women; but her robust, matter-of-fact Scotch common sense could not always understand a temperament like my laddie's. What was lacking in her you have supplied. Between you, I think Paul's training in these two past years has been as nearly ideal as a motherless boy's could be."

Everybody likes to be appreciated. Under Mr. Irving's praise Anne's face "burst flower-like into rosy bloom," and the busy, weary man of the world, looking at her, thought he had never seen a fairer, sweeter slip of girlhood than this little "down east" schoolteacher with her red hair and wonderful eyes.

Paul sat between them blissfully happy.

"I never dreamed father was coming," he said radiantly. "Even Grandma didn't know it. It was a great surprise. As a general thing . . ." Paul shook his brown curls gravely . . . "I don't like to be surprised. You lose all the fun of expecting things when you're surprised. But in a case like this it is all right. Father came last night after I had gone to bed. And after Grandma and Mary Joe had stopped being surprised he and Grandma came upstairs to look at me, not meaning to wake me up till morning. But I woke right up and saw father. I tell you I just sprang at him."

"With a hug like a bear's," said Mr. Irving, putting his arm around Paul's shoulder smilingly. "I hardly knew my boy, he had grown so big and brown and sturdy."

"I don't know which was the most pleased to see father, Grandma or I," continued Paul. "Grandma's been in kitchen all day making the things father likes to eat. She wouldn't trust Mary Joe, she says. That's *her* way of showing gladness. *I* like best just to sit and talk to father. But I'm going to leave you for a little while now if you'll excuse me. I must get the cows for Mary Joe. That is one of my daily duties."

When Paul had scampered away to do his "daily duty" Mr. Irving talked to Anne of various matters. But Anne felt that he was thinking of something else underneath all the time. Presently it came to the surface.

"In Paul's last letter he spoke of going with you to visit an old . . . friend of mine . . . Miss Lewis at the stone house in Grafton. Do you know her well?"

"Yes, indeed, she is a *very* dear friend of mine," was Anne's demure reply, which gave no hint of the sudden thrill that tingled over her from head to foot at Mr. Irving's question. Anne "felt instinctively" that romance was peeping at her around a corner.

Mr. Irving rose and went to the window, looking out on a great, golden, billowing sea where a wild wind was harping. For a few moments there was silence in the little, dark-walled room. Then he turned and looked down into Anne's sympathetic face with a smile, half-whimsical, half-tender.

"I wonder how much you know," he said.

"I know all about it," replied Anne promptly. "You see," she explained hastily, "Miss Lavendar and I are very intimate. She wouldn't tell things of such a sacred nature to everybody. We are kindred spirits."

"Yes, I believe you are. Well, I am going to ask a favor of you. I would like to go and see Miss Lavendar if she will let me. Will you ask her if I may come?"

Would she not? Oh, indeed she would! Yes, this was romance, the very, the real thing, with all the charm of rhyme and story and dream. It was a little belated, perhaps, like a rose blooming in October which should have bloomed in June; but nonetheless a rose, all sweetness and fragrance, with the gleam of gold in its heart. Never did Anne's feet bear her on a more willing errand than on that walk through the beechwoods to Grafton the next morning. She found Miss Lavendar in the garden. Anne was fearfully excited. Her hands grew cold and her voice trembled.

"Miss Lavendar, I have something to tell you . . . something very important. Can you guess what it is?"

Anne never supposed that Miss Lavendar *could* guess; but Miss Lavendar's face grew very pale and Miss Lavendar said in a quiet, still voice, from which all the color and sparkle that Miss Lavendar's voice usually suggested had faded,

"Stephen Irving is home?"

"How did you know? Who told you?" cried Anne disappointedly, vexed that her great revelation had been anticipated.

"Nobody. I knew that must be it, just from the way you spoke."

"He wants to come and see you," said Anne. "May I send him word that he may?"

"Yes, of course," fluttered Miss Lavendar. "There is no reason why he shouldn't. He is only coming as any old friend might."

Anne had her own opinion about that as she hastened into the house to write a note at Miss Lavendar's desk.

"Oh, it's delightful to be living in a story-book," she thought gaily. "It will come out all right of course . . . it must . . . and Paul will have a mother after his own heart and everybody will be happy. But Mr. Irving will take Miss Lavendar away . . . and dear knows what will happen to the little stone house . . . and so there are two sides to everything in this world."

The important note was written and Anne herself carried it to the Grafton post office, where she waylaid the mail-carrier and asked him to leave it at the Avonlea office.

"It's so very important," Anne assured him anxiously. The mail carrier was a rather grumpy old personage who did not at all look the part of a messenger of Cupid; and Anne was none too certain that his memory was to be trusted. But he said he would do his best to remember and she had to be contented with that.

Charlotta the Fourth felt that some mystery pervaded the stone house that afternoon . . . a mystery from which she was excluded. Miss Lavendar roamed about the garden in a distracted fashion. Anne, too, seemed possessed by a demon of unrest, and walked to and fro and went up and down. Charlotta the Fourth endured it till patience ceased to be a virtue; then she confronted Anne on the occasion of that romantic young person's third aimless peregrination through the kitchen.

"Please, Miss Shirley, ma'am," said Charlotta the Fourth, with an indignant toss of her very blue bows, "it's plain to be seen you and Miss Lavendar have got a secret and I think, begging your pardon if I'm too forward, Miss Shirley, ma'am, that it's real mean not to tell me when we've all been such chums."

"Oh, Charlotta dear, I'd have told you all about it if it were my secret . . . but it's Miss Lavendar's, you see. However, I'll tell you this much . . . and if nothing comes of it you must never breathe a word about it to a living soul. You see, Prince Charming is coming tonight. He came long ago, but in a foolish moment went away and wandered afar and forgot the secret of the magic pathway to the enchanted castle, where the princess was weeping her faithful heart out for him. But at last he remembered it again and the princess is waiting still . . . because nobody but her own dear prince could carry her off."

"Oh, Miss Shirley, ma'am, what is that in prose?" gasped the mystified Charlotta.

Anne laughed.

"In prose, an old friend of Miss Lavendar's is coming to see her tonight."

"Do you mean an old beau of hers?" demanded the literal Charlotta.

"That is probably what I do mean . . . in prose," answered Anne gravely. "It is Paul's father . . . Stephen Irving. And goodness knows what will come of it, but let us hope for the best, Charlotta."

"I hope that he'll marry Miss Lavendar," was Charlotta's unequivocal response. "Some women's intended from the start to be old maids, and I'm afraid I'm one of them, Miss Shirley, ma'am, because I've awful little patience with the men. But Miss Lavendar never was. And I've been awful worried, thinking what on earth she'd do when I got so big I'd *have* to go to Boston. There ain't any more girls in our family and dear knows what she'd do if she got some stranger that might laugh at her pretendings and leave things lying out of their place and not be willing to be called Charlotta the Fifth. She might get someone who wouldn't be as unlucky as me in breaking dishes but she'd never get anyone who'd love her better."

And the faithful little handmaiden dashed to the oven door with a sniff.

They went through the form of having tea as usual that night at Echo Lodge; but nobody really ate anything. After tea Miss Lavendar went to her room and put on her new forget-me-not organdie, while Anne did her hair for her. Both were dreadfully excited; but Miss Lavendar pretended to be very calm and indifferent.

"I must really mend that rent in the curtain tomorrow," she said anxiously, inspecting it as if it were the only thing of any importance just then. "Those curtains have not worn well as they should, considering the price I paid. Dear me, Charlotta has forgotten to dust the stair railing *again*. I really *must* speak to her about it."

Anne was sitting on the porch steps when Stephen Irving came down and across the garden.

"This is the one place where time stands still," he said, looking around him with delighted eyes. "There is nothing changed about this house or garden since I was here twenty-five years ago. It makes me feel young again."

"You know time always does stand still in an enchanted palace," said Anne seriously. "It is only when the prince comes that things begin to happen."

Mr. Irving smiled a little sadly into her uplifted face, all astar with its youth and promise.

"Sometimes the prince comes too late," he said. He did not ask Anne to translate her remark into prose. Like all kindred spirits he "understood."

"Oh, no, not if he is the real prince coming to the true princess," said Anne, shaking her red head decidedly, as she opened the parlor door. When he had gone in she shut it tightly behind him and turned to confront Charlotta the Fourth, who was in the hall, all "nods and becks and wreathed smiles."

"Oh, Miss Shirley, ma'am," she breathed, "I peeked from the kitchen window . . . and he's awful handsome . . . and just the right age for Miss Lavendar. And oh, Miss Shirley, ma'am, do you think it would be much harm to listen at the door?"

"It would be dreadful, Charlotta," said Anne firmly, "so just you come away with me out of the reach of temptation."

"I can't do anything, and it's awful to hang round just waiting," sighed Charlotta. "What if he don't propose after all, Miss Shirley, ma'am? You can never be sure of them men. My oldest sister, Charlotta the First, thought she was engaged to one once. But it turned out *he* had a different opinion and she says she'll never trust one of them again. And I heard of another case where a man thought he wanted one girl awful bad when it was really her sister he wanted all the time. When a man don't know his own mind, Miss Shirley, ma'am, how's a poor woman going to be sure of it?"

"We'll go to the kitchen and clean the silver spoons," said Anne.

"That's a task which won't require much thinking fortunately . . . for I *couldn't* think tonight. And it will pass the time."

It passed an hour. Then, just as Anne laid down the last shining spoon, they heard the front door shut. Both sought comfort fearfully in each other's eyes.

"Oh, Miss Shirley, ma'am," gasped Charlotta, 'if he's going away this early there's nothing into it and never will be."

They flew to the window. Mr. Irving had no intention of going away. He and Miss Lavendar were strolling slowly down the middle path to the stone bench.

"Oh, Miss Shirley, ma'am, he's got his arm around her waist," whispered Charlotta the Fourth delightedly. "He *must* have proposed to her or she'd never allow it."

Anne caught Charlotta the Fourth by her own plump waist and danced her around the kitchen until they were both out of breath.

"Oh, Charlotta," she cried gaily, "I'm neither a prophetess nor the daughter of a prophetess but I'm going to make a prediction. There'll be a wedding in this old stone house before the maple leaves are red. Do you want that translated into prose, Charlotta?"

"No, I can understand that," said Charlotta. "A wedding ain't poetry. Why, Miss Shirley, ma'am, you're crying! What for?"

"Oh, because it's all so beautiful . . . and story bookish . . . and romantic . . . and sad," said Anne, winking the tears out of her eyes. "It's all perfectly lovely . . . but there's a little sadness mixed up in it too, somehow."

"Oh, of course there's a resk in marrying anybody," conceded Charlotta the Fourth, "but, when all's said and done, Miss Shirley, ma'am, there's many a worse thing than a husband."

CHAPTER 29

POETRY AND PROSE

FOR THE next month Anne lived in what, for Avonlea, might be called a whirl of excitement. The preparation of her own modest outfit for Redmond was of secondary importance. Miss Lavendar was getting ready to be married and the stone house was the scene of endless consultations and plannings and discussions, with Charlotta the Fourth hovering on the outskirts of things in agitated delight and wonder. Then the dressmaker came, and there was the rapture and wretchedness of choosing fashions and being fitted. Anne and Diana spent half their time at Echo Lodge and there were nights when Anne could not sleep for wondering whether she had done right in advising Miss Lavendar to select brown rather than navy blue for her traveling dress, and to have her gray silk made princess.

Everybody concerned in Miss Lavendar's story was very happy. Paul Irving rushed to Green Gables to talk the news over with Anne as soon as his father had told him.

"I knew I could trust father to pick me out a nice little second mother," he said proudly. "It's a fine thing to have a father you can depend on, teacher. I just love Miss Lavendar. Grandma is pleased, too. She says she's real glad father didn't pick out an American for his second wife, because, although it turned out all right the first time, such a thing wouldn't be likely to happen twice. Mrs. Lynde says she thoroughly approves of the match and thinks it likely Miss Lavendar will give up her queer notions and be like other people, now that she's going to be married. But I hope she won't give her queer notions up, teacher, because I like them. And I don't want her to be like other people. There are too many other people around as it is. *You* know, teacher."

Charlotta the Fourth was another radiant person.

"Oh, Miss Shirley, ma'am, it has all turned out so beautiful. When Mr. Irving and Miss Lavendar come back from their tower I'm to go up to Boston to live with them . . . and me only fifteen, and the other girls never went till they were sixteen. Ain't Mr. Irving splendid? He just worships the ground she treads on and it makes me feel so queer sometimes to see the look in his eyes when he's watching her. It beggars description, Miss Shirley, ma'am. I'm awful thankful they're so fond of each other. It's the best way, when all's said and done, though some folks can get along without it. I've got an aunt who has been married three times and she says she married the first time for love and the last two times strictly for business, and was happy with all three except at the times of the funerals. But I think she took a resk, Miss Shirley, ma'am."

"Oh, it's all so romantic," breathed Anne to Marilla that night. "If I hadn't taken the wrong path that day we went to Mr. Kimball's I'd never have known Miss Lavendar; and if I hadn't met her I'd never have taken Paul there . . . and he'd never have written to his father about visiting Miss Lavendar just as Mr. Irving was starting for San Francisco. Mr. Irving says whenever he got that letter he made up his mind to send his partner to San Francisco and come here instead. He hadn't heard anything of Miss Lavendar for fifteen years. Somebody had told him then that she was to be married and he thought she was and never asked anybody anything about her. And now everything has come right. And I had a hand in bringing it about. Perhaps, as Mrs. Lynde says, everything is foreordained and it was bound to happen anyway. But even so, it's nice to think one was an instrument used by predestination. Yes indeed, it's very romantic.''

"I can't see that it's so terribly romantic at all," said Marilla rather crisply. Marilla thought Anne was too worked up about it and had plenty to do with getting ready for college without "traipsing" to Echo Lodge two days out of every three helping Miss Lavendar. "In the first place two young fools quarrel and turn sulky; then Steve Irving goes to the States and after a spell gets married up there and is perfectly happy from all accounts. Then his wife dies and after a decent interval he thinks he'll come home and see if his first fancy'll have him. Meanwhile, she's been living single, probably because nobody nice enough came along to want her, and they meet and agree to be married after all. Now, where is the romance in all that?"

"Oh, there isn't any, when you put it that way," gasped Anne, rather as if somebody had thrown cold water over her. "I suppose that's how it looks in prose. But it's very different if you look at it through poetry . . . and *I* think it's nicer . . ." Anne recovered herself and her eyes shone and her cheeks flushed . . . "to look at it through poetry."

Marilla glanced at the radiant young face and refrained from further sarcastic comments. Perhaps some realization came to her that after all it was better to have, like Anne, "the vision and the faculty devine" . . . that gift which the world cannot bestow or take away, of looking at life through some transfiguring . . . or revealing? . . . medium, whereby everything seemed apparelled in celestial light, wearing a glory and freshness not visible to those who, like herself and Charlotta the Fourth, looked at things only through prose.

"When's the wedding to be?" she asked after a pause.

"The last Wednesday in August. They are to be married in the garden under the honeysuckle trellis . . . the very spot where Mr.

Irving proposed to her twenty-five years ago. Marilla, that *is* romantic, even in prose. There's to be nobody there except Mrs. Irving and Paul and Gilbert and Diana and I, and Miss Lavendar's cousins. And they will leave on the six o'clock train for a trip to the Pacific coast. When they come back in the fall Paul and Charlotta the Fourth are to go up to Boston to live with them. But Echo Lodge is to be left just as it is . . . only of course they'll sell the hens and cow, and board up the windows . . . and every summer they're coming down to live in it. I'm so glad. It would have hurt me dreadfully next winter at Redmond to think of that dear stone house all stripped and deserted, with empty rooms . . . or far worse still, with other people living in it. But I can think of it now, just as I've always seen it, waiting happily for the summer to bring life and laughter back to it again.''

There was more romance in the world than that which had fallen to the share of the middle-aged lovers of the stone house. Anne stumbled suddenly on it one evening when she came over to Orchard Slope by the wood cut and came out into the Barry garden. Diana Barry and Fred Wright were standing together under the big willow. Diana was leaning against the gray trunk, her lashes cast down on very crimson cheeks. One hand was held by Fred, who stood with his face bent towards her, stammering something in low earnest tones. There were no other people in the world except their two selves at that magic moment; so neither of them saw Anne, who, after one dazed glance of comprehension, turned and sped noiselessly back through the spruce wood, never stopping till she gained her own gable room, where she sat breathlessly down by her window and tried to collect her scattered wits.

"Diana and Fred are in love with each other," she gasped. "Oh, it does seem so . . . so . . . so *hopelessly* grown up."

Anne, of late, had not been without her suspicions that Diana was proving false to the melancholy Byronic hero of her early dreams. But as "things seen are mightier than things heard," or suspected, the realization that it was actually so came to her with almost the shock of perfect surprise. This was succeeded by a queer, little lonely feeling . . . as if, somehow, Diana had gone forward into a new world, shutting a gate behind her, leaving Anne on the outside.

"Things are changing so fast it almost frightens me," Anne thought, a little sadly. "And I'm afraid that this can't help making some difference between Diana and me. I'm sure I can't tell her all my secrets after this . . . she might tell Fred. And what *can* she see in Fred? He's very nice and jolly . . . but he's just Fred Wright.''

It is always a very puzzling question . . . what can somebody see in somebody else? But how fortunate after all that it is so, for if everybody saw alike . . . well, in that case, as the old Indian said, ''Everybody would want my squaw.'' It was plain that Diana *did* see something in Fred Wright, however Anne's eyes might be holden. Diana came to Green Gables the next evening, a pensive, shy young lady, and told Anne the whole story in the dusky seclusion of the east gable. Both girls cried and kissed and laughed.

''I'm so happy,'' said Diana, ''but it does seem ridiculous to think of me being engaged.''

''What is it really like to be engaged?'' asked Anne curiously.

''Well, that depends on who you're engaged to,'' answered Diana, with that maddening air of superior wisdom always assumed by those who are engaged over those who are not. ''It's perfectly lovely to be engaged to Fred . . . but I think it would be simply horrid to be engaged to anyone else.''

''There's not much comfort for the rest of us in that, seeing that there is only one Fred,'' laughed Anne.

''Oh, Anne, you don't understand,'' said Diana in vexation. ''I didn't mean *that* . . . it's so hard to explain. Never mind, you'll understand sometime, when your own turn comes.''

''Bless you, dearest of Dianas, I understand now. What is an imagination for if not to enable you to peep at life through other people's eyes?''

''You must be my bridesmaid, you know, Anne. Promise me that . . . wherever you may be when I'm married.''

''I'll come from the ends of the earth if necessary,'' promised Anne solemnly.

''Of course, it won't be for ever so long yet,'' said Diana, blushing. ''Three years at the very least . . . for I'm only eighteen and mother says no daughter of hers shall be married before she's twenty-one. Besides, Fred's father is going to buy the Abraham Fletcher farm for him and he says he's got to have it two thirds paid for before he'll give it to him in his own name. But three years isn't any to much time to get ready for housekeeping, for I haven't a speck of fancy work made yet. But I'm going to begin crocheting doilies tomorrow. Myra Gillis had thirty-seven doilies when she was married and I'm determined I shall have as many as she had.''

"I suppose it would be perfectly impossible to keep house with only thirty-six doilies," conceded Anne, with a solemn face but dancing eyes.

Diana looked hurt.

"I didn't think you'd make fun of me, Anne," she said reproachfully.

"Dearest, I wasn't making fun of you," cried Anne repentantly. "I was only teasing you a bit. I think you'll make the sweetest little housekeeper in the world. And I think it's perfectly lovely of you to be planning already for your home o' dreams."

Anne had no sooner uttered the phrase, "home o' dreams," than it captivated her fancy and she immediately began the erection of one of her own. It was, of course, tenanted by an ideal master, dark, proud, and melancholy; but oddly enough, Gilbert Blythe persisted in hanging about too, helping her arrange pictures, lay out gardens, and accomplish sundry other tasks which a proud and melancholy hero evidently considered beneath his dignity. Anne tried to banish Gilbert's image from her castle in Spain but, somehow, he went on being there, so Anne, being in a hurry, gave up the attempt and pursued her aerial architecture with such success that her "home o' dreams" was built and furnished before Diana spoke again.

"I suppose, Anne, you must think it's funny I should like Fred so well when he's so different from the kind of man I've always said I would marry . . . the tall, slender kind? But somehow I wouldn't want Fred to be tall and slender . . . because, don't you see, he wouldn't be Fred then. Of course," added Diana rather dolefully, "we will be a dreadfully pudgy couple. But after all that's better than one of us being short and fat and the other tall and lean, like Morgan Sloane and his wife. Mrs. Lynde says it always makes her think of the long and short of it when she sees them together."

"Well," said Anne to herself that night, as she brushed her hair before her gilt framed mirror, "I am glad Diana is so happy and satisfied. But when my turn comes . . . if it ever does . . . I do hope there'll be something a little more thrilling about it. But then Diana thought so too, once. I've heard her say time and again she'd never get engaged any poky commonplace way . . . he'd *have* to do something splendid to win her. But she has changed. Perhaps I'll change too. But I won't . . . I'm determined I won't. Oh, I think these engagements are dreadfully unsettling things when they happen to your intimate friends."

CHAPTER 30

A WEDDING AT THE STONE HOUSE

THE LAST week in August came. Miss Lavendar was to be married in it. Two weeks later Anne and Gilbert would leave for Redmond College. In a week's time Mrs. Rachel Lynde would move to Green Gables and set up her lares and penates in the erstwhile spare room, which was already prepared for her coming. She had sold all her superfluous household plenishings by auction and was at present revelling in the congenial occupation of helping the Allans pack up. Mr. Allan was to preach his farewell sermon the next Sunday. The old order was changing rapidly to give place to the new, as Anne felt with a little sadness threading all her excitement and happiness.

"Changes ain't totally pleasant but they're excellent things," said Mr. Harrison philosophically. "Two years is about long enough for things to stay exactly the same. If they stayed put any longer they might grow mossy."

Mr. Harrison was smoking on his veranda. His wife had self-sacrificingly told him that he might smoke in the house if he took care to sit by an open window. Mr. Harrison rewarded this concession by going outdoors altogether to smoke in fine weather, and so mutual goodwill reigned.

Anne had come over to ask Mrs. Harrison for some of her yellow dahlias. She and Diana were going through to Echo Lodge that evening to help Miss Lavendar and Charlotta the Fourth with their final preparations for the morrow's bridal. Miss Lavendar herself never had dahlias; she did not like them and they would not have suited the fine retirement of her old-fashioned garden. But flowers of any kind were rather scarce in Avonlea and the neighboring districts that summer, thanks to Uncle Abe's storm; and Anne and Diana thought that a certain old cream-colored stone jug, usually kept sacred to doughnuts, brimmed over with yellow dahlias, would be just the thing to set in a dim angle of the stone house stairs, against the dark background of red hall paper.

"I s'pose you'll be starting off for college in a fortnight's time?" continued Mr. Harrison. "Well, we're going to miss you an awful lot, Emily and me. To be sure, Mrs. Lynde'll be over there in your place. There ain't nobody but a substitute can be found for them."

441

The irony of Mr. Harrison's tone is quite untransferable to paper. In spite of his wife's intimacy with Mrs. Lynde, the best that could be said of the relationship between her and Mr. Harrison, even under the new regime, was that they preserved an armed neutrality.

"Yes, I'm going," said Anne. "I'm very glad with my head . . . and very sorry with my heart."

"I s'pose you'll be scooping up all the honors that are lying round loose at Redmond."

"I may try for one or two of them," confessed Anne, "but I don't care so much for things like that as I did two years ago. What I want to get out of college course is some knowledge of the best way of living life and doing the most and best with it. I want to learn to understand and help other people and myself."

Mr. Harrison nodded.

"That's the idea exactly. That's what college ought to be for, instead of for turning out a lot of B.A.s, so chock full of book-learning and vanity that there ain't room for anything else. You're all right. College won't be able to do you much harm, I reckon."

Diana and Anne drove over to Echo Lodge after tea, taking with them all the flowery spoil that several predatory expeditions in their own and their neighbor's gardens had yielded. They found the stone house agog with excitement. Charlotta the Fourth was flying around with such vim and briskness that her blue bows seemed really to possess the power of being everywhere at once. Like the helmet of Navarre, Charlotta's blue bows waved ever in the thickest of the fray.

"Praise be to goodness you've come," she said devoutly, "for there's heaps of things to do . . . and the frosting on that cake *won't* harden . . . and there's all the silver to be rubbed up yet . . . and the horsehair trunk to be packed . . . and the roosters for the chicken salad are running out there beyant the henhouse yet, *crowing*, Miss Shirley, ma'am. And Miss Lavendar ain't to be trusted to do a thing. I was thankful when Mr. Irving came a few minutes ago and took her off for a walk in the woods. Courting's all right in its place, Miss Shirley, ma'am, but if you try to mix it up with cooking and scouring everything's spoiled. That's *my* opinion, Miss Shirley, ma'am."

Anne and Diana worked so heartily that by ten o'clock even Charlotta the Fourth was satisfied. She braided her hair in innumerable plaits and took her weary little bones off to bed.

"But I'm sure I shan't sleep a blessed wink, Miss Shirley, ma'am, for fear that something'll go wrong at the last minute . . . the cream won't whip . . . or Mr. Irving'll have a stroke and not be able to come.''

''He isn't in the habit of having strokes, is he?'' asked Diana, the dimpled corners of her mouth twitching. To Diana, Charlotta the Fourth was, if not exactly a thing of beauty, certainly a joy forever.

''They're not things that go by habit,'' said Charlotta the Fourth with dignity. ''They just *happen* . . . and there you are. *Anybody* can have a stroke. You don't have to learn how. Mr. Irving looks a lot like an uncle of mine that had one once just as he was sitting down to dinner one day. But maybe everything'll go all right. In this world you've just got to hope for the best and prepare for the worst and take whatever God sends.''

''The only thing I'm worried about is that it won't be fine tommorrow,'' said Diana. ''Uncle Abe predicted rain for the middle of the week, and ever since the big storm I can't help believing there's a good deal in what Uncle Abe says.''

Anne, who knew better than Diana just how much Uncle Abe had to do with the storm, was not much disturbed by this. She slept the sleep of the just and weary, and was roused at an unearthly hour by Charlotta the Fourth.

''Oh, Miss Shirley, ma'am, it's awful to call you so early,'' came wailing through the keyhole, ''but there's so much to do yet . . . and oh, Miss Shirley, ma'am, I'm skeered it's going to rain and I wish you'd get up and tell me you think it ain't.''

Anne flew to the window, hoping against hope that Charlotta the Fourth was saying this merely by way of rousing her effectively. But alas, the morning did look unpropitious. Below the window Miss Lavendar's garden, which should have been a glory of pale virgin sunshine, lay dim and windless; and the sky over the firs was dark with moody clouds.

''Isn't it too mean!'' said Diana.

''We must hope for the best,'' said Anne determinedly. ''If it only doesn't exactly rain, a cool, pearly gray day like this would really be nicer than hot sunshine.''

''But it will rain,'' mourned Charlotta, creeping into the room, a figure of fun, with her many braids wound about her head, the ends, tied up with white thread, sticking out in all directions. ''It'll hold off till the last minute and then pour cats and dogs. And all the folks will get sopping . . . and track mud all over the house . . . and they won't be able to be married under the honeysuckle . . . and it's awful unlucky for no sun to shine on a bride, say what you will, Miss

Shirley, ma'am. I *knew* things were going too well to last."

Charlotta the Fourth seemed certainly to have borrowed a leaf out of Miss Eliza Andrew's book.

It did not rain, though it kept on looking as if it meant to. By noon the rooms were decorated, the table beautifully laid; and upstairs was waiting a bride, "adorned for her husband."

"You do look sweet," said Anne rapturously.

"Lovely," echoed Diana.

"Everything's ready, Miss Shirley, ma'am, and nothing dreadful has happened *yet*," was Charlotta's cheerful statement as she betook herself to her little back room to dress. Out came all the braids; the resultant rampant crinkliness was plaited into two tails and tied, not with two bows alone, but with four, of brand-new ribbon, brightly blue. The two upper bows rather gave the impression of overgrown wings sprouting from Charlotta's neck, somewhat after the fashion of Raphael's cherubs. But Charlotta the Fourth thought them very beautiful, and after she had rustled into a white dress, so stiffly starched that it could stand alone, she surveyed herself in her glass with great satisfaction . . . a satisfaction which lasted until she went out in the hall and caught a glimpse through the spare room of a tall girl in some softly clinging gown, pinning white, star-like flowers on the smooth ripples of her ruddy hair.

"Oh, I'll *never* be able to look like Miss Shirley," thought poor Charlotta despairingly. "You just have to be born so, I guess . . . don't seem's if any amount of practice could give you that *air*."

By one o'clock the guests had come, including Mr. and Mrs. Allan, for Mr. Allan was to perform the ceremony in the absence of the Grafton minister on his vacation. There was no formality about the marriage. Miss Lavendar came down the stairs to meet her bridegroom at the foot, and as he took her hand she lifted her big brown eyes to his with a look that made Charlotta the Fourth, who intercepted it, feel queerer than ever. They went out to the honeysuckle arbor, where Mr. Allan was awaiting them. The guests grouped themselves as they pleased. Anne and Diana stood by the old stone bench, with Charlotta the Fourth between them, desperately clutching their hands in her cold, tremulous little paws.

Mr. Allan opened his blue book and the ceremony proceeded. Just as Miss Lavendar and Stephen Irving were pronounced man and wife a very beautiful and symbolic thing happened. The sun suddenly burst through the gray and poured a flood of radiance on the happy bride. Instantly the garden was alive with dancing shadows and flickering lights.

"What a lovely omen," thought Anne, as she ran to kiss the bride. Then the three girls left the rest of the guests laughing around the bridal pair while they flew into the house to see that all was in readiness for the feast.

"Thanks be to goodness, it's over, Miss Shirley, ma'am," breathed Charlotta the Fourth, "and they're married safe and sound, no matter what happens now. The bags of rice are in the pantry, ma'am, and the old shoes are behind the door, and the cream for whipping is on the sullar steps."

At half past two Mr. and Mrs. Irving left, and everybody went to Bright River to see them off on the afternoon train. As Miss Lavendar . . . I beg her pardon, Mrs. Irving . . . stepped from the door of her old home Gilbert and the girls threw the rice and Charlotta the Fourth hurled an old shoe with such excellent aim that she struck Mr. Allan squarely on the head. But it was reserved for Paul to give the prettiest send-off. He popped out of the porch ringing furiously a huge old brass dinner bell which had adorned the dining room mantel. Paul's only motive was to make a joyful noise; but as the clangor died away, from point and curve and hill across the river came the chime of "fairy wedding bells," ringing clearly, sweetly, faintly and more faint, as if Miss Lavendar's beloved echoes were bidding her greeting and farewell. And so, amid this benediction of sweet sounds, Miss Lavendar drove away from the old life of dreams and make-believes to a fuller life of realities in the busy world beyond.

Two hours later Anne and Charlotta the Fourth came down the lane again. Gilbert had gone to West Grafton on an errand and Diana had to keep an engagement at home. Anne and Charlotta had come back to put things in order and lock up the little stone house. The garden was a pool of late golden sunshine, with butterflies hovering and bees booming; but the little house had already that indefinable air of desolation which always follows a festivity.

"Oh dear me, don't it look lonesome?" sniffed Charlotta the Fourth, who had been crying all the way home from the station. "A wedding ain't much cheerfuller than a funeral after all, when it's all over, Miss Shirley, ma'am."

A busy evening followed. The decorations had to be removed, the dishes washed, the uneaten delicacies packed into a basket for the delectation of Charlotta the Fourth's young brothers at home. Anne would not rest until everything was in apple pie order; after Charlotta had gone home with her plunder Anne went over the still rooms, feeling like one who trod alone some banquet hall deserted, and closed the blinds. Then she locked the door and sat down under the silver poplar to wait for Gilbert, feeling very tired but still unweariedly thinking "long, long thoughts."

"What are you thinking of, Anne?" asked Gilbert, coming down the walk. He had left his horse and buggy out at the road.

"Of Miss Lavendar and Mr. Irving," answered Anne dreamily. "Isn't it beautiful to think how everything has turned out . . . how they have come together again after all the years of separation and misunderstanding?"

"Yes, it's beautiful," said Gilbert looking steadily down into Anne's uplifted face, "but wouldn't it have been more beautiful still, Anne, if there had been *no* separation or misunderstanding . . . if they had come hand in hand all the way through life, with no memories behind them but those which belonged to each other?"

For a moment Anne's heart fluttered queerly and for the first time her eyes faltered under Gilbert's gaze and a rosy flush stained the paleness of her face. It was as if a veil that had hung before her inner consciousness had been lifted, giving to her view a revelation of unsuspected feelings and realities. Perhaps, after all, romance did not come into one's life with pomp and blare, like a gay knight riding down; perhaps it crept to one's side like an old friend through quiet ways; perhaps it revealed itself in seeming prose, until some sudden shaft of illumination flung athwart its pages betrayed the rhythm and the music; perhaps . . . perhaps . . . love unfolded naturally out of a beautiful friendship, as a golden-hearted rose slipping from its green sheath.

Then the veil dropped again; but the Anne who walked up the dark lane was not quite the same Anne who had driven gaily down it the evening before. The page of girlhood had been turned, as if by an unseen finger, and the page of womanhood was before her with all its charm and mystery, its pain and gladness.

Gilbert wisely said nothing more; but in his silence he read the history of the next four years in the light of Anne's remembered blush. Four years of earnest, happy work . . . and then the guerdon of a useful knowledge gained and a sweetheart won.

Behind them in the garden the little stone house brooded among the shadows. It was lonely but not forsaken. It had not yet done with dreams and laughter and the joy of life; there were to be future summers for the little stone house; meanwhile, it could wait. And over the river in the purple durance the echoes bided their time.

Anne's House of Dreams

CHAPTER 1

IN THE GARRET OF GREEN GABLES

"THANKS BE, I'm done with geometry, learning or teaching it," said Anne Shirley, a trifle vindictively, as she thumped a somewhat battered volume of Euclid into a big chest of books, banged the lid in triumph, and sat down upon it, looking at Diana Wright across the Green Gables garret, with gray eyes that were like a morning sky.

The garret was a shadowy, suggestive, delightful place, as all garrets should be. Through the open window, by which Anne sat, blew the sweet, scented, sun-warm air of the August afternoon; outside, poplar boughs rustled and tossed in the wind; beyond them were the woods, where Lover's Lane wound its enchanted path, and the old apple orchard which still bore its rosy harvests munificently. And, over all, was a great mountain range of snowy clouds in the blue southern sky. Through the other window was glimpsed a distant, white-capped, blue sea—the beautiful St. Lawrence Gulf, on which floats, like a jewel, Abegweit, whose softer, sweeter Indian name has long been forsaken for the more prosaic one of Prince Edward Island.

Diana Wright, three years older than when we last saw her, had grown somewhat matronly in the intervening time. But her eyes were as black and brilliant, her cheeks as rosy, and her dimples as enchanting, as in the long-ago days when she and Anne Shirley had vowed eternal friendship in the garden at Orchard Slope. In her arms she held a small, sleeping, black-curled creature, who for two happy years had been known to the world of Avonlea as "Small Anne

449

Cordelia.'' Avonlea folks knew why Diana had called her Anne, of course, but Avonlea folks were puzzled by the Cordelia. There had never been a Cordelia in the Wright or Barry connections. Mrs. Harmon Andrews said she supposed Diana had found the name in some trashy novel, and wondered that Fred hadn't more sense than to allow it. But Diana and Anne smiled at each other. They knew how Small Anne Cordelia had come by her name.

"You always hated geometry," said Diana with a retrospective smile. "I should think you'd be real glad to be through with teaching, anyhow."

"Oh, I've always liked teaching, apart from geomtery. These past three years in Summerside have been very pleasant ones. Mrs. Harmon Andrews told me when I came home that I wouldn't likely find married life as much better than teaching as I expected. Evidently Mrs. Harmon is of Hamlet's opinion that it may be better to bear the ills that we have than fly to others that we know not of.''

Anne's laugh, as blithe and irresistible as of yore, with an added note of sweetness and maturity, rang through the garret. Marilla in the kitchen below, compounding blue plum preserve, heard it and smiled; then sighed to think how seldom that dear laugh would echo through Green Gables in the years to come. Nothing in her life had ever given Marilla so much happiness as the knowledge that Anne was going to marry Gilbert Blythe; but every joy must bring with it its little shadow of sorrow. During the three Summerside years Anne had been home often for vacations and weekends; but, after this, a bi-annual visit would be as much as could be hoped for.

"You needn't let what Mrs. Harmon says worry you," said Diana, with the calm assurance of the four-years matron. "Married life has its ups and downs, of course. You mustn't expect that everything will always go smoothly. But I can assure you, Anne, that it's a happy life, when you're married to the right man."

Anne smothered a smile. Diana's airs of vast experience always amused her a little.

"I daresay I'll be putting them on too, when I've been married four years," she thought. "Surely my sense of humor will preserve me from it, though."

"Is it settled yet where you are going to live?" asked Diana, cuddling Small Anne Cordelia with the inimitable gesture of motherhood which always sent through Anne's heart, filled with sweet, unuttered dreams and hopes, a thrill that was half pure pleasure and half a strange, ethereal pain.

"Yes. That was what I wanted to tell you when I 'phoned to you to come down today. By the way, I can't realize that we really have telephones in Avonlea now. It sounds so preposterously up-to-date and modernish for this darling, leisurely old place.''

"We can thank the A. V. I. S. for them," said Diana. "We should never have got the line if they hadn't taken the matter up and carried it through. There was enough cold water thrown to discourage any society. But they stuck to it, nevertheless. You did a splendid thing for Avonlea when you founded that society, Anne. What fun we did have at our meetings! Will you ever forget the blue hall and Judson Parker's scheme for painting medicine advertisements on his fence?''

"I don't know that I'm wholly grateful to the A. V. I. S. in the matter of the telephone," said Anne. "Oh, I know it's most convenient—even more so than our old device of signalling to each other by flashes of candlelight! And, as Mrs. Rachel says, 'Avonlea must keep up with the procession, that's what.' But somehow I feel as if I didn't want Avonlea spoiled by what Mr. Harrison, when he wants to be witty, calls 'modern inconveniences.' I should like to have it kept always just as it was in the dear old years. That's foolish—and sentimental—and impossible. So I shall immediately become wise and practical and possible. The telephone, as Mr. Harrison concedes, is 'a buster of a good thing'—even if you do know that probably half a dozen interested people are listening along the line.''

"That's the worst of it," sighed Diana. "It's so annoying to hear the receivers going down whenever you ring anyone up. They say Mrs. Harmon Andrews insisted that their 'phone should be put in their kitchen just so that she could listen whenever it rang and keep an eye on the dinner at the same time. Today, when you called me, I distinctly heard that queer clock of the Pyes' striking. So no doubt Josie or Gertie was listening.''

"Oh, so that is why you said, 'You've got a new clock at Green Gables, haven't you?' I couldn't imagine what you meant. I heard a vicious click as soon as you had spoken. I suppose it was the Pye receiver being hung up with profane energy. Well, never mind the Pyes. As Mrs. Rachel says, 'Pyes they always were and Pyes they always will be, world without end, amen.' I want to talk of pleasanter things. It's all settled as to where my new home shall be.''

"Oh, Anne, where? I do hope it's near here.''

"No-o-o, that's the drawback. Gilbert is going to settle at Four Winds Harbor—sixty miles from here.''

"Sixty! It might as well be six hundred," sighed Diana. "I never can get further from home now than Charlottetown.''

"You'll have to come to Four Winds. It's the most beautiful

harbor on the Island. There's a little village called Glen St. Mary at its head, and Dr. David Blythe has been practicing there for fifty years. He is Gilbert's great-uncle, you know. He is going to retire, and Gilbert is to take over his practice. Dr. Blythe is going to keep his house, though, so we shall have to find a habitation for ourselves. I don't know yet what it is, or where it will be in reality, but I have a little house o'dreams all furnished in my imagination—a tiny, delightful castle in Spain.''

''Where are you going for your wedding tour?'' asked Diana.

''Nowhere. Don't look horrified, Diana dearest. You suggest Mrs. Harmon Andrews. She, no doubt, will remark condescendingly that people who can't afford wedding 'towers' are real sensible not to take them; and then she'll remind me that Jane went to Europe for hers. I want to spend *my* honeymoon at Four Winds in my own dear house of dreams.''

''And you've decided not to have any bridesmaid?''

''There isn't any one to have. You and Phil and Priscilla and Jane all stole a march on me in the matter of marriage; and Stella is teaching in Vancouver. I have no other 'kindred soul' and I won't have a bridesmaid who isn't.''

''But you are going to wear a veil, aren't you?'' asked Diana, anxiously.

''Yes, indeedy. I shouldn't feel like a bride without one. I remember telling Matthew, that evening when he brought me to Green Gables, that I never expected to be a bride because I was so homely no one would ever want to marry me—unless some foreign missionary did. I had an idea then that foreign missionaries couldn't afford to be finicky in the matter of looks if they wanted a girl to risk her life among cannibals. You should have seen the foreign missionary Priscilla married. He was as handsome and inscrutable as those daydreams we once planned to marry ourselves, Diana; he was the best dressed man I ever met, and he raved over Priscilla's 'ethereal, golden beauty.' But of course there are no cannibals in Japan.''

''Your wedding dress is a dream, anyhow,'' sighed Diana rapturously. ''You'll look like a perfect queen in it—you're so tall and slender. How *do* you keep so slim, Anne? I'm fatter than ever—I'll soon have no waist at all.''

''Stoutness and slimness seem to be matters of predestination,'' said Anne. ''At all events, Mrs. Harmon Andrews can't say to you what she said to me when I came home from Summerside, 'Well, Anne, you're just about as skinny as ever.' It sounds quite romantic to be 'slender,' but 'skinny' has a very different tang.''

"Mrs. Harmon has been talking about your trousseau. She admits it's as nice as Jane's, although she says Jane married a millionaire and you are only marrying a 'poor young doctor without a cent to his name.'"

Anne laughed.

"My dresses *are* nice. I love pretty things. I remember the first pretty dress I ever had—the brown gloria Matthew gave me for our school concert. Before that everything I had was so ugly. It seemed to me that I stepped into a new world that night."

"That was the night Gilbert recited 'Bingen on the Rhine,' and looked at you when he said, 'There's another, *not* a sister.' And you were so furious because he put your pink tissue rose in his breast pocket! You didn't much imagine then that you would ever marry him."

"Oh, well, that's another instance of predestination," laughed Anne, as they went down the garret stairs.

CHAPTER 2

THE HOUSE OF DREAMS

THERE WAS more excitement in the air of Green Gables than there had ever been before in all its history. Even Marilla was so excited that she couldn't help showing it—which was little short of being phenomenal.

"There's never been a wedding in this house," she said, half apologetically, to Mrs. Rachel Lynde. "When I was a child I heard an old minister say that a house was not a real home until it had been consecrated by a birth, a wedding and a death. We've had deaths here—my father and mother died here as well as Matthew; and we've even had a birth here. Long ago, just after we moved into this house, we had a married hired man for a little while, and his wife had a baby here. But there's never been a wedding before. It does seem so strange to think of Anne being married. In a way she just seems to me the little girl Matthew brought home here fourteen years ago. I can't realize that she's grown up. I shall never forget what I felt when I saw Matthew bringing in a *girl*. I wonder what became of the boy we would have got if there hadn't been a mistake. I wonder what *his* fate was.''

"Well, it was a fortunate mistake," said Mrs. Rachel Lynde, "though, mind you, there was a time I didn't think so—that evening I came up to see Anne and she treated us to such a scene. Many things have changed since then, that's what."

Mrs. Rachel sighed, and then brisked up again. When weddings were in order Mrs. Rachel was ready to let the dead past bury its dead.

"I'm going to give Anne two of my cotton warp spreads," she resumed. "A tobacco-stripe one and an apple-leaf one. She tells me they're getting to be real fashionable again. Well, fashion or no fashion, I don't believe there's anything prettier for a spare-room bed than a nice apple-leaf spread, that's what. I must see about getting them bleached. I've had them sewed up in cotton bags ever since Thomas died, and no doubt they're an awful color. But there's a month yet, and dew-bleaching will work wonders."

Only a month! Marilla sighed and then said proudly:

"I'm giving Anne that half dozen braided rugs I have in the garret. I never supposed she'd want them—they're so old-fashioned, and nobody seems to want anything but hooked mats now. But she asked me for them—said she'd rather have them than anything else for her floors. They *are* pretty. I made them of the nicest rags, and braided them in stripes. It was such company these last few winters. And I'll make her enough blue plum preserve to stock her jam closet for a year. It seems real strange. Those blue plum trees hadn't even a blossom for three years, and I thought they might as well be cut down. And this last spring they were white, and such a crop of plums I never remember at Green Gables."

"Well, thank goodness that Anne and Gilbert really are going to be married after all. It's what I've always prayed for," said Mrs. Rachel, in the tone of one who is comfortably sure that her prayers have availed much. "It was a great relief to find out that she really didn't mean to take the Kingsport man. He was rich, to be sure, and Gilbert is poor—at least, to begin with; but then he's an Island boy."

He's Gilbert Blythe," said Marilla contentedly. Marilla would have died the death before she would have put into words the thought that was always in the background of her mind whenever she had looked at Gilbert from his childhood up—the thought that, had it not been for her own wilful pride long, long ago, he might have been *her* son. Marilla felt that, in some strange way, his marriage with Anne would put right that old mistake. Good had come out of the evil of the ancient bitterness.

As for Anne herself, she was so happy that she almost felt frightened. The gods, so says the old superstition, do not like to behold too happy mortals. It is certain, at least, that some human beings do not. Two of that ilk descended upon Anne one violet dusk and proceeded to do what in them lay to prick the rainbow bubble of her satisfaction. If she thought she was getting any particular prize in young Dr. Blythe, or if she imagined that he was still as infatuated with her as he might have been in his salad days, it was surely their duty to put the matter before her in another light. Yet these two worthy ladies were not enemies of Anne; on the contrary, they were really quite fond of her, and would have defended her as their own young had anyone else attacked her. Human nature is not obliged to be consistent.

Mrs. Inglis—*née* Jane Andrews, to quote from the *Daily Enterprise*—came with her mother and Mrs. Jasper Bell. But in Jane the milk of human kindness had not been curdled by years of matrimonial bickerings. Her lines had fallen in pleasant places. In spite of the fact—as Mrs. Rachel Lynde would say—that she had married a millionaire, her marriage had been happy. Wealth had not spoiled her. She was still the placid, amiable, pink-cheeked Jane of the old quartette, sympathising with her old chum's happiness and as keenly interested in all the dainty details of Anne's trousseau as if it could rival her own silken and bejewelled splendors. Jane was not brilliant, and had probably never made a remark worth listening to in her life; but she never said anything that would hurt anyone's feelings—which may be a negative talent but is likewise a rare and enviable one.

"So Gilbert didn't go back on you after all," said Mrs. Harmon Andrews, contriving to convey an expression of surprise in her tone. "Well, the Blythes generally keep their word when they've once passed it, no matter what happens. Let me see—you're twenty-five, aren't you, Anne? When I was a girl twenty-five was the first corner. But you look quite young. Red-headed people always do."

"Red hair is very fashionable now," said Anne, trying to smile, but speaking rather coldly. Life had developed in her a sense of humor which helped her over many difficulties; but as yet nothing had availed to steel her against a reference to her hair.

"So it is—so it is," conceded Mrs. Harmon. "There's no telling what queer freaks fashion will take. Well, Anne, your things are very pretty, and very suitable to your position in life, aren't they, Jane? I hope you'll be very happy. You have my best wishes, I'm sure. A long engagement doesn't often turn out well. But, of course, in your case it couldn't be helped."

"Gilbert looks very young for a doctor. I'm afraid people won't have much confidence in him," said Mrs. Jasper Bell gloomily. Then she shut her mouth tightly, as if she had said what she considered it her duty to say and held her conscience clear. She belonged to the type which always has a stringy black feather in its hat and straggling locks of hair on its neck.

Anne's surface pleasure in her pretty bridal things was temporarily shadowed; but the deeps of happiness below could not thus be disturbed; and the little stings of Mesdames Bell and Andrews were forgotten when Gilbert came later, and they wandered down to the birches of the brook, which had been saplings when Anne had come to Green Gables, but were now tall, ivory columns in a fairy palace of twilight and stars. In their shadows Anne and Gilbert talked in lover-fashion of their new home and their new life together.

"I've found a nest for us, Anne."

"Oh, where? Not right in the village, I hope. I wouldn't like that altogether."

"No. There was no house to be had in the village. This is a little white house on the harbor shore, half way between Glen St. Mary and Four Winds Point. It's a little out of the way, but when we get a 'phone in that won't matter so much. The situation is beautiful. It looks to the sunset and has the great blue harbor before it. The sand-dunes aren't very far away—the sea winds blow over them and the sea spray drenches them."

"But the house itself, Gilbert,—*our* first home? What is it like?"

"Not very large, but large enough for us. There's a splendid living room with a fireplace in it downstairs, and a dining room that looks out on the harbor, and a little room that will do for my office. It is about sixty years old—the oldest house in Four Winds. But it has been kept in pretty good repair, and was all done over about fifteen years ago—shingled, plastered and re-floored. It was well built to begin with. I understand that there was some romantic story connected with its building, but the man I rented it from didn't know it. He said Captain Jim was the only one who could spin that old yarn now."

"Who is Captain Jim?"

"The keeper of the lighthouse on Four Winds Point. You'll love that Four Winds light, Anne. It's a revolving one, and it flashes like a magnificent star through the twilights. We can see it from our living room windows and our front door."

"Who owns the house?"

"Well, it's the property of the Glen St. Mary Presbyterian Church now, and I rented it from the trustees. But it belonged until lately to a very old lady, Miss Elizabeth Russell. She died last spring, and as she had no near relatives she left her property to the Glen St. Mary Church. Her furniture is still in the house, and I bought most of it—for a mere song you might say, because it was all so old-fashioned that the trustees despaired of selling it. Glen St. Mary folks prefer plush brocade and sideboards with mirrors and ornamentations, I fancy. But Miss Russell's furniture is very good and I feel sure you'll like it, Anne."

"So far, good," said Anne, nodding cautious approval. "But, Gilbert, people cannot live by furniture alone. You haven't yet mentioned one very important thing. Are there *trees* about this house?"

"Heaps of them, oh, dryad! There is a big grove of fir trees behind it, two rows of Lombardy poplars down the lane, and a ring of white birches around a very delightful garden. Our front door opens right into the garden, but there is another entrance—a little gate hung between two firs. The hinges are on one trunk and the catch on the other. Their boughs form an arch overhead."

"Oh, I'm so glad! I couldn't live where there were no trees—something vital in me would starve. Well, after that, there's no use asking you if there's a brook anywhere near. *That* would be expecting too much."

"But there *is* a brook—and it actually cuts across one corner of the garden."

"Then," said Anne, with a long sigh of supreme satisfaction, "this house you have found *is* my house of dreams and none other."

CHAPTER 3

THE LAND OF DREAMS AMONG

"HAVE YOU made up your mind who you're going to have to the wedding, Anne?" asked Mrs. Rachel Lynde, as she hemstitched table napkins industriously. "It's time your invitations were sent, even if they are to be only informal ones."

"I don't mean to have very many," said Anne. "We just want those we love best to see us married. Gilbert's people, and Mr. and Mrs. Allan, and Mr. and Mrs. Harrison."

"There was a time when you'd hardly have numbered Mr. Harrison among your dearest friends," said Marilla drily.

"Well, I wasn't *very* strongly attracted to him at our first meeting," acknowledged Anne, with a laugh over the recollection. "But Mr. Harrison has improved on acquaintance, and Mrs. Harrison is really a dear. Then, of course, there are Miss Lavendar and Paul."

"Have they decided to come to the Island this summer? I thought they were going to Europe."

"They changed their minds when I wrote them I was going to be married. I had a letter from Paul today. He says he *must* come to my wedding, no matter what happens to Europe."

"That child always idolised you," remarked Mrs. Rachel.

"That 'child' is a young man of nineteen now, Mrs. Lynde."

"How time does fly!" was Mrs. Lynde's brilliant and original response.

"Charlotta the Fourth may come with them. She sent word by Paul that she would come if her husband would let her. I wonder if she still wears those enormous blue bows, and whether her husband calls her Charlotta or Leonora. I should love to have Charlotta at my wedding. Charlotta and I were at a wedding long syne. They expect to be at Echo Lodge next week. Then there are Phil and the Reverend Jo——"

"It sounds awful to hear you speaking of a minister like that, Anne," said Mrs. Rachel severely.

"His wife calls him that."

"She should have more respect for his holy office, then," retorted Mrs. Rachel.

"I've heard you criticise ministers pretty sharply yourself," teased Anne.

"Yes, but I do it reverently," protested Mrs. Lynde. "You never heard me *nickname* a minister."

Anne smothered a smile.

"Well, there are Diana and Fred and little Fred and Small Anne Cordelia—and Jane Andrews. I wish I could have Miss Stacey and Aunt Jamesina and Priscilla and Stella. But Stella is in Vancouver, and Pris is in Japan, and Miss Stacey is married in California, and Aunt Jamesina has gone to India to explore her daughter's mission field, in spite of her horror of snakes. It's really dreadful—the way people get scattered over the globe.''

"The Lord never intended it, that's what," said Mrs. Rachel authoritatively. "In my young days people grew up and married and settled down where they were born, or pretty near it. Thank goodness you've stuck to the Island, Anne. I was afraid Gilbert would insist on rushing off to the ends of the earth when he got through college, and dragging you with him.''

"If everybody stayed where he was born places would soon be filled up, Mrs. Lynde.''

"Oh, I'm not going to argue with you, Anne. *I* am not a B.A. What time of the day is the ceremony to be?''

"We have decided on noon—high noon, as the society reporters say. That will give us time to catch the evening train to Glen St. Mary.''

"And you'll be married in the parlor?''

"No—not unless it rains. We mean to be married in the orchard—with the blue sky over us and the sunshine around us. Do you know when and where I'd like to be married, if I could? It would be at dawn—a June dawn, with a glorious sunrise, and roses blooming in the gardens; and I would slip down and meet Gilbert and we would go together to the heart of the beech woods,—and there, under the green arches that would be like a splendid cathedral, we would be married.''

Marilla sniffed scornfully and Mrs. Lynde looked shocked.

"But that would be terrible queer, Anne. Why, it wouldn't really seem legal. And what would Mrs. Harmon Andrews say?''

"Ah, there's the rub,'' sighed Anne. "There are so many things in life we cannot do because of the fear of what Mrs. Harmon Andrews would say. ''Tis true, 'tis pity, and pity 'tis, 'tis true.' What delightful things we might do were it not for Mrs. Harmon Andrews!''

"By times, Anne, I don't feel quite sure that I understand you altogether,'' complained Mrs. Lynde.

"Anne was always romantic, you know,'' said Marilla apologetically.

"Well, married life will most likely cure her of that,'' Mrs. Rachel responded comfortingly.

Anne laughed and slipped away to Lover's Lane, where Gilbert found her; and neither of them seemed to entertain much fear, or hope, that their married life would cure them of romance.

The Echo Lodge people came over the next week, and Green Gables buzzed with the delight of them. Miss Lavendar had changed so little that the three years since her last Island visit might have been a watch in the night; but Anne gasped with amazement over Paul. Could this splendid six feet of manhood be the little Paul of Avonlea schooldays?

"You really make me feel old, Paul," said Anne. "Why, I have to look up to you!"

"You'll never grow old, Teacher," said Paul. "You are one of the fortunate mortals who have found and drunk from the Fountain of Youth,—you and Mother Lavendar. See here! When you're married I *won't* call you Mrs. Blythe. To me you'll always be 'Teacher'—the teacher of the best lessons I ever learned. I want to show you something."

The "something" was a pocketbook full of poems. Paul had put some of his beautiful fancies into verse, and magazine editors had not been as unappreciative as they are sometimes supposed to be. Anne read Paul's poems with real delight. They were full of charm and promise.

"You'll be famous yet, Paul. I always dreamed of having one famous pupil. He was to be a college president—but a great poet would be even better. Some day I'll be able to boast that I whipped the distinguished Paul Irving. But then I never did whip you, did I, Paul? What an opportunity lost! I think I kept you in at recess, however."

"You may be famous yourself, Teacher. I've seen a good deal of your work these last three years."

"No. I know what I can do. I can write pretty, fanciful little sketches that children love and editors send welcome cheques for. But I can do nothing big. My only chance for earthly immortality is a corner in your Memoirs."

Charlotta the Fourth had discarded the blue bows but her freckles were not noticeably less.

"I never did think I'd come down to marrying a Yankee, Miss Shirley, ma'am," she said. "But you never know what's before you, and it isn't his fault. He was born that way."

"You're a Yankee yourself, Charlotta, since you've married one."

"Miss Shirley, ma'am, I'm *not!* And I wouldn't be if I was to marry a dozen Yankees! Tom's kind of nice. And besides, I thought I'd better not be too hard to please, for I mightn't get another chance. Tom don't drink and he don't growl because he has to work between meals, and when all's said and done I'm satisfied, Miss Shirley, ma'am."

"Does he call you Leonora?" asked Anne.

"Goodness, no, Miss Shirley, ma'am. I wouldn't know who he meant if he did. Of course, when we got married he had to say, 'I take thee, Leonora,' and I declare to you, Miss Shirley, ma'am, I've had the most dreadful feeling ever since that it wasn't me he was talking to and I haven't been rightly married at all. And so you're going to be married yourself, Miss Shirley, ma'am? I always thought I'd like to marry a doctor. It would be so handy when the children had measles and croup. Tom is only a bricklayer, but he's real good-tempered. When I said to him, says I, 'Tom, can I go to Miss Shirley's wedding? I mean to go anyhow, but I'd like to have your consent,' he just says, 'Suit yourself, Charlotta, and you'll suit me.' That's a real pleasant kind of husband to have, Miss Shirley, ma'am."

Philippa and her Reverend Jo arrived at Green Gables the day before the wedding. Anne and Phil had a rapturous meeting which presently simmered down to a cosy, confidential chat over all that had been and was about to be.

"Queen Anne, you're as queenly as ever. I've got fearfully thin since the babies came. I'm not half so good-looking; but I think Jo likes it. There's not such a contrast between us, you see. And oh, it's perfectly magnificent that you're going to marry Gilbert. Roy Gardner wouldn't have done at all, at all. I can see that now, though I was horribly disappointed at the time. You know, Anne, you did treat Roy very badly."

"He has recovered, I understand," smiled Anne.

"Oh, yes. He is married and his wife is a sweet little thing and they're perfectly happy. Everything works together for good. Jo and the Bible say that, and they are pretty good authorities."

"Are Alec and Alonzo married yet?"

"Alec is, but Alonzo isn't. How those dear old days at Patty's Place come back when I'm talking to you, Anne! What fun we had!"

"Have you been to Patty's Place lately?"

"Oh, yes, I go often. Miss Patty and Miss Maria still sit by the fireplace and knit. And that reminds me—we've brought you a wedding gift from them, Anne. Guess what it is."

"I never could. How did they know I was going to be married?"

"Oh, I told them. I was there last week. And they were so interested. Two days ago Miss Patty wrote me a note asking me to call; and then she asked if I would take her gift to you. What would you wish most from Patty's Place, Anne?"

'You can't mean that Miss Patty has sent me her china dogs?"

"Go up head. They're in my trunk this very moment. And I've a letter for you. Wait a moment and I'll get it."

"Dear Miss Shirley," Miss Patty had written, "Maria and I were very much interested in hearing of your approaching nuptials. We send you our best wishes. Maria and I have never married, but we have no objection to other people doing so. We are sending you the china dogs. I intended to leave them to you in my will, because you seemed to have sincere affection for them. But Maria and I expect to live a good while yet (D.V.), so I have decided to give you the dogs while you are young. You will not have forgotten that Gog looks to the right and Magog to the left."

"Just fancy those lovely old dogs sitting by the fireplace in my house of dreams," said Anne rapturously. "I never expected anything so delightful."

That evening Green Gables hummed with preparations for the following day; but in the twilight Anne slipped away. She had a little pilgrimage to make on this last day of her girlhood and she must make it alone. She went to Matthew's grave, in the little poplar-shaded Avonlea graveyard, and there kept a silent tryst with old memories and immortal loves.

"How glad Matthew would be tomorrow if he were here," she whispered. "But I believe he does know and is glad of it—somewhere else. I've read somewhere that 'our dead are never dead until we have forgotten them.' Matthew will never be dead to me, for I can never forget him."

She left on his grave the flowers she had brought and walked slowly down the long hill. It was a gracious evening, full of delectable lights and shadows. In the west was a sky of mackerel clouds—crimson and amber-tinted, with long strips of apple-green sky between. Beyond was the glimmering radiance of a sunset sea, and the ceaseless voice of many waters came up from the tawny shore. All around her, lying in the fine, beautiful country silence, were the hills and fields and woods she had known and loved so long.

"History repeats itself," said Gilbert, joining her as she passed the Blythe gate. "Do you remember our first walk down this hill, Anne—our first walk together anywhere, for that matter?"

"I was coming home in the twilight from Matthew's grave—and you came out of the gate; and I swallowed the pride of years and spoke to you."

"And all heaven opened before me," supplemented Gilbert. "From that moment I looked forward to tomorrow. When I left you

ALL AROUND HER WERE THE HILLS AND FIELDS AND WOODS
SHE HAD KNOWN AND LOVED SO LONG.

at your gate that night and walked home I was the happiest boy in the world. Anne had forgiven me.''

"I think you had the most to forgive. I was an ungrateful little wretch—and after you had really saved my life that day on the pond, too. How I loathed that load of obligation at first! I don't deserve the happiness that has come to me.''

Gilbert laughed and clasped tighter the girlish hand that wore his ring. Anne's engagement ring was a circlet of pearls. She had refused to wear a diamond.

"I've never really liked diamonds since I found out they weren't the lovely purple I had dreamed. They will always suggest my old disappointment.''

"But pearls are for tears, the old legend says," Gilbert had objected.

"I'm not afraid of that. And tears can be happy as well as sad. My very happiest moments have been when I had tears in my eyes— when Marilla told me I might stay at Green Gables—when Matthew gave me the first pretty dress I ever had—when I heard that you were going to recover from the fever. So give me pearls for our troth ring, Gilbert, and I'll willingly accept the sorrow of life with its joy.''

But tonight our lovers thought only of joy and never of sorrow. For the morrow was their wedding day, and their house of dreams awaited them on the misty, purple shore of Four Winds Harbor.

CHAPTER 4

THE FIRST BRIDE OF GREEN GABLES

ANNE WAKENED on the morning of her wedding day to find the sunshine winking in at the window of the little porch gable and a September breeze frolicking with her curtains.

"I'm so glad the sun will shine on me," she thought happily.

She recalled the first morning she had wakened in that little porch room, when the sunshine had crept in on her through the blossom-drift of the old Snow Queen. That had not been a happy wakening, for it brought with it the bitter disappointment of the preceding night.

But since then the little room had been endeared and consecrated by years of happy childhood dreams and maiden visions. To it she had come back joyfully after all her absences; at its window she had knelt through that night of bitter agony when she believed Gilbert dying, and by it she had sat in speechless happiness the night of her betrothal. Many vigils of joy and some of sorrow had been kept there; and today she must leave it forever. Henceforth it would be hers no more; fifteen-year-old Dora was to inherit it when she had gone. Nor did Anne wish it otherwise; the little room was sacred to youth and girlhood—to the past that was to close today before the chapter of wifehood opened.

Green Gables was a busy and joyous house that forenoon. Diana arrived early, with little Fred and Small Anne Cordelia, to lend a hand. Davy and Dora, the Green Gables twins, whisked the babies off to the garden.

"Don't let Small Anne Cordelia spoil her clothes," warned Diana anxiously.

"You needn't be afraid to trust her with Dora," said Marilla. "That child is more sensible and careful than most of the mothers I've known. She's really a wonder in some ways. Not much like that other harum-scarum I brought up."

Marilla smiled across her chicken salad at Anne. It might even be suspected that she liked the harum-scarum best after all.

"Those twins are real nice children," said Mrs. Rachel, when she was sure they were out of earshot. "Dora is so womanly and helpful, and Davy is developing into a very smart boy. He isn't the holy terror for mischief he used to be."

"I never was so distracted in my life as I was the first six months he was here," acknowledged Marilla. "After that I suppose I got used to him. He's taken a great notion to farming lately, and wants me to let him try running the farm next year. I may, for Mr. Barry doesn't think he'll want to rent it much longer, and some new arrangement will have to be made."

"Well, you certainly have a lovely day for your wedding, Anne," said Diana, as she slipped a voluminous apron over her silken array. "You couldn't have had a finer one if you'd ordered it from Eaton's."

"Indeed, there's too much money going out of this Island to that same Eaton's," said Mrs. Lynde indignantly. She had strong views on the subject of octopus-like department stores, and never lost an opportunity of airing them. "And as for those catalogues of theirs, they're the Avonlea girls' Bible now, that's what. They pore over them on Sundays instead of studying the Holy Scriptures.''

"Well, they're splendid to amuse children with," said Diana. "Fred and Small Anne look at the pictures by the hour."

"*I* amused ten children without the aid of Eaton's catalogue," said Mrs. Rachel severely.

"Come, you two, don't quarrel over Eaton's catalogue," said Anne gaily. "This is my day of days, you know. I'm so happy I want every one else to be happy, too."

"I'm sure I hope your happiness will last, child," sighed Mrs. Rachel. She did hope it truly, and believed it, but she was afraid it was in the nature of a challenge to Providence to flaunt your happiness too openly. Anne, for her own good, must be toned down a trifle.

But it was a happy and beautiful bride who came down the old, homespun-carpeted stairs that September noon—the first bride of Green Gables, slender and shining-eyed, in the mist of her maiden veil, with her arms full of roses. Gilbert, waiting for her in the hall below, looked up at her with adoring eyes. She was his at last, this evasive, long-sought Anne, won after years of patient waiting. It was to him she was coming in the sweet surrender of the bride. Was he worthy of her? Could he make her as happy as he hoped? If he failed her—if he could not measure up to her standard of manhood—then, as she held out her hand, their eyes met and all doubt was swept away in a glad certainty. They belonged to each other; and, no matter what life might hold for them, it could never alter that. Their happiness was in each other's keeping and both were unafraid.

They were married in the sunshine of the old orchard, circled by the loving and kindly faces of long-familiar friends. Mr. Allan married them, and the Reverend Jo made what Mrs. Rachel Lynde afterwards pronounced to be the "most beautiful wedding prayer" she had ever heard. Birds do not often sing in September, but one sang sweetly from some hidden bough while Gilbert and Anne repeated their deathless vows. Anne heard it and thrilled to it; Gilbert heard it, and wondered only that all the birds in the world had not burst into jubilant song; Paul heard it and later wrote a lyric about it which was one of the most admired in his first volume of verse; Charlotta the Fourth heard it and was blissfully sure it meant good luck for her adored Miss Shirley. The bird sang until the ceremony was ended and then it wound up with one mad little, glad little trill. Never had the old gray-green house among its enfolding orchards known a blither, merrier afternoon. All the old jests and quips that must have done duty at weddings since Eden were served up, and seemed as new and brilliant and mirth-provoking as if they had never been uttered before. Laughter and joy had their way; and when Anne and Gilbert left to catch the Carmody train, with Paul as driver, the twins were ready with rice and old shoes, in the throwing of which Charlotta the Fourth and Mr. Harrison bore a valiant part. Marilla stood at the gate and watched the carriage out of sight down the long lane with its banks of goldenrod. Anne turned at its end to wave her last good-bye. She was gone—Green Gables was her home no more; Marilla's face looked very gray and old as she turned to the house which Anne had filled for fourteen years, and even in her absence, with light and life.

But Diana and her small fry, the Echo Lodge people and the Allans, had stayed to help the two old ladies over the loneliness of the first evening; and they contrived to have a quietly pleasant little supper time, sitting long around the table and chatting over all the details of the day. While they were sitting there Anne and Gilbert were alighting from the train at Glen St. Mary.

CHAPTER 5

THE HOME COMING

DR. DAVID BLYTHE had sent his horse and buggy to meet them, and the urchin who had brought it slipped away with a sympathetic grin, leaving them to the delight of driving alone to their new home through the radiant evening.

Anne never forgot the loveliness of the view that broke upon them when they had driven over the hill behind the village. Her new home could not yet be seen; but before her lay Four Winds Harbor like a great, shining mirror of rose and silver. Far down, she saw its entrance between the bar of sand dunes on one side and a steep, high, grim, red sandstone cliff on the other. Beyond the bar the sea, calm and austere, dreamed in the afterlight. The little fishing village, nestled in the cove where the sand-dunes met the harbor shore, looked like a great opal in the haze. The sky over them was like a jewelled cup from which the dusk was pouring; the air was crisp with the compelling tang of the sea, and the whole landscape was infused with the subtleties of a sea evening. A few dim sails drifted along the darkening, fir-clad harbor shores. A bell was ringing from the tower of a little white church on the far side; mellowly and dreamily sweet, the chime floated across the water blent with the moan of the sea. The great revolving light on the cliff at the channel flashed warm and golden against the clear northern sky, a trembling, quivering star of good hope. Far out along the horizon was the crinkled gray ribbon of a passing steamer's smoke.

"Oh, beautiful, beautiful," murmured Anne. "I shall love Four Winds, Gilbert. Where is our house?"

"We can't see it yet—the belt of birch running up from that little cove hides it. It's about two miles from Glen St. Mary, and there's another mile between it and the light-house. We won't have many neighbors, Anne. There's only one house near us and I don't know who lives in it. Shall you be lonely when I'm away?"

"Not with that light and that loveliness for company. Who lives in that house, Gilbert?"

"I don't know. It doesn't look—exactly—as if the occupants would be kindred spirits, Anne, does it?"

The house was a large, substantial affair, painted such a vivid green that the landscape seemed quite faded by contrast. There was an orchard behind it, and a nicely kept lawn before it, but, somehow, there was a certain bareness about it. Perhaps its neatness was responsible for this; the whole establishment, house, barns, orchard, garden, lawn and lane, was so starkly neat.

"It doesn't seem probable that anyone with that taste in paint could be *very* kindred," acknowledged Anne, "unless it were an accident—like our blue hall. I feel certain there are no children there, at least. It's even neater than the old Copp place on the Tory road, and I never expected to see anything neater than that."

They had not met anybody on the moist, red road that wound along the harbor shore. But just before they came to the belt of birch which hid their home, Anne saw a girl who was driving a flock of snow-white geese along the crest of a velvety green hill on the right. Great, scattered firs grew along it. Between their trunks one saw glimpses of yellow harvest fields, gleams of golden sand-hills, and bits of blue sea. The girl was tall and wore a dress of pale blue print. She walked with a certain springiness of step and erectness of bearing. She and her geese came out of the gate at the foot of the hill as Anne and Gilbert passed. She stood with her hand on the fastening of the gate, and looked steadily at them, with an expression that hardly attained to interest, but did not descend to curiosity. It seemed to Anne, for a fleeting moment, that there was even a veiled hint of hostility in it. But it was the girl's beauty which made Anne give a little gasp—a beauty so marked that it must have attracted attention anywhere. She was hatless, but heavy braids of burnished hair, the hue of ripe wheat, were twisted about her head like a coronet; her eyes were blue and star-like; her figure, in its plain print gown, was magnificent; and her lips were as crimson as the bunch of blood-red poppies she wore at her belt.

"Gilbert, who is the girl we have just passed?" asked Anne, in a low voice.

"I didn't notice any girl," said Gilbert, who had eyes only for his bride.

"She was standing by that gate—no, don't look back. She is still watching us. I never saw such a beautiful face."

"I don't remember seeing any very handsome girls while I was here. There are some pretty girls up at the Glen, but I hardly think they could be called beautiful."

"This girl is. You can't have seen her, or you would remember her. Nobody could forget her. I never saw such a face except in pictures. And her hair! It made me think of Browning's 'cord of gold' and 'gorgeous snake'!"

"Probably she's some visitor in Four Winds—likely some one from that big summer hotel over the harbor."

"She wore a white apron and she was driving geese."

"She might do that for amusement. Look, Anne—there's our house."

Anne looked and forgot for a time the girl with the splendid, resentful eyes. The first glimpse of her new home was a delight to eye and spirit—it looked so like a big, creamy seashell stranded on the harbor shore. The rows of tall Lombardy poplars down its lane stood out in stately, purple silhouette against the sky. Behind it, sheltering its garden from the too keen breath of sea winds, was a cloudy fir wood, in which the winds might make all kinds of weird and haunting music. Like all woods, it seemed to be holding and enfolding secrets in its recesses,—secrets whose charm is only to be won by entering in and patiently seeking. Outwardly, dark green arms keep them inviolate from curious or indifferent eyes.

The night winds were beginning their wild dances beyond the bar and the fishing hamlet across the harbor was gemmed with lights as Anne and Gilbert drove up the poplar lane. The door of the little house opened, and a warm glow of firelight flickered out into the dusk. Gilbert lifted Anne from the buggy and led her into the garden, through the little gate between the ruddy-tipped firs, up the trim, red path to the sandstone step.

"Welcome home," he whispered, and hand in hand they stepped over the threshold of their house of dreams.

CHAPTER 6

CAPTAIN JIM

"OLD DOCTOR DAVE" and "Mrs. Doctor Dave" had come down to the little house to greet the bride and groom. Doctor Dave was a big, jolly, white-whiskered old fellow, and Mrs. Doctor was a trim, rosy-cheeked, silver-haired little lady who took Anne at once to her heart, literally and figuratively.

"I'm so glad to see you, dear. You must be real tired. We've got a bite of supper ready, and Captain Jim brought up some trout for you. Captain Jim—where are you? Oh, he's slipped out to see to the horse, I suppose. Come upstairs and take your things off."

Anne looked about her with bright, appreciative eyes as she followed Mrs. Doctor Dave upstairs. She liked the appearance of her new home very much. It seemed to have the atmosphere of Green Gables and the flavor of her old traditions.

"I think I would have found Miss Elizabeth Russell a 'kindred spirit,' " she murmured when she was alone in her room. There were two windows in it; the dormer one looked out on the lower harbor and the sand-bar and the Four Winds light.

> *"A magic casement opening on the foam*
> *Of perilous seas in fairy lands forlorn,"*

quoted Anne softly. The gable window gave a view of a little harvest-hued valley through which a brook ran. Half a mile up the brook was the only house in sight—an old, rambling, gray one surrounded by huge willows through which its windows peered, like shy, seeking eyes, into the dusk. Anne wondered who lived there; they would be her nearest neighbors and she hoped they would be nice. She suddenly found herself thinking of the beautiful girl with the white geese.

"Gilbert thought she didn't belong here," mused Anne, "but I feel sure she does. There was something about her that made her part of the sea and the sky and the harbor. Four Winds is in her blood."

When Anne went downstairs Gilbert was standing before the fireplace talking to a stranger. Both turned as Anne entered.

"Anne, this is Captain Boyd. Captain Boyd, my wife."

It was the first time Gilbert had said "my wife" to anybody but Anne, and he narrowly escaped bursting with the pride of it. The old captain held out a sinewy hand to Anne; they smiled at each other and were friends from that moment. Kindred spirit flashed recognition to kindred spirit.

"I'm right down pleased to meet you, Mistress Blythe; and I hope you'll be as happy as the first bride was who came here. I can't wish you no better than *that*. But your husband doesn't introduce me jest exactly right. 'Captain Jim' is my week-a-day name and you might as well begin as you're sartain to end up—calling me that. You sartainly are a nice little bride, Mistress Blythe. Looking at you sorter makes me feel that I've jest been married myself."

Amid the laughter that followed Mrs. Doctor Dave urged Captain Jim to stay and have supper with them.

"Thank you kindly. 'Twill be a real treat, Mistress Doctor. I mostly has to eat my meals alone, with the reflection of my ugly old phiz in a looking-glass opposite for company. 'Tisn't often I have a chance to sit down with two such sweet, purty ladies."

Captain Jim's compliments may look very bald on paper, but he paid them with such a gracious, gentle deference of tone and look that the woman upon whom they were bestowed felt that she was being offered a queen's tribute in a kingly fashion.

Captain Jim was a high-souled, simple-minded old man, with eternal youth in his eyes and heart. He had a tall, rather ungainly figure, somewhat stooped, yet suggestive of great strength and endurance; a clean-shaven face deeply lined and bronzed; a thick mane of iron-gray hair falling quite to his shoulders, and a pair of remarkably blue, deep-set eyes, which sometimes twinkled and sometimes dreamed, and sometimes looked out seaward with a wistful quest in them, as of one seeking something precious and lost. Anne was to learn one day what it was for which Captain Jim looked.

It could not be denied that Captain Jim was a homely man. His spare jaws, rugged mouth, and square brow were not fashioned on the lines of beauty; and he had passed through many hardships and sorrows which had marked his body as well as his soul; but though at first sight Anne thought him plain she never thought anything more about it—the spirit shining through that rugged tenement beautified it so wholly.

They gathered gaily around the supper table. The hearth fire banished the chill of the September evening, but the window of the dining room was open and sea breezes entered at their own sweet will. The view was magnificent, taking in the harbor and the sweep of low, purple hills beyond. The table was heaped with Mrs. Doctor's delicacies but the *pièce de resistance* was undoubtedly the big platter of sea trout.

"Thought they'd be sorter tasty after travelling," said Captain Jim. "They're fresh as trout can be, Mistress Blythe. Two hours ago they were swimming in the Glen Pond."

"Who is attending to the light tonight, Captain Jim?" asked Doctor Dave.

"Nephew Alec. He understands it as well as I do. Well, now, I'm real glad you asked me to stay to supper. I'm proper hungry—didn't have much of a dinner today."

"I believe you half starve yourself most of the time down at that light," said Mrs. Doctor Dave severely. "You won't take the trouble to get up a decent meal."

"Oh, I do, Mistress Doctor, I do," protested Captain Jim. "Why, I live like a king gen'rally. Last night I was up to the Glen and took home two pounds of steak. I meant to have a spanking good dinner today."

"And what happened to the steak?" asked Mrs. Doctor Dave. "Did you lose it on the way home?"

"No." Captain Jim looked sheepish. "Just at bedtime a poor, ornery sort of dog came along and asked for a night's lodging. Guess he belonged to some of the fishermen 'long shore. I couldn't turn the poor cur out—he had a sore foot. So I shut him in the porch, with an old bag to lie on, and went to bed. But somehow I couldn't sleep. Come to think it over, I sorter remembered that the dog looked hungry."

"And you got up and gave him that steak—*all* that steak," said Mrs. Doctor Dave, with a kind of triumphant reproof.

"Well, there wasn't anything else *to* give him," said Captain Jim deprecatingly. "Nothing a dog'd care for, that is. I reckon he *was* hungry, for he made about two bites of it. I had a fine sleep the rest of the night but my dinner had to be sorter scanty—potatoes and point, as you might say. The dog, he lit out for home this morning. I reckon *he* weren't a vegetarian."

"The idea of starving yourself for a worthless dog!" sniffed Mrs. Doctor.

"You don't know but he may be worth a lot to somebody," protested Captain Jim. "He didn't *look* of much account, but you can't go by looks in jedging a dog. Like meself, he might be a real beauty inside. The First Mate didn't approve of him, I'll allow. His language was right down forcible. But the First Mate is prejudiced. No use in taking a cat's opinion of a dog. 'Tennyrate, I lost my dinner, so this nice spread in this dee-lightful company is real pleasant. It's a great thing to have good neighbors."

"Who lives in the house among the willows up the brook?" asked Anne.

"Mrs. Dick Moore," said Captain Jim—"and her husband," he added, as if by way of an afterthought.

Anne smiled, and deduced a mental picture of Mrs. Dick Moore from Captain Jim's way of putting it; evidently a second Mrs. Rachel Lynde.

"You haven't many neighbors, Mistress Blythe," Captain Jim went on. "This side of the harbor is mighty thinly settled. Most of the land belongs to Mr. Howard up yander past the Glen, and he rents it out for pasture. The other side of the harbor, now, is thick with folks—'specially MacAllisters. There's a whole colony of Mac-Allisters—you can't throw a stone but you hit one. I was talking to old Leon Blacquiere the other day. He's been working on the harbor all summer. 'Dey're nearly all MacAllisters over thar,' he told me. 'Dare's Neil MacAllister and Sandy MacAllister and William Mac-Allister and Alec MacAllister and Angus MacAllister—and I believe dare's de Devil MacAllister.'"

"There are nearly as many Elliotts and Crawfords," said Doctor Dave, after the laughter had subsided. "You know, Gilbert, we folk on this side of Four Winds have an old saying—'From the conceit of the Elliotts, the pride of the MacAllisters, and the vainglory of the Crawfords, good Lord deliver us.'"

"There's a plenty of fine people among them, though," said Captain Jim. "I sailed with William Crawford for many a year, and for courage and endurance and truth that man hadn't an equal. They've got brains over on that side of Four Winds. Mebbe that's why this side is sorter inclined to pick on 'em. Strange, ain't it, how folks seem to resent anyone being born a mite cleverer than they be.''

Doctor Dave, who had a forty years' feud with the over-harbor people, laughed and subsided.

''Who lives in that brilliant emerald house about half a mile up the road?'' asked Gilbert.

Captain Jim smiled delightedly.

''Miss Cornelia Bryant. She'll likely be over to see you soon, seeing you're Presbyterians. If you were Methodists she wouldn't come at all. Cornelia has a holy horror of Methodists.''

''She's quite a character,'' chuckled Doctor Dave. ''A most inveterate man-hater!''

''Sour grapes?'' queried Gilbert, laughing.

''No, 'tisn't sour grapes,'' answered Captain Jim seriously. ''Cornelia could have had her pick when she was young. Even yet she's only to say the word to see the old widowers jump. She jest seems to have been born with a sort of chronic spite agin men and Methodists. She's got the bitterest tongue and the kindest heart in Four Winds. Wherever there's any trouble, that woman is there, doing everything to help in the tenderest way. She never says a harsh word about another woman, and if she likes to card us poor scala-wags of men down I reckon our tough old hides can stand it.''

''She always speaks well of you, Captain Jim,'' said Mrs. Doctor.

''Yes, I'm afraid so. I don't half like it. It makes me feel as if there must be something sorter unnateral about me.''

CHAPTER 7

THE SCHOOLMASTER'S BRIDE

''WHO WAS the first bride who came to this house, Captain Jim?'' Anne asked, as they sat around the fireplace after supper.

''Was she a part of the story I've heard was connected with this house?'' asked Gilbert. ''Somebody told me you could tell it, Captain Jim.''

"Well, yes, I know it. I reckon I'm the only person living in Four Winds now that can remember the schoolmaster's bride as she was when she come to the Island. She's been dead this thirty year, but she was one of them women you never forget."

"Tell us the story," pleaded Anne. "I want to find out all about the women who have lived in this house before me."

"Well, there's jest been three—Elizabeth Russell, and Mrs. Ned Russell, and the schoolmaster's bride. Elizabeth Russell was a nice, clever little critter, and Mrs. Ned was a nice woman, too. But they weren't ever like the schoolmaster's bride.

"The schoolmaster's name was John Selwyn. He came out from the Old Country to teach school at the Glen when I was a boy of sixteen. He wasn't much like the usual run of derelicts who used to come out to P.E.I. to teach school in them days. Most of them were clever, drunken critters who taught the children the three R's when they were sober, and lambasted them when they wasn't. But John Selwyn was a fine, handsome young fellow. He boarded at my father's, and he and me were cronies, though he was ten years older'n me. We read and walked and talked a heap together. He knew about all the poetry that was ever written, I reckon, and he used to quote it to me along shore in the evenings. Dad thought it an awful waste of time, but he sorter endured it, hoping it'd put me off the notion of going to sea. Well, nothing could do *that*—mother come of a race of sea-going folk and it was born in me. But I loved to hear John read and recite. It's almost sixty years ago, but I could repeat yards of poetry I learned from him. Nearly sixty years!"

Captain Jim was silent for a space, gazing into the glowing fire in a quest of the bygones. Then, with a sigh, he resumed his story.

"I remember one spring evening I met him on the sand-hills. He looked sorter uplifted—jest like you did, Dr. Blythe, when you brought Mistress Blythe in tonight. I thought of him the minute I seen you. And he told me that he had a sweetheart back home and that she was coming out to him. I wasn't more'n half pleased, ornery young lump of selfishness that I was; I thought he wouldn't be as much my friend after she came. But I'd enough decency not to let him see it. He told me all about her. Her name was Persis Leigh, and she would have come out with him if it hadn't been for her old uncle. He was sick, and he'd looked after her when her parents died and she wouldn't leave him. And now he was dead and she was coming out to marry John Selwyn. 'Twasn't no easy journey for a woman in them days. There weren't no steamers, you must ricollect.

"'When do you expect her?' says I.

" 'She sails on the *Royal William,* the 20th of June,' says he, 'and so she should be here by mid-July. I must set Carpenter Johnson to building me a home for her. Her letter come today. I know before I opened it that it had good news for me. I saw her a few nights ago.'

"I didn't understand him, and then he explained—though I didn't understand *that* much better. He said he had a gift—or a curse. Them was his words, Mistress Blythe—a gift or a curse. He didn't know which it was. He said a great-great-grandmother of his had had it, and they burned her for a witch on account of it. He said queer spells—trances, I think was the name he give 'em—come over him now and again. Are there such things, Doctor?"

"There are people who are certainly subject to trances," answered Gilbert. "The matter is more in the line of psychical research than medical. What were the trances of this John Selwyn like?"

"Like dreams," said the old Doctor skeptically.

"He said he could see things in them," said Captain Jim slowly. "Mind you, I'm telling you jest what *he* said—things that were happening—things that were *going* to happen. He said they were sometimes a comfort to him and sometimes a horror. Four nights before this he'd been in one—went into it while he was sitting looking at the fire. And he saw an old room he knew well in England, and Persis Leigh in it, holding out her hands to him and looking glad and happy. So he knew he was going to hear good news of her."

"A dream—a dream," scoffed the old Doctor.

"Likely—likely," conceded Captain Jim. "That's what *I* said to him at the time. It was a vast more comfortable to think so. I didn't like the idea of him seeing things like that—it was real uncanny.

" 'No,' says he, 'I didn't dream it. But we won't talk of this again. You won't be so much my friend if you think much about it.'

"I told him nothing could make me any less his friend. But he jest shook his head and says, says he:

" 'Lad, I know. I've lost friends before because of this. I don't blame them. There are times when I feel hardly friendly to myself because of it. Such a power has a bit of divinity in it—whether of a good or an evil divinity who shall say? And we mortals all shrink from too close contact with God or devil.'

"Them was his words. I remember them as if 'twas yesterday, though I didn't know jest what he meant. What do you s'pose he *did* mean, doctor?"

"I doubt if he knew what he meant himself," said Doctor Dave testily.

"I think I understand," whispered Anne. She was listening in her old attitude of clasped lips and shining eyes. Captain Jim treated himself to an admiring smile before he went on with his story.

"Well, purty soon all the Glen and Four Winds people knew the schoolmaster's bride was coming, and they were all glad because they thought so much of him. And everybody took an interest in his new house—*this* house. He picked this site for it, because you could see the harbor and hear the sea from it. He made the garden out there for his bride, but he didn't plant the Lombardies. Mrs. Ned Russell planted *them*. But there's a double row of rose-bushes in the garden that the little girls who went to the Glen school set out there for the schoolmaster's bride. He said they were pink for her cheeks and white for her brow and red for her lips. He'd quoted poetry so much that he sorter got into the habit of talking it, too, I reckon.

"Almost everybody sent him some little present to help out the furnishing of the house. When the Russells came into it they were well-to-do and furnished it real handsome, as you can see; but the first furniture that went into it was plain enough. This little house was rich in love, though. The women sent in quilts and tablecloths and towels, and one man made a chest for her, and another a table and so on. Even blind old Aunt Margaret Boyd wove a little basket for her out of the sweet-scented sand-hill grass. The schoolmaster's wife used it for years to keep her handkerchiefs in.

"Well, at last everything was ready—even to the logs in the big fireplace ready for lighting. 'Twasn't exactly *this* fireplace, though 'twas in the same place. Miss Elizabeth had this put in when she made the house over fifteen years ago. It was a big, old-fashioned fireplace where you could have roasted an ox. Many's the time I've sat here and spun yarns, same's I'm doing tonight."

Again there was a silence, while Captain Jim kept a passing tryst with visitants Anne and Gilbert could not see—the folks who had sat with him around that fireplace in the vanished years, with mirth and bridal joy shining in eyes long since closed forever under churchyard sod or heaving leagues of sea. Here on olden nights children had tossed laughter lightly to and fro. Here on winter evenings friends had gathered. Dance and music and jest had been here. Here youths and maidens had dreamed. For Captain Jim the little house was tenanted with shapes entreating remembrance.

"It was the first of July when the house was finished. The schoolmaster began to count the days then. We used to see him walking along the shore, and we'd say to each other, 'She'll soon be with him now.'

"She was expected the middle of July, but she didn't come then.

Nobody felt anxious. Vessels were often delayed for days and mebbe weeks. The *Royal William* was a week overdue—and then two—and then three. And at last we began to be frightened, and it got worse and worse. Fin'lly I couldn't bear to look into John Selwyn's eyes. D'ye know, Mistress Blythe''—Captain Jim lowered his voice—''I used to think that they looked just like what his old great-great-grandmother's must have been when they were burning her to death. He never said much but he taught school like a man in a dream and then hurried to the shore. Many a night he walked there from dark to dawn. People said he was losing his mind. Everybody had given up hope—the *Royal William* was eight weeks overdue. It was the middle of September and the schoolmaster's bride hadn't come—never would come, we thought.

''There was a big storm then that lasted three days, and on the evening after it died away I went to the shore. I found the schoolmaster there, leaning with his arms folded against a big rock, gazing out to sea.

''I spoke to him but he didn't answer. His eyes seemed to be looking at something I couldn't see. His face was set, like a dead man's.

'''John—John,' I called out—jest like that—jest like a frightened child, 'wake up—wake up.'

''That strange, awful look seemed to sorter fade out of his eyes. He turned his head and looked at me. I've never forgot his face—never will forget it till I ships for my last voyage.

'''All is well, lad,' he says. 'I've seen the *Royal William* coming around East Point. She will be here by dawn. Tomorrow night I shall sit with my bride by my own hearth-fire.'

''Do you think he did see it?'' demanded Captain Jim abruptly.

''God knows,'' said Gilbert softly. ''Great love and great pain might compass we know not what marvels.''

''I am sure he did see it,'' said Anne earnestly.

''Fol-de-rol,'' said Doctor Dave, but he spoke with less conviction than usual.

''Because, you know,'' said Captain Jim solemnly, ''the *Royal William* came into Four Winds Harbor at daylight the next morning. Every soul in the Glen and along the shore was at the old wharf to meet her. The schoolmaster had been watching there all night. How we cheered as she sailed up the channel.''

Captain Jim's eyes were shining. They were looking at the Four

Winds Harbor of sixty years agone, with a battered old ship sailing through the sunrise splendor.

"And Persis Leigh was on board?" asked Anne.

"Yes—her and the captain's wife. They'd had an awful passage—storm after storm—and their provisions give out, too. But there they were at last. When Persis Leigh stepped onto the old wharf John Selwyn took her in his arms—and folks stopped cheering and begun to cry. I cried myself, though 'twas years, mind you, afore I'd admit it. Ain't it funny how ashamed boys are of tears?"

"Was Persis Leigh beautiful?" asked Anne.

"Well, I don't know that you'd call her beautiful exactly—I—don't—know," said Captain Jim slowly. "Somehow, you never got so far along as to wonder if she was handsome or not. It jest didn't matter. There was something so sweet and winsome about her that you had to love her, that was all. But she was pleasant to look at—big, clear, hazel eyes and heaps of glossy brown hair, and an English skin. John and her were married at our house that night at early candle-lighting; everybody from far and near was there to see it and we all brought them down here afterwards. Mistress Selwyn lighted the fire, and we went away and left them sitting here, jest as John had seen in that vision of his. A strange thing—a strange thing! But I've seen a turrible lot of strange things in my time."

Captain Jim shook his head sagely.

"It's a dear story," said Anne, feeling that for once she had got enough romance to satisfy her. "How long did they live here?"

"Fifteen years. I ran off to sea soon after they were married, like the young scalawag I was. But every time I come back from a voyage I'd head for here, even before I went home, and tell Mistress Selwyn all about it. Fifteen happy years! They had a sort of talent for happiness, them two. Some folks are like that, if you've noticed. They *couldn't* be unhappy for long, no matter what happened. They quarrelled once or twice, for they was both high-sperrited. But Mistress Selwyn says to me once, says she, laughing in that pretty way of hers, 'I felt dreadful when John and I quarrelled, but underneath it all I was very happy because I had such a nice husband to quarrel with and make it up with.' Then they moved to Charlottetown, and Ned Russell bought this house and brought his bride here. They were a gay young pair, as I remember them. Miss Elizabeth Russell was Alec's sister. She came to live with them a year or so later, and she was a creature of mirth, too. The walls of this house must be sorter *soaked* with laughing and good times. You're the third bride I've seen come here, Mistress Blythe—and the handsomest.''

Captain Jim contrived to give his sunflower compliment the delicacy of a violet, and Anne wore it proudly. She was looking her best that night, with the bridal rose on her cheeks and the love-light in her eyes; even gruff old Doctor Dave gave her an approving glance, and told his wife, as they drove home together, that that red-headed wife of the boy's was something of a beauty.

''I must be getting back to the light,'' announced Captain Jim. ''I've enj'yed this evening something tremenjus.''

''You must come often to see us,'' said Anne.

''I wonder if you'd give that invitation if you knew how likely I'll be to accept it,'' Captain Jim remarked whimsically.

''Which is another way of saying you wonder if I mean it,'' smiled Anne. ''I do, 'cross my heart,' as we used to say at school.''

''Then I'll come. You're likely to be pestered with me at any hour. And I'll be proud to have you drop down and visit me now and then, too. Gin'rally I haven't anyone to talk to but the First Mate, bless his sociable heart. He's a mighty good listener, and has forgot more'n any MacAllister of them all ever knew, but he isn't much of a conversationalist. You're young and I'm old, but our souls are about the same age, I reckon. We both belong to the race that knows Joseph, as Cornelia Bryant would say.''

''The race that knows Joseph?'' puzzled Anne.

''Yes. Cornelia divides all the folks in the world into two kinds—the race that knows Joseph and the race that don't. If a person sorter sees eye to eye with you, and has pretty much the same ideas about things, and the same taste in jokes—why, then he belongs to the race that knows Joseph.''

''Oh, I understand,'' exclaimed Anne, light breaking in upon her. ''It's what I used to call—and still call in quotation marks—'kindred spirits.' ''

''Jest so—jest so,'' agreed Captain Jim. ''We're *it*, whatever it is. When you come in tonight, Mistress Blythe, I says to myself, says I, 'Yes, she's of the race that knows Joseph.' And mighty glad I was, for if it wasn't so we couldn't have had any real satisfaction in each other's company. The race that knows Joseph is the salt of the airth, I reckon.''

The moon had just risen when Anne and Gilbert went to the door with their guests. Four Winds Harbor was beginning to be a thing of dream and glamour and enchantment—a spellbound haven where no tempest might ever ravin. The Lombardies down the lane, tall and sombre as the priestly forms of some mystic band, were tipped with silver.

"Always liked Lombardies," said Captain Jim, waving a long arm at them. "They're the trees of princesses. They're out of fashion now. Folks complain that they die at the top and get ragged-looking. So they do—so they do, if you don't risk your neck every spring climbing up a light ladder to trim them out. I always did it for Miss Elizabeth, so her Lombardies never got out-at-elbows. She was especially fond of them. She liked their dignity and stand-offishness. *They* don't hobnob with every Tom, Dick and Harry. If it's maples for company, Mistress Blythe, it's Lombardies for society."

"What a beautiful night," said Mrs. Doctor Dave, as she climbed into the Doctor's buggy.

"Most nights are beautiful," said Captain Jim. "But I 'low that moonlight over Four Winds makes me sorter wonder what's left for heaven. The moon's a great friend of mine, Mistress Blythe. I've loved her ever since I can remember. When I was a little chap of eight I fell asleep in the garden one evening and wasn't missed. I woke up along in the night and I was most scared to death. What shadows and queer noises there was! I dursn't move. Jest crouched there quaking, poor small mite. Seemed 'sif there weren't anyone in the world but meself and it was mighty big. Then all at once I saw the moon looking down at me through the apple boughs, jest like an old friend. I was comforted right off. Got up and walked to the house as brave as a lion, looking at her. Many's the night I've watched her from the deck of my vessel, on seas far away from here. Why don't you folks tell me to take in the slack of my jaw and go home?"

The laughter of the goodnights died away. Anne and Gilbert walked hand in hand around their garden. The brook that ran across the corner dimpled pellucidly in the shadows of the birches. The poppies along its banks were like shallow cups of moonlight. Flowers that had been planted by the hands of the schoolmaster's bride flung their sweetness on the shadowy air, like the beauty and blessing of sacred yesterdays. Anne paused in the gloom to gather a spray.

"I love to smell flowers in the dark," she said. "You get hold of their soul then. Oh, Gilbert, this little house is all I've dreamed it. And I'm so glad that we are not the first who have kept bridal tryst here!"

CHAPTER 8

MISS CORNELIA BRYANT COMES TO CALL

THAT SEPTEMBER was a month of golden mists and purple hazes at Four Winds Harbor—a month of sun-steeped days and of nights that were swimming in moonlight, or pulsating with stars. No storm marred it, no rough wind blew. Anne and Gilbert put their nest in order, rambled on the shores, sailed on the harbor, drove about Four Winds and the Glen, or through the ferny, sequestered roads of the woods around the harbor head; in short, had such a honeymoon as any lovers in the world might have envied them.

"If life were to stop short just now it would still have been richly worth while, just for the sake of these past four weeks, wouldn't it?" said Anne. "I don't suppose we will ever have four such perfect weeks again—but we've *had* them. Everything—wind, weather, folks, house of dreams—has conspired to make our honeymoon delightful. There hasn't even been a rainy day since we came here."

"And we haven't quarrelled once," teased Gilbert.

"Well, 'that's a pleasure all the greater for being deferred,'" quoted Anne. "I'm so glad we decided to spend our honeymoon here. Our memories of it will always belong here, in our house of dreams, instead of being scattered about in strange places."

There was a certain tang of romance and adventure in the atmosphere of their new home which Anne had never found in Avonlea. There, although she had lived in sight of the sea, it had not entered intimately into her life. In Four Winds it surrounded her and called to her constantly. From every window of her new home she saw some varying aspect of it. Its haunting murmur was ever in her ears. Veseels sailed up the harbor every day to the wharf at the Glen, or sailed out again through the sunset, bound for ports that might be half way round the globe. Fishing boats went white-winged down the channel in the mornings, and returned laden in the evenings. Sailors and fisher-folk travelled the red, winding harbor roads, light-hearted and content. There was always a certain sense of things going to happen—of adventures and farings-forth. The ways of Four Winds were less staid and settled and grooved than those of Avonlea; winds of change blew over them; the sea called ever to the dwellers on shore, and even those who might not answer its call felt the thrill and unrest and mystery and possibilities of it.

"I understand now why some men must go to sea," said Anne. "That desire which comes to us all at times—'to sail beyond the bourne of sunset'—must be very imperious when it is born in you. I don't wonder Captain Jim ran away because of it. I never see a ship sailing out of the channel, or a gull soaring over the sand-bar, without wishing I were on board the ship or had wings, not like a dove 'to fly away and be at rest,' but like a gull, to sweep out into the very heart of a storm."

"You'll stay right here with me, Anne-girl," said Gilbert lazily. "I won't have you flying away from me into the hearts of storms."

They were sitting on their red sand-stone doorstep in the late afternoon. Great tranquillities were all about them in land and sea and sky. Silvery gulls were soaring over them. The horizons were laced with long trails of frail, pinkish clouds. The hushed air was threaded with a murmurous refrain of minstrel winds and waves. Pale asters were blowing in the sere and misty meadows between them and the harbor.

"Doctors who have to be up all night waiting on sick folk don't feel very adventurous, I suppose," Anne said indulgently. "If you had had a good sleep last night, Gilbert, you'd be as ready as I am for a flight of imagination."

"I did good work last night, Anne," said Gilbert quietly. "Under God, I saved a life. This is the first time I could ever really claim that. In other cases I may have helped; but, Anne, if I had not stayed at Allonby's last night and fought death hand to hand, that woman would have died before morning. I tried an experiment that was certainly never tried in Four Winds before. I doubt if it was ever tried anywhere before outside of a hospital. It was a new thing in Kingsport hospital last winter. I could never have dared try it here if I had not been absolutely certain that there was no other chance. I risked it—and it succeeded. As a result, a good wife and mother is saved for long years of happiness and usefulness. As I drove home this morning, while the sun was rising over the harbor, I thanked God that I had chosen the profession I did. I had fought a good fight and won—think of it, Anne, *won,* against the Great Destroyer. It's what I dreamed of doing long ago when we talked together of what we wanted to do in life. That dream of mine came true this morning."

"Was that the only one of your dreams that has come true?" asked Anne, who knew perfectly well what the substance of his answer would be, but wanted to hear it again.

"*You* know, Anne-girl," said Gilbert, smiling into her eyes. At that moment there were certainly two perfectly happy people sitting on the doorstep of a little white house on the Four Winds Harbor shore.

Presently Gilbert said, with a change of tone, "Do I or do I not see a full-rigged ship sailing up our lane?"

Anne looked and sprang up.

"That must be either Miss Cornelia Bryant or Mrs. Moore coming to call," she said.

"I'm going into the office, and if it is Miss Cornelia I warn you that I'll eavesdrop," said Gilbert. "From all I've heard regarding Miss Cornelia I conclude that her conversation will not be dull, to say the least."

"It may be Mrs. Moore."

"I don't think Mrs. Moore is built on those lines. I saw her working in her garden the other day, and, though I was too far away to see clearly, I thought she was rather slender. She doesn't seem very socially inclined when she has never called on you yet, although she's your nearest neighbor."

"She can't be like Mrs. Lynde, after all, or curiosity would have brought her," said Anne. "This caller is, I think, Miss Cornelia."

Miss Cornelia it was; moreover, Miss Cornelia had not come to make any brief and fashionable wedding call. She had her work under her arm in a substantial parcel, and when Anne asked her to stay she promptly took off her capacious sun-hat, which had been held on her head, despite irreverent September breezes, by a tight elastic band under her hard little knob of fair hair. No hat pins for Miss Cornelia, an it please ye! Elastic bands had been good enough for her mother and they were good enough for *her*. She had a fresh, round, pink-and-white face, and jolly brown eyes. She did not look in the least like the traditional old maid, and there was something in her expression which won Anne instantly. With her old instinctive quickness to discern kindred spirits she knew she was going to like Miss Cornelia, in spite of uncertain oddities of opinion, and certain oddities of attire.

Nobody but Miss Cornelia would have come to make a call arrayed in a striped blue-and-white apron and a wrapper of chocolate print, with a design of huge, pink roses scattered over it. And nobody but Miss Cornelia could have looked dignified and suitably garbed in it. Had Miss Cornelia been entering a palace to call on a prince's bride, she would have been just as dignified and just as wholly mistress of the situation. She would have trailed her rose-spattered flounce over the marble floors just as unconcernedly, and she would have proceeded just as calmly to disabuse the mind of the princess of any idea that the possession of a mere man, be he prince or peasant, was anything to brag of.

"I've brought my work, Mrs. Blythe, dearie," she remarked, unrolling some dainty material. "I'm in a hurry to get this done, and there isn't any time to lose."

Anne looked in some surprise at the white garment spread over Miss Cornelia's ample lap. It was certainly a baby's dress, and it was most beautifully made, with tiny frills and tucks. Miss Cornelia adjusted her glasses and fell to embroidering with exquisite stitches.

"This is for Mrs. Fred Proctor up at the Glen," she announced. "She's expecting her eighth baby any day now, and not a stitch has she ready for it. The other seven have wore out all she made for the first, and she's never had time or strength or spirit to make any more. That woman is a martyr, Mrs. Blythe, believe *me*. When she married Fred Proctor *I* knew how it would turn out. He was one of your wicked, fascinating men. After he got married he left off being fascinating and just kept on being wicked. He drinks and he neglects his family. Isn't that like a man? I don't know how Mrs. Proctor would ever keep her children decently clothed if her neighbors didn't help her out."

As Anne was afterwards to learn, Miss Cornelia was the only neighbor who troubled herself much about the decency of the young Proctors.

"When I heard this eighth baby was coming I decided to make some things for it," Miss Cornelia went on. "This is the last and I want to finish it today."

"It's certainly very pretty," said Anne. "I'll get my sewing and we'll have a little thimble party of two. You are a beautiful sewer, Miss Bryant."

"Yes, I'm the best sewer in these parts," said Miss Cornelia in a matter-of-fact tone. "I ought to be! Lord, I've done more of it than if I'd had a hundred children of my own, believe *me!* I s'pose I'm a fool, to be putting hand embroidery on this dress for an eighth baby. But, Lord, Mrs. Blythe, dearie, it isn't to blame for being the eighth, and I kind of wished it to have one real pretty dress, just as if it *was* wanted. Nobody's wanting the poor mite—so I put some extra fuss on its little things just on that account."

"Any baby might be proud of that dress," said Anne, feeling still more strongly that she was going to like Miss Cornelia.

"I s'pose you've been thinking I was never coming to call on you," resumed Miss Cornelia. "But this is harvest month, you know, and I've been busy—and a lot of extra hands hanging round, eating more'n they work, just like the men. I'd have come yesterday, but I went to Mrs. Roderick MacAllister's funeral. At first I thought my head was aching so badly I couldn't enjoy myself if I did go. But she was a hundred years old, and I'd always promised myself that I'd go to her funeral."

"Was it a successful function?" asked Anne, noticing that the office door was ajar.

"What's that? Oh, yes, it was a tremendous funeral. She had a very large connection. There was over one hundred and twenty carriages in the procession. There was one or two funny things happened. I thought that die I would to see old Joe Bradshaw, who is an infidel and never darkens the door of a church, singing 'Safe in the Arms of Jesus' with great gusto and fervor. He glories in singing—that's why he never misses a funeral. Poor Mrs. Bradshaw didn't look much like singing—all wore out slaving. Old Joe starts out once in a while to buy her a present and brings home some new kind of farm machinery. Isn't that like a man? But what else would you expect of a man who never goes to church, even a Methodist one? I was real thankful to see you and the young Doctor in the Presbyterian church your first Sunday. No doctor for me who isn't a Presbyterian."

"We were in the Methodist church last Sunday evening," said Anne wickedly.

"Oh, I s'pose Dr. Blythe has to go to the Methodist church once in a while or he wouldn't get the Methodist practice."

"We liked the sermon very much," declared Anne boldly. "And I thought the Methodist minster's prayer was one of the most beautiful I ever heard."

"Oh, I've no doubt he can pray. I never heard anyone make more beautiful prayers than old Simon Bentley, who was always drunk, or hoping to be, and the drunker he was the better he prayed."

"The Methodist minister is very fine looking," said Anne, for the benefit of the office door.

"Yes, he's quite ornamental," agreed Miss Cornelia. "Oh, and *very* ladylike. And he thinks that every girl who looks at him falls in love with him—as if a Methodist minister, wandering about like any Jew, was such a prize! If you and the young doctor take *my* advice, you won't have much to do with the Methodists. My motto is—if you *are* a Presbyterian, *be* a Presbyterian."

"Don't you think that Methodists go to heaven as well as Presbyterians?" asked Anne smilelessly.

"That isn't for *us* to decide. It's in higher hands than ours," said Miss Cornelia solemnly. "But I ain't going to associate with them on earth whatever I may have to do in heaven. *This* Methodist minister isn't married. The last one they had was, and his wife was the silliest, flightiest little thing I ever saw. I told her husband once that he should have waited till she was grown up before he married her. He said he wanted to have the training of her. Wasn't that like a man?"

"It's rather hard to decide just when people *are* grown up," laughed Anne.

"That's a true word, dearie. Some are grown up when they're born, and others ain't grown up when they're eighty, believe *me*. That same Mrs. Roderick I was speaking of never grew up. She was as foolish when she was a hundred as when she was ten."

"Perhaps that was why she lived so long," suggested Anne.

"Maybe 'twas. *I*'d rather live fifty sensible years than a hundred foolish ones."

"But just think what a dull world it would be if everyone was sensible," pleaded Anne.

Miss Cornelia disdained any skirmish of flippant epigram.

"Mrs. Roderick was a Milgrave, and the Milgraves never had much sense. Her nephew, Ebenezer Milgrave, used to be insane for years. He believed he was dead and used to rage at his wife because she wouldn't bury him. *I*'d a-done it."

Miss Cornelia looked so grimly determined that Anne could almost see her with a spade in her hand.

"Don't you know *any* good husbands, Miss Bryant?"

"Oh, yes, lots of them—over yonder," said Miss Cornelia, waving her hand through the open window towards the little graveyard of the church across the harbor.

"But living—going about in the flesh?" persisted Anne.

"Oh, there's a few, just to show that with God all things are possible," acknowledged Miss Cornelia reluctantly. "I don't deny that an odd man here and there, if he's caught young and trained up proper, and if his mother has spanked him well beforehand, may turn out a decent being. *Your* husband, now, isn't so bad, as men go, from all I hear. I s'pose"—Miss Cornelia looked sharply at Anne over her glasses—"you think there's nobody like him in the world."

"There isn't," said Anne promptly.

"Ah, well, I heard another bride say that once," sighed Miss

Cornelia. "Jennie Dean thought when she married that there wasn't anybody like *her* husband in the world. And she was right—there wasn't! And a good thing, too, believe *me!* He led her an awful life—and he was courting his second wife while Jennie was dying. Wasn't that like a man? However, I hope *your* confidence will be better justified, dearie. The young doctor is taking real well. I was afraid at first he mightn't, for folks hereabouts have always thought old Doctor Dave the only doctor in the world. Doctor Dave hadn't much tact, to be sure—he was always talking of ropes in houses where someone had hanged himself. But folks forgot their hurt feelings when they had a pain in their stomachs. If he'd been a minister instead of a doctor they'd never have forgiven him. Soul-ache doesn't worry folks near as much as stomach-ache. Seeing as we're both Presbyterians and no Methodists around, will you tell me your candid opinion of *our* minister?"

"Why—really—I—well," hesitated Anne.

Miss Cornelia nodded.

"Exactly. I agree with you, dearie. We made a mistake when we called *him*. His face just looks like one of those long, narrow stones in the graveyard, doesn't it? 'Sacred to the memory' ought to be written on his forehead. I shall never forget the first sermon he preached after he came. It was on the subject of everyone doing what they were best fitted for—a very good subject, of course; but such illustrations as he used! He said, 'If you had a cow and an apple tree, and if you tied the apple tree in your stable and planted the cow in your orchard, with her legs up, how much milk would you get from the apple tree, or how many apples from the cow?' Did you ever hear the like in your born days, dearie? I was so thankful there were no Methodists there that day—they'd never have been done hooting over it. But what I dislike most in him is his habit of agreeing with everybody, no matter what is said. If you said to him, 'You're a scoundrel,' he'd say, with that smooth smile of his, 'Yes, that's so.' A minister should have more backbone. The long and the short of it is, I consider him a reverend jackass. But, of course, this is just between you and me. When there are Methodists in hearing I praise him to the skies. Some folks think his wife dresses too gay, but *I* say when she has to live with a face like that she needs something to cheer her up. You'll never hear *me* condemning a woman for her dress. I'm only too thankful when her husband isn't too mean and miserly to allow it. Not that I bother much with dress myself. Women just dress to please the men, and I'd never stoop to *that*. I have had a real placid, comfortable life, dearie, and it's just because I never cared a cent what the men thought.''

"Why do you hate the men so, Miss Bryant?''

"Lord, dearie, I don't hate them. They aren't worth it. I just sort of despise them. I think I'll like *your* husband if he keeps on as he has begun. But apart from him about the only men in the world I've much use for are the old doctor and Captain Jim.''

"Captain Jim is certainly splendid,'' agreed Anne cordially.

"Captain Jim is a good man, but he's kind of vexing in one way. You *can't* make him mad. I've tried for twenty years and he just keeps on being placid. It does sort of rile me. And I s'pose the woman he should have married got a man who went into tantrums twice a day.''

"Who was she?''

"Oh, I don't know, dearie. I never remember of Captain Jim making up to anybody. He was edging on old as far as my memory goes. He's seventy-six, you know. I never heard any reason for his staying a bachelor, but there must be one, believe *me*. He sailed all his life till five years ago, and there's no corner of the earth he hasn't poked his nose into. He and Elizabeth Russell were great cronies, all their lives, but they never had any notion of sweet-hearting. Elizabeth never married, though she had plenty of chances. She was a great beauty when she was young. The year the Prince of Wales came to the Island she was visiting her uncle in Charlottetown and he was a Government official, and so she got invited to the great ball. She was the prettiest girl there, and the Prince danced with her, and all the other women he didn't dance with were furious about it, because their social standing was higher than hers and they said he shouldn't have passed them over. Elizabeth was always very proud of that dance. Mean folks said that was why she never married—she couldn't put up with an ordinary man after dancing with a prince. But that wasn't so. She told me the reason once—it was because she had such a temper that she was afraid she couldn't live peaceably with any man. She *had* an awful temper—she used to have to go upstairs and bite pieces out of her bureau to keep it down by times. But I told her that wasn't any reason for not marrying if she wanted to. There's no reason why we should let the men have a monopoly of temper, is there, Mrs. Blythe, dearie?''

"I've a bit of temper myself,'' sighed Anne.

"It's well you have, dearie. You won't be half so likely to be trodden on, believe *me!* My, how that golden glow of yours is blooming! Your garden looks fine. Poor Elizabeth always took such care of it.''

"I love it," said Anne. "I'm glad it's so full of old-fashioned flowers. Speaking of gardening, we want to get a man to dig up that little lot beyond the fir grove and set it out with strawberry plants for us. Gilbert is so busy he will never get time for it this fall. Do you know anyone we can get?''

"Well, Henry Hammond up at the Glen goes out doing jobs like that. He'll do, maybe. He's always a heap more interested in his wages than in his work, just like a man, and he's so slow in the uptake that he stands still for five minutes before it dawns on him that he's stopped. His father threw a stump at him when he was small. Nice gentle missile, wasn't it? So like a man! Course, the boy never got over it. But he's the only one I can recommend at all. He painted my house for me last spring. It looks real nice now, don't you think?''

Anne was saved by the clock striking five.

"Lord, is it that late?" exclaimed Miss Cornelia. "How time does slip by when you're enjoying yourself! Well, I must betake myself home.''

"No, indeed! You are going to stay and have tea with us," said Anne eagerly.

"Are you asking me because you think you ought to, or because you really want to?'' demanded Miss Cornelia.

"Because I really want to.''

"Then I'll stay. *You* belong to the race that knows Joseph.''

"I know we are going to be friends," said Anne, with the smile that only they of the household of faith ever saw.

"Yes, we are, dearie. Thank goodness, we can choose our friends. We have to take our relatives as they are, and be thankful if there are no penitentiary birds among them. Not that I've many— none nearer than second cousins. I'm a kind of lonely soul, Mrs. Blythe.''

There was a wistful note in Miss Cornelia's voice.

"I wish you would call me Anne," exclaimed Anne impulsively. "It would seem more *homey.* Everyone in Four Winds, except my husband, calls me Mrs. Blythe, and it makes me feel like a stranger. Do you know that your name is very near being the one I yearned after when I was a child. I hated 'Anne' and I called myself 'Cordelia' in imagination.''

"I like Anne. It was my mother's name. Old-fashioned names are the best and sweetest in my opinion. If you're going to get tea you might send the young doctor to talk to me. He's been lying on the sofa in that office ever since I came, laughing fit to kill over what I've been saying."

"How did you know?" cried Anne, too aghast at this instance of Miss Cornelia's uncanny prescience to make a polite denial.

"I saw him sitting beside you when I came up the lane, and I know men's tricks," retorted Miss Cornelia. "There, I've finished my little dress, dearie, and the eighth baby can come as soon as it pleases."

CHAPTER 9

AN EVENING AT FOUR WINDS POINT

IT WAS late September when Anne and Gilbert were able to pay Four Winds light their promised visit. They had often planned to go, but something always occurred to prevent them. Captain Jim had "dropped in" several times at the little house.

"I don't stand on ceremony, Mistress Blythe," he told Anne. "It's a real pleasure to me to come here, and I'm not going to deny myself jest because you haven't got down to see me. There oughtn't to be no bargaining like that among the race that knows Joseph. I'll come when I can, and you come when you can, and so long's we have our pleasant little chat it don't matter a mite what roof's over us."

Captain Jim took a great fancy to Gog and Magog, who were presiding over the destinies of the hearth in the little house with as much dignity and aplomb as they had done at Patty's Place.

"Aren't they the cutest little cusses?" he would say delightedly; and he bade them greeting and farewell as gravely and invariably as he did his host and hostess. Captain Jim was not going to offend household deities by any lack of reverence and ceremony.

"You've made this little house just about perfect," he told Anne. "It never was so nice before. Mistress Selwyn had your taste and she did wonders; but folks in those days didn't have the pretty little curtains and pictures and nicknacks you have. As for Elizabeth, she lived in the past. You've kinder brought the future into it, so to speak. I'd be real happy even if we couldn't talk at all, when I come here—jest to sit and look at you and your pictures and your flowers would be enough of a treat. It's beautiful—beautiful.''

Captain Jim was a passionate worshipper of beauty. Every lovely thing heard or seen gave him a deep, subtle, inner joy that irradiated his life. He was quite keenly aware of his own lack of outward comeliness and lamented it.

"Folks say I'm good," he remarked whimsically upon one occasion, "but I sometimes wish the Lord had made me only half as good and put the rest of it into looks. But there, I reckon He knew what He was about, as a good Captain should. Some of us have to be homely, or the purty ones—like Mistress Blythe here—wouldn't show up so well.''

One evening Anne and Gilbert finally walked down to the Four Winds light. The day had begun sombrely in gray cloud and mist, but it had ended in a pomp of scarlet and gold. Over the western hills beyond the harbor were amber deeps and crystalline shallows, with the fire of sunset below. The north was a mackerel sky of little, fiery golden clouds. The red light flamed on the white sails of a vessel gliding down the channel, bound to a southern port in a land of palms. Beyond her, it smote upon and incarnadined the shining, white, grassless faces of the sand dunes. To the right, it fell on the old house among the willows up the brook, and gave it for a fleeting space casements more splendid than those of an old cathedral. They glowed out of its quiet and grayness like the throbbing, blood-red thoughts of a vivid soul imprisoned in a dull husk of environment.

"That old house up the brook always seems so lonely," said Anne. "I never see visitors there. Of course, its lane opens on the upper road—but I don't think there's much coming and going. It seems odd we've never met the Moores yet, when they live within fifteen minutes' walk of us. I may have seen them in church, of course, but if so I didn't know them. I'm sorry they are so unsociable, when they are our only near neighbors.''

"Evidently they don't belong to the race that knows Joseph," laughed Gilbert. "Have you ever found out who that girl was whom you thought so beautiful?''

"No. Somehow I have never remembered to ask about her. But I've never seen her anywhere, so I suppose she must have been a stranger. Oh, the sun has just vanished—and there's the light.''

As the dusk deepened, the great beacon cut swathes of light through it, sweeping in a circle over the fields and the harbor, the sandbar and the gulf.

"I feel as if it might catch me and whisk me leagues out to sea," said Anne, as one drenched them with radiance; and she felt rather relieved when they got so near the Point that they were inside the range of those dazzling, recurrent flashes.

As they turned into the little lane that led across the fields to the Point they met a man coming out of it—a man of such extraordinary appearance that for a moment they both frankly stared. He was a decidedly fine-looking person—tall, broad-shouldered, well-featured, with a Roman nose and frank gray eyes; he was dressed in a prosperous farmer's Sunday best; in so far he might have been any inhabitant of Four Winds or the Glen. But, flowing over his breast nearly to his knees, was a river of crinkly brown beard; and adown his back, beneath his commonplace felt hat, was a corresponding cascade of thick, wavy, brown hair.

"Anne," murmured Gilbert, when they were out of earshot, "you didn't put what Uncle Dave calls 'a little of the Scott Act' in that lemonade you gave me just before we left home, did you?"

"No, I didn't," said Anne, stifling her laughter, lest the retreating enigma should hear here. "Who in the world can he be?"

"I don't know; but if Captain Jim keeps apparitions like that down at this Point I'm going to carry cold iron in my pocket when I come here. He wasn't a sailor, or one might pardon his eccentricity of appearance; he must belong to the over-harbor clans. Uncle Dave says they have several freaks over there."

"Uncle Dave is a little prejudiced, I think. You know all the over-harbor people who come to the Glen Church seem very nice. Oh, Gilbert, isn't this beautiful?"

The Four Winds light was built on a spur of red sand-stone cliff jutting out into the gulf. On one side, across the channel, stretched the silvery sand shore of the bar; on the other, extended a long, curving beach of red cliffs, rising steeply from the pebbled coves. It was a shore that knew the magic and mystery of storm and star. There is a great solitude about such a shore. The woods are never solitary—they are full of whispering, beckoning, friendly life. But the sea is a mighty soul, forever moaning of some great, unshareable sorrow, which shuts it up into itself for all eternity. We can never pierce its infinite mystery—we may only wander, awed and spellbound, on the outer fringe of it. The woods call to us with a hundred voices, but the sea has one only—a mighty voice that drowns our souls in its majestic music. The woods are human, but the sea is of the company of the archangels.

Anne and Gilbert found Uncle Jim sitting on a bench outside the lighthouse, putting the finishing touches to a wonderful, full-rigged, toy schooner. He rose and welcomed them to his abode with the gentle, unconscious courtesy that became him so well.

"This has been a purty nice day all through, Mistress Blythe, and now, right at the last, it's brought its best. Would you like to sit down here outside a bit, while the light lasts? I've just finished this bit of a plaything for my little grand nephew, Joe, up at the Glen. After I promised to make it for him I was kinder sorry, for his mother was vexed. She's afraid he'll be wanting to go to sea later on and she doesn't want the notion encouraged in him. But what could I do, Mistress Blythe? I'd *promised* him, and I think it's sorter real dastardly to break a promise you make to a child. Come, sit down. It won't take long to stay an hour."

The wind was off shore, and only broke the sea's surface into long, silvery ripples, and sent sheeny shadows flying out across it, from every point and headland, like transparent wings. The dusk was hanging a curtain of violet gloom over the sand dunes and the head-lands where gulls were huddling. The sky was faintly filmed over with scarfs of silken vapor. Cloud fleets rode at anchor along the horizons. An evening star was watching over the bar.

"Isn't that a view worth looking at?" said Captain Jim, with a loving, proprietary pride. "Nice and far from the market-place, ain't it? No buying and selling and getting gain. You don't have to pay anything—all that sea and sky free—'without money and without price.' There's going to be a moonrise purty soon, too—I'm never tired of finding out what a moonrise can be over them rocks and sea and harbor. There's a surprise in it every time."

They had their moonrise, and watched its marvel and magic in a silence that asked nothing of the world or each other. Then they went up into the tower, and Captain Jim showed and explained the mechanism of the great light. Finally they found themselves in the dining room, where a fire of driftwood was weaving flames of wavering, elusive, sea-born hues in the open fireplace.

"I put this fireplace in myself," remarked Captain Jim. "The Government don't give lighthouse keepers such luxuries. Look at the colors that wood makes. If you'd like some driftwood for your fire, Mistress Blythe, I'll bring you up a load some day. Sit down. I'm going to make you a cup of tea."

Captain Jim placed a chair for Anne, having first removed therefrom a huge, orange-colored cat and a newspaper.

"Get down, Matey. The sofa is your place. I must put this paper away safe till I can find time to finish the story in it. It's called *A Mad Love*. 'Tisn't my favorite brand of fiction, but I'm reading it jest to see how long she can spin it out. It's at the sixty-second chapter now, and the wedding ain't any nearer than when it begun, far's I can see. When little Joe comes I have to read him pirate yarns. Ain't it strange how innocent little creatures like children like the blood-thirstiest stories?"

"Like my lad Davy at home," said Anne. "He wants tales that reek with gore."

Captain Jim's tea proved to be nectar. He was pleased as a child with Anne's compliments, but he affected a fine indifference.

"The secret is I don't skimp the cream," he remarked airily. Captain Jim had never heard of Oliver Wendell Holmes, but he evidently agreed with that writer's dictum that "big heart never liked little cream pot."

"We met an odd-looking personage coming out of your lane," said Gilbert as they sipped. "Who was he?"

Captain Jim grinned.

"That's Marshall Elliott—a mighty fine man with jest one streak of foolishness in him. I s'pose you wondered what his object was in turning himself into a sort of dime museum freak."

"Is he a modern Nazarite or a Hebrew prophet left over from olden times?" asked Anne.

"Neither of them. It's politics that's at the bottom of his freak. All those Elliotts and Crawfords and MacAllisters are dyed-in-the-wool politicians. They're born Grit or Tory, as the case may be, and they live Grit or Tory, and they die Grit or Tory; and what they're going to do in heaven, where there's probably no politics, is more than I can fathom. This Marshall Elliott was born a Grit. I'm a Grit myself in moderation, but there's no moderation about Marshall. Fifteen years ago there was a specially bitter general election. Marshall fought for his party tooth and nail. He was dead sure the Liberals would win—so sure that he got up at a public meeting and vowed that he wouldn't shave his face or cut his hair until the Grits were in power. Well, they didn't go in—and they've never got in yet—and you saw the result today for yourselves. Marshall stuck to his word."

"What does his wife think of it?" asked Anne.

"He's a bachelor. But if he had a wife I reckon she couldn't make him break that vow. That family of Elliotts has always been more stubborn than natteral. Marshall's brother Alexander had a dog he set great store by, and when it died the man actilly wanted to have it buried in the graveyard, 'along with the other Christians,' he said. Course, he wasn't allowed to; so he buried it just outside the grave-yard fence, and never darkened the church door again. But Sundays he'd drive his family to church and sit by that dog's grave and read his Bible all the time service was going on. They say when he was dying he asked his wife to bury him beside the dog; she was a meek little soul but she fired up at *that*. She said *she* wasn't going to be buried beside no dog, and if he'd rather have his last resting place beside the dog than beside her, jest to say so. Alexander Elliott was a stubborn mule, but he was fond of his wife, so he give in and said, 'Well, durn it, bury me where you please. But when Gabriel's trump blows I expect my dog to rise with the rest of us, for he had as much soul as any durned Elliott or Crawford or MacAllister that ever strutted.' Them was *his* parting words. As for Marshall, we're all used to him, but he must strike strangers as right down peculiar-looking. I've known him ever since he was ten—he's about fifty now—and I like him. Him and me was out cod-fishing today. That's about all I'm good for now—catching trout and cod occasional. But 'tweren't always so—not by no manner of means. I used to do other things, as you'd admit if you saw my life-book."

Anne was just going to ask what his life-book was when the First Mate created a diversion by springing upon Captain Jim's knee. He was a gorgeous beastie, with a face as round as a full moon, vivid green eyes, and immense, white, double paws. Captain Jim stroked his velvet back gently.

"I never fancied cats much till I found the First Mate," he remarked, to the accompaniment of the Mate's tremendous purrs. "I saved his life, and when you've saved a creature's life you're bound to love it. It's next thing to giving life. There's some turrible thoughtless people in the world, Mistress Blythe. Some of them city folks who have summer homes over the harbor are so thought-less that they're cruel. It's the worst kind of cruelty—the thoughtless kind. You can't cope with it. They keep cats there in the summer, and feed and pet 'em, and doll 'em up with ribbons and collars. And then in the fall they go off and leave 'em to starve or freeze. It makes my blood boil, Mistress Blythe. One day last winter I found a poor old mother cat dead on the shore, lying against the skin-and-bone bodies of her three little kittens. She'd died trying to shelter 'em. She had her poor stiff paws around 'em. Master, I cried. Then I swore. Then I carried them poor little kittens home and fed 'em up and found good homes for 'em. I knew the woman who left the cat and when she come back this summer I jest went over the harbor and told her my opinion of her. It was rank meddling, but I do love meddling in a good cause.''

"How did she take it?'' asked Gilbert.

"Cried and said she 'didn't think.' I says to her, says I, 'Do you s'pose that'll be held for a good excuse in the day of Jedgment, when you'll have to account for that poor old mother's life? The Lord'll ask you what He give you your brains for if it wasn't to think, I reckon.' I don't fancy she'll leave cats to starve another time.''

"Was the First Mate one of the forsaken?'' asked Anne, making advances to him which were responded to graciously, if condescendingly.

"Yes. I found *him* one bitter cold day in winter, caught in the branches of a tree by his durn-fool ribbon collar. He was almost starving. If you could have seen his eyes, Mistress Blythe! He was nothing but a kitten, and he'd got his living somehow since he'd been left until he got hung up. When I loosed him he gave my hand a pitiful swipe with his little red tongue. He wasn't the able seaman you see now. He was meek as Moses. That was nine years ago. His life has been long in the land for a cat. He's a good old pal, the First Mate is.''

"I should have expected you to have a dog,'' said Gilbert.

Captain Jim shook his head.

"I had a dog once. I thought so much of him that when he died I couldn't bear the thought of getting another in his place. He was a *friend*—you understand, Mistress Blythe? Matey's only a pal. I'm fond of Matey—all the fonder on account of the spice of devilment that's in him—like there is in all cats. But I *loved* my dog. I always had a sneaking sympathy for Alexander Elliott about *his* dog. There isn't any devil in a good dog. That's why they're more lovable than cats, I reckon. But I'm darned if they're as interesting. Here I am, talking too much. Why don't you check me? When I do get a chance to talk to anyone I run on turrible. If you've done your tea I've a few little things you might like to look at—picked 'em up in the queer corners I used to be poking my nose into.''

Captain Jim's "few little things'' turned out to be a most interesting collection of curios, hideous, quaint and beautiful. And almost every one had some striking story attached to it.

Anne never forgot the delight with which she listened to those old tales that moonlit evening by that enchanted driftwood fire, while the silver sea called to them through the open window and sobbed against the rocks below them.

Captain Jim never said a boastful word, but it was impossible to help seeing what a hero the man had been—brave, true, resourceful, unselfish. He sat there in his little room and made those things live again for his hearers. By a lift of the eyebrow, a twist of the lip, a gesture, a word, he painted a whole scene or character so that they saw it as it was.

Some of Captain Jim's adventures had such a marvellous edge that Anne and Gilbert secretly wondered if he were not drawing a rather long bow at their credulous expense. But in this, as they found later, they did him injustice. His tales were all literally true. Captain Jim had the gift of the born storyteller, whereby "unhappy, far-off things" can be brought vividly before the hearer in all their pristine poignancy.

Anne and Gilbert laughed and shivered over his tales, and once Anne found herself crying. Captain Jim surveyed her tears with pleasure shining from his face.

"I like to see folks cry that way," he remarked. "It's a compliment. But I can't do justice to the things I've seen or helped to do. I've 'em all jotted down in my life-book, but I haven't got the knack of writing them out properly. If I could hit on jest the right words and string 'em together proper on paper I could make a great book. It would beat *A Mad Love* holler, and I believe Joe'd like it as well as the pirate yarns. Yes, I've had some adventures in my time; and, do you know, Mistress Blythe, I still lust after 'em. Yes, old and useless as I be, there's an awful longing sweeps over me at times to sail out—out—out there—forever and ever."

"Like Ulysses, you would

> *Sail beyond the sunset and the baths*
> *Of all the western stars until you die,"*

said Anne dreamily.

"Ulysses? I've read of him. Yes, that's just how I feel—jest how all us old sailors feel, I reckon. I'll die on land after all, I s'pose. Well, what is to be will be. There was old William Ford at the Glen who never went on the water in his life, 'cause he was afraid of being drowned. A fortune-teller had predicted he would be. And one day he fainted and fell with his face in the barn trough and was drowned. Must you go? Well, come soon and come often. The doctor is to do the talking next time. He knows a heap of things I want to find out. I'm sorter lonesome here by times. It's been worse since Elizabeth Russell died. Her and me was such cronies."

Captain Jim spoke with the pathos of the aged, who see their old friends slipping from them one by one—friends whose place can never be quite filled by those of a younger generation, even of the race that knows Joseph. Anne and Gilbert promised to come soon and often.

"He's a rare old fellow, isn't he?" said Gilbert, as they walked home.

"Somehow, I can't reconcile his simple, kindly personality with the wild, adventurous life he has lived," mused Anne.

"You wouldn't find it so hard if you had seen him the other day down at the fishing village. One of the men of Peter Gautier's boat made a nasty remark about some girl along the shore. Captain Jim fairly scorched the wretched fellow with the lightning of his eyes. He seemed a man transformed. He didn't say much—but the way he said it! You'd have thought it would strip the flesh from the fellow's bones. I understand that Captain Jim will never allow a word against any woman to be said in his presence."

"I wonder why he never married," said Anne. "He should have sons with their ships at sea now, and grandchildren climbing over him to hear his stories—he's that kind of a man. Instead, he has nothing but a magnificent cat."

But Anne was mistaken. Captain Jim had more than that. He had a memory.

CHAPTER 10

LESLIE MOORE

"I'M GOING for a walk to the outside shore tonight," Anne told Gog and Magog one October evening. There was no one else to tell, for Gilbert had gone over the harbor. Anne had her little domain in the speckless order one would expect of anyone brought up by Marilla

Cuthbert, and felt that she could gad shoreward with a clear conscience. Many and delightful had been her shore rambles, sometimes with Gilbert, sometimes with Captain Jim, sometimes alone with her own thoughts and new, poignantly-sweet dreams that were beginning to span life with their rainbows. She loved the gentle, misty harbor shore and the silvery, wind-haunted sand shore, but best of all she loved the rock shore, with its cliffs and caves and piles of surf-worn boulders, and its coves where the pebbles glittered under the pools; and it was to this shore she hied herself tonight.

There had been an autumn storm of wind and rain, lasting for three days. Thunderous had been the crash of billows on the rocks, wild the white spray and spume that blew over the bar, troubled and misty and tempest-torn the erstwhile blue peace of Four Winds Harbor. Now it was over, and the shore lay clean-washed after the storm; not a wind stirred, but there was still a fine surf on, dashing on sand and rock in a splendid white turmoil—the only restless thing in the great, pervading stillness and peace.

"Oh, this is a moment worth living through weeks of storm and stress for," Anne exclaimed, delightedly sending her far gaze across the tossing waters from the top of the cliff where she stood. Presently she scrambled down the steep path to the little cove below, where she seemed shut in with rocks and sea and sky.

"I'm going to dance and sing," she said. "There's no one here to see me—the seagulls won't carry tales of the matter. I may be as crazy as I like."

She caught up her skirt and pirouetted along the hard strip of sand just out of reach of the waves that almost lapped her feet with their spent foam. Whirling round and round, laughing like a child, she reached the little headland that ran out to the east of the cove; then she stopped suddenly, blushing crimson; she was not alone; there had been a witness to her dance and laughter.

The girl of the golden hair and sea-blue eyes was sitting on a boulder of the headland, half-hidden by a jutting rock. She was looking straight at Anne with a strange expression—part wonder, part sympathy, part—could it be?—envy. She was bare-headed, and her splendid hair, more than ever like Browning's "gorgeous snake," was bound about her head with a crimson ribbon. She wore a dress of some dark material, very plainly made; but swathed about her waist, outlining its fine curves, was a vivid girdle of red silk. Her hands, clasped over her knee, were brown and somewhat work-hardened; but the skin of her throat and cheeks was as white as cream. A flying gleam of sunset broke through a low-lying western cloud and fell across her hair. For a moment she seemed the spirit of the sea personified—all its mystery, all its passion, all its elusive charm.

"You—you must think me crazy," stammered Anne, trying to recover her self-possession. To be seen by this stately girl in such an abandon of childishness—she, Mrs. Dr. Blythe, with all the dignity of the matron to keep up—it was too bad!

"No," said the girl, "I don't."

She said nothing more; her voice was expressionless; her manner slightly repellent; but there was something in her eyes—eager yet shy, defiant yet pleading—which turned Anne from her purpose of walking away. Instead, she sat down on the boulder beside the girl.

"Let's introduce ourselves," she said, with the smile that had never yet failed to win confidence and friendliness. "I am Mrs. Blythe—and I live in that little white house up the harbor shore."

"Yes, I know," said the girl. "I am Leslie Moore—Mrs. Dick Moore," she added stiffly.

Anne was silent for a moment from sheer amazement. It had not occurred to her that this girl was married—there seemed nothing of the wife about her. And that she should be the neighbor whom Anne had pictured as a commonplace Four Winds housewife! Anne could not quickly adjust her mental focus to this astonishing change.

"Then—then you live in that gray house up the brook," she stammered.

"Yes. I should have gone over to call on you long ago," said the other. She did not offer any explanation or excuse for not having gone.

"I wish you *would* come," said Anne, recovering herself somewhat. "We're such near neighbors we ought to be friends. That is the sole fault of Four Winds—there aren't quite enough neighbors. Otherwise it is perfection."

"You like it?"

"*Like* it! I love it. It is the most beautiful place I ever saw."

"I've never seen many places," said Leslie Moore, slowly, "but I've always thought it was very lovely here. I—I love it, too."

She spoke, as she looked, shyly, yet eagerly. Anne had an odd impression that this strange girl—the word "girl" would persist—could say a good deal if she chose.

"I often come to the shore," she added.

"So do I," said Anne. "It's a wonder we haven't met here before."

"Probably you come earlier in the evening than I do. It is generally late—almost dark—when I come. And I love to come just after a storm—like this. I don't like the sea so well when it's calm and quiet. I like the struggle—and the crash—and the noise.''

"I love it in all its moods," declared Anne. "The sea at Four Winds is to me what Lover's Lane was at home. Tonight it seemed so free—so untamed—something broke loose in me, too, out of sympathy. That was why I danced along the shore in that wild way. I didn't suppose anybody was looking, of course. If Miss Cornelia Bryant had seen me she would have forboded a gloomy prospect for poor young Dr. Blythe.''

"You know Miss Cornelia?" said Leslie, laughing. She had an exquisite laugh; it bubbled up suddenly and unexpectedly with something of the delicious quality of a baby's. Anne laughed, too.

"Oh, yes. She has been down to my house of dreams several times.''

"Your house of dreams?''

"Oh, that's a dear, foolish little name Gilbert and I have for our home. We just call it that between ourselves. It slipped out before I thought.''

"So Miss Russell's little white house is *your* house of dreams," said Leslie wonderingly. "*I* had a house of dreams once—but it was a palace," she added, with a laugh, the sweetness of which was marred by a little note of derision.

"Oh, I once dreamed of a palace, too," said Anne. "I suppose all girls do. And then we settle down contentedly in eight-room houses that seem to fulfill all the desires of our hearts—because our prince is there. *You* should have had your palace really, though—you are so beautiful. You *must* let me say it—it *has* to be said—I'm nearly bursting with admiration. You are the loveliest thing I ever saw, Mrs. Moore.''

"If we are to be friends you must call me Leslie," said the other with an odd passion.

"Of course I will. And *my* friends call me Anne.''

"I suppose I am beautiful," Leslie went on, looking stormily out to sea. "I hate my beauty. I wish I had always been as brown and plain as the brownest and plainest girl at the fishing village over there. Well, what do you think of Miss Cornelia?''

The abrupt change of subject shut the door on any further confidences.

"Miss Cornelia is a darling, isn't she?" said Anne. "Gilbert and I were invited to her house to a state tea last week. You've heard of groaning tables.''

"I seem to recall seeing the expression in the newspaper reports of weddings," said Leslie, smiling.

"Well, Miss Cornelia's groaned—at least, it creaked—positively. You couldn't have believed she would have cooked so much for two ordinary people. She had every kind of pie you could name, I think—except lemon pie. She said she had taken the prize for lemon pies at the Charlottetown Exhibition ten years ago and had never made any since for fear of losing her reputation for them."

"Were you able to eat enough pie to please her?"

"*I* wasn't. Gilbert won her heart by eating—I won't tell you how much. She said she never knew a man who didn't like pie better than his Bible. Do you know, I love Miss Cornelia."

"So do I," said Leslie. "She is the best friend I have in the world."

Anne wondered secretly why, if this were so, Miss Cornelia had never mentioned Mrs. Dick Moore to her. Miss Cornelia had certainly talked freely about every other individual in or near Four Winds.

"Isn't that beautiful?" said Leslie, after a brief silence, pointing to the exquisite effect of a shaft of light falling through a cleft in the rock behind them, across a dark green pool at its base. "If I had come here—and seen nothing but just that—I would go home satisfied."

"The effects of light and shadow all along these shores are wonderful," agreed Anne. "My little sewing room looks out on the harbor, and I sit at its window and feast my eyes. The colors and shadows are never the same two minutes together."

"And you are never lonely?" asked Leslie abruptly. "Never—when you are alone?"

"No. I don't think I've ever been really lonely in my life," answered Anne. "Even when I'm alone I have real good company—dreams and imaginations and pretendings. I *like* to be alone now and then, just to think over things and *taste* them. But I love friendship—and nice, jolly little times with people. Oh, *won't* you come to see me—often? Please do. I believe," Anne added, laughing, "that you'd like me if you knew me."

"I wonder if *you* would like *me,*" said Leslie seriously. She was not fishing for a compliment. She looked out across the waves that were beginning to be garlanded with blossoms of moonlit foam, and her eyes filled with shadows.

"I'm sure I would," said Anne. "And please don't think I'm utterly irresponsible because you saw me dancing on the shore at sunset. No doubt I shall be dignified after a time. You see, I haven't been married very long. I feel like a girl, and sometimes like a child, yet.''

"I have been married twelve years," said Leslie.

Here was another unbelievable thing.

"Why, you can't be as old as I am!" exclaimed Anne. "You must have been a child when you were married."

"I was sixteen," said Leslie, rising, and picking up the cap and jacket lying beside her. "I am twenty-eight now. Well, I must go back."

"So must I. Gilbert will probably be home. But I'm so glad we both came to the shore tonight and met each other."

Leslie said nothing, and Anne was a little chilled. She had offered friendship frankly but it had not been accepted very graciously, if it had not been absolutely repelled. In silence they climbed the cliffs and walked across a pasture-field of which the feathery, bleached, wild grasses were like a carpet of creamy velvet in the moonlight. When they reached the shore lane Leslie turned.

"I go this way, Mrs. Blythe. You will come over and see me some time, won't you?"

Anne felt as if the invitation had been thrown at her. She got the impression that Leslie Moore gave it reluctantly.

"I will come if you really want me to," she said a little coldly.

"Oh, I do—I do," exclaimed Leslie, with an eagerness which seemed to burst forth and beat down some restraint that had been imposed on it.

"Then I'll come. Good-night—Leslie."

"Good-night, Mrs. Blythe."

Anne walked home in a brown study and poured out her tale to Gilbert.

"So Mrs. Dick Moore isn't one of the race that knows Joseph?" said Gilbert teasingly.

"No—o—o, not exactly. And yet—I think she *was* one of them once, but has gone or got into exile," said Anne musingly. "She is certainly very different from the other women about here. You can't talk about eggs and butter to *her*. To think I've been imagining her a second Mrs. Rachel Lynde! Have you ever seen Dick Moore, Gilbert?"

"No. I've seen several men working about the fields of the farm, but I don't know which was Moore."

"She never mentioned him. I *know* she isn't happy."

"From what you tell me I suppose she was married before she was old enough to know her own mind or heart, and found out too late that she had made a mistake. It's a common tragedy enough, Anne.

A fine woman would have made the best of it. Mrs. Moore has evidently let it make her bitter and resentful.''

''Don't let us judge her till we know,'' pleaded Anne. ''I don't believe her case is so ordinary. You will understand her fascination when you meet her, Gilbert. It is a thing quite apart from her beauty. I feel that she possesses a rich nature, into which a friend might enter as into a kingdom; but for some reason she bars every one out and shuts all her possibilities up in herself, so that they cannot develop and blossom. There, I've been struggling to define her to myself ever since I left her, and that is the nearest I can get to it. I'm going to ask Miss Cornelia about her.''

CHAPTER 11

THE STORY OF LESLIE MOORE

''YES, THE eighth baby arrived a fortnight ago,'' said Miss Cornelia, from a rocker before the fire of the little house one chilly October afternoon. ''It's a girl. Fred was ranting mad—said he wanted a boy—when the truth is he didn't want it at all. If it had been a boy he'd have ranted because it wasn't a girl. They had four girls and three boys before, so I can't see that it made much difference what this one was, but of course he'd have to be cantankerous, just like a man. The baby is real pretty, dressed up in its nice little clothes. It has black eyes and the dearest, tiny hands.''

''I must go and see it. I just love babies,'' said Anne, smiling to herself over a thought too dear and sacred to be put into words.

''I don't say but what they're nice,'' admitted Miss Cornelia. ''But some folks seem to have more than they really need, believe *me*. My poor cousin Flora up at the Glen had eleven, and such a slave as she is! Her husband suicided three years ago. Just like a man!''

''What made him do that?'' asked Anne, rather shocked.

''Couldn't get his way over something, so he jumped into the well. A good riddance! He was a born tyrant. But of course it spoiled the well. Flora could never abide the thought of using it again, poor thing! So she had another dug and a frightful expense it was, and the water as hard as nails. If he *had* to drown himself there was plenty of water in the harbor, wasn't there? I've no patience with a man like that. We've only had two suicides in Four Winds in my recollection. The other was Frank West—Leslie Moore's father. By the way, has Leslie ever been over to call on you yet?''

"No, but I met her on the shore a few nights ago and we scraped an acquaintance," said Anne, pricking up her ears.

Miss Cornelia nodded.

"I'm glad, dearie. I was hoping you'd foregather with her. What do you think of her?''

"I thought her very beautiful."

"Oh, of course. There was never anybody about Four Winds could touch her for looks. Did you ever see her hair? It reaches to her feet when she lets it down. But I meant how did you like her?''

"I think I could like her very much if she'd let me," said Anne slowly.

"But she wouldn't let you—she pushed you off and kept you at arm's length. Poor Leslie! You wouldn't be much surprised if you knew what her life has been. It's been a tragedy—a tragedy!'' repeated Miss Cornelia emphatically.

"I wish you would tell me all about her—that is, if you can do so without betraying any confidence.''

"Lord, dearie, everybody in Four Winds knows poor Leslie's story. It's no secret—the *outside*, that is. Nobody knows the *inside* but Leslie herself, and she doesn't take folks into her confidence. I'm about the best friend she has on earth, I reckon, and she's never uttered a word of complaint to me. Have you ever seen Dick Moore?''

"No."

"Well, I may as well begin at the beginning and tell you everything straight through, so you'll understand it. As I said, Leslie's father was Frank West. He was clever and shiftless—just like a man. Oh, he had heaps of brains—and much good they did him! He started to go to college, and he went for two years, and then his health broke down. The Wests were all inclined to be consumptive. So Frank came home and started farming. He married Rose Elliott from over harbor. Rose was reckoned the beauty of Four Winds—Leslie takes her looks from her mother, but she has ten times the spirit and go that Rose had, and a far better figure. Now you know, Anne, I always take the ground that us women ought to stand by each other. We've got enough to endure at the hands of the men, the Lord knows, so I hold we hadn't ought to clapper-claw one another, and it isn't often you'll find me running down another woman. But I never had much use for Rose Elliott. She was spoiled to begin with, believe *me*, and she was nothing but a lazy, selfish, whining creature. Frank was no hand to work, so they were poor as Job's turkey. Poor! They lived on potatoes and point, believe *me*. They had two children—Leslie and Kenneth. Leslie had her mother's looks and her father's brains, and something she didn't get from either of them. She took after her Grandmother West—a splendid old lady. She was the brightest, friendliest, merriest thing when she was a child, Anne. Everybody liked her. She was her father's favorite and she was awful fond of him. They were 'chums,' as she used to say. She couldn't see any of his faults—and he *was* a taking sort of man in some ways.

"Well, when Leslie was twelve years old, the first dreadful thing happened. She worshipped little Kenneth—he was four years younger than her, and he *was* a dear little chap. And he was killed one day—fell off a big load of hay just as it was going into the barn, and the wheel went right over his little body and crushed the life out of it. And mind you, Anne, Leslie saw it. She was looking down from the loft. She gave one screech—the hired man said he never heard such a sound in all his life—he said it would ring in his ears till Gabriel's trump drove it out. But she never screeched or cried again about it. She jumped from the loft onto the load and from the load to the floor, and caught up the little bleeding, warm, dead body, Anne—they had to tear it from her before she would let it go. They sent for me—I can't talk of it."

Miss Cornelia wiped the tears from her kindly brown eyes and sewed in bitter silence for a few minutes.

"Well," she resumed, "it was all over—they buried little Kenneth in that graveyard over the harbor, and after a while Leslie went back to her school and her studies. She never mentioned Kenneth's name—I've never heard it cross her lips from that day to this. I reckon that old hurt still aches and burns at times; but she was only a child and time is real kind to children, Anne, dearie. After a while she began to laugh again—she had the prettiest laugh. You don't often hear it now."

"I heard it once the other night," said Anne. "It *is* a beautiful laugh."

"Frank West began to go down after Kenneth's death. He wasn't strong and it was a shock to him, because he was real fond of the child, though, as I've said, Leslie was his favorite. He got mopy and melancholy, and couldn't or wouldn't work. And one day, when Leslie was fourteen years of age, he hanged himself—and in the parlor, too, mind you, Anne, right in the middle of the parlor from the lamp hook in the ceiling. Wasn't that like a man? It was the anniversary of his wedding day, too. Nice, tasty time to pick for it, wasn't it? And, of course, that poor Leslie had to be the one to find him. She went into the parlor that morning, singing, with some fresh flowers for the vases, and there she saw her father hanging from the ceiling, his face as black as a coal. It was something awful, believe *me!*''

"Oh, how horrible!'' said Anne, shuddering. "The poor, poor child!''

"Leslie didn't cry at her father's funeral any more then she had cried at Kenneth's. Rose whooped and howled for two, however, and Leslie had all she could do trying to calm and comfort her mother. I was disgusted with Rose and so was everyone else, but Leslie never got out of patience. She loved her mother. Leslie is clannish—her own could never do wrong in her eyes. Well, they buried Frank West beside Kenneth, and Rose put up a great big monument to him. It was bigger than his character, believe *me!* Anyhow, it was bigger than Rose could afford, for the farm was mortgaged for more than its value. But not long after Leslie's old grandmother West died and she left Leslie a little money—enough to give her a year at Queen's Academy. Leslie had made up her mind to pass for a teacher if she could, and then earn enough to put herself through Redmond College. That had been her father's pet scheme—he wanted her to have what he had lost. Leslie was full of ambition and her head was chock full of brains. She went to Queen's, and she took two years' work in one year and got her First; and when she came home she got the Glen school. She was so happy and hopeful and full of life and eagerness. When I think of what she was then and what she is now, I say—drat the men!''

Miss Cornelia snipped her thread off as viciously as if, Nero-like, she was severing the neck of mankind by the stroke.

"Dick Moore came into her life that summer. His father, Abner Moore, kept store at the Glen, but Dick had a sea-going streak in him from his mother; he used to sail in summer and clerk in his father's store in winter. He was a big, handsome fellow, with a little ugly soul. He was always wanting something till he got it, and then he stopped wanting it—just like a man. Oh, he didn't growl at the weather when it was fine, and he was mostly real pleasant and agreeable when everything went right. But he drank a good deal, and there were some nasty stories told of him and a girl down at the fishing village. He wasn't fit for Leslie to wipe her feet on, that's the long and short of it. And he was a Methodist! But he was clean mad about her—because of her good looks in the first place, and because she wouldn't have anything to say to him in the second. He vowed he'd have her—and he got her!''

"How did he bring it about?"

"Oh, it was an iniquitous thing! I'll never forgive Rose West. You see, dearie, Abner Moore held the mortgage on the West farm, and the interest was overdue some years, and Dick just went and told Mrs. West that if Leslie wouldn't marry him he'd get his father to foreclose the mortgage. Rose carried on terrible—fainted and wept, and pleaded with Leslie not to let her be turned out of her home. She said it would break her heart to leave the home she'd come to as a bride. I wouldn't have blamed her for feeling dreadful bad over it—but you wouldn't have thought she'd be so selfish as to sacrifice her own flesh and blood because of it, would you? Well, she was. And Leslie gave in—she loved her mother so much she would have done anything to save her pain. She married Dick Moore. None of us knew why at the time. It wasn't till long afterward that I found out how her mother had worried her into it. I was sure there was something wrong, though, because I knew how she had snubbed him time and again, and it wasn't like Leslie to turn face-about like that. Besides, I knew that Dick Moore wasn't the kind of man Leslie could ever fancy, in spite of his good looks and dashing ways. Of course, there was no wedding, but Rose asked me to go and see them married. I went, but I was sorry I did. I'd seen Leslie's face at her brother's funeral and at her father's funeral—and now it seemed to me I was seeing it at her own funeral. But Rose was smiling as a basket of chips, believe *me!*

"Leslie and Dick settled down on the West place—Rose couldn't bear to part with her dear daughter!—and lived there for the winter. In the spring Rose took pneumonia and died—a year too late! Leslie was heart-broken enough over it. Isn't it terrible the way some unworthy folks are loved, while others that deserve it far more, you'd think, never get much affection? As for Dick, he'd had enough of quiet married life—just like a man. He was for up and off. He went over to Nova Scotia to visit his relations—his father had come from Nova Scotia—and he wrote back to Leslie that his cousin, George Moore, was going on a voyage to Havana and he was going too. The name of the vessel was the *Four Sisters* and they were to be gone about nine weeks.

"It must have been a relief to Leslie. But she never said anything. From the day of her marriage she was just what she is now—cold and proud, and keeping everyone but me at a distance. I won't *be* kept at a distance, believe *me!* I've just stuck to Leslie as close as I knew how in spite of everything.''

"She told me you were the best friend she had," said Anne.

"Did she?" exclaimed Miss Cornelia delightedly. "Well, I'm real thankful to hear it. Sometimes I've wondered if she really did want me around at all—she never let me think so. You must have thawed her out more than you think, or she wouldn't have said that much itself to you. Oh, that poor, heart-broken girl! I never see Dick Moore but I want to run a knife clean through him."

Miss Cornelia wiped her eyes again and having relieved her feelings by her blood-thirsty wish, took up her tale.

"Well, Leslie was left over there alone. Dick had put in the crop before he went, and old Abner looked after it. The summer went by and the *Four Sisters* didn't come back. The Nova Scotia Moores investigated, and found she had got to Havana and discharged her cargo and took on another and left for home; and that was all they ever found out about her. By degrees people began to talk of Dick Moore as one that was dead. Almost everyone believed that he was, though no one felt certain, for men have turned up here at the harbor after they'd been gone for years. Leslie never thought he was dead—and she was right. A thousand pities too! The next summer Captain Jim was in Havana—that was before he gave up the sea, of course. He thought he'd poke round a bit—Captain Jim was always meddlesome, just like a man—and he went to inquiring round among the sailors' boarding houses and places like that, to see if he could find out anything about the crew of the *Four Sisters*. He'd better have let sleeping dogs lie, in my opinion! Well, he went to one out-of-the-way place, and there he found a man he knew at first sight it was Dick Moore, though he had a big beard. Captain Jim got it shaved off and then there was no doubt—Dick Moore it was—his body at least. His mind wasn't there—as for his soul, in my opinion he never had one!"

"What had happened to him?"

"Nobody knows the rights of it. All the folks who kept the boarding house could tell was that about a year before they had found him lying on their doorstep one morning in an awful condition—his head battered to a jelly almost. They supposed he'd got hurt in some drunken row, and likely that's the truth of it. They took him in, never thinking he could live. But he did—and he was just like a child when he got well. He hadn't memory or intellect or reason. They tried to find out who he was but they never could. He couldn't even tell them his name—he could only say a few simple words. He had a letter on him beginning 'Dear Dick' and signed 'Leslie,' but there was no address on it and the envelope was gone.

They let him stay on—he learned to do a few odd jobs about the place—and there Captain Jim found hm. He brought him home—I've always said it was a bad day's work, though I s'pose there was nothing else he could do. He thought maybe when Dick got home and saw his old surroundings and familiar faces his memory would wake up. But it hadn't any effect. There he's been at the house up the brook ever since. He's just like a child, no more nor less. Takes fractious spells occasionally, but mostly he's just vacant and good humored and harmless. He's apt to run away if he isn't watched. That's the burden Leslie has had to carry for eleven years—and all alone. Old Abner Moore died soon after Dick was brought home and it was found he was almost bankrupt. When things were settled up there was nothing for Leslie and Dick but the old West farm. Leslie rented it to John Ward, and the rent is all she has to live on. Sometimes in summer she takes a boarder to help out. But most visitors prefer the other side of the harbor where the hotels and summer cottages are. Leslie's house is too far from the bathing shore. She's taken care of Dick and she's never been away from him for eleven years—she's tied to that imbecile for life. And after all the dreams and hopes she once had! You can imagine what it has been like for her, Anne, dearie—with her beauty and spirit and pride and cleverness. It's just been a living death.''

''Poor, poor girl!'' said Anne again. Her own happiness seemed to reproach her. What right had she to be so happy when another human soul must be so miserable?

''Will you tell me just what Leslie said and how she acted the night you met her on the shore?'' asked Miss Cornelia.

She listened intently and nodded her satisfaction.

''*You* thought she was stiff and cold, Anne, dearie, but I can tell you she thawed out wonderful for her. She must have taken to you real strong. I'm so glad. You may be able to help her a good deal. I was thankful when I heard that a young couple was coming to this house, for I hoped it would mean some friends for Leslie; especially if you belonged to the race that knows Joseph. You *will* be her friend, won't you, Anne, dearie?''

''Indeed I will, if she'll let me,'' said Anne, with all her own sweet, impulsive earnestness.

''No, you must be her friend, whether she'll let you or not,'' said Miss Cornelia resolutely. ''Don't you mind if she's stiff by times—don't notice it. Remember what her life has been—and is—and must always be, I suppose, for creatures like Dick Moore live forever, I understand. You should see how fat he's got since he came home. He used to be lean enough. Just *make* her be friends—you can do it—you're one of those who have the knack. Only you mustn't be sensitive. And don't mind if she doesn't seem to want you to go over there much. She knows that some women don't like to be where Dick is—they complain he gives them the creeps. Just get her to come over here as often as she can. She can't get away so very much—she can't leave Dick long, for the Lord knows what he'd do—burn the house down most likely. At nights, after he's in bed and asleep, is about the only time she's free. He always goes to bed early and sleeps like the dead till next morning. That is how you came to meet her at the shore likely. She wanders there considerable.''

"I will do everything I can for her,'' said Anne. Her interest in Leslie Moore, which had been vivid ever since she had seen her driving her geese down the hill, was intensified a thousand fold by Miss Cornelia's narration. The girl's beauty and sorrow and loneliness drew her with an irresistible fascination. She had never known anyone like her; her friends had hitherto been wholesome, normal, merry girls like herself, with only the average trials of human care and bereavement to shadow their girlish dreams. Leslie Moore stood apart, a tragic, appealing figure of thwarted womanhood. Anne resolved that she would win entrance into the kingdom of that lonely soul and find there the comradeship it could so richly give, were it not for the cruel fetters that held it in a prison not of its own making.

"And mind you this, Anne, dearie,'' said Miss Cornelia, who had not yet wholly relieved her mind, "You mustn't think Leslie is an infidel because she hardly ever goes to church—or even that she's a Methodist. She can't take Dick to church, of course—not that he ever troubled church much in his best days. But you just remember that she's a real strong Presbyterian at heart, Anne, dearie.''

--- CHAPTER 12 ---

LESLIE COMES OVER

LESLIE CAME over to the house of dreams one frosty October night, when moonlit mists were hanging over the harbor and curling like silver ribbons along the seaward glens. She looked as if she repented coming when Gilbert answered her knock; but Anne flew past him, pounced on her, and drew her in.

"I'm so glad you picked tonight for a call," she said gaily. "I made up a lot of extra good fudge this afternoon and we want someone to help us eat it—before the fire—while we tell stories. Perhaps Captain Jim will drop in, too. This is his night."

"No. Captain Jim is over home," said Leslie. "He—he made me come here," she added, half defiantly.

"I'll say a thank-you to him for that when I see him," said Anne, pulling easy chairs before the fire.

"Oh, I don't mean that I didn't want to come," protested Leslie, flushing a little. "I—I've been thinking of coming—but it isn't always easy for me to get away."

"Of course it must be hard for you to leave Mr. Moore," said Anne, in a matter-of-fact tone. She had decided that it would be best to mention Dick Moore occasionally as an accepted fact, and not give undue morbidness to the subject by avoiding it. She was right, for Leslie's air of constraint suddenly vanished. Evidently she had been wondering how much Anne knew of the conditions of her life and was relieved that no explanations were needed. She allowed her cap and jacket to be taken, and sat down with a girlish snuggle in the big armchair by Magog. She was dressed prettily and carefully, with the customary touch of color in the scarlet geranium at her white throat. Her beautiful hair gleamed like molten gold in the warm firelight. Her sea-blue eyes were full of soft laughter and allurement. For the moment, under the influence of the little house of dreams, she was a girl again—a girl forgetful of the past and its bitterness. The atmosphere of the many loves that had sanctified the little house was all about her; the companionship of two healthy, happy, young folks of her own generation encircled her; she felt and yielded to the magic of her surroundings—Miss Cornelia and Captain Jim would scarcely have recognized her; Anne found it hard to believe that this was the cold, unresponsive woman she had met on the shore—this animated girl who talked and listened with the eagerness of a starved soul. And how hungrily Leslie's eyes looked at the bookcases between the windows!

"Our library isn't very extensive," said Anne, "but every book in it is a *friend*. We've picked our books up through the years, here and there, never buying one until we had first read it and knew that it belonged to the race of Joseph."

Leslie laughed—beautiful laughter that seemed akin to all the mirth that had echoed through the little house in the vanished years.

"I have a few books of father's—not many," she said. "I've read them until I know them almost by heart. I don't get many books. There's a circulating library at the Glen store—but I don't think the committee who pick the books for Mr. Parker know what books are of Joseph's race—or perhaps they don't care. It was so seldom I got one I really liked that I gave up getting any."

"I hope you'll look on our bookshelves as your own," said Anne. "You are entirely and wholeheartedly welcome to the loan of any book on them."

"You are setting a feast of fat things before me," said Leslie, joyously. Then, as the clock struck ten, she rose, half unwillingly.

"I must go. I didn't realise it was so late. Captain Jim is always saying it doesn't take long to stay an hour. But I've stayed two—and oh, but I've enjoyed them," she added frankly.

"Come often," said Anne and Gilbert. They had risen and stood together in the firelight's glow. Leslie looked at them—youthful, hopeful, happy, typifying all she had missed and must forever miss. The light went out of her face and eyes; the girl vanished; it was the sorrowful, cheated woman who answered the invitation almost coldly and got herself away with a pitiful haste.

Anne watched her until she was lost in the shadows of the chill and misty night. Then she turned slowly back to the glow of her own radiant hearthstone.

"Isn't she lovely, Gilbert? Her hair fascinates me. Miss Cornelia says it reaches to her feet. Ruby Gillis had beautiful hair—but Leslie's is *alive*—every thread of it is living gold."

"She is very beautiful," agreed Gilbert, so heartily that Anne almost wished he were a *little* less enthusiastic.

"Gilbert, would you like my hair better if it were like Leslie's?" she asked wistfully.

"I wouldn't have your hair any color but just what it is for the world," said Gilbert, with one or two convincing accompaniments. "You wouldn't be *Anne* if you had golden hair—or hair of any color but"—

"Red," said Anne, with gloomy satisfaction.

"Yes, red—to give warmth to that milk-white skin and those shining gray-green eyes of yours. Golden hair wouldn't suit you at all, Queen Anne—*my* Queen Anne—queen of my heart and life and home."

"Then you may admire Leslie's all you like," said Anne magnanimously.

CHAPTER 13

A GHOSTLY EVENING

ONE EVENING, a week later, Anne decided to run over the fields to the house up the brook for an informal call. It was an evening of gray fog that had crept in from the gulf, swathed the harbor, filled the glens and valleys, and clung heavily to the autumnal meadows. Through it the sea sobbed and shuddered. Anne saw Four Winds in a new aspect, and found it weird and mysterious and fascinating; but it also gave her a little feeling of loneliness. Gilbert was away and would be away until the morrow, attending a medical pow-wow in Charlottetown. Anne longed for an hour of fellowship with some girl friend. Captain Jim and Miss Cornelia were "good fellows" each, in their own way; but youth yearned to youth.

"If only Diana or Phil or Pris or Stella could drop in for a chat," she said to herself, "how delightful it would be! This is such a *ghostly* night. I'm sure all the ships that ever sailed out of Four Winds to their doom could be seen tonight sailing up the harbor with their drowned crews on their decks, if that shrouding fog could suddenly be drawn aside. I feel as if it concealed innumerable mysteries—as if I were surrounded by the wraiths of old generations of Four Winds people peering at me through that gray veil. If ever the dear dead ladies of this little house came back to revisit it they would come on just such a night as this. If I sit here any longer I'll see one of them there opposite me in Gilbert's chair. This place isn't exactly canny tonight. Even Gog and Magog have an air of pricking up their ears to hear the footsteps of unseen guests. I'll run over to see Leslie before I frighten myself with my own fancies, as I did long ago in the matter of the Haunted Wood. I'll leave my house of dreams to welcome back its old inhabitants. My fire will give them my good-will and greeting—they will be gone before I come back, and my house will be mine once more. Tonight I am sure it is keeping a tryst with the past."

Laughing a little over her fancy, yet with something of a creepy sensation in the region of her spine, Anne kissed her hand to Gog and Magog and slipped out into the fog, with some of the new magazines under her arm for Leslie.

"Leslie's wild for books and magazines," Miss Cornelia had told her, "and she hardly ever sees one. She can't afford to buy them or subscribe for them. She's really pitifully poor, Anne. I don't see how she makes out to live at all on the little rent the farm brings in. She never even hints a complaint on the score of poverty, but I know what it must be. She's been handicapped by it all her life. She didn't mind it when she was free and ambitious, but it must gall now, believe *me*. I'm glad she seemed so bright and merry the evening she spent with you. Captain Jim told me he had fairly to put her cap and coat on and push her out of the door. Don't be too long going to see her either. If you are she'll think it's because you don't like the sight of Dick, and she'll crawl into her shell again. Dick's a great, big, harmless baby, but that silly grin and chuckle of his do get on some people's nerves. Thank goodness, I've no nerves myself. I like Dick Moore better now than I ever did when he was in his right senses—though the Lord knows that isn't saying much. I was down there one day in housecleaning time helping Leslie a bit, and I was frying doughnuts. Dick was hanging round to get one, as usual, and all at once he picked up a scalding hot one I'd just fished out and dropped it on the back of my neck when I was bending over. Then he laughed and laughed. Believe *me,* Anne, it took all the grace of God in my heart to keep me from just whisking up that stew-pan of boiling fat and pouring it over his head."

Anne laughed over Miss Cornelia's wrath as she sped through the darkness. But laughter accorded ill with that night. She was sober enough when she reached the house among the willows. Everything was very silent. The front part of the house seemed dark and deserted, so Anne slipped round to the side door, which opened from the veranda into a little sitting room. There she halted noiselessly.

The door was open. Beyond, in the dimly lighted room, sat Leslie Moore, with her arms flung out on the table and her head bent upon them. She was weeping horribly—with low, fierce, choking sobs, as if some agony in her soul were trying to tear itself out. An old black dog was sitting by her, his nose resting on his lap, his big doggish eyes full of mute, imploring sympathy and devotion. Anne drew back in dismay. She felt that she could not intermeddle with this bitterness. Her heart ached with a sympathy she might not utter. To go in now would be to shut the door forever on any possible help or friendship. Some instinct warned Anne that the proud, bitter girl would never forgive the one who thus surprised her in her abandonment of despair.

Anne slipped noiselessly from the veranda and found her way

across the yard. Beyond, she heard voices in the gloom and saw the dim glow of a light. At the gate she met two men—Captain Jim with a lantern, and another who she knew must be Dick Moore—a big man, badly gone to fat, with a broad, round, red face, and vacant eyes. Even in the dull light Anne got the impession that there was something unusual about his eyes.

"Is this you, Mistress Blythe?" said Captain Jim. "Now, now, you hadn't oughter be roaming about alone on a night like this. You could get lost in this fog easier than not. Jest you wait till I see Dick safe inside the door and I'll come back and light you over the fields. I ain't going to have Dr. Blythe coming home and finding that you walked clean over Cape Leforce in the fog. A woman did that once, forty years ago.

"So you've been over to see Leslie," he said, when he rejoined her.

"I didn't go in," said Anne, and told what she had seen. Captain Jim sighed.

"Poor, poor, little girl! She don't cry often, Mistress Blythe—she's too brave for that. She must feel terrible when she does cry. A night like this is hard on poor women who have sorrows. There's something about it that kinder brings up all we've suffered—or feared."

"It's full of ghosts," said Anne, with a shiver. "That was why I came over—I wanted to clasp a human hand and hear a human voice. There seem to be so many *inhuman* presences about tonight. Even my own dear house was full of them. They fairly elbowed me out. So I fled over here for companionship of my kind."

"You were right not to go in, though, Mistress Blythe. Leslie wouldn't have liked it. She wouldn't have liked me going in with Dick, as I'd have done if I hadn't met you. I had Dick down with me all day. I keep him with me as much as I can to help Leslie a bit."

"Isn't there something odd about his eyes?" asked Anne.

"You noticed that? Yes, one is blue and t'other is hazel—his father had the same. It's a Moore peculiarity. That was what told me he was Dick Moore when I saw him first down in Cuby. If it hadn't a-bin for his eyes I mightn't a-known him, with his beard and fat. You know, I reckon, that it was me found him and brought him home. Miss Cornelia always says I shouldn't have done it, but I can't agree with her. It was the *right* thing to do—and so 'twas the only thing. There ain't no question in my mind about *that*. But my old heart aches for Leslie. She's only twenty-eight and she's eaten more bread with sorrow than most women do in eighty years.''

They walked on in silence for a little while. Presently Anne said, ''Do you know, Captain Jim, I never like walking with a lantern. I have always the strangest feeling that just outside the circle of light, just over its edge in the darkness, I am surrounded by a ring of furtive, sinister things, watching me from the shadows with hostile eyes. I've had that feeling from childhood. What is the reason? I never feel like that when I'm really in the darkness—when it is close all around me—I'm not the least frightened.''

''I've something of that feeling myself,'' admitted Captain Jim. ''I reckon when the darkness is close to us it is a friend. But when we sorter push it away from us—divorce ourselves from it, so to speak, with lantern light—it becomes an enemy. But the fog is lifting. There's a smart west wind rising, if you notice. The stars will be out when you get home.''

They were out; and when Anne re-entered her house of dreams the red embers were still glowing on the hearth, and all the haunting presences were gone.

CHAPTER 14

NOVEMBER DAYS

THE SPLENDOR of color which had glowed for weeks along the shores of Four Winds Harbor had faded out into the soft gray-blue of late autumnal hills. There came many days when fields and shores were dim with misty rain, or shivering before the breath of a melancholy sea-wind—nights, too, of storm and tempest, when Anne sometimes wakened to pray that no ship might be beating up the grim north shore, for if it were so not even the great, faithful light whirling through the darkness unafraid, could avail to guide it into safe haven.

''In November I sometimes feel as if spring could never come again,'' she sighed, grieving over the hopeless unsightliness of her frosted and bedraggled flower-plots. The gay little garden of the schoolmaster's bride was rather a forlorn place now, and the Lombardies and birches were under bare poles, as Captain Jim said. But the fir-wood behind the little house was forever green and staunch; and even in November and December there came gracious days of sunshine and purple hazes, when the harbor danced and sparkled as blithely as in midsummer, and the gulf was so softly blue and tender that the storm and the wild wind seemed only things of a long-past dream.

Anne and Gilbert spent many an autumn evening at the lighthouse. It was always a cheery place. Even when the east wind sang in minor and the sea was dead and gray, hints of sunshine seemed to be lurking all about it. Perhaps this was because the First Mate always paraded it in panoply of gold. He was so large and effulgent that one hardly missed the sun, and his resounding purrs formed a pleasant accompaniment to the laughter and conversation which went on around Captain Jim's fireplace. Captain Jim and Gilbert had many long discussions and high converse on matters beyond the ken of cat or king.

"I like to ponder on all kinds of problems, though I can't solve 'em," said Captain Jim. "My father held that we should never talk of things we couldn't understand, but if we didn't, doctor, the subjects for conversation would be mighty few. I reckon the gods laugh many a time to hear us, but what matters so long as we remember that we're only men and don't take to fancying that we're gods ourselves, really, knowing good and evil. I reckon our pow-wows won't do us or anyone much harm, so let's have another whack at the whence, why and whither this evening, doctor."

While they "whacked," Anne listened or dreamed. Sometimes Leslie went to the lighthouse with them, and she and Anne wandered along the shore in the eerie twilight, or sat on the rocks below the lighthouse until the darkness drove them back to the cheer of the driftwood fire. Then Captain Jim would brew them tea and tell them

> *"tales of land and sea*
> *And whatsoever might betide*
> *The great forgotten world outside."*

Leslie seemed always to enjoy those lighthouse carousals very much, and bloomed out for the time being into ready wit and beautiful laughter, or glowing-eyed silence. There was a certain tang and savor in the conversation when Leslie was present which they missed when she was absent. Even when she did not talk she seemed to inspire others to brilliancy. Captain Jim told his stories better, Gilbert was quicker in argument and repartee, Anne felt little gushes and trickles of fancy and imagination bubbling to her lips under the influence of Leslie's personality.

"That girl was born to be a leader in social and intellectual circles, far away from Four Winds," she said to Gilbert as they walked home one night. "She's just wasted here—wasted."

"Weren't you listening to Captain Jim and yours truly the other night when we discussed that subject generally? We came to the comforting conclusion that the Creator probably knew how to run His universe quite as well as we do, and that, after all, there are no such things as 'wasted' lives, saving and except when an individual wilfully squanders and wastes his own life—which Leslie Moore certainly hasn't done. And some people might think that a Redmond B.A., whom editors were beginning to honor, was 'wasted' as the wife of a struggling country doctor in the rural community of Four Winds."

"Gilbert!"

"If you had married Roy Gardner, now," continued Gilbert mercilessly, "*you* could have been 'a leader in social and intellectual circles far away from Four Winds.'"

"Gilbert *Blythe!*"

"You *know* you were in love with him at one time, Anne."

"Gilbert, that's mean—'pisen mean, just like all the men,' as Miss Cornelia says. I *never* was in love with him. I only imagined I was. *You* know that. You *know* I'd rather be your wife in our house of dreams and fulfillment than a queen in a palace."

Gilbert's answer was not in words; but I am afraid that both of them forgot poor Leslie speeding her lonely way across the fields to a house that was neither a palace nor the fulfillment of a dream.

The moon was rising over the sad, dark sea behind them and transfiguring it. Her light had not yet reached the harbor, the further side of which was shadowy and suggestive, with dim coves and rich glooms and jewelling lights.

"How the home lights shine out tonight through the dark!" said Anne. " That string of them over the harbor looks like a necklace. And what a coruscation there is up at the Glen! Oh, look, Gilbert, there is ours. I'm so glad we left it burning. I hate to come home to a dark house. *Our* homelight, Gilbert! Isn't it lovely to see?"

"Just one of earth's many millions of homes, Anne-girl—but ours— *ours*—our beacon in 'a naughty world.' When a fellow has a home and a dear, little, red-haired wife in it what more need he ask of life?''

''Well, he might ask *one* thing more,'' whispered Anne happily. ''Oh, Gilbert, it seems as if I just *couldn't* wait for the spring.''

CHAPTER 15

CHRISTMAS AT FOUR WINDS

AT FIRST Anne and Gilbert talked of going home to Avonlea for Christmas; but eventually they decided to stay in Four Winds. ''I want to spend the first Christmas of our life together in our own home,'' decreed Anne.

So it fell out that Marilla and Mrs. Rachel Lynde and the twins came to Four Winds for Christmas. Marilla had the face of a woman who had circumnavigated the globe. She had never been sixty miles away from home before; and she had never eaten a Christmas dinner anywhere save at Green Gables.

Mrs. Rachel had made and brought with her an enormous plum pudding. Nothing could have convinced Mrs. Rachel that a college graduate of the younger generation could make a Christmas plum pudding properly; but she bestowed approval on Anne's house.

''Anne's a good housekeeper,'' she said to Marilla in the spare room the night of their arrival. ''I've looked into her bread box and her scrap pail. I always judge a housekeeper by those, that's what. There's nothing in the pail that shouldn't have been thrown away, and no stale pieces in the bread box. Of course, she was trained up with you—but, then, she went to college afterwards. I notice she's got my tobacco stripe quilt on the bed here, and that big round braided mat of yours before her living-room fire. It makes me feel right at home.''

Anne's first Christmas in her own house was as delightful as she could have wished. The day was fine and bright; the first skim of snow had fallen on Christmas Eve and made the world beautiful; the harbor was still open and glittering.

Captain Jim and Miss Cornelia came to dinner. Leslie and Dick had been invited, but Leslie made excuse; they always went to her

Uncle Isaac West's for Christmas, she said.

"She'd rather have it so," Miss Cornelia told Anne. "She can't bear taking Dick where there are strangers. Christmas is always a hard time for Leslie. She and her father used to make a lot of it."

Miss Cornelia and Mrs. Rachel did not take a very violent fancy to each other. "Two suns hold not their courses in one sphere." But they did not clash at all, for Mrs. Rachel was in the kitchen helping Anne and Marilla with the dinner, and it fell to Gilbert to entertain Captain Jim and Miss Cornelia,—or rather to be entertained by them, for a dialogue between those two old friends and antagonists was assuredly never dull.

"It's many a year since there was a Christmas dinner here, Mistress Blythe," said Captain Jim. "Miss Russell always went to her friends in town for Christmas. But I was here to the first Christmas dinner that was ever eaten in this house—and the schoolmaster's bride cooked it. That was sixty years ago today, Mistress Blythe—and a day very like this—just enough snow to make the hills white, and the harbor as blue as June. I was only a lad, and I'd never been invited out to dinner before, and I was too shy to eat enough. I've got all over *that*."

"Most men do," said Miss Cornelia, sewing furiously. Miss Cornelia was not going to sit with idle hands, even on Christmas. Babies come without any consideration for holidays, and there was one expected in a poverty-stricken household at Glen St. Mary. Miss Cornelia had sent that household a substantial dinner for its little swarm, and so meant to eat her own with a comfortable conscience.

"Well, you know, the way to a man's heart is through his stomach, Cornelia," explained Captain Jim.

"I believe you—when he *has* a heart," retorted Miss Cornelia. "I suppose that's why so many women kill themselves cooking—just as poor Amelia Baxter did. She died last Christmas morning, and she said it was the first Christmas since she was married that she didn't have to cook a big, twenty-plate dinner. It must have been a real pleasant change for her. Well, she's been dead a year, so you'll soon hear of Horace Baxter taking notice."

"I heard he was taking notice already," said Captain Jim, winking at Gilbert. "Wasn't he up to your place one Sunday lately, with his funeral blacks on, and a boiled collar?"

"No, he wasn't. And he needn't come neither. I could have had him long ago when he was fresh. I don't want any second-hand goods, believe *me*. As for Horace Baxter, he was in financial difficulties a year ago last summer, and he prayed to the Lord for help; and when his wife died and he got her life insurance he said he believed it was the answer to his prayer. Wasn't that like a man?''

"Have you really proof that he said that, Cornelia?"

"I have the Methodist minister's word for it—if you call *that* proof. Robert Baxter told me the same thing too, but I admit *that* isn't evidence. Robert Baxter isn't often known to tell the truth."

"Come, come, Cornelia, I think he generally tells the truth, but he changes his opinion so often it sometimes sounds as if he didn't."

"It sounds like it mighty often, believe *me*. But trust one man to excuse another. I have no use for Robert Baxter. He turned Methodist just because the Presbyterian choir happened to be singing 'Behold the bridegroom cometh' for a collection piece when him and Margaret walked up the aisle the Sunday after they were married. Served him right for being late! He always insisted the choir did it on purpose to insult him, as if he was of that much importance. But that family always thought they were much bigger potatoes than they really were. His brother Eliphalet imagined the devil was always at his elbow—but *I* never believed the devil wasted that much time on him."

"I—don't—know," said Captain Jim thoughtfully. "Eliphalet Baxter lived too much alone—hadn't even a cat or dog to keep him human. When a man is alone he's mighty apt to be with the devil—if he ain't with God. He has to choose which company he'll keep, I reckon. If the devil always was at Life Baxter's elbow it must have been because Life liked to have him there."

"Man-like," said Miss Cornelia, and subsided into silence over a complicated arrangement of tucks until Captain Jim deliberately stirred her up again by remarking in a casual way:

"I was up to the Methodist church last Sunday morning."

"You'd better have been home reading your Bible," was Miss Cornelia's retort.

"Come, now, Cornelia, *I* can't see any harm in going to the Methodist church when there's no preaching in your own. I've been a Presbyterian for seventy-six years, and it isn't likely my theology will hoist anchor at this late day."

"It's setting a bad example," said Miss Cornelia grimly.

"Besides," continued wicked Captain Jim, "I wanted to hear some good singing. The Methodists have a good choir; and you can't deny, Cornelia, that the singing in our church is awful since the split in the choir."

"What if the singing isn't good? They're doing their best, and God sees no difference between the voice of a crow and the voice of a nightingale."

"Come, come, Cornelia," said Captain Jim mildly, "I've a better opinion of the Almighty's ear for music than *that*."

"What caused the trouble in our choir?" asked Gilbert, who was suffering from suppressed laughter.

"It dates back to the new church, three years ago," answered Captain Jim. "We had a fearful time over the building of that church—fell out over the question of a new site. The two sites wasn't more'n two hundred yards apart, but you'd have thought they was a thousand by the bitterness of that fight. We was split up into three factions—one wanted the east site and one the south, and one held to the old. It was fought out in bed and at board, and in church and at market. All the old scandals of three generations were dragged out of their graves and aired. Three matches was broken up by it. And the meetings we had to try to settle the question! Cornelia, will you ever forget the one when old Luther Burns got up and made a speech? *He* stated his opinions forcibly."

"Call a spade a spade, Captain. You mean he got red-mad and raked them all, fore and aft. They deserved it too—a pack of incapables. But what would you expect of a committee of men? That building committee held twenty-seven meetings, and at the end of the twenty-seventh weren't no nearer having a church than when they begun—not so near, for a fact, for in one fit of hurrying things along they'd gone to work and tore the old church down, so there we were, without a church, and no place but the hall to worship in."

"The Methodists offered us their church, Cornelia."

"The Glen St. Mary church wouldn't have been built to this day," went on Miss Cornelia, ignoring Captain Jim, "if we women hadn't just started in and took charge. We said *we* meant to have a church, if the men meant to quarrel till doomsday, and we were tired of being a laughing-stock for the Methodists. We held *one* meeting and elected a committee and canvassed for subscriptions. We got them, too. When any of the men tried to sass us we told them they'd tried for two years to build a church and it was our turn now. We shut them up close, believe *me*, and in six months we had our church. Of course, when the men saw we were determined they stopped fighting and went to work, man-like, as soon as they saw they had to, or quit bossing. Oh, women can't preach or be elders; but they can build churches and scare up the money for them.''

"The Methodists allow women to preach,'' said Captain Jim.

Miss Cornelia glared at him.

"I never said the Methodists hadn't common sense, Captain. What I say is, I doubt if they have much religion.''

"I suppose you are in favor of votes for women, Miss Cornelia,'' said Gilbert.

"I'm not hankering after the vote, believe *me*,'' said Miss Cornelia scornfully. "*I* know what it is to clean up after the men. But some of these days, when the men realize they've got the world into a mess they can't get it out of, they'll be glad to give us the vote, and shoulder their troubles over on us. That's *their* scheme. Oh, it's well that women are patient, believe *me!*''

"What about Job?'' suggested Captain Jim.

"Job! It was such a rare thing to find a patient man that when one was really discovered they were determined he shouldn't be forgotten,'' retorted Miss Cornelia triumphantly. "Anyhow, the virtue doesn't go with the name. There never was such an impatient man born as old Job Taylor over harbor.''

"Well, you know, he had a good deal to try him, Cornelia. Even you can't defend his wife. I always remember what old William MacAllister said of her at her funeral, 'There's nae doot she was a Chreestian wumman, but she had the de'il's own temper.' ''

"I suppose she *was* trying,'' admitted Miss Cornelia reluctantly, "but that didn't justify what Job said when she died. He rode home from the graveyard the day of the funeral with my father. He never said a word till they got near home. Then he heaved a big sigh and said, 'You may not believe it, Stephen, but this is the happiest day of my life!' Wasn't that like a man?''

"I s'pose poor old Mrs. Job did make life kinder uneasy for him,'' reflected Captain Jim.

"Well, there's such a thing as decency, isn't there? Even if a man is rejoicing in his heart over his wife being dead, he needn't proclaim it to the four winds of heaven. And happy day or not, Job Taylor wasn't long in marrying again, you might notice. His second wife could manage him. She made him walk Spanish, believe me! The first thing she did was to make him hustle round and put up a tombstone to the first Mrs. Job—and she had a place left on it for her own name. She said there'd be nobody to make Job put up a monument to *her*.''

"Speaking of Taylors, how is Mrs. Lewis Taylor up at the Glen, doctor?" asked Captain Jim.

"She's getting better slowly—but she has to work too hard," replied Gilbert.

"Her husband works hard too—raising prize pigs," said Miss Cornelia. "He's noted for his beautiful pigs. He's a heap prouder of his pigs than of his children. But then, to be sure, his pigs are the best pigs possible, while his children don't amount to much. He picked a poor mother for them, and starved her while she was bearing and rearing them. His pigs got the cream and his children got the skim milk."

"There are times, Cornelia, when I have to agree with you, though it hurts me," said Captain Jim. "That's just exactly the truth about Lewis Taylor. When I see those poor, miserable children of his, robbed of all children ought to have, it p'isens my own bite and sup for days afterwards."

Gilbert went out to the kitchen in response to Anne's beckoning. Anne shut the door and gave him a connubial lecture.

"Gilbert, you and Captain Jim must stop baiting Miss Cornelia. Oh, I've been listening to you—and I just won't allow it."

"Anne, Miss Cornelia is enjoying herself hugely. You know she is."

"Well, never mind. You two needn't egg her on like that. Dinner is ready now, and, Gilbert, *don't* let Mrs. Rachel carve the geese. I know she means to offer to do it because she doesn't think you can do it properly. Show her you can."

"I ought to be able to. I've been studying A-B-C-D diagrams of carving for the past month," said Gilbert. "Only don't talk to me while I'm doing it, Anne, for if you drive the letters out of my head I'll be in a worse predicament than you were in old geometry days when the teacher changed them."

Gilbert carved the geese beautifully. Even Mrs. Rachel had to admit that. And everybody ate of them and enjoyed them. Anne's first Christmas dinner was a great success and she beamed with housewifely pride. Merry was the feast and long; and when it was over they gathered around the cheer of the red hearth flame and Captain Jim told them stories until the red sun swung low over Four Winds Harbor, and the long blue shadows of the Lombardies fell across the snow in the lane.

"I must be getting back to the light," he said finally. "I'll jest have time to walk home before sundown. Thank you for a beautiful Christmas, Mistress Blythe. Bring Master Davy down to the light some night before he goes home.

"I want to see those stone gods," said Davy with a relish.

CHAPTER 16

NEW YEAR'S EVE AT THE LIGHT

THE GREEN GABLES folk went home after Christmas, Marilla under solemn covenant to return for a month in the spring. More snow came before New Year's, and the harbor froze over, but the gulf still was free, beyond the white, imprisoned fields. The last day of the old year was one of those bright, cold, dazzling winter days, which bombard us with their brilliancy, and command our admiration but never our love. The sky was sharp and blue; the snow diamonds sparkled insistently; the stark trees were bare and shameless, with a kind of brazen beauty; the hills shot assaulting lances of crystal. Even the shadows were sharp and stiff and clear-cut, as no proper shadows should be. Everything that was handsome seemed ten times handsomer and less attractive in the glaring splendor; and everything that was ugly seemed ten times uglier, and everything was either handsome or ugly. There was no soft blending, or kind obscurity, or elusive mistiness in that searching glitter. The only things that held their own individuality were the firs—for the fir is the tree of mystery and shadow, and yields never to the encroachments of crude radiance.

But finally the day began to realise that she was growing old. Then a certain pensiveness fell over her beauty which dimmed yet intensified it; sharp angles, glittering points, melted away into curves and enticing gleams. The white harbor put on soft grays and pinks; the far-away hills turned amethyst.

"The old year is going away beautifully," said Anne.

She and Leslie and Gilbert were on their way to the Four Winds Point, having plotted with Captain Jim to watch the New Year in at the light. The sun had set and in the southwestern sky hung Venus, glorious and golden, having drawn as near to her earth-sister as is possible for her. For the first time Anne and Gilbert saw the shadow cast by that brilliant star of evening, that faint, mysterious shadow, never seen save when there is white snow to reveal it, and then only with averted vision, vanishing when you gaze at it directly.

"It's like the spirit of a shadow, isn't it?" whispered Anne. "You can see it so plainly haunting your side when you look ahead; but when you turn and look at it—it's gone."

"I have heard that you can see the shadow of Venus only once in a lifetime, and that within a year of seeing it your life's most wonderful gift will come to you," said Leslie. But she spoke rather hardly; perhaps she thought that even the shadow of Venus could bring her no gift of life. Anne smiled in the soft twilight; she felt quite sure what the mystic shadow promised her.

They found Marshall Elliott at the lighthouse. At first Anne felt inclined to resent the intrusion of this long-haired, long-bearded eccentric into the familiar little circle. But Marshall Elliott soon proved his legitimate claim to membership in the household of Joseph. He was a witty, intelligent, well-read man, rivalling Captain Jim himself in the knack of telling a good story. They were all glad when he agreed to watch the old year out with them.

Captain Jim's small nephew Joe had come down to spend New Year's with his great-uncle, and had fallen asleep on the sofa with the First Mate curled up in a huge golden ball at his feet.

"Ain't he a dear little man?" said Captain Jim gloatingly. "I do love to watch a little child asleep, Mistress Blythe. It's the most beautiful sight in the world, I reckon. Joe does love to get down here for a night, because I have him sleep with me. At home he has to sleep with the other two boys, and he doesn't like it. "Why can't I sleep with father, Uncle Jim?" says he. 'Everybody in the Bible slept with their fathers.' As for the questions he asks, the minister himself couldn't answer them. They fair swamp me. 'Uncle Jim, if I wasn't *me* who'd I be?' and, 'Uncle Jim, what would happen if God died?' He fired them two off at me tonight, afore he went to sleep. As for his imagination, it sails away from everything. He makes up the most remarkable yarns—and then his mother shuts him up in the closet for telling stories. And he sits down and makes up another one, and has it ready to relate to her when she lets him out. He had one for me when he come down tonight. 'Uncle Jim,' says he, solemn as a tombstone, 'I had a 'venture in the Glen today.' 'Yes, what was it?' says I, expecting something quite startling, but nowise prepared for what I really got. 'I met a wolf in the street,' says he, 'a 'normous wolf with a big, red mouf and *awful* long teeth, Uncle Jim.' 'I didn't know there was any wolves up at the Glen,' says I. 'Oh, he comed there from far, far away,' says Joe, 'and I fought he was going to eat me up, Uncle Jim.' 'Were you scared?' says I. 'No, 'cause I had a big gun,' says Joe, 'and I shot the wolf dead, Uncle Jim,—solid dead—and then he went up to heaven and bit God,' says he. Well, I was fair staggered, Mistress Blythe.''

The hours bloomed into mirth around the driftwood fire. Captain Jim told tales, and Marshall Elliott sang old Scotch ballads in a fine tenor voice; finally Captain Jim took down his old brown fiddle from the wall and began to play. He had a tolerable knack of fiddling, which all appreciated save the First Mate, who sprang from the sofa as if he had been shot, emitted a shriek of protest, and fled wildly up the stairs.

"Can't cultivate an ear for music in that cat nohow," said Captain Jim. "He won't stay long enough to learn to like it. When we got the organ up at the Glen church old Elder Richards bounced up from his seat the minute the organist began to play and scuttled down the aisle and out of the church at the rate of no-man's-business. It reminded me so strong of the First Mate tearing loose as soon as I begin to fiddle that I come nearer to laughing out loud in church than I ever did before or since."

There was something so infectious in the rollicking tunes which Captain Jim played that very soon Marshall Elliott's feet began to twitch. He had been a noted dancer in his youth. Presently he started up and held out his hands to Leslie. Instantly she responded. Round and round the firelit room they circled with a rhythmic grace that was wonderful. Leslie danced like one inspired; the wild, sweet abandon of the music seemed to have entered into and possessed her. Anne watched her in fascinated admiration. She had never seen her like this. All the innate richness and color and charm of her nature seemed to have broken loose and overflowed in crimson cheek and glowing eye and grace of motion. Even the aspect of Marshall Elliott, with his long beard and hair, could not spoil the picture. On the contrary, it seemed to enhance it. Marshall Elliott looked like a Viking of elder days, dancing with one of the blue-eyed, golden-haired daughters of the Northland.

"The purtiest dancing I ever saw, and I've seen some in my time," declared Captain Jim, when at last the bow fell from his tired hand. Leslie dropped into her chair, laughing, breathless.

"I love dancing," she said apart to Anne. "I haven't danced since

I was sixteen—but I love it. The music seems to run through my veins like quicksilver and I forget everything—everything—except the delight of keeping time to it. There isn't any floor beneath me, or walls about me, or roof over me—I'm floating amid the stars."

Captain Jim hung his fiddle up in its place, beside a large frame enclosing several banknotes.

"Is there anybody else of your acquaintance who can afford to hang his walls with banknotes for pictures?" he asked. "There's twenty ten-dollar notes there, not worth the glass over them. They're old Bank of P. E. Island notes. Had them by me when the bank failed, and I had 'em framed and hung up, partly as a reminder not to put your trust in banks, and partly to give me a real luxurious, millionairy feeling. Hullo, Matey, don't be scared. You can come back now. The music and revelry is over for tonight. The old year has just another hour to stay with us. I've seen seventy-six New Years come in over that gulf yonder, Mistress Blythe."

"You'll see a hundred," said Marshall Elliott.

Captain Jim shook his head.

"No; and I don't want to—at least, I think I don't. Death grows friendlier as we grow older. Not that one of us really wants to die though, Marshall. Tennyson spoke truth when he said that. There's old Mrs. Wallace up at the Glen. She's had heaps of trouble all her life, poor soul, and she's lost almost everyone she cared about. She's always saying that she'll be glad when her time comes, and she doesn't want to sojourn any longer in this vale of tears. But when she takes a sick spell there's a fuss! Doctors from town, and a trained nurse, and enough medicine to kill a dog. Life may be a vale of tears, all right, but there are some folks who enjoy weeping, I reckon."

They spent the old year's last hour quietly around the fire. A few minutes before twelve Captain Jim rose and opened the door.

"We must let the New Year in," he said.

Outside was a fine blue night. A sparkling ribbon of moonlight garlanded the gulf. Inside the bar the harbor shone like a pavement of pearl. They stood before the door and waited—Captain Jim with his ripe, full experience, Marshall Elliott in his vigorous but empty middle life, Gilbert and Anne with their precious memories and exquisite hopes, Leslie with her record of starved years and her hopeless future. The clock on the little shelf above the fireplace struck twelve.

"Welcome, New Year," said Captain Jim, bowing low as the last stroke died away. "I wish you all the best year of your lives, mates. I reckon that whatever the New Year brings us will be the best the Great Captain has for us—and somehow or other we'll all make port in a good harbor.''

CHAPTER 17

A FOUR WINDS WINTER

WINTER SET in vigorously after New Year's. Big, white drifts heaped themselves about the little house, and palms of frost covered its windows. The harbor ice grew harder and thicker, until the Four Winds people began their usual winter travelling over it. The safe ways were "bushed" by a benevolent Government, and night and day the gay tinkle of the sleigh-bells sounded on it. On moonlit nights Anne heard them in her house of dreams like fairy chimes. The gulf froze over, and the Four Winds light flashed no more. During the months when navigation was closed Captain Jim's office was a sinecure.

"The First Mate and I will have nothing to do till spring except keep warm and amuse ourselves. The last lighthouse keeper used always to move up to the Glen in winter; but I'd rather stay at the Point. The First Mate might get poisoned or chewed up by dogs at the Glen. It's a mite lonely, to be sure, with neither the light nor the water for company, but if our friends come to see us often we'll weather it through.''

Captain Jim had an ice boat, and many a wild, glorious spin Gilbert and Anne and Leslie had over the glib harbor ice with him. Anne and Leslie took long snowshoe tramps together, too, over the fields, or across the harbor after storms, or through the woods beyond the Glen. They were very good comrades in their rambles and their fireside communings. Each had something to give the other—each felt life the richer for friendly exchange of thought and friendly silence; each looked across the white fields between their homes with a pleasant consciousness of a friend beyond. But, in spite of all this, Anne felt that there was always a barrier between Leslie and herself—a constraint that never wholly vanished.

"I don't know why I can't get closer to her," Anne said one

evening to Captain Jim. "I like her so much—I admire her so much—I *want* to take her right into my heart and creep right into hers. But I can never cross the barrier."

"You've been too happy all your life, Mistress Blythe," said Captain Jim thoughtfully. "I reckon that's why you and Leslie can't get real close together in your souls. The barrier between you is her experience of sorrow and trouble. She ain't responsible for it and you ain't; but it's there and neither of you can cross it."

"My childhood wasn't very happy before I came to Green Gables," said Anne, gazing soberly out of the window at the still, sad, dead beauty of the leafless tree-shadows on the moonlit snow.

"Mebbe not—but it was just the usual unhappiness of a child who hasn't anyone to look after it properly. There hasn't been any *tragedy* in your life, Mistress Blythe. And poor Leslie's has been almost *all* tragedy. She feels, I reckon, though mebbe she hardly knows she feels it, that there's a vast deal in her life you can't enter nor understand—and so she has to keep you back from it—hold you off, so to speak, from hurting her. You know if we've got anything about us that hurts we shrink from anyone's touch on or near it. It holds good with our souls as well as our bodies, I reckon. Leslie's soul must be near raw—it's no wonder she hides it away."

"If that were really all, I wouldn't mind, Captain Jim. I would understand. But there are times—not always, but now and again—when I almost have to believe that Leslie doesn't—doesn't like me. Sometimes I surprise a look in her eyes that seems to show resentment and dislike—it goes so quickly—but I've seen it, I'm sure of that. And it hurts me, Captain Jim. I'm not used to being disliked—and I've tried so hard to win Leslie's friendship."

"You have won it, Mistress Blythe. Don't you go cherishing any foolish notion that Leslie don't like you. If she didn't she wouldn't have anything to do with you, much less chumming with you as she does. I know Leslie Moore too well not to be sure of that."

"The first time I ever saw her, driving her geese down the hill on the day I came to Four Winds, she looked at me with the same expression," persisted Anne. "I felt it, even in the midst of my admiration of her beauty. She looked at me resentfully—she did, indeed, Captain Jim."

"The resentment must have been about something else, Mistress Blythe, and you jest come in for a share of it because you happened past. Leslie *does* take sullen spells now and again, poor girl. I can't blame her, when I know what she has to put up with. I don't know why it's permitted. The doctor and I have talked a lot abut the origin of evil, but we haven't quite found out all about it yet. There's a vast of onunderstandable things in life, ain't there, Mistress Blythe? Sometimes things seem to work out real proper-like, same as with you and the doctor. And then again they all seem to go catawampus. There's Leslie, so clever and beautiful you'd think she was meant for a queen, and instead she's cooped up over there, robbed of almost everything a woman'd value, with no prospect except waiting on Dick Moore all her life. Though, mind you, Mistress Blythe, I daresay she'd choose her life now, such as it is, rather than the life she lived with Dick before he went away. *That's* something a clumsy old sailor's tongue mustn't meddle with. But you've helped Leslie a lot—she's a different creature since you come to Four Winds. Us old friends see the difference in her, as you can't. Miss Cornelia and me was talking it over the other day, and it's one of the mighty few p'ints that we see eye to eye on. So jest you throw overboard any idea of her not liking you.''

Anne could hardly discard it completely, for there were undoubtedly times when she felt, with an instinct that was not to be combated by reason, that Leslie harbored a queer, indefinable resentment towards her. At times, this secret consciousness marred the delight of their comradeship; at others it was almost forgotten; but Anne always felt the hidden thorn was there, and might prick her at any moment. She felt a cruel sting from it on the day when she told Leslie of what she hoped the spring would bring to the little house of dreams. Leslie looked at her with hard, bitter, unfriendly eyes.

''So you are to have *that,* too,'' she said in a choked voice. And without another word she had turned and gone across the fields homeward. Anne was deeply hurt; for the moment she felt as if she could never like Leslie again. But when Leslie came over a few evenings later she was so pleasant, so friendly, so frank, and witty, and winsome, that Anne was charmed into forgiveness and forgetfulness. Only, she never mentioned her darling hope to Leslie again; nor did Leslie ever refer to it. But one evening, when late winter was listening for the word of spring, she came over to the little house for a twilight chat; and when she went away she left a small, white box on the table. Anne found it after she was gone and opened it wonderingly. In it was a tiny white dress of exquisite workmanship— delicate embroidery, wonderful tucking, sheer loveliness. Every stitch in it was handwork; and the little frills of lace at neck and sleeves were of real Valenciennes. Lying on it was a card—''with Leslie's love.''

''What hours of work she must have put on it,'' said Anne. ''And the material must have cost more than she could really afford.

It is very sweet of her.''

But Leslie was brusque and curt when Anne thanked her, and again the latter felt thrown back upon herself.

Leslie's gift was not alone in the little house. Miss Cornelia had, for the time being, given up sewing for unwanted, unwelcome eighth babies, and fallen to sewing for a very much wanted first one, whose welcome would leave nothing to be desired. Philippa Blake and Diana Wright each sent a marvellous garment; and Mrs. Rachel Lynde sent several, in which good material and honest stitches took the place of embroidery and frills. Anne herself made many, desecrated by no touch of machinery, spending over them the happiest hours of the happy winter.

Captain Jim was the most frequent guest of the little house, and none was more welcome. Every day Anne loved the simple-souled, true-hearted old sailor more and more. He was as refreshing as a sea breeze, as interesting as some ancient chronicle. She was never tired of listening to his stories, and his quaint remarks and comments were a continual delight to her. Captain Jim was one of those rare and interesting people who ''never speak but they say something.'' The milk of human kindness and the wisdom of the serpent were mingled in his composition in delightful proportions.

Nothing ever seemed to put Captain Jim out or depress him in any way.

''I've kind of contracted a habit of enj'ying things,'' he remarked once, when Anne had commented on his invariable cheerfulness. ''It's got so chronic that I believe I even enj'y the disagreeable things. It's great fun thinking they can't last. 'Old rheumatiz,' says I, when it grips me hard, 'you've *got* to stop aching sometime. The worse you are the sooner you'll stop, mebbe. I'm bound to get the better of you in the long run, whether in the body or out of the body.' ''

One night, by the fireside at the light Anne saw Captain Jim's ''life-book.'' He needed no coaxing to show it and proudly gave it to her to read.

''I writ it to leave to little Joe,'' he said. ''I don't like the idea of everything I've done and seen being clean forgot after I've shipped for my last v'yage. Joe, he'll remember it, and tell the yarns to his children.''

It was an old leather-bound book filled with the record of his voyages and adventures. Anne thought what a treasure trove it would be to a writer. Every sentence was a nugget. In itself the book had no literary merit; Captain Jim's charm of storytelling failed him when he came to pen and ink; he could only jot roughly down the outline of his famous tales, and both spelling and grammar were sadly askew. But Anne felt that if anyone possessed of the gift could take that simple record of a brave, adventurous life, reading between the bald lines the tales of dangers staunchly faced and duty manfully done, a wonderful story might be made from it. Rich comedy and thrilling tragedy were both lying hidden in Captain Jim's "life-book," waiting for the touch of the master hand to waken the laughter and grief and horror of thousands.

Anne said something of this to Gilbert as they walked home.

"Why don't you try your hand at it yourself, Anne?"

Anne shook her head.

"No. I only wish I could. But it's not in the power of my gift. You know what my forte is, Gilbert—the fanciful, the fairylike, the pretty. To write Captain Jim's life-book as it should be written one should be a master of vigorous yet subtle style, a keen psychologist, a born humorist and a born tragedian. A rare combination of gifts is needed. Paul might do it if he were older. Anyhow, I'm going to ask him to come down next summer and meet Captain Jim."

"Come to this shore," wrote Anne to Paul. "I am afraid you cannot find here Nora or the Golden Lady or the Twin Sailors; but you will find one old sailor who can tell you wonderful stories."

Paul, however wrote back, saying regretfully that he could not come that year. He was going abroad for two year's study.

"When I return I'll come to Four Winds, dear Teacher," he wrote.

"But meanwhile, Captain Jim is growing old," said Anne, sorrowfully, "and there is nobody to write his life-book."

CHAPTER 18

SPRING DAYS

THE ICE in the harbor grew black and rotten in the March suns; in April there were blue waters and a windy, white-capped gulf again; and again the Four Winds light begemmed the twilights.

"I'm so glad to see it once more," said Anne, on the first evening of its reappearance. "I've missed it so all winter. The northwestern sky has seemed blank and lonely without it.''

The land was tender with brand-new, golden-green, baby leaves. There was an emerald mist on the woods beyond the Glen. The seaward valleys were full of fairy mists at dawn.

Vibrant winds came and went with salt foam in their breath. The sea laughed and flashed and preened and allured, like a beautiful, coquettish woman. The herring schooled and the fishing village woke to life. The harbor was alive with white sails making for the channel. The ships began to sail outward and inward again.

''On a spring day like this,'' said Anne, ''I know exactly what my soul will feel like on the resurrection morning.''

''There are times in spring when I sorter feel that I might have been a poet if I'd been caught young,'' remarked Captain Jim. ''I catch myself conning over old lines and verses I heard the school-master reciting sixty years ago. They don't trouble me at other times. Now I feel as if I had to get out on the rocks or the fields or the water and spout them.''

Captain Jim had come up that afternoon to bring Anne a load of shells for her garden, and a little bunch of sweet-grass which he had found in a ramble over the sand dunes.

''It's getting real scarce along this shore now,'' he said. ''When I was a boy there was a-plenty of it. But now it's only once in a while you'll find a plot—and never when you're looking for it. You jest have to stumble on it—you're walking along on the sand hills, never thinking of sweet-grass—and all at once the air is full of sweetness— and there's the grass under your feet. I favor the smell of sweet-grass. It always makes me think of my mother.''

''She was fond of it?'' asked Anne.

''Not that I knows on. Dunno's she ever saw any sweet-grass. No, it's because it has a kind of motherly perfume—not too young, you understand—something kind of seasoned and wholesome and dependable—jest like a mother. The schoolmaster's bride always kept it among her handkerchiefs. You might put that little bunch among yours, Mistress Blythe. I don't like these boughten scents— but a whiff of sweet-grass belongs anywhere a lady does.''

Anne had not been especially enthusiastic over the idea of sur-rounding her flower beds with quahog shells; as a decoration they did not appeal to her on first thought. But she would not have hurt Captain Jim's feelings for anything; so she assumed a virtue she did not at first feel, and thanked him heartily. And when Captain Jim had proudly encircled every bed with a rim of the big, milk-white shells,

Anne found to her surprise that she liked the effect. On a town lawn, or even up at the Glen, they would not have been in keeping, but here, in the old-fashioned, sea-bound garden of the little house of dreams, they *belonged*.

"They *do* look nice," she said sincerely.

"The schoolmaster's bride always had cowhawks round her beds," said Captain Jim. "She was a master hand with flowers. She *looked* at 'em—and touched 'em—*so*—and they grew like mad. Some folks have that knack—I reckon you have it, too, Mistress Blythe."

"Oh, I don't know—but I love my garden, and I love working in it. To potter with green, growing things, watching each day to see the dear, new sprouts come up, is like taking a hand in creation, I think. Just now my garden is like faith—the substance of things hoped for. But bide a wee."

"It always amazes me to look at the little, wrinkled brown seeds and think of the rainbows in 'em," said Captain Jim. "When I ponder on them seeds I don't find it nowise hard to believe that we've got souls that'll live in other worlds. You couldn't hardly believe there was life in them tiny things, some no bigger than grains of dust, let alone color and scent, if you hadn't seen the miracle, could you?"

Anne, who was counting her days like silver beads on a rosary, could not now take the long walk to the lighthouse or up the Glen road. But Miss Cornelia and Captain Jim came very often to the little house. Miss Cornelia was the joy of Anne's and Gilbert's existence. They laughed side-splittingly over her speeches after every visit. When Captain Jim and she happened to visit the little house at the same time there was much sport for the listening. They waged wordy warfare, she attacking, he defending. Anne once reproached the Captain for his baiting of Miss Cornelia.

"Oh, I do love to set her going, Mistress Blythe," chuckled the unrepentant sinner. "It's the greatest amusement I have in life. That tongue of hers would blister a stone. And you and that young dog of a doctor enj'y listening to her as much as I do."

Captain Jim came along another evening to bring Anne some mayflowers. The garden was full of the moist, scented air of a maritime spring evening. There was a milk-white mist on the edge of the sea, with a young moon kissing it, and a silver gladness of stars over the Glen. The bell of the church across the harbor was ringing dreamily sweet. The mellow chime drifted through the dusk to mingle with the soft spring-moan of the sea. Captain Jim's mayflowers added the last completing touch to the charm of the night.

"I haven't seen any this spring, and I've missed them," said Anne, burying her face in them.

"They ain't to be found around Four Winds, only in the barrens away behind the Glen up yander. I took a little trip today to the Land-of-nothing-to-do, and hunted these up for you. I reckon they're the last you'll see this spring, for they're nearly done."

"How kind and thoughtful you are, Captain Jim. Nobody else— not even Gilbert"—with a shake of her head at him—"remembered that I always long for mayflowers in spring."

"Well, I had another errand, too—I wanted to take Mr. Howard back yander a mess of trout. He likes one occasional, and it's all I can do for a kindness he did me once. I stayed all the afternoon and talked to him. He likes to talk to me, though he's a highly eddicated man and I'm only an ignorant old sailor, because he's one of the folks that's *got* to talk or they're miserable, and he finds listeners scarce around here. The Glen folks fight shy of him because they think he's an infidel. He ain't that far gone exactly—few men is, I reckon—but he's what you might call a heretic. Heretics are wicked, but they're mighty int'resting. It's jest that they've got sorter lost looking for God, being under the impression that He's hard to find—which He ain't never. Most of 'em blunder to Him after awhile, I guess. I don't think listening to Mr. Howard's arguments is likely to do *me* much harm. Mind you, I believe what I was brought up to believe. It saves a vast of bother—and back of it all, God is good. The trouble with Mr. Howard is that he's a leetle *too* clever. He thinks that he's bound to live up to his cleverness, and that it's smarter to thrash out some new way of getting to heaven than to go by the old track the common, ignorant folks is travelling. But he'll get there sometime all right, and then he'll laugh at himself."

"Mr. Howard was a Methodist to begin with," said Miss Cornelia, as if she thought he had not far to go from that to heresy.

"Do you know, Cornelia," said Captain Jim gravely, "I've often thought that if I wasn't a Presbyterian I'd be a Methodist."

"Oh, well," conceded Miss Cornelia, "if you weren't a Presbyterian it wouldn't matter much what you were. Speaking of heresy, reminds me, doctor—I've brought back that book you lent me—that *Natural Law in the Spiritual World*—I didn't read more'n a third of it. I can read sense, and I can read nonsense, but that book is neither the one nor the other."

"It *is* considered rather heretical in some quarters," admitted

Gilbert, "but I told you that before you took it, Miss Cornelia."

"Oh, I wouldn't have minded its being heretical. I can stand wickedness, but I can't stand foolishness," said Miss Cornelia calmly, and with the air of having said the last thing there was to say about *Natural Law*.

"Speaking of books, *A Mad Love* come to an end at last two weeks ago," remarked Captain Jim musingly. "It run to one hundred and three chapters. When they got married the book stopped right off, so I reckon their troubles were all over. It's real nice that that's the way in books anyhow, isn't it, even if 'tistn't so anywhere else?"

"I never read novels," said Miss Cornelia. "Did you hear how Geordie Russell was today, Captain Jim?"

"Yes, I called in on my way home to see him. He's getting round all right—but stewing in a broth of trouble, as usual, poor man. 'Course he brews up most of it for himself, but I reckon that don't make it any easier to bear."

"He's an awful pessimist," said Miss Cornelia.

"Well, no, he ain't a pessimist exactly, Cornelia. He only jest never finds anything that suits him."

"And isn't that a pessimist?"

"No, no. A pessimist is one who never expects to find anything to suit him. Geordie hain't got *that* far yet."

"You'd find something good to say of the devil himself, Jim Boyd."

"Well, you've heard the story of the old lady who said he was persevering. But no, Cornelia, I've nothing good to say of the devil."

"Do you believe in him at all?" asked Miss Cornelia seriously.

"How can you ask that when you know what a good Presbyterian I am, Cornelia? How could a Presbyterian get along without a devil?"

"*Do* you?" persisted Miss Cornelia.

Captain Jim suddenly became grave.

"I believe in what I heard a minister once call 'a mighty and malignant and *intelligent* power of evil working in the universe,'" he said solemnly. "I do *that*, Cornelia. You can call it the devil, or the 'principle of evil,' or the Old Scratch, or any name you like. It's *there*, and all the infidels and heretics in the world can't argue it away, any more'n they can argue God away. It's there, and it's working. But, mind you, Cornelia, I beleive it's going to get the worst of it in the long run."

"I am sure I hope so," said Miss Cornelia, none too hopefully.

''But speaking of the devil, I am positive that Billy Booth is possessed by him now. Have you heard of Billy's latest performance?''

''No, what was that?''

''He's gone and burned up his wife's new, brown broadcloth suit, that she paid twenty-five dollars for in Charlottetown, because he declares the men looked too admiring at her when she wore it to church the first time. Wasn't that like a man?''

''Mistress Booth *is* mighty pretty, and brown's her color,'' said Captain Jim reflectively.

''Is that any good reason why he should poke her new suit into the kitchen stove? Billy Booth is a jealous fool, and he makes his wife's life miserable. She's cried all the week about her suit. Oh, Anne, I wish I could write like you, believe *me*. Wouldn't I score some of the men round here!''

''Those Booths are all a mite queer,'' said Captain Jim. ''Billy seemed the sanest of the lot till he got married and then this queer jealous streak cropped out in him. His brother Daniel, now, was always odd.''

''Took tantrums every few days or so and wouldn't get out of bed,'' said Miss Cornelia with a relish. ''His wife would have to do all the barn work till he got over his spell. When he died people wrote her letters of condolence; if I'd written anything it would have been one of congratulation. Their father, old Abram Booth, was a disgusting old sot. He was drunk at his wife's funeral, and kept reeling round and hiccuping 'I didn't dri—i—i—nk much but I feel a—a—awfully que—e—e—r.' I gave him a good jab in the back with my umbrella when he came near me, and it sobered him up until they got the casket out of the house. Young Johnny Booth was to have been married yesterday, but he couldn't be because he's gone and got the mumps. Wasn't that like a man?''

''How could he help getting the mumps, poor fellow?''

''I'd poor fellow him, believe *me*, if I was Kate Sterns. I don't know how he could help getting the mumps, but I *do* know the wedding supper was all prepared and everything will be spoiled before he's well again. Such a waste! He should have had the mumps when he was a boy.''

''Come, come, Cornelia, don't you think you're a mite unreasonable?''

Miss Cornelia disdained to reply and turned instead to Susan Baker, a grim-faced, kind-hearted elderly spinster of the Glen, who had been installed as maid-of-all-work at the little house for some weeks. Susan had been up to the Glen to make a sick call, and had just returned.

"How is poor old Aunt Mandy tonight?" asked Miss Cornelia.

Susan sighed.

"Very poorly—very poorly, Cornelia. I am afraid she will soon be in heaven, poor thing!"

"Oh, surely, it's not so bad as that!" exclaimed Miss Cornelia, sympathetically.

Captain Jim and Gilbert looked at each other. Then they suddenly rose and went out.

"There are times," said Captain Jim, between spasms, "when it would be a sin *not* to laugh. Them two excellent women!"

CHAPTER 19

DAWN AND DUSK

IN EARLY June, when the sand hills were a great glory of pink wild roses, and the Glen was smothered in apple blossoms, Marilla arrived at the little house, accompanied by a black horsehair trunk, patterned with brass nails, which had reposed undisturbed in the Green Gables garret for half a century. Susan Baker, who, during her few weeks' sojourn in the little house, had come to worship "young Mrs. Doctor," as she called Anne, with blind fervor, looked rather jealously askance at Marilla at first. But as Marilla did not try to interfere in kitchen matters, and showed no desire to interrupt Susan's ministrations to young Mrs. Doctor, the good handmaiden became reconciled to her presence, and told her cronies at the Glen that Miss Cuthbert was a fine old lady and knew her place.

One evening, when the sky's limpid bowl was filled with a red glory, and the robins were thrilling the golden twilight with jubilant hymns to the stars of evening, there was a sudden commotion in the little house of dreams. Telephone messages were sent up to the Glen, Doctor Dave and a white-capped nurse came hastily down, Marilla paced the garden walks between the quahog shells, murmuring prayers between her set lips, and Susan sat in the kitchen with cotton wool in her ears and her apron over her head.

Leslie, looking out from the house up the brook, saw that every window of the little house was alight, and did not sleep that night.

The June night was short; but it seemed an eternity to those who waited and watched.

"Oh, will it *never* end?" said Marilla; then she saw how grave the nurse and Doctor Dave looked, and she dared ask no more questions. Suppose Anne—but Marilla could not suppose it.

"Do not tell me," said Susan fiercely, answering the anguish in Marilla's eyes, "that God could be so cruel as to take that darling lamb from us when we all love her so much."

"He has taken others as well beloved," said Marilla hoarsely.

But at dawn, when the rising sun rent apart the mists hanging over the sandbar, and made rainbows of them, joy came to the little house. Anne was safe, and a wee, white lady, with her mother's big eyes, was lying beside her. Gilbert, his face gray and haggard from his night's agony, came down to tell Marilla and Susan.

"Thank God," shuddered Marilla.

Susan got up and took the cotton wool out of her ears.

"Now for breakfast," she said briskly. "I am of the opinion that we will all be glad of a bite and sup. You tell young Mrs. Doctor not to worry about a single thing—Susan is at the helm. You tell her just to think of her baby."

Gilbert smiled rather sadly as he went away. Anne, her pale face blanched with its baptism of pain, her eyes aglow with the holy passion of motherhood, did not need to be told to think of her baby. She thought of nothing else. For a few hours she tasted of happiness so rare and exquisite that she wondered if the angels in heaven did not envy her.

"Little Joyce," she murmured, when Marilla came in to see the baby. "We planned to call her that if she were a girlie. There were so many we would have liked to name her for; we couldn't choose between them, so we decided on Joyce—we can call her Joy for short—Joy—it suits so well. Oh, Marilla, I thought I was happy before. Now I know that I just dreamed a pleasant dream of happiness. *This* is the reality."

"You mustn't talk, Anne—wait till you're stronger," said Marilla warningly.

"You know how hard it is for me *not* to talk," smiled Anne.

At first she was too weak and too happy to notice that Gilbert and the nurse looked grave and Marilla sorrowful. Then, as subtly, and coldly, and remorselessly as a sea-fog stealing landward, fear crept into her heart. Why was not Gilbert gladder? Why would he not talk about the baby? Why would they not let her have it with her after that first heavenly-happy hour? Was—was there anything wrong?

"Gilbert," whispered Anne imploringly, "the baby—is all right—isn't she? Tell me—tell me."

Gilbert was a long while in turning round; then he bent over Anne and looked in her eyes. Marilla, listening fearfully outside the door, heard a pitiful, heartbroken moan, and fled to the kitchen where Susan was weeping.

"Oh, the poor lamb—the poor lamb! How can she bear it, Miss Cuthbert? I am afraid it will kill her. She has been that built up and happy, longing for that baby, and planning for it. Cannot anything be done nohow, Miss Cuthbert?"

"I'm afraid not, Susan. Gilbert says there is no hope. He knew from the first the little thing couldn't live."

"And it is such a sweet baby," sobbed Susan. "I never saw one so white—they are mostly red or yallow. And it opened its big eyes as if it was months old. The little, little thing! Oh, the poor, young Mrs. Doctor!"

At sunset the little soul that had come with the dawning went away, leaving heartbreak behind it. Miss Cornelia took the wee, white lady from the kindly but stranger hands of the nurse, and dressed the tiny waxen form in the beautiful dress Leslie had made for it. Leslie had asked her to do that. Then she took it back and laid it beside the poor, broken, tear-blinded little mother.

"The Lord has given and the Lord has taken away, dearie," she said through her own tears. "Blessed be the name of the Lord."

Then she went away, leaving Anne and Gilbert alone together with their dead.

The next day, the small white Joy was laid in a velvet casket which Leslie had lined with apple-blossoms, and taken to the grave-yard of the church across the harbor. Miss Cornelia and Marilla put all the little love-made garments away, together with the ruffled basket which had been befrilled and belaced for dimpled limbs and downy head. Little Joy was never to sleep there; she had found a colder, narrower bed.

"This has been an awful disappointment to me," sighed Miss Cornelia. "I've looked forward to this baby—and I did want it to be a girl, too."

"I can only be thankful that Anne's life was spared," said Marilla, with a shiver, recalling those hours of darkness when the girl she loved was passing through the valley of the shadow.

"Poor, poor lamb! Her heart is broken," said Susan.

"I *envy* Anne," said Leslie suddenly and fiercely, "and I'd envy her even if she had died! She was a mother for one beautiful day. I'd gladly give my life for *that*!"

"I wouldn't talk like that, Leslie, dearie," said Miss Cornelia deprecatingly. She was afraid that the dignified Miss Cuthbert would think Leslie quite terrible.

Anne's convalescence was long, and made bitter for her by many things. The bloom and sunshine of the Four Winds world grated harshly on her; and yet, when the rain fell heavily, she pictured it beating so mercilessly down on that little grave across the harbor; and when the wind blew around the eaves she heard sad voices in it she had never heard before.

Kindly callers hurt her, too, with the well-meant platitudes with which they strove to cover the nakedness of bereavement. A letter from Phil Blake was an added sting. Phil had heard of the baby's birth, but not of its death, and she wrote Anne a congratulatory letter of sweet mirth which hurt her horribly.

"I would have laughed over it so happily if I had my baby," she sobbed to Marilla. "But when I haven't it just seems like wanton cruelty—though I know Phil wouldn't hurt me for the world. Oh, Marilla, I don't see how I can *ever* be happy again—*everything* will hurt me all the rest of my life."

"Time will help you," said Marilla, who was racked with sympathy but could never learn to express it in other than age-worn formulas.

"It doesn't seem *fair*," said Anne rebelliously. "Babies are born and live where they are not wanted—where they will be neglected—where they will have no chance. I would have loved my baby so—and cared for it so tenderly—and tried to give her every chance for good. And yet I wasn't allowed to keep her."

"It was God's will, Anne," said Marilla, helpless before the riddle of the universe—the *why* of undeserved pain. "And little Joy is better off."

"I can't believe *that*," cried Anne bitterly. Then, seeing that Marilla looked shocked, she added passionately, "Why should she be born at all—why should any one be born at all—if she's better off dead? I *don't* believe it is better for a child to die at birth than to live its life out—and love and be loved—and enjoy and suffer—and do its work—and develop a character that would give it a personality in eternity. And how do you know it was God's will? Perhaps it was just a thwarting of His purpose by the Power of Evil. We can't be expected to be resigned to *that*."

"Oh, Anne, don't talk so," said Marilla, genuinely alarmed lest Anne were drifting into deep and dangerous waters. "We can't understand—but we must have faith—we *must* believe that all is for the best. I know you find it hard to think so, just now. But try to be brave—for Gilbert's sake. He's so worried about you. You aren't getting strong as fast as you should."

"Oh, I know I've been very selfish," sighed Anne. "I love Gilbert more than ever—and I want to live for his sake. But it seems as if part of me was buried over there in that little harbor graveyard— and it hurts so much that I'm afraid of life."

"It won't hurt so much always, Anne."

"The thought that it may stop hurting sometimes hurts me worse than all else, Marilla."

"Yes, I know, I've felt that too, about other things. But we all love you, Anne. Captain Jim has been up every day to ask for you—and Mrs. Moore haunts the place—and Miss Bryant spends most of her time, I think, cooking up nice things for you. Susan doesn't like it very well. She thinks she can cook as well as Miss Bryant."

"Dear Susan! Oh, everybody has been so dear and good and lovely to me, Marilla. I'm not ungrateful—and perhaps—when this horrible ache grows a little less—I'll find that I can go on living."

CHAPTER 20

LOST MARGARET

ANNE FOUND that she could go on living; the day came when she even smiled again over one of Miss Cornelia's speeches. But there was something in the smile that had never been in Anne's smile before and would never be absent from it again.

On the first day she was able to go for a drive Gilbert took her down to Four Winds Point, and left her there while he rowed over the channel to see a patient at the fishing village. A rollicking wind was scudding across the harbor and the dunes, whipping the water into white-caps and washing the sandshore with long lines of silvery breakers.

"I'm real proud to see you here again, Mistress Blythe," said Captain Jim. "Sit down—sit down. I'm afeared it's mighty dusty here today—but there's no need of looking at dust when you can look at such scenery, is there?"

"I don't mind the dust," said Anne, "but Gilbert says I must keep in the open air. I think I'll go and sit on the rocks down there."

"Would you like company or would you rather be alone?"

"If by company you mean yours I'd much rather have it than be alone," said Anne, smiling. Then she sighed. She had never before minded being alone. Now she dreaded it. When she was alone now she felt so dreadfully alone.

"Here's a nice little spot where the wind can't get at you," said Captain Jim, when they reached the rocks. "I often sit here. It's a great place jest to sit and dream."

"Oh—dreams," sighed Anne. "I can't dream now, Captain Jim—I'm done with dreams."

"Oh, no, you're not, Mistress Blythe—oh, no, you're not," said Captain Jim meditatively. "I know how you feel jest now—but if you keep on living you'll get glad again, and the first thing you know you'll be dreaming again—thank the good Lord for it! If it wasn't for our dreams they might as well bury us. How'd we stand living if it wasn't for our dream of immortality? And that's a dream that's *bound* to come true, Mistress Blythe. You'll see your little Joyce again some day."

"But she won't be my baby," said Anne, with trembling lips. "Oh, she may be, as Longfellow says, 'a fair maiden clothed with celestial grace'—but she'll be a stranger to me."

"God will manage better'n *that,* I believe," said Captain Jim.

They were both silent for a little time. Then Captain Jim said very softly:

"Mistress Blythe, may I tell you about lost Margaret?"

"Of course," said Anne gently. She did not know who "lost Margaret" was, but she felt that she was going to hear the romance of Captain Jim's life.

"I've often wanted to tell you about her," Captain Jim went on. "Do you know why, Mistress Blythe? It's because I want somebody to remember and think of her sometime after I'm gone. I can't bear that her name should be forgotten by all living souls. And now nobody remembers lost Margaret but me."

Then Captain Jim told the story—an old, old forgotten story, for it was over fifty years since Margaret had fallen asleep one day in her father's dory and drifted—or so it was supposed, for nothing was ever certainly known as to her fate—out of the channel, beyond the bar, to perish in the black thundersquall which had come up so suddenly that long-ago summer afternoon. But to Captain Jim those fifty years were but as yesterday when it is past.

"I walked the shore for months after that," he said sadly, "looking to find her dear, sweet little body; but the sea never give her back to me. But I'll find her sometime, Mistress Blythe—I'll find her sometime. She's waiting for me. I wish I could tell you jest how she looked, but I can't. I've seen a fine, silvery mist hanging over the bar at sunrise that seemed like her—and then again I've seen a white birch in the woods back yander that made me think of her. She had pale, brown hair and a little white, sweet face, and long slender fingers like yours, Mistress Blythe, only browner, for she was a shore girl. Sometimes I wake up in the night and hear the sea calling to me in the old way, and it seems as if lost Margaret called in it. And when there's a storm and the waves are sobbing and moaning I hear her lamenting among them. And when they laugh on a gay day it's *her* laugh—lost Margaret's sweet, roguish, little laugh. The sea took her from me, but some day I'll find her. Mistress Blythe. It can't keep us apart forever."

"I am glad you have told me about her," said Anne. "I have often wondered why you had lived all your life alone."

"I couldn't ever care for anyone else. Lost Margaret took my heart with her—out there," said the old lover, who had been faithful for fifty years to his drowned sweetheart. "You won't mind if I talk a good deal about her, will you, Mistress Blythe? It's a pleasure to me—for all the pain went out of her memory years ago and jest left its blessing. I know you'll never forget her, Mistress Blythe. And if the years, as I hope, bring other little folks to your home, I want you to promise me that you'll tell *them* the story of lost Margaret, so that her name won't be forgotten among humankind."

CHAPTER 21

BARRIERS SWEPT AWAY

"ANNE," SAID Leslie, breaking abruptly a short silence, "you don't know how *good* it is to be sitting here with you again—working—and talking—and being silent together."

They were sitting among the blue-eyed grasses on the bank of the brook in Anne's garden. The water sparkled and crooned past them; the birches threw dappled shadows over them; roses bloomed along the walks. The sun was beginning to be low, and the air was full of woven music. There was one music of the wind in the firs behind the house, and another of the waves on the bar, and still another from the distant bell of the church near which the wee, white lady slept. Anne loved that bell, though it brought sorrowful thoughts now.

She looked curiously at Leslie, who had thrown down her sewing and spoken with a lack of restraint that was very unusual with her.

"On that horrible night when you were so ill," Leslie went on, "I kept thinking that perhaps we'd have no more talks and walks and *works* together. And I realised just what your friendship had come to mean to me—just what *you* meant—and just what a hateful little beast I had been."

"Leslie! Leslie! I never allow anyone to call my friends names."

"It's true. That's exactly what I am—a hateful little beast. There's something I've *got* to tell you, Anne. I suppose it will make you despise me, but I *must* confess it. Anne, there have been times this past winter and spring when I have *hated* you."

"I knew it," said Anne calmly.

"You *knew* it?"

"Yes, I saw it in your eyes."

"And yet you went on liking me and being my friend."

"Well, it was only now and then you hated me, Leslie. Between times you loved me, I think."

"I certainly did. But that other horrid feeling was always there, spoiling it, back in my heart. I kept it down—sometimes I forgot it—but sometimes it would surge up and take possession of me. I hated you because I *envied* you—oh, I was sick with envy of you at times. You had a dear little home—and love—and happiness—and glad dreams—everything I wanted—and never had—and never could have. Oh, never could have! *That* was what stung. I wouldn't have

548

envied you, if I had had any *hope* that life would ever be different for me. But I hadn't—I hadn't—and it didn't seem *fair*. It made me rebellious—and it hurt me—and so I hated you at times. Oh, I was so ashamed of it—I'm dying of shame now—but I couldn't conquer it. That night, when I was afraid you mightn't live—I thought I was going to be punished for my wickedness—and I loved you so then. Anne, Anne, I never had anything to love since my mother died, except Dick's old dog—and it's so dreadful to have nothing to love—life is so *empty*—and there's *nothing* worse than emptiness— and I might have loved you so much—and that horrible thing had spoiled it—''

Leslie was trembling and growing almost incoherent with the violence of her emotion.

"Don't, Leslie," implored Anne, "oh, don't. I understand— don't talk of it any more."

"I must—I must. When I knew you were going to live I vowed that I would tell you as soon as you were well—that I wouldn't go on accepting your friendship and companionship without telling you how unworthy I was of it. And I've been so afraid—it would turn you against me."

"You needn't fear that, Leslie."

"Oh, I'm so glad—so glad, Anne." Leslie clasped her brown, work-hardened hands tightly together to still their shaking. "But I want to tell you everything, now I've begun. You don't remember the first time I saw you, I suppose—it wasn't that night on the shore—"

"No, it was the night Gilbert and I came home. You were driving your geese down the hill. I should think I *do* remember it! I thought you were so beautiful—I longed for weeks after to find out who you were."

"I knew who *you* were, although I had never seen either of you before. I had heard of the new doctor and his bride who were coming to live in Miss Russell's little house. I—I hated you that very moment, Anne."

"I felt the resentment in your eyes—then I doubted—I thought I must be mistaken—because *why* should it be?"

"It was because you looked so happy. Oh, you'll agree with me now that I *am* a hateful beast—to hate another woman just because she was happy,—and when her happiness didn't take anything from me! That was why I never went to see you. I knew quite well I ought to go—even our simple Four Winds customs demanded that. But I couldn't. I used to watch you from my window—I could see you and your husband strolling about your garden in the evening—or you running down the poplar lane to meet him. And it hurt me. And yet in another way I wanted to go over. I felt that, if I were not so miserable, I could have liked you and found in you what I've never had in my life—an intimate, *real* friend of my own age. And then you remember that night at the shore? You were afraid I would think you crazy. You must have thought *I* was.''

"No, but I couldn't understand you, Leslie. One moment you drew me to you—the next you pushed me back.''

''I was very unhappy that evening. I had had a hard day. Dick had been very—very hard to manage that day. Generally he is quite good-natured and easily controlled, you know, Anne. But some days he is very different. I was so heartsick—I ran away to the shore as soon as he went to sleep. It was my only refuge. I sat there thinking of how my poor father had ended his life, and wondering if I wouldn't be driven to it some day. Oh, my heart was full of black thoughts! And then you came dancing along the cove like a glad, light-hearted child. I—I hated you more then than I've ever done since. And yet I craved your friendship. The one feeling swayed me one moment; the other feeling the next. When I got home that night I cried for shame of what you must think of me. But it's always been just the same when I came over here. Sometimes I'd be happy and enjoy my visit. And at other times that hideous feeling would mar it all. There were times when everything about you and your house hurt me. You had so many dear little things I couldn't have. Do you know—it's ridiculous—but I had an especial spite at those china dogs of yours. There were times when I wanted to catch up Gog and Magog and bang their pert black noses together! Oh, you smile, Anne—but it was never funny to me. I would come here and see you and Gilbert with your books and your flowers, and your household goods, and your little family jokes—and your love for each other showing in every look and word, even when you didn't know it—and I would go home to—you know what I went home to! Oh, Anne, I don't believe I'm jealous and envious by nature. When I was a girl I lacked many things my schoolmates had, but I never cared—I never disliked them for it. But I seem to have grown so hateful—''

"Leslie, dearest, stop blaming yourself. You are *not* hateful or jealous or envious. The life you have to live has warped you a little, perhaps—but it would have ruined a nature less fine and noble than yours. I'm letting you tell me all this because I believe it's better for you to talk it out and rid your soul of it. But don't blame yourself any more."

"Well, I won't. I just wanted you to know me as I am. That time you told me of your darling hope for the spring was the worst of all, Anne. I shall never forgive myself for the way I behaved then. I repented it with tears. And I *did* put many a tender and loving thought of you into the little dress I made. But I might have known that anything I made could only be a shroud in the end."

"Now, Leslie, that *is* bitter and morbid—put such thoughts away. I was so glad when you brought the little dress; and since I had to lose little Joyce I like to think that the dress she wore was the one you made for her when you let yourself love me."

"Anne, do you know, I believe I shall always love you after this. I don't think I'll ever feel that dreadful way about you again. Talking it all out seems to have done away with it, somehow. It's very strange —and I thought it so real and bitter. It's like opening the door of a dark room to show some hideous creature you've believed to be there—and when the light streams in your monster turns out to have been just a shadow, vanishing when the light comes. It will never come between us again."

"No, we are real friends now, Leslie, and I am very glad."

"I hope you won't misunderstand me if I say something else. Anne, I was grieved to the core of my heart when you lost your baby; and if I could have saved her for you by cutting off one of my hands I would have done it. But your sorrow has brought us closer together. Your perfect happiness isn't a barrier any longer. Oh, don't misunderstand, dearest—I'm *not* glad that your happiness isn't perfect any longer—I can say that sincerely; but since it isn't, there isn't such a gulf between us."

"I *do* understand that, too, Leslie. Now, we'll just shut up the past and forget what was unpleasant in it. It's all going to be different. We're both of the race of Joseph now. I think you've been wonderful —wonderful. And, Leslie, I can't help believing that life has something good and beautiful for you yet."

Leslie shook her head.

"No," she said dully. "There isn't any hope. Dick will never be better—and even if his memory were to come back—oh, Anne, it would be worse, even worse, than it is now. *This* is something you can't understand, you happy bride. Anne, did Miss Cornelia ever tell you how I came to marry Dick?''

"Yes."

"I'm glad—I wanted you to know—but I couldn't bring myself to talk of it if you hadn't known. Anne, it seems to me that ever since I was twelve years old life has been bitter. Before that I had a happy childhood. We were very poor—but we didn't mind. Father was so splendid—so clever and loving and sympathetic. We were chums as far back as I can remember. And mother was so sweet. She was very, very beautiful. I look like her, but I am not so beautiful as she was.''

"Miss Cornelia says you are far more beautiful.''

"She is mistaken—or prejudiced. I think my figure *is* better—mother was slight and bent by hard work—but she had the face of an angel. I used just to look up at her in worship. We all worshipped her,—father and Kenneth and I.''

Anne remembered that Miss Cornelia had given her a very different impression of Leslie's mother. But had not love the truer vision? Still, it *was* selfish of Rose West to make her daughter marry Dick Moore.

"Kenneth was my brother,'' went on Leslie. "Oh, I can't tell you how I loved him. And he was cruelly killed. Do you know how?''

"Yes."

"Anne, I saw his little face as the wheel went over him. He fell on his back. Anne—Anne—I can see it now. I shall always see it. Anne, all I ask of heaven is that that recollection shall be blotted out of my memory. O my God!''

"Leslie, don't speak of it. I know the story—don't go into details that only harrow your soul up unavailingly. It *will* be blotted out.''

After a moment's struggle, Leslie regained a measure of self-control.

"Then father's health got worse and he grew despondent—his mind became unbalanced—you've heard all that, too?''

"Yes."

"After that I had just mother to live for. But I was very ambitious. I meant to teach and earn my way through college. I meant to climb to the very top—oh, I won't talk of that either. It's no use. You know what happened. I couldn't see my dear little heart-broken mother, who had been such a slave all her life, turned out of her home. Of course, I could have earned enough for us to live on. But mother *couldn't* leave her home. She had come there as a bride—and she had loved father so—and all her memories were there. Even yet,

Anne, when I think that I made her last year happy I'm not sorry for what I did. As for Dick—I didn't hate him when I married him—I just felt for him the indifferent, friendly feeling I had for most of my schoolmates. I knew he drank some—but I had never heard the story of the girl down at the fishing cove. If I had, I *couldn't* have married him, even for mother's sake. Afterwards—I *did* hate him—but mother never knew. She died—and then I was alone. I was only seventeen and I was alone. Dick had gone off in the *Four Sisters*. I hoped he wouldn't be home very much more. The sea had always been in his blood. I had no other hope. Well, Captain Jim brought him home, as you know—and that's all there is to say. You know me now, Anne—the worst of me—the barriers are all down. And you still want to be my friend?''

Anne looked up through the birches, at the white paper-lantern of a half moon drifing downwards to the gulf of sunset. Her face was very sweet.

''I am your friend and you are mine, for always,'' she said. ''Such a friend as I never had before. I have had many dear and beloved friends—but there is a something in you, Leslie, that I never found in anyone else. You have more to offer me in that rich nature of yours, and I have more to give you than I had in my careless girlhood. We are both women—and friends forever.''

They clasped hands and smiled at each other through the tears that filled the gray eyes and the blue.

CHAPTER 22

MISS CORNELIA ARRANGES MATTERS

GILBERT INSISTED that Susan should be kept on at the little house for the summer. Anne protested at first.

''Life here with just the two of us is so sweet, Gilbert. It spoils it a little to have anyone else. Susan is a dear soul, but she is an outsider. It won't hurt me to do the work here.''

''You must take your doctor's advice,'' said Gilbert. ''There's an old proverb to the effect that shoemakers' wives go barefoot and doctors' wives die young. I don't mean that it shall be true in my household. You will keep Susan until the old spring comes back into your step, and those little hollows on your cheeks fill out.''

"You just take it easy, Mrs. Doctor, dear,'' said Susan, coming abruptly in. "Have a good time and do not worry about the pantry. Susan is at the helm. There is no use in keeping a dog and doing your own barking. I am going to take your breakfast up to you every morning.''

"Indeed you are not,'' laughed Anne. "I agree with Miss Cornelia that it's a scandal for a woman who isn't sick to eat her breakfast in bed, and almost justifies the men in any enormities.''

"Oh, Cornelia!'' said Susan, with ineffable contempt. "I think you have better sense, Mrs. Doctor, dear, than to heed what Cornelia Bryant says. I cannot see why she must be always running down the men, even if she is an old maid. *I* am an old maid, but you never hear *me* abusing the men. I like 'em. I would have married one if I could. Is it not funny nobody ever asked me to marry him, Mrs. Doctor, dear? I am no beauty, but I am as good-looking as most of the married women you see. But I never had a beau. What do you suppose is the reason?''

"It may be predestination,'' suggested Anne, with unearthly solemnity.

Susan nodded.

"That is what I have often thought, Mrs. Doctor, dear, and a great comfort it is. I do not mind nobody wanting me if the Almighty decreed it so for His own wise purposes. But sometimes doubt creeps in, Mrs. Doctor, dear, and I wonder if maybe the Old Scratch has not more to do with it than anyone else. I cannot feel resigned *then*. But maybe,'' added Susan, brightening up, "I will have a chance to get married yet. I often and often think of the old verse my aunt used to repeat:

There never was a goose so gray but sometime soon or late
Some honest gander came her way and took her for his mate!

A woman cannot ever be sure of not being married till she is buried, Mrs. Doctor, dear, and meanwhile I will make a batch of cherry pies. I notice the doctor favors 'em, and I *do* like cooking for a man who appreciates his victuals.''

Miss Cornelia dropped in that afternoon, puffing a little.

"I don't mind the world or the devil much, but the flesh *does* rather bother me," she admitted. "You always look as cool as a cucumber, Anne, dearie. Do I smell cherry pie? If I do, ask me to stay to tea. Haven't tasted a cherry pie this summer. My cherries have all been stolen by those scamps of Gilman boys from the Glen."

"Now, now, Cornelia," remonstrated Captain Jim, who had been reading a sea novel in a corner of the living room, "you shouldn't say that about those two poor, motherless Gilman boys, unless you've got certain proof. Jest because their father ain't none too honest isn't any reason for calling them thieves. It's more likely it's been the robins took your cherries. They're turrible thick this year."

"Robins!" said Miss Cornelia disdainfully. "Humph! Two-legged robins, believe *me!*"

"Well, most of the Four Winds robins *are* constructed on that principle," said Captain Jim gravely.

Miss Cornelia stared at him for a moment. Then she leaned back in her rocker and laughed long and ungrudgingly.

"Well, you *have* got one on me at last, Jim Boyd, I'll admit. Just look how pleased he is, Anne, dearie, grinning like a Chessy-cat. As for the robins' legs if robins have great, big, bare, sunburned legs, with ragged trousers hanging on 'em, such as I saw up in my cherry tree one morning at sunrise last week, I'll beg the Gilman boys' pardon. By the time I got down they were gone. I couldn't understand how they had disappeared so quick, but Captain Jim has enlightened me. They flew away, of course."

Captain Jim laughed and went away, regretfully declining an invitation to stay to supper and partake of cherry pie.

"I'm on my way to see Leslie and ask her if she'll take a boarder," Miss Cornelia resumed. "I'd a letter yesterday from a Mrs. Daly in Toronto, who boarded a spell with me two years ago. She wanted me to take a friend of hers for the summer. His name is Owen Ford, and he's a newspaper man, and it seems he's a grandson of the schoolmaster who built this house. John Selwyn's oldest daughter married an Ontario man named Ford, and this is her son. He wants to see the old place his grandparents lived in. He had a bad spell of typhoid in the spring and hasn't got rightly over it, so his doctor has ordered him to the sea. He doesn't want to go to the hotel—he just wants a quiet home place. I can't take him, for I have to be away in August. I've been appointed a delegate to the W.F.M.S. convention in Kingsport and I'm going. I don't know whether Leslie'll want to be bothered with him, either, but there's no one else. If she can't take him he'll have to go over the harbor.''

''When you've seen her come back and help us eat our cherry pies,'' said Anne. ''Bring Leslie and Dick, too, if they can come. And so you're going to Kingsport? What a nice time you will have. I must give you a letter to a friend of mine there—Mrs. Jonas Blake.''

''I've prevailed on Mrs. Thomas Holt to go with me,'' said Miss Cornelia complacently. ''It's time she had a little holiday, believe *me*. She has just about worked herself to death. Tom Holt can crochet beautifully, but he can't make a living for his family. He never seems to be able to get up early enough to do any work, but I notice he can always get up early to go fishing. Isn't that like a man?''

Anne smiled. She had learned to discount largely Miss Cornelia's opinions of the Four Winds men. Otherwise she must have believed them the most hopeless assortment of reprobates and ne'er-do-wells in the world, with veritable slaves and martyrs for wives. This particular Tom Holt, for example, she knew to be a kind husband, a much loved father, and an excellent neighbor. If he were rather inclined to be lazy, liking better the fishing he had been born for than the farming he had not, and if he had a harmless eccentricity for doing fancy work, nobody save Miss Cornelia seemed to hold it against him. His wife was a ''hustler,'' who gloried in hustling; his family got a comfortable living off the farm; and his strapping sons and daughters, inheriting their mother's energy, were all in a fair way to do well in the world. There was not a happier household in Glen St. Mary than the Holts'.

Miss Cornelia returned satisfied from the house up the brook.

''Leslie's going to take him,'' she announced. ''She jumped at the chance. She wants to make a little money to shingle the roof of her house this fall, and she didn't know how she was going to manage it. I expect Captain Jim'll be more than interested when he hears that a grandson of the Selwyns' is coming here. Leslie said to tell you she hankered after cherry pie, but she couldn't come to tea because she has to go and hunt up her turkeys. They've strayed away. But she said, if there was a piece left, for you to put it in the pantry and she'd run over in the cat's light, when prowling's in order, to get it. You don't know, Anne, dearie, what good it did my heart to hear Leslie send you a message like that, laughing like she used to long ago. There's a great change come over her lately. She laughs and jokes like a girl, and from her talk I gather she's here real often."

"Every day—or else I'm over there," said Anne. "I don't know what I'd do without Leslie, especially just now when Gilbert is so busy. He's hardly ever home except for a few hours in the wee sma's. He's really working himself to death. So many of the over-harbor people send for him now."

"They might better be content with their own doctor," said Miss Cornelia. "Though to be sure I can't blame them, for he's a Methodist. Ever since Dr. Blythe brought Mrs. Allonby round folks think he can raise the dead. I believe Dr. Dave is a mite jealous—just like a man. He thinks Dr. Blythe has too many new-fangled notions! 'Well,' I says to him, 'it was a new-fangled notion saved Rhoda Allonby. If *you'd* been attending her she'd have died, and had a tombstone saying it had pleased God to take her away.' Oh, I *do* like to speak my mind to Dr. Dave! He's bossed the Glen for years, and he thinks he's forgotten more than other people ever knew. Speaking of doctors, I wish Dr. Blythe'd run over and see to that boil on Dick Moore's neck. It's getting past Leslie's skill. I'm sure I don't know what Dick Moore wants to start in having boils for—as if he wasn't enough trouble without that!"

"Do you know, Dick has taken quite a fancy to me," said Anne. "He follows me round like a dog, and smiles like a pleased child when I notice him."

"Does it make you creepy?"

"Not at all. I rather like poor Dick Moore. He seems so pitiful and appealing, somehow."

"You wouldn't think him very appealing if you'd see him on his cantankerous days, believe *me*. But I'm glad you don't mind him—it's all the nicer for Leslie. She'll have more to do when her boarder comes. I hope he'll be a decent creature. You'll probably like him—he's a writer."

"I wonder why people so commonly suppose that if two individuals are both writers they must therefore be hugely congenial," said Anne, rather scornfully. "Nobody would expect two blacksmiths to be violently attracted toward each other merely because they were both blacksmiths."

Nevertheless, she looked forward to the advent of Owen Ford with a pleasant sense of expectation. If he were young and likeable he might prove a very pleasant addition to society in Four Winds. The latch-string of the little house was always out for the race of Joseph.

CHAPTER 23

OWEN FORD COMES

ONE EVENING Miss Cornelia telephoned down to Anne.

"The writer man has just arrived here. I'm going to drive him down to your place, and you can show him the way over to Leslie's. It's shorter than driving round by the other road, and I'm in a mortal hurry. The Reese baby has gone and fallen into a pail of hot water at the Glen, and got nearly scalded to death and they want me right off—to put a new skin on the child, I presume. Mrs. Reese is always so careless, and then expects other people to mend her mistakes. You won't mind, will you, dearie? His trunk can go down tomorrow."

"Very well," said Anne. "What is he like, Miss Cornelia?"

"You'll see what he's like outside when I take him down. As for what he's like inside only the Lord who made him knows *that*. I'm not going to say another word, for every receiver in the Glen is down."

"Miss Cornelia evidently can't find much fault with Mr. Ford's looks, or she would find it in spite of the receivers," said Anne. "I conclude therefore, Susan, that Mr. Ford is rather handsome than otherwise."

"Well, Mrs. Doctor, dear, I *do* enjoy seeing a well-looking man," said Susan candidly. "Had I not better get up a snack for him? There is a strawberry pie that would melt in your mouth."

"No, Leslie is expecting him and has his supper ready. Besides, I want that strawberry pie for my own poor man. He won't be home till late, so leave the pie and a glass of milk out for him, Susan."

"That I will, Mrs. Doctor, dear. Susan is at the helm. After all, it is better to give pie to your own men than to strangers, who may be only seeking to devour, and the doctor himself is as well-looking a man as you often come across."

When Owen Ford came Anne secretly admitted, as Miss Cornelia towed him in, that he was very "well-looking" indeed. He was tall and broad-shouldered, with thick, brown hair, finely-cut nose and chin, large and brilliant dark-gray eyes.

"And did you notice his ears and his teeth, Mrs. Doctor, dear?" queried Susan later on. "He has got the nicest-shaped ears I ever saw on a man's head. I am choice about ears. When I was young I was scared that I might have to marry a man with ears like flaps. But I need not have worried, for never a chance did I have with any kind of ears."

Anne had not noticed Owen Ford's ears, but she did see his teeth, as his lips parted over them in a frank and friendly smile. Unsmiling, his face was rather sad and absent in expression, not unlike the melancholy, inscrutable hero of Anne's own early dreams; but mirth and humor and charm lighted it up when he smiled. Certainly, on the outside, as Miss Cornelia said, Owen Ford was a very presentable fellow.

"You cannot realise how delighted I am to be here, Mrs. Blythe," he said, looking around him with eager, interested eyes. "I have an odd feeling of coming home. My mother was born and spent her childhood here, you know. She used to talk a great deal to me of her old home. I know the geography of it as well as of the one I lived in, and, of course, she told me the story of the building of the house, and of my grandfather's agonised watch for the *Royal William*. I had thought that so old a house must have vanished years ago, or I should have come to see it before this."

"Old houses don't vanish easily on this enchanted coast," smiled Anne. "This is a 'land where all things always seem the same'— nearly always, at least. John Selwyn's house hasn't even been much changed, and outside the rose-bushes your grandfather planted for his bride are blooming this very minute."

"How the thought links me with them! With your leave I must explore the whole place soon."

"Our latch-string will always be out for you," promised Anne. "And do you know that the old sea captain who keeps the Four Winds light knew John Selwyn and his bride well in his boyhood? He told me their story the night I came here—the third bride of the old house."

"Can it be possible? This *is* a discovery. I must hunt him up."

"It won't be difficult; we are all cronies of Captain Jim. He will be as eager to see you as you could be to see him. Your grandmother shines like a star in his memory. But I think Mrs. Moore is expecting you. I'll show you our 'cross-lots' road."

Anne walked with him to the house up the brook, over a field that was as white as snow with daisies. A boat-load of people were singing far across the harbor. The sound drifted over the water like faint, unearthly music wind-blown across a starlit sea. The big light flashed and beaconed. Owen Ford looked around him with satisfaction.

"And so this is Four Winds," he said. "I wasn't prepared to find it quite so beautiful, in spite of all mother's praises. What colors— what scenery—what charm! I shall get as strong as a horse in no time. And if inspiration comes from beauty, I should certainly be able to begin my great Canadian novel here.''

"You haven't begun it yet?" asked Anne.

"Alack-a-day, no. I've never been able to get the right central idea for it. It lurks beyond me—it allures—and beckons—and recedes—I almost grasp it and it is gone. Perhaps amid this peace and loveliness, I shall be able to capture it. Miss Bryant tells me that you write.''

"Oh, I do little things for children. I haven't done much since I was married. And I have no designs on a great Canadian novel,'' laughed Anne. ''That is quite beyond me.''

Owen Ford laughed too.

"I dare say it is beyond me as well. All the same I mean to have a try at it some day, if I can ever get time. A newspaper man doesn't have much chance for that sort of thing. I've done a good deal of short story writing for the magazines, but I've never had the leisure that seems to be necessary for the writing of a book. With three months of liberty I ought to make a start, though—if I could only get the necessary *motif* for it—the *soul* of the book.''

An idea whisked through Anne's brain with a suddenness that made her jump. But she did not utter it, for they had reached the Moore house. As they entered the yard Leslie came out on the veranda from the side door, peering through the gloom for some sign of her expected guest. She stood just where the warm yellow light flooded her from the open door. She wore a plain dress of cheap, cream-tinted cotton voile, with the usual girdle of crimson. Leslie was never without her touch of crimson. She had told Anne that she never felt satisfied without a gleam of red somewhere about her, if it were only a flower. To Anne, it always seemed to symbolise Leslie's glowing, pent-up personality, denied all expression save in that flaming glint. Leslie's dress was cut a little away at the neck and had short sleeves. Her arms gleamed like ivory-tinted marble. Every exquisite curve of her form was outlined in soft darkness against the light. Her hair shone in it like flame. Beyond her was a purple sky, flowering with stars over the harbor.

Anne heard her companion give a gasp. Even in the dusk she could see the amazement and admiration on his face.

"Who is that beautiful creature?" he asked.

"That is Mrs. Moore," said Anne. "She is very lovely, isn't she?"

"I—I never saw anything like her," he answered, rather dazedly. "I wasn't prepared—I didn't expect—good heavens, one *doesn't* expect a goddess for a landlady! Why, if she were clothed in a gown of sea-purple, with a rope of amethysts in her hair, she would be a veritable sea-queen. And she takes in boarders!''

''Even goddesses must live,'' said Anne. ''And Leslie isn't a goddess. She's just a very beautiful woman, as human as the rest of us. Did Miss Bryant tell you about Mr. Moore?''

''Yes,—he's mentally deficient, or something of the sort, isn't he? But she said nothing about Mrs. Moore, and I supposed she'd be the usual hustling country housewife who takes in boarders to earn an honest penny.''

''Well, that's just what Leslie is doing,'' said Anne crisply. ''And it isn't altogether pleasant for her, either. I hope you won't mind Dick. If you do, please don't let Leslie see it. It would hurt her horribly. He's just a big baby, and sometimes a rather annoying one.''

''Oh, I won't mind him. I don't suppose I'll be much in the house anyhow, except for meals. But what a shame it all is! Her life must be a hard one.''

''It is. But she doesn't like to be pitied.''

Leslie had gone back into the house and now met them at the front door. She greeted Owen Ford with cold civility, and told him in a business-like tone that his room and his supper were ready for him. Dick, with a pleased grin, shambled upstairs with the valise, and Owen Ford was installed as an inmate of the old house among the willows.

CHAPTER 24

THE LIFE-BOOK OF CAPTAIN JIM

''I HAVE a little brown cocoon of an idea that may possibly expand into a magnificent moth of fulfilment,'' Anne told Gilbert when she reached home. He had returned earlier than she had expected, and was enjoying Susan's cherry pie. Susan herself hovered in the background, like a rather grim but beneficent guardian spirit, and found as much pleasure in watching Gilbert eat pie as he did in eating it.

"What is your idea?" he asked.

"I sha'n't tell you just yet—not till I see if I can bring the thing about."

"What sort of a chap is Ford?"

"Oh, very nice, and quite good-looking."

"Such beautiful ears, doctor, dear," interjected Susan with a relish.

"He is about thirty or thirty-five, I think, and he meditates writing a novel. His voice is pleasant and his smile delightful, and he knows how to dress. He looks as if life hadn't been altogether easy for him, somehow."

Owen Ford came over the next evening with a note to Anne from Leslie; they spent the sunset time in the garden and then went for a moonlit sail on the harbor, in the little boat Gilbert had set up for summer outings. They liked Owen immensely and had that feeling of having known him for many years which distinguishes the free-masonry of the house of Joseph. "He is as nice as his ears, Mrs. Doctor, dear," said Susan, when he had gone. He had told Susan that he had never tasted anything like her strawberry shortcake and Susan's susceptible heart was his forever.

"He has got a way with him." she reflected, as she cleared up the relics of the supper. "It is real queer he is not married, for a man like that could have anybody for the asking. Well, maybe he is like me, and has not met the right one yet."

Susan really grew quite romantic in her musings as she washed the supper dishes.

Two nights later Anne took Owen Ford down to Four Winds Point to introduce him to Captain Jim. The clover fields along the harbor shore were whitening in the western wind, and Captain Jim had one of his finest sunsets on exhibition. He himself had just returned from a trip over the harbor.

"I had to go over and tell Henry Pollack he was dying. Everybody else was afraid to tell him. They expected he'd take on turrible, for he's been dreadful determined to live, and been making no end of plans for the fall. His wife thought he oughter be told and that I'd be the best one to break it to him that he couldn't get better. Henry and me are old cronies—we sailed in the *Gray Gull* for years together. Well, I went over and sat down by Henry's bed and I says to him, says I, jest right out plain and simple, for if a thing's got to be told it may as well be told first as last, says I, 'Mate, I reckon you've got your sailing orders this time,' I was sorter quaking inside, for it's an

awful thing to have to tell a man who hain't any idea he's dying that
he is. But lo and behold, Mistress Blythe, Henry looks up at me, with
those bright old black eyes of his in his wizened face and says, says
he, 'Tell me something I don't know, Jim Boyd, if you want to give
me information. I've known *that* for a week.' I was too astonished to
speak, and Henry, he chuckled. 'To see you coming in here,' says
he, 'with your face as solemn as a tombstone and sitting down there
with your hands clasped over your stomach, and passing me out a
blue-mouldy old item of news like that! It'd make a cat laugh, Jim
Boyd,' says he. 'Who told you?' says I, stupid like. 'Nobody,' says
he. 'A week ago Tuesday night I was lying here awake—and I jest
knew. I'd suspicioned it before, but then I *knew*. I've been keepng up
for the wife's sake. And I'd *like* to have got that barn built, for
Eben'll never get it right. But anyhow, now that you've eased your
mind, Jim, put on a smile and tell me something interestng,' Well,
there it was. They'd been so scared to tell him and he knew it all the
time. Strange how nature looks out for us, ain't it, and lets us know
what we should know when the time comes? Did I never tell you the
yarn about Henry getting the fish hook in his nose, Mistress
Blythe?''

''No.''

''Well, him and me had a laugh over it today. It happened nigh
unto thirty years ago. Him and me and several more was out mackerel fishing one day. It was a great day—never saw such a school of
mackerel in the gulf—and in the general excitement Henry got quite
wild and contrived to stick a fish hook clean through one side of his
nose. Well, there he was; there was barb on one end and a big piece
of lead on the other, so it couldn't be pulled out. We wanted to take
him ashore at once, but Henry was game; he said he'd be jiggered if
he'd leave a school like that for anything short of lockjaw; then he
kept fishing away, hauling in hand over fist and groaning between
times. Fin'lly the school passed and we come in with a load; I got a
file and begun to try to file through that hook. I tried to be as
easy as I could, but you should have heard Henry—no, you
shouldn't either. It was well no ladies were around. Henry wasn't a
swearing man, but he'd heard some few matters of that sort along
shore in his time, and he fished 'em all out of his recollection and
hurled 'em at me. Fin'lly he declared he couldn't stand it and I had no
bowels of compassion. So we hitched up and I drove him to a doctor
in Charlottetown, thirty-five miles—there weren't none nearer in
them days—with that blessed hook still hanging from his nose.

When we got there old Dr. Crabb jest took a file and filed that hook jest the same as I'd tried to do, only he weren't a mite particular about doing it easy!''

Captain Jim's visit to his old friend had revived many recollections and he was now in the full tide of reminiscences.

"Henry was asking me today if I remembered the time old Father Chiniquy blessed Alexander MacAllister's boat. Another odd yarn—and true as gospel. I was in the boat myself. We went out, him and me, in Alexander MacAllister's boat one morning at sunrise. Besides, there was a French boy in the boat—Catholic of course. You know old Father Chiniquy had turned Protestant, so the Catholics hadn't much use for him. Well, we sat out in the gulf in the broiling sun till noon, and not a bite did we get. When we went ashore old Father Chiniquy had to go, so he said in that polite way of his, 'I'm very sorry I cannot go out with you dis afternoon, Mr. MacAllister, but I leave you my blessing. You will catch a t'ousand dis afternoon.' Well, we did not catch a thousand, but we caught exactly nine hundred and ninety-nine—the biggest catch for a small boat on the whole north shore that summer. Curious, wasn't it? Alexander MacAllister, he says to Andrew Peters, 'Well, and what do you think of Father Chiniquy now?' 'Vell,' growled Andrew, 'I t'ink de old devil has got a blessing left yet.' Laws, how Henry did laugh over that today!''

"Do you know who Mr. Ford is, Captain Jim?" asked Anne, seeing that Captain Jim's fountain of reminiscence had run out for the present. "I want you to guess."

Captain Jim shook his head.

"I never was any hand at guessing, Mistress Blythe, and yet somehow when I come in I thought, 'Where have I seen them eyes before?'—for I *have* seen 'em."

"Think of a September morning many years ago," said Anne, softly. "Think of a ship sailing up the harbor—a ship long waited for and despaired of. Think of the day the *Royal William* came in and the first look you had at the schoolmaster's bride."

Captain Jim sprang up.

"They're Persis Selwyn's eyes," he almost shouted. "You can't be her son—you must be her—"

"Grandson; yes, I am Alice Selwyn's son."

Captain Jim swooped down on Owen Ford and shook his hand over again.

"Alice Selwyn's son! Lord, but you're welcome! Many's the time

I've wondered where the descendants of the schoolmaster were living. I knew there was none on the Island. Alice—Alice—the first baby ever born in that little house. No baby ever brought more joy! I've dandled her a hundred times. It was from my knee she took her first steps alone. Can't I see her mother's face watching her—and it was near sixty years ago. Is she living yet?''

"No, she died when I was only a boy.''

"Oh, it doesn't seem right that I should be living to hear that,'' sighed Captain Jim. "But I'm heart-glad to see you. It's brought back my youth for a little while. You don't know yet what a boon *that* is. Mistress Blythe here has the trick—she does it quite often for me.''

Captain Jim was still more excited when he discovered that Owen Ford was what he called a "real writing man.'' He gazed at him as at a superior being. Captain Jim knew that Anne wrote, but he had never taken that fact very seriously. Captain Jim thought women were delightful creatures, who ought to have the vote, and everything else they wanted, bless their hearts; but he did not believe they could write.

"Jest look at *A Mad Love*,'' he would protest. "A woman wrote that and jest look at it—one hundred and three chapters when it could all have been told in ten. A writing woman never knows when to stop; that's the trouble. The p'int of good writing is to know when to stop.''

"Mr. Ford wants to hear some of your stories, Captain Jim'' said Anne. "Tell him the one about the captain who went crazy and imagined he was the Flying Dutchman.''

This was Captain Jim's best story. It was a compound of horror and humor, and though Anne had heard it several times she laughed as heartily and shivered as fearsomely over it as Mr. Ford did. Other tales followed, for Captain Jim had an audience after his own heart. He told how his vessel had been run down by a steamer; how he had been boarded by Malay pirates; how his ship had caught fire; how he helped a political prisoner escape from a South African republic; how he had been wrecked one fall on the Magdalens and stranded there for the winter; how a tiger had broken loose on board ship; how his crew had mutinied and marooned him on a barren island—these and many other tales, tragic or humorous or grotesque, did Captain Jim relate. The mystery of the sea, the fascination of far lands, the lure of adventure, the laughter of the world—his hearers felt and realised them all. Owen Ford listened, with his head on his hand, and the First Mate purring on his knee, his brillint eyes fastened on

Captain Jim's rugged, eloquent face.

"Won't you let Mr. Ford see your life-book, Captain Jim?" asked Anne, when Captain Jim finally declared that yarn-spinning must end for the time.

"Oh, he don't want to be bothered with *that*," protested Captain Jim, who was secretly dying to show it.

"I should like nothing better than to see it, Captain Boyd," said Owen. "If it is half as wonderful as your tales it will be worth seeing."

With pretended reluctance Captain Jim dug his life-book out of his old chest and handed it to Owen.

"I reckon you won't care to wrastle long with my old hand o' write. I never had much schooling," he observed carelessly. "Just wrote that there to amuse my nephew Joe. He's always wanting stories. Comes here yesterday and says to me, reproachful-like, as I was lifting a twenty-pound codfish out of my boat, 'Uncle Jim, ain't a codfish a dumb animal?' I'd been a-telling him, you see, that he must be real kind to dumb animals, and never hurt 'em in any way. I got out of the scrape by saying a codfish was dumb enough but it wasn't an animal, but Joe didn't look satisfied, and I wasn't satisfied myself. You've got to be mighty careful what you tell them little critters. *They* can see through you."

While talking, Captain Jim watched Owen Ford from the corner of his eye as the latter examined the life-book; and presently observing that his guest was lost in its pages, he turned smilingly to his cupboard and proceeded to make a pot of tea. Owen Ford separated himself from the life-book, with as much reluctance as a miser wrenches himself from his gold, long enough to drink his tea, and then returned to it hungrily.

"Oh, you can take that thing home with you if you want to," said Captain Jim, as if the "thing" were not his most treasured possession. "I must go down and pull my boat up a bit on the skids. There's a wind coming. Did you notice the sky tonight?

> *Mackerel skies and mares' tails*
> *Make tall ships carry short sails.*"

Owen Ford accepted the offer of the life-book gladly. On their way home Anne told him the story of lost Margaret.

"That old captain is a wonderful old fellow," he said. "What a life he has led! Why, the man had more adventures in one week of his life than most of us have in a lifetime. Do you really think his tales are all true?''

"I certainly do. I am sure Captain Jim could not tell a lie; and besides, all the people about here say that everything happened as he relates it. There used to be plenty of his old shipmates alive to corroborate him. He's one of the last of the old type of P.E. Island sea-captains. They are almost extinct now.''

CHAPTER 25

THE WRITING OF THE BOOK

OWEN FORD came over to the little house the next morning in a state of great excitement. "Mrs. Blythe, this is a wonderful book—absolutely wonderful. If I could take it and use the material for a book I feel certain I could make the novel of the year out of it. Do you suppose Captain Jim would let me do it?''

"Let you! I'm sure he would be delighted,'' cried Anne. "I admit that it was what was in my head when I took you down last night. Captain Jim has always been wishing he could get somebody to write his life-book properly for him.''

"Will you go down to the Point with me this evening, Mrs. Blythe? I'll ask him about that life-book myself, but I want you to tell him that you told me the story of lost Margaret and ask him if he will let me use it as a thread of romance with which to weave the stories of the life-book into a harmonious whole.''

Captain Jim was more excited than ever when Owen Ford told him of his plan. At last his cherished dream was to be realized and his "life-book'' given to the world. He was also pleased that the story of lost Margaret should be woven into it.

"It will keep her name from being forgotten,'' he said wistfully. "That's why I want it put in.''

"We'll collaborate,'' cried Owen delightedly. "You will give the soul and I the body. Oh, we'll write a famous book between us,

Captain Jim. And we'll get right to work.''

"And to think my book is to be writ by the schoolmaster's grandson!" exclaimed Captain Jim. "Lad, your grandfather was my dearest friend. I thought there was nobody like him. I see now why I had to wait so long. It couldn't be writ till the right man come. You *belong* here—you've got the soul of this old north shore in you— you're the only one who *could* write it.''

It was arranged that the tiny room off the living room at the lighthouse should be given over to Owen for a workshop. It was necessary that Captain Jim should be near him as he wrote, for consultation upon many matters of sea-faring and gulf lore of which Owen was quite ignorant.

He began work on the book the very next morning, and flung himself into it heart and soul. As for Captain Jim, he was a happy man that summer. He looked upon the little room where Owen worked as a sacred shrine. Owen talked everything over with Captain Jim, but he would not let him see the manuscript.

"You must wait until it is published," he said. "Then you'll get it all at once in its best shape.''

He delved into the treasures of the life-book and used them freely. He dreamed and brooded over lost Margaret until she became a vivid reality to him and lived in his pages. As the book progressed it took possession of him and he worked at it with feverish eagerness. He let Anne and Leslie read the manuscript and criticise it; and the concluding chapter of the book, which the critics, later on, were pleased to call idyllic, was modelled upon a suggestion of Leslie's.

Anne fairly hugged herself with delight over the success of her idea.

"I knew when I looked at Owen Ford that he was the very man for it," she told Gilbert. "Both humor and passion were in his face, and that, together with the art of expression, was just what was necessary for the writing of such a book. As Mrs. Rachel would say, he was predestined for the part.''

Owen Ford wrote in the mornings. The afternoons were generally spent in some merry outing with the Blythes. Leslie often went, too, for Captain Jim took charge of Dick frequently, in order to set her free. They went boating on the harbor and up the three pretty rivers that flowed into it; they had clambakes on the bar and mussel-bakes on the rocks; they picked strawberries on the sand-dunes; they went out cod-fishing with Captain Jim; they shot plover in the shore fields and wild ducks in the cove—at least, the men did. In the evenings they rambled in the low-lying, daisied, shore fields under a golden moon, or they sat in the living room at the little house where often the coolness of the sea breeze justified a driftwood fire, and talked of the thousand and one things which happy, eager, clever young people can find to talk about.

Ever since the day on which she had made her confession to Anne Leslie had been a changed creature. There was no trace of her old coldness and reserve, no shadow of her old bitterness. The girlhood of which she had been cheated seemed to come back to her with the ripeness of womanhood; she expanded like a flower of flame and perfume; no laugh was readier than hers, no wit quicker, in the twilight circles of that enchanted summer. When she could not be with them all felt that some exquisite savor was lacking in their intercourse. Her beauty was illumined by the awakened soul within, as some rosy lamp might shine through a flawless vase of alabaster. There were hours when Anne's eyes seemed to ache with the splendor of her. As for Owen Ford, the "Margaret" of his book, although she had the soft brown hair and elfin face of the real girl who had vanished so long ago, "pillowed where lost Atlantis sleeps," had the personality of Leslie Moore, as it was revealed to him in those halcyon days at Four Winds Harbor.

All in all, it was a never-to-be-forgotten summer—one of those summers which come seldom into any life, but leave a rich heritage of beautiful memories in their going—one of those summers which, in a fortunate combination of delightful weather, delightful friends and delightful doings, come as near to perfection as anything can come in this world.

"Too good to last," Anne told herself with a little sigh, on the September day when a certain nip in the wind and a certain shade of intense blue on the gulf water said that autumn was hard by.

That evening Owen Ford told them that he had finished his book and that his vacation must come to an end.

"I have a good deal to do to it yet—revising and pruning and so forth," he said, "but in the main it's done. I wrote the last sentence this morning. If I can find a publisher for it it will probably be out next summer or fall."

Owen had not much doubt that he would find a publisher. He knew that he had written a great book—a book that would score a wonderful success—a book that would *live*. He knew that it would bring him both fame and fortune; but when he had written the last line of it he had bowed his head on the manuscript and so sat for a long time. And his thoughts were not of the good work he had done.

CHAPTER 26

OWEN FORD'S CONFESSION

"I'M SO sorry Gilbert is away," said Anne. "He had to go—Allan Lyons at the Glen has met with a serious accident. He will not likely be home till very late. But he told me to tell you he'd be up and over early enough in the morning to see you before you left. It's too provoking. Susan and I had planned such a nice little jamboree for your last night here."

She was sitting beside the garden brook on the little rustic seat Gilbert had built. Owen Ford stood before her, leaning against the bronze column of a yellow birch. He was very pale and his face bore the marks of the preceding sleepless night. Anne, glancing up at him, wondered if, after all, his summer had brought him the strength it should. Had he worked too hard over his book? She remembered that for a week he had not been looking well.

"I'm rather glad the doctor is away," said Owen slowly. "I wanted to see you alone, Mrs. Blythe. There is something I must tell somebody, or I think it will drive me mad. I've been trying for a week to look it in the face—and I can't. I know I can trust you—and, besides, you will understand. A woman with eyes like yours always understands. You are one of the folks people instinctively tell things to. Mrs. Blythe, I love Leslie. *Love* her! That seems too weak a word!"

His voice suddenly broke with the suppressed passion of his utterance. He turned his head away and hid his face on his arm. His whole form shook. Anne sat looking at him, pale and aghast. She had never thought of this! And yet—how was it she had never thought of it? It now seemed a natural and inevitable thing. She wondered at her own blindness. But—but—things like this did not happen in Four Winds. Elsewhere in the world human passions might set at defiance human conventions and laws—but not *here*, surely. Leslie had kept summer boarders off and on for ten years, and nothing like this had happened. But perhaps they had not been like Owen Ford; and the vivid, *living* Leslie of this summer was not the cold, sullen girl of other years. Oh, *somebody* should have thought of this! Why hadn't Miss Cornelia thought of it? Miss Cornelia was always ready enough to sound the alarm where men were concerned. Anne felt an unreasonable resentment against Miss Cornelia. Then she gave a little inward groan. No matter who was to blame the mischief was done. And Leslie—what of Leslie? It was for Leslie Anne felt most concerned.

"Does Leslie know this, Mr. Ford?" she asked quietly.

"No—no,—unless she has guessed it. You surely don't think I'd be cad and scoundrel enough to tell her, Mrs. Blythe. I couldn't help loving her—that's all—and my misery is greater than I can bear."

"Does *she* care?" asked Anne. The moment the question crossed her lips she felt that she should not have asked it. Owen Ford answered it with overeager protest.

"No—no, of course not. But I could make her care if she were free—I know I could."

"She does care—and he knows it," thought Anne. Aloud she said, sympathetically but decidedly:

"But she is not free, Mr. Ford. And the only thing you can do is to go away in silence and leave her to her own life."

"I know—I know," groaned Owen. He sat down on the grassy bank and stared moodily into the amber water beneath him. "I know there's nothing to do—nothing but to say conventionally, 'Good-bye, Mrs. Moore. Thank you for all your kindness to me this summer,' just as I would have said it to the sonsy, bustling, keen-eyed housewife I expected her to be when I came. Then I'll pay my board money like any honest boarder and go! Oh, it's very simple. No doubt—no perplexity—a straight road to the end of the world! And I'll walk it—you needn't fear that I won't, Mrs. Blythe. But it would be easier to walk over red-hot ploughshares."

Anne flinched with the pain of his voice. And there was so little she could say that would be adequate to the situation. Blame was out of the question—advice was not needed—sympathy was mocked by the man's stark agony. She could only feel with him in a maze of compassion and regret. Her heart ached for Leslie! Had not that poor girl suffered enough without this?

"It wouldn't be so hard to go and leave her if she were only happy," resumed Owen passionately. "But to think of her living death—to realise what it is to which I do leave her! *That* is the worst of all. I would give my life to make her happy—and I can do nothing even to help her—nothing. She is bound forever to that poor wretch—with nothing to look forward to but growing old in a succession of empty, meaningless, barren years. It drives me mad to think of it. But I must go through my life, never seeing her, but always knowing what she is enduring. It's hideous—hideous!"

"It is very hard," said Anne sorrowfully. "We—her friends here—all know how hard it is for her."

"And she is so richly fitted for life," said Owen rebelliously. "Her beauty is the least of her dower—and she is the most beautiful woman I've ever known. That laugh of hers! I've angled all summer to evoke that laugh, just for the delight of hearing it. And her eyes— they are as deep and blue as the gulf out there. I never saw such blueness—and gold! Did you ever see her hair down, Mrs. Blythe?"

"No."

"I did—once. I had gone down to the Point to go fishing with Captain Jim but it was too rough to go out, so I came back. She had taken the opportunity of what she expected to be an afternoon alone to wash her hair, and she was standing on the veranda in the sunshine to dry it. It fell all about her to her feet in a fountain of living gold. When she saw me she hurried in, and the wind caught her hair and swirled it all around her—Danae in her cloud. Somehow, just then the knowledge that I loved her came home to me—and realised that I had loved her from the moment I first saw her standing against the darkness in that glow of light. And she must live on here—petting and soothing Dick, pinching and saving for a mere existence, while I spend my life longing vainly for her, and debarred, by that very fact, from even giving her the little help a friend might. I walked the shore last night, almost till dawn, and thrashed it all out over and over again. And yet, in spite of everything, I can't find it in my heart to be sorry that I came to Four Winds. It seems to me that, bad as everything is, it would be still worse never to have known Leslie. It's burning, searing pain to love her and leave her—but not to have loved her is unthinkable. I suppose all this sounds very crazy—all these terrible emotions always do sound foolish when we put them into our inadequate words. They are not meant to be spoken—only felt and endured. I shouldn't have spoken—but it has helped— some. At least, it has given me strength to go away respectably tomorrow morning, without making a scene. You'll write me now and then, won't you, Mrs. Blythe, and give me what news there is to give of her?"

"Yes, " said Anne. "Oh, I'm so sorry you are going—we'll miss you so—we've all been such friends! If it were not for this you could come back other summers. Perhaps, even yet—by-and-by—when you've forgotten, perhaps—"

"I shall never forget—and I shall never come back to Four Winds," said Owen briefly.

Silence and twilight fell over the garden. Far away the sea was lapping gently and monotonously on the bar. The wind of evening in the poplars sounded like some sad, weird, old rune—some broken dream of old memories. A slender shapely young aspen rose up before them against the fine maize and emerald and paling rose of the western sky, which brought out every leaf and twig in dark, tremulous, elfin loveliness.

"Isn't that beautiful?" said Owen, pointing to it with the air of a man who puts a certain conversation behind him.

"It's so beautiful that it hurts me," said Anne softly. "Perfect things like that always did hurt me—I remember I called it 'the queer ache' when I was a child. What is the reason that pain like this seems inseparable from perfection? Is it the pain of finality—when we realise that there can be nothing beyond but retrogression?"

"Perhaps," said Owen dreamily, "it is the prisoned infinite in us calling out to its kindred infinite as expressed in that visible perfection."

"You seem to have a cold in the head. Better rub some tallow on your nose when you go to bed," said Miss Cornelia, who had come in through the little gate between the firs in time to catch Owen's last remark. Miss Cornelia liked Owen; but it was a matter of principle with her to visit any "high-falutin" language from a man with a snub.

Miss Cornelia personated the comedy that ever peeps around the corner at the tragedy of life. Anne, whose nerves had been rather strained, laughed hysterically, and even Owen smiled. Certainly, sentiment and passion had a way of shrinking out of sight in Miss Cornelia's presence. And yet to Anne nothing seemed quite as hopeless and dark and painful as it had seemed a few moments before. But sleep was far from her eyes that night.

CHAPTER 27

ON THE SAND-BAR

OWEN FORD left Four Winds the next morning. In the evening Anne went over to see Leslie, but found nobody. The house was locked and there was no light in any window. It looked like a home left soulless. Leslie did not run over on the following day—which Anne thought a bad sign.

Gilbert having occasion to go in the evening to the fishing cove, Anne drove with him to the Point, intending to stay awhile with Captain Jim. But the great light, cutting its swathes through the fog of the autumn evening, was in care of Alec Boyd and Captain Jim was away.

"What will you do?" asked Gilbert. "Come with me?"

"I don't want to go to the cove—but I'll go over the channel with you, and roam about on the sand shore till you come back. The rock shore is too slippery and grim tonight."

Alone on the sands of the bar Anne gave herself up to the eerie charm of the night. It was warm for September, and the late afternoon had been very foggy; but a full moon had in part lessened the fog and transformed the harbor and the gulf and the surrounding shores into a strange, fantastic, unreal world of pale silver mist, through which everything loomed phantom-like. Captain Josiah Crawford's black schooner sailing down the channel, laden with potatoes for Bluenose ports, was a spectral ship bound for a far uncharted land, ever receding, never to be reached. The calls of unseen gulls overhead were the cries of the souls of doomed seamen. The little curls of foam that blew across the sand were elfin things stealing up from the sea-caves. The big, round-shouldered sand-dunes were the sleeping giants of some old northern tale. The lights that glimmered palely across the harbor were the delusive beacons on some coast of fairyland. Anne pleased herself with a hundred fancies as she wandered through the mist. It was delightful—romantic— mysterious to be roaming here alone on this enchanted shore.

But was she alone? Something loomed in the mist before her—took shape and form—suddenly moved towards her across the wave-rippled sand.

"Leslie!" exclaimed Anne in amazement. "Whatever are you doing—*here*—tonight?"

"If it comes to that, whatever are *you* doing here?" said Leslie, trying to laugh. The effort was a failure. She looked very pale and tired; but the love locks under her scarlet cap were curling about her face and eyes like little sparkling rings of gold.

"I'm waiting for Gilbert—he's over at the Cove. I intended to stay at the light, but Captain Jim is away."

"Well, *I* came here because I wanted to walk—and walk—and *walk*," said Leslie restlessly. "I couldn't on the rock shore—the tide was too high and the rocks prisoned me. I had to come here—or I should have gone mad, I think. I rowed myself over the channel in Captain Jim's flat. I've been here for an hour. Come—come—let us walk. I can't stand still. Oh, Anne!''

"Leslie, dearest, what is the trouble?" asked Anne, though she knew too well already.

"I can't tell you—don't ask me. I wouldn't mind your knowing— I wish you did know—but I can't tell you—I can't tell anyone. I've been such a fool, Anne—and oh, it hurts so terribly to be a fool. There's nothing so painful in the world.''

She laughed bitterly. Anne slipped her arm around her.

"Leslie, is it that you have learned to care for Mr. Ford?"

Leslie turned herself about passionately.

"How did you know?" she cried. "Anne, how did you know? Oh, is it written in my face for everyone to see? Is it as plain as that?"

"No, no. I—I can't tell you how I knew. It just came into my mind, somehow. Leslie, don't look at me like that!''

"Do you despise me?" demanded Leslie in a fierce, low tone. "Do you think I'm wicked—unwomanly? Or do you think I'm just plain fool?"

"I don't think you any of those things. Come, dear, let's just talk it over sensibly, as we might talk over any other of the great crises of life. You've been brooding over it and let yourself drift into a morbid view of it. You know you have a little tendency to do that about everything that goes wrong, and you promised me that you would fight against it.''

"But—oh, it's so—so shameful," murmured Leslie. "To love him—unsought—and when I'm not free to love anybody.''

"There's nothing shameful about it. But I'm very sorry that you have learned to care for Owen, because, as things are, it will only make you more unhappy.''

"I didn't *learn* to care," said Leslie, walking on and speaking passionately. "If it had been like that I could have prevented it. I never dreamed of such a thing until that day, a week ago, when he told me he had finished his book and must soon go away. Then— then I knew. I felt as if someone had struck me a terrible blow. I didn't say anything—I couldn't speak—but I don't know what I looked like. I'm so afraid my face betrayed me. Oh, I would die of shame if I thought he knew—or suspected.''

Anne was miserably silent, hampered by her deductions from her conversation with Owen. Leslie went on feverishly, as if she found relief in speech.

"I was so happy all this summer, Anne—happier than I ever was in my life. I thought it was because everything had been made clear between you and me, and that it was our friendship which made life seem so beautiful and full once more. And it *was*, in part—but not all—oh, not nearly all. I know now why everything was so different. And now it's all over—and he has gone. How can I live, Anne? When I turned back into the house this morning after he had gone the solitude struck me like a blow in the face."

"It won't seem so hard by and by, dear," said Anne, who always felt the pain of her friends so keenly that she could not speak easy, fluent words of comforting. Besides, she remembered how well-meant speeches had hurt her in her own sorrow and was afraid.

"Oh, it seems to me it will grow harder all the time," said Leslie miserably. "I've nothing to look forward to. Morning will come after morning—and he will not come back—he will never come back. Oh, when I think that I will never see him again I feel as if a great brutal hand had twisted itself among my heartstrings, and was wrenching them. Once, long ago, I dreamed of love—and I thought it must be beautiful—and *now*—its like *this*. When he went away yesterday morning he was so cold and indifferent. He said 'Good-bye, Mrs. Moore' in the coldest tone in the world—as if we had not even been friends—as if I meant absolutely nothing to him. I know I don't—I didn't want him to care—but he *might* have been a little kinder."

"Oh, I wish Gilbert would come," thought Anne. She was racked between her sympathy for Leslie and the necessity of avoiding anything that would betray Owen's confidence. She knew why his good-bye had been so cold—why it could not have the cordiality that their good-comradeship demanded—but she could not tell Leslie.

"I couldn't help it, Anne—I couldn't help it," said poor Leslie.

"I know that."

"Do you blame me so very much?"

"I don't blame you at all."

"And you won't—you won't tell Gilbert?"

"Leslie! Do you think I would do such a thing?"

"Oh, I don't know—you and Gilbert are such *chums*. I don't see how you could help telling him everything."

"Everything about my own concerns—yes. But not my friends' secrets."

"I couldn't have *him* know. But I'm glad *you* know. I would feel guilty if there were anything I was ashamed to tell you. I hope Miss

Cornelia won't find out. Sometimes I feel as if those terrible, kind brown eyes of hers read my very soul. Oh, I wish this mist would never lift—I wish I could just stay in it forever, hidden away from every living being. I don't see how I can go on with life. This summer has been so full. I never was lonely for a moment. Before Owen came there used to be horrible moments—when I had been with you and Gilbert—and then had to leave you. You two would walk away together and I would walk away *alone*. After Owen came he was always there to walk home with me—we would laugh and talk as you and Gilbert were doing—there were no more lonely, envious moments for me. And *now!* Oh, yes, I've been a fool. Let's have done talking about my folly. I'll never bore you with it again."

"Here is Gilbert, and you are coming back with us," said Anne, who had no intention of leaving Leslie to wander alone on the sand-bar on such a night and in such a mood. "There's plenty of room in our boat for three, and we'll tie the flat on behind."

"Oh, I suppose I must reconcile myself to being the odd one again," said poor Leslie with another bitter laugh. "Forgive me, Anne—that was hateful. I ought to be thankful—and I *am*—that I have two good friends who are glad to count me in as a third. Don't mind my hateful speeches. I just seem to be one great pain all over and everything hurts me."

"Leslie seemed very quiet tonight, didn't she?" said Gilbert, when he and Anne reached home. "What in the world was she doing over there on the bar alone?"

"Oh, she was tired—and you know she likes to go to the shore after one of Dick's bad days."

"What a pity she hadn't met and married a fellow like Ford long ago," ruminated Gilbert. "They'd have made an ideal couple, wouldn't they?"

"For pity's sake, Gilbert, don't develop into a match-maker. It's an abominable profession for a man," cried Anne rather sharply, afraid that Gilbert might blunder on the truth if he kept on in this strain.

"Bless us, Anne-girl, I'm not matchmaking," protested Gilbert, rather surprised at her tone. "I was only thinking of one of the might-have-beens."

"Well, don't. It's a waste of time," said Anne. Then she added suddenly:

"Oh, Gilbert, I wish everybody could be as happy as we are."

CHAPTER 28

ODDS AND ENDS

"I'VE BEEN reading obituary notices," said Miss Cornelia, laying down the *Daily Enterprise* and taking up her sewing.

The harbor was lying black and sullen under a dour November sky; the wet, dead leaves clung drenched and sodden to the window sills; but the little house was gay with firelight and spring-like with Anne's ferns and geraniums.

"It's always summer here, Anne," Leslie had said one day; and all who were the guests of that house of dreams felt the same.

"The *Enterprise* seems to run to obituaries these days," quoth Miss Cornelia. "It always has a couple of columns of them, and I read every line. It's one of my forms of recreation, especially when there's some original poetry attached to them. Here's a choice sample for you:

> *She's gone to be with her Maker,*
> *Never more to roam.*
> *She used to play and sing with joy*
> *The song of Home, Sweet Home.*

Who says we haven't any poetical talent on the Island! Have you ever noticed what heaps of good people die, Anne, dearie? It's kind of pitiful. Here's ten obituaries, and every one of them saints and models, even the men. Here's old Peter Stimson, who has 'left a large circle of friends to mourn his untimely loss.' Lord, Anne, dearie, that man was eighty, and everybody who knew him had been wishing him dead these thirty years. Read obituaries when you're blue, Anne, dearie—especially the ones of folks you know. If you've any sense of humor at all they'll cheer you up, believe *me*. I just wish *I* had the writing of the obituaries of some people. Isn't 'obituary' an awful ugly word? This very Peter I've been speaking of had a face exactly like one. I never saw it but I thought of the word *obituary* then and there. There's only one uglier word that I know of, and that's *relict*. Lord, Anne, dearie, I may be an old maid, but there's this comfort in it—I'll never be any man's 'relict.' "

"It *is* an ugly word," said Anne, laughing. "Avonlea graveyard was full of old tombstones 'sacred to the memory of So-and-So, *relict* of the late So-and So.' It always made me think of something worn out and moth eaten. Why is it that so many of the words connected with death are so disagreeable? I do wish that the custom of calling a dead body 'the remains' could be abolished. I positively shiver when I hear the undertaker say at a funeral,' All who wish to see the remains please step this way.' It always gives me the horrible impression that I am about to view the scene of a cannibal feast.''

''Well, all I hope,'' said Miss Cornelia calmly, ''is that when I'm dead nobody will call me 'our departed sister.' I took a scunner at this sister-and-brothering business five years ago when there was a travelling evangelist holding meetings at the Glen. I hadn't any use for him from the start. I felt in my bones that there was something wrong with him. And there was. Mind you, he was pretending to be a Presbyterian—Presby*tar*ian, *he* called it—and all the time he was a Methodist. He brothered and sistered everybody. He had a large circle of relations, that man had. He clutched my hand fervently one night, and said imploringly, 'My *dear* sister Bryant, are you a Christian?' I just looked him over a bit, and then I said calmly, 'The only brother I ever had, *Mr*. Fiske, was buried fifteen years ago, and I haven't adopted any since. As for being a Christian, I was that, I hope and believe, when you were crawling about the floor in pet- ticoats.' *That* squelched him, believe *me*. Mind you, Anne dearie, I'm not down on all evangelists. We've had some real fine, earnest men, who did a lot of good and made the old sinners squirm. But this Fiske-man wasn't one of them. I had a good laugh all to myself one evening. Fiske had asked all who were Christians to stand up. *I* didn't, believe *me!* I never had any use for that sort of thing. But most of them did, and then he asked all who wanted to be Christians to stand up. Nobody stirred for a spell, so Fiske started up a hymn at the top of his voice. Just in front of me poor little Ikey Baker was sitting in the Millison pew. He was a home boy, ten years old, and Millison just about worked him to death. The poor little creature was always so tired he fell asleep right off whenever he went to church or anywhere he could sit still for a few minutes. He'd been sleeping all through the meeting, and I was thankful to see the poor child getting a rest, believe *me*. Well, when Fiske's voice went soaring skyward and the rest joined in, poor Ikey wakened with a start. He thought it was just an ordinary singing and that everybody ought to stand up, so he scrambled to his feet mighty quick, knowing he'd get a combing down from Maria Millison for sleeping in meeting. Fiske saw him, stopped and shouted, 'Another soul saved! Glory Hallelujah!' And there was poor, frightened Ikey, only half awake and yawning, never thinking about his soul at all. Poor child, he never had time to think of anything but his tired, overworked little body.

"Leslie went one night and the Fiske-man got right after her—oh, he was especially anxious about the souls of the nice-looking girls, believe me!—and he hurt her feelings so she never went again. And then he prayed every night after that, right in public, that the Lord would soften her hard heart. Finally I went to Mr. Leavitt, our minister then, and told him if he didn't make Fiske stop that I'd just rise up the next night and throw my hymn book at him when he mentioned that 'beautiful but unrepentant young woman.' I'd have done it too, believe *me*. Mr. Leavitt did put a stop to it, but Fiske kept on with his meetings until Charley Douglas put an end to his career in the Glen. Mrs. Charley had been out in California all winter. She'd been real melancholy in the fall—religious melancholy—it ran in her family. Her father worried so much over believing that he had committed the unpardonable sin that he died in the asylum. So when Rose Douglas got that way Charley packed her off to visit her sister in Los Angeles. She got perfectly well and came home just when the Fiske revival was in full swing. She stepped off the train at the Glen, real smiling and chipper, and the first thing she saw staring her in the face on the black, gable-end of the freight shed, was the question, in big white letters, two feet high, 'Whither goest thou—to heaven or hell?' That had been one of Fiske's ideas, and he had got Henry Hammond to paint it. Rose just gave a shriek and fainted; and when they got her home she was worse than ever. Charley Douglas went to Mr. Leavitt and told him that every Douglas would leave the church if Fiske was kept there any longer. Mr. Leavitt had to give in, for the Douglases paid half his salary, so Fiske departed, and we had to depend on our Bibles once more for instructions on how to get to heaven. After he was gone Mr. Leavitt found out he was just a masquerading Methodist, and he felt pretty sick, believe *me*. Mr. Leavitt fell short in some ways, but he was a good, sound Presbyterian."

"By the way, I had a letter from Mr. Ford yesterday," said Anne. "He asked me to remember him kindly to you."

"I don't want his remembrances," said Miss Cornelia, curtly.

"Why?" said Anne, in astonishment. "I thought you liked him."

"Well, so I did, in a kind of way. But I'll never forgive him for what he done to Leslie. There's that poor child eating her heart out about him—as if she hadn't had trouble enough—and him ranting round Toronto, I've no doubt, enjoying himself same as ever. Just like a man.''

"Oh, Miss Cornelia, how did you find out?''

"Lord, Anne, dearie, I've got eyes, haven't I? And I've known Leslie since she was a baby. There's been a new kind of heartbreak in her eyes all the fall, and I know that writer-man was behind it somehow. I'll never forgive myself for being the means of bringing him here. But I never expected he'd be like he was. I thought he'd just be like the other men Leslie had boarded—conceited young asses, every one of them, that she never had any use for. One of them did try to flirt with her once and she froze him out—so bad, I feel sure he's never got himself thawed since. So I never thought of any danger.''

"Don't let Leslie suspect you know her secret,'' said Anne hurriedly. "I think it would hurt her.''

"Trust me, Anne, dearie. *I* wasn't born yesterday. Oh, a plague on all the men! One of them ruined Leslie's life to begin with, and now another of the tribe comes and makes her still more wretched. Anne, this world is an awful place, believe *me*.''

> *"There's something in the world amiss*
> *Will be unriddled by and by,"*

quoted Anne dreamily.

"If it is, it'll be in a world where there aren't any men,'' said Miss Cornelia gloomily.

"What have the men been doing now?'' asked Gilbert, entering.

"Mischief—mischief! What else did they ever do?''

"It was Eve ate the apple, Miss Cornelia.''

" 'Twas a he-creature tempted her,'' retorted Miss Cornelia triumphantly.

Leslie, after her first anguish was over, found it possible to go on with life after all, as most of us do, no matter what our particular form of torment has been. It is even possible that she enjoyed moments of it, when she was one of the gay circle in the little house of dreams. But if Anne ever hoped that she was forgetting Owen Ford she would have been undeceived by the furtive hunger in Leslie's eyes whenever his name was mentioned. Pitiful to that hunger, Anne always contrived to tell Captain Jim or Gilbert bits of news from Owen's letters when Leslie was with them. The girl's flush and pallor at such moments spoke all too eloquently of the emotion that filled her being. But she never spoke of him to Anne, or mentioned that night on the sand-bar.

One day her old dog died and she grieved bitterly over him.

"He's been my friend so long," she said sorrowfully to Anne. "He was Dick's old dog, you know—Dick had him for a year or so before we were married. He left him with me when he sailed on the *Four Sisters*. Carlo got very fond of me—and his dog-love helped me through that first dreadful year after mother died, when I was alone. When I heard that Dick was coming back I was afraid Carlo wouldn't be so much mine. But he never seemed to care for Dick, though he had been so fond of him once. He would snap and growl at him as if he were a stranger. I was glad. It was nice to have one thing whose love was all mine. That old dog has been such a comfort to me, Anne. He got so feeble in the fall that I was afraid he couldn't live long—but I hoped I could nurse him through the winter. He seemed pretty well this morning. He was lying on the rug before the fire; then, all at once, he got up and crept over to me; he put his head on my lap and gave me one loving look out of his big, soft, dog eyes—and then he just shivered and died. I shall miss him so."

"Let me give you another dog, Leslie," said Anne. "I'm getting a lovely Gordon setter for a Christmas present for Gilbert. Let me give you one too."

Leslie shook her head.

"Not just now, thank you, Anne. I don't feel like having another dog yet. I don't seem to have any affection left for another. Perhaps—in time—I'll let you give me one. I really need one as a kind of protection. But there was something almost human about Carlo—it wouldn't be *decent* to fill his place too hurriedly, dear old fellow."

Anne went to Avonlea a week before Christmas and stayed until after the holidays. Gilbert came up for her, and there was a glad New Year celebration at Green Gables, when Barrys and Blythes and Wrights assembled to devour a dinner which had cost Mrs. Rachel and Marilla much careful thought and preparation. When they went back to Four Winds the little house was almost drifted over, for the third storm of a winter that was to prove phenomenally stormy had whirled up the harbor and heaped huge snow mountains about everything it encountered. But Captain Jim had shovelled out doors and paths, and Miss Cornelia had come down and kindled the hearth-fire.

"It's good to see you back, Anne, dearie! But did you ever see such drifts? You can't see the Moore place at all unless you go upstairs. Leslie'll be so glad you're back. She's almost buried alive over there. Fortunately Dick can shovel snow, and thinks it's great fun. Susan sent me word to tell you she would be on hand tomorrow. Where are you off to now, Captain?''

"I reckon I'll plough up to the Glen and sit a bit with old Martin Strong. He's not far from his end and he's lonesome. He hasn't many friends—been too busy all his life to make any. He's made heaps of money, though."

"Well, he thought that since he couldn't serve God and Mammon he'd better stick to Mammon," said Miss Cornelia crisply. "So he shouldn't complain if he doesn't find Mammon very good company now."

Captain Jim went out, but remembered something in the yard and turned back for a moment.

"I'd a letter from Mr. Ford, Mistress Blythe, and he says the life-book is accepted and is going to be published next fall. I felt fair uplifted when I got the news. To think that I'm to see it in print at last."

"That man is clean crazy on the subject of his life-book," said Miss Cornelia compassionately. "For my part, I think there's far too many books in the world now."

CHAPTER 29

GILBERT AND ANNE DISAGREE

GILBERT LAID down the ponderous medical tome over which he had been poring until the increasing dusk of the March evening made him desist. He leaned back in his chair and gazed meditatively out of the window. It was early spring—probably the ugliest time of the year. Not even the sunset could redeem the dead, sodden landscape and rotten black harbor ice upon which he looked. No sign of life was visible, save a big black crow winging his solitary way across a leaden field. Gilbert speculated idly concerning that crow. Was he a family crow, with a black but comely crow wife awaiting him in the woods beyond the Glen? Or was he a glossy young buck of a crow on courting thoughts intent? Or was he a cynical bachelor crow, believing that he travels the fastest who travels alone? Whatever he was, he soon disappeared in congenial gloom and Gilbert turned to the cheerier view indoors.

The firelight flickered from point to point, gleaming on the white and green coats of Gog and Magog, on the sleek, brown head of the beautiful setter basking on the rug, on the picture frames on the walls, on the vaseful of daffodils from the window garden, on Anne herself, sitting by her little table, with her sewing beside her and her hands clasped over her knee while she traced out pictures in the fire—Castles in Spain whose airy turrets pierced moonlit cloud and sunset bar—ships sailing from the Haven of Good Hopes straight to Four Winds Harbor with precious burthen. For Anne was again a dreamer of dreams, albeit a grim shape of fear went with her night and day to shadow and darken her visions.

Gilbert was accustomed to refer to himself as "an old married man." But he still looked upon Anne with the incredulous eyes of a lover. He couldn't wholly believe yet that she was really his. It *might* be only a dream after all, part and parcel of this magic house of dreams. His soul still went on tip-toe before her, lest the charm be shattered and the dream dispelled.

"Anne," he said slowly, "lend me your ears. I want to talk with you about something."

Anne looked across at him through the fire-lit gloom.

"What is it?" she asked gaily. "You look fearfully solemn, Gilbert. I really haven't done anything naughty today. Ask Susan."

"It's not of you—or ourselves—I want to talk. It's about Dick Moore."

"Dick Moore?" echoed Anne, sitting up alertly. "Why, what in the world have you to say about Dick Moore?"

"I've been thinking a great deal about him lately. Do you remember that time last summer I treated him for those carbuncles on his neck?"

"Yes—yes."

"I took the opportunity to examine the scars on his head thoroughly. I've always thought Dick was a very interesting case from a medical point of view. Lately I've been studying the history of trephining and the cases where it has been employed. Anne, I have come to the conclusion that if Dick Moore were taken to a good hospital and the operation of trephining performed on several places in his skull, his memory and faculties might be restored."

"Gilbert!" Anne's voice was full of protest. "Surely you don't mean it!"

"I do, indeed. And I have decided that it is my duty to broach the subject to Leslie."

"Gilbert Blythe, you shall *not* do any such thing," cried Anne vehemently. "Oh, Gilbert, you won't—you won't. You couldn't be so cruel. Promise me you won't."

"Why, Anne-girl, I didn't suppose you would take it like this. Be reasonable—"

"I won't be reasonable—I can't be reasonable—I *am* reasonable. It is you who are unreasonable. Gilbert, have you ever once thought what it would mean for Leslie if Dick Moore were to be restored to his right senses? Just stop and think! She's unhappy enough now; but life as Dick's nurse and attendant is a thousand times easier for her than life as Dick's wife. I know—I *know!* It's unthinkable. Don't you meddle with the matter. Leave well enough alone."

"I *have* thought over that aspect of the case thoroughly, Anne. But I believe that a doctor is bound to set the sanctity of a patient's mind and body above all other considerations, no matter what the consequences may be. I believe it his duty to endeavor to restore health and sanity, if there is any hope whatever of it."

"But Dick isn't your patient in that respect," cried Anne, taking another tack. "If Leslie had asked you if anything could be done for him, *then* it might be your duty to tell her what you really thought. But you've no right to meddle."

"I don't call it meddling. Uncle Dave told Leslie twelve years ago that nothing could be done for Dick. She believes that, of course."

"And why did Uncle Dave tell her that, if it wasn't true?" cried Anne, triumphantly. "Doesn't he know as much about it as you?"

"I think not—though it may sound conceited and presumptuous to say it. And you know as well as I that he is rather prejudiced against what he calls 'these new-fangled notions of cutting and carving.' He's even opposed to operating for appendicitis."

"He's right," exclaimed Anne, with a complete change of front. 'I believe myself that you modern doctors are entirely too fond of making experiments with human flesh and blood."

"Rhoda Allonby would not be a living woman today if I had been afraid of making a certain experiment," argued Gilbert. "I took the risk—and saved her life."

"I'm sick and tired of hearing about Rhoda Allonby," cried Anne—most unjustly, for Gilbert had never mentioned Mrs. Allonby's name since the day he had told Anne of his success in regard to her. And he could not be blamed for other people's discussion of it.

Gilbert felt rather hurt.

"I had not expected you to look at the matter as you do, Anne," he said a little stiffly, getting up and moving towards the office door. It was their first approach to a quarrel.

But Anne flew after him and dragged him back.

"Now, Gilbert, you are not 'going off mad.' Sit down here and I'll apologise bee-*yew*-ti-fully, I shouldn't have said that. But—oh, if you knew—"

Anne checked herself just in time. She had been on the very verge of betraying Leslie's secret.

"Knew what a woman feels about it," she concluded lamely.

"I think I do know. I've looked at the matter from every point of view—and I've been driven to the conclusion that it is my duty to tell Leslie that I believe it is possible that Dick can be restored to himself; there my responsibility ends. It will be for her to decide what she will do."

"I don't think you've any right to put such a responsibility on her. She has enough to bear. She is poor—how could she afford such an operation?"

"That is for her to decide," persisted Gilbert stubbornly.

"You say you think that Dick can be cured. But are you *sure* of it?"

"Certainly not. Nobody could be sure of such a thing. There may have been lesions of the brain itself, the effect of which can never be removed. But if, as I believe, his loss of memory and other faculties is due merely to the pressure on the brain centers of certain depressed areas of bone, then he can be cured."

"But it's only a possibility!" insisted Anne. "Now, suppose you tell Leslie and she decides to have the operation. It will cost a great deal. She will have to borrow the money, or sell her little property. And suppose the operation is a failure and Dick remains the same. How will she be able to pay back the money she borrows, or make a living for herself and that big helpless creature if she sells the farm?"

"Oh, I know—I know. But it is my duty to tell her. I can't get away from that conviction."

"Oh, I know the Blythe stubbornness," groaned Anne. "But don't do this solely on your own responsibility. Consult Doctor Dave."

"I *have* done so," said Gilbert reluctantly.

"And what did he say?"

"In brief—as you say—leave well enough alone. Apart from his prejudice against new-fangled surgery, I'm afraid he looks at the case from your point of view—don't do it, for Leslie's sake."

"There now," cried Anne triumphantly. "I do think, Gilbert, that you ought to abide by the judgment of a man nearly eighty, who has seen a great deal and saved scores of lives himself—surely his opinion ought to weigh more than a mere boy's."

"Thank you."

"Don't laugh. It's too serious."

"That's just my point. It *is* serious. Here is a man who is a helpless burden. He may be restored to reason and usefulness—"

"He was so very useful before," interjected Anne witheringly.

"He may be given a chance to make good and redeem the past. His wife doesn't know this. I do. It is therefore my duty to tell her that there is such a possibility. That, boiled down, is my decision."

"Don't say 'decision' yet, Gilbert. Consult somebody else. Ask Captain Jim what he thinks about it."

"Very well. But I'll not promise to abide by his opinion, Anne. This is something a man must decide for himself. My conscience would never be easy if I kept silent on the subject."

"Oh, your conscience!" moaned Anne. "I suppose that Uncle Dave has a conscience too, hasn't he?"

"Yes. But I am not the keeper of his conscience. Come, Anne, if this affair did not concern Leslie—if it were a purely abstract case, you would agree with me,—you know you would."

"I wouldn't," vowed Anne, trying to believe it herself. "Oh, you can argue all night, Gilbert, but you won't convince me. Just you ask Miss Cornelia what she thinks of it."

"You're driven to the last ditch, Anne, when you bring up Miss Cornelia as a reinforcement. She will say, 'Just like a man,' and rage furiously. No matter. This is no affair for Miss Cornelia to settle. Leslie alone must decide it."

"You know very well how she will decide it," said Anne, almost in tears. "She has ideals of duty, too. I don't see how you can take such a responsibility on your shoulders. *I* couldn't."

> *"Because right is right to follow right*
> *Were wisdom in the scorn of consequence,"*

quoted Gilbert.

"Oh, you think a couplet of poetry a convincing argument!" scoffed Anne. "That is so like a man."

And then she laughed in spite of herself. It sounded so like an echo of Miss Cornelia.

"Well, if you won't accept Tennyson as an authority, perhaps you will believe the words of a Greater than he,'' said Gilbert seriously. '' 'Ye shall know the truth and the truth shall make you free.' I believe that, Anne, with all my heart. It's the greatest and grandest verse in the Bible—or in any literature—and the *truest*, if there are comparative degrees of trueness. And it's the first duty of a man to tell the truth, as he sees it and believes it.''

"In this case the truth won't make poor Leslie free," sighed Anne. "It will probably end in still more bitter bondage for her. Oh, Gilbert, I *can't* think you are right."

CHAPTER 30

LESLIE DECIDES

A SUDDEN outbreak of a virulent type of influenza at the Glen and down at the fishing village kept Gilbert so busy for the next fortnight that he had no time to pay the promised visit to Captain Jim. Anne hoped against hope that he had abandoned the idea about Dick Moore, and, resolving to let sleeping dogs lie, she said no more about the subject. But she thought of it incessantly.

"I wonder if it would be right for me to tell him that Leslie cares for Owen," she thought. "He would never let her suspect that he knew, so her pride would not suffer, and it *might* convince him that he should let Dick Moore alone. Shall I—shall I? No, after all, I cannot. A promise is sacred, and I've no right to betray Leslie's secret. But oh, I never felt so worried over anything in my life as I do over this. It's spoiling the spring—it's spoiling everything."

One evening Gilbert abruptly proposed that they go down and see Captain Jim. With a sinking heart Anne agreed, and they set forth. Two weeks of kind sunshine had wrought a miracle in the bleak landscape over which Gilbert's crow had flown. The hills and fields were dry and brown and warm, ready to break into bud and blossom; the harbor was laughter-shaken again; the long harbor road was lke a gleaming red ribbon; down on the dunes a crowd of boys, who were out smelt fishing, were burning the thick, dry sandhill grass of the preceding summer. The flames swept over the dunes rosily, flinging their cardinal banners against the dark gulf beyond, and illuminating the channel and the fishing village. It was a picturesque scene which would at other times have delighted Anne's eyes; but she was not enjoying this walk. Neither was Gilbert. Their usual good-comrade-ship and Josephian community of taste and viewpoint were sadly lacking. Anne's disapproval of the whole project showed itself in the haughty uplift of her head and the studied politeness of her remarks. Gilbert's mouth was set in all the Blythe obstinacy, but his eyes were troubled. He meant to do what he believed to be his duty; but to be at outs with Anne was a high price to pay. Altogether, both were glad when they reached the light—and remorseful that they should be glad.

Captain Jim put away the fishing net upon which he was working, and welcomed them joyfully. In the searching light of the spring evening he looked older than Anne had ever seen him. His hair had grown much grayer, and the strong old hand shook a little. But his blue eyes were clear and steady, and the staunch soul looked out through them gallant and unafraid.

Captain Jim listened in amazed silence while Gilbert said what he had come to say. Anne, who knew how the old man worshipped Leslie, felt quite sure that he would side with her, although she had not much hope that this would influence Gilbert. She was therefore surprised beyond measure when Captain Jim, slowly and sorrow-fully, but unhesitatingly, gave it as his opinion that Leslie should be told.

"Oh, Captain Jim, I didn't think you'd say that," she exclaimed reproachfully. "I thought you wouldn't want to make more trouble for her."

Captain Jim shook his head.

"I don't want to. I know how you feel about it, Mistress Blythe— just as I feel meself. But it ain't our feelings we have to steer by through life—no, no, we'd make shipwreck mighty often if we did that. There's only the one safe compass and we've got to set our course by that—what it's right to do. I agree with the doctor. If there's a chance for Dick, Leslie should be told of it. There's no two sides to that, in my opinion."

"Well," said Anne, giving up in despair, "wait until Miss Cor-nelia gets after you two men."

"Cornelia'll rake us fore and aft, no doubt," assented Captain

Jim. "You women are lovely critters, Mistress Blythe, but you're just a mite illogical. You're a highly eddicated lady and Cornelia isn't, but you're like as two peas when it comes to that. I dunno's you're any the worse for it. Logic is a sort of hard, merciless thing, I reckon. Now, I'll brew a cup of tea and we'll drink it and talk of pleasant things, jest to calm our minds a bit."

At least, Captain Jim's tea and conversation calmed Anne's mind to such an extent that she did not make Gilbert suffer so acutely on the way home as she had deliberately intended to do. She did not refer to the burning question at all, but she chatted amiably of other matters, and Gilbert understood that he was forgiven under protest.

"Captain Jim seems very frail and bent this spring. The winter has aged him," said Anne sadly. "I am afraid that he will soon be going to seek lost Margaret. I can't bear to think of it."

"Four Winds won't be the same place when Captain Jim 'sets out to sea,'" agreed Gilbert.

The following evening he went to the house up the brook. Anne wandered dismally around until his return.

"Well, what did Leslie say?" she demanded when he came in.

"Very little. I think she felt rather dazed."

"And is she going to have the operation?"

"She is going to think it over and decide very soon."

Gilbert flung himself wearily into the easy chair before the fire. He looked tired. It had not been an easy thing for him to tell Leslie. And the terror that had sprung into her eyes when the meaning of what he told her came home to her was not a pleasant thing to remember. Now, when the die was cast, he was beset with doubts of his own wisdom.

Anne looked at him remorsefully; then she slipped down on the rug beside him and laid her glossy red head on his arm.

"Gilbert, I've been rather hateful over this. I won't be any more. Please just call me red-headed and forgive me."

By which Gilbert understood that, no matter what came of it, there would be no I-told-you-so's. But he was not wholly comforted. Duty in the abstract is one thing; duty in the concrete is quite another, especially when the doer is confronted by a woman's stricken eyes.

Some instinct made Anne keep away from Leslie for the next three days. On the third evening Leslie came down to the little house and told Gilbert that she had made up her mind; she would take Dick to Montreal and have the operation.

She was very pale and seemed to have wrapped herself in her old mantle of aloofness. But her eyes had lost the look which had haunted Gilbert; they were cold and bright; and she proceeded to discuss details with him in a crisp, business-like way. There were plans to be made and many things to be thought over. When Leslie had got the information she wanted she went home. Anne wanted to walk part of the way with her.

"Better not," said Leslie curtly. "Today's rain has made the ground damp. Good-night."

"Have I lost my friend?" said Anne with a sigh. "If the operation is successful and Dick Moore finds himself again Leslie will retreat into some remote fastness of her soul where none of us can ever find her."

"Perhaps she will leave him," said Gilbert.

"Leslie would never do that, Gilbert. Her sense of duty is very strong. She told me once that her Grandmother West always impressed upon her the fact that when she assumed any responsibility she must never shirk it, no matter what the consequences might be. That is one of her cardinal rules. I suppose it's very old-fashioned."

"Don't be bitter, Anne-girl. You know you don't think it old-fashioned—you know you have the very same idea of sacredness of assumed responsibilities yourself. And you are right. Shirking responsibilities is the curse of our modern life—the secret of all the unrest and discontent that is seething in the world."

"Thus saith the preacher," mocked Anne. But under the mockery she felt that he was right; and she was very sick at heart for Leslie.

A week later Miss Cornelia descended like an avalanche upon the little house. Gilbert was away and Anne was compelled to bear the shock of the impact alone.

Miss Cornelia hardly waited to get her hat off before she began.

"Anne, do you mean to tell me it's true what I've heard—that Dr. Blythe has told Leslie Dick can be cured, and that she is going to take him to Montreal to have him operated on?"

"Yes, it is quite true, Miss Cornelia," said Anne bravely.

"Well, it's inhuman cruelty, that's what it is," said Miss Cornelia, violently agitated. "I did think Dr. Blythe was a decent man. I didn't think he could have been guilty of this."

"Dr. Blythe thought it was his duty to tell Leslie that there was a chance for Dick," said Anne with spirit, "and," she added, loyalty to Gilbert getting the better of her, "I agree with him."

"Oh, no, you don't, dearie," said Miss Cornelia. "No person with any bowels of compassion could."

"Captain Jim does."

"Don't quote that old ninny to me," cried Miss Cornelia. "And I don't care who agrees with him. Think—*think* what it means to that poor hunted, harried girl."

"We *do* think of it. But Gilbert believes that a doctor should put the welfare of a patient's mind and body before all other considerations."

"That's just like a man. But I expected better things of you, Anne," said Miss Cornelia, more in sorrow than in wrath; then she proceeded to bombard Anne with precisely the same arguments with which the latter had attacked Gilbert; and Anne valiantly defended her husband with the weapons he had used for his own protection. Long was the fray, but Miss Cornelia made an end at last.

"It's an iniquitous shame," she declared, almost in tears. "That's just what it is—an iniquitous shame. Poor, poor Leslie!"

"Don't you think Dick should be considered a little too?" pleaded Anne.

"Dick! Dick Moore! *He's* happy enough. He's a better behaved and more reputable member of society now than he ever was before. Why, he was a drunkard and perhaps worse. Are you going to set him loose again to roar and to devour?"

"He may reform," said poor Anne, beset by foe without and traitor within.

"Reform your grandmother!" retorted Miss Cornelia. "Dick Moore got the injuries that left him as he is in a drunken brawl. He *deserves* his fate. It was sent on him for a punishment. I don't believe the doctor has any business to tamper with the visitations of God."

"Nobody knows how Dick was hurt, Miss Cornelia. It may not have been in a drunken brawl at all. He may have been waylaid and robbed."

"Pigs *may* whistle, but they've poor mouths for it," said Miss Cornelia. "Well, the gist of what you tell me is that the thing is settled and there's no use in talking. If that's so I'll hold my tongue. I don't propose to wear *my* teeth out gnawing files. When a thing has to be I give in to it. But I like to make mighty sure first that it *has* to be. Now, I'll devote *my* energies to comforting and sustaining Leslie. And after all," added Miss Cornelia, brightening up hopefully. "perhaps nothing can be done for Dick."

CHAPTER 31

THE TRUTH MAKES FREE

LESLIE, HAVING once made up her mind what to do, proceeded to do it with characteristic resolution and speed. House-cleaning must be finished with first, whatever issues of life and death might await beyond. The gray house up the brook was put into flawless order and cleanliness, with Miss Cornelia's ready assistance. Miss Cornelia, having said her say to Anne, and later on to Gilbert and Captain Jim—sparing neither of them, let it be assured—never spoke of the matter to Leslie. She accepted the fact of Dick's operaton, referred to it when necessary in a business-like way, and ignored it when it was not. Leslie never attempted to discuss it. She was very cold and quiet during these beautiful spring days. She seldom visited Anne, and though she was invariably courteous and friendly, that very courtesy was as an icy barrier between her and the people of the little house. The old jokes and laughter and chumminess of common things could not reach her over it. Anne refused to feel hurt. She knew that Leslie was in the grip of a hideous dread—a dread that wrapped her away from all little glimpses of happiness and hours of pleasure. When one great passion seizes possession of the soul all other feelings are crowded aside. Never in all her life had Leslie Moore shuddered away from the future with more intolerable terror. But she went forward as unswervingly in the path she had elected as the martyrs of old walked their chosen way, knowing the end of it to be the fiery agony of the stake.

The financial question was settled with greater ease than Anne had feared. Leslie borrowed the necessary money from Captain Jim, and, at her insistence, he took a mortgage on the little farm.

"So that is one thing off the poor girl's mind," Miss Cornelia told Anne, "and off mine too. Now, if Dick gets well enough to work again he'll be able to earn enough to pay the interest on it; and if he doesn't I know Captain Jim'll manage someway that Leslie won't have to. He said as much to me. 'I'm getting old, Cornelia,' he said, 'and I've no chick or child of my own. Leslie won't take a gift from a living man, but mebbe she will from a dead one.' So it will be all right as far as *that* goes. I wish everything else might be settled as satisfactorily. As for that wretch of a Dick, he's been awful these last few days. The devil was in him, believe *me!* Leslie and I couldn't get on with our work for the tricks he'd play. He chased all her ducks one day around the yard till most of them died. And not one thing would he do for us. Sometimes, you know, he'll make himself quite handy, bringing in pails of water and wood. But this week if we sent him to the well he'd try to climb down into it. I thought once, 'If you'd only shoot down there head-first everything would be nicely settled.'"

"Oh, Miss Cornelia!"

"Now, you needn't Miss Cornelia me, Anne, dearie. *Anybody* would have thought the same. If the Montreal doctors can make a rational creature out of Dick Moore they're wonders."

Leslie took Dick to Montreal early in May. Gilbert went with her, to help her, and make the necessary arrangements for her. He came home with the report that the Montreal surgeon whom they had consulted agreed with him that there was a good chance of Dick's restoration.

"Very comforting," was Miss Cornelia's sarcastic comment.

Anne only sighed. Leslie had been very distant at their parting. But she had promised to write. Ten days after Gilbert's return the letter came. Leslie wrote that the operation had been successfully performed and that Dick was making a good recovery.

"What does she mean by 'successfully?'" asked Anne. "Does she mean that Dick's memory is really restored?"

"Not likely—since she says nothing of it," said Gilbert. "She uses the word 'successfully' from the surgeon's point of view. The operation has been performed and followed by normal results. But it is too soon to know whether Dick's faculties will be eventually restored, wholly or in part. His memory would not be likely to return to him all at once. The process will be gradual, if it occurs at all. Is that all she says?"

"Yes—there's her letter. It's very short. Poor girl, she must be under a terrible strain. Gilbert Blythe, there are heaps of things I long to say to you, only it would be mean."

"Miss Cornelia says them for you," said Gilbert with a rueful smile. "She combs me down every time I encounter her. She makes it plain to me that she regards me as little better than a murderer, and that she thinks it a great pity that Dr. Dave ever let me step into his shoes. She even told me that the Methodist doctor over the harbor was to be preferred before me. With Miss Cornelia the force of condemnation can no further go."

"If Cornelia Bryant was sick, it would not be Doctor Dave or the Methodist doctor she would send for," sniffed Susan. "She would have you out of your hard-earned bed in the middle of the night, doctor, dear, if she took a spell of misery, that she would. And then she would likely say your bill was past all reason. But do not mind her, doctor, dear. It takes all kinds of people to make a world."

No further word came from Leslie for some time. The May days crept away in a sweet succession and the shores of Four Winds Harbor greened and bloomed and purpled. One day in late May Gilbert came home to be met by Susan in the stable yard.

"I am afraid something has upset Mrs. Doctor, doctor, dear," she said mysteriously. "She got a letter this afternoon and since then she has just been walking round the garden and talking to herself. You know it is not good for her to be on her feet so much, doctor, dear. She did not see fit to tell me what her news was, and I am no pry, doctor, dear, and never was, but it is plain something has upset her. And it is not good for her to be upset."

Gilbert hurried rather anxiously to the garden. Had anything happened at Green Gables? But Anne, sitting on the rustic seat by the brook, did not look troubled, though she was certainly much excited. Her eyes were their grayest, and scarlet spots burned on her cheeks.

"What has happened, Anne?"

Anne gave a queer little laugh.

"I think you'll hardly believe it when I tell you, Gilbert. *I* can't believe it yet. As Susan said the other day, 'I feel like a fly coming to live in the sun—dazed-like.' It's all so incredible. I've read the letter a score of times and every time it's just the same—I can't believe my own eyes. Oh, Gilbert, you were right—so right. I can see that clearly enough now—and I'm so ashamed of myself—and will you ever really forgive me?"

"Anne, I'll shake you if you don't grow coherent. Redmond would be ashamed of you. *What* has happened?"

"You won't believe it—you won't believe it—"

"I'm going to phone for Uncle Dave," said Gilbert, pretending to start for the house.

"Sit down, Gilbert. I'll try to tell you. I've had a letter, and oh, Gilbert, it's all so amazing—so incredibly amazing—we never thought—not one of us ever dreamed—"

"I suppose," said Gilbert, sitting down with a resigned air, "the only thing to do in a case of this kind is to have patience and go at the matter categorically. Whom is your letter from?"

"Leslie—and, oh, Gilbert—"

"Leslie! Whew! What has she to say? What's the news about Dick?"

Anne lifted the letter and held it out, calmly dramatic in a moment.

"There is *no* Dick! The man we have thought Dick Moore—whom everybody in Four Winds has believed for twelve years to be Dick Moore—is his cousin, George Moore, of Nova Scotia, who, it seems, always resembled him very strikingly. Dick Moore died of yellow fever thirteen years ago in Cuba.''

CHAPTER 32

MISS CORNELIA DISCUSSES THE AFFAIR

"AND DO you mean to tell me, Anne, dearie, that Dick Moore has turned out not to be Dick Moore at all but somebody else? Is *that* what you phoned up to me today?''

"Yes, Miss Cornelia. It is very amazing, isn't it?''

"It's—it's—just like a man," said Miss Cornelia helplessly. She took off her hat with trembling fingers. For once in her life Miss Cornelia was undeniably staggered.

"I can't seem to sense it, Anne," she said. "I've heard you say it—and I believe you—but I can't take it in. Dick Moore is dead—has been dead all these years—and Leslie is free?''

"Yes. The truth has made her free. Gilbert was right when he said that verse was the grandest in the Bible.''

"Tell me everything, Anne, dearie. Since I got your phone I've been in a regular muddle, believe *me*. Cornelia Bryant was never so kerflummuxed before.''

"There isn't a very great deal to tell. Leslie's letter was short. She didn't go into particulars. This man—George Moore—has recovered his memory and knows who he is. He says Dick took yellow fever in Cuba, and the *Four Sisters* had to sail without him. George stayed behind to nurse him. But he died very shortly afterwards. George did not write Leslie because he intended to come right home and tell her himself.''

"And why didn't he?''

"I suppose his accident must have intervened. Gilbert says it is quite likely that George Moore remembers nothing of his accident, or what led to it, and may never remember it. It probably happened very soon after Dick's death. We may find out more particulars when Leslie writes again.''

"Does she say what she is going to do? When is she coming home?''

"She says she will stay with George Moore until he can leave the hospital. She has written to his people in Nova Scotia. It seems that George's only near relative is a married sister much older than himself. She was living when George sailed on the *Four Sisters,* but of course we do not know what may have happened since. Did you ever see George Moore, Miss Cornelia?''

"I did. It is all coming back to me. He was here visiting his Uncle Abner eighteen years ago, when he and Dick would be about seventeen. They were double cousins, you see. Their fathers were brothers and their mothers were twin sisters, and they did look a terrible lot alike. Of course," added Miss Cornelia scornfully, "it wasn't one of those freak resemblances you read of in novels where two people are so much alike that they can fill each other's places and their nearest and dearest can't tell between them. In those days you could tell easy enough which was George and which was Dick, if you saw them together and near at hand. Apart, or some distance away, it wasn't so easy. They played lots of tricks on people and thought it great fun, the two scamps. George Moore was a little taller and a good deal fatter than Dick—though neither of them was what you would call fat—they were both of the lean kind. Dick had higher color than George, and his hair was a shade lighter. But their features were just alike, and they both had that queer freak of eyes—one blue and one hazel. They weren't much alike in any other way, though. George was a real nice fellow, though he was a scalawag for mischief, and some said he had a liking for a glass even then. But everybody liked him better than Dick. He spent about a month here. Leslie never saw him; she was only about eight or nine then and I remember now that she spent that whole winter over harbor with her grandmother West. Captain Jim was away, too—that was the winter he was wrecked on the Magdalens. I don't suppose either he or Leslie had ever heard about the Nova Scotia cousin looking so much like Dick. Nobody ever thought of him when Captain Jim brought Dick—George, I should say—home. Of course, we all thought Dick had changed considerable—he'd got so lumpish and fat. But we put that down to what had happened to him, and no doubt that was the reason, for, as I've said, George wasn't fat to begin with either. And there was no other way we could have guessed, for the man's senses were clean gone. I can't see that it is any wonder we were all deceived. But it's a staggering thing. And Leslie has sacrificed the best years of her life to nursing a man who hadn't any claim on her! Oh, drat the men! No matter what they do, it's the wrong thing. And no matter who they are, it's somebody they shouldn't be. They do exasperate me.''

"Gilbert and Captain Jim are men, and it is through them that the truth has been discovered at last," said Anne.

"Well, I admit that," conceded Miss Cornelia reluctantly. "I'm sorry I raked the doctor off so. It's the first time in my life I've ever felt ashamed of anything I said to a man. I don't know as I shall tell him so, though. He'll just have to take it for granted. Well, Anne, dearie, it's a mercy the Lord doesn't answer all our prayers. I've been praying hard right along that the operation wouldn't cure Dick. Of course I didn't put it just quite so plain. But that was what was in the back of my mind, and I have no doubt the Lord knew it.''

"Well, He has answered the spirit of your prayer. You really wished that things shouldn't be made any harder for Leslie. I'm afraid that in my secret heart I've been hoping the operation wouldn't succeed, and I am wholesomely ashamed of it.''

"How does Leslie seem to take it?''

"She writes like one dazed. I think that, like ourselves, she hardly realises it yet. She says, 'It all seems like a strange dream to me, Anne.' That is the only reference she makes to herself.''

"Poor child! I suppose when the chains are struck off a prisoner he'd feel queer and lost without them for a while. Anne, dearie, here's a thought keeps coming into my mind. What about Owen Ford? We both know Leslie was fond of him. Did it ever occur to you that he was fond of her?''

"It—did—once," admitted Anne, feeling that she might say so much.

"Well, I hadn't any reason to think he was, but it just appeared to me he *must* be. Now, Anne, dearie, the Lord knows I'm not a match-maker, and I scorn all such doings. But if I were you and writing to that Ford man I'd just mention, casual-like, what has happened. That is what *I'd* do.''

"Of course I will mention it when I write him," said Anne, a trifle distantly. Somehow, this was a thing she could not discuss with Miss Cornelia. And yet, she had to admit that the same thought had been lurking in her mind ever since she had heard of Leslie's freedom. But she would not desecrate it by free speech.

"Of course there is no great rush, dearie. But Dick Moore's been dead for thirteen years and Leslie has wasted enough of her life for him. We'll just see what comes of it. As for this George Moore, who's gone and come back to life when everyone thought he was dead and done for, just like a man, I'm real sorry for him. He won't seem to fit in anywhere.''

''He is still a young man, and if he recovers completely, as seems likely, he will be able to make a place for himself again. It must be very strange for him, poor fellow. I suppose all these years since his accident will not exist for him.''

CHAPTER 33

LESLIE RETURNS

A FORTNIGHT later Leslie Moore came home alone to the old house where she had spent so many bitter years. In the June twilight she went over the fields to Anne's, and appeared with ghost-like suddenness in the scented garden.

''Leslie!'' cried Anne in amazement. ''Where have you sprung from? We never knew you were coming. Why didn't you write? We would have met you.''

''I couldn't write somehow, Anne. It seemed so futile to try to say anything with pen and ink. And I wanted to get back quietly and unobserved.''

Anne put her arms about Leslie and kissed her. Leslie returned the kiss warmly. She looked pale and tired, and she gave a little sigh as she dropped down on the grasses beside a great bed of daffodils that were gleaming through the pale, silvery twilight like golden stars.

''And you have come home alone, Leslie?''

''Yes. George Moore's sister came to Montreal and took him home with her. Poor fellow, he was sorry to part with me—though I was a stranger to him when his memory first came back. He clung to me in those first hard days when he was trying to realise that Dick's death was not the thing of yesterday that it seemed to him. It was all very hard for him. I helped him all I could. When his sister came it was easier for him, because it seemed to him only the other day that he had seen her last. Fortunately she had not changed much, and that helped him, too.''

''It is all so strange and wonderful, Leslie. I think we none of us realise it yet.''

"I cannot. When I went into the house over there an hour ago, I felt that it *must* be a dream—that Dick must be there, with his childish smile, as he had been for so long. Anne, I seem stunned yet. I'm not glad or sorry—or *anything*. I feel as if something had been torn suddenly out of my life and left a terrible hole. I feel as if I couldn't be *I*—as if I must have changed into somebody else and couldn't get used to it. It gives me a horrible lonely, dazed, helpless feeling. It's good to see you again—it seems as if you were a sort of anchor for my drifting soul. Oh, Anne, I dread it all—the gossip and wonderment and questioning. When I think of that, I wish that I need not have come home at all. Dr. Dave was at the station when I came off the train—he brought me home. Poor old man, he feels very badly because he told me years ago that nothing could be done for Dick. 'I honestly thought so, Leslie,' he said to me today. 'But I should have told you not to depend on my opinion—I should have told you to go to a specialist. If I had, you would have been saved many bitter years, and poor George Moore many wasted ones. I blame myself very much, Leslie.' I told him not to do that—he had done what he thought right. He has always been so kind to me—I couldn't bear to see him worrying over it."

"And Dick—George, I mean? Is his memory fully restored?"

"Practically. Of course, there are a great many details he can't recall yet—but he remembers more and more every day. He went out for a walk on the evening after Dick was buried. He had Dick's money and watch on him; he meant to bring them home to me, along with my letter. He admits he went to a place where the sailors resorted—and he remembers drinking—and nothing else. Anne, I shall never forget the moment he remembered his own name. I saw him looking at me with an intelligent but puzzled expression. I said, 'Do you know me, Dick?' He answered, 'I never saw you before. Who are you? And my name is not Dick. I am George Moore, and Dick died of yellow fever yesterday! Where am I? What has happened to me?' I—I fainted, Anne. And ever since I have felt as if I were in a dream."

"You will soon adjust yourself to this new state of things, Leslie. And you are young—life is before you—you will have many beautiful years yet."

"Perhaps I shall be able to look at it in that way after a while, Anne. Just now I feel too tired and indifferent to think about the future. I'm—I'm—Anne, I'm lonely. I miss Dick. Isn't it all very strange? Do you know, I was really fond of poor Dick—George, I suppose I should say—just as I would have been fond of a helpless child who depended on me for everything. I would never have admitted it—I was really ashamed of it—because, you see, I had hated and despised Dick so much before he went away. When I heard that Captain Jim was bringing him home I expected I would just feel. the same to him. But I never did—although I continued to loathe him as I remembered him before. From the time he came home I felt only pity—a pity that hurt and wrung me. I supposed then that it was just because his accident had made him so helpless and changed. But now I believe it was because there was really a different personality there. Carlo knew it, Anne—I know now that Carlo knew it. I always thought it strange that Carlo shouldn't have known Dick. Dogs are usually so faithful. But *he* knew it was not his master who had come back, although none of the rest of us did. I had never seen George Moore, you know. I remember now that Dick once mentioned casually that he had a cousin in Nova Scotia who looked as much like him as a twin; but the thing had gone out of my memory, and in any case I would never have thought it of any importance. You see, it never occurred to me to question Dick's identity. Any change in him seemed to me just the result of the accident.

"Oh, Anne, that night in April when Gilbert told me he thought Dick might be cured! I can never forget it. It seemed to me that I had once been a prisoner in a hideous cage of torture, and then the door had been opened and I could get out. I was still chained to the cage but I was not in it. And that night I felt that a merciless hand was drawing me back into the cage—back to a torture even more terrible than it had once been. I didn't blame Gilbert. I felt he was right. And he had been very good—he said that if, in view of the expense and uncertainty of the operation, I should decide not to risk it, he would not blame me in the least. But I knew how I ought to decide—and I couldn't face it. All night I walked the floor like a mad woman, trying to compel myself to face it. I couldn't, Anne—I thought I couldn't—and when morning broke I set my teeth and resolved that I *wouldn't*. I would let things remain as they were. It was very wicked, I know. It would have been just punishment for such wickedness if I had just been left to abide by that decision. I kept to it all day. That afternoon I had to go up to the Glen to do some shopping. It was one of Dick's quiet, drowsy days, so I left him alone. I was gone a little longer than I had expected, and he missed me. He felt lonely. And when I got home, he ran to meet me just like a child, with such a pleased smile on his face. Somehow, Anne, I just gave way then. That smile on his poor vacant face was more than I could endure. I felt as if I were denying a child the chance to grow and develop. I knew that I must give him his chance, no matter what the consequences might be. So I came over and told Gilbert. Oh, Anne, you must have thought me hateful in those weeks before I went away. I didn't mean to be—but I couldn't think of anything except what I had to do, and everything and everybody about me were like shadows."

"I know—I understood, Leslie. And now it is all over—your chain is broken—there is no cage."

"There is no cage," repeated Leslie absently, plucking at the fringing grasses with her slender, brown hands. "But—it doesn't seem as if there were anything else, Anne. You—you remember what I told you of my folly that night on the sand-bar? I find one doesn't get over being a fool very quickly. Sometimes I think there are people who are fools forever. And to be a fool—of that kind—is almost as bad as being a—a dog on a chain."

"You will feel very differently after you get over being tired and bewildered," said Anne, who, knowing a certain thing that Leslie did not know, did not feel herself called upon to waste overmuch sympathy.

Leslie laid her splendid golden head against Anne's knee.

"Anyhow, I have *you*," she said. "Life can't be altogether empty with such a friend. Anne, pat my head—just as if I were a little girl—*mother* me a bit—and let me tell you while my stubborn tongue is loosed a little just what you and your comradeship have meant to me since that night I met you on the rock shore."

CHAPTER 34

THE SHIP O' DREAMS COMES TO HARBOR

ONE MORNING, when a windy golden sunrise was billowing over the gulf in waves of light, a certain weary stork flew over the bar of Four Winds Harbor on his way from the Land of Evening Stars. Under his wing was tucked a sleepy, starry-eyed, little creature. The stork was tired, and he looked wistfully about him. He knew he was somewhere near his destination, but he could not yet see it. The big, white light-house on the red sandstone cliff had its good points; but no stork possessed of any gumption would leave a new, velvet baby there. An old gray house, surrounded by willows, in a blossomy brook valley, looked more promising, but did not seem quite the thing either. The staring green abode further on was manifestly out of the question. Then the stork brighened up. He had caught sight of the very place—a little white house nestled against a big, whispering fir-wood, with a spiral of blue smoke winding up from its kitchen chimney—a house which just looked as if it were meant for babies. The stork gave a sigh of satisfaction, and softly alighted on the ridge-pole.

Half an hour later Gilbert ran down the hall and tapped on the spare-room door. A drowsy voice answered him and in a moment Marilla's pale, scared face peeped out from behind the door.

"Marilla, Anne has sent me to tell you that a certain young gentleman has arrived here. He hasn't brought much luggage with him, but he evidently means to stay."

"For pity's sake!" said Marilla blankly. "You don't mean to tell me, Gilbert, that it's all over. Why wasn't I called?"

"Anne wouldn't let us disturb you when there was no need. Nobody was called until about two hours ago. There was no 'passage perilous' this time."

"And—and —Gilbert—will this baby live?"

"He certainly will. He weighs ten pounds and—why, listen to him. Nothing wrong with his lungs, is there? The nurse says his hair will be red. Anne is furious with her, and I'm tickled to death."

That was a wonderful day in the little house of dreams.

"The best dream of all has come true," said Anne, pale and rapturous. "Oh, Marilla, I hardly dare believe it, after that horrible day last summer. I have had a heartache ever since then—but it is gone now."

"This baby will take Joy's place," said Marilla.

"Oh, no, no, *no*, Marilla. He can't—nothing can ever do that. He has his own place, my dear, wee man-child. But little Joy has hers, and always will have it. If she had lived she would have been over a year old. She would have been toddling around on her tiny feet and lisping a few words. I can see her so plainly, Marilla. Oh, I know now that Captain Jim was right when he said God would manage better than that my baby would seem a stranger to me when I found her Beyond. I've learned *that* this past year. I've followed her development day by day and week by week—I always shall. I shall know just how she grows from year to year—and when I meet her again I'll know her—she won't be a stranger. Oh, Marilla, *look* at his dear, darling toes! Isn't it strange they should be so perfect?"

"It would be stranger if they weren't," said Marilla crisply. Now that all was safely over, Marilla was herself again.

"Oh, I know—but it seems as if they couldn't be quite *finished*, you know—and they are, even to the tiny nails. And his hands—*just* look at his hands, Marilla."

"They appear to be a good deal like hands," Marilla conceded.

"See how he clings to my finger. I'm sure he knows me already. He cries when the nurse takes him away. Oh, Marilla, do you think—you don't think, do you—that his hair is going to be red?"

"I don't see much hair of any color," said Marilla. "I wouldn't worry about it, if I were you, until it becomes visible."

"Marilla, he *has* hair—look at that fine little down all over his head. Anyway, nurse says his eyes will be hazel and his forehead is exactly like Gilbert's."

"And he has the nicest little ears, Mrs. Doctor, dear," said Susan. "The first thing I did was to look at his ears. Hair is deceitful and noses and eyes change, and you cannot tell what is going to come of them, but ears is ears from start to finish, and you always know where you are with them. Just look at their shape—and they are set right back against his precious head. You will never need to be ashamed of his ears, Mrs. Doctor, dear."

Anne's convalescence was rapid and happy. Folks came and worshipped the baby, as people have bowed before the kingship of the new-born since long before the Wise Men of the East knelt in homage to the Royal Babe of the Bethlehem manger. Leslie, slowly finding herself amid the new conditions of her life, hovered over it, like a beautiful, golden-crowned Madonna. Miss Cornelia nursed it as knackily as could any mother in Israel. Captain Jim held the small creature in his big brown hands and gazed tenderly at it, with eyes that saw the children who had never been born to him.

"What are you going to call him?" asked Miss Cornelia.

"Anne has settled his name," answered Gilbert.

"James Matthew—after the two finest gentlemen I've ever known—not even saving your presence," said Anne with a saucy glance at Gilbert.

Gilbert smiled.

"I never knew Matthew very well; he was so shy we boys couldn't get acquainted with him—but I quite agree with you that Captain Jim is one of the rarest and finest souls God ever clothed in clay. He is so delighted over the fact that we have given his name to our small lad. It seems he has no other namesake.''

''Well, James Matthew is a name that will wear well and not fade in the washing,'' said Miss Cornelia. ''I'm glad you didn't load him down with some highfalutin, romantic name that he'd be ashamed of when he gets to be a grandfather. Mrs. William Drew at the Glen has called her baby Bertie Shakespeare. Quite a combination, isn't it? And I'm glad you haven't had much trouble picking on a name. Some folks have an awful time. When the Stanley Flaggs' first boy was born there was so much rivalry as to who the child should be named for that the poor little soul had to go for two years without a name. Then a brother came along and there it was—'Big Baby' and 'Little Baby.' Finally they called Big Baby Peter and Little Baby Isaac, after the two grandfathers, and had them both christened together. And each tried to see if it couldn't howl the other down. You know that Highland Scotch family of MacNabs back of the Glen? They've got twelve boys and the oldest and the youngest are both called Neil—Big Neil and Little Neil in the same family. Well, I s'pose they ran out of names.''

''I have read somewhere,'' laughed Anne, ''that the first child is a poem but the tenth is very prosy prose. Perhaps Mrs. MacNab thought that the twelfth was merely an old tale re-told.''

''Well, there's something to be said for large families,'' said Miss Cornelia, with a sigh. ''I was an only child for eight years and I did long for a brother and sister. Mother told me to pray for one—and pray I did, believe *me*. Well, one day Aunt Nellie came to me and said, 'Cornelia, there is a little brother for you upstairs in your ma's room. You can go up and see him.' I was so excited and delighted I just flew upstairs. And old Mrs. Flagg lifted up the baby for me to see. Lord, Anne, dearie, I never was so disappointed in my life. You see, I'd been praying for *a brother two years older than myself*.''

''How long did it take you to get over your disappointment?'' asked Anne, amid her laughter.

''Well, I had a spite at Providence for a good spell, and for weeks I wouldn't even look at the baby. Nobody knew why, for I never told. Then he began to get real cute, and held out his wee hands to me and I began to get fond of him. But I didn't get really reconciled to him until one day a school chum came to see him and said she thought he was awful small for his age. I just got boiling mad, and I sailed right into her, and told her she didn't know a nice baby when she saw one, and ours was the nicest baby in the world. And after that I just worshipped him. Mother died before he was three years old and I was sister and mother to him both. Poor little lad, he was never strong, and he died when he wasn't much over twenty. Seems to me I'd have given anything on earth, Anne, dearie, if he'd only lived.''

Miss Cornelia sighed. Gilbert had gone down and Leslie, who had been crooning over the small James Matthew in the dormer window, laid him asleep in his basket and went her way. As soon as she was safely out of earshot, Miss Cornelia bent forward and said in a conspirator's whisper:

''Anne, dearie, I'd a letter from Owen Ford yesterday. He's in Vancouver just now, but he wants to know if I can board him for a month later on. *You* know what that means. Well, I hope we're doing right.''

''We've nothing to do with it—we couldn't prevent him from coming to Four Winds if he wanted to,'' said Anne quickly. She did not like the feeling of match-making Miss Cornelia's whispers gave her; and then she weakly succumbed herself.

''Don't let Leslie know he is coming until he is here,'' she said. ''If she found out I feel sure she would go away at once. She intends to go in the fall anyhow—she told me so the other day. She is going to Montreal to take up nursing and make what she can of her life.''

''Oh, well, Anne, dearie,'' said Miss Cornelia, nodding sagely, ''that is all as it may be. You and I have done our part and we must leave the rest to Higher Hands.''

CHAPTER 35

POLITICS AT FOUR WINDS

WHEN ANNE came downstairs again, the Island, as well as all Canada, was in the throes of a campaign preceding a general election. Gilbert, who was an ardent Conservative, found himself caught in the vortex, being much in demand for speech-making at the various county rallies. Miss Cornelia did not approve of his mixing up in politics and told Anne so.

"Dr. Dave never did it. Dr. Blythe will find he is making a mistake, believe *me*. Politics is something no decent man should meddle with."

"Is the government of the country to be left solely to the rogues then?" asked Anne.

"Yes—so long as it's Conservative rogues," said Miss Cornelia, marching off with the honors of war. "Men and politicians are all tarred with the same brush. The Grits have it laid on thicker than the Conservatives, that's all—*considerably* thicker. But Grit or Tory, my advice to Dr. Blythe is to steer clear of politics. First thing you know, he'll be running an election himself, and going off to Ottawa for half the year and leaving his practice to go to the dogs."

"Ah, well, let's not borrow trouble," said Anne. "The rate of interest is too high. Instead, let's look at Little Jem. It should be spelled with a G. Isn't he perfectly beautiful? Just see the dimples in his elbows. We'll bring him up to be a good Conservative, you and I, Miss Cornelia."

"Bring him up to be a good man," said Miss Cornelia. "They're scarce and valuable; though, mind you, I wouldn't like to see him a Grit. As for the election, you and I may be thankful we don't live over harbor. The air there is blue these days. Every Elliott and Crawford and MacAllister is on the warpath, loaded for bear. This side is peaceful and calm, seeing there's so few men. Captain Jim's a Grit, but it's my opinion he's ashamed of it, for he never talks politics. There isn't any earthly doubt that the Conservatives will be returned with a big majority again."

Miss Cornelia was mistaken. On the morning after the election Captain Jim dropped in at the little house to tell the news. So virulent is the microbe of party politics, even in a peaceable old man, that Captain Jim's cheeks were flushed and his eyes were flashing with all his old-time fire.

"Mistress Blythe, the Liberals are in with a sweeping majority. After eighteen years of Tory mismanagement this down-trodden country is going to have a chance at last."

"I never heard you make such a bitter partisan speech before, Captain Jim. I didn't think you had so much political venom in you," laughed Anne, who was not much excited over the tidings. Little Jem had said "Wow-ga" that morning. What were principalities and powers, the rise and fall of dynasties, the overthrow of Grit or Tory, compared with that miraculous occurrence?

"It's been accumulating for a long while," said Captain Jim, with a deprecating smile. "I thought I was only a moderate Grit, but when the news came that we were in I found out how Gritty I really was."

"You know the doctor and I are Conservatives."

"Ah, well, it's the only bad thing I know of either of you, Mistress Blythe. Cornelia is a Tory, too. I called in on my way from the Glen to tell her the news."

"Didn't you know you took your life in your hands?"

"Yes, but I couldn't resist the temptation."

"How did she take it?"

"Comparatively calm, Mistress Blythe, comparatively calm. She says, says she, 'Well, Providence sends seasons of humiliation to a country, same as to individuals. You Grits have been cold and hungry for many a year. Make haste to get warmed and fed, for you won't be in long.' 'Well, now Cornelia,' I says, 'mebbe Providence thinks Canada needs a real long spell of humiliation.' Ah, Susan, have *you* heard the news? The Liberals are in."

Susan had just come in from the kitchen, attended by the odor of delectable dishes which always seemed to hover around her.

"Now, are they?" she said, with beautiful unconcern. "Well, I never could see but that my bread rose just as light when Grits were in as when they were not. And if any party, Mrs. Doctor, dear, will make it rain before the week is out, and save our kitchen garden from entire ruination, that is the party Susan will vote for. In the meantime, will you just step out and give me your opinion on the meat for dinner? I am fearing that it is very tough, and I think that we had better change our butcher as well as our government."

One evening, a week later, Anne walked down to the Point, to see if she could get some fresh fish from Captain Jim, leaving Little Jem for the first time. It was quite a tragedy. Suppose he cried? Suppose Susan did not know just exactly what to do for him? Susan was calm and serene.

"I have had as much experience with him as you, Mrs. Doctor, dear, have I not?"

"Yes, with him—but not with other babies. Why, I looked after three pairs of twins, when I was a child, Susan. When they cried, I gave them peppermint or castor oil quite coolly. It's quite curious now to recall how lightly I took all those babies and their woes."

"Oh, well, if Little Jem cries, I will just clap a hot water bag on his little stomach," said Susan.

"Not too hot, you know," said Anne anxiously. Oh, was it really wise to go?

"Do not you fret, Mrs. Doctor, dear. Susan is not the woman to burn a wee man. Bless him, he has no notion of crying."

Anne tore herself away finally and enjoyed her walk to the Point after all, through the long shadows of the sun-setting. Captain Jim was not in the living room of the lighthouse, but another man was—a handsome, middle-aged man, with a strong, clean-shaven chin, who was unknown to Anne. Nevertheless, when she sat down, he began to talk to her with all the assurance of an old acquaintance. There was nothing amiss in what he said or the way he said it, but Anne rather resented such a cool taking-for-granted in a complete stranger. Her replies were frosty, and as few as decency required. Nothing daunted, her companion talked on for several minutes, then excused himself and went away. Anne could have sworn there was a twinkle in his eye and it annoyed her. Who was the creature? There was something vaguely familiar about him but she was certain she had never seen him before.

"Captain Jim, who was that who just went out?" she asked, as Captain Jim came in.

"Marshall Elliott," answered the captain.

"Marshall Elliott!" cried Anne. "Oh, Captain Jim—it wasn't— yes, it *was* his voice—oh, Captain Jim, I didn't know him—and I was quite insulting to him! *Why* didn't he tell me? He must have seen I didn't know him."

"He wouldn't say a word about it—he'd just enjoy the joke. Don't worry over snubbing him—he'll think it fun. Yes, Marshall's shaved off his beard at last and cut his hair. His party is in, you know. I didn't know him myself first time I saw him. He was up in Carter Flagg's store at the Glen the night after election day, along with a crowd of others, waiting for the news. About twelve the 'phone came through—the Liberals were in. Marshall just got up and walked out—he didn't cheer or shout—he left the others to do that, and they nearly lifted the roof off Carter's store, I reckon. Of course, all the Tories were over in Raymond Russell's store. Not much cheering *there*. Marshall went straight down the street to the side door of Augustus Palmer's barber shop. Augustus was in bed asleep, but Marhall hammered on the door until he got up and come down, wanting to know what all the racket was about.

"Come into your shop and do the best job you ever did in your life,

Gus,' said Marshall. 'The Liberals are in and you're going to barber a good Grit before the sun rises.'

"Gus was mad as hops—partly because he'd been dragged out of bed, but more because he's a Tory. He vowed he wouldn't shave any man after twelve at night.

" 'You'll do what I want you to do, sonny,' said Marshall, 'or I'll jest turn you over my knee and give you one of those spankings your mother forgot.'

"He'd have done it, too, and Gus knew it, for Marshall is as strong as an ox and Gus is only a midget of a man. So he gave in and towed Marshall in to the shop and went to work. 'Now,' says he, 'I'll barber you up, but if you say one word to me about the Grits getting in while I'm doing it I'll cut your throat with this razor,' says he. You wouldn't have thought mild little Gus could be so bloodthirsty, would you? Shows what party politics will do for a man. Marshall kept quiet and got his hair and beard disposed of and went home. When his old housekeeper heard him come upstairs she peeked out of her bedroom door to see whether 'twas him or the hired boy. And when she saw a strange man striding down the hall with a candle in his hand she screamed blue murder and fainted dead away. They had to send for the doctor before they could bring her to, and it was several days before she could look at Marshall without shaking all over.''

Captain Jim had no fish. He seldom went out in his boat that summer, and his long tramping expeditions were over. He spent a great deal of his time sitting by his seaward window, looking out over the gulf, with his swiftly-whitening head leaning on his hand. He sat there tonight for many silent minutes, keeping some tryst with the past which Anne would not disturb. Presently he pointed to the iris of the West:

"That's beautiful, isn't, it, Mistress Blythe? But I wish you could have seen the sunrise this morning. It was a wonderful thing—wonderful. I've seen all kinds of sunrises come over that gulf. I've been all over the world, Mistress Blythe, and take it all in all, I've never seen a finer sight than a summer sunrise over the gulf. A man can't pick his time for dying, Mistress Blythe—jest got to go when the Great Captain gives His sailing orders. But if I could I'd go out when the morning comes across that water. I've watched it many a time and thought what a thing it would be to pass out through that great white glory to whatever was waiting beyant, on a sea that ain't mapped out on any airthly chart. I think, Mistress Blythe, that I'd find lost Margaret there.''

Captain Jim had often talked to Anne of lost Margaret since he had told her the old story. His love for her trembled in every tone—that love that had never grown faint or forgetful.

"Anyway, I hope when my time comes I'll go quick and easy. I don't think I'm a coward, Mistress Blythe—I've looked an ugly death in the face more than once without blenching. But the thought of a lingering death does give me a queer, sick feeling of horror.''

"Don't talk about leaving us, dear, *dear* Captain, Jim,'' pleaded Anne, in a choked voice, patting the old brown hand, once so strong, but now grown very feeble. "What would we do without you?''

Captain Jim smiled beautifully.

"Oh, you'd get along nicely—nicely—but you wouldn't forget the old man altogether, Mistress Blythe—no, I don't think you'll ever quite forget him. The race of Joseph always remembers one another. But it'll be a memory that won't hurt—I like to think that my memory won't hurt my friends—it'll always be kind of pleasant to them, I hope and believe. It won't be very long now before lost Margaret calls me, for the last time. I'll be all ready to answer. I jest spoke of this because there's a little favor I want to ask you. Here's this poor old Matey of mine''—Captain Jim reached out a hand and poked the big, warm, velvety, golden ball on the sofa. The First Mate uncoiled himself like a spring with a nice, throaty, comfortable sound, half purr, half meow, stretched his paws in air, turned over and coiled himself up again. "*He*'ll miss me when I start on the Long V'yage. I can't bear to think of leaving the poor critter to starve, like he was left before. If anything happens to me will you give Matey a bite and a corner, Mistress Blythe?''

"Indeed I will.''

"Then that is all I had on my mind. Your Little Jem is to have the few curious things I picked up—I've seen to that. And now I don't like to see tears in those pretty eyes, Mistress Blythe. I'll mebbe hang on for quite a spell yet. I heard you reading a piece of poetry one day last winter—one of Tennyson's pieces. I'd sorter like to hear it again, if you could recite it for me.''

Softly and clearly, while the seawind blew in on them, Anne repeated the beautiful lines of Tennyson's wondersul swan song—"Crossing the Bar.'' The old captain kept time gently with his sinewy hand.

"Yes, yes, Mistress Blythe," he said, when she had finished, "that's it, that's it. He wasn't a sailor, you tell me—I dunno how he could have put an old sailor's feelings into words like that, if he wasn't one. He didn't want any 'sadness o' farewells' and neither do I, Mistress Blythe—for all will be well with me and mine beyant the bar."

CHAPTER 36

BEAUTY FOR ASHES

"ANY NEWS from Green Gables, Anne?"

"Nothing very especial," replied Anne, folding up Marilla's letter. "Jake Donnell has been there shingling the roof. He is a full-fledged carpenter now, so it seems he has had his own way in regard to the choice of a life-work. You remember his mother wanted him to be a college professor. I shall never forget the day she came to the school and rated me for failing to call him St. Clair."

"Does anyone ever call him that now?"

"Evidently not. It seems that he has completely lived it down. Even his mother has succumbed. I always thought that a boy with Jake's chin and mouth would get his own way in the end. Diana writes me that Dora has a beau. Just think of it—that child!"

"Dora is seventeen," said Gilbert. "Charlie Sloane and I were both mad about you when you were seventeen, Anne."

"Really, Gilbert, we must be getting on in years," said Anne, with a half-rueful smile, "when children who were six when we thought ourselves grown up are old enough now to have beaux. Dora's is Ralph Andrews—Jane's brother. I remember him as a little, round, fat, white-headed fellow who was always at the foot of his class. But I understand he is quite a fine-looking young man now."

"Dora will probably marry young. She's of the same type as Charlotta the Fourth—she'll never miss her first chance for fear she might not get another."

"Well, if she marries Ralph I hope he will be a little more

up-and-coming than his brother Billy," mused Anne.

"For instance," said Gilbert, laughing, "let us hope he will be able to propose on his own account. Anne, would you have married Billy if he had asked you himself, instead of getting Jane to do it for him?"

"I might have." Anne went off into a shriek of laughter over the recollection of her first proposal. "The shock of the whole thing might have hypnotized me into some such rash and foolish act. Let us be thankful he did it by proxy."

"I had a letter from George Moore yesterday," said Leslie, from the corner where she was reading.

"Oh, how is he?" asked Anne interestedly, yet with an unreal feeling that she was inquiring about some one whom she did not know.

"He is well, but he finds it very hard to adapt himself to all the changes in his old home and friends. He is going to sea again in the spring. It's in his blood, he says, and he longs for it. But he told me something that made me glad for him, poor fellow. Before he sailed on the *Four Sisters* he was engaged to a girl at home. He did not tell me anything about her in Montreal, because he said he supposed she would have forgotten him and married someone else long ago, and with him, you see, his engagement and love was still a thing of the present. It was pretty hard on him, but when he got home he found she had never married and still cared for him. They are to be married this fall. I'm going to ask him to bring her over here for a little trip; he says he wants to come and see the place where he lived so many years without knowing it."

"What a nice little romance," said Anne, whose love for the romantic was immortal. "And to think," she added with a sigh of self-reproach, "that if I had had my way George Moore would never have come up from the grave in which his identity was buried. How I did fight against Gilbert's suggestion! Well, I am punished: I shall never be able to have a different opinion from Gilbert's again! If I try to have, he will squelch me by casting George Moore's case up to me!"

"As if even that would squelch a woman!" mocked Gilbert. "At least do not become my echo, Anne. A little opposition gives spice to life. I do not want a wife like John MacAllister's over the harbor. No matter what he says, she at once remarks in that drab, lifeless little voice of hers, 'That is very true, John, dear me!' "

Anne and Leslie laughed. Anne's laughter was silver and Leslie's golden, and the combination of the two was as satisfactory as a perfect chord in music.

Susan, coming in on the heels of the laughter, echoed it with a resounding sigh.

"Why, Susan, what is the matter?" asked Gilbert.

"There's nothing wrong with little Jem, is there, Susan?" cried Anne, starting up in alarm.

"No, no, calm yourself, Mrs. Doctor, dear. Something has happened, though. Dear me, everything has gone catawampus with me this week. I spoiled the bread, as you know too well—and I scorched the doctor's best shirt bosom—and I broke your big platter. And now, on the top of all this, comes word that my sister Matilda has broken her leg and wants me to go and stay with her for a spell."

"Oh, I'm very sorry—sorry that your sister has met with such an accident, I mean," exclaimed Anne.

"Ah, well, man was made to mourn, Mrs. Doctor, dear. That sounds as if it ought to be in the Bible, but they tell me a person named Burns wrote it. And there is no doubt that we are born to trouble as the sparks fly upward. As for Matilda, I do not know what to think of her. None of our family ever broke their legs before. But whatever she has done she is still my sister, and I feel that it is my duty to go and wait on her, if you can spare me for a few weeks, Mrs. Doctor, dear."

"Of course, Susan, of course. I can get someone to help me while you are gone."

"If you cannot I will not go, Mrs. Doctor, dear, Matilda's leg to the contrary notwithstanding. I will not have you worried, and that blessed child upset in consequence, for any number of legs."

"Oh, you must go to your sister at once, Susan. I can get a girl from the cove, who will do for a time."

"Anne, will you let me come and stay with you while Susan is away?" exclaimed Leslie. "Do! I'd love to—and it would be an act of charity on your part. I'm so horribly lonely over there in that big barn of a house. There's so little to do—and at night I'm worse than lonely—I'm frightened and nervous in spite of locked doors. There was a tramp around two days ago."

Anne joyfully agreed, and next day Leslie was installed as an inmate of the little house of dreams. Miss Cornelia warmly approved of the arrangement.

"It seems Providential," she told Anne in confidence. "I'm sorry for Matilda Clow, but since she had to break her leg it couldn't have happened at a better time. Leslie will be here while Owen Ford is in Four Winds, and those old cats up at the Glen won't get the chance to meow, as they would if she was living over there alone and Owen going to see her. They are doing enough of it as it is, because she doesn't put on mourning. I said to one of them, 'If you mean she should put on mourning for George Moore, it seems to me more like his resurrection than his funeral; and if it's Dick you mean, I confess *I* can't see the propriety of going into weeds for a man who died thirteen years ago and good riddance then!' And when old Louisa Baldwin remarked to me that she thought it very strange that Leslie should never have suspected it wasn't her own husband *I* said, *'You* never suspected it wasn't Dick Moore, and you were next-door neighbor to him all his life, and by nature you're ten times as suspicious as Leslie.' But you can't stop some people's tongues, Anne, dearie, and I'm real thankful Leslie will be under your roof while Owen is courting her.''

Owen Ford came to the little house one August evening when Leslie and Anne were absorbed in worshipping the baby. He paused at the open door of the living room, unseen by the two within, gazing with greedy eyes at the beautiful picture. Leslie sat on the floor with the baby in her lap, making ecstatic dabs at his fat little hands as he fluttered them in the air.

''Oh, you dear, beautiful, beloved baby,'' she mumbled, catching one wee hand and covering it with kisses.

''Isn't him ze darlingest itty sing,'' crooned Anne, hanging over the arm of her chair adoringly. ''Dem itty wee pads are ze very tweetest handies in ze whole big world, isn't dey, you darling itty man.''

Anne, in the months before Little Jem's coming, had pored diligently over several wise volumes, and pinned her faith to one in especial, ''Sir Oracle on the Care and Training of Children.'' Sir Oracle implored parents by all they held sacred never to talk ''baby talk'' to their children. Infants should invariably be addressed in classical language from the moment of their birth. So should they learn to speak English undefiled from their earliest utterance. ''How,'' demanded Sir Oracle, ''can a mother reasonably expect her child to learn correct speech, when she continually accustoms its impressionable gray matter to such absurd expressions and distortions of our noble tongue as thoughtless mothers inflict every day on the helpless creatures committed to their care? Can a child who is constantly called 'tweet itty wee singie' ever attain to any proper conception of his own being and possibilities and destiny?''

Anne was vastly impressed with this, and informed Gilbert that ¦ meant to make it an inflexible rule never, under any circumnces, to talk "baby talk" to her children. Gilbert agreed with her, ¦d they made a solemn compact on the subject—a compact which ¦ne shamelessly violated the very first moment Little Jem was laid ¦ her arms. "Oh, the darling itty wee sing!" she had exclaimed. ¦nd she had continued to violate it ever since. When Gilbert teased ¦er she laughed Sir Oracle to scorn.

"He never had any children of his own, Gilbert—I am positive he ¦adn't or he would never have written such rubbish. You just can't ¦elp talking baby talk to a baby. It comes natural—and it's *right*. It would be inhuman to talk to those tiny, soft, velvety little creatures as we do to great big boys and girls. Babies want love and cuddling and all the sweet baby talk they can get, and Little Jem is going to have it, bless his dear itty heartums."

"But you're the worst I ever heard, Anne," protested Gilbert, who, not being a mother but only a father, was not wholly convinced yet that Sir Oracle was wrong. "I never heard anything like the way you talk to that child."

"Very likely you never did. Go away—go away. Didn't I bring up three pairs of Hammond twins before I was eleven? You and Sir Oracle are nothing but cold-blooded theorists. Gilbert, *just* look at him! He's smiling at me—he knows what we're talking about. And oo dest agwees wif evy word muzzer says, don't oo, angel-lover?"

Gilbert put his arm about them. "Oh you mothers!" he said. "You mothers! God knew what He was about when He made you."

So Little Jem was talked to and loved and cuddled; and he throve as became a child of the house of dreams. Leslie was quite as foolish over him as Anne was. When their work was done and Gilbert was out of the way, they gave themselves over to shameless orgies of love-making and ecstasies of adoration, such as that in which Owen Ford had surprised them.

Leslie was the first to become aware of him. Even in the twilight Anne could see the sudden whiteness that swept over her beautiful face, blotting out the crimson of lip and cheeks.

Owen came forward, eagerly, blind for a moment to Anne.

"Leslie!" he said, holding out his hand. It was the first time he had ever called her by her name; but the hand Leslie gave him was cold; and she was very quiet all the evening, while Anne and Gilbert and Owen laughed and talked together. Before his call ended she excused herself and went upstairs. Owen's gay spirits flagged and he went away soon after with a downcast air.

Gilbert looked at Anne.

"Anne, what are you up to? There's something going on that I don't understand. The whole air here tonight has been charged with electricity. Leslie sits like the muse of tragedy; Owen Ford jokes and laughs on the surface, and watches Leslie with the eyes of his soul. You seem all the time to be bursting with some suppressed excitement. Own up. What secret have you been keeping from your deceived husband?"

"Don't be a goose, Gilbert," was Anne's conjugal reply. "As for Leslie, she is absurd and I'm going up to tell her so."

Anne found Leslie at the dormer window of her room. The little place was filled with the rhythmic thunder of the sea. Leslie sat with locked hands in the misty moonshine—a beautiful, accusing presence.

"Anne," she said in a low, reproachful voice, "did you know Owen Ford was coming to Four Winds?"

"I did," said Anne brazenly.

"Oh, you should have told me, Anne," Leslie cried passionately. "If I had known I would have gone away—I wouldnt' have stayed here to meet him. You should have told me. It wasn't fair of you, Anne—oh, it wasn't fair!"

Leslie's lips were trembling and her whole form was tense with emotion. But Anne laughed heartlessly. She bent over and kissed Leslie's upturned reproachful face.

"Leslie, you are an adorable goose. Owen Ford didn't rush from the Pacific to the Atlantic from a burning desire to see *me*. Neither do I believe that he was inspired by any wild and frenzied passion for Miss Cornelia. Take off your tragic airs, my dear friend, and fold them up and put them away in lavender. You'll never need them again. There are some people who can see through a grindstone when there is a hole in it, even if you cannot. I am not a prophetess, but I shall venture on a prediction. The bitterness of life is over for you. After this you are going to have the joys and hopes—and I daresay the sorrows, too—of a happy woman. The omen of the shadow of Venus did come true for you, Leslie. The year in which you saw it brought your life's best gift for you—your love for Owen Ford. Now, go right to bed and have a good sleep."

Leslie obeyed orders in so far that she went to bed: but it may be questioned if she slept much. I do not think she dared to dream wakingly; life had been so hard for this poor Leslie, the path on which she had had to walk had been so strait, that she could not whisper to her own heart the hopes that might wait on the future. But she watched the great revolving light bestarring the short hours of the summer night, and her eyes grew soft and bright and young once more. Nor, when Owen Ford came next day, to ask her to go with him to the shore, did she say him nay.

CHAPTER 37

MISS CORNELIA MAKES
A STARTLING ANNOUNCEMENT

MISS CORNELIA sailed down to the little house one drowsy afternoon, when the gulf was the faint, bleached blue of the August seas, and the orange lilies at the gate of Anne's garden held up their imperial cups to be filled with the molten gold of August sunshine. Not that Miss Cornelia concerned herself with painted oceans or sun-thirsty lilies. She sat in her favorite rocker in unusual idleness. She sewed not, neither did she spin. Nor did she say a single derogatory word concerning any portion of mankind. In short, Miss Cornelia's conversation was singularly devoid of spice that day, and Gilbert, who had stayed home to listen to her, instead of going a-fishing, as he had intended, felt himself aggrieved. What had come over Miss Cornelia? She did not look cast down or worried. On the contrary, there was a certain air of nervous exultation about her.

"Where is Leslie?" she asked—not as if it mattered much either.

"Owen and she went raspberrying in the woods back of her farm," answered Anne. "They won't be back before supper time—if then."

"They don't seem to have any idea that there is such a thing as a clock," said Gilbert. "I can't get to the bottom of that affair. I'm certain you women pulled strings. But Anne, undutiful wife, won't tell me. Will you, Miss Cornelia?"

"No, I shall not. But," said Miss Cornelia, with the air of one determined to take the plunge and have it over, "I will tell you something else. I came today on purpose to tell it. I am going to be married."

Anne and Gilbert were silent. If Miss Cornelia had announced her intention of going out to the channel and drowning herself the thing might have been believable. This was not. So they waited. Of course Miss Cornelia had made a mistake.

"Well, you both look sort of kerflummexed," said Miss Cornelia, with a twinkle in her eyes. Now that the awkward moment of revelation was over, Miss Cornelia was her own woman again. "Do you think I'm too young and inexperienced for matrimony?"

"You know—it *is* rather staggering," said Gilbert, trying to gather his wits together. "I've heard you say a score of times that you wouldn't marry the best man in the world."

"I'm not going to marry the best man in the world," retorted Miss Cornelia. "Marshall Elliott is a long way from being the best."

"Are you going to marry Marshall Elliott?" exclaimed Anne, recovering her power of speech under this second shock.

"Yes. I could have had him any time these twenty years if I'd lifted my finger. But do you suppose I was going to walk into church beside a perambulating haystack like that?"

"I am sure we are very glad—and we wish you all possible happiness," said Anne, very flatly and inadequately, as she felt. She was not prepared for such an occasion. She had never imagined herself offering betrothal felicitations to Miss Cornelia.

"Thanks, I knew you would," said Miss Cornelia. "You are the first of my friends to know it."

"We shall be so sorry to lose you, though, dear Miss Cornelia," said Anne, beginning to be a little sad and sentimental.

"Oh, you won't lose me," said Miss Cornelia unsentimentally. "You don't suppose I would live over harbor with all those MacAllisters and Elliotts and Crawfords, do you? 'From the conceit of the Elliotts, the pride of the MacAllisters and the vain-glory of the Crawfords, good Lord deliver us.' Marshall is coming to live at my place. I'm sick and tired of hired men. That Jim Hastings I've got this summer is positively the worst of the species. He would drive anyone to getting married. What do you think? He upset the churn yesterday and spilled a big churning of cream over the yard. And not one whit concerned about it was he! Just gave a foolish laugh and said cream was good for the land. Wasn't that like a man? I told him I wasn't in the habit of fertilising my back yard with cream."

"Well, I wish you all manner of happiness too, Miss Cornelia," said Gilbert, solemnly; "but," he added, unable to resist the temptation to tease Miss Cornelia, despite Anne's imploring eyes, "I fear your day of independence is done. As you know, Marshall Elliott is a very determined man."

"I like a man who can stick to a thing," retorted Miss Cornelia. "Amos Grant, who used to be after me long ago, couldn't. You never saw such a weather-vane. He jumped into the pond to drown himself once and then changed his mind and swum out again. Wasn't that like a man? Marshall would have stuck to it and drowned."

"And he has a bit of a temper, they tell me," persisted Gilbert.

"He wouldn't be an Elliott if he hadn't. I'm thankful he has. It will be real fun to make him mad. And you can generally do something with a tempery man when it comes to repenting time. But you can't do anything with a man who just keeps placid and aggravating."

"You know he's a Grit, Miss Cornelia."

"Yes, he *is*," admitted Miss Cornelia rather sadly. "And of course there is no hope of making a Conservative of him. But at least he is a Presbyterian. So I suppose I shall have to be satisfied with that."

"Would you marry him if he were a Methodist, Miss Cornelia?"

"No, I would not. Politics is for this world, but religion is for both."

"And you may be a 'relict' after all, Miss Cornelia."

"Not I. Marshall will live me out. The Elliotts are long-lived, and the Bryants are not."

"When are you to be married?" asked Anne.

"In about a month's time. My wedding dress is to be navy blue silk. And I want to ask you, Anne, dearie, if you think it would be all right to wear a veil with a navy blue dress. I've always thought I'd like to wear a veil if I ever got married. Marshall says to have it if I want to. Isn't that like a man?"

"Why shouldn't you wear it if you want to?" asked Anne.

"Well, one doesn't want to be different from other people," said Miss Cornelia, who was not noticeably like anyone else on the face of the earth. "As I say, I do fancy a veil. But maybe it shouldn't be worn with any dress but a white one. Please tell me, Anne, dearie, what you really think. I'll go by your advice."

"I don't think veils are usually worn with any but white dresses," admitted Anne, "but that is merely a convention; and I am like Mr. Elliott, Miss Cornelia. I don't see any good reason why you shouldn't have a veil if you want one."

But Miss Cornelia, who made her calls in calico wrappers, shook her head.

"If it isn't the proper thing I won't wear it," she said, with a sigh of regret for a lost dream.

"Since you are determined to be married, Miss Cornelia," said Gilbert solemnly, "I shall give you the excellent rules for the management of a husband which my grandmother gave my mother when she married my father."

"Well, I reckon I can manage Marshall Elliott," said Miss Cornelia placidly. "But let us hear your rules."

"The first one is, catch him."

"He's caught. Go on."

"The second one is, feed him well."

"With enough pie. What next?"

"The third and fourth are—keep your eye on him."

"I believe you," said Miss Cornelia emphatically.

CHAPTER 38

RED ROSES

THE GARDEN of the little house was a haunt beloved of bees and reddened by late roses that August. The little house folk lived much in it, and were given to taking picnic suppers in the grassy corner beyond the brook and sitting about in it through the twilights when great night moths sailed athwart the velvet gloom. One evening Owen Ford found Leslie alone in it. Anne and Gilbert were away, and Susan, who was expected back that night, had not yet returned.

The northern sky was amber and pale green over the fir tops. The air was cool, for August was nearing September, and Leslie wore a crimson scarf over her white dress. Together they wandered through the little, friendly, flower-crowded paths in silence. Owen must go soon. His holiday was nearly over. Leslie found her heart beating wildly. She knew that this beloved garden was to be the scene of the binding words that must seal their as yet unworded understanding.

"Some evenings a strange odor blows down the air of this garden, like a phantom perfume," said Owen. "I have never been able to discover from just what flower it comes. It is elusive and haunting and wonderfully sweet. I like to fancy it is the soul of Grandmother Selwyn passing on a little visit to the old spot she loved so well. There should be a lot of friendly ghosts about this little old house.''

''I have lived under its roof only a month,'' said Leslie, ''but I love it as I never loved the house over there where I have lived all my life.''

''This house was builded and consecrated by love,'' said Owen. ''Such houses, *must* exert an influence over those who live in them. And this garden—it is over sixty years old and the history of a thousand hopes and joys is written in its blossoms. Some of those flowers were actually set out by the schoolmaster's bride, and she has been dead for thirty years. Yet they bloom on every summer. Look at those red roses, Leslie—how they queen it over everything else!''

''I love the red roses,'' said Leslie. ''Anne likes the pink ones best, and Gilbert likes the white. But I want the crimson ones. They satisfy some craving in me as no other flower does.''

''These roses are very late—they bloom after all the others have gone—and they hold all the warmth and soul of the summer come to fruition,'' said Owen, plucking some of the glowing, half-opened buds.

''The rose is the flower of love—the world has acclaimed it so for centuries. The pink roses are love hopeful and expectant—the white roses are love dead or forsaken—but the red roses—ah, Leslie, what are the red roses?''

''Love triumphant,'' said Leslie in a low voice.

''Yes—love triumphant and perfect. Leslie, you know—you understand. I have loved you from the first. And I *know* you love me—I don't need to ask you. But I want to hear you say it—my darling—my darling!''

Leslie said something in a very low and tremulous voice. Their hands and lips met; it was life's supreme moment for them and as they stood there in the old garden, with its many years of love and delight and sorrow and glory, he crowned her shining hair with the red, red rose of a love triumphant.

Anne and Gilbert returned presently, accompanied by Captain Jim. Anne lighted a few sticks of driftwood in the fireplace, for love of the pixy flames, and they sat around it for an hour of good fellowship.

''When I sit looking at a driftwood fire it's easy to believe I'm young again,'' said Captain Jim.

''Can you read futures in the fire, Captain Jim?'' asked Owen.

Captain Jim looked at them all affectionately and then back again at Leslie's vivid face and glowing eyes.

''I don't need the fire to read your futures,'' he said. ''I see happiness for all of you—all of you—for Leslie and Mr. Ford—and the doctor here and Mistress Blythe—and Little Jem—and children that ain't born yet but will be. Happiness for you all—though, mind you, I reckon you'll have your troubles and worries and sorrows, too. They're bound to come—and no house, whether it's a palace or a little house of dreams, can bar 'em out. But they won't get the better of you if you face 'em *together* with love and trust. You can weather any storm with them two for compass and pilot.''

The old man rose suddenly and placed one hand on Leslie's head and one on Anne's.

''Two good, sweet women,'' he said. ''True and faithful and to be depended on. Your husbands will have honor in the gates because of you—your children will rise up and call you blessed in the years to come.''

There was a strange solemnity about the little scene. Anne and Leslie bowed as those receiving a benediction. Gilbert suddenly brushed his hand over his eyes; Owen Ford was rapt as one who can see visions. All were silent for a space. The little house of dreams added another poignant and unforgettable moment to its store of memories.

''I must be going now,'' said Captain Jim slowly at last. He took up his hat and looked lingeringly about the room.

''Good night, all of you,'' he said, as he went out.

Anne, pierced by the unusual wistfulness of his farewell, ran to the door after him.

''Come back soon, Captain Jim,'' she called, as he passed through the little gate hung between the firs.

''Ay, ay,'' he called cheerily back to her. But Captain Jim had sat by the old fireside of the house of dreams for the last time.

Anne went slowly back to the others.

''It's so—so pitiful to think of him going all alone down to that lonely Point,'' she said. ''And there is no one to welcome him there.''

''Captain Jim is such good company for others that one can't imagine him being anything but good company for himself,'' said Owen. ''But he must often be lonely. There was a touch of the seer about him tonight—he spoke as one to whom it had been given to speak. Well, I must be going, too."

Anne and Gilbert discreetly melted away; but when Owen had gone Anne returned, to find Leslie standing by the hearth.

"Oh, Leslie—I know—and I'm so glad, dear," she said, putting her arms about her.

"Anne, my happiness frightens me," whispered Leslie. "It seems too great to be real—I'm afraid to speak of it—to think of it. It seems to me that it must just be another dream of this house of dreams and it will vanish when I leave here."

"Well, you are not going to leave here—until Owen takes you. You are going to stay with me until that times comes. Do you think I'd let you go over to that lonely, sad place again?"

"Thank you, dear. I meant to ask you if I might stay with you. I didn't want to go back there—it would seem like going back into the chill and dreariness of the old life again. Anne, Anne, what a friend you've been to me—'a good, sweet woman—true and faithful and to be depended on'—Captain Jim summed you up."

"He said 'women,' not 'woman,' " smiled Anne. "Perhaps Captain Jim sees us both through the rose-colored spectacles of his love for us. But we can try to live up to his belief in us, at least."

"Do you remember, Anne," said Leslie slowly, "that I once said—that night we met on the shore—that I hated my good looks? I did—then. It always seemed to me that if I had been homely Dick would never have thought of me. I hated my beauty because it had attracted him, but now—oh, I'm glad that I have it. It's all I have to offer Owen,—his artist soul delights in it. I feel as if I do not come to him quite empty-handed."

"Owen loves your beauty, Leslie. Who would not? But it's foolish of you to say or think that that is all you bring him. *He* will tell you that—I needn't. And now I must lock up. I expected Susan back tonight, but she has not come."

"Oh, yes, here I am, Mrs. Doctor, dear," said Susan, entering unexpectedly from the kitchen, "and puffing like a hen drawing rails at that! It's quite a walk from the Glen down here."

"I'm glad to see you back, Susan. How is your sister?"

"She is able to sit up, but of course she cannot walk yet. However, she is very well able to get on without me now, for her daughter has come home for her vacation. And I am thankful to be back, Mrs. Doctor, dear. Matilda's leg was broken and no mistake, but her tongue was not. She would talk the legs off an iron pot, that she would, Mrs. Doctor, dear, though I grieve to say it of my own sister.

She was always a great talker and yet she was the first of our family to get married. She really did not care much about marrying James Clow, but she could not bear to disoblige him. Not but what James is a good man—the only fault I have to find with him is that he always starts in to say grace with such an unearthly groan, Mrs. Doctor, dear. It always frightens my appetite clear away. And speaking of getting married, Mrs. Doctor, dear, is it true that Cornelia Bryant is going to be married to Marshall Elliott?''

"Yes, quite true, Susan."

"Well, Mrs. Doctor, dear, it does *not* seem to me fair. Here is me, who never said a word against the men, and I cannot get married nohow. And there is Cornelia Bryant, who is never done abusing them, and all she has to do is to reach out her hand and pick one up, as it were. It is a very strange world, Mrs. Doctor, dear."

"There's another world, you know, Susan."

"Yes," said Susan with a heavy sigh, "but, Mrs. Doctor, dear, there is neither marrying nor giving in marriage there."

--------------------- CHAPTER 39 ---------------------

CAPTAIN JIM CROSSES THE BAR

ONE DAY in late September Owen Ford's book came at last. Captain Jim had gone faithfully to the Glen post office every day for a month, expecting it. This day he had not gone, and Leslie brought his copy home with hers and Anne's.

"We'll take it down to him this evening," said Anne, excited as a schoolgirl.

The long walk to the Point on that clear, beguiling evening along the red harbor road was very pleasant. Then the sun dropped down behind the western hills into some valley that must have been full of lost sunsets, and at the same instant the big light flashed out on the white tower of the point.

"Captain Jim is never late by the fraction of a second," said Leslie.

Neither Anne nor Leslie ever forgot Captain Jim's face when they gave him the book—*his* book, transfigured and glorified. The cheeks that had been blanched of late suddenly flamed with the color of boyhood; his eyes glowed with all the fire of youth; but his hands trembled as he opened it.

It was called simply *The Life-Book of Captain Jim,* and on the title page the names of Owen Ford and James Boyd were printed as collaborators. The frontispiece was a photograph of Captain Jim himself, standing at the door of the lighthouse, looking across the gulf. Owen Ford had "snapped" him one day while the book was being written. Captain Jim had known this, but he had not known that the picture was to be in the book.

"Just think of it," he said, "the old sailor right there in a real printed book. This is the proudest day of my life. I'm like to bust, girls. There'll be no sleep for me tonight. I'll read my book clean through before sun-up."

"We'll go right away and leave you free to begin it," said Anne.

Captain Jim had been handling the book in a kind of reverent rapture. Now he decidedly closed it and laid it aside.

"No, no, you're not going away before you take a cup of tea with the old man," he protested. "I couldn't hear to that—could you, Matey? The life-book will keep, I reckon. I've waited for it this many a year. I can wait a little longer while I'm enjoying my friends."

Captain Jim moved about getting his kettle on to boil, and setting out his bread and butter. Despite his excitement he did not move with his old briskness. His movements were slow and halting. But the girls did not offer to help him. They knew it would hurt his feelings.

"You just picked the right evening to visit me," he said, producing a cake from his cupboard. "Leetle Joe's mother sent me down a big basket full of cakes and pies today. A blessing on all good cooks, says I. Look at this purty cake, all frosting and nuts. 'Tain't often I can entertain in such style. Set in, girls, set in! We'll 'tak a cup o' kindness yet for auld lang syne.'"

The girls "set in" right merrily. The tea was up to Captain Jim's best brewing. Little Joe's mother's cake was the last word in cakes; Captain Jim was the prince of gracious hosts, never even permitting his eyes to wander to the corner where the life-book lay, in all its bravery of green and gold. But when his door finally closed behind Anne and Leslie they knew that he went straight to it, and as they walked home they pictured the delight of the old man poring over the printed pages wherein his own life was portrayed with all the charm and color of reality itself.

"I wonder how he will like the ending—the ending I suggested," said Leslie.

She was never to know. Early the next morning Anne awakened to find Gilbert bending over her, fully dressed, and with an expression of anxiety on his face.

"Are you called out?" she asked drowsily.

"No. Anne, I'm afraid there's something wrong at the Point. It's an hour after sunrise now, and the light is still burning. You know it has always been a matter of pride with Captain Jim to start the light the moment the sun sets, and put it out the moment it rises."

Anne sat up in dismay. Through her window she saw the light blinking palely against the blue skies of dawn.

"Perhaps he has fallen asleep over his life-book," she said anxiously, "or become so absorbed in it that he has forgotten the light."

Gilbert shook his head.

"That wouldn't be like Captain Jim. Anyway, I'm going down to see."

"Wait a minute and I'll go with you," exclaimed Anne. "Oh, yes, I must—Little Jem will sleep for an hour yet, and I'll call Susan. You may need a woman's help if Captain Jim is ill."

It was an exquisite morning, full of tints and sounds at once ripe and delicate. The harbor was sparkling and dimpling like a girl; white gulls were soaring over the dunes; beyond the bar was a shining, wonderful sea. The long fields by the shore were dewy and fresh in that first fine, purely-tinted light. The wind came dancing and whistling up the channel to replace the beautiful silence with a music more beautiful still. Had it not been for the baleful star on the white tower that early walk would have been a delight to Anne and Gilbert. But they went softly with fear.

Their knock was not responded to. Gilbert opened the door and they went in.

The old room was very quiet. On the table were the remnants of the little evening feast. The lamp still burned on the corner stand. The First Mate was asleep in a square of sunshine by the sofa.

Captain Jim lay on the sofa, with his hands clasped over the life-book, open at the last page, lying on his breast. His eyes were closed and on his face was a look of the most perfect peace and happiness—the look of one who has long sought and found at last.

"He is asleep?" whispered Anne tremulously.

Gilbert went to the sofa and bent over him for a few moments. Then he straightened up.

''Yes, he sleeps—well,'' he added quietly. ''Anne, Captain Jim has crossed the bar.''

They could not know precisely at what hour he had died, but Anne always believed that he had had his wish, and went out when the morning came across the gulf. Out on that shining tide his spirit drifted, over the sunrise sea of pearl and silver, to the haven where lost Margaret waited, beyond the storms and calms.

———————— CHAPTER 40 ————————

FAREWELL TO THE HOUSE OF DREAMS

CAPTAIN JIM was buried in the little over-harbor graveyard, very near to the spot where the wee white lady slept. His relatives put up a very expensive, very ugly ''monument''—a monument at which he would have poked sly fun had he seen it in life. But his real monument was in the hearts of those who knew him, and in the book that was to live for generations.

Leslie mourned that Captain Jim had not lived to see the amazing success of it.

''How he would have delighted in the reviews—they are almost all so kindly. And to have seen his life-book heading the lists of the best sellers—oh, if he could just have lived to see it, Anne!''

But Anne, despite her grief, was wiser.

''It was the book itself he cared for, Leslie—not what might be said of it—and he had it. He had read it all through. That last night must have been one of the greatest happiness for him—with the quick, painless ending he had hoped for in the morning. I am glad for Owen's sake and yours that the book is such a success—but Captain Jim was satisfied—I *know*.''

The lighthouse star still kept a nightly vigil; a substitute keeper had been sent to the Point, until such time as an all-wise government could decide which of many applicants was best fitted for the place—or had the strongest pull. The First Mate was at home in the little house, beloved by Anne and Gilbert and Leslie, and tolerated by a Susan who had small liking for cats.

"I can put up with him for the sake of Captain Jim, Mrs. Doctor, dear, for I liked the old man. And I will see that he gets bite and sup, and every mouse the traps account for. But do not ask me to do more than that, Mrs. Doctor, dear. Cats is cats, and take my word for it, they will never be anything else. And at least, Mrs. Doctor, dear, do keep him away from the blessed wee man. Picture to yourself how awful it would be if he was to suck the darling's breath."

"That might be fitly called a *cat*-astrophe," said Gilbert.

"Oh, you may laugh, doctor, dear, but it would be no laughing matter."

"Cats never suck babies' breaths," said Gilbert. "That is only an old superstition, Susan."

"Oh, well, it may be a superstition or it may not, doctor, dear. All that I know is, it has happened. My sister's husband's nephew's wife's cat sucked their baby's breath, and the poor innocent was all but gone when they found it. And superstition or not, if I find that yellow beast lurking near our baby I will whack him with the poker, Mrs. Doctor, dear."

Mr. and Mrs. Marshall Elliott were living comfortably and harmoniously in the green house. Leslie was busy with sewing, for she and Owen were to be married at Christmas. Anne wondered what she would do when Leslie was gone.

"Changes come all the time. Just as soon as things get really nice they change," she said with a sigh.

"The old Morgan place up at the Glen is for sale," said Gilbert, apropos of nothing in especial.

"Is it?" asked Anne indifferently.

"Yes. Now that Mr. Morgan has gone, Mrs. Morgan wants to go to live with her children in Vancouver. She will sell cheaply, for a big place like that in a small village like the Glen will not be very easy to dispose of."

"Well, it's certainly a beautiful place, so it is likely she will find a purchaser," said Anne, absently, wondering whether she should hemstitch or feather-stitch little Jem's "short" dresses. He was to be shortened the next week, and Anne felt ready to cry at the thought of it.

"Suppose we buy it, Anne?" remarked Gilbert quietly.

Anne dropped her sewing and stared at him.

"You're not in earnest, Gilbert?"

"Indeed I am, dear."

"And leave this darling spot—our house of dreams?" said Anne incredulously. "Oh, Gilbert, it's—it's unthinkable!"

"Listen patiently to me, dear. I know just how you feel about it. I feel the same. But we've always known we would have to move some day."

"Oh, but not so soon, Gilbert—not just yet."

"We may never get such a chance again. If we don't buy the Morgan place someone else will—and there is no other house in the Glen we would care to have, and no other really good site on which to build. This little house is—well, it is and has been what no other house can ever be to us, I admit, but you know it is out-of-the-way down here for a doctor. We have felt the inconvenience, though we've made the best of it. And it's a tight fit for us now. Perhaps, in a few years, when Jem wants a room of his own, it will be entirely too small."

"Oh, I know—I know," said Anne, tears filling her eyes. "I know all that can be said against it, but I love it so—and it's so beautiful here."

"You would find it very lonely here after Leslie goes—and Captain Jim has gone too. The Morgan place is beautiful, and in time we would love it. You know you have always admired it, Anne."

"Oh, yes, but—but—this has all seemed to come up so suddenly, Gilbert. I'm dizzy. Ten minutes ago I had no thought of leaving this dear spot. I was planning what I meant to do for it in the spring— what I meant to do in the garden. And if we leave this place who will get it? It *is* out-of-the-way, so it's likely some poor, shiftless, wandering family will rent it—and over-run it—and oh, that would be desecration. It would hurt me horribly."

"I know. But we cannot sacrifice our own interests to such considerations, Anne-girl. The Morgan place will suit us in every essential particular—we really can't afford to miss such a chance. Think of that big lawn with those magnificent old trees; and of that splendid hardwood grove behind it—twelve acres of it. What a play place for our children! There's a fine orchard, too, and you've always admired that high brick wall around the garden with the door in it—you've thought it was so like a story-book garden. And there is almost as fine a view of the harbor and the dunes from the Morgan place as from here."

"You can't see the lighthouse star from it."

"Yes, You can see it from the attic window. *There's* another advantage, Anne-girl—you love big garrets."

"There's no brook in the garden."

"Well, no, but there is one running through the maple grove into the Glen pond. And the pond itself isn't far away. You'll be able to fancy you have your own Lake of Shining Waters again."

"Well, don't say anything more about it just now, Gilbert. Give me time to think—to get used to the idea."

"All right. There is no great hurry, of course. Only—if we decide to buy, it would be well to be moved in and settled before winter."

Gilbert went out, and Anne put away Little Jem's short dresses with trembling hands. She could not sew any more that day. With tear-wet eyes she wandered over the little domain where she had reigned so happy a queen. The Morgan place was all that Gilbert claimed. The grounds were beautiful, the house old enough to have dignity and repose and traditions, and new enough to be comfortable and up-to-date. Anne had always admired it; but admiring is not loving; and she loved this house of dreams so much. She loved *everything* about it—the garden she had tended, and which so many women had tended before her—the gleam and sparkle of the little brook that crept so roguishly across the corner—the gate between the creaking fir trees—the old red sandstone step—the stately Lombardies—the two tiny quaint glass cupboards over the chimney-piece in the living-room—the crooked pantry door in the kitchen—the two funny dormer windows upstairs—the little jog in the staircase—why, these things were a part of her! How could she leave them?

And how this little house, consecrated aforetime by love and joy, had been re-consecrated for her by her happiness and sorrow! Here she had spent her bridal moon; here wee Joyce had lived her one brief day; here the sweetness of motherhood had come again with Little Jem; here she had heard the exquisite music of her baby's cooing laughter; here beloved friends had sat by her fireside. Joy and grief, birth and death, had made sacred forever this little house of dreams.

And now she must leave it. She knew that, even while she had contended against the idea to Gilbert. The little house was outgrown. Gilbert's interests made the change necessary; his work, successful though it had been, was hampered by his location. Anne realised that the end of their life in this dear place drew nigh, and that she must face the fact bravely. But how her heart ached!

"It will be just like tearing something out of my life," she sobbed. "And oh, if I could hope that some nice folk would come here in our place—or even that it would be left vacant. That itself would be better than having it overrun with some horde who know nothing of the geography of dreamland, and nothing of the history that has given this house its soul and its identity. And if such a tribe come here the place will go to rack and ruin in no time—an old place goes down so quickly if it is not carefully attended to. They'll tear up my garden—and let the Lombardies get ragged—and the paling will come to look like a mouth with half the teeth missing—and the roof will leak—and the plaster fall—and they'll stuff pillows and rags in broken window panes—and everything will be out-at-elbows.''

Anne's imagination pictured forth so vividly the coming degeneration of her dear little house that it hurt her as severely as if it had already been an accomplished fact. She sat down on the stairs and had a long, bitter cry. Susan found her there and enquired with much concern what the trouble was.

"You have not quarrelled with the doctor, have you now, Mrs. Doctor, dear? But if you have, do not worry. It is a thing quite likely to happen to married couples, I am told, although I have had no experience that way myself. He will be sorry, and you can soon make it up.''

"No, no, Susan, we haven't quarrelled. It's only—Gilbert is going to buy the Morgan place, and we'll have to go and live at the Glen. And it will break my heart.''

Susan did not enter into Anne's feelings at all. She was, indeed, quite rejoiced over the prospect of living at the Glen. Her one grievance against her place in the little house was its lonesome location.

"Why, Mrs. Doctor, dear, it will be splendid. The Morgan hous׳ is such a fine, big one.''

"I hate big houses,'' sobbed Anne.

"Oh, well, you will not hate them by the time you have half a dozen children,'' remarked Susan calmly. "And this house is too small already for us. We have no spare room, since Mrs. Moore is here, and that pantry is the most aggravating place I ever tried to work in. There is a corner every way you turn. Besides, it is out-of-the-world down here. There is really nothing at all but scenery.''

"Out of your world perhaps, Susan—but not out of mine,'' said Anne with a faint smile.

"I do not quite understand you, Mrs. Doctor, dear, but of course I am not well educated. But if Dr. Blythe buys the Morgan place he will make no mistake, and that you may tie to. They have water in it, and the pantries and closets are beautiful, and there is not another such cellar in P. E. Island, so I have been told. Why, the cellar here, Mrs. Doctor, dear, has been a heart-break to me, as well you know."

"Oh, go away, Susan, go away," said Anne forlornly. "Cellars and pantries and closets don't make a *home*. Why don't you weep with those who weep?"

"Well, I never was much hand for weeping, Mrs. Doctor, dear. I would rather fall to and cheer people up than weep with them. Now, do not you cry and spoil your pretty eyes. This house is very well and has served your turn, but it is high time you had a better."

Susan's point of view seemed to be that of most people. Leslie was the only one who sympathised understandingly with Anne. She had a good cry, too, when she heard the news. Then they both dried their tears and went to work at the preparations for moving.

"Since we must go let us go as soon as we can and have it over," said poor Anne with bitter resignation.

"You know you will like that lovely old place at the Glen after you have lived in it long enough to have dear memories woven about it," said Leslie. "Friends will come there, as they have come here—happiness will glorify it for you. Now, it's just a house to you—but the years will make it a home."

Anne and Leslie had another cry the next week when they shortened Little Jem. Anne felt the tragedy of it until evening when in his long nightie she found her own dear baby again.

"But it will be rompers next—and then trousers—and in no time he will be grown-up," she sighed.

"Well, you would not want him to stay a baby always, Mrs. Doctor, dear, would you?" said Susan. "Bless his innocent heart, he looks too sweet for anything in his little short dresses, with his dear feet sticking out. And think of the save in the ironing, Mrs. Doctor, dear."

"Anne, I have just had a letter from Owen," said Leslie, entering with a bright face. "And, oh! I have such good news. He writes me that he is going to buy this place from the church trustees and keep it to spend our summer vacations in. Anne, are you not glad?"

"Oh, Leslie, 'glad' isn't the word for it! It seems almost too good to be true. I sha'n't feel half so badly now that I know this dear spot will never be desecrated by a vandal tribe, or left to tumble down in decay. Why, it's lovely! It's lovely!"

One October morning Anne wakened to the realisation that she had slept for the last time under the roof of her little house. The day was too busy to indulge regret and when evening came the house was stripped and bare. Anne and Gilbert were alone in it to say farewell. Leslie and Susan and Little Jem had gone to the Glen with the last load of furniture. The sunset light streamed in through the curtainless windows.

"It has all such a heart-broken, reproachful look, hasn't it?" said Anne. "Oh, I shall be so homesick at the Glen tonight!"

"We have been very happy here, haven't we, Anne-girl?" said Gilbert, his voice full of feeling.

Anne choked, unable to answer. Gilbert waited for her at the fir-tree gate, while she went over the house and said farewell to every room. She was going away; but the old house would still be there, looking seaward through its quaint windows. The autumn winds would blow around it mournfully, and the gray rain would beat upon it and the white mists would come in from the sea to enfold it; and the moonlight would fall over it and light up the old paths where the schoolmaster and his bride had walked. There on that old harbor shore the charm of story would linger; the wind would still whistle alluringly over the silver sand-dunes; the waves would still call from the red rock-coves.

"But we will be gone," said Anne through her tears.

She went out, closing and locking the door behind her. Gilbert was waiting for her with a smile. The lighthouse star was gleaming northward. The little garden, where only marigolds still bloomed, was already hooding itself in shadows.

Anne knelt down and kissed the worn old step which she had crossed as a bride.

"Good-bye, dear little house of dreams," she said.